SKOKIE PUBLIC LIBRARY

S0-AHA-819

MAY   2005

DARKWITCH RISING

By Sara Douglass

From Tom Doherty Associates

Beyond the Hanging Wall

Threshold

The Wayfarer Redemption Series

The Wayfarer Redemption

Enchanter

Starman

The Troy Game Series

Hades' Daughter

Gods' Concubine

Darkwitch Rising

DARKWITCH RISING

BOOK THREE OF THE TROY GAME

⚏ Sara Douglass ⚏

A TOM DOHERTY ASSOCIATES BOOK
NEW YORK

SKOKIE PUBLIC LIBRARY

This is a work of fiction. All the characters and events portrayed in this novel are either fictitious or are used fictitiously.

DARKWITCH RISING: BOOK THREE OF THE TROY GAME

Copyright © 2005 by Sara Douglass Enterprises Pty Ltd.

All rights reserved, including the right to reproduce this book, or portions thereof, in any form.

This book is printed on acid-free paper.

Edited by Claire Eddy

A Tor Book
Published by Tom Doherty Associates, LLC
175 Fifth Avenue
New York, NY 10010

www.tor.com

Tor® is a registered trademark of Tom Doherty Associates, LLC.

Library of Congress Cataloging-in-Publication Data

Douglass, Sara.
    Darkwitch rising / Sara Douglass.
        p. cm.—(Troy game; bk. 3)
    "A Tom Doherty Associates book."
    ISBN 0-765-30542-9
    EAN 978-0765-30542-8
    1. Great Britain—History—Civil War, 1642–1649—Fiction. 2. Charles II, King of England, 1630–1685—Fiction. 3. Brutus the Trojan (Legendary character)—Fiction. I. Title.

    PR9619.3.D672D68 2005
    823'.914—dc22

                                                                            2005041719

First Edition: May 2005

Printed in the United States of America

0 9 8 7 6 5 4 3 2 1

SCIENCE
FICTION

*This book remembers John Warneke, merchant, and
Frederick Warneke, Gentleman of the Tower of London.
I've met some strange people in London,
but you two have proved the most surprising.*

AUTHOR'S NOTE

This is a very special book to me. Firstly because when I began the research for this book, I never expected to knock on the door of the seventeenth-century Tower of London and find there inhabiting one of my German ancestors, and on the right side of the bars for once. So I gave him Ariadne. I thought he'd enjoy her.

Secondly, the book recalls a remarkable stillness in the most remarkable of cities. On Sunday, May 4, 2003, I was in London, exploring the back alleys of the southeastern quadrant of the City. The City was empty, as it usually is on a Sunday. I was walking up St. Mary-at-Hill, following the steeple trail. To my right I saw a tiny laneway—Idol Lane—and I caught a glimpse of something intriguing lurking amid the warehouses.

So I walked up Idol Lane, mildly curious, found an open churchyard gate . . . and walked through. I'm never one to refuse such an invitation.

I found . . . No. I'm not going to tell you. If ever you're in London on a sunny Sunday (don't go there during a weekday when the City office workers will be enjoying the magic), eschew the lure of Buckingham Palace, or the Tower. Instead take a packed lunch and a bottle of wine, and perhaps even some company, and walk up Idol Lane and through the open churchyard gate.

You'll find there one of the reasons I love London so greatly: a living piece of *real* London, and a very special silence.

Acknowledgments

Many thanks to Lavinia Wellecombe, curator of Woburn Abbey; to Janine Barton for driving me about so much of Llangarlia; and to Polly and Robert Arnold, for providing a comfortable place to stay so near to where Caela hid one of the Kingship bands.

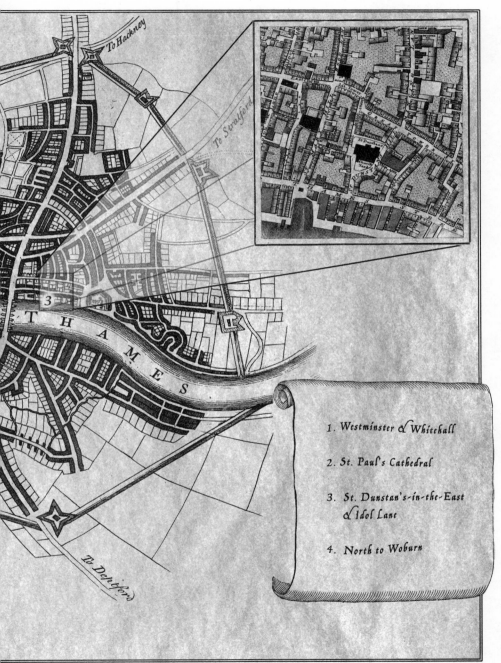

To Hackney

To Stratford

THAMES

3

To Deptford

1. Westminster & Whitehall

2. St. Paul's Cathedral

3. St. Dunstan's-in-the-East
   & Idol Lane

4. North to Woburn

G. Vertue Sc. 1738.

PROLOGUE

ATOP THE NAKED IN
THE REALM OF THE FAERIE

HE TWO GIANTS WALKED SLOWLY AND MAJESTI-cally up the gentle incline of the hill. Each was almost eight feet tall and five in girth, each wore long garments of chain mail, and each had wild long curls of reddish brown hair that escaped from under their smooth, conical helmets, and thick, tangled beards. One grasped a spear, the other a sword.

Although they moved smoothly, and while their limbs swung freely and their curls fluttered in stringy tangles behind them, each looked as though they had been carved from wood. If you came upon them in the dusk, when they were still and watchful, you would think them nothing more than massive tree trunks, denuded of their leaves.

Their names were Gog and Magog, and they had once been Sidlesaghes. Now they were the legendary defenders of London, the sprawling seventeenth-century city which occupied the Veiled Hills, the sacred heart of the ancient land of Llangarlia. While the giants spent most of their time resting motionless in the Guildhall of the city, they remained true creatures of the Faerie, and it was to the Faerie that they came this night.

After lying quiescent for tens of thousands of years, the Faerie was waking, and the creatures of the Faerie stirring. Eaving, the goddess of the waters, had been reborn, and soon her lover, the Stag God, would also awaken from his long death.

There was one other to rise back into warmth and life and breath—the Lord of the Faerie, the master of both Eaving and the Stag God, and all the creatures of the Faerie large and small. It was for news of him that the giants had left the Guildhall and entered the Realm of the Faerie.

The smooth-grassed hill Gog and Magog climbed was one of many. It rose some three hundred feet from the valley floor to a smooth flattened peak. To either side, and to the north beyond the valley, rose many similar hills, although these were all wooded. Mist drifted in the valleys and dips between the hills, scarlet and blue birds dipping languidly in and out of its billowing vapors. It was a tranquil scene, but only at first glance. When one looked closer, as Gog and Magog did as they paused for breath ten or so paces from the summit of the hill, flashes of movement could be discerned amid the trees of all the surrounding hills: creatures of the Faerie, converging toward the hill which the giants climbed. This hill was the only one clear of all vegetation save grass. For this reason it was known among the Faerie as The Naked.

The Naked was one of the great holy sites within the Realm of the Faerie, for it was here that its lord sat his Faerie throne.

Tonight, the Faerie who gathered atop The Naked hoped to hear the news toward which they'd been yearning for ten thousand years: that the Faerie throne, so long bare and cold, would soon be filled again.

GOG AND MAGOG HALTED AS THEY ATTAINED THE summit, looking about. Despite the fact that the hill was only relatively small, the summit appeared roomy enough to hold several ten thousands of the Faerie folk. The giants were not the first to arrive. They were greeted by a small, dark fey woman who walked over to them, her hands outstretched.

"Gog, Magog," she said, reaching up to kiss each one on the cheek (a feat which had to be aided by Gog, who lifted her up to so she could kiss Magog's cheek, and then his, before he set her down). "It has been so long."

"Mag," rumbled Magog. "We are glad-hearted that you are here."

"I, and all my sisters and predecessors," said Mag, the once goddess of the waters of the land.

"Is it . . ." Gog could not finish, for emotion had choked him.

Mag smiled, her face gentle and serene. "Aye," she said. "It is time. The Lord of the Faerie approaches."

The giants each drew in deep breaths of joy.

"Where?" said Magog. "When?"

"Not here," she said. "Not yet. But soon. Before too many more years have passed."

She stood back, and the giants saw that now many thousands of creatures thronged the summit: Sidlesaghes, water-sprites, snow-ghosts, wood-sylphs, gray-and-black lumpens who were the souls of the mountains, badgers and moles (the most mystical and royal of those animals who trod the mortal world), moon-shadows and sun-dapples, and the strange low, pallid-skinned creatures who inhabited the caverns of the land, but who, since the beginning of creation, had refused to tell anyone their names.

Most of the Faerie simply called them cavelings.

One of the Sidlesaghes walked toward where Mag stood with the giants. It was Long Tom, the Sidlesaghe who best knew Eaving, the newborn goddess of the waters. The giants greeted him cheerfully, for Long Tom had once been their brother.

"Is it true," said Gog, "that the Lord of the Faerie shall be returning to us?"

"Yes," said Long Tom. He stood back a little, and gestured toward the eastern part of the summit.

As if at his command, the creatures that thronged the summit stepped back, and the giants had a clear sight through to the eastern aspect of the summit where stood a great carved throne of faerie wood, known to mortals as burr elm.

On the seat of the throne rested a crown made of twisted twigs and sprigs of red berries, and as the giants stared, a beam of light illumed the crown of twigs.

"Do you remember the day that Eaving sat atop Pen Hill?" said Long Tom.

"Aye," said Gog. "That was when Harold came to her, and the beam of light crowned him."

Long Tom's smile grew broader, and his eyes twinkled. Mag stared at him. "No!" she said. "Truly?"

"Oh, aye," said Long Tom. "The Lord of the Faerie shall reawake in Coelreborn, for he has proved himself a great man, a fair king, and, most important of all, a man of true faerie-heart."

Mag closed her eyes briefly. "I am so very glad," she whispered.

PART ONE

THE GATHERING

LONDON, 1939

MAJOR JACK SKELTON CHECKED HIS TIE ONE LAST *time in the mirror of Frank and Violet Bentley's drab spare bedroom, then he grabbed his bag and, as Frank sounded the motor's horn outside, ran lightly down the stairs.*

Violet stood at their foot, her pretty face uncertain. "I hope you enjoy your stay in England, Major," she said as Skelton stopped before her.

He raised an eyebrow. "I've come to prepare for war, Mrs. Bentley. It's not an enjoyable business."

She flushed, her hands twisting a little within her floral apron. Skelton knew she couldn't wait to be rid of him.

Outside Frank sounded the horn once again, but Skelton didn't move, nor shift his eyes from Violet's face. "I'd move from London, if I was you," he said. "Hell lies just around the corner, and if you don't have the taste for that kind of thing"—now his eyes traveled slowly about the garish, cheap furnishings of the hall—"I suggest you find yourself a quiet corner somewhere far from London."

"Major," Violet whispered, her eyes now huge. "Frank's waiting. You've got to go."

Skelton's mouth twitched. He lifted his hand, and Violet shook it too quickly, her grip clammy and soft.

Skelton touched his cap, and then he was gone.

Frank Bentley had the motor of his small car turning over, and he gestured impatiently out the window as he saw Skelton emerge from the front door. "Come on, old chap! We're late as it is!"

Skelton paused halfway down the front path, looking at the house next door. The curtains in the front bay window parted, and for a moment Skelton had a view of the two women within: Mrs. Ecub and Mrs. Matilda Flanders, watching.

Again he touched his hat, but this time his eyes twinkled, and a small smile lifted his mouth.

"Major!" Frank yelled.

I'm off to war, Skelton said to the two women.

We know, *Matilda replied.* We'll hold a Circle. Be well.

For an instant Skelton's mind was overwhelmed with memories of the Circles he'd held with these two women, with the intimacy, both sexual and emotional, and his eyes softened.

Then he was gone, running down the path toward Frank and his motor.

Chapter One

Gog Magog Hills, Cambridgeshire, and Oatlands Palace, Weybridge, England

SIMON GAUTIER, MARQUIS DE LONQUEFORT, gripped the armrests of the wildly rocking carriage and grinned lasciviously at his current mistress, Mademoiselle Helene Gardien, sitting across from him. She was sixteen, with the face of an angel and the body of a whore, and she was shrieking with feigned terror, although whether at the wild movement of the carriage or at the wanton expression on his face, Lonquefort didn't particularly know—nor did he particularly care. Outside the driver had whipped the team of horses into a frenzy, and they plunged recklessly down the forest track, their hooves and the abused wheels of the carriage marking each dip, each hole, and each rock that pitted their way.

Lonquefort was a man who disdained sedateness, in every aspect of his life.

His uncle, and his guardian since the death of his father, had sent Lonquefort for a season to the austere colleges of Cambridge in an effort to wean him from the fleshly delights of his native Paris. But Lonquefort was a man not to be outwitted, and in July of this year of our Lord 1629 he arranged for the passage of Helene across to England. She was young, pliable, tender and fresh, and she shrieked delightfully whenever Lonquefort buried himself within her pleasures.

Which explained why Lonquefort had hired carriage and driver for this day expedition to the Gog Magog Hills four miles south of the university city: the Cambridge dons were starting to complain about the noise. What better to calm their shattered nerves and to indulge his own wanton desires than to take Helene in the center of some stubbled field, or the incline of some gentle hillside slope, where she could scream to her heart's content and he could . . .

Oh, God, he was going to have to stop the carriage soon!

As Helene pursed her sweet lips for yet another shriek, Lonquefort glanced outside. He'd been told the Gog Magog Hills were gentle rolling hills, cleared by years of grazing, yet the view which met his eyes contradicted all reports he'd heard.

Forests crowded about, thick and dark.

Lonquefort frowned.

Helene shrieked.

Lonquefort looked at her.

She gave another cry, and jumped slightly in her seat, her breasts jiggling just enough that her nipples slipped briefly, tantalizingly, into view above the frothy lace of her bodice.

Lonquefort forgot the strangeness of the forests.

"Stop!" he cried, his voice so thick with desire he could barely manage the word. "Stop, I command you!" He lifted his cane, banging its golden head against the roof of the carriage.

Outside the driver swore as he hauled on the reins in an effort to stop the violent, plunging motion of the horses.

Lonquefort couldn't tear his mind away from the violent, plunging efforts *he* would soon be engaged in. As the horses finally came to a halt, he leaned forward, grabbed Helene by the hand, flung open the carriage door, and hauled her outside.

"Wait here," he said to the driver.

Lonquefort managed to get Helene twenty or thirty paces inside the tree line before his lust overcame him. He pulled her to him and tore her bodice apart. He grabbed at her breasts, bruising them, then pushed her first against the broad trunk of a tree, then down so that she lay beneath him amid the leaf litter of the forest. He bit at her neck, and her breasts, and his hands grabbed at her skirts, fumbling in his haste.

Oh, God, oh, God, he'd never wanted her this badly. Never! Never!

Helene cried out, but he took no notice, and did not realize that the tone of her voice had changed from the provocative to the terrified.

She beat at his back and his shoulders, trying to push him away.

He took no notice.

Helene grabbed at his hair, intending to pull it until he pulled away from her, but instead her fingers encountered not fine, powdered brown hair, but the soft velvet of antlers.

Lonquefort thrust deep, and Helene, gasping with horror, felt not her lover, but the heat and strangeness of a wild beast. No, no, of a beast so un-tamed she felt as if she would die from the force and horror of it.

Lonquefort's movements became frenzied, and Helene lay quiescent beneath him, shocked beyond resistance. Her face was devoid of its usual rosy color, her eyes wide and staring, her injured breasts heaved, her breath whistled in her throat, her hands now clutched behind her at the bark of the tree, preferring to find comfort there before the pelt of the creature that was mating her.

Then, suddenly, wondrously, she was at peace, and she sighed and closed her eyes. While the beast above and inside her still felt wild, he no longer seemed strange, or frightening, and she lifted down her hands from the bark of the tree, and buried them within his pelt, and she whispered, "Anything for you. Anything."

And she felt then, within the pit of her belly, the beginning of something incredible, and Helene knew that her life as a girl was done for.

She sighed once more, and was replete.

"MADAM?"

Henrietta Maria, queen of England, looked up from her embroideries, and put a practiced smile on her face.

"My good lord," she said, rising, then sinking in a deep curtsy, "I had not expected you."

Charles I looked at his wife, repressed a sigh, then instantly hated himself for his impatience. Other men managed with wives they found difficult to love, and so must he. Besides, she had been ill, had miscarried of a child, and doubtless some of her coolness could be ascribed to her aches both of body and of spirit.

At this thought Charles looked a little more closely at his wife. Sweet Lord Christ, she was only sixteen, and yet her face was drawn and lined almost as if she had lived through twice those many years. There were shadows under her dark eyes, her cheeks were pallid, and her hair had lost the luminosity that he remembered from their awkward, fraught wedding night.

What kind of man were he, then, to have brought a girl to this extreme of weariness? What kind of husband, to look in irritation on a woman, and judge her unkindly, when she had just lost a precious child? What kind of king, if he could not care for this most important of his subjects? What kind of lover, if he could not make her smile?

Now Charles smiled himself, and the expression was unexpectedly kind and warm, wiping away much of the aloofness which Henrietta Maria found so intimidating.

"You and I have made a poor start to our marriage," he said, "and I am sorry for it."

The false smile froze on Henrietta Maria's face, and Charles could see the confusion in her eyes. They had spoken nothing but banalities to each other in the entire first year of their marriage. This degree of forthrightness, *and* spoken so winsomely from a man prone to the most frightful bouts of stuttering, patently had caught her off guard.

Charles suddenly felt a most unexpected wave of mischievousness wash through him. She *was* but a girl, after all. Why had he not remembered that? His smile warmed, his entire face relaxed, and he was rewarded with the slightest of thaws in his wife's own expression.

Charles glanced behind him. "We would be alone," he said, and with those words, and a wave of his hand, he dismissed from the royal presence the entire bevy of ladies-in-waiting, valets, diplomats, secretaries, and courtiers who normally attended every waking moment of king and queen.

Henrietta Maria's face grew uncertain.

"Am I so unkind a husband," he asked, holding out his arm for her, "that you must look so suspiciously upon me when I seek a moment or two alone with you?"

"You are not unkind," she said, slipping her arm through his as he led her for a gentle stroll down the splendid gallery of Oatlands palace.

"Then, if I am not unkind then I have most certainly been—" He paused awkwardly, his speech struggling to master the word. "—ungracious."

She did not reply.

He stopped, and turned to her, cupping her small face between his hands.

Her muscles tensed beneath his fingers.

He lowered his face until it was but a finger's distance above hers. "I have no doubt that as I speak, our courtiers and ladies, indeed, half the realm, stand huddled against the other side of the far door, ears pressed against its hardness, wondering what we do alone in here. What do *you* think they imagine?"

His voice was light and teasing, and as its reward, he felt her face relax slightly.

"Perhaps that we discuss great matters of state," she said, her voice low.

"Perhaps, but, no. I think not. What else might they consider?"

"Perhaps that you rebuke me for some childish wrong."

"I hope not," he said, his voice and face now sober, "for that would be a stain on my soul, and I am most sorry I should ever have given them the fodder to imagine such a thing.

"*I think*"—he lowered his face that final distance between them and planted a soft kiss on her mouth—"that they imagine we sit in silence on our cold thrones, and stare out the windows at the stiff, formal gardens, and wish to ourselves that we were anywhere else but in each other's presence."

"I sincerely hope not," she said, "for that is *not* what I wish right now."

"Then perhaps they imagine that I have been so overcome by my desire for you—"

Her cheeks stained even rosier.

"—that I have begged for solitude so that I might enjoy my wife's love."

"My lord—"

"Perhaps even now they think I have borne you to that bench by the window—"

She giggled.

"—and there avail myself," his voice grew deeper, a little hoarser, and she could hear real admiration within it, "of your sweet, wondrous white flesh. What say you, wife? Shall I?"

"My lord! It lacks but an hour until noon. We cannot—"

"Parliament may plot to make my life a misery," he said, "but it has not yet passed that act which forbids the nation's monarch from making love to his much-admired wife during the daylight hours."

"You admire me?"

"Most particularly during this beautiful hour before noon. What say you, wife. Shall we? That bench looks right inviting."

"But . . . But they'll *know*!"

His only answer was to kiss her neck, and lay his hand on her bosom.

"Charles . . ." she said, and he heard the weakness in her voice, and it encouraged him to turn tease into reality.

And so, atop a beautiful brocaded bench set into one of the great windows of the gallery at Oatlands, Charles I of England made love to his young wife while their courtiers crowded the door outside and a shaft of sunlight broke through the clouds and clothed the couple's soft movements in gold.

Although this was not Charles and Henrietta Maria's marriage night, it *was* the day on which they made their marriage, and it was also the day during which they conceived one of the greatest kings that England would ever know.

FAR AWAY IN LONDON A FAIR-HAIRED, HAZEL-EYED boy in his midteens raised his face to the sky. He was tall for his age, and too thin for his height, but he held himself gracefully nonetheless, and his face already held hints of the handsomeness it would assume in maturity. He stood in one of London's innumerable back alleys, hidden in shadow. At his side stood a solemn-faced toddling girl of some eighteen months. She was a pretty little thing, with soft brown eyes and silvery hair, but her prettiness was marred by a blank look of terror in those dark eyes, and she stood tense and fearful, as if expecting a blow at any moment.

The boy held her by the hand, and, as he lowered his face, he gave her flesh a squeeze, painful enough that the girl gave a low gasp, her eyes filling with tears.

"Do you feel it, Jane?" said the boy. "Do you know what has happened?"

She made no reply save for two great fat tears that rolled down her cheeks.

The boy squatted so he could look directly into her eyes. "You *do* feel it, don't you? Brutus is back, your lover when you were Genvissa. He's reborn, and growing contentedly in a queen's womb. Not a bastard, *this* life. Tell me, pretty Jane, do you think he'll want you? Do you think he'll ever stoop to love *you*, dirty street urchin, Asterion's whore?"

More tears flowed, and the boy nodded slowly. "Aye. You know he's back, and you know he'll never touch you. So sad, pretty Jane."

She spoke, this tiny girl, with the voice of a child much, much older. "Let me go, Weyland."

"Never," Weyland whispered. "You're mine, now. You and all your talents."

CHAPTER TWO

PARIS, FRANCE, AND ST. JAMES'S PALACE, LONDON

ON THE TWENTY-NINTH OF MAY IN 1630 HELENE Gardien went into labor at daybreak, delivering her child six hours later. Her lover, Simon Gautier, the marquis de Lonquefort, was in residence at the Parisian townhouse where he'd installed his mistress and visited Helene two hours after he'd been informed of her safe delivery.

This was his first child, and he was curious, if somewhat apprehensive and more than a little annoyed. All he'd wanted from Helene was sex, not responsibility.

"Well?" he said as he inched up to the bed.

"A boy," Helene said, not looking up from the child's face. "See, he has neither your eyes, nor mine, but those of a poet."

Neither your eyes nor mine. Lonquefort instantly seized on her words. Could he claim the child wasn't his? Not his responsibility?

Then he looked at the baby, and was lost. The baby's eyes *were* different, for while both Lonquefort and Helene had blue eyes, this infant had the deepest-black eyes Lonquefort thought he'd ever seen in a face. But it wasn't their color that immediately captivated Lonquefort. The boy's eyes *were* those of a poet, Lonquefort decided, for they seemed to contain knowledge and suffering that stretched back aeons, rather than the two hours this boy had lived in this painful world.

"He will be a great man," Lonquefort pronounced, and Helene smiled.

"I will call him Louis," she said, then hesitated. Poet or not, the boy was a bastard, and Helene was not sure whether she should name him for his father.

But who was his father, she wondered as the awkward silence stretched out between them. Lonquefort, or that strange beast she'd envisioned riding her in the forest?

"Louis," Lonquefort said, then he grinned. "Louis de Silva, for the forest where we made him."

Helene laughed, her doubts gone. The forest had made him, indeed, and so he should be named.

"I shall settle a pension on him, and you," said Lonquefort. "You shall not want."

"Thank you," Helene said softly, and bent her head back to her poet-son.

AS HELENE RELAXED IN RELIEF, ANOTHER WOMAN, far distant, arched her back and cried out in the extremities of her own labor.

Henrietta Maria, queen of England, lay writhing in the great bed draped with forest-green silk within her lying-in chamber off the Color Court of St. James's Palace. About her hovered midwives and physicians, privy councillors and lords, all there either to ensure a safe delivery or to witness the birth of an heir.

Elsewhere within the palace Charles I paced up and down, praying silently. He was riven with anxiety, more for Henrietta Maria than for concern over the arrival of a healthy heir. Over the course of the past nine months, as his wife's body had swelled, so also had waxed Charles's regard and love for her. Now he could not bear the thought that she might suffer in childbed.

As the palace clocks chimed noon, one of the privy councillors hurried toward Charles.

"Well?" demanded Charles.

"You have a healthy son," the man said. "An heir!"

"And my wife?"

"She is well," said the councillor, and Charles finally allowed himself to relax, and smile.

"A son," he said. "He shall be named Charles."

"Of course," said the councillor.

Charles went to his wife, assured for himself that she was indeed well, then turned to look at the child one of the midwives held.

He studied the baby curiously, then folded back his wrappings.

"By Jesus!" Charles exclaimed, and looked back at Henrietta Maria. "Are you sure you *are* well, my love?"

She grinned wanly. "He was an effort, my lord. But, yes, I am well. He did not injure me."

Charles looked back to the baby. *By God, look at the size of him!* He was a giant, surely, with great strong limbs and a head of long, tight black curls. Charles reached down a hand and, as he did so, the baby reached up his own right hand and snatched at a golden crown embroidered on Charles's sleeve.

"Observe!" said the midwife. "He was born a king, truly! See how he grasps for what shall be his!"

Then both the midwife and Charles cried out, for the baby's hand tightened about the crown, and tugged at it, tearing it away from his father's sleeve.

"I shall have to watch my back, surely," Charles said with a forced laugh, "in case this son of mine decides to snatch my crown before his time."

The midwife prised the torn piece of material out of the infant's fist, and he began to wail.

"You shall surely die abed, an aged and beloved king," murmured one of the physicians. "This is no omen to be feared."

"Of course not," said Charles, but at that moment the room darkened as a cloud covered the sun, and the only one in the chamber who did not shiver in dread was the baby.

WEYLAND ORR BROUGHT HIS LITTLE SISTER JANE TO stand outside the octagonal-towered gatehouse of St James's Palace among the other crowds awaiting news of the queen's delivery. Most of the crowd prayed for a prince; Weyland and Jane *knew* the child would be a prince. A king reborn.

Weyland hoisted Jane in his arms so that she could see through the gates into the Color Court off which, the crowd was reliably informed, the queen labored in her chamber.

See, Genvissa, in that tumbled mess of ancient buildings Brutus-reborn draws his first breath, while you sit, caught in the arms of Asterion, knowing you'll never feel Brutus' arms about you again. Will he come looking for you, do you think, once he has control of those infant legs of his?

Weyland laughed, softly, tormenting Jane with his thoughts. *No, of course not. He'll want his precious princess, Cornelia. He won't want you, particularly after what I have planned.*

Weyland sent a series of images skidding through Jane's mind, and the girl began to cry.

Weyland hugged her to him. "There, there," he whispered, playing the part of the affectionate brother to perfection. "All will be well. I shall look after you."

Then he lifted his head. A nobleman had walked to the gates, and now shouted to the crowds.

"A son! A son! The queen has been safely delivered of a healthy son!"

The crowd roared, and Weyland cheered with the best of them.

In his arms, the little girl wept.

Chapter Three

QUEEN HENRIETTA MARIA OF ENGLAND STOOD IN the center of the hall of Pendinnis Castle, holding the letter in trembling hands. She looked about the great chamber, first at her beloved fifteen-year-old son, Charles, and then to their advisers and protectors, Sir Edward Hyde, John Colepeper, and Thomas Howard, earl of Berkshire. Honest men all, and loyal in an age when it seemed to Henrietta Maria that loyalty was a forgotten concept.

"It comes from my lord, my husband," she said, unnecessarily.

Hyde bowed his head, hiding his impatience. "Majesty, what does our king command?"

Tears filled Henrietta Maria's eyes, and Charles moved to her side, resting a hand on her arm. Even at fifteen he towered over his mother, and his physical presence was such that Henrietta Maria instinctively leaned against him.

"He commands," she said, "that I take our son Charles and flee this realm."

There was an appalled silence. King Charles must think matters desperate indeed.

"No!" Charles said. "This is *my* land! I will not be exiled because some rogues say my father has lost his right to rule!"

"Charles . . ." his mother murmured.

Charles was so angry he visibly shook, his long black curls trembling in the weak candlelight, his darkly handsome face flushed. "I will not leave—"

"You father thinks you will die if you don't," Henrietta Maria said.

Charles took the letter from his mother, and all could see the effort it took him to take it gently from her.

"You are your father's heir," Hyde said softly. "*One* of you needs to live."

"No," said Charles, but his voice had dropped, and he had to dash away the tears so he could read the letter. His eyes skimmed the lines, then he read one line aloud. "'I sense a malevolent, ungodly hand behind all this treachery,'" Charles quoted, then looked up, although he did not focus on any of those standing about him. "Oh, aye, malevolent and ungodly *indeed*."

There was a further silence as all thought on the crisis that had gripped the realm. Charles I had always endured an uneasy relationship with Parliament which was now determined to curb his power. He'd tried to rule without it, had been forced to recall it, and had then been subjected to humiliation after humiliation by the rebellious parliamentarians until war erupted. The country had divided between those who supported the king, and those who supported the Parliament. For years the armies of king and Parliament had battled each other the length and breadth of the country until, some ten months previously, Charles I's forces had been disastrously defeated by Parliament's New Model Army. Henrietta Maria and her son had held out hope for months, but now . . .

"He tells us to flee," the queen said, "so that *you* may live."

"For what?" said Charles. "My father has no kingdom to leave me. Not a one. He's lost them all: Scotland, Ireland, and now *England*."

"Then you must rely on your wits to retrieve them," said Hyde.

"And retrieve them you most surely shall!" Berkshire said loyally, and with a little too much bravado.

"As I have had to previously," Charles muttered, "from this 'malevolent and ungodly hand.'"

"My prince?" said Colepeper.

"Nothing," Charles said, and sighed. "My younger brother and sisters are safe?" he asked of his mother.

"Yes. I received word this morning that James and Henriette-Anne are in France. Mary, of course, sits and frets with her husband in the Netherlands. We shall be the last to abandon your father."

"Parliament will kill him!" Charles said.

"They dare not!" said his mother, but all heard the uncertainty in her voice.

"My queen, prince," Hyde said. "We *must* go. I can ready a ship within the hour."

"Where?" asked Charles, his voice harsh and bitter.

"The Scilly Isles," said Hyde.

"So my inheritance is to be reduced to the Scilly Isles," Charles said. "How . . . quaint."

* * *

THAT NIGHT, AS HYDE HURRIED CHARLES AND HIS
mother toward the hastily readied ship, Charles leaned down and snatched at
a piece of turf.

"I will not leave it *all* behind," he said to Hyde, who looked on incredulously as the young prince pocketed the crumbling handful of turf and soil.

WEYLAND SLOUCHED ON THE SINGLE CHAIR IN THE
small, cramped room. In his mind's eye he watched as Charles was jostled
aboard the ship.

How comical. Brutus-reborn, exiled with nothing more to show for his almost three thousand years of effort to control the Troy Game than a pocketful
of dirt.

There came a sound at the door, and it opened.

Weyland tensed, his vision of Charles slipping away.

A woman of some seventeen or eighteen years of age entered. She was tall,
and lithe, and with pretty dark-blonde hair over brown eyes. Most men might
have found her attractive were it not for the hard cast to her features, or the
practiced blankness in her eyes.

"My pet," said Weyland. "Did you manage to find my plums at market?"

She held up a small package silently, and Weyland nodded. "Good. I shall
allow you one or two, for this is an auspicious day and I am feeling gracious."

Jane tipped the plums into a wooden bowl. If she was curious at Weyland's
words she didn't show it.

"Brutus has gone," Weyland said. "Fled. Brutus . . . *Charles* . . . is not a
happy boy. His father is about to lose his head, his kingdom is lost, and his
kingship bands are so out of reach they might as well not exist at all. He
should have tried to snatch them while he had the chance, eh? Too late, now."

Jane walked over, her every movement stiff, and held out the bowl of
plums.

"I thank you, sweetheart," Weyland said, then smiled as he watched Jane's
features harden at the endearment.

He'd raped her at nine, and prostituted her the next year. For nigh on eight
years now Jane had spent the best part of each day on her back—or in whatever
position her client demanded—being skewered by what Weyland imagined
must by now have been at least half of the male population of London. Oh,
she'd tried to escape many a time, particularly in the early years. But Weyland
always hauled her back, and set her once more to her humiliation.

Genvissa, MagaLlan and Mistress of the Labyrinth. Swanne, highborn wife
of Harold, king of England.

Jane, world-weary prostitute. In their previous life Weyland had made her love him. In this life he did not bother. Jane could loathe him all she liked, so long as she continued to do his bidding.

Weyland had prostituted her for a number of reasons. Foremost, her degradation amused him while keeping her under some degree of control—Weyland could always use the imp he put in Jane's womb in her previous life to restrain her, but he'd seen how badly the imp had affected her health as Swanne, and Weyland didn't think Jane would survive too many years of constant intra-uterine nibbling. Weyland also enjoyed watching Jane suffer, enjoyed watching the light die in her eyes, enjoyed seeing her struggle, enjoyed knowing he had the power to so degrade a woman, to bring her under his control.

Weyland would one day have to bring Cornelia-reborn under his control, and he wanted to be sure he had the skill down to a fine art by then. Cornelia-reborn was important. She knew where the kingship bands were, and Weyland needed those bands if ever he were to gain ascendancy over the Troy Game.

But Weyland didn't need Cornelia-reborn only to acquire those tiresome kingship bands. He knew that she wanted to learn the skills of the Mistress of the Labyrinth so that she could conclude the Game with her Kingman. Weyland had no argument with that desire. He wanted Cornelia-reborn to learn the arts of the Labyrinth as well. She was the goddess of the land reborn . . . Imagine the power she would bring to the Game as its Mistress.

Imagine the power *he*, Weyland, would control, when such a talented Mistress of the Labyrinth had danced that final dance with him, and the Game was his.

Thus the final reason for so humiliating Jane. She was the only one who currently had the skills of the Mistress of the Labyrinth. Once Mistresses had dotted the ancient Aegean world, controlling the Game in whichever city it had been constructed. Now Jane was the very last of her breed. Weyland needed her to be so under his control that by the time he also had Cornelia-reborn with him, he could just snap his fingers, and Jane would hand on her knowledge without a murmur.

Weyland sighed. All this was very many years into the future. Cornelia-reborn was still only a girl. She had years yet in which she needed to grow.

And the bands. Weyland couldn't approach the bands until Brutus-reborn was close to his thirtieth year. There was no point. This consideration was what had dictated William's return in the previous life, as well. When the Game had first begin, so many thousands of years ago, Brutus had been in his early thirties and Genvissa a few years older. Somehow this affected when the bands could be taken, and the Game completed. The Kingman and the Mistress of the Labyrinth had to be about the same age now as they had been two and a half thousand years ago. The power of the Game relied almost entirely on harmonies, and the ages of the Mistress of the Labyrinth and the Kingman had to be in harmony with their first lives.

Thus Weyland had to wait for years. At least fifteen. And there was no point rushing anything until the time was literally ripe.

Furthermore, Weyland was more cautious than ever. In the last life he was the one who'd controlled everyone's rebirth. This life he'd not been able to manage it. Weyland had wanted to come back long before this, and had intended to command back everyone else he needed—but something had held him back. That "something" had held back *everyone*'s rebirth until now—and the only entity capable of this was the Troy Game itself. *It* had grown and matured since their last lives in the eleventh century.

And, by the gods, it had grown so powerful.

And so dangerous.

Weyland meant nothing to get in his way of success in this life, not even the Game itself, and he resolved not to put a foot wrong in the doing. The Troy Game was as much his enemy as was Brutus-reborn.

Weyland slowly ate his plums as he watched Jane moving about the room. She was clearly on guard, waiting for whatever torment he decided to toss her way. Weyland smiled to himself. Would Cornelia-reborn be as manageable as Jane, once *she'd* been humiliated and broken?

All Weyland needed of Cornelia-reborn was that she do as he wished, without question, and at the instant he required it of her.

He didn't need her to be happy. He just needed her alive.

And compliant.

CHAPTER FOUR

THE ISLAND OF JERSEY

CHARLES WALKED BRISKLY ACROSS THE CLIFF-TOPS of Jersey, heading toward a hill a mile or two distant, glad not only to get away from the depressive company of his minders but to get the chance to speak alone with the person he strode to meet. Far below, the sea pounded, about him grasses and flowers nodded in the hot summer sun; it might have been a beautiful day save for the anger and worry in his heart. Charles was dressed only in heavy linen breeches, such as a tradesman might wear, knee-high boots, and a snowy-white linen shirt that was patched at both elbow and collar. His long, curling black hair was tied loosely with a thong at the nape of his neck.

He looked like a nondescript tradesman and, by God, he felt like one. Prince of the realm, indeed! He and his mother had spent but a few weeks in the Scilly Isles before warning had reached them of the approach of Parliament's fleet. They'd fled once more, Henrietta Maria to her native France and Charles to Jersey (it being felt that the heir to the English throne should, perhaps, keep his feet on English soil for as long as possible) where, for the moment, he was safe.

Safe. The concept was anathema to him. All Charles wanted was to get England back, to return to London, to grab that crown that was slowly toppling from his father's head, and to find Cornelia-reborn and, somehow, *somehow,* protect her from Asterion's malevolence.

But Charles could do none of those things. If he stepped so much as a toe back inside mainland England he would be seized and face the same fate as his father likely would: death. He would certainly be thrown in close prison.

"I need an *army!*" Charles seethed to himself as he continued his walk. But there was no army. Royalist supporters were scattered far and wide, the people of England had been too seduced by wicked whispers to support anyone that

Parliament openly despised, and the only retinue that Charles had about him here in Jersey was a ragtag court comprising varied servants, a few members of his father's council and some fiercely loyal, but ultimately helpless, noblemen. Charles had taken refuge in Elizabeth Castle, the domain of the island's governor, Sir George Carteret, where Charles had done all he could to ensure that he and his retinue would not cause undue strain on the thin resources of the island and its inhabitants.

Five weeks ago Charles had celebrated his sixteenth birthday. The islanders had done their best to mark the occasion, but their well-meaning efforts had served only to deepen Charles's despair.

He should be in England . . . He should be in London.

What was happening to Cornelia-reborn? Where was she? *How* was she?

The answers to these questions he hoped could be answered within the hour.

He continued to stride through the grasses, wishing he'd been able to bring a horse. But the only way he'd managed to escape the castle unnoticed was via its orchard—the stables were on the other side of the castle complex, and the mere fact of the prince asking for a horse to be readied would have brought numerous murmured concerns about where he was going, and offers to accompany him.

So he had to make do with his feet and legs and, to be honest, Charles appreciated the release of tension that walking afforded him.

He stopped abruptly, and stared. Ahead rose the hill that was his destination, and on that hill he could see a riderless saddled horse, its head bent down to the grass. It shifted slightly, and a figure came into view behind it.

Tall, graceful, fair hair blowing in the wind.

"Marguerite," Charles muttered, and started forward at a jog.

By the time he topped the hill he was breathing hard, and Marguerite Carteret, twenty-year-old daughter of the governor, laughed at him as she held out her hands.

"Oh, would-be king of England, if only your subjects could see you now, all red-faced and sweaty!"

He took her hands, then kissed her on the cheek. "Mother Ecub," he said. "I had never thought you ever to be young, and delicious."

Marguerite's light-brown eyes snapped with humor. "You only ever knew me as an old woman. But even then, I had been young, once." Her mouth curved a little. "But, my, look at you. So dark and handsome, so *vital*. I imagine every girl in England mourns your loss."

He let her hands drop. "What do you know?"

"What do I know? Why, that the sun shines, and that the wind is gentle, and that the lord my prince has managed to escape his minders so that—"

"*Damn you!* What do you know?"

"That you are too impatient a young man, and that this exile shall doubt-less encourage the growth of patience and circumspection without which you shall never regain England!" she snapped back at him.

He drew a deep breath, and Marguerite felt instantly contrite when she saw how it caught in his throat.

"What do I know?" she said softly. "That we are all back, and that many of us, this time, are exiled. But I know also that we shall return, and that *you* are the one about whom we shall coalesce."

He nodded, accepting that statement as if his right. "And Cornelia?" he said. "Where is she?"

"In England. Not in London. Safe, for the moment."

"For the moment." Charles turned away. "I should be there for her. Dammit, Marguerite, I *love* her."

"What can a sixteen-year-old boy do for her, Charles?"

Now he swung back to her. "I am *far* more than a sixteen-year-old boy!"

"And where has that 'far more' got you in this life thus far?"

Charles gave no answer to that. He stared beyond Marguerite to where the sea foamed, then he suddenly reached into the pocket of his breeches, and pulled forth a dried piece of dirt and turf.

Marguerite drew in a sharp breath. "What is that?"

He said nothing, but held it out to her in his open hand.

She reached out, and touched it briefly. "It is *land*."

"Asterion shall not have exiled me entirely." He pocketed the piece of turf, Marguerite's eyes following it hungrily, knowing that someday, somehow, that piece of turf would be very important to them. "Asterion is stronger," Charles said. "Stronger than ever."

"Aye. I can feel him, even from here. Whispering evil into the hearts and minds of Englishmen."

"Cornelia—"

"Cornelia shall have to shift for herself. She is not so weak and helpless that you must spend every waking moment fretting for her. She has strength, too."

"To face what confronts her?"

"Aye," said Marguerite. "To face even Asterion. She can do it."

Charles sighed again, this time easier. "Aye. She *can* do it, but she will need aid."

"Thus I, here and now. All of Eaving's Sisters will gather to you, Charles. The more of us with you, the greater your power." She studied him, a slight frown lining her forehead. "You have greater power than ever before, Charles." Again her mouth curved. "Very heady indeed. I can see that I shall enjoy your company."

They stood for a long moment, staring at each other, thinking of all that had gone before, of all the opportunities that had been lost, and all the mistakes that had been made.

And of all that *could* be accomplished, if they could manage to weld their powers.

"All of us will gather to you, Charles," Marguerite said again. Her hands slipped behind the back of her gown, and Charles realized she was loosening the laces that bound her bodice. "And then somehow we will find a way to aid Cornelia-reborn. But until then, there is but you and I, and all we can do is to wait, and to comfort each other."

A thrill went down his spine at her words, but still Charles held back from her. "Everything I do is noted. We must be circumspect."

"To a point." The gown slid free of her shoulders, and Charles saw that the fair skin over her shoulders and the rise of her breasts was dusted with soft freckles. "Asterion will expect nothing less of you. Brutus has ever gathered women to him. Charles, if you worry that . . . Well, Cornelia will not mind."

"I know that." The gown was around her waist, now catching about her hips before she shook herself free of it.

She wore no chemise or underskirt underneath. "I am the first of Eaving's Sisters to come to you. Will you accept me, Charles?"

He stared at her, hardly able to reconcile the Ecub he had known in his two previous lives with this beautiful, sexual creature.

"For the love of England, man, how long are you going to stand there and think about it?"

He laughed. "Ah, *there* speaks Ecub!" Charles put his hands gently about her waist, pulling her toward him, and this time when he kissed her, it was no chaste peck on the cheek. His hand slid upward to her breasts, and Ecub tipped back her head so he could run his mouth down her neck.

"Cornelia once told me," Marguerite said, laughing a little breathlessly now as he lowered his face to one of her breasts, "how good a lover you were."

He laughed, then let her go and stood back a little as he stripped away his clothes. "Now you can judge the truthfulness of her relation for yourself, Ecub."

She leaned forward, putting the palm of her hand flat against his mouth. "My name is Marguerite. We need to be careful."

Naked now, he pushed away her hand and pulled her back to him. "Not this afternoon," he said. "Not here."

ChAPTER FIVE

EASTHILL, ESSEX

Noah Speaks

*J*THINK I PUZZLED THE ENTIRE PARISH OF EASTHILL;
I know I certainly puzzled my parents. *What is this child,* they thought,
who seems so unchildlike? I remember lying in my cot, a baby only a few
months old, and *knowing.* Remembering all that had gone before. This life,
praise all gods who lived, I *remembered.* I would not repeat Caela's mistakes.

I think I distressed my mother with my unbabyish gaze. I recall her leaning
down to study me, bewilderment all over her honest, lovely face. I didn't cry, I
didn't burble. I rarely laughed.

I watched.

My father, a local vicar, insisted I be named Noah. He'd wanted a son, desperately, and the disappointment of a daughter was not enough for him to
abandon his cherished name. In any case, he loved me despite my femininity,
and I loved the name. Noah. *Survivor.* I hoped it bode well for the future.

So I grew through my childhood, puzzling everyone who beheld me. I took
part in no children's games, I played no mischief, I did not cry, I rarely
laughed. (Who could laugh, remembering Asterion's grip on my flesh, and his
taunting words, "*Not God's Concubine at all, but* mine"?)

I learned to read faster than any child hitherto, and displayed an uncomfortable knowledge both of Greek and of Latin.

How could my poor parents have known I drew on the knowledge of two
previous lives to aid me in traversing this one?

My mother faded away when I was four. I felt sadness for her, but more for
my father who had loved her dearly. He continued another nine years, writing
his sermons in the sunlit front room of our parsonage, distributing the parish
poor relief as best he could, and all the while lost in puzzlement at his strange,
unsettling daughter.

Poor Father, what would he have felt if I had said to him one day over our lonely supper table, "Father, I am far more than just Noah Banks, daughter of Parson Banks of Easthill. I am Eaving, great mother goddess of this land, inheritor of more troubles and sorcery than you could possibly imagine."

But I could not say that. I merely watched as he, too, faded away. He died in the early summer of 1646, peacefully and gently: that, at least, I could grant him. He had tried, and I had loved him in my own way.

I was left into the care of Bess Felton. Mistress Felton was . . . Oh, I suppose she was the local parish "good woman." She concerned herself in everyone's affairs, which could be a great irritant, but she aided and advised, and was a comforting presence. I certainly did not mind when she bustled me away from my father's grave into her own home (the parsonage could no longer be my home, for my right to its comforts died with my father). I could not stay there long, for Bess had her own husband, and five children, all packed into a three-roomed cottage, but Bess made me welcome and, so soon as I was seated before the grate, began to make plans to ensure my future.

How, Mistress Felton? Can you keep me from Asterion's grip? Can you show me the twisted path I must endure if all is to be well?

"We will write your mother's cousin," Mistress Felton said firmly, by which I understood her to mean *I* would write, as Mistress Felton knew no more of the alphabet than I knew of childhood playfulness and innocence. My mother's second cousin, Anne Carr, was the wife of William Russell, earl of Bedford, and reigned as the chatelaine of Woburn Abbey, one of England's great houses. All of Easthill had shared in my mother's pride in her second cousin's achievement; the parish viewed this tenuous link with the aristocracy as a great personal achievement for every one of its inhabitants.

Surely, Bess Felton thought, *Lady Bedford could find room for one small child amid all the abbey's chambers.*

So Mistress Felton set me to composing a letter, which she dictated and which I tactfully reinterpreted in my written words, and which we sent on its way.

Six weeks passed, then came a reply. Lady Bedford would be glad to have me as a companion. A textile merchant, a certain Samuel Bescamp, would be passing by Easthill in a week or so, and I was to ready myself and a small bag of possessions to sit atop Bescamp's cart of textiles for the three-day journey to Woburn Abbey.

Thus it came to pass that, having endured Mistress Felton's embraces and tears, I found myself, one bright Wednesday morning, sitting on a great pile of bolts of woolen cloth atop Bescamp's lurching cart. Bescamp himself sat at the front of the cart, with his apprentice beside him. (We were not introduced, and I realized Bescamp was a little irritated that Lady Bedford had asked him to take this detour.) I had little in the way of possessions with me: a small canvas bag with a change of underthings, a shawl against the chill, a cloak against unexpected cold, a clean apron, and a carefully knotted cloth which held my greatest possession—a gold-and-ruby bracelet.

It amazed me that this bracelet had survived three thousand years. I'd worn it as Cornelia, spoiled princess of Mesopotama. I'd worn it also as Caela, unloved wife of Edward the Confessor. And here it was again. Still gleaming, its joints sharp and tight. I'd found it two autumns ago in the parsonage's small orchard. As I walked underneath an apple tree, one of the summer's fruit fell to the ground before me. The apple split open on impact, and inside lay the bracelet.

I'd sighed, deeply (the land was not going to let me forget), then bent to retrieve it. My greatest challenge from that point on had been to keep it from prying eyes. (How could the daughter of a poor country parson explain such a fabulous jewel?)

I wondered if ever I might find a chance to wear it in this life.

We were passing through some of the most beautiful of England's countryside and, whatever this life might hold in store for me, I could not help but enjoy the chance to commune with the land. The summer's rural activities were well under way: men swung scythes in line through meadows, laying out the winter's hay for their livestock; women raked and tedded; children herded geese and ducks; the land *sunned*. I cannot think how else to describe it. The land lay underneath all this activity, and enjoyed the day as much as I did.

There was little other traffic on the lanes and byways through which we passed. Several farm laborers, a country wife or two, a stray pig grunting happily to itself as it trotted down the road. I was so relaxed I think I may have been drifting toward sleep when the sound of heavy footfalls roused me to full awareness.

I looked first to Bescamp and his apprentice. They showed no sign of hearing the footfalls, for they sat relaxed at the front of the cart, conversing in low tones.

I looked behind me—and my entire body tensed.

Running up the road behind the cart, his long strides eating the distance between us, came Long Tom.

My instant, gut reaction, was to think: *Dear Lady Moon, here comes trouble!*

Ah, I loved Long Tom, surely I did, but his presence signified nothing but woe. None of the Sidlesaghes had yet appeared to me in this life; that Long Tom did so now meant that life and trouble was waking about me.

Yet what else should I have expected? The death of my remaining parent, my removal from the village of my birth into a far more aristocratic household, and, last week, the appearance of the first of my menstrual cycles for this life, meant that I now grew into something far larger and darker than mere womanhood.

My inheritance. All of it, troubles and joys, both.

"Eaving," said Long Tom on a grunt as he grabbed at the back of the cart and hauled himself in.

Bescamp and his apprentice took no notice. Magical appearances in the back of their cart were beyond their perception and experience of life, and so Long Tom's visit passed by unnoticed.

"Long Tom," I said gravely.

Long Tom settled himself atop a wrapped bundle of silks and studied me carefully. "You grow prettier with each passing life."

"My appearance was of concern to my parents, for they, of fair aspect themselves, did not know from where they bred this darkness."

Long Tom extended one of his long arms, and his fingers lifted a braid of my dark brown hair. It had glints of copper through it, and it glowed as it caught the sunlight. Together with my pale skin and my (as always) dark-blue eyes, I knew I was an arresting sight.

"Is it time?" I said, and I am afraid my voice shook slightly.

"No." My braid fell back to my shoulder, and he withdrew his hand. "There are years to pass yet before Asterion calls. But I have come . . ."

"My womanhood is upon me," I said, referring to the beginning of my menstrual cycle.

Long Tom nodded. "It is time to talk, you and I, and this land."

I bowed my head.

"Eaving," he said, very gentle, "there can be no errors this life."

I laid my hand on my belly. Asterion's imp rested in there, waiting. It had caused me no trouble, not yet, but I knew it was a lethal nightmare, just waiting to be woken at the call of its master.

If only I had not succumbed to Asterion's sorcery in my last life. If only . . . If only . . .

"I remember you saying to me one night in the last life, when you took me underground through the Game's strange twistings," I said, "that there were many possibilities for my future lives, and that in one of them I would be Asterion's whore."

"In this life," he said, his voice horribly expressionless, "you shall achieve that."

I closed my eyes, trying not to succumb to the horror.

"You cannot escape it," he continued.

I lifted my hand away from my belly. *Thank you, Long Tom, for that piece of comfort.*

"Eaving, you *must* contend with it."

Ah, to hear that put so baldly. "And thus I will," I said, my voice a little harder than I'd meant.

"Good," said Long Tom. "I am here for both land and Game. I am here to tell you what must be achieved in this life." He paused. "Old wounds must be healed. All of them."

Now he had caught me unawares. "Old wounds?"

"The wounds caused during your first life: not those caused only by you, but those caused and suffered by everyone caught in the Game."

"The wounds between Brutus and I," I said. "And the suffering caused when Genvissa murdered my daughter."

"Aye," he said. "As well as your murder of Genvissa, and *her* daughter."

I closed my eyes briefly, my conscience stinging at the memory. Cornelia, standing atop Og's Hill, driving the knife into the heavily pregnant Genvissa's neck as she was about to complete the Game with her lover, Brutus.

"Brutus' murder of his father," Long Tom said.

"*I* cannot redeem that!"

"You must facilitate it. You must encourage it."

"And Coel's murder?" I said.

"That wound has been healed."

Of course. In our last life Coel-Harold took the life of Swanne, who was Genvissa reborn. And . . . "He and Brutus healed the rift between them in our last life," I said. "They became friends, and shared respect."

Long Tom nodded. "Wounds can be healed," he said. "They *must*. Matters must be righted between you and Brutus, between you and Genvissa-reborn, and between Brutus and his father, or else no one can move forward."

If I did not heal the rift between Genvissa and myself, then she would never hand to me her powers as Mistress of the Labyrinth. And if Brutus could not heal the guilt and tragedy of his own father's murder, then he could not move forward into what he needed to become, either.

"Wounds must be healed," I said. "What else?"

"The stag must be raised."

I drew in a sharp breath. "Is it possible?"

"Yes. He was bred in this land this life."

I found I was trembling, and I clutched my hands tight together. "Where is he?"

"In exile. But he will return."

I nodded. "If the stag is to be raised, then I must learn the dances and intricacies of the Labyrinth. I must become the Mistress of the Labyrinth."

He nodded. "But neither of these tasks, the raising of the stag, and the handing to you of the powers of Mistress of the Labyrinth, can be accomplished if the first is not achieved. Old wounds *must* be healed, Eaving. They must, for Asterion is growing powerful beyond measure. Give him another life beyond this one, and if you don't have the weapons and power needed to destroy him, then he will best you . . ."

He stopped, and took a moment to compose himself. "There is one more thing," he said.

I closed my eyes briefly. I was not sure if I wanted to hear it.

"Eaving," he said, "you have been reborn. The Stag God shall rise. There is one more who shall walk again."

I thought. I was still so much the novice as Eaving. When I'd been Caela I'd lingered in unknowing for years, and once I had known who I was, and accepted it . . . well, then I'd died all too soon. There was still so much for me to know . . . to remember . . .

"Who?" I said, hoping Long Tom would just tell me.

"The Lord of the Faerie," he said. "The one the peoples venerate as the Green Man."

And then he was gone, and I was left rigid with shock and ancient memory.

CHAPTER SIX

IDOL LANE, LONDON

E WAS A GROWN MAN NOW, THIRTY-THREE YEARS old, and successful without being flamboyant or overly noticeable within the great bustling community that was London. Weyland Orr had risen from street boy to entrepreneur essentially by becoming a procurer. Whatever it was that a man or woman wanted, then Weyland Orr could discover and deliver it. Fine linens, dainties, jewels, horse- and woman-flesh— none of it was beyond the remarkable skills of Weyland. Whatever a Londoner wanted, Weyland could deliver—so long as there was coin enough to pay at the end of the transaction.

Weyland was totally discreet. Not merely in the procuring of dreams, but in keeping himself as unnoticeable as possible. People requested, Weyland discovered and delivered, and after a day or so the customer tended to forget *who* precisely it was had procured the goods. There had been a man . . . but, oh, his face, it was too difficult to recall, and his name . . . No . . . that had gone, as well. Weyland drifted through London, discovering its secrets, indulging its whims, pandering to its excesses, and yet few ever noticed or remembered him. He was merely one of the city's more spectral inhabitants, slipping silently and unobserved through back alleys and lanes.

Jane was far better known than Weyland. He'd come to regret prostituting her so early. He'd overused her during her early years, offering her without thought to sailor and laborer and clerk alike, until a year or so previously when Weyland had noticed the early signs of the pox in her—the open sore on her forehead which would not heal, the ache in her long bones as the disease took hold. Weyland lamented the onset of this disease. Not because it made Jane suffer, and would eventually disfigure her, but Weyland did not want her to die before she managed that which he needed more than anything else in this life: to pass on the mysteries of the Labyrinth to Cornelia-reborn.

Diseased and thus useless as an earning woman, Jane no longer prostituted for Weyland, but managed the homeless, friendless girls that Weyland took from the streets. These girls Jane fed and bathed, and taught some of the sexual skills that she had learned as a Mistress of the Labyrinth, as well a woman who had managed great experience through her several lives. Once the girls were fed, cleaned, and trained, Weyland offered them to his clients, whether sailor or bishop, so long as the girls' freshness and looks lasted.

All this activity took place in a single, discreet room Weyland leased from a tavern keeper just off Cheapside. Here Weyland ate and slept, kept Jane, and worked his girls. Weyland could have afforded quarters more commodious, but for years he had preferred discretion to comfort, anonymity to open brazenness.

He was, after all, a highly cautious man, and he didn't want to bring himself to the attention of the Troy Game, which was more powerful in this life than ever before. Weyland would have vastly preferred the opulence of a palace; but that, he did not dare.

But, oh, how difficult it was to live in such close confines with Jane. Not surprisingly, Jane loathed Weyland, and her tongue was becoming more tart with each passing year (even with the beatings Weyland dealt her). It had now got to the point where Weyland had decided that it was high time to find more commodious quarters. Somewhere discreet, somewhere dark, somewhere overlooked (Weyland still meant to keep himself as unnoticeable as possible), but somewhere *larger*, where he could live separated by a wall or two from Jane.

Thus, in the autumn of 1646, Weyland set about discovering suitable accommodation for himself, Jane, whatever number of girls he had working for him at any given time, and for Cornelia-reborn—Noah—once he brought her to join them. Nothing ostentatious, nothing that might draw him to the attention of the Troy Game. Just something that had more than one room.

So as Weyland wandered the streets about his business, he also kept on alert for some unassuming, darkened house that might serve both as a prison for Jane (as well as Noah) and as a sanctuary for himself. London afforded many narrow alleys and winding, tiny lanes into which were crowded a host of tenement dwellings. Given his now not-inconsiderable resources, Weyland could have had his pick of fifty of them.

And yet none of them felt right.

Weyland had not thought he would be so fastidious. He found fault with this house, and then that, and then the one after. This one was too gloomy, this too airy; this had too many doors. After all, what was a house? A shelter, only— yet why should he care so greatly about finding the *right* shelter? To his disgust, as his hunt for a house extended into the months, Weyland found himself *dreaming* of shelter; of finding the perfect and most unexpected shelter; of falling into a space so comforting and beloved that he could finally feel safe. Contented. Fulfilled.

These dreams worried Weyland. Yearning dreams of a comforting and safe shelter were so unlike him that Weyland wondered if he'd somehow managed to fall under the influence of some dark, malign planet. *Damn it!* All he needed was something vaguely upright, with at least two rooms, and secreted down some dark alleyway.

How difficult could that be in a city composed of almost nothing else?

Finally, just when Weyland thought he would drive himself insane with the looking, he wandered down Idol Lane.

IDOL LANE WAS A NARROW, CROOKED, DARK, MAL-odorous lane in Tower Street Ward that ran from Thames Street north uphill to the junction of Tower and Little Tower Streets. It was relatively insignificant, save that halfway up the lane bordered the jumbled buildings and churchyard of St. Dunstan's-in-the-East; everything else in the lane was either dank warehouse or tumbledown tenement. Barely nine feet wide, the lane was cobbled with slippery, slime-covered stones and existed in a permanent state of semi-darkness as both the church buildings and warehouses reared so high into the sky that all sunlight was effectively blocked out.

As it was, the lane was much the same as hundreds of other malodorous, narrow lanes in the city, and as he stepped into it Weyland did not give it much thought. He was due to meet with a wealthy wool merchant in the church nave who required a small item that no one but Weyland could procure for him.

That the small item had needed to be stolen from the bedchamber of one of the great nobles in the realm had vastly increased its already not-inconsiderable value, and Weyland was looking forward to a payment that would—should he ever find the right house—furnish his new home quite nicely.

Weyland slipped into the churchyard and then through a small door in the northern face of the church into the nave. St. Dunstan's-in-the-East once had been a quite magnificent church but was now greatly decayed. Its once beautiful floor of luminous green tiles was marred with a myriad of cracks. The banners hanging from the ceiling were moth-eaten and so faded their armorial shields were impossible to read. Two of the stained-glass windows were broken. Most of the golden plate from the altar been pawned, and the majority of the stone memorials and tombs in the church (of which there were close to a hundred) were water-stained and crumbled.

Weyland hated it the instant he stepped inside. The church was unbearably dismal, and he resolved to have done with his business as quickly as he might.

The wool merchant was waiting as planned in a side chapel.

"You have it?" the merchant asked as Weyland joined him.

"Aye," Weyland said. "You have the coin?"

The merchant grimaced, as if he found the subject of money repellent. That annoyed Weyland, for how else had this merchant managed to scrabble together enough for his stolen bauble if not by money-dealing?

"Aye," the merchant mumbled.

"Give it to me," said Weyland.

"Show *it* to me," said the merchant.

Weyland sighed, but drew from a pocket a small leather-wrapped bundle. Glancing about to make sure they were unobserved, Weyland unfolded the leather, and showed the merchant that which he craved—a stunning ruby ring which the merchant wanted to give to his nubile young lover.

His eyes unable to remove themselves from the ring with which he would purchase a few short nights in his lover's bed, the merchant unclipped his purse and tipped a pile of gold coins into Weyland's outstretched hand.

"Don't spend it all at once," the merchant said, snatching the ring from Weyland's other hand.

"I need to purchase a house," said Weyland. "No doubt this shall prove more than useful for the purpose."

That comment finally drew the merchant's eyes from ring to Weyland's face. "You? A house?" The merchant gave a small mirthless chuckle. "What do *your* sort need with houses? All you need is a rat-hole, surely."

Weyland's mouth thinned, but before he could retort the merchant continued.

"Use the money to buy the godforsaken ruin attached to the bone house of this church. It's no idyll, to be sure, but it has enough damp spots and shadowy corners within which to hide your deceitfulness."

And then he was gone, and Weyland was left standing, looking at the spot where he'd been, his mouth open in astonishment.

It's no idyll, to be sure, but it has enough damp spots and shadowy corners within which to hide your deceitfulness.

Weyland did not know what it was about those words, but *something* about them called to him. He stood a moment longer, then he strode out the church and turned right up Idol Lane to the jumble of buildings that had once housed the medieval monks of St. Dunstan's.

They were all built solidly enough—made of stone, which in a city of timbered houses was unusual enough—if showing evidence of the same decay that the church itself did. At the extreme northern boundary of the church buildings stood the bone house where the clergy of St. Dunstan's stored the bones they dug up from their increasingly full churchyard.

The northern wall of the bone house abutted onto a four-storied house made of the same stone as the rest of the church and outbuildings. A small alleyway ran down the northern side of the house. Weyland had no idea to what purpose the house had once been put, but now it had an air of neglect and loneliness that bespoke its emptiness.

No doubt the clergy of St. Dunstan's wished to sell it to raise enough money for repairs to the church itself.

Weyland walked slowly to the front door and turned the handle.

It opened, and he walked inside.

The door opened directly into a large, unfurnished, and dusty parlor which Weyland could see then led into a kitchen. Three paces away from the door rose a staircase, and it was to this that Weyland walked. Hesitating a moment at its base—briefly laying a hand against the shared wall with the bone house to feel the souls lost and moaning on its other side—Weyland climbed the stairs.

HE DID NOT COME DOWN FOR OVER FIVE HOURS, and when he did, it was to walk directly out the door and back down Idol Lane to the church to open negotiations with the vicar.

Chapter Seven

Elizabeth Castle, Jersey

October 1649

ROM JERSEY, CHARLES HAD GONE TO FRANCE, wandered through parts of the Netherlands, and then in the late summer of 1649 he had returned to Jersey. He had wanted to go home, home to England, but now only this small island was all that remained of his kingdom. Yes, *his* kingdom now, for Parliament had taken his father on a cold January day to an even colder block, and there, to the accompaniment of the groans of the watching crowd, taken from him his head. Charles had been in the Netherlands, and had learned of his father's death only when his chaplain, Stephen Goffe, had entered the chamber and said, haltingly, "Majesty . . ." before bursting into tears.

The crown was his, but it was a fragile and ephemeral thing. What use a crown with no realm? Parliament had gone mad, declared a Commonwealth, abolished the monarchy, and Charles was left with nothing save the memories and ambitions of several lives, and the knowledge that it was likely Asterion who had caused all of this. Charles had thought of invasion, but there was little hope of that. He had no monies with which to raise an army (he had hardly the monies to feed himself and his companions), and, besides, he knew that England was sick of war and would not tolerate yet another.

So Charles had come back to Jersey if only for the reason that it was the closest he could come to his land and to London.

In Jersey, Charles loitered in chamber and hall, grew another three inches, rode to the hunt, made love to Marguerite, and, in his most despairing of moments, listened to the bravado of his courtiers and advisers as they plotted and planned about him: Invade through Scotland, through Ireland, invoke the aid of the French, the Dutch, and even the faeries, if they could help.

Nothing could aid him against Asterion. Nothing, save his own wits.

In July of 1649 Charles was seated in his private chamber within Elizabeth Castle. The sun streamed in through the windows, and Charles thought idly that perhaps he could make use of this autumn sunshine and call for his horse and ride along the cliff-tops, listening to the screaming of the seagulls and pretend that they were the screams of his supporters, or the cheers of the Londoners as they welcomed him back into his city and his heritage, or even the acclaim of the assembled nobility (those who had survived Parliament's hatred) as the archbishop of Canterbury lowered the crown to his head in Westminster Abbey.

His mind shied away from what had happened the last time an archbishop had laid the crown on his head.

Charles was almost completely lost in his daydreams of restoration when there was a discreet knock at the door, and Sir Edward Hyde, friend, supporter, and counselor, entered.

"Aye?" said Charles.

"Majesty," said Hyde, who always managed to make that word sound something other than cynically pointless. He inclined his head, one knee slightly bent, and managed to make that action look truly deferential instead of stupidly pointless.

"What is it?" said Charles.

"There is a man who came across from France yesterday, Majesty. He claims to bear a message for you, for your ears only."

Charles raised an eyebrow.

"He has no weapon, majesty, and no poisons secreted about his person or clothes. He is well-spoken and -bred, although he bears but a common name and a base ancestry."

"And that is . . . ?"

"Louis de Silva, bastard son of the marquis de Lonquefort."

Charles started to shrug in disinterest, but then paused. "De Silva?" *Of the forest?*

"Aye."

"Tell me of him—his appearance, his aspect, his humor."

"He is of your age, and as dark, although not so well built, nor with your height. He speaks well, in quiet and pleasing tones. He has the eyes of a poet . . . and the impatience of one, too."

Charles very slowly smiled, and for a moment Hyde thought he'd never seen his young king look happier.

"Then send him in, my friend. Send him in!"

* * *

HYDE HAD ONLY TO STEP TO THE DOOR AND MUR-
mur a few words to admit the man: Hyde must have been certain of Charles's
reaction.

As soon as Louis de Silva had entered, Hyde exited, closing the door behind him.

De Silva stared at the young king sitting on the chest by the window, then
he bowed, deep and formal, sweeping off the hat from his head so that it
brushed the floor.

"Charles," he said. "Majesty."

Charles rose slowly, looking intently at the newcomer. The man had dark
hair, as dark as Charles's own, but straight, and worn much shorter, slicked
back from his face. His build was less muscular than Charles's own, but
nonetheless gave the impression of wiry strength and grace, as if he would be
as useful on the dance floor as on the battlefield. His hands, where they
emerged from the lace cuffs of his doublet, were long and slender, yet with the
same implied strength as his build and bearing.

De Silva was a stunning man, not simply in his dark, fine-boned handsomeness or in his graceful carriage, but in the depth of his dark eyes, and the
wildness that lurked there.

De Silva . . . of the forest.

Louis de Silva watched Charles stare at him, and then he slowly smiled.
"Greetings, Brutus," he said.

Charles took a halting step forward, then another, and then one more before he embraced de Silva fiercely. "Oh, gods, I am glad you are here!" He
pulled back, and took de Silva's face between his hands. "Poet Coel? Is that
you I see in there?"

"Who else?" said de Silva.

For a moment both men stared at each other, then they burst into laughter,
and embraced once more, even more fiercely than previously.

"I had not believed that Asterion could be bested until now, this moment,
when I laid eyes on you," Louis de Silva said, finally pulling back.

"Careful," Charles said, and laid a hand on Louis's mouth. "Words are
powerful, and they can also be enemies."

"But not you and I, not anymore."

"We were not enemies in our last life, Louis. Not then, and most certainly
not now."

Again they stared at each other, hands resting on each other's shoulders,
wordless, their eyes brimming with tears.

"Who else?" said Louis eventually, and Charles knew instantly what he
meant.

"Mother Ecub is here with me," he said, and then grinned at the expression on Louis face. "A *younger* Mother Ecub, called Marguerite Carteret now, and the delectable daughter of the governor of this island."

"Delectable? You have *tasted* her? *Mother Ecub?*"

"Why is it you always think me old, and arthritic?" said a woman's voice from the doorway, and Charles and Louis turned to see the woman who stood there.

Marguerite entered, closed the door, and curtsied prettily first to Charles and then to Louis. "Demure and sensible, and always at service," she murmured, and Louis chuckled, stepped forward, and kissed her hand.

"The first among Eaving's Sisters," he said, all humor now gone from his voice, and Marguerite shuddered at the depth and blackness in his eyes. "Where is she, Marguerite?"

"We don't know precisely," Marguerite said. "She is in England, but further than that . . ." She shrugged.

"Is she with Asterion?" said Louis.

Charles shook his head. "We would have felt it," he said. "All of us."

Louis sighed. "Any others?" he said.

Charles and Marguerite exchanged glances.

"Well?" Louis snapped. "Who?"

"Loth is back," said Marguerite.

"Born my younger brother," Charles said.

"James?" said Louis. "The duke of York?"

Charles nodded. "Aye." He paused, and looked at Louis steadily. "He calls me Brutus, and hates me."

Louis's mouth slowly dropped open. "He doesn't . . . ?"

"You will meet him soon enough, and judge for yourself," said Marguerite. "He came to Jersey recently, although he now says he wants to return to France and to his mother."

"He has . . ." Charles said slowly, as if he had to force the words out. "He has taken greatly to Catholic priests."

If possible, Louis's jaw dropped even further open. "Christianity? *Loth?*"

"Charles and I think," Marguerite said, taking Charles's hand, a gesture that Louis did not miss, "that perhaps he has lost purpose."

"Or has had it lost for him," said Charles.

"What do you mean?" said Louis.

"That perhaps the Game has no more use for him."

Louis raised his eyebrows, blowing out the breath slowly from his cheeks. "I still cannot reconcile the idea of Loth, taking to Christianity."

"Is that idea any stranger than what some of us have taken to?" asked Charles with a grin, and Louis smiled back.

"No, I suppose not."

Charles waved Louis to a chair, then sat back down on the chest under the window, Marguerite beside him. "Genvissa?" he said, once Louis had seated himself.

Louis shrugged. "I have no interest. I cannot bear the thought of her. No. I do not know where she is, or what her estate. I imagine that she has found herself a comfortable magnate to take her as wife, and that she lives somewhere in London, in comfort, and plotting with . . . well, with whomever suits her purpose for the moment."

"We are merely glad she has not yet touched our lives," said Marguerite.

At that Charles leaned forward, changing the subject, and thus they sat for many hours, talking of this and that, renewing friendship, and staying away from the one subject that ate at all three of them.

Cornelia, where was she? *How* was she?

Chapter Eight

Elizabeth Castle, Jersey

MARGUERITE TOSSED IN HER SLEEP. IT WAS A warm night, and Charles more than half lay over her, but neither the oppressive heat nor her lover's weight caused her restlessness.

Instead, Marguerite dreamed of Pen Hill, where, during her last life, she'd spent so much time as prioress of St. Margaret the Martyr.

At least, Marguerite *thought* this was Pen Hill.

It was of a similar height and aspect, with the same gentle rounded grassy knoll ringed by the standing stones (Sidlesaghes). But the hill did not overlook London, as had Pen Hill, and there was something very different about the stones, and Marguerite knew she had to concentrate on them.

Pen Hill had a score or more of stones on its peak, but now that Marguerite focused, she saw that this hill only had two stones, standing on opposite edges of the summit. Marguerite could feel the wind rush through them, and she knew she was being shown the rushing of this wind for some reason.

Something changed. A third stone materialized at the edge of the knoll, and the two stones already there somehow shifted their position so that there was now an equidistance between all three.

The wind no longer rushed through.

The dream stilled, and Marguerite knew that at this point an understanding was being demanded of her.

The wind no longer rushed through.

Where two stones had formed no barrier at all, the presence of a third *had* formed a barrier. The wind no longer rushed through, but was contained within the grassy knoll.

Contained within the circle of the stones.

Two cannot form a circle.

Three can.

The wind was power . . . held within the Circle.

Marguerite gasped, her body jerking in its sleep so that Charles murmured and shifted.

Now something was happening within the Circle on the hill. Something momentous.

Something in the grass.

Something in the *turf*.

A face was forming . . . a girl's face on the verge of womanhood.

Marguerite woke with a half-shriek, sitting up so abruptly that Charles rolled away to the other side of the vast bed.

"Gods, Marguerite . . . what's—"

"Get Louis," she said. "Get him *now!*"

Charles slid out of the bed and stood, staring at her. "Marguerite?"

"Get Louis. *Now*. Please, Charles, please. Get him now!"

He gave her one more uncomprehending look, then he strode to the door, flung it open, and shouted his valet awake. "Fetch Monsieur de Silva. Now! Fetch him to this chamber!"

When Louis entered the chamber, confused, more than a little concerned, and still blinking away the sleep from his eyes, he saw that Charles stood naked by the shuttered window, staring at the bed where sat Marguerite, similarly naked.

"Thank the gods," she said as Louis closed the door behind him.

"Charles?" said Louis.

Charles shrugged. "Marguerite will not tell me what ails her. She insisted you come to this chamber."

Marguerite made a gesture of impatience. "I know how to reach Cornelia," she said.

"*What?*" said both men together, each taking a step toward the bed.

"We have a hill," said Marguerite, patting the bed. "And Louis makes the third we need to form a Circle. James would never have done. But Louis will."

Now the men looked at each other, bewildered.

"A Circle," said Marguerite. "A Circle of power, drawn from the land itself."

The men continued to stare at her, then Charles's face, finally, showed some comprehension. "The turf . . ." he said.

"Aye," said Marguerite. "That piece of turf. Where is it?"

"Where is *what*?" said Louis.

"This," said Charles, who bent down to a chest, opened it, and pulled forth a small box. "When I was forced to flee England, I brought this with me." He opened the box, and held it out.

Louis walked over, looking inside where lay a lump of browned turf still attached to a clod of crumbly dirt.

Louis lifted his eyes to Charles. "England."

"The *land*," said Charles. "Aye."

"We form a Circle on this bed, this hill," said Marguerite, again patting the sheets, "and we use the turf, the *land*, to find Cornelia-reborn."

Louis looked uncertain. "Are you sure that *I* should be here . . ."

"Never more sure," said Marguerite. "You are welcomed among us, Louis."

"But the land, its power . . . I am not . . ."

"It was the *land* which showed me the way, Louis," she said. "The land was waiting for you to join us."

"You have as much right to touch Cornelia-reborn as any of us, Louis," Charles said very gently. "Marguerite is right. The land waited only for you to join us before it showed Marguerite the way."

Louis sighed, then nodded. "What is this Circle, then?"

"It is the living embodiment of the Stone Dances," Marguerite said. "It commands the same power."

"And as prime among Eaving's Sisters, and the one who watched over Pen Hill in our last life," said Charles, "you are the one to lead the Circle."

"Yes," she said. "Louis, you shall need to disrobe. We come into this naked, as do the stones. Charles, bring me the box."

Louis removed his shoes, then shrugged off his hastily donned shirt and breeches, dropped them to the floor, then walked naked to the bed, climbed into it, and sat cross-legged where Marguerite indicated.

She and Charles also sat, cross-legged, equidistant from Louis and each other, and Marguerite took the box, opened it, and removed the turf.

Taking a deep breath, she held it reverently in her hands, then suddenly cast it upward, toward the ceiling, calling out at the same time a word that the two men could not quite make out.

The turf hit the plaster with a distinct thud, then fell back toward the bed and, as it did so, transformed.

Marguerite, Charles, and Louis gasped. The turf shimmered, then flattened and expanded all at once until it became a large circle of lustrous emerald-green silk, fluttering gently toward the bed.

It settled in the center of the Circle, stilled for a single heartbeat, and then began to rumple, rising and falling into hills and valleys, moors and fields, until it represented a relief of the land of England.

Marguerite reached out a hand. It trembled a little, and she had to clutch it momentarily in order to still it. Then she said, "Eaving? Eaving? Where are you?"

The emerald silk again moved, now forming a lake, and then it shimmered once more, and its surface became opaque, then clear until an image formed within it.

A great house that sat nestled in rolling hills.

"Woburn Abbey," Charles said.

"You know it?" said Louis.

Charles nodded. "Aye. I've been there twice as a child. Woburn Abbey is home to the earls of Bedford. Gods . . . *Eaving?* Are you there?"

Again the silk shimmered, and the image of the house rushed toward them until a single window occupied the entire silken lake, and in the window . . . in that window . . .

In that window a girl of some sixteen years lay in a bed. As if she felt the weight of their regard, she woke, and rose so that she sat staring out of the window. She was beautiful, her heavy hair framing a face made almost luminous by its pale, translucent skin, and containing the most wondrous pair of deep-blue eyes.

Her mouth moved, forming soundless words, but each of the three watchers heard them in their minds.

Brutus? Brutus? Is that you, Brutus?

THE IMAGE FADED, AND CHARLES PUT HIS FACE INTO his hands, and groaned.

Marguerite hesitated, then picked up the silk and folded it into a tiny square in her hands where, once again, it became the piece of browned turf and crumbled soil.

They sat a very long time in silence, each lost in his own thoughts, until finally Charles stirred himself.

"She is in Woburn Abbey in Bedfordshire," he said.

"Far from London," said Louis.

"Far from Asterion," said Marguerite. "For now."

She put the turf back in its box, put the box into the center of the Circle they still formed, and for the rest of the night they sat there, staring at it, their thoughts filled with Eaving.

Chapter Nine

WOBURN ABBEY, BEDFORDSHIRE

Noah Speaks

*A*H, GODS, TO WAKE UP AND FEEL HIM STARING
through the window at me! Not even Asterion suddenly appearing
all leering and lecherous beneath the sheets could have killed the
joy of that single, fleeting moment.

I felt Mother Ecub there, too, and Coel. All three of them, close, bonded
with a deep friendship and loyalty and something else . . . a sexual intimacy, I
think. Their shared closeness reached out and touched me, comforted me.
Their care enveloped me, nurtured me. All in that instant.

But of all of it, of all that love and care and intimacy that had reached me,
what I remembered long into the night as I sat there in my third-floor bedroom, arms about my knees, was how Brutus had felt as his presence had
merged so fleetingly with mine. He felt . . . Oh, I don't know. *Distant* perhaps,
but then Brutus was always distant. *Uncertain,* and that was something new.
Unsure, and that heartened me.

I sat there through the long night, my arms wrapped about my legs, my
chin resting on my knees, and wept for sheer joy.

I HAD BEEN THREE YEARS AT WOBURN ABBEY, AND IT
had been a good three years for me. Lady Anne, the countess of Bedford, was
a kind woman, if a trifle reserved to the point where she sometimes gave the
entirely wrong impression of distance. But she was kindhearted and she loved
me in her own way, and had accepted this poor, distant cousin into her family
as one of her own.

She put me to school with her children where I tried not to befuddle the tutor, the Reverend John Thornton, with my knowledge of history, as well as several ancient languages. Lady Anne had dressed me in clothes that her own children wore: sober clothing during my early years with her, but now, in my seventeenth year, she allowed me more brightly colored and daringly cut textiles. I loved the clothes! Oh, this was Cornelia emerging all over again, and I did not begrudge her this delight: the stiff-boned bodices, the full skirts, the embroideries, the silks and satins, the cascading lace of chemises and underskirts, and the delightful brocaded slippers with their daring scarlet heels. Cornelia reveled, and so did I, for which I felt no guilt. The earl and his wife were Protestants, and toed the public line when it came to parliamentary-imposed Puritan prudery, but at home, among friends, they still delighted in rich fabrics and the occasional daring neckline. The ivory swell of breast by candlelight was still an indulgence much appreciated by the earl, and I (as Lady Anne) was not one to deny him it.

As I had grown older, beyond the reach of childhood, I would sit with the earl and the countess at night, often with John Thornton joining us, and enjoyed the conversation. I remember one night arguing the point that a saint may be canonized for his good works and service to the Church, but none of that mattered when he remained a tyrant at home.

That night we had been discussing Edward the Confessor, and I suppose that both the Bedfords and Thornton were a little put-out by my vehemence.

As I grew older I became Lady Anne's companion. Not quite one of the intimate family, but much closer than a servant. I ate with the family, was educated with the family, and traveled with the family on their various excursions about their estates, and to the estates and house parties of their neighbours.

But not to London. When the earl and countess made the occasional trip (and it *was* occasional, now that the king was dead, and his heir exiled) to their London townhouse, I always made the excuse to remain behind. To watch over one of the babies, perhaps, or to attend to one of the more difficult Latin translations that John Thornton had set me. I know this irritated Lady Anne and her husband, but there was little I could do about that.

I could not go to London. Not with Asterion undoubtedly haunting its streets and byways.

I might avoid London, but over the years, and particularly since Long Tom came to me on my journey to Woburn, I had come to terms with what my fate would be.

Asterion's whore. So be it. I could accept that, I could use it, and I would not allow it to defeat me. I had seen how Genvissa-reborn, Swanne, had allowed it to consume her in our previous life, and I had learned from her error.

The Minotaur (and his dreadful imp) might choose to dictate the boundaries of my life, but they did not own me, and they could not touch who I essentially was: *Eaving*.

That Asterion's imp lived inside my womb in this life was undoubted. It was quiescent, but I could feel its *life* inside me, like some dark child. Caela had not realized its presence, but I did. My monthly cycles were bloody and painful: Asterion's curse, I had no doubt. But I did not allow those to defeat me; I did not allow them to depress me. Instead, I embraced them. *I was Eaving, and I would survive.*

I knew what I had to do. Long Tom had been very clear on that point. I had to make amends with both Brutus and Genvissa-reborn, and I had to learn the duties and steps of the Mistress of the Labyrinth.

Those amends would be difficult, and in their own way I dreaded them, but that other thing that Long Tom had told me—that the Lord of the Faerie would walk once more—delighted me beyond measure. The Lord of the Faerie was an ancient memory bequeathed to me by Mag. From her memories I knew that Mag had never met him during her long lifetime, but she certainly had known about him, and because I now carried her knowledge, so also did I. Both myself and my lover reborn as the Stag God were citizens of two worlds: this mortal one, but also the Faerie world. When the Sidlesaghes had taken myself and Harold to the water cathedral, there to meet and talk with Mag, they had taken us through the Realm of the Faerie to the very borderlands of this life and the next. The Sidlesaghes themselves were inhabitants of both worlds, mortal and Faerie, but more creature of Faerie than mortal.

I—as also the soon-to-rise Stag God—draw most of our power and knowledge and comfort from the Realm of the Faerie. It is our nourishment, and our ultimate home.

The Realm of the Faerie is ruled over by that strange creature known as the Lord of the Faerie. The Lord of the Faerie was not exactly my lord and master, but he was most certainly my senior, and I would owe to him both deference and respect.

As I grew in Woburn Abbey, and reveled in the peace and stillness, I tried to recall all I could of the Lord of the Faerie from Mag's memories. He had not walked during her lifetime, nor during that of three or four of her predecessors. The Lord of the Faerie was ancient beyond measure, a part of the primeval earth, a being who had literally grown with the island of Great Britain, and was one with it as neither myself nor the Stag God could be.

The Lord of the Faerie was magic beyond knowing—if you can describe that strange power of the faerie as "magic," which is such a cumbersome and overused word. Even thinking about the Lord of the Faerie and his eventual rise made my spine tingle. Every time thoughts of Asterion depressed me, I only had to turn my mind to the Lord of the Faerie, to that wonderful day when I might finally meet with him face-to-face, and I would rise from my misery, and smile.

Apart from what Long Tom had told me, there was one other duty for me to accomplish. Something I needed to realize in order to achieve my full power and understanding as Eaving.

A duty which pleased me very, very much.

I sat through that night when Brutus, Coel, and Ecub had reached out to me, and while I thought on Brutus most of the time, and what lay ahead of us through this lifetime, I also thought on the intimacy that I had felt between the three of them. I envied them that intimacy, both sexual and emotional, and it made me realize that, as Eaving, there was something I needed to do so I could truly fulfill my potential and give me the strength to survive whatever Asterion had awaiting me.

An easy task, and not one I would mismanage as I had done when I was Caela.

Thus it was, that harvest season of 1649, I took myself a lover.

CHAPTER TEN

WOBURN ABBEY, BEDFORDSHIRE

ONE OF THE REVEREND JOHN THORNTON'S FA-
vorite rituals was to sit by his window, all but one of the candles ex-
tinguished in his chamber, and watch the night settle over Woburn
Park as he sipped a small glass of wine. It relaxed him for his bed, enabling his
mind to let go the myriad little worries and irritations that had beset it during
the day: one of the children refused to pay attention; the eldest son, Francis,
was weaker than usual and unable to attend his studies; the new translation of
Machiavelli (never to be displayed in the schoolroom) had yet to arrive even
though he'd ordered it six months past; and Noah Banks . . .

Noah Banks. Invariably, during this nightly peaceful ritual, Thornton found
his mind returning to the strange girl-woman that the countess had brought
into the household. Noah was a insolvable puzzle. How had she become so
learned in ancient languages and in history and the manner of conquerors and
saints, when, by all accounts, her father had barely enough learning to write
his sermons each week, and her mother could only sign her name with a cross?
From where had she received her wit and her perception?

And at such a young age?

She was sixteen years old, yet she had the maturity and demeanor of a
woman far older. During his thirty-two years Thornton had met women who,
although young, had been old far beyond their years. Women who had suffered, woman who had been debased—the wretched of street and alleyway.
These women wore their experience and knowledge poorly; hardness glittered
from their eyes, and spilled in brittle and bitter words from their mouths.
These were women who had been spoiled; not allowed to ease from innocence
into experienced womanhood with gentleness and guidance of either a parental
or spousal hand.

Noah Banks was not one of these hard, ruined women. She wore her experience and knowledge easily. It did not emerge in her demeanor as co-quettishness, which Thornton would have despised, or as pride, which he would have loathed even more thoroughly, but as a deep peacefulness of which he was—he sighed, admitting it to himself—deeply envious.

She was a girl (*a woman*) who Thornton suspected had such boundless compassion combined with her strange store of knowledge and experience that she would, to whoever loved her, become an endless source of comfort.

Of shelter.

Thornton slouched in the wooden chair, his half-drunk glass of wine resting on his chest. This was a rare moment of relaxation for him. The Reverend Thornton was a man who never relaxed in another's company, only in his own. He was a tall man, his long legs now stretched out before him, crossed at their ankles, with shoulder-length wavy dark-brown hair worn swept back from his brow. He had a thin humorous mouth, and dark eyes that sparkled with what might appear to be mischief—save that Thornton so habitually clothed himself in the dark tones of Puritan garb that the humor of his mouth and the mischief of his eyes was (thankfully, for the reverend's public persona) quite obscured and shadowed. Thornton had dedicated himself to God and to instructing the knowledge of God into his young charges; his humor and mischief he tried to bury or to ignore.

Now, relaxed, at ease, Thornton's eyes drifted lazily over the deep twilight outside. The rolling hills of the park were almost completely obscured: the still of the gathering night broken only by the movement of a small group of deer toward the shelter of a stand of great oaks, and the haunting cry of an owl, out hunting mice and kittens.

There was a movement—the sudden sweep of the owl's wings as it launched itself from one of the trees—and Thornton sighed, and sipped his wine.

Outside, the only reminder of the day past was the line of gentle light sinking across the horizon of the hills. It was a beautiful sight, peaceful and powerful, and Thornton imagined for a moment that the land was about to rise up and reach out to him, seeping in through the window until it embraced him and made him part of its earthiness . . .

"Do you feel it, John?" she said, and her voice seemed so much a part of the gathering night and of the gentle landscape beyond the windows, that Thornton was not perturbed, nor even overly surprised, to hear her speak, here, within the inner sanctum of his private chambers.

He turned his head, slowly, almost lazily, but otherwise did not move.

She was standing a pace or two inside the door, and Thornton, so given over to the magic of the twilit landscape, found himself thinking that she had not entered the chamber as any mortal person would have done, through the door, but had instead just materialized where now she stood, just as the night slowly fell outside without any discernible movement of arrival.

Then his reserve roared to the fore.

"Noah!" Thornton said, rising so abruptly from his chair that the remnants of his wine spilled from the glass. He suddenly realized that he stood before her in bare feet, clad only in breeches and a linen shirt that he'd unbuttoned in the warmth of the night, and he almost dropped the glass in his haste to set it to one side so he could pull the shirt closed about his chest.

"John," she said, and smiled.

It was very gentle, that smile, and so unexpected in a sixteen-year-old girl, so comforting, so *deep*, that Thornton's hands stilled as they fumbled at the shirt.

Noah was still dressed as she had been this evening, when she'd sat with Thornton and the earl and countess for an hour after supper. In the past year she'd taken to wearing the costume of a woman rather than a girl, and this evening she was wearing one of her favorite costumes: a full skirt of green silk topped with a bodice of green-and-ivory–striped silk, its square neckline low-cut over the swell of her breasts, the lacy cuffs of her chemise tumbling from its elbow-length sleeves. On most sixteen-year-old girls the costume would have looked ridiculously and horribly provocative, but on Noah it looked perfect, perhaps because she eschewed the overbearing ringleted hairstyle so beloved of women of fashion, and wore her sleek dark hair loosely piled atop the crown of her head where it made an outfit that would otherwise have been overly flirtatious and almost insulting to Noah's youth, merely an adornment to the beauty of the girl herself.

"The land," she said, her head inclining very slightly toward the window. "Do you feel it?'

"What?" he said, stupidly.

By the Lord, what would happen if the earl or countess discovered their charge in his room? What if a servant happened by, and heard Noah's warm, rich voice issuing forth from beneath the door?

He knew he should be demanding she leave. He knew he should be furiously stoking the fires of his indignant anger, of his moral outrage . . . of his concern for *her* innocence, for sweet Jesus' sake, but Thornton could do none of this.

He could only stand, and stare at her.

"The land," she said yet again, and he marveled at how calm her voice was; how assured. "You were sitting in the chair, being at one with the land. It is why I am here."

"Noah . . ."

She walked forward, as if her presence within his chamber were the most natural and expected thing, until she stood directly before Thornton, then she turned calmly about, and presented her back to him.

If she had had been coquettish, if she had been hard, or abrasive, if she had shown wantonness or lewdness, if she had shown herself to be overly practiced . . . if Noah had done or shown any of these things, Thornton would have found it easy to open his mouth and speak scathing or condemnatory words, or perhaps to have taken her arm in a gentle hand, and spoken to her words of wise caution as he escorted her to the door (and, in both instances, to have presented the earl with his regretful resignation in the morning).

Instead, he found himself staring transfixed as his hand, moving as if it were controlled by a mind other than his own, raised itself to the bare skin of her shoulders above the neckline of her bodice, and rested itself there, its palm flat against her soft warmth.

She drew in a slow, deep breath, her head tilting back very slightly, and Thornton heard joy in that breath. He moved his hand across the rise at the back of her neck, where the column of her neck joined her shoulders, and realized that he was caressing her.

And then realized that his other hand had raised itself to the laces of her bodice and was pulling them loose, one by one.

One of her hands raised itself, as if to pull at the sleeve of the bodice.

"No," he whispered, and, kissing the back of her neck with a soft, gentle mouth, pulled her bodice free himself.

She caught it the instant before it fell to the floor, and draped it over a nearby coffer.

Her chemise was made of a very fine linen, a lawn, and Thornton could see the gleam of her skin through it.

Sweet Jesus, her skin . . . it glows in the night, as if it were lit within by a soft ivory fire.

Then the chemise was unlaced, seemingly of its own accord, and was falling away, and Thornton's hands had slipped about her body, and were now caressing her breasts.

She turned within the circle of his arms, and lifted her face for his kiss.

Her breasts brushed against the skin of his chest, and Thornton groaned as he bent down to her, and kissed her with more abandon and passion than he had ever thought himself capable of.

"Do I taste foul to you?" she said, pulling her mouth away just enough to speak the words.

"Foul?" he said. "How could that be?"

"A man said to me once, as he kissed me, that he could taste the foulness of corruption in my mouth."

"I taste no foulness," he said, and it was true, for he could taste many things in her mouth—warmth, comfort, tenderness, knowledge beyond knowing, peace—and not one of them was in any manner a close cousin to foulness.

"John Thornton," she said as his mouth slipped down her neck, and his hands fumbled with the ties first of her skirt and then of her underskirt, "you are a very good man, which is why I am here."

Suddenly everything seemed *right* in John Thornton's mind: why she was here, and why he reacted to her with as much abandonment and lack of care as he did. He felt somehow privileged, and graced by the privilege she bestowed upon him.

He did not feel like the earl's trusted tutor, taking terrible advantage of one of his charges.

He did not feel like a man of God who had abandoned every tenet of his belief and righteousness at the first sight (*taste and feel*) of a tender, swelling breast.

She was unclothed now, and Thornton pulled back from her so he could disrobe. She smiled as his clothes fell away, and pulled him back to her, and she did not seem perturbed or frightened by the feel of his hardness against her belly, and *he* did not feel perturbed at her lack of fear of his nakedness and arousal.

He sighed, content, and lifted her to the bed.

Thornton had slept with two women in his thirty-two years. The first woman had been the kind of woman he both despised and feared: a hard, brazen woman, a widow, who took into her bed young students from the nearby Cambridge colleges for a few pennies scattered across the sheets once they had done.

He had gone to her three times, driven by the rising, almost uncontrollable desires of youth, and he had despised himself far more than he did her as he'd risen hastily from her bed and self-consciously tossed the pennies on the sheets.

The second woman Thornton had lain with was another widow, but this time a woman that Thornton had hoped to wed. He'd been twenty-five, newly graduated but not yet a full member of the Church of England—she, twenty-nine—and they had spent a few months in the summer believing that perhaps they had a future together. Their two brief, hurried couplings had been cumbersome, awkward and guilt-ridden, and likely had been the reason the woman and Thornton had decided, finally, to go their separate ways.

But this, *this*, this was the first time in his life that Thornton felt as if his sexual union with a woman was also a complete union of body and soul with another human being. There was no awkwardness for either of them, not even in her virginity: no fumbling, no guilt, no desperation.

Only sweetness, joy, and a warmth and comfort that Thornton had never imagined could exist.

All this, he wondered at one moment, as she arched her body into his, and laughed, and told him how wonderful he was, *in a girl only sixteen*.

But, oh, in sinking into her he felt as if he sank into generations. It was as if he were being invited home after years spent wandering lost, as if he had found *himself* deep within her.

"John Thornton," she whispered to him as she caught at his hips with her hands, and encouraged him into a slower and deeper rhythm, "do you feel it?"

And yes, he did feel it. He felt the rise and fall of the land as it rolled away over hill and dale, he felt the joy in the waters of the streams and lakes as they tossed and turned under the sway of the moon, he felt the blessed peace of the night give way to the gentle joy of the morning, and then slip away again into twilight and mystery.

And he felt her, *all* of her, and knew that there was nothing else awaiting him in this life that would give him any greater sense of joy and blessing than this woman could.

LATER, WHEN THEY LAY QUIETLY SIDE BY SIDE, HE kissed the beauty of her shoulder and said, "Be my wife." What more could he ask but that she be beside him, and be the mother of his children?

"I cannot," she said.

"Why?"

She did not immediately reply, and Thornton felt for the first time a great sadness within her.

"I would destroy you," she whispered, "for eventually I would have to leave you."

And he could see how that would be so. If she married him, and then left him, it would destroy him so completely she might as well have stabbed him deep within the heart before she had walked out the door.

"I will be your lover for a while," she said.

"It will be enough," he said, knowing it never would be, but that he would need to content himself with it.

She sighed, and rolled over so that she faced him, and took his face between her hands.

"Can you feel it, John Thornton?" she said again, and he could, as before: the rise and fall of the land, and all the strange faerie creatures that were somehow associated with this woman, and he knew that she was no real woman at all, but a rare, magical being who had, for whatever reason, decided to stay awhile at Woburn Abbey, and there, to bless his life with her presence.

"Be my lover," she said, and he nodded, the movement brushing his mouth against hers.

"Yes," he whispered, and he felt then the land itself sigh, content.

* * *

INSIDE THE STONE HALL THE IMP STIRRED, MADE mildly uncomfortable by the woman's closeness with the man she lay with. It sent a query to its master, but because the imp itself was merely mildly put-out, and only mildly curious, its master dismissed the event.

"It is of no matter," he told the imp. "She can whore with whomever she wants. It will give her no respite, no relief, no escape."

The imp grinned, and settled back for that day when its master would need more of it than the occasional report on the activities of the woman the imp inhabited.

Then the imp's grin faded, for this stone hall was a cold and barren place (or so it appeared to the imp), and it sighed, and wished its master would find a need and a purpose for the imp soon, for it grew lonely and bored.

CHAPTER ELEVEN

THE REALM OF THE FAERIE

E TWISTED IN SLEEP, HIS MIND CONSUMED WITH
images of Cornelia.

Of Cornelia—with a man who he did not recognize. Jealousy
rippled through him, and for a moment threatened to wake him.

But he overcame it, and slid so deep into dream that when he slipped into
the Faerie it was so effortless a transition he barely realized it.

He woke, and he was no longer in his borrowed bedchamber in the governor's castle on Jersey.

Instead he stood atop a hill. He felt as though he stood on an island, for
while the hill on which he stood was bare of anything save a smooth carpet of
grass, all the other hills which rolled away into the distance were covered with
forest. Mist drifted about the valleys between the hills, but his summit was
bathed in sunshine.

"Greetings, Coel."

Coel turned about.

A tall, pale spindly creature with a long, expressive face and melancholy
eyes stood a few paces away. He wore nothing but some poorly made leather
jerkins and trousers, from which poked overly large hands and bare feet.

Coel frowned, and then memory filtered back to him, and he smiled.
"Greetings, Long Tom," he said.

Long Tom held out both his hands, and Coel walked forward and took
them.

"Why am I here?" said Coel.

"What is 'here,' Coel?" said Long Tom.

Coel looked about him. Then he gasped, and color flooded his face. "I am
in the Realm of the Faerie!"

Long Tom laughed in delight, and squeezed Coel's hands. "Yes! You stand in the land of the Faerie. I remember when I came to you that day I pointed you toward Pen Hill, and Caela. Then you thought I'd led you into the Realm of the Faerie, but this time I have, truly, and this day waits an even greater blessing than Caela."

"Why *am* I here, Long Tom?"

Long Tom gave his hands another squeeze, then let them go. "Look," he said, pointing.

Coel turned. A throne stood on the eastern segment of the summit, and on the seat of the throne lay a crown of twisted twigs and sprigs of red berries. As he watched, the sunshine which bathed the summit became particularly intense above the throne, and Coel frowned as the crown of twigs turned a rich gold.

"What is that?" he said.

"Your crown," said Long Tom.

For a long moment Coel said nothing. He stared at the throne with its crown, before finally looking back at Long Tom.

"How is this so?" he said.

"How can it not be so?"

"I am not . . ." Coel's voice drifted off.

"You cannot deny it," said Long Tom. "You are unable to."

"I . . ."

"You made Eaving atop Pen Hill. Do you not remember?"

Coel's brow furrowed.

"You were the land," said Long Tom. "You *made* Eaving."

"I made love with her."

"You *made* her. You *were* the land. You always have been."

Coel did not answer. He studied the grass, as if it could somehow reveal to him all the answers for the questions which flooded his mind.

"When you return to England," said Long Tom, his voice now low and vibrant with power, "will you accept the crown? Will you stand forth as the Lord of the Faerie, the land's first and last defense?"

Coel kept his face turned to the grass for a very long time, but finally he lifted it, and looked at Long Tom. For so long he had felt directionless, unwanted, unfulfilled.

Now . . .

His face flooded with joy as, finally, he realized he had found his purpose. "Yes," he said. "I will take the crown."

chapter twelve

IDOL LANE

Two Years Later

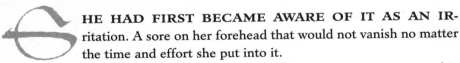

SHE HAD FIRST BECAME AWARE OF IT AS AN IR-ritation. A sore on her forehead that would not vanish no matter the time and effort she put into it.

Then came a rash, then a fever, then more reddened, weeping sores, and in more intimate places.

The day Jane Orr confronted the truth of what had happened to her was one of the worst days of her life, of *all* of her lives, and she thought she had suffered unendurably before this.

But this . . . the pox. She had contracted the pox. This was to what her pride and ambition, her heritage and promise, her power and beauty had brought her.

The pox.

Given to her no doubt by one of the sailors Weyland had forced on her.

A whore, and now a *poxy* whore.

MagaLlan, Darkwitch, Mistress of the Labyrinth, inheritor of a heritage so proud and so stunning that few could have comprehended it, and this is to what it had brought her.

A poxy whore. Despised by all who laid eyes on her. That Jane no longer worked the mattresses was of no consequence. Everyone who saw her knew her profession from the open weeping sores on her face. All would despise and pity her, men and women alike.

How could she—MagaLlan, Darkwitch, and Mistress of the Labyrinth—have come to this, a poxy whore?

The temptation was there to blame Asterion for all of it, for her downfall, for her degradation, for her daily humiliations, but Jane no longer had the energy to evade the truth. She was as much to blame for this as he: her blindness, her stupidity, her damned arrogance . . .

Oh gods, her ambition to rule the world through the Troy Game . . . Rather than hate Weyland, perversely, Jane found herself hating Brutus. If it wasn't for him . . . If only they hadn't attempted to create the Troy Game . . . If only they hadn't ignored the danger of Asterion . . .

If only she had never met Brutus, and had lived out her life as MagaLlan and Darkwitch and nothing else. Gods, *then* she'd had the respect of all who had beheld her.

She lived her life in the house that Weyland had purchased in Idol Lane. She was its mistress, a fact Weyland often remarked upon with a small smile on his face. *You are the mistress only of a whorehouse, Jane.* And after that, generally some crude jest upon the labyrinthine ways of the whore's bed.

Jane ran the house, as well as those pitiable girls that Weyland dragged in from the streets to work out a few years for him. She wasn't sure where he found them, but find them Weyland did, and he gave them to Jane to feed, wash, manage, and advise. They lived and worked in Idol Lane for a year or two, perhaps three, and then Weyland grew tired of them, and set them loose back into the streets. Where they went from there Jane did not know, but she worried about it from time to time, wondering what kind of lives these girls faced, alone and friendless. Weyland might do many terrible things to those girls, but at least he'd fed them, and put a roof over their heads.

Weyland had no financial need to run a brothel, but Jane suspected that it amused him. Most certainly he enjoyed humiliating and tormenting Jane, and grew fat on her despair.

At least now Jane lived in some manner of comfort. Weyland had moved her here from that terrible, stinking, tiny room they had shared for so many years. It was a strange house, growing almost organically as it did out of the bone house of St. Dunstan's-in-the-East, and in a state of disrepair when first they'd moved in. But Weyland had hired men to fix the roof, and to replace the floors, and to glass the hitherto unglazed windows, and now the house was not only more than comfortable, but a comfort in itself. Here there were many rooms, places where Jane could exist for hours at a time in some solitude and in some manner of peace.

Her favorite room was the kitchen. How Genvissa and Swanne would have laughed! That they had come to this, a whore who took pride in her kitchen. Kitchen it might be, but the room was one of the largest in the house, and it was comfortable, and warm, and it did not stink of sex for sale. The girls (three at the moment) that Weyland had working for him, lived in a tavern cellar on Tower Street (he would not keep them at the house), and fulfilled their duties to Weyland and to every lustful carter and sailor and ironmonger in two rooms on the first floor. They came to the kitchen to eat, and to rest, and to sit in silence, partaking of the same comfort in the room as did Jane.

Weyland often joined them. He ate in the kitchen, and he usually tormented either Jane or one of the girls while he was there, but generally Weyland was either out in the city, or he was upstairs on the top floor of the house, where he had constructed something . . . strange.

WEYLAND HAD FELT IT SO SOON AS HE HAD CLIMBED the stairs on that first day he'd wandered into the house from Idol Lane. The first floor was nothing, merely a collection of small rooms that would serve well as bedchambers, the next floor no different, but the top floor of the house . . . well, that was something special. It was one large open space, and it stank of magic and power. Weyland had spent hours up here that initial day, firstly searching the space out with both eyes and his own darkcraft, making sure it could be what he needed, and secondly, trying to scry out the source of the attic's power. In the end, after hours of trying, he could not manage to discover the source, but that did not trouble him, for he felt that the power was not only not antagonistic to him, but in some strange way was highly sympathetic.

This was the place he'd been searching out for so many years.

This would be his home, his sanctuary.

His Idyll.

The instant that damned wool merchant had spoken the word "idyll" Weyland had realized the house had been calling out to him.

Here I am! Here I am!

And here it was indeed. Once the house had been repaired and Weyland had moved in, he'd made it abundantly clear to Jane and the other girls that the attic space was out-of-bounds.

"It is my den," Weyland said to them as they stood in a line before him, faces solemn, hands clasped behind their backs. "My lair, my nest, my shadowy corner of hell. Keep away from it."

They had. Weyland had infused enough threat into his voice to impress even Jane. He had the top floor of the house in Idol Lane to himself, and out of it Weyland had fashioned his Idyll.

It took him over a year, and he needed most every particle of his darkcraft to accomplish it. Weyland knew that expenditure of power would bring him to the Troy Game's attention, and he had been worried for many months. But nothing had happened. The Troy Game had continued, apparently quiescent.

And the Idyll had grown.

It was better by far than Weyland had expected. It *was* his hidey-hole and his sanctuary, but it was also something far deeper. It was Weyland's expression of self, of what perhaps he might be, given the chance . . . and the kingship bands.

It was his kingdom.

Yet with all this, Weyland was somehow dissatisfied with his Idyll. Oh, it was pleasant enough and beautiful enough to keep him happy and contented for many a long night. But there was still something missing, some tiny element that Weyland could not quite put his finger on, and that irritated him. He wanted his Idyll to be perfect, and to have perfection evade him by just one tiny fraction, and to not know what it was that he needed to fill that small, missing space . . . Well, that was frustration incarnate, and those days when Weyland spent hours in his Idyll, studying it, and fretting over what it might be he needed to complete his Idyll, those days were the ones when his temper too often frayed, and either Jane or one other of his whores was likely to feel the full force of his temper in her face.

Weyland understood that he had years to wait until the time was right to make a play for the kingship bands, and he was furious that he might have to spend those years fretting over what probably was no more than a small detail of decoration.

He was greater than that, surely.

PART TWO

THE POWER OF THE CIRCLE

LONDON, 1939

*J*ACK SKELTON THREW HIS BAG INTO THE BOOT OF the car, then jumped in the passenger seat, silently cursing the British preoccupation with tiny vehicles. He slouched down in the seat, reaching for his cigarettes just as Frank threw the car into gear.

"It'll take us at least half an hour," Frank said. "The Old Man'll be furious. We were supposed to report in at—"

"I'll take responsibility," Skelton said, drawing deeply on his cigarette, relishing the smoke in his lungs. There were very few things he liked about this twentieth-century world, but this was one of them.

"But you are my responsibility," Frank said. "The Old Man told me to—"

"Oh, for God's sake, Frank! Calm down. The 'Old Man' will cope if we're twenty minutes late. Now, get this damned conveyance moving, why don't you, before we're twenty hours late."

Frank's mouth thinned. He crouched over the steering wheel in that peculiar manner he had and pushed his foot down on the accelerator.

The car moved forward, and Skelton slouched down even further. He was getting very tired of Frank, and hoped he didn't have to work too closely with him at—

Ahead a huge black four-door sedan hurtled around the corner and screeched to a halt before them. Frank slammed his foot on the brakes, and Skelton muttered an obscenity as he was thrown forward against the dashboard.

"Jesus, Frank! Where did the English learn to drive?"

A slight, fair-haired woman in the uniform of a WREN leapt out of the sedan.

Frank groaned. "Christ. It's Piper."

The WREN, Piper, hurried to Frank's window, leaning down to peer first at Frank and then, more curiously, at Skelton. "Hello, Frank!" Piper said, her eyes again slipping to Skelton, who studiously ignored her. "There's been change of plans. I'm so glad to have caught you!"

"Yes?" snapped Frank. Patently he didn't like Piper much, which perversely made Skelton like her immensely.

"*The Old Man's left London,*" *said Piper, her voice breathless.* "*Gone up to his weekend place. Wants to see you and*"—*yet again she looked curiously at Skelton*—"*the major there. You're to report to him for lunch.*"

"*The weekend house, eh?*" *murmured Skelton, throwing Piper a grin.* "*If I'd known, I'd have brought my tweeds.*"

"*Very well, Piper,*" *said Frank.* "*Are you coming as well?*"

"*Oh, yes,*" *said Piper, and her mouth twisted.* "*I've 'the Spiv' in the back.*"

"*The Spiv,*" *Skelton thought.* "*The Old Man.*" *Do the British not once use a cursed* name? *He looked ahead again, trying to see into the backseat of the black sedan, but cigarette smoke obscured his vision, and all he could make out was the vague form of a man, partly hidden behind the newspaper he was reading.*

Piper was walking back to her sedan, and Frank once more put his own car into gear, waiting for Piper to drive off.

"*So, where is it we're going?*" *said Skelton.* "*Where is this weekend house?*"

"*Epping Forest,*" *said Frank, unaware that Skelton had stiffened at the information.* "*The Old Man's got a house there, inherited from some boffin in his family. It's called Faerie Hill Manor.*"

CHAPTER ONE

THE HEART OF THE TROY GAME
Antwerp, the Netherlands

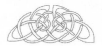

*L*ONG TOM, OLDEST AND WISEST OF THE SIDLE-*saghes, sat by the prostrate white form of the Stag God, Og, as he lay in the glade in the heart of the forest. The flanks of the stag rose and fell in discernible breaths, and his heart beat, not once in millennia, but now at least once an hour, close enough that the watching eye might catch it.*

Og was waking, moving toward rebirth.

Long Tom kept watch this night, as he did many nights, but this night, that of the first of May, became something unexpected.

As he sat, something moved in the forests which surrounded the glade.

Long Tom raised his head and looked about as he heard a noise coming from behind the trees.

"Who goes there?" he called, wondering if Asterion had gained enough power to dare this heart of the Game.

Then the stag moaned, and something most unexpected walked free of the forest.

Long Tom stared.

The being that had stepped forth smiled, and then it spoke.

Long Tom listened, his large mouth dropped ever so slightly open. When the being had stopped speaking, Long Tom frowned, but then nodded.

"I will see that it is done," he said.

THE CHAMBER, LIKE THE HOUSE WHICH CONTAINED it, was large yet sparsely furnished. The floorboards were well swept, but bare save for a single rug sprawled before the fire. There were two plain elm-wood chests pushed against a far wall, and a table of similar material to one side of the room with the remains of a meal scattered over it. Candles sat on both the table and on the chest. A fire burned brightly in the grate, and before it, and slightly away from the direct heat, stood five large copper urns, steam rising gently from their openings.

A huge full tester bed, again of plain unadorned wood, dominated the room. The bedcurtains which hung down from the tester, threadbare and dulled with years of use, had been pushed back toward the head of the bed. The creamy linens and the single blanket—both linens and blanket expertly patched here and there—were piled toward the foot of the bed.

Three people lay on the bed, two women and a man. The younger of the women, perhaps of some twenty-five or twenty-six years, and of a fair beauty, lay stretched out naked on her side, watching the other woman and man make love, occasionally reaching out to stroke the man down the length of his back, or the woman over her breasts. This younger woman watched with gleaming eyes, seeming to receive as much pleasure from watching the lovemaking as she would have had she been the recipient of the man's attention's herself. That she had been the recipient of some man's attentions, if perhaps not this one's, was evident in the gentle rounding of her stomach, showing a five- or six-month pregnancy.

The lovemaking between the other two intensified, and the younger woman stretched sensuously, her hand now running softly over her distended belly. When the man cried out, and then his partner, so also did this younger woman, her breasts rising and falling as rapidly as did those of her companions.

A long moment passed, then the man, Charles, now King Charles II in exile, raised himself from Marguerite's body, leaned over, kissed Kate's mouth lingeringly, then pulled himself free of both women, rolled over to the side of the bed, and sat there, laughing softly.

"You will tire me out," he said, "before we have accomplished what we must this night."

Marguerite, slowly rousing from her state of postcoital languor, ignored her lover for the moment, and instead rolled onto her side so she could kiss and fondle Kate. Catherine Pegge, called Kate by all who knew her well, had joined Charles's court in exile some eighteen months earlier.

She was Erith-reborn, the second of Eaving's Sisters to join Charles, and the second of the triumvirate which would eventually give Charles so much of his power. These three greater sisters, Ecub-reborn, Erith-reborn, and Matilda-reborn—who had yet to join the group—were the core among the larger community of Eaving's Sisters. The three most important, the three most powerful, the three greatest in the Circle about Charles.

And the most unknown. Charles had now spent almost thirteen years in exile, much of it spent traveling western Europe seeking financial, moral, and military support for his always-in-the-planning invasion of England, to snatch it back from the archtraitor Oliver Cromwell. Charles had gathered little in the way of any such support, save muttered sympathies, and the occasional embarrassed handout from this prince or that, mortified to have the ragtag king begging at his court.

What Charles *did* have extreme success in collecting, was women. Tall, darkly handsome, charming, and exuding an aura of undefinable power, Charles was well known for his score of mistresses, most of them highborn, all of them willing to part with whatever virtue they had, to share a night, a month, or a season in Charles's bed.

But this night, Charles was secluded with that tiny, inner circle of "mistresses," his unknown coterie of Eaving's Sisters. These women shared not only Charles's bed, but his heart and soul and ambition as well. They knew his innermost secrets, and gloried in them.

Marguerite rolled onto her back, smiling in contentment, her eyes staring at but not seeing the shabby bedcurtains about her. The twelve years since she had joined Charles had treated her well. Her beauty had mellowed from that of the young girl to that of the mature woman: her hair was darker, but just as thick and luxurious; her form was a little thicker, but the more sensual because of it; her softly rounded belly showed the marks of the three children she had borne Charles. Without looking, she raised a hand and rested it on Kate's pregnant belly. This was Kate's first child, a daughter, and growing well.

"Matters are stirring," said Charles, rising and walking to the curtained window. He twitched one of the curtains back, staring out into the night. It was May Day (May Night, now), and spring celebrations would be well under way across Europe.

It was one of the nights of power in the annual cycle of seasons, the night of the land's rebirth and reawakening. It was one of those four or five nights during the year that Charles always spent closely closeted with this magical, powerful inner coterie, Eaving's Sisters, as well as . . .

"Louis?" he said.

Both the women sighed, and Charles repressed a grin, hearing their disappointment in the lack of Louis's presence.

"He said he would attend as soon as possible," said Marguerite. "Edward Hyde kept him awhile, to go over some detail regarding money, I believe."

"Where would we have been without Louis and his money?" asked Charles, his tone indicating he expected no reply. The marquis de Lonquefort had kept his bastard son well supplied from the Lonquefort coffers, which in turn had kept the wolf from the door of Charles's court. Well might he bear a pretty title, and even prettier pretensions, but Charles was a king without a kingdom, and without the money with which to support a court. His mother had done her best (the sale of the crown jewels had kept them in bread and wine for a few months), as had Charles's relatives spread about Europe.

But there comes a point when relatives grow tired of supporting what appears to be a pointless cause, and over the past few years Charles had literally existed from hand to mouth on those handouts his loyal supporters were able to secure. If this chamber was plainly furnished, then it was because Charles had no money to spare.

That they could actually *eat* was due almost entirely to de Silva money; Louis had offered more, but Charles had refused. He had given up many things over the past thirteen years, but his pride was not one of them.

"There is something happening," Charles said. "Not just in the land. I can feel darkness closing about, and I can feel the Game moving." He raised both his hands, resting them on his biceps, as if he could feel the golden kingship bands of Troy there. "Something will happen tonight. Something powerful."

Both Marguerite and Kate shivered as they stared at Charles. Their intimacy with him greatly increased their respect, not only for his intuition, but also for his power. If Charles said something was going to happen tonight, then tonight would be a night of power, indeed.

And not necessarily a *benevolent* power.

"Asterion?" said Marguerite.

Charles shrugged. "I don't know. It is just a tightness in my belly. An intuition only."

"Will we be safe?" Kate said, resting her hand on her belly.

"I can never guarantee safety," Charles said. "You have always known that. If you want safety, then leave now. Leave me, leave this house, leave this Circle."

Kate had joined the Circle that Charles, Marguerite, and Louis had first formed twelve years earlier as a matter of course. She was one of Eaving's Sisters, she was sworn to Eaving's protection, and she had the power. The group used the Circle to reach out to Eaving where she lived at Woburn Abbey, to ensure that she was safe, and to send her all the well-being they could muster.

It was not much, but it was enough, and it was all they could do to help her until they were back in England, back with their feet touching the Troy Game.

It was also potentially dangerous. They all feared that somehow Asterion might sense the power of the Circle, sense the reaching-out to Eaving, and, in so sensing, that he might *leap*. They had all imagined, and then discussed, the nightmarish possibility that one day Asterion himself would rise up from beneath the piece of turf that Marguerite had transformed into the circle of emerald silk.

There had been no indication yet that Asterion was aware of their activities in any way, but they were apprehensive nonetheless.

Everyone had learned from their previous life that it was murderously foolish to underestimate the Minotaur.

Kate dropped her eyes, chastened. "I'm sorry. I was concerned for the child, only."

Charles's stern gaze did not turn away from her. "Then you should not have conceived it. Kate, the child is as much a part of this as you or I, or Marguerite, or Louis, or Cornelia-reborn. Fate has us all caught in its whim. If we don't have the courage to dare it, then we will never succeed."

Kate raised her eyes, moving her hand away from her belly. "I know."

"We *must* be strong, Kate," Marguerite said.

Even more chastened now that Marguerite had spoken, Kate colored, then nodded. "I have endured too much to walk away now," she said. "I will be strong."

"Cornelia-reborn needs you," Marguerite said. "As she needs all of us."

As Marguerite spoke, the door opened, and Louis de Silva entered.

He looked drawn and tired, as if Hyde's undoubtedly anxious queries about money had sapped his strength, but he smiled as he set eyes on the women and Charles, and the smile lifted away much of the tiredness from his face.

"Louis," Kate breathed, and stretched naked across the bed in a display of almost feline grace. Her hand was back on her belly, for on the night she had conceived this child she had lain with both Charles and Louis, and to be honest she had no idea which of the men had fathered the child, or if, in some magical way, the baby was an amalgam of both men's seeds. She hoped it was the latter, and knew in her heart that it was entirely possible. Charles and Louis were inseparable friends (if it hadn't been for Hyde, Louis would have joined the recent shared bedsport with as much enthusiasm as the other three), and when it came to conception, Kate thought her body would have accepted the seeds of both men as indistinguishable.

"I am glad you are here, Louis," Charles said. "It is almost time."

"And Charles is worried," Marguerite said. "He feels . . ."

"He feels what?" said Louis. He had strolled over to the bed, kissed both Marguerite and Kate softly on their mouths in greeting, then stepped over to Charles, who he also kissed softly. "What is wrong?"

"There is a disturbance tonight," Charles said. "An . . . expectation, almost. Something is waiting for us."

Louis stilled, his dark eyes riveted into Charles's. "Then perhaps we should not form the Circle."

"We must," said Marguerite and Charles together.

"I will *not* be frightened off," said Charles.

"Those are the words of the thwarted king, not of the wise man," said Louis. "Charles, we—"

"I *must*," said Charles. "*We* must. That I feel, too. Ah"—he made a frustrated gesture with a hand—"I cannot say why, but this night is both unknown and yet vitally important. Who knows, it may be Noah herself who is reaching out to us. It might be Asterion, yes, but it might also be Noah." They had learned Cornelia-reborn's name, not through the efforts of the Circle, but through discreet inquiries back in England. *Who is the young girl living at Woburn Abbey? She of the lustrous hair and vivid eyes?*

"Or a myriad of other unknown entities," muttered Louis.

"I wish Matilda-reborn was here," Marguerite said. "The Circle would be so much more powerful with her presence."

Matilda-reborn, unlike Marguerite and Kate, had been born far distant and into high aristocracy—the daughter of the king of Portugal, no less. Catharine of Braganza, as Matilda was known in this life, was young and of great marriageable value. Her father, already aware of her attachment to the exiled Charles, was firm that she could not join him, unless as his wife.

Negotiations were under way, but Charles had little hope of winning Catharine until he had his kingdom firmly in hand; the king of Portugal was not going to let his beloved daughter marry a penniless, if prettily titled, exile.

In all save a few details it was history repeating itself: William the Bastard of Normandy had endured more than a few years of hardship in winning Matilda of Flanders, and Charles supposed he would need to do the winning all over again in this life.

Well, Matilda was worth it.

But until she was with them, and the Circle of the three most powerful of Eaving's Sisters about Charles complete, then they must make do with what they had.

In the silence Louis turned away and disrobed, as he had the first night Marguerite had shown them how to form the Circle.

As Louis folded his clothes neatly and placed them on one of the chests, and Kate poured out water from the copper urns so that all could ritually cleanse themselves, Charles thought about the ever-increasing power and influence of the Troy Game itself.

In their last lives, the Game had showed that it was remarkably aware and capable of influencing the course of lives. It had decided it wanted Cornelia, reborn as Eaving the goddess of the waters, to become the Mistress of the Labyrinth, and to dance out the final steps of the Game with the resurrected Stag God, Og, as Kingman. Brutus and Genvissa, the originators of the Game, were to be discarded.

In this life, Eaving's Sisters—Marguerite, Kate, and Catharine—had been reborn with vastly more power than they'd ever commanded previously, and Charles suspected that was as much the Game's doing as it was the women's connection with Eaving herself. Eaving needed protection, and, together with Charles and Louis, Eaving's Sisters were to provide it.

It was, Charles had realized years ago, the Game's means of counteracting Asterion's malevolence.

The women had done washing and now Louis and Charles took their turn. Although the sexual intimacy the four shared further cemented the ties that bound them, to work the Circle they needed to come to it clean and naked, as they had been born. All the sexual tension that had permeated the room now dissipated; the four worked silently, the women stripping and remaking the bed with clean linens, the men sponging down before drying themselves. Their nakedness was no longer arousing, but binding and solidifying.

Once the bed was made, and the men dry, then Charles stood in the center of the chamber, and held out his hands. Marguerite came to his right hand, Louis to his left, Kate took Louis's and Marguerite's other hands.

"We must name ourselves," said Charles, and thus they did, using the names of their first lives, to bind themselves not only to the past, but to wherever the Game and the land needed them to go. *Brutus, Coel, Ecub, Erith.* Even now, after all of these lives, it felt strange accepting Brutus among them, but then . . . he had changed, hadn't he? More than any of them.

They dropped their hands, and moved to the bed. There they sat cross-legged on its vast expanse, forming a circle, in the same order that they had named themselves when they were standing, and sitting an equidistance apart.

"What is it we wish to view?" asked Marguerite quietly. As she had with Charles and Louis when they had made the first Circle together so many years ago, so she took the lead here.

"We wish to view Eaving," the others whispered, as one.

"What is it we wish to accomplish?" Marguerite said.

"To send Eaving our love and support, to let her know that she is not alone."

Marguerite reached behind her and lifted something from a box she had earlier put on one of the pillows. It was that same lump of turf and dirt that Charles had torn from the Cornish coast that night he and his mother had fled the land.

Now even more browned and crumbly than it had been when Marguerite had first held it, it nonetheless held together as one piece as Marguerite hefted it in one hand.

"The land," she whispered, then threw the piece of turf high into the air. It hit the ceiling plaster with a distinct *thud,* then fell back toward the bed.

As it did so, it changed.

The watchers gasped in wonder, as they never failed to do. Even Kate's baby twisted a little in the womb, awed at what she saw through her mother's eyes.

The crumbled piece of turf and dirt shimmered, then in the blink of an eye flattened and spread out, its very nature changing as it fell (slower now, as both its nature changed and the magic which bound it took hold). It turned from turf into a large circle of lustrous emerald silk that rippled and glimmered in the candlelight as it continued to fall.

It settled to the bed in the center of the Circle with a sigh, and as it did so, once more it changed its contour, this time into the shape of the island that was the land. Its form undulated as it settled against the linen sheets, and mountains rose and moors spread out, and the lay of the land was revealed.

Llangarlia, the ancient land to which they were all bound by magic, murder, and love.

"Noah," said Charles, and as he spoke, he moved his hand so that it pointed toward Woburn Abbey to the north of London.

The emerald silk flattened, as if it had become a great lake, and then it clouded, and shapes began to form within its center.

But not of Noah, nor of Woburn Abbey, as it normally did.

The watchers gasped, and might have broken the Circle, had not Charles held out a stern hand in warning. "*Watch,*" he commanded. "Whatever appears is for a reason. *Watch!*"

The view within the circle of silk resolved into that of the interior of a great hall, stacked with chairs and pews.

"The House of Commons," Charles muttered, for the others here had not ever seen it.

The House was empty, save for a man who sat in the grandest chair of them all, the Speaker's chair. He had a powerful presence, his dark eyes looking about the hall as if he knew he was being watched, and his hands where they rested the arms of the chair were tense, ready for action.

"Cromwell," Charles said, his voice tight. "My father's murderer."

"No," Louis said. "Asterion was your father's murderer, Charles. Never forget that."

Charles's eyes flickered Louis's way, then settled back on the figure the silk showed them.

Cromwell was still, and very, very watchful.

Almost as if he expected someone, or something.

"Look!" Kate said, one hand pointing.

They all saw it, a miasma of blackness that crept under the great closed doors of the House and slid toward Cromwell.

He did not appear to notice it.

"Asterion?" said Marguerite.

"Death," said Charles, "whether at Asterion's hand, or that of the Game . . . Death . . . finally."

"And thus we are being shown this," said Louis. "Your time has almost come, Charles. England awaits. For *all* of us."

The scene changed again, Cromwell sitting on his lonely throne fading first into a murky grayness, and then into . . . into . . .

A great roiling mass of silk as it suddenly heaved away from the bed. Its center rose, as if it contained something underneath, while its edges remained flat on the bed.

"No!" Kate cried, reeling back, one hand on her belly. "Something comes!" *Something comes!*

"Asterion," Louis said flatly.

CHAPTER TWO

*N*O!"

Marguerite's voice cracked across the Circle, stalling all who had been in the process of rising.

"No," she said, more softly now, and there was a hint of a smile about her face. "It is not Asterion at all, but . . ."

She leaned forward, gave the silk a tug and, before the other three's astounded gazes, revealed Long Tom.

"You have given us a surprise, Long Tom," Marguerite said.

Long Tom bowed to her, then to Charles, to Kate, and finally to Louis. Then, as the others watched, he moved out from the silken circle and sat down between Kate and Louis; the rest of the Circle shifted about so that, again, there rested an equidistance between all members.

"Long Tom," Charles said, inclining his head respectfully. "Why have you come? And how? I had not thought you had the power to manage this transference."

"To the second of your questions first," Long Tom said. "It was not my power which has accomplished this transference, but yours." He nodded at them, as if a teacher particularly proud of his pupils' accomplishments. "You are potent, indeed."

Marguerite flushed with pleasure. "Was it you who directed our sight to Cromwell?"

Long Tom nodded. "Yes. I, and the Game."

"As one, now," said Charles.

Long Tom shrugged his shoulders very slightly, which could have meant anything. "Cromwell is touched with death," said Long Tom. "He will not last beyond the autumn."

"Is this your doing—the *Game's*? Or Asterion's?" said Charles.

"Does it matter?" said Long Tom. "Cromwell's death will herald your return, Charles. Your invitation back to the throne. There shall be no invasion needed *this* time. England shall be yours for the asking. You shall be welcomed with roses and cheers and grants of heavy gold coin."

Charles grunted. "Roses and coin, eh?" He met Louis's eyes, and both men smiled a little. "Better that, than battle, I suppose."

"Cromwell's death not only heralds your return, Charles," said Long Tom, "as that of all within the chambers, but also . . ."

"Asterion," said Louis, and the bleakness in his tone killed all remaining humor among the Circle. "Asterion will make his move."

"Aye," said Long Tom. "The instant you set foot back on the English mainland," he said to Charles, "then Asterion will seize Noah. She bears Asterion's imp within her. She *will* answer his summons. It is a reality we cannot change."

"But for *what* does everyone wait?" said Marguerite. "I don't understand this. Asterion could take Noah anytime he wants, and, once he has her, then he can take the bands. Frankly, Asterion could have had the bands many years ago."

"No," Charles said, shaking his head slightly. "It is a great deal more complex than that, now. This contest between ourselves and Asterion has now gone on over three lifetimes. *Everyone* who is reborn time after time is caught up in the struggle. No single person or entity controls events; we are all a part of this complex and dangerous dance." He paused. "*I* think that the true tussle cannot begin until everyone is in place. *Everyone.*" He looked about the Circle. "And Catharine is still missing. Her father won't allow her to come to me until I am certain of the throne, and that won't happen until Cromwell dies."

"But events *are* moving," said Louis. "Cromwell is dying. It shall not be long before Catharine is with us, and then—"

"Then Asterion shall seize Noah," said Marguerite.

"No!" said Louis. "We cannot allow this."

"You must," said Long Tom. "None of you can prevent it. She is his whore in this life. You know that. She—"

"We find that difficult to accept, Long Tom," said Charles.

"You *must* accept it!" Long Tom barked, and everyone went rigid at the command in his voice. "This was one of Eaving's many possibilities for her future, and, because of the misstep she took in her previous life, now this has become a reality in this life. Accept it," he finished softly. "She *will* become Asterion's whore."

For a moment there was silence, then Charles spoke softly. "This is truly a bitter message you bear."

"And yet there is more of it, I think," said Marguerite, watching Long Tom closely.

"Aye," he said. "Indeed there is. I talked to Noah, years ago now, as she was entering her womanhood and thus her powers as Eaving. I am going to tell you part of what I told her—the rest of what I said to her concerns her ears only—and I am going to tell you one more thing. First, to what I told Noah. There is something which must be accomplished in this life if there is to be any hope that Asterion can be defeated.

"Old wounds must be healed." Long Tom looked down at his hands folded before him, as if he could not bear to study the faces of his listeners. "Brutus must make amends to his father; the wound of patricide must be healed."

Charles gave a soft, disbelieving laugh. "Silvius shall demand a high price for *that* wound to be healed, my friend."

"Then it must be paid," said Long Tom. "If it isn't, then the stag cannot be raised."

Charles shook his head, then moved on. "What other wounds must be healed, Sidlesaghe?"

"The deep fissures between Noah and Genvissa-reborn," said Long Tom. "These healings, if they are ever to be accomplished, you can have no say in. It shall be between Noah, and Jane Orr."

"*Jane Orr?*" Louis said. "That is her name?" None of them had ever been able to scry out Genvissa-reborn's identity.

Long Tom nodded. "She is born sister to Asterion, who masquerades as a man called Weyland Orr. He prostitutes women for his enjoyment, and as practice for what one day he shall do to Noah. He has debased Jane, humiliated her, and keeps her as his slave."

"In Jane's last life as Swanne she thought herself in love with Asterion, and plotted with him for her own gain, as she then thought," said Louis. "Is she still so misguided?"

"Nay," said Long Tom. "Her life is a misery, and she loathes Asterion. I believe she has come to regret her actions of past lives."

Charles snorted. "That I find hard to believe. Genvissa has ever managed to justify her actions."

"Enough of Genvissa-reborn," said Louis. "It is Noah who occupies *my* thoughts. You say that she needs to endure the certain misery of Asterion's ill-treatment? Why? *Why?*"

"I think I understand," said Marguerite slowly. "Noah, *Eaving,* and Jane must be reduced to the same circumstances. To the same degree of baseness so that they may begin anew. Perhaps suffering shall bond them as nothing else has."

"You are a perceptive woman," Long Tom said. "Yes, Noah and Jane shall be reduced to a new beginning. We must hope they take the opportunities it offers."

"I cannot sit here and accept this," Louis said. "You say that the instant Charles sets foot on England again Asterion shall seize Noah and you want us *to do nothing about it?*"

Long Tom dropped his head and studied his hands. When finally he looked up, there was a strange light in his eyes, and everyone else within the Circle felt a chill run down their spines.

"We can prepare her as best we can," he said, his voice very low and very commanding. "We can give her every support possible to endure her time with Asterion, and to allow her to believe that, eventually, all will be well."

"But we do this already," said Charles, "with our Circle."

Long Tom smiled very slowly. "I want you to do *more*," he said. "There is something you need to accomplish. Something which can aid Noah, and heal the greatest wound of all—that between her, and you, Brutus-reborn. Listen."

Long Tom talked for a long time, explaining to them what they must do on the night of the summer solstice, one of the most powerful nights of the year, and which was the next time they could form the Circle within the annual cycle of seasons. He talked for so long, and what he had said both so disturbed and so excited the group, that their power was almost gone by the time Long Tom was done.

Their power and endurance depleted, there was no chance to see Noah, nor to send her their support.

"She will know there has been good reason you could not do so," said Long Tom as he prepared to leave.

"She will worry," said Marguerite.

"She will know there was good reason," the Sidlesaghe repeated. "Besides, she has a lover, John Thornton, to keep her company and to give her comfort."

Complete silence met this pronouncement.

"What?" said Long Tom. "You thought you could take your pleasure in your shared bed, and in the comfort of your shared intimacies, and she not?"

"We have sent her our support," said Charles, his voice tight.

"She is a living, breathing woman," said Long Tom. "She needed more than the knowledge that you were all having a good time and wished her well."

To that no one had anything to say.

THE GROUP WAS VERY SUBDUED AS THEY FIRST folded the emerald cloth, then handed it into Marguerite's hands, where it became once more the piece of crumbled turf. She put this away in its box, and the box carefully away in one of Charles's chests.

Then she rejoined the other three on the bed.

"I wish we had seen Noah," she said.

"Aye," said Charles. He looked exhausted, for it was mostly his power which had held the Circle together, and he rubbed at his eyes and forehead, as if he could soothe away his tiredness.

"Charles," said Louis. "We need to—"

Charles gave him no chance to finish. He caught Louis's eye, and gave a small nod. "I know. Wait a moment." He rose from the bed, and gave Marguerite and Kate each a kiss. "Go to sleep," he said. "Louis and I shall be with you shortly."

The women looked at each other, then at Charles's face, then nodded themselves, pulling back the coverlets and slipping beneath.

"Do not be long," said Kate, and then fell into sleep almost immediately.

Louis smiled and, leaning over the bed, tucked in the coverlets about her shoulders. He straightened and looked at Charles, who tipped his head toward the door.

THEY STOOD BY A SHADOWED WINDOW, SPEAKING IN whispers.

"I do not care for what Long Tom has told us," said Charles. "*I*, for one, cannot countenance the thought that we must sit idly back and watch Noah go to Asterion."

"I am with you," said Louis.

Charles held Louis's gaze. "We must prevent it."

"Aye. How?"

"One of us must—"

"*How?*"

Charles put a hand on Louis's shoulder. "Ah, my friend. I am too weary to hold a single thought in my head. I cannot think of the 'how.' Not tonight. But a 'how' you and I shall find. We *must*."

Louis relaxed a little. "After what Long Tom has told us tonight, after what he has told us we must do, we have no choice."

Charles's hand tightened a little. "We will not tell Marguerite or Kate of our plans. It would only worry them."

Louis nodded. "I wish . . ."

"We have wished on the stars and moon and sun for over two and a half thousand years already, my friend. I am sick to death of 'wishes.' Now, we must *act*."

Chapter Three

Idol Lane, London

WEYLAND BROUGHT TWO NEW GIRLS TO IDOL Lane. They replaced the three who had worked for him since he'd first moved into this house, and who had, separately over the past six months, grown so tired and dispirited that Weyland had let them go.

Each had walked out the front door, their heads low, their faces wretched, with nothing but enough coin to keep them fed for a week. Weyland felt he owed them nothing more. They had the skills to earn themselves more coin if they so desired, and there were enough men in the city who would take in a girl willing to exchange her body for food and a roof over her head.

These two new girls were the best Weyland had ever found. Both from Essex, and from neighboring villages, they'd separately come to London seeking work in one of the great mansions of the Strand.

They had, of course, found no work at all, for they had few skills and no experience, but they *had* found each other and, in time, Weyland had found them—sheltering under one of the small bridges crossing Fleet River, cold, hungry, and destitute.

Willing to do whatever they needed to, in order to survive.

They were called Elizabeth and Frances. They had surnames, but Weyland had forgotten them so soon as he'd heard them. Surnames were of no importance to whores. What was important was that they were pretty enough, young enough, and, within an hour or two of being taken back to Idol Lane, terrified enough to do whatever Weyland told them.

At fifteen, Frances was the younger of the two by a year. She had a strong, lithe body and abundant red hair: Weyland could use that to market her as a firebrand, although less a firebrand Weyland thought he had yet to meet. Her face was round and pretty with pale, creamy skin, lightly spattered with freckles. Those who didn't like firebrands could be tempted with her sweet innocent air.

Weyland found Frances somewhat dreary, but the other one, Elizabeth, attracted him markedly. She was tall and slim, and with fine dark hair, elegant features, translucent skin, and pale-green eyes. Elizabeth had an exotic look about her which bespoke a fathering by one of the dark, quiet men who wandered the country's highways and byways, and whose bloodlines stretched back many thousands of years into England's ancient past. As attractive as Weyland found these mysterious looks, there was something else about her . . . Weyland wasn't entirely sure what it was, although he wondered if it might be her intelligence, for Elizabeth had a wit about her that most of the girls Weyland brought to his house completely lacked. Unlike Frances, Elizabeth had been a virgin when she entered Idol Lane.

Weyland made certain that she had lost that virginity within the hour.

Elizabeth had wept, and afterward curled up about herself. Jane had gone to the girl, and wrapped arms about her, and tried to comfort her, all the time shooting Weyland dark looks that, had they been arrows, would certainly have seen Weyland skewered in forty different places.

But looks didn't touch Weyland, and the next day both girls were hauled upstairs, and set to entertaining the men who came to the front door.

Within a week both Frances and Elizabeth had acquired the hard, blank facial expression of all whores, and somehow Weyland found that disquieting. Especially whenever he regarded Elizabeth.

At odd moments, when he was alone in his Idyll, Weyland regretted the fact that he'd set Elizabeth to whoring so soon.

Perhaps he could have brought her here, to the Idyll.

Perhaps she could have been a companion for him.

Perhaps . . .

When his thoughts drifted this way, Weyland found himself yearning for that *something*—that one, small, insignificant thing—that he needed to complete his Idyll. No matter how hard he'd tried, he'd never managed to identify the Idyll's lack. But when he thought on Elizabeth, and thought on bringing her to the Idyll, then somehow . . . perhaps . . . maybe even . . .

Ah! It was just out of his reach.

But Weyland kept thinking of Elizabeth, and he began to spend more of his time in the kitchen when he knew that Elizabeth would be there.

THREE WEEKS AFTER ELIZABETH HAD COME TO IDOL Lane, Weyland came down the stairs, walked through the parlor into the kitchen, and there found Elizabeth alone, sitting at the table.

Elizabeth looked up, and a strange expression came over her face as she saw him standing there. To his discomfort, Weyland realized it was fear.

Why did *that* realization discomfort him?

"Where are Jane and Frances?" he said.

"Gone to Smithfield," she said. "Jane said we needed meat."

Weyland nodded, and sat down next to her on the bench.

She smelt fresh, as if she had just bathed. The fact Elizabeth was not staled with the sweat of men made Weyland feel extraordinarily cheerful. It made him think of the Idyll, and then of its incompleteness.

"Are you happy?" he said.

She looked at him in disbelief. "I want to go home," she said.

"This is your home, now."

To Weyland's deepening discomfort, Elizabeth's beautiful eyes filled with tears. "Home to my *village*," she said. "Home to my sister, and her husband."

"You need to earn to pay your way."

"I would crawl there on my hands and knees, if you would but let me go."

Weyland didn't know what to say. He lifted a hand, and touched gently Elizabeth's cheek.

She flinched.

"Elizabeth," he said. "I wish . . ."

She tensed, and Weyland wondered if she were terrified.

The thought gave him no joy, and that unsettled him more than ever.

He thought again of his Idyll, waiting upstairs, and of Elizabeth's sweetness and intelligence. Without thinking, Weyland slid his hand behind Elizabeth's neck, holding her head still, and leaned forward and kissed her. She tensed even further, but then managed to relax a little, and that gave Weyland hope.

His free hand now picking at the buttons of her bodice, Weyland kissed Elizabeth ever more deeply. He ran his hand beneath her bodice, and caressed her breasts.

A moment later he lifted her onto the kitchen table, pulled up her skirts, fumbled at his own breeches, and then slid contentedly into her.

"Elizabeth . . ." he whispered, working his hips gently, wanting to tell her how much he liked her, how much he was attracted by her, and how much he wanted to invite her into his Idyll, so that they might—

"Finish and be done," the girl said, her face now averted from him, her voice harsh. "I wish not to share my hell with the likes of *you*."

Her words hit Weyland with the strength of a woodsman's mallet. He lurched backward, pulling himself free from her, and awkwardly pulled closed his breeches.

She lay there on the table, not moving to cover her bare flesh, her face still averted from him.

He remembered another woman, long ago, who had rejected him. Who had taunted him with a new lover. Who had laughed at him, and then set her lover to murder him.

She had been a whore, too. That's all women ever were.

Whores.

Without thinking, Weyland reached forward, grabbed one of Elizabeth's ankles, and pulled her off the table so hard she cried out in pain as she hit the floor.

"Coldhearted bitch," Weyland said, and then left the kitchen, retreating up the stairs to his haven, his desperately incomplete sanctuary.

Chapter Four

Antwerp, the Netherlands

L OUIS."

Louis turned. Charles had entered the small walled garden of their house, and now stood a pace or two away. Louis had been so lost in his thoughts he hadn't even heard him enter. He tried a smile of welcome, and, failing, turned back to the apple tree at which he'd been staring sightlessly before Charles entered.

Charles stepped close and put a hand on Louis's shoulder, making the man turn back to him. "Louis, I know how you feel."

"Sweet gods, Charles, we must find a way to save Noah from Asterion . . . this *Weyland.*"

"Louis, what can we do? The instant I set foot back in England, Asterion will seize Noah and—"

"Then let *me* go to England. Let *me* save her."

Now it was Charles whose gaze hardened. "And what will happen if *you* set foot back in England, eh? What happens then? We lose everything. In our peculiar circumstance, my friend, your foot is as dangerous as mine."

Louis finally dropped his eyes away from Charles's face. "There must be a way."

"Then, if there is, we shall find it. Louis, I do not like what Long Tom had to say. *I* do not want to see Noah made Asterion's whore."

There was a silence for a few minutes, both men walking to a bench and sitting down.

"What about James?" Charles said eventually.

Louis grunted derisively. "James might aid her. *Might.* But I do not trust him to it. Besides, I do not think he would be able to act secretively. The entire nation would know James, duke of York, had returned to England within the hour of his so doing. After that he would not be able to secrete away a mouse, let alone Noah."

"Nay . . . And if I sent another? A man experienced in the arts both of action and of most secret diplomacy?"

"*I* would be best!"

"Aye, but . . ." Charles allowed his voice to drift away, and again silence fell between the two men.

"Charles . . ." Louis said after a moment.

"Aye?"

"The problem is that you and I are so closely connected that if either of us set foot in England, Weyland would know, and seize Noah before we could get to her."

"Aye. So . . ."

"But what if I set foot back in England a day or so before you? Just a day or so, hid amid all the excitement generated by your imminent arrival. Would Asterion then realize my presence? Or would he think what he felt was just your impending arrival?"

Charles's eyes narrowed as he thought. "Maybe, Louis. But, dear gods, you'd have to move fast. You'd have a day, perhaps two. Anything more, and Weyland would be able to tell that what he felt was not *only* my impending arrival. You'd have but a breath in which to snatch her."

"A breath is all I would need."

Charles thought, chewing the inside of his cheek.

"Charles, let me do it, I beg you! A day or two, and I would have her. Damn it! We *know* where she is! Even if Weyland does summon Noah, then I could find her on the road to London, or even as she enters London."

"Gods, my friend, we'd have to time this so carefully . . ."

"Charles . . ." Louis almost growled the word.

Charles finally nodded, and sighed. "If we fail . . ."

"I will not fail."

Clearly troubled, Charles stared at Louis, then nodded again. "You will need to be ready to move at a moment's notice."

Louis grinned, relieved. He put a hand on Charles's shoulder. "I *will* rescue her, Charles. Have no doubt."

CDAPTER FIVE

WOBURN ABBEY, BEDFORDSHIRE

THE REVEREND JOHN THORNTON WALKED VERY slowly behind and to one side of Lady Anne Bedford and Noah Banks.

It was a beautiful late-spring morning. The sun beat down with an unseasonable warmth, and the air had a languid quality about it, as if it contained all the heaviness of midsummer instead of the usual sprightliness of spring. Those deer and rabbits who saw the walkers, moved away only sluggishly, as if they were too exhausted to be bothered with panic.

The women wore broad-brimmed straw hats against the sun, and light, summery clothes: Thornton guessed they'd spent half the morning finding and then airing last summer's bodices and skirts. But Lady Anne had been insistent; the moment she'd looked out upon the sun-swathed park she'd proclaimed that the day was too beautiful for anyone to spend indoors.

His position to one side and slightly behind, gave Thornton the opportunity to study the two women.

Lady Anne, now in her sixth month of yet another pregnancy, looked drawn and tired, and Thornton wondered why she'd insisted on this walk. The day was beautiful, yes, but she might have been better off instructing one of the footmen to set a chair on the lawns for her leisure rather than insisting on this meander through the parklands.

On the other hand, Noah looked as lovely as ever. She was a special woman, as Thornton had every reason to know. For the past nine or ten years she'd been his lover, gracing him with her body and presence on two or three nights a week. He was in love with her. Worse, he was addicted to her. Whenever they lay together he embraced not only Noah, but also the land.

Always, when they made love, Thornton could feel the land rise up to meet him.

Do you feel it, John Thornton? she would whisper to him, and he would weep, and hold her, and say, *Yes, I feel it.*

Thornton had lost count of the number of times he'd begged Noah to marry him. He was desperate for her, and he was plagued by nightmares of losing her. *Marry me,* he would beg, *Marry me, and never leave me.*

She cried whenever he said that, and laid a hand to his cheek. *I cannot,* she would say. *And I must leave, eventually.*

Thornton was not sure how their love affair had kept itself secret for so long. He wondered if the countess suspected; she certainly knew Thornton loved Noah. She had once asked him directly if he held a "special affection" for Noah. He replied truthfully that he did, but that she would not have him.

Noah later told him that the countess had taxed her with Thornton's apparently unrequited love, and that Noah had told Lady Anne what she so often told Thornton.

She could not marry him. She could not marry any man, for she would eventually have to leave.

The countess was as perplexed as Thornton was increasingly desperate.

He studied Noah now as he strolled along, hands clasped behind his back, eyes heavy-lidded against the sun.

At sixteen Noah had been lovely.

At twenty-five she was stunning.

Her glossy brunette hair had darkened a little more with age, but it was still striking. When they made love Thornton would sink his hands into its thick, cool mass, and often fantasized about losing himself within it completely. Her pale, luminescent skin was as exquisite now as it had been at sixteen, and her eyes, ah, those eyes . . . when she smiled at him, slow and warm, those eyes glowed with such intensity that Thornton imagined he could feel their heat burning into his face.

And yet, sometimes, after they had made love and she lay in his arms, he would hear her sigh, and turn her head slightly as if she were looking for someone in the dark of the chamber. At these moments he would feel the sense of a falling-away, whether of Noah herself, or of that remarkable sense of land she brought with her, he did not know.

At these moments he would wonder how many other men Noah had left bereft in her wake. How many other men, desperately in love with her, had heard her sigh like that, and turn her eyes to stare into the unknown dark? Noah had been a virgin when she'd first come to Thornton's bed, but Thornton was intuitive enough (and certainly intuitive enough after all these close years with this faerie-woman) to understand that his might not have been the first heart she'd ever broken.

"Reverend," Lady Anne said, pausing to turn slightly to wave Thornton forward. "Why lag so? I would speak with you, and Noah."

As Thornton drew abreast of Lady Anne, she resumed speaking.

"I have decided to travel to a healing spring. This child discomforts me greatly, and I need to partake of mineral waters."

"I am sorry to hear of that, madam," Thornton said. "To where do you travel? And when?"

"As to the 'when,' in a few weeks, perhaps, when my husband can spare me. And as to 'where' . . . , Well . . . I have heard good reports of the springs at Hampstead."

Thornton saw Noah stiffen, and he thought he knew what was coming.

"I would have you stay and continue the children's education," Lady Anne said to Thornton, then she turned and laid a gloved hand on Noah's arm. "But I would have you with me, Noah, for no one soothes my aches and discomforts as well as you. Between you and the waters, I have no doubt I shall feel well again in but a short while."

"Madam . . ." Noah said, and Thornton saw panic well in her eyes.

For some reason, Noah loathed London. The earl and countess traveled to London at least once a year to oversee their interests there. They always asked Noah to travel with them; Noah just as regularly declined, citing this reason or that.

"I *will* have you with me," the countess said, her voice like ice.

"Madam—" Noah began again.

"The waters of Hampstead are renowned for their curative powers," Lady Anne continued. "I *must* go, Noah, and you shall accompany me."

Thornton was sure that he saw tears in Noah's eyes, and he started forward, thinking that if he did not grasp her hand then she would bolt for the cover of the forests like a terrified deer.

But just as Thornton had stepped forward and raised his hand, Noah looked toward a tree, and gasped, her already pale skin losing what little color it had.

Thornton looked in the direction of her eyes, and felt his own mouth drop open in wonder.

A tall thin creature in rough leather breeches and jerkin had stepped forward, and if his dealings with Noah had taught Thornton anything, it was that he could recognize a faerie creature when he saw one.

CHAPTER SIX

J AM NOT SURE WHAT STUNNED ME THE MOST: LONG
Tom's precipitous appearance from behind the tree, or the fact that
John Thornton could see him as well as I could. It was then, at that
precise moment, that I knew my intimacy with Thornton had gone too far. I
had taught him too much, or *he* had learned too much.

Lady Anne was completely unaware of Long Tom's presence. She had a
slightly distracted expression in her eyes, and her breathing was still to the
point of nonexistence: I realized Long Tom had cast some kind of enchantment upon her.

Long Tom stepped forward, nodded at Thornton, then looked beseechingly
at me, as only a Sidlesaghe could do.

"Eaving," he said. "Go to Hampstead. Please."

I shook my head slowly from side to side, although I was not sure what I
was denying. I think my thoughts were more with John than they were with
whatever Long Tom was trying to say to me.

"'Eaving'?" said John. Then, "Noah, who *is* this?"

"I am Long Tom," said the Sidlesaghe, most obligingly. He held out his hand.

John looked at it, looked at me, then shook Long Tom's hand.

"Well met," said Long Tom.

"Aye," said John, somewhat doubtfully.

"Eaving," Long Tom's attention had switched back to me, "you must go to
Hampstead."

"It is time?" I whispered. *Time to take my place as Asterion's whore?*

"No, no!" Long Tom said, and his face wrinkled up almost as if his anxiety
to soothe me had reduced him nigh to tears. "Not at all. It is time to heal the
wounds between you and Brutus."

Time to heal the first wound.

Time to bridge those terrible rifts Brutus and I had created between us. Could it be done?

"Of course," said Long Tom.

"But why Hampstead?"

"Hampstead is where it needs to be."

"It is too dangerous," I said. London was only a few miles southeast from Hampstead. Asterion would be close. "*He* will know I am there."

"We will distract him," said Long Tom. "Eaving, this wound *needs* to be healed, and it needs to be done now."

Why now? I wondered into Long Tom's mind. Thornton must be having a hard-enough time of this conversation, and I thought the less said verbally, the better.

While Long Tom understood me well enough, he ignored the implicit request.

"It must be now," he said. "It is as the Game asks."

"Noah?" John said.

"All is well, John," I said, trying to give him a smile, and, I am afraid, failing miserably. "Long Tom is an old friend and he only wants to aid me."

"Why does he call you Eaving?"

"It is an old and dear name to me."

"And as an old and dear friend," Long Tom said, "I am asking you, Eaving, to agree with your lady companion—"

Oh, how I like that! Lady Anne was my companion, rather than I hers. I suppose Long Tom could see it no other way.

"—and to travel with her to Hampstead."

The imp? I spoke into Long Tom's mind. (This of all things could not be said before John!) The imp had lain quiescent thus far, but I had no idea what it would do if I transported it suddenly closer to its master. I well knew it would not lie quiescent *all* this life. It had a task, and it would attend to it the moment its master informed it of its necessity.

We will manage the imp, Long Tom replied, and I blessed him that this time, at least, he had not spoken the words aloud.

Gods, I hoped so. I felt the first flutter of excitement. *Brutus will be in Hampstead. Somehow. Somewhere.*

"Will it be safe for *him* as well?" I said. *How in the world will Brutus manage to travel to meet me there? Does he think he can wander the roads unrecognized?*

From the corner of my eye I could see John frown, and I wished I had not said that verbally.

Long Tom hesitated, which reassured me not at all. "You shall both need to take risks. There is no other way."

I nodded, finally; although frankly, I was almost as nervous about meeting with Brutus-reborn than I was about being so close to Asterion. Would Brutus *want* to reconcile with me? Did he not hate me still? I remembered his anger when he had confronted me in our ancient tomb under Tower Hill and told me that I had been duped by Asterion, and turned into his whore. I had felt Brutus' presence whenever Coel, Ecub, and Erith and he had formed the Circle they used to reach out to me, but I'd never been able to glean more. They were there, they were intimate, they wanted me to know they loved me . . . but what did *Brutus* want me to know? Did he merely acquiesce to the group in these matters, or did he truly wish me well, too?

Well, how would I ever discover how he felt, save by meeting him?

"I shall go to Hampstead," I said, and Long Tom smiled.

SOMEHOW WE GOT THROUGH THE REST OF THAT walk through the park, Lady Anne blinking back into awareness the instant Long Tom vanished. I smiled, and said that of course I would accompany her to Hampstead; Lady Anne professed herself well pleased; and John, the dear man, kept his own counsel although I felt his eyes boring into my back as we made our way back to the abbey.

That night I went to him, for I owed him that much at least. Far more, truly, but I did not know how I could ever repay him.

Unusually, he did not move instantly to disrobe me and make love to me. We often talked far into the night, but always the physical intimacy came first, so that we might the more easily establish the greater intimacy later.

Instead John took my face between his hands, and regarded me soberly.

"I have put many things to one side for you," he said. "My loyalty to my patron, the earl. My moral righteousness. My duty to God. My very *faith* in God! Everything you are, and everything you have shown me over the past years, has turned my world upside down . . . and what do I have for that? Your love? No, I do not have that. Your hand in marriage? No, that even less. I have merely been a dalliance for you—"

His voice had turned black with bitterness, and I went rigid and tears filled my eyes.

"—a means by which to pass the time."

"No! You have given me so much comfort and friendship—"

"'Comfort and friendship'? *'Comfort and friendship'*? For almost ten years you have twisted my heart and wrung it dry, and yet for that you will give me nothing in return. Not your love, not—"

"I do . . ." I stopped. I couldn't lie to him.

He saw it, and his mouth twisted even more than it had done thus far. "You *do* love me?" He shook his head. "Nay. You don't. You wanted a lover, and so you took me. I was *convenient,* Noah. Admit it."

I said nothing, admitting everything with my silence.

"Marry me," he whispered. "Please. Don't leave me."

"I would destroy you if I did that. I'm so sorry, John."

John pulled my face toward his, but he did not kiss me. Instead he rested his forehead against mine, his eyes closed, and for a long time we stood there like that, leaning into each other, silent.

"Will you come back from Hampstead?" he said eventually, so softly I could barely hear him.

"I hope so," I said. "More than you can imagine."

MUCH LATER, AFTER WE HAD MADE LOVE WITH A desperation that made me weep, we lay sleepless. He was as lost in his own thoughts as I was in mine, I think.

I was thankful he did not inquire as to what I pondered, for I thought of nothing but Brutus.

Brutus would be there, in Hampstead.

I'd had time to think how his presence might be accomplished, and I'd reached the conclusion that Brutus-reborn would not travel physically to Hampstead. Brutus would not dare to set foot in England for the same reason I was terrified of setting foot in London: Asterion. The Minotaur had more power than ever, and I don't think Brutus had the power, now, to confront him.

Brutus would use the power of the Circle to come to me. It was dangerous, but it could be done.

I didn't think it was a coincidence that Long Tom had come to me and told me to go to Hampstead just after the Circle had failed to reach out to me on May Night. I'd been worried about that, but now I think I knew the answer.

Long Tom had gone to them, probably using their power as they formed the Circle to catapult himself into their midst. They'd formed the Circle, intending to touch me, and instead had received Long Tom for their troubles.

I smiled a little to myself in the dark. Had Brutus been disappointed?

At this further thought of Brutus, I stiffened in excitement, fool that I was, and John felt it.

"Who is he?" he whispered in my ear, one hand on my breast. "Who is he that you long for so desperately? Who is it you are going to Hampstead to meet?"

What could I say?

Chapter Seven

Antwerp, the Netherlands
Hampstead, Middlesex, and London

*I*T WAS MIDSUMMER DAY, THE NATIVITY OF SAINT John the Baptist, and England and western Europe sweltered under a hot sun and the shared headache of a splendidly celebrated Midsummer Eve the previous night. In the afternoon of the day just gone, men and women had danced into the forests and taken from there branches which they hauled back to their dwellings to place over their front doors. To any priest who asked, this ritual was to honor the nativity of Saint John the Baptist, but in hearts and memories, this ritual recalled a time long past, when there was something more to be celebrated in the forests at the solstice than the nativity of Christian martyrs.

Deadwood was collected for the night, and piled into great bonfires, recalling the ancient bone-fires designed to frighten away witches. Once twilight set in, all across Europe men set these massive bonfires alight. Once the fires were burning well, and the men and women present well-fueled with alcohol, then there began great dances. People grasped hands and formed concentric rings about the fires, moving first this way and then that, with the occasional foolhardy youth breaking free of the ring to leap through the flames.

Most of the dancers didn't even pretend to associate these fire dances with the Baptist. Instead, they remembered the circling dance as Ringwalker's Dance and, if asked what that meant, the only reply to be received was a sly look and a cunning smile.

Londoners, dancing about fires in both East and West Smithfield, called their dances the Troy Game, although one or two were heard to refer to it as "Ringwalker's Troy."

Lady Anne and Noah occupied a townhouse in Highgate Village, some four miles to the northwest of London and just on the edge of Hampstead Heath. They had been at Highgate some two weeks now, and Lady Anne was pleased to see that Noah's initial nervousness at being so close to London had abated, so that Noah now appeared as relaxed as was Lady Anne herself.

Every day they rode in a trap pulled by a small pony from their rented townhouse to the spring-fed ponds on the eastern reaches of the heath, and there Lady Anne took of the waters, either orally or—when she dared and when she felt it seemly—by clothing herself in a voluminous linen garment and immersing herself in the waters themselves. Noah generally sat with Lady Anne, or assisted her in whatever way she could, but on Midsummer Day, as Lady Anne settled into a chair by the side of one of the ponds under the shade of a spreading oak tree, the countess told Noah that she might amuse herself as she pleased, for she, Lady Anne, felt so lethargic she wanted only to doze the day away.

Noah smiled, ensured that Lady Anne was comfortable and wanting for nothing, then wandered off toward Parliament Hill which rose in the western near-distance.

IN ANTWERP, CHARLES CONVENED THE CIRCLE IN HIS bedchamber at one hour past midday. Normally it would have been difficult for him to have acquired several hours free during the day, but such had been the celebrations of Midsummer Eve the previous night, that few people begrudged the king a few hours' rest within his chamber.

They sat on his bed, five of them, for Long Tom had materialized just as they were forming the Circle—using his own power this time—and was wordlessly accepted. Charles sat in the center head of the bed, Marguerite to his right, Kate to his left, then Louis to Marguerite's right, then Long Tom between Louis and Kate. All were naked, save Long Tom who, apparently, was incapable of shedding his clothes.

All were quiet and introspective.

"All depends on our strength today," Charles said eventually, looking at each in turn, his eyes resting fractionally longer on Louis than on any of the others.

There was silent acceptance for a reply. They all knew it.

"Asterion will feel something, and wonder," Charles continued. He lifted his hands and touched his biceps briefly, as if feeling there the golden bands of Troy. "I will be here for him, to ease his worry."

"It is not Asterion I worry so much about," said Louis, "but Noah's imp. Are you sure—"

"It will sleep, along with Noah," said Long Tom. "I am sure of it."

"'Sure' is not quite the extent of reassurance I was seeking," Louis muttered. He was tense, and very nervous, and Long Tom smiled at him and reached out a hand, resting it momentarily on his shoulder.

"We will do all we can," Long Tom said. "There is risk, yes, but once 'done is done,' then the imp will . . ." His voice trailed off.

The imp will be deceived, everyone finished, in their own minds, and prayed that it might be so.

"It is time," said Charles, and Marguerite reached for the box and the small piece of browned turf it contained.

NOAH WANDERED TO THE LOWER REACHES OF PARliament Hill. She did not want to climb to its peak, mainly because she had a fear of standing there, outlined against the clear blue sky for any who cared to lift their eyes and see, so she walked slowly about the base of the hill to a gigantic elm tree that someone in the village had mentioned to her.

It was almost thirty feet in girth, and was so old that its center was quite hollowed out with age. Almost forty years earlier some enterprising local villager had built a circular wooden staircase within, comprising forty-two steps, leading to a platform built among the branches of the tree.

Noah stood at the base of the tree, considered, then entered. The platform was shrouded in leaves, affording her some concealment, and she could hear no voices or laughter, so she knew she would be alone.

She climbed.

IN LONDON, IN THE KITCHEN OF THE HOUSE IN IDOL
Lane, Jane reached for a basket and looked to where Weyland sat at the table, counting his hoard of gold and silver.

"I am going to fetch some fish," she said, and Weyland grunted.

"Don't be too long," he said, then went back to his pile of coins.

Jane stared at him a moment, then turned and left the house, closing the door quietly behind her.

JANE HAD ONLY BEEN ALLOWED TO LEAVE THE
house in the past three or four years. Before then, she'd been Weyland's prisoner, hardly able even to see the light without his constant presence. But now Jane's pox had progressed to the point no one would listen to what she had to say. She was so greatly the outcast—hated by the men who had used her and hated by those men's wives and daughters—that Weyland felt comfortable in

allowing her to leave the house. There was no one within London who would lift a finger to aid her or offer her sanctuary. Jane had two choices: Weyland's comfortable house, or to live as a beggar beyond the walls of London.

Jane hated it—*hated herself*—that Weyland knew she would always come home. There was nowhere else for her to go.

Besides, it was hardly as if Jane walked the streets *quite* unescorted. There was always Weyland's imp deep within her, ready to bite and gnaw and chew and create such agony it would drive Jane to her knees in despair the instant it felt that she had overstepped in some manner.

Jane would be a good girl in her brief time away from Weyland, and well Weyland knew it.

MARGUERITE THREW THE TURF TOWARD THE CEIL-ing, rejoining her hands into the Circle as she did so, then all five watched as the turf metamorphosed into the circle of emerald silk as it fell.

"Noah," Charles said in a tight, hungry voice as the silk settled to the bed. *"Noah!"*

SHE STOOD ATOP THE PLATFORM IN THE ELM, FEEL-ing completely relaxed for the first time in weeks. The sun's rays were hot, but here the branches of the elm created a lovely dappled shade about her, and a gentle wind stirred through the tree and eased away some of the heat.

She yawned, and thought that perhaps she would sit for a few minutes before she climbed down and back to Lady Anne.

As she sat down, and her head started to nod sleepily, Noah realized that she was very close to the ancient Mag's Pond where, as foolish Cornelia, she had gone to beg Mag to give her a daughter so she would bind Brutus to her through a child.

Brutus, she thought, and slipped into unconsciousness.

JANE HAD REACHED BILLINGSGATE FISH MARKET BE-fore she realized that something strange was happening. The market was almost empty—this was a holiday, and there were only a very few stalls open for those needing to purchase fresh food—but Jane had a sudden sense of something *impending*. Something that made no sense in the sleepy quiet of the market.

"Brutus?" she whispered, and then almost immediately fought away the thought, and kept her mind blank.

But still Jane's face turned north, and still her lips formed a single word. *Brutus!*

AT THE KITCHEN TABLE, WEYLAND RAISED HIS HEAD, and frowned.

HIGH WITHIN HER ELM, NOAH SLIPPED DEEPLY INTO an enchanted sleep. But even so, she remained aware.

She found herself standing at the edge of Mag's Pond, with her glossy hair falling unbound down her back, and dressed in nothing save a long, simple white linen wrap draped about her hips.

"Brutus!" she said, and stepped into the pond.

Chapter Eight

MAG'S POND, HAMPSTEAD, MIDDLESEX
Noah Speaks

I WAS SHAKING WITH NERVOUSNESS. I KNEW WHAT had happened: My friends had formed the Circle, almost certainly with the aid of Long Tom—for I could feel Sidlesaghe power in this—and had "arranged" for me to meet with Brutus here, in the magical waters of Mag's Pond. I was both exhilarated and horribly nervous all at the same moment. Would he speak loving words to me?

Or would he condemn me?

We'd always parted life with such bitterness. In our first lives he'd hated me so deeply he had refused to speak to me for almost twenty years. In our second lives he had finally kissed me, but then spat at me, and said I tasted corrupt, and that I had allowed myself to become Asterion's whore.

Now, here we were to meet again, through the magic of the Circle, and of Mag's Pond.

I was terrified, more of my own appalling hope than of what he might do or say. I cared not about healing old wounds or bridging ancient rifts. All I wanted was for Brutus to love me, and I was almost panicked that this could never be.

THE WATER WAS COOL AS I STEPPED INTO IT, ITS WET-ness tugging at the hem of my linen skirt, but as I stepped farther into its depths that water took on a faint sheen, and became as if dry, and the linen of my skirt wrapped about my legs as if driven by a breeze rather than by the weight of water.

I walked through the water, and I stepped into . . . I stepped into . . .

Oh gods, I stepped into the chamber that had been mine in Mesopotama when I had been the spoiled princess Cornelia; and Brutus . . . Well, when Brutus had been Brutus.

It was fitting, somehow, that we had to try to heal this wound in the place where it had first opened.

The chairs where Brutus and I had sat to sup of our first meal together were there, the food still spread upon the table between them. The bath that Brutus had caused the servants to pour was there, steaming gently. The bed where Brutus had raped me was there, its covers smooth and pristine, as if once again they awaited the press of our struggling bodies.

My throat felt dry, my heart was pounding so fast I thought my entire chest must be shaking with its effort.

"Noah," said a voice, and I started.

The voice had come from the windows, and I turned to look.

He was there, and had been for some time, I think. He must have observed my arriving through whatever magic portal had carried me here.

"Noah," he said again, and I thought I heard a catch in his voice. Nervousness, almost, if I could believe that from him. I tried to arrange my face into a smile, but I was too anxious to make any great success of it. I must have looked pale and apprehensive and likely to run at any moment, and I thought this was not a good start.

He moved, and I tried to focus more clearly on him.

This was difficult, for the light was behind him, and so I could not immediately discern his features. I could, however, see that he was dressed as I had originally known him, in a white hip-wrap and with sandals upon his feet.

His limbs were bare of their kingship bands, but I could just make out the paler flesh where once they had been.

"You *are* Brutus?" I said, calling him for some reason by his original name and not the one he bore now (it seemed fitting, somehow). My voice struggled as much as had his, and I had to gather my strength in order to continue. "You are not some terrible glamour come to trap me?"

Gods, I couldn't believe I had said that. I sounded accusatory where I thought I had meant to sound humorous. What a fool I was, to try and jest at this moment.

He made a soft sound. (. . . of exasperation?)

"I am truly Brutus," he said. Then, "Is there someone else you'd prefer to be here?"

Oh, this *was* Brutus well enough. Here we were, making all the same mistakes all over again, letting our mouths say words our hearts denied.

"There is no one I would prefer to be here more than you," I said, and I was relieved to hear that this time my voice had a level of sincerity and emotion underscoring it.

He smiled—at least, I saw the flash of white teeth as he walked a little closer to me. Finally I could more clearly see his features. His hair was as black as ever it was, falling over his shoulders and partway down his back. His eyes were very dark, black mysteries, as they always had been. But there were differences. In this rebirth his build was finer, not so muscular as he had been in his two previous lives, but he was just as tall and just as beautiful to me.

"You grow more lovely with each life," he said, and he smiled again; now I could see that it *was* a smile. "Noah . . ."

Terrified of what he *might* say, I rushed in. "Long Tom said we must heal the wounds between us. Brutus, I am so sorry that I ever denied you the right to kiss me, or that I said to you such foul words about Melanthus, or that—"

"Noah, do you loathe me?" He seemed to have disregarded every word I'd said, which made me cross, because it had taken all my effort to force them out. Gods, they'd been sitting unsaid in my mouth for two and a half thousand years, and they had not easily leapt forth into voice.

Finally, what he said sank into my consciousness. "*Loathe* you? Why?" How could he possibly think that? Hadn't I spent two lifetimes throwing myself at him in one form or another?

"After what I said to you, when last we parted. After what I did."

"Brutus, I *begged* you to kill me. I thought you loathed me. You said—"

"I said stupid things." He suddenly reached out a hand and ran it through my hair. I shuddered, and I knew he felt it, for his eyes widened in an almost stunned disbelief.

He hadn't thought I would respond so readily to him. He *had* been scared, and *was* scared. Could it possibly be that he was as apprehensive as I? As terrified of failure as I?

His hand came to a halt at the back of my neck, his fingers so warm and strong.

"I have always said stupid and hateful things to you," he repeated, "because I was so frightened of you."

"Frightened of me? Why?" His fingers were now stroking at the back of my neck, and I wished to every god in heaven and hell that they would never stop.

"I was frightened of you because I felt too deeply for you. I was scared of loving you. I was terrified of you the moment I first laid eyes on you, I think. You stood there so proud and sure in your father's megaron"—he half laughed—"having just kicked one of my guards in the shins. I was scared of you, and of your father, and *that* is why I acted as I did. I demanded you as my wife, for I think I knew even then that I could not bear to lose you to another."

I could say nothing. I could hardly believe I was hearing these words.

"I would murder the world, if ever I lost you to another," he whispered, and I shivered.

He was so close now, and our bodies touched briefly with this breath and that, at breast and chest. I could feel his heat, see his heart skittering in his rib cage, and without thinking, acting only on instinct, I put out a hand and rested it on his chest.

His skin jumped under my fingers. "I am sick of being scared of loving you," he said. "Noah, please . . ."

And then I knew that he truly *was* scared, and I could stand it no longer. If he wanted a new beginning, then so be it. I did the one thing I had denied him in this chamber so long ago, the one thing our relationship had foundered on for so many lives.

I leaned against him, pressing my breasts against his chest, ran my hands down to his hips, and raised my face to his.

His hand tightened against the back of my skull, and somehow we were doing so easily what we had never allowed ourselves to do before: kiss.

It began gently and nervously, trembling tentative movements of mouth against mouth, each of us almost too scared to touch the other, but then suddenly he grabbed at me with his hands and body and mouth. Oh, gods, this was not like the kiss he had given me in the death chamber under Tower Hill. *This* was the kind of kiss that could found empires and tear down skies all at the same time.

I would settle merely for the founding of an empire.

"Do I still taste foul?" I asked eventually, pulling my mouth away from his.

He paused, as if thinking through what he *had* felt.

"I tasted you, and all that you are," he said, kissing me softly on the top of my nose, and then again behind my left ear.

Ah, I almost melted at those brief caresses.

"I tasted the land and its rivers and the tug of the moon, all this in your mouth."

Again he kissed me, more deeply this time, and with enough passion that I moaned. Suddenly all this kissing was not quite enough for me.

"And, yes," he said, pulling away just enough so that his words could play across my upturned face. "Yes, I can taste that imp within you, but in you it does not taste foul. What you *are* overcomes all that the imp represents. When I kissed Swanne, then I tasted all that she had become, and *it* was foul."

"But you said that I also—"

"I was a *fool.* I tasted only what I wanted. I was so angered, so terrified, and so *lost* when I realized how Asterion had tricked you, that all I could taste was foulness. But that foulness was *my* foulness, not yours."

"But this imp remains within me, even in this enchanted place. Are you not afraid of it?"

"Oh, gods, Noah. I am afraid for *you*. Long Tom has told me that you are destined to become Asterion's whore in this life, and—"

"Hush," I said, laying fingers against his mouth. "Do not speak of that now."

"I cannot allow it."

"You must, my love."

"I will save you. Somehow. I *will*."

His fervor touched me deeply. I knew that he could hate well. I had never realized until now how well, also, he could love.

"That is far into the future," I whispered. "Pray, let us not talk of it now. But . . . we do need to speak of the imp. I need to know if you are willing to—"

"I am *not* willing to allow this imp to keep me from you," he said. "Not ever again. If it snatches, then so be it."

"That is not the Brutus I knew and loved," I whispered.

"Then can you know and love this one?"

"Truly," I said, "I think I might be able to manage."

And with that, he picked me up, and carried me to the bed. "Cornelia," he said, naming me by my ancient and first name as he laid me softly down. "Will you be my wife?"

"Yes!" I said.

"Cornelia," he said, "will you love me?"

"Yes!" I said.

"Cornelia—Caela—Noah," he said, and he was laughing and weeping all at the same moment, "and Eaving, too, if she wants to hear it, the depth of love that I feel for you has been exceeded only by the stupidity I have shown in not realizing it."

"You love me?" I wished he'd just say it, three simple words, and not wrap them about with all this elegant courtspeak.

"Most exceedingly," he said.

"Then, dear gods, just say it!"

He laughed, and kissed me, softly. "Aye, I do love you, Noah. I always have."

"Well, that is good," I said, but I felt my voice choke up as I spoke those practical words. "For I happen to discover that I love you, too." I paused, then continued in a whisper. "And always have."

Then I reached out and undid the knots of his linen waistcloth, then allowed him to divest me of my skirt, and then he lay down beside me and cradled me in his arms.

"Asterion be damned," I whispered, and he laughed, and kissed me, and all was very well.

When, eventually, he rose above me, and entered me, I ran my hands through his hair and pulled his face back to mine, and let him kiss me all he wanted.

"Shelter me," he whispered, raising his face slightly, and I did, and so much of my worry and apprehension slid away as, together, in this place that was both Mag's Pond and the bedchamber where we had originally made so many mistakes, we finally did something right.

CHAPTER NINE

IDOL LANE, LONDON

Hampstead, Middlesex, and Antwerp, the Netherlands

*J*ANE FELT IT, *KNEW* IT, THE INSTANT THAT CORNELIA-reborn and Brutus-reborn met. She stood in the center of the fish market, staring northward, and gaped.

And then felt agony as the imp within her womb bit deep.

Come home! Weyland's voice seethed through her mind. *Come home! I command it!*

Jane dropped the basket she held over one arm, tore her mind free of whatever it was that Brutus and Cornelia were doing, and half sank to her knees in pain, her arms wrapped about her belly.

"For Christ's sake!" she whispered. "Allow me to walk and I *will* return to you!"

The pain abated somewhat, and Jane straightened. A few people had turned to stare at her, but none had moved to aid her. Instead they turned aside, presenting Jane with the cold hardness of their backs.

She was "the Harlot of Idol Lane," and if she had succumbed to whatever sinful disease beset her, then it was no concern of theirs.

Jane took a deep breath, steeled herself against both the pain she suffered now and which she expected once she returned to Weyland, and hobbled, as fast as she was able, back to the house in Idol Lane.

THE INSTANT SHE WAS WITHIN THE DOOR, WEYLAND grabbed her shoulder, spun her about, and slammed her back against the now closed door.

"There is magic about," he hissed, "and it involves Brutus!"

Jane's loathing of Weyland had by now far outstripped her fear, and she was able to regard him with a modicum of composure. "It is Midsummer, the solstice. There is magic about everywhere."

"Don't spin me tales about Midsummer. This is something else. It involves Brutus."

There was fear in his eyes, and Jane almost smiled at it. *You're still afraid of him, aren't you?* "Brutus is in Antwerp," she said. "You would have known if he had returned."

Weyland's eyes narrowed. "Have you been in contact with him?'

Now Jane did allow a cold smile to emerge. How, as Swanne, had she ever been fooled into thinking she loved *this*? "'In contact'? With Brutus? How can that be so? I am your slave, your whore, and I speak to no one without your consent."

His fingers dug into her, his hazel eyes more intense than she'd ever seen them previously. When he spoke, his voice was dangerously calm. "You stupid bitch, Jane. Speaking to me as if I were a simpleton is no way to bolster your own position."

"I can sink no farther," Jane snapped. "Threats of further degradation have no power over *me*!"

He stared intently at her, then nodded. His face relaxed a little, and he raised a hand to run one finger slowly about the line of her jaw. "You'll never escape me, Jane. You know that, don't you?"

All the defiance drained from Jane's face, and she sagged slightly. "I know that."

He leaned very close to her so that their mouths were almost touching. "Good," he said, so soft that it was little more than a whisper of breath against her lips.

He stood back, and jerked his head toward the kitchen. Jane straightened, thinking that Weyland had done with her, and walked through the parlor into the kitchen, aware every moment of Weyland following close behind.

As she entered the kitchen, Jane moved toward the hearth, thinking Weyland would want something to eat, but was stopped dead as he siezed at her arm, spinning her round to face him.

He hadn't finished with her, after all.

"Don't think I've forgotten Brutus," he said. "I can still smell his stink as though he were standing next to me." With his other hand Weyland grabbed painfully at Jane's chin. "You and I are going to make sure that Brutus is still in Antwerp. If he isn't, then all hell is going to break loose, my dear."

There was a flash of fear in Jane's eyes, and Weyland smiled.

* * *

"THE IMP HAS NOT HARMED YOU," NOAH SAID, WITH immeasurable relief as they lay relaxed and entangled amid the sweat-dampened sheets of the bed. Their hands were loosely entwined, their faces very close.

"The imp sleeps," he said. "Coel's power has done this."

She half smiled. "I have felt some of his power in this life. He is greatly blessed, I think."

"I would have lain with you no matter what. I meant what I said. If the imp snatches, then so be it. I am tied to you . . . Dammit, Noah, *I love you,* and if my death is a result of that . . ." He shrugged.

"How I have longed for you to say that."

His only answer was to stroke her face with gentle fingers. "Whatever you need, Noah, I will do it."

Her eyes became very dark. "And if what I need is for you to hand over your powers as Kingman to the Stag God new-risen, then you will do it?"

"Noah, who *shall* be this stag-reborn?"

"It is not for me to say who the Stag God is to be, Brutus."

"Why not?"

"You must hand your powers as Kingman to whomever the land picks, Brutus. Whoever it is. Can you do this?"

He moved away from her very slightly, little more than a tensing of his body, but it was enough, and she sighed.

Brutus tensed even further. "Is it to be this John Thornton whom you have taken as your lover? Is he who you have picked as your Kingman?"

Noah's eyes widened and he could see he had shocked her with his knowledge. Well, so be it. Let her guilt match the hurt he felt.

"John Thornton is as important to me," she said, her voice low but forceful, "as Marguerite is to you. How important is *that,* Brutus?"

"Is Thornton to be your Kingman?"

She sighed. "Brutus—"

But he had rolled away, and was no longer listening.

WEYLAND'S FINGERS TIGHTENED AGONIZINGLY ABOUT Jane's chin. "You're bound to Brutus," Weyland said. "You were his Mistress of the Labyrinth and his lover. You can reach him, and, by God, *I'm* going to reach out and touch him through you. God help you, Jane, if he *isn't* in Antwerp."

Then power seethed through her, taking control of her, and Jane gasped and sagged to the floor, her eyes rolling back in her head.

Weyland sank to the floor with her until they faced each other on their knees, and he took both of her wrists in his hard hands.

"Take me to Brutus, Jane Orr, Mistress of the Labyrinth. Take me to your Kingman!"

NOAH SAT UP, ANGRY. "I CANNOT ALWAYS BE WHO YOU want me to be, Brutus."

"Most apparently."

"Brutus—"

He sighed, and rolled back to face her. "Noah, I am sorry. Can we not talk of this? I am more worried about you."

Now Brutus was sitting up as well, and took Noah's shoulders in gentle hands. "Noah, you cannot go to Asterion."

"I must."

"Why?"

"If for no other reason than he has Jane in his thrall, and she is the only one who can teach me the ways of the Labyrinth."

"Then I will snatch Jane, and bring her to you, and—"

"Brutus. Enough." She laid her hand on her belly. "I have his imp inside me. I cannot escape this fate. I must live it through, in whatever manner Fate dictates."

"Then I curse fate, for—" Brutus suddenly stiffened, his hands dropping away from Noah. "Gods!" he said. "Asterion is scrying out for me! I have to return. Now!" He leaned forward, kissed Noah hard but briefly on the mouth. "I will do everything I can to protect you," he said. "You shall *not* be trapped by Asterion!"

And then he vanished before Noah could make any reply.

EVERYONE IN THE CIRCLE TWITCHED, AND MARGUE-rite and Kate both moaned.

Charles, who had been bent over from his waist to such an extent that his nose was almost touching the circle of emerald silk, gave a great, strangled cry and jerked himself upright, his eyes blinking, their pupils dilated as if he were disorientated.

"He's coming," he whispered, his voice very dry. "Asterion."

Kate made as if to pull away from the Circle, but Charles almost snarled at her. "No! We must let him enter. We must let him see that I am here!"

The circle of silk rippled, then a noxious black stain spread out from its center. Just before the stain reached the outer edges of the silk, the material reared up, taking on the shape of the Minotaur's head.

It slowly revolved, looking about the Circle with eyes black and luminous.

"Well, well," it hissed. "How pretty. How sweet."

Suddenly its head swiveled about and stared at Charles. "And how help-less, eh, Brutus? What are you up to, then?"

Charles extended his arms to his sides and then raised his hands, Mar-guerite's and Kate's still held within them, until they were just below shoulder height.

"Sending *you* my very own best wishes," he said, and abruptly he let the women's hands go and flung his own fists toward the apparition in the center of the silk, opening his fingers just as his arms extended fully.

Everyone in the Circle save Charles gasped in shock, for as Charles opened his hands, so then a storm of leaves and twigs erupted from his palms, flinging themselves at the apparition of Asterion.

The Minotaur cried out, then vanished, and the silk fluttered, flaccid, to the bed, resuming its emerald aspect.

Charles slowly retracted his hands, and rubbed at his biceps. "You weren't expecting *that*, were you, my friend?" he said.

WEYLAND LET GO OF JANE SO ABRUPTLY SHE FELL senseless to the floor. He rose to his feet, staring at her prone form, although it was not Jane that he saw, but Brutus.

Brutus, hands outstretched, a sly grin on his face, flinging such power at Asterion that the Minotaur had never expected.

The power of the forests?

Weyland cursed, low and foul. Brutus' transformation was far further ad-vanced than he had thought.

LOUIS SCRAMBLED ABOUT THE NOW BROKEN CIRCLE and laid his hands on Charles's shoulders. "Charles, are you well? By God, I never expected . . ." His voice trailed off.

"And Asterion 'never expected,' either," Charles said. "He will think twice about trying to scry me out next time."

He glanced at Long Tom, who was regarding him with a smile.

Then Marguerite sighed, and she reached for the silk circle, and folded it back into its original turf.

The Circle was disbanded.

NOAH WOKE WITH A START, FINDING HERSELF LYING, arms and legs akimbo, in a corner of the wooden platform in the elm.

She scrambled to her feet, her face red, wondering if someone had climbed the steps and seen her thus.

But there was nothing but quiet, no voices, no sound save for the gentle rustling of the leaves of the elm.

She stood for a few minutes, reorientating herself, hardly daring to believe in what had just happened, then she descended the steps in the elm and made her way back to the edge of Hampstead Heath where Lady Anne was more than pleased to see her.

THAT NIGHT MARGUERITE CAME TO CHARLES. "DO you wish me to stay?" she asked, her fingers already at the laces of her bodice.

Charles reached forward and stilled them. "No," he said. "I am sorry, Marguerite, but I think you and I can no more . . ."

She kissed him briefly on the mouth, and smiled to show that he had not wounded her feelings. "I understand," she said.

And then she turned, and left him alone.

IN THE STONE HALL THE IMP SAT, LEGS SPLAYED OUT, resting his weight on his hands.

He was feeling very groggy.

Then came a noise, very faint, but a noise nonetheless, and the imp sprang to his feet, wavering a little until he caught his balance.

For a moment he saw nothing; then, as his eyes focused and became their usual bright points of bleakness, he saw that something moved in the shadows at the very far end of the hall.

"Come out!" he hissed. "Come out, whatever you be!"

Another noise, as if of the scraping of a foot against stone, and then something, did emerge from the shadows at the very hard end of the hall.

The imp squinted, his small round face layering up in myriad lines of concern. He took a step forward, and squinted all the harder.

"Oh," he said, deflated that the intruder was merely a very small girl.

She walked forward, a child of some six or seven years. She was very pretty, with long black curly hair, very pale skin—fine as only a child's can be—and with sparkling, deep-blue eyes.

In her hands she carried a long loop of red wool.

"Would you like to play a Game?" she said to the imp.

The imp chewed his lip, thinking. He really should tell his master about this . . .

"If you win, then you may tell the world of my presence if you wish," said the girl, "but if I win, then you shall do whatever I say in this matter."

"No one ever bests me in a game," said the imp, his pride dented by the very idea that a child could outwit him.

The little girl smiled.

"Very well," said the imp, and squatted down on the marble floor of the stone hall. *"Show me this game of yours, then."*

ON THE NEXT DAY, LOUIS AND CHARLES MANAGED A few quiet words. Both had been shaken deeply by what had happened the previous day. Of the two, Charles looked by far the worse; he'd been exhausted both physically and emotionally by his exertions of the last twenty-four hours.

"She is fatalistic about Weyland," said Charles. "I cannot believe she can be so calm about her fate. *Damn* it!"

"She needs to be saved from him," Louis said. "After yesterday, neither of us can just let her walk into what Weyland has waiting for her."

"But Noah needs Jane to teach her the skills of Mistress of the Labyrinth, and Weyland has Jane, so—"

"Then we snatch Jane as well. But at the very least we do *not* allow Noah to fall into Weyland's power. What he might do to her beggars the imagination."

"Aye," Charles said. "I agree. I've been thinking on what you said earlier . . . that perhaps you can return to England a day or so before I do, and take Noah before Weyland has a chance to snatch at her."

"So," Louis said, "you agree that I can return to England immediately before you? Snatch Noah before Weyland manages it?"

Charles gave a single, curt nod. "Just make sure that Weyland doesn't snatch *you*, my friend, for then all would indeed be lost."

"How long?" Louis asked. "How long before . . . ?"

Charles sighed. "Who can tell? Cromwell must die, England must set aside its experiment with parliamentary democracy, and the people must invite me home. Only then, as I prepare for my grand restoration, can you embark for England."

"It will not be soon enough," said Louis.

CHAPTER TEN

WOBURN ABBEY, BEDFORDSHIRE
Noah Speaks

*I*T SEEMED LIKE A DREAM, THAT AFTERNOON SPENT
in my Mesopotamian bedchamber, but four or five weeks after we'd
returned to Woburn Abbey I had ample evidence for the reality of
that meeting between Brutus and myself.

I woke one morning feeling ill, an indisposition which did not depart me
the entire day, and by evening I could no longer ignore all the evidence my
body had been screaming at me for the past month.

I was pregnant.

The reality of that hit me in the evening when, thankfully, I was alone in my
bedchamber.

I was pregnant.

My instant reaction as that realization dawned in my mind was one of
sheer joy. *I was carrying Brutus' child!*

My second reaction, following almost instantly upon that first, was one of
horror. *My child shared my womb with Asterion's imp!*

I was, in essence, pregnant with twins. One I hated and feared; one I
yearned for almost more than life itself.

I was sitting on a chair by my bed, dressed in a nightgown, when all this
was rushing through my mind. Once I had calmed myself, I stood and, standing before the mirror, removed the nightgown.

I gazed at myself, my hands on my belly. I no longer believed in coinci-
dences in life. Certainly not in mine.

In my dream I had stepped into Mag's Pond to enter my ancient bedchamber in Mesopotama.

Mag's Pond, where I had gone with Erith and Loth to beg Mag for a child
so Brutus would return to me.

My daughter . . .

She whom I had seen so often within the stone hall. Seen as if she was meant to live again.

My daughter!

Joy emerged victorious over horror, and I literally sagged a little as I stood there, my hands now trembling, my eyes misting with tears. My daughter, once so brutally torn from me, had been given back to me. I had no idea whether I had been blessed by the Troy Game, by some benevolent gods I was not aware of, or by Fate itself. Whoever had gifted me this daughter, I knew it *was* my daughter, reconceived within the magic of the sacred waters of Mag's Pond.

My daughter. Brutus and I had reconceived our daughter.

The tears were trickling down my face now, but I didn't care. I just stood there, gazing stupidly at my reflection in the mirror. I had my daughter back. *She* had her life back.

"I will protect you," I whispered, still staring at my reflection's belly. "You may share my womb with Asterion's hateful imp, but I *will* protect you."

If it was the last thing I did, I would protect her.

I managed to tear myself away from my reflection and sat on the edge of the bed. Tentatively, I reached my power inside my own body, touching my child.

And felt nothing.

Oh, I could feel the child there, feel her warmth and life, but I could not feel *her*. I could remember my daughter, remember how she felt and smelt, even in death when I had held her, and I was sure I should be able to sense her now. After all, I was infinitely more powerful now than I'd ever been as Cornelia.

I should be able to touch her, shouldn't I?

Ah, perhaps it was too early. I forced my mind away from the problem, and instead thought of Brutus-reborn, and of that act which had re-created this child.

"Brutus," I whispered. *Brutus.* He needed to know. I smiled. He would surely be as joyful as I.

THE IMP FROWNED, THEN HISSED A LITTLE IN HIS FRUS-tration. The girl sat before him, cross-legged, her pretty face serene, her splayed hands held out before her, the red wool stretched in a complicated pattern between her fingers.

The imp raised a blackened, clawed finger and traced yet again the route from the center of the pattern to the exterior gate.

But, as always, his finger stalled at this dead end or that, or lost itself amid the myriad twisting paths of the pattern.

"You cannot find your way out," said the little girl.

"A moment more," snapped the imp.

"You cannot find your way out."

"It is tricky!"

"Yes. This was designed to trick and trap. And, see, you cannot find your way out."

"It is a tricky little game for such a little girl!"

She smiled, apparently truly delighted. "So," she said, "do you acknowledge your defeat?"

"Aye, you have bested me," he grumbled, venting his frustration by twisting his finger about in the red wool until it was thoroughly tangled. "I don't know what your mother has been murmuring on about . . . it's not as if you need any protection."

The girl laughed, the sound a beautiful rill within the stone hall.

"I win!" she said. "Again."

The imp pulled his finger free, and glared at her. "I have a brother," he said. "Bigger and nastier than me."

"Of course you do," said the girl.

"He shall be able to defeat you."

The girl raised an eyebrow, the expression on her face that of a much older and experienced person than a six-year-old girl. "Shall we ask him, then?" she said.

THE NEXT NIGHT I WENT TO JOHN THORNTON. I HAD not been to him, been *with* him, for almost three months, not since that night Long Tom had appeared to us in the park. A great coolness had sprung up between he and I, for which I was very sad. I liked John greatly, and had a vast respect for him, and I knew I had treated him poorly. He had come to love me, and even so, I had let our affair continue when it would have been better and kinder to have stopped it before he came to feel too deeply for me.

In my hands I carried a sealed letter.

He was asleep, for it was very late, and he jerked awake with a start when he realized my presence in his chamber.

"Noah? Lord Jesus, Noah, what do you here?"

I smiled, sadly. "May I sit on the bed for a while, John?"

He sat up, propping up the pillows behind his back. "What do you want?"

Ah, how sad. Just those four short words. *What do you want?* Well, what I wanted would hurt him immeasurably, and I could hardly bear to do it.

I sat down. I drew in a deep breath, took one of his hands, and rested it on my belly. "I am carrying a child," I said, and then regretted the words the instant I saw the look of wonder and hope in his eyes.

His hand tightened about my belly, and he leaned closer to me. "My child?" he said, and although he had phrased it as a question, I knew it wasn't. John truly thought that this was his baby—and what else should he have thought?

"No," I whispered, then winced as he flinched away from me, his hand snatched back as if it had been touching evil.

"Who else have you been whoring with?"

"I'm sorry, John. I—"

He had started to cry, and nothing could have made me feel worse. "What have I done to you, Noah, that you should treat me this way? What have I done, that I must be punished by your presence here, resting *my* hand on your belly, and your saying you carry another man's baby? My God, Noah . . ." His voice broke, and now I also began to weep. "My God, I had wanted you to be my wife."

Suddenly wild hope shone from his eyes. "Is that what you want? A husband, to save you from the shame of a lover who has deserted you?"

"No, John," I whispered.

"Then what *do* you want?" he said, his voice horribly hard. He used one of his hands, which shook badly, to dash away the tears from his cheeks. "What *do* you want?" he repeated.

I raised the hand in which I held the letter. "I need you to help me send this to . . . to . . ." *Gods, how to say it?*

"To the child's father?"

I nodded miserably.

He gave a hollow laugh, riddled with anguish. "Send it yourself. If you could find him well enough to get that baby in you, then you can find the wherewithal to send him *this* hateful piece of correspondence!"

"He is out of my reach, now. John . . . John, he is in Antwerp."

There was a silence. Then: "At *King Charles's* court?"

I nodded. No need to make it any worse for him with additional information.

"Who?" he snarled. "*Who?*"

"It does not matter," I said.

"It matters to *me!*"

"A man whom I love more than life itself."

That broke his anger, finally. He gave a harsh sob, and turned his face away from me.

"I do not know the means to get correspondence to Charles's court," I hurried on. "In Cromwell's Commonwealth it is death to send it publicly. But

I know the earl has contacts with the court, and I thought you might know how . . ." I drifted off. John was no fool. He would know what I meant.

There was a far longer silence than previously.

"Will you allow me to help you?" he said, eventually, and I knew he meant far more than the letter.

I nodded.

He reached out and took the letter from me, holding it between forefinger and thumb as if it were Pilate's death warrant for Christ.

"I will not read it," he said.

"I know that," I said.

He put it to one side, then he shifted forward in the bed, wrapped his arms about me, and rested his face in the hollow of my neck and shoulder.

I could feel his tears wet upon my skin.

"I will never stop loving you," he whispered.

"I know."

One of his hands crept around to my belly. "How I wish this were my child."

"I know." My tears were flowing again. Gods, I hated hurting this man!

"If it helps," he said, a terrible hope in his voice, "I can tell the Bedfords that this *is* my child. Once they discover you're with child, they will ask you to leave . . ."

"No," I said. I needed to stop this now. He wanted to claim the child, knowing the earl and countess would force me to marry him. "No, John. We will *not* say this is your child. I will face them myself, and I will not mention your name. This is my burden, my child, and I will carry all responsibility for it."

"Whatever you want from me," he whispered, "*ask*. I will give you anything you ask for."

"I will," I said. "I promise."

We sat in silence for a while, then he sighed softly.

"I hope this child is everything you want it to be," he said.

"Oh," I said, "she will be. I have wanted this daughter . . . oh, for so long."

"Daughter? You know it is a daughter?"

How to explain? I hesitated, then decided to speak as much of the truth as I could. John deserved that much, at least. "I carried a child many years ago, John. When I was seven months pregnant, a woman who wished me much harm forced the child from me, and murdered her. This child is my daughter reconceived, a second chance for her to live, and for me to love her."

Again, a period of quiet before John spoke. "A child you carried many years ago? How can this be? You were a virgin when first we bedded. My God, you were *thirteen* when you came to Woburn Abbey. When did you manage a child?"

How could I explain *that* to him? Once more, I spoke the truth. "I lost my daughter in a life I lived many, many years past. This child's father . . . I loved him then, too."

John was still upset enough that he ignored the reference to a past life. "Then what have *I* ever been to you, Noah, if all this time at Woburn you have been doing nothing but pining for this lover and, apparently, his daughter?"

"You have been my lifeblood, John," I said. Then I rose, kissed him once, gently, on the mouth, and left.

THE IMP SAT BEFORE THE GIRL, HIS FINGER TRACING A *painfully slow path through the labyrinthine tangle of red wool before him.*

To one side sat his brother, his wrinkled blackened face bright with hope that his sibling might succeed where he had failed.

But the second imp had no more luck than the first, and, after this, his thirty-third attempt to reach the outer gate of the labyrinth of red wool stretched between the girl's hands, he snatched his hand away and spat on the floor.

The girl, unperturbed, raised her eyebrow in that peculiarly mature expression of hers.

"You admit defeat?" she asked the imp sitting before her.

To the other side, the already vanquished imp sighed in resignation.

"Aye," muttered the imp sitting before the girl. "I suppose I do."

"This means I have bested the both of you, and, therefore, you must do as I say. Yes?"

Silence.

"Yes?" she said again, her tone more insistent.

"Yes," both imps mumbled.

She laughed again, the sound chilling. "Good! But no need for such long faces. I have a proposition for you. One sure to please."

PART THREE

CATLING

LONDON, 1939

CHEY DROVE NORTHWARD TOWARD EPPING FOREST *for only a few minutes before Piper's sedan made an unexpected turn to the left.*

"Where's she going?" Frank said, leaning even closer to his steering wheel and peering ahead. "The woman's addled!"

Skelton sat up straighter in his seat, a newly lit cigarette burning unnoticed in his right hand. "This isn't the road?"

"No. No." Frank leaned the heel of his left hand on the horn, giving it three long blasts.

In front of them, the man in the backseat of the sedan, "the Spiv," raised a hand and gave a nonchalant wave.

Follow us, Jack. There's something I want to show you.

"Just follow him, Frank," Skelton said quietly.

"What? I mean . . . Sir? The Old Man expects us to report for lunch, and—"

"Just follow him, Frank!"

Frank scowled, but he did as Skelton ordered.

PIPER PULLED HER SEDAN TO A HALT BY THE SIDE OF A *small hill not five minutes later. The area was completely built up—nondescript brick houses lined streets to either side of the hill, which was fenced off with six-foot-high iron railings.*

As Frank pulled in behind the black sedan, its passenger-side door opened and a figure in an expensive civilian suit climbed out. He paused just before he stood up, speaking to Piper, waving her back into her seat.

Then he stood up and, without looking behind him, strolled toward the iron railings, studying the hill, his hands in the pockets of his trousers.

"Stay here, Frank," Skelton said, then climbed out of the car, shutting the car door gently behind him.

He looked to where "the Spiv" stood, waiting for him, and felt a shiver go down his spine.

He knew who he was.

Skelton took a deep breath, then walked forward, clasping then unclasping his hands as he went.

He walked up to the man, then looked up at the hill. "What is it?" Skelton said.

The man turned his head to look at Skelton. He had a strong, angular face under well-cut fair hair, and a dapper air, as if he was at home among the upper-class salons of London society.

"Do you know what this hill is, Skelton?" the man said.

"No, Weyland," said Skelton. "Why don't you tell me?"

Weyland Orr gave a half-smile. "Light me one of your smokes, old chap, and I will."

CHAPTER ONE

IDOL LANE, LONDON

JANE WORKED SILENTLY IN THE KITCHEN AS SHE prepared the evening meal. Every so often she paused to rub at either one of her legs or at her forehead. Both legs and head ached abominably. In the past six months her pox had become infinitely worse. Large sores covered her forehead and cheekbones, fermenting, laying open her flesh to the bone, and constantly weeping foul fluids. The pain of the sores was made much worse by the terrible aches in her lower spine and legs: her bones suppurated as vigorously as did her outer flesh. The flesh over her thigh bones was now hard and reddened and extremely painful to the touch; Jane was terrified that soon lesions would open up there, too; great abscesses which would ooze right down to the bone.

Jane spent a great deal of her time either weeping or wishing she were dead. *Anything*, to escape this horror.

There was a step in the doorway which led to the parlor, and Jane turned about slowly.

Elizabeth stood there, her face drawn and weary. "Do you need any help, Jane?" she asked.

"You have finished for the day?"

Elizabeth's mouth twisted. "There are no more men waiting."

There was such quiet resignation in Elizabeth's voice that Jane felt a moment of sympathy. She liked Elizabeth, for the girl never averted her gaze from Jane's ruined face, nor regarded her with disdain. Elizabeth did not try to avoid Jane, nor did she try to curry favor with her.

She regarded Jane with what Jane had—eventually, and very surprisingly—recognized as a respectful friendship.

"Leave, Elizabeth," Jane said. "There is no need for you to stay the rest of the day."

"Weyland will not want me to go so early."

"I will tell him I sent you back to the tavern cellar. That you were ill. Go now. There is no need for you to . . ." Jane stopped, unable to complete the sentence. *There is no need for you to suffer as I do.*

Elizabeth nodded, hesitated, then walked over to Jane and gave her a quick kiss on her cheek. "Thank you," she said, and then she was gone.

Jane stood motionless for a long time after Elizabeth had left, stunned at the simple gesture of affection.

WEYLAND RETURNED WITHIN THE HOUR.

"Where's Elizabeth?" he said as he sat himself down at the table. "I saw Frances cleaning the stairs, but no sign of the other."

"I sent her home. Her head ached, and her back."

He grunted.

Jane looked at him in surprise. She had expected far worse of Weyland than a mere grunt.

But then, Weyland had been distracted and distant ever since Midsummer Day. Despite finding Brutus-reborn still in Antwerp, the day's events had patently unsettled him.

Due to the suffering she'd received at Weyland's hands during that day, Jane herself remembered little save for snatches of extraordinary vision. Brutus and Cornelia (and she dressed as the Mistress of the Labyrinth, as if she had already taken over that office), kissing, making love. Brutus-reborn, throwing a forest into Weyland's face.

A tiny girl, playing with imps.

Imps? There were more than hers?

"It's time," Weyland said, fairly softly. "His thirtieth year approaches."

"Time for what?"

"Time for Charles to get his throne back, I think."

Jane's breath caught a moment in her chest. "Time to bring *Brutus* back?"

Weyland said nothing, not even acknowledging her question with his eyes.

"But you're afraid of him!"

He roared to his feet, and struck her the terrible blow she'd been expecting ever since she'd sent Elizabeth home. "I am not afraid of him!"

You're terrified of him! But Jane kept her shoulders bowed, her face averted, and Weyland returned to his seat at the table.

"I have a means of controlling him," he said.

"Cornelia-reborn," Jane murmured, shuffling closer to the hearth.

"Yes. Noah Banks, now. Living a life of luxury at Woburn Abbey. Well, I hope she enjoys it while she may."

It took Jane a moment to realize what Weyland meant. "You're going to bring her *here*?"

"Aye. And Charles will do anything to keep her safe."

"How do you think you can control Cornelia . . . 'Noah'?"

"Have I never told you? I put an imp in her, too, in our last lives."

Jane gaped, and for a moment she could not speak. *In the name of heaven . . . that is why she'd seen two imps in her visions!* "Why? Why? Why torment her as you have me?"

"Because I want the Game, Jane, and Noah is going to give it to me."

"You want her to find the bands for you."

Weyland regarded her thoughtfully. "Aye. And I want you to teach her the ways of the Labyrinth."

Jane went cold. Her death lay revealed in that simple sentence. That Weyland might want Noah before he wanted her did not surprise Jane (in all of their lives, *everyone* seemed to want Noah before Jane). That he wanted Jane to teach Noah the ways of the Labyrinth, and to induct her into the mysteries of the Mistress of the Labyrinth did not surprise her. Jane wasn't even shocked by the idea that Weyland might kill her once he had what he wanted in Noah. What *did* stun Jane was that she should care so much about death.

She didn't want to die. Even after all these years of torment and humiliation, she didn't want to die.

"Of course, I'll let you go once I have what I need in Noah," said Weyland, still watching Jane carefully.

Jane swallowed, her mouth so dry she was unable to speak. *Of course he would* not. *She was dead the instant Noah passed the Great Ordeal in the Great Founding Labyrinth.*

She blinked, and became aware that Weyland was grinning at her.

Bastard! He undoubtedly knew every thought that was screaming through her head. She spun around, pretending to concentrate on the pot hanging over the hearth.

"Can't you wait," said Weyland softly behind her, "to see Noah in my arms? To hear *her* scream? To know that she shall suffer the same torment which has tormented you all these years?"

Strangely, Jane felt no satisfaction at the thought.

The pox, she decided, must have finally eaten its way through to her brain.

CHAPTER TWO

ANTWERP, THE NETHERLANDS

THE LETTER REACHED CHARLES WHEN HE WAS surrounded by a roomful of people: Sir Edward Hyde; Louis de Silva; several chaplains, courtiers, and sundry servants.

The sealed letter was one of only several that had made their way to Charles from his land of birth that day, and it was the last that Charles had picked up. He broke the seal, paying the letter little mind as he laughed at some jest one of the courtiers had made, then cast his eyes quickly over the contents.

He went still, horribly still, and his face paled.

"Majesty?" Hyde said, bending close.

Charles laid the letter against his chest so that Hyde could not read its contents.

"A sudden indisposition," Charles said. "No more."

"Do you need—" Hyde began.

"Some quiet, I think," Charles said, and Hyde obediently turned and began to usher people from the royal presence.

"Louis, if you will . . ." Charles murmured, and Louis halted just inside the door, waited until Hyde had closed it behind him, then walked back to Charles's side.

"What is it?" Louis's voice was tense.

Charles at first made no response, save to more diligently read the letter, then he handed it to Louis.

He noted without surprise the horror that spread across Louis's face as he read.

"She's carrying a child," Louis whispered.

"We *must* act now," said Charles. "To allow her to fall into Weyland's hands while pregnant, or with a child in her arms . . ."

"Aye," said Louis. The letter trembled a little in his hand, and he was about to speak again when the door to the chamber opened and closed. Both men jumped, but they relaxed as they saw Marguerite hurrying toward them.

"I heard . . ." she said, then her eyes fell upon the letter in Louis's hand, and she all but snatched it from him.

Her reaction was very different to that of the two men. A broad smile broke out across her face as she read the letter.

"How she must be pleased!" she said as, finally, she gave the letter back to Charles.

"'Pleased'?" Louis said. "That child . . . and the imp . . . and soon . . ."

"Weyland," Charles said.

"The child will be a great comfort to her," said Marguerite. "And what did you expect? Going to her and loving her? It is the way children are made."

"I should go to her now," said Charles.

"You can't," said Louis. "But I . . ."

"Neither of you can," said Marguerite, and both men glanced at each other before as quickly looking away.

"*I* shall go to her," Marguerite continued, "and Kate, for she is well enough after her daughter's birth. Weyland shall never suspect our presence. He does not know of us. He does not suspect us. Charles, you may write to the earl of Bedford, and ask him to expect us to stay. A small house in Woburn village, perhaps, will do well for Charles's mistresses and whatever of their children they bring with them. I am sure the earl shall be glad to comply."

"Yes, Majesty," Charles said wryly, but there was no amusement in his face, and when he looked back to Louis, there was nothing shared between the men but desperate worry.

"It is time," said Marguerite, softly, "that the first of Eaving's Sisters returns to her side."

CDapCer CDRee

Hoogstraeten, on the Border of the
Netherlands

M AJESTY! MAJESTY!"

Charles's racquet missed the ball, and he swore. He was on the tennis court at Hoogstraeten, deep in battle with Louis, and the interruption had just cost him a game.

"What is it?" he snapped at Sir Stephen Fox, who by now was standing at the side of the court, breathless from his run.

"Cromwell is dead."

Charles stared at Fox. "Say again, man?"

"Cromwell is *dead*. A fever, some say, although another rumor whispers poison. But what care we? Cromwell is dead!"

"I hope not poison, for the sake of your reputation, Majesty," said Louis, who had come to Charles's side. Both men were sweating heavily, the linen of their shirts stuck in patches to their backs and chests, their breeches stained at groin and waistbands.

"Cromwell is truly *dead*?" Charles said.

"Aye," said Fox. "And aye and aye again. A week now. He died on the third."

Charles and Louis locked eyes; there was a great deal which needed to be said, and none of it here, with other ears listening.

The news had spread. Men were running from the house toward the tennis court, cheers announcing their forthcoming joyous arrival.

"What do we now, Majesty?" said Fox, a great grin splitting his face.

"We play it more carefully then ever we have before," said Charles, and Sir Edward Hyde, who had just arrived, nodded.

"Aye, Majesty. Now is not the time to put a single foot wrong."

"No invasion," Charles said slowly, and again his eyes met Louis's. *Not this time.* "We wait for the invitation."

Hyde looked at Fox, and around at the other men who had gathered in an excited circle about Charles. *Exile . . . finally, finally, over!*

Almost.

"Cromwell's son, Richard?" said Charles. "Has he been proclaimed Protector, d'you know?"

Fox nodded. "On his father's deathbed. The Council of State have ratified it."

"That isn't worth the hot air it took them to expel the blessing," said Louis.

"Nay," Charles said. "Richard must now prove himself, and I think he shall not have the nerve for it. My friends, the world turned upside down fifteen years ago, but now I think the mighty tide of revolution has passed along with Cromwell. Rebellion has exhausted itself, and we—*we*—shall return on the ebbing tide of its strength."

"*Who,* then?" said Louis. "Who holds the power? Who holds the key to your"—*our*—"return?"

Charles looked at Sir Edward Hyde.

"General George Monck," Hyde said, and Charles nodded. Monck was the leading general in Cromwell's army, controlling over half of its total forces. He was virtually the most powerful man in Britain at the moment; not in title, but in influence and might of weapons.

"But Monck has been ever loyal to Cromwell," said Fox. "He has never said a word in your favor, Majesty."

"It is what he doesn't want that is more important," said Hyde. "And what Monck *doesn't* want is for England to dissolve into chaos, which is likely with Richard Cromwell at its helm."

"He is an astute man," said Charles. "He will be amenable to . . . discussion."

"Promises of titles? Lands?" said Fox.

"No!" snapped Charles. "*That* is just what we must *not* do. Hyde, de Silva, my private chamber, if you please."

THEY RECONVENED WITHIN CHARLES'S CHAMBER within the half-hour, giving both Louis and Charles time to bathe and change their clothes.

Hyde had gathered several sheets of paper, and a pen and inkwell lay to one side of his right hand.

Charles sat down at the table; Louis also, setting down a large flask of ale and three cups. He filled the cups and passed them about.

"Lord God," Charles said quietly, "pray I do not make a misstep now."

"It will take time," said Hyde. "Months, likely, if not longer."

"I know," said Charles. "I am a patient man." He laughed shortly. "After all, I have had the time and the opportunity to perfect my patience."

Louis caught Charles's eye. *More than enough time, eh, my friend? Over two lifetimes' worth of patience.*

"What steps *do* we take now?" said Louis.

"We approach Monck," said Hyde. "Quietly and gently and humbly. Your crown literally rests in his hand, Majesty."

Charles briefly wiped a hand over his eyes. *Pray to all gods, Christian included, that Weyland doesn't think of that.*

"What should I say?" Charles said. "What words do I use to beg my throne back?"

"Use words of truth," said Louis. "He is a general. He has no time for the dissimulation of courtiers."

"Perhaps," Hyde said, picking up his pen and dipping it into the inkwell, "after a general salutation, we might say something in the manner of: 'I know too well the power you have, to do me good or harm, not to desire you should be my friend.'"

Charles grunted. "Are those the kinds of words a general would wish to hear, my friend?" he said to Louis.

"They are truth, and they are straight," said Louis. "He will accept them, and not think you the weaker for speaking them."

"Then perhaps some words stating my desire above all else for peace and happiness for all Englishmen," said Charles to Hyde. "I am sure you can find something suitable to express my meaning."

"Make sure, also," said Louis, "to ensure Monck knows that, should he hear anything to the contrary, then it be a falsehood. The king desires peace for his country, nothing else. He does not send this missive with a sword in his hand."

Hyde nodded, intent on his scribbling.

They passed to and fro some more suggestions, then Hyde had a suitable draft before him. "How should I end it, Majesty?" he asked.

Charles sipped his ale, thinking, then dictated: "'I must say, that I will take all the ways I may, to let the world see that I have an entire trust in you, and as much kindness for you, as can be expressed by your affectionate friend, Charles R.'"

Louis grinned. "A final flourish, Majesty, to let him know the courtier is not quite dead?"

"'Affectionate friend'?" queried Hyde. "He was Cromwell's man, after all."

"Monck was not one of the men who signed my father's death warrant,

Hyde. He was not one of the murderers. He came later to Cromwell's cause, and then worked with him for England's sake. If his *had* been one of the signatures on my father's warrant of murder"—Charles shuddered—"then what I have just written would damn me. I would rather invade than grovel to one of my father's murderers."

Louis and Hyde exchanged glances. No one who had put his name to that warrant would live long once Charles was firmly back on his throne.

"How shall we send it to him?" said Hyde. "If we send it directly we may well endanger Monck. We cannot know the full subtleties of the situation in England at this moment."

"He has a brother, a clergyman in Cornwall, I believe. We can send the communication to him, and he can pass it to his brother."

"Very well," said Hyde. "I shall retire and write this more neatly, and without these schoolboy blotches." He rose. "If I may have leave to retire . . ."

Charles nodded, and Hyde left the chamber.

"England!" Louis said, emotion rippling through his voice.

"Aye. Finally."

"Noah . . ." Louis said.

"Marguerite and Kate left yesterday. They are better placed than I'd thought, with this welcome news. Bedford now cannot refuse me. Not his probable future king. Ah, Louis, Noah is my life. I wish *I* could be going to her now."

"I know," said Louis, gently. "I know, Charles. At least, now that Cromwell has died, it should not be too long before *I* can be with her."

Charles shot him a dark look.

CHAPTER FOUR

WOBURN ABBEY, BEDFORDSHIRE

*L*ADY ANNE SAT, HER FACE ASHEN, STARING AT Noah Banks who, at least, had the grace to keep *her* eyes cast down to her hands folded in her lap. The countess flashed a look at her husband, and noted that he looked as shocked as she herself felt.

"I had not thought it of you," Lady Anne managed, her eyes once more on Noah.

Noah inclined her head, which could have meant anything. In counterpoint to the Bedfords, *she* was looking radiant.

"Who is the father?" Lord Bedford said.

Noah at last raised her face. It was very calm. "A man I love very much."

"Patently," said Bedford, "to have so lost your virtue to him! *Who?*"

Noah kept her eyes steady on the earl, but she said nothing.

"John Thornton," said the countess. "It must be. He and Noah have ever had an affection for each—"

"No," said Noah. "The father of this child is not John Thornton."

"You have dallied with *another*?" Lady Anne said.

Noah lowered her face again.

There came the sound of a horse's hooves outside, although no one in the gallery paid it the least mind.

"You cannot stay here," said Lady Anne. "My daughters . . ."

"I have not in the least harmed them," said Noah. Now, when she raised her face to look Lady Anne directly in the eye, there were two visible patches of color in Noah's cheeks. "It is not as if I have poisoned them with this pregnancy."

The earl opened his mouth to speak but was prevented by the arrival of a footman, carrying in his hand a sealed letter.

"My lord," the footman said, bowing. "This has just arrived. The courier said it was most urgent."

"It can wait," said Lady Anne—but the earl, who by this point had the let-ter in his hand, and had seen the handwriting, waved her to silence.

"No," he said. "It can't." He nodded the footman a dismissal, waited until the man had left the room, then looked at first his wife, then to Noah.

His wife's face was a muddle of confusion and hurt, but the earl was shocked at what he saw on Noah's face. She was staring at the letter, and there was both wild hope and joy in that face.

A man I love very much, she had said, and the earl felt his chest tighten at the logical connection of that remark and her expression at the sight of this letter in his hand.

But the pregnancy . . . How? *How?*

"It comes from Hoogstraeten," the earl said slowly. "From the king."

And how much more *the king, eh?* A bare fortnight ago Cromwell had caught a fever, and died within the day. A bare fortnight ago the earl might have been able to dismiss this letter. Not now.

Never, now.

His hands trembling very slightly, Lord Bedford broke the seal and read the contents of the letter, slowly.

Twice, to make sure he'd understood it.

Then he looked back at Noah. "It seems you have a very powerful protec-tor," he said.

"Husband?" said Lady Anne. "What is it? What does the king wish of us? And what does this have to do with Noah?"

"Charles has a request of us," he said. "'A small one,' he says. Two dear friends of his, the mademoiselles Marguerite Carteret and Catherine Pegge, as well what children cling to their skirts, are returning to England within the week. They wish to stay in Woburn village—they do not wish to impose on us at the abbey—and Charles asks that we provide them with a comfortable house. He says the ladies have the means by which to pay us for the privi-lege."

"Carteret? And Catherine Pegge?" Lady Anne said. "Aren't they among—" She broke off suddenly, coloring.

"Among the king's many and varied mistresses," Lord Bedford said. "Yes. And the children they bring, undoubtedly of the king's many and varied bas-tards. What these *women*"—he said that word with a disdainful twist of his lips—"could possibly want to do with Woburn I have little idea, *save,*" again he looked at Noah, "the ladies wish that Mistress Noah Banks stay with them as their companion."

Noah's face broke into a broad smile, and in all the years he'd known her, the earl thought he'd never seen her look so joyous.

"Charles writes," Lord Bedford continued, his words very measured, his eyes never leaving Noah's face, "that Marguerite and his Kate, as well Mistress Noah, are highly important to him." His eyes dropped to the letter, and he read a section of it: "'I would you do this favor for me, my lord of Bedford, which I shall greatly remember, and much favorably, when circumstances allow.'"

Lady Anne stared at her husband. "He hadn't heard of Cromwell's death when he wrote this."

Bedford checked the date. "No. This predates Cromwell's death by several days." Whatever power lay behind any directive Charles had asked for *before* Cromwell's death, was ten times as potent *after* Cromwell's death. Charles had not yet been proclaimed king in this land, but Bedford had every expectation that he would be, before very much time had passed. The Protectorship had passed to Cromwell's son Richard, but he was nothing but a weak seedling grown in the shadow of his father's strong stem. Richard Cromwell would never be able to hold England together.

Everyone who had any interests at all to protect in England would now be aligning themselves very quietly with the exiled king.

"What is Charles to you, Noah?" Bedford asked.

"A most-loved lord and king," she replied.

"And this . . . Marguerite Carteret? And 'Kate' Pegge?"

"Women whom I love as sisters."

"Who is the father of your child, Noah? Charles?"

"How can this be, my lord? My king is in exile, many miles distant, and I have never left Woburn in all my years here."

"Save for accompanying me to Hampstead," said Lady Anne. "How far gone *are* you?"

"Three months, my lady."

"Then that child *was* conceived at Hampstead!" said Lady Anne.

"But not by our lord king," said Bedford. "Unless he has powers of trickery we are unaware of."

Noah's face stayed perfectly expressionless.

Bedford sighed. "I cannot see how we can deny Charles, my sweet," he said to Lady Anne. "And it does solve a dilemma for us."

"The house two from the village church stands vacant," said Lady Anne. She looked at Noah. "You may remove yourself there so soon as these '*Ladies*' Carteret and Pegge arrive."

THE STONE HALL HAD VANISHED, AND THE GIRL LED the two imps through a bewildering maze of alleys and laneways. Houses and warehouses reared to either side, blocking out the sun, and the three had to pick their way through piles of refuse and worse, the girl delicately holding her nose against the stench.

"Where is this?" asked one of the imps.

"Your new home," said the girl. "Eventually."

The imps glanced at each other. "We like it better where we are," one said.

"You'll not stay there," said the girl. "You'll get your freedom, soon enough. Then . . . this awaits you."

"There's no freedom. You've won us," said an imp.

"True enough," said the girl. "But what if, besides your loyalty, I earned your love?"

"How?"

"By giving you true freedom," said the girl. "Now, pay attention. Do you know who I am yet?"

"Our enemy," said one of the imps, and the girl laughed.

"Oh, yes, your enemy indeed. But your liberator as well. I have the power to both trap you and free you. I have done the first. Do you want the second?"

ChAPTER FIVE

WOBURN ABBEY, BEDFORDSHIRE

"THEY ARRIVED LATE LAST NIGHT, AND HAVE SENT word this morning they shall arrive to collect you in the hour before noon."

Lady Anne, standing with Noah in the great entrance hall of the abbey, wondered at the sheer joy which the woman didn't even attempt to disguise at this news. Had she no shame? Carrying a bastard child herself, Noah was *happy* to house with two of the most notorious women of English gossip? A product of a strict disciplinarian upbringing herself, the countess simply could not understand why Noah had thrown away everything she could have had— John Thornton, for instance—for some light, immoral tumble.

"I find no sin and no shame in this child," Noah said, one hand on her still-flat belly and her eyes steady on those of the countess.

Lady Anne's jaw tightened. "You are packed?"

"Yes. I take little with me. My lady, may I farewell your children? They have meant much to—"

"No. I forbid you to have contact with them."

"I am no danger to them!"

Lady Anne did not reply to that. Not verbally, but the anger and distress in her eyes was response enough.

Noah sighed, then she turned away and walked up the great staircase toward her chamber.

Within moments one of the servants announced that a coach approached down the long road through Woburn Park, and the countess, still greatly disturbed by her exchange with Noah, settled herself on a chair near the fire in the gallery and requested that her husband join her to greet the arrivals.

I will meet with them this once, she thought, *and then dismiss them from my mind.*

There came the faint flurry of noises and voices from the entrance to the abbey, which intensified as the footman showed the (presumably two) women into the front hall. Just then the earl came into the gallery, taking a chair next to his wife.

Lady Anne felt some of the tension leave her shoulders. They would face these shameful women, she and her husband, with the combined weight of their aristocracy and their virtue. King Charles be damned, if he thought they would grovel to *these* women!

"I shall both be glad and sorry for Noah's departure," the earl said softly as footsteps sounded up the stairs toward the gallery. "She has been a delightful companion to both of us, as to our children, over the past years."

Rebuked, the countess made no reply. As the far double-doors opened, she stiffened a little, and raised her chin.

A footman bowed, then two women swept past him.

They were both pretty enough, Lady Anne conceded, though doubtless that prettiness had caused their fall from grace into immorality, and they bore themselves well—which bearing they had undoubtedly observed at whatever manner of court Charles had managed to gather about him in exile. The older of the women had dark-blonde hair, worn simply enough in a twist at the crown of her head, a figure somewhat thickened at the waist by childbearing, yet still graceful and supple. The younger woman was darker, much slimmer (although the thickness at *her* waist suggested to the countess that she had recently risen from childbed), and more vivacious, with bright eyes and a ready smile.

The women reached the earl and his countess, and both curtsied demurely enough.

The earl and countess inclined their heads.

"My lord, lady," said the older woman, Marguerite Carteret, "my companion and I are much obliged by your generosity in permitting us to lease such a well-equipped house within Woburn village."

"Our king required it of us," said the earl.

"In our current, sad climate," said Marguerite, "you were not obliged to King Charles in any manner. Yet you acquiesced to his request. That was well done of you."

"We will take up no more of your time," said the younger woman, Kate Pegge, "but ask only that we may make reacquaintance with our friend Noah Banks—"

Reacquaintance? The countess frowned.

"—for we have left our children waiting below in the carriage, and we would return to them speedily."

A carriageful of Stuart bastards, Lady Anne thought bemusedly, *at our front door.* "Then, you may collect Noah and—" she began, but just then there came a footfall from the doorway, and both Marguerite Carteret and Kate Pegge spun about, their faces alive with joy.

The countess and the earl looked at each other. What *was* Noah to these two?

Noah had entered through the far door and, abandoning any pretensions to decorum, she picked up her heavy skirts, and ran toward the two women.

"Ecub!" she cried. "Erith!"

The countess looked at her husband. *Ecub? Erith?*

The three women met in a flurry of skirts and kisses and embraces halfway between where the Bedfords sat and the door. After their initial greeting, Marguerite Carteret and Kate Pegge further stunned and bewildered the earl and countess by stepping back from Noah, then sinking into such deep curtsies before her that anyone might have thought her the most ancient and venerable of empresses.

"For the Lord's sake," the earl whispered to his wife, "has Charles somehow managed to wed Noah in secret, that these two make obeisance to her as if she *were* queen?"

Lady Anne had a sudden and appalling vision of a Charles restored; and she, visiting court, to be forced to curtsy before Noah.

"Surely not," Lady Anne said.

Noah came to stand before the earl and his wife. "Lady Anne, Lord Bedford . . . I am most sorry that I must leave you in this manner. You have been good to me, and Woburn the best of homes. I—"

Lady Anne sighed, and rubbed a little at her eyes as if she were distracted. "I wish you well, Noah, but I wish you had done better." She hesitated, then reached out and gave Noah's hand a brief squeeze.

The earl rose, and kissed Noah's cheek. "Go with our blessings, Noah. I pray that your life shall be a good one."

The gestures of both Bedfords plainly touched Noah, for her cheeks colored and she smiled tremulously, as if close to tears.

She nodded, curtsied to both the earl and his wife, then turned.

Just before Noah reached the door, Lady Anne spoke once more. "The children are waiting for you in the vestibule, Noah. Say goodbye if you wish."

Noah stopped, turned, and looked at the countess with shining eyes. "Thank you," she said.

ONCE NOAH HAD SAID HER FAREWELLS TO THE BED-
ford children, and had kissed each one in turn, she, Marguerite, and Kate went outside. There was a driver and a coach drawn by two horses waiting outside

the steps leading to the entrance of Woburn Abbey. Two children, one a boy of about ten years, another a girl of some six years, were sitting inside with a well-wrapped baby secured between them.

"My children," said Marguerite proudly, introducing the boy and the girl to Noah. "You may call her 'madam'," Marguerite said to the children, "and treat her as if she were your queen."

"They have their father's look about them," said Noah, kissing each child gently on the cheek. Then, leaning into the carriage, she picked up the baby and cradled it in her arms. "Yours, Kate?" she said.

"Aye," Kate replied, love and pride evident in equal amounts on her face.

"Just born, too," said Noah. "Ah, she's beautiful, Kate. You are well?"

At Kate's nod, Noah handed the baby back into the care of the two children, and looked at the women. "You know that . . ."

"Yes," Marguerite said, kissing Noah yet one more time. "Charles showed us your letter. He fears for you, Noah."

"And thus you have come to me," said Noah, laying a hand briefly on each woman's cheek. "We should speak of—"

She stopped suddenly, her face losing all expression as a man came slowly down the steps toward the carriage and the group of women beside it.

"John," Noah said, and Marguerite and Kate could hear clearly the tension in her voice.

Noah recovered somewhat, and introduced John Thornton to Marguerite and Kate.

John smiled, and kissed each woman's hand graciously, but his attention returned almost immediately to Noah.

"I had to . . ."

"I know," she said, finally smiling a little at him.

"I could not let you go without . . ."

"I know."

There was a silence, then John looked at Marguerite and Kate. "Will you look after her well? I cannot bear to think of her suffering for her loss of home."

"For every loss of home, another is gained," said Kate. "We will watch her well, John Thornton, and we thank *you* for such care in farewelling Noah."

"I have loved her," said John, once again looking at Noah, "and will do so again, should she allow it."

Noah was now close to tears, and so patently incapable of replying, that Marguerite did so for her. "You are a man with farseeing eyes," she said. "You shall live a charmed life."

Thornton's mouth twisted sadly. "Without Noah? I cannot think it." Then he suddenly leaned forward, kissed Noah very softly on the mouth. "Farewell, beloved. May the land rise to meet you."

Marguerite's eyes glowed at this remark, and, as Thornton turned abruptly to go, she reached out a hand and stopped him. "You *will* live a charmed life," she said. "Believe it."

Thornton looked once more at Noah, as if he wanted to commit her face to memory, then turned and ran lightly up the steps and into the abbey.

"He is a good man," Noah said softly, watching his retreating back, "and I have treated him poorly."

To that, neither Marguerite nor Kate had anything to say.

CHAPTER SIX

WOBURN VILLAGE, BEDFORDSHIRE
Noah Speaks

SUCH LOVE AND COMFORT! I REVELED IN IT. THE depth of companionship between women beloved of each other is so vastly different to that which exists between a man and a woman that, I must confess, I allowed myself to luxuriate within it.

I chatted with Marguerite's two children as we rode toward Woburn village (there was a third, older girl, but she was happily ensconced within her father's court and had not accompanied her mother to England), and held Kate's baby. For the first time since realizing my own pregnancy, I felt relaxed and happy. I felt *safe*. Not merely physically secure, but safe *emotionally*. Marguerite and Kate and their children represented only joy and loving and companionship.

Their children delighted me. They had so much of their father within them that they were a pleasure merely to watch. They had his darkness of hair and of eye, even Kate's tiny baby daughter; and I was joyful, not only for their mothers, but for Charles as well, that he had children such as these. "Bastards" they might be in this world's tiny, cramped morality, but they came of a line so kingly, so powerful, that I knew they would consistently shine in every aspect of their lives. Blessed, indeed.

"I cannot think that your father could bear to allow you out of his sight," I said to the boy, and he grinned.

"He would not disallow us this adventure," he replied, "and he said we had mothers who could keep us safe through whatever travails might beset us."

"Aye," I said, smiling now at Marguerite and Kate, "you have extraordinary mothers, indeed."

And so, in warmth and love and joy, we arrived at our house. Woburn village was one of the prettiest English villages I had ever seen, and it was no tragedy for me that I should now find myself living there. The house stood on the gently sloping main street, two doors up from the church: a large, substantial brick-and-stone building of some three floors that could accommodate, with ease, all of us—Marguerite, Kate, myself, and all our children . . . born or still waiting for birth. The earl had sent along two servants for us, but Marguerite told me she had sent them back to the abbey.

"We three women can manage for ourselves nicely," she said as we drove into the village. "And besides, what we shall manage within the house, no Christian eyes should witness."

I smiled, content, and took Marguerite's hand as we walked into the house.

Marguerite and Kate had traveled well. They had brought with them a vast quantity of books and fabrics and carpets and chests and lamps and *everything* that might make a home.

"Where did the coin come from, for all of these riches?" I said, aghast, for I had heard of Charles's penury, the difficulties of his life in exile, and I did not want to think that he had sent himself even further into poverty, that we three might live in comfort.

"Not Charles," said Kate, "but Louis de Silva. His own father was generous with him, even though Louis is himself a bastard, and so Louis was generous with us."

"He said," Marguerite said, and I turned my head to regard her, "that he would do anything for you. Anything. This"—she spread a hand, indicating the vast expanse of opened chests and coffers—"is but a fraction of what he says he gifts to you."

"And for England?" I whispered. "What will he do for this land?"

Anything. Everything.

I heard the words whispered in the air about me, and I shivered.

Marguerite took my hand again, then she and Kate showed me the house. They had only just arrived themselves, so all was in chaos, but it was easy enough to see how comfortable we should be. There were two large reception rooms, a kitchen, pantry, and two small storerooms on the ground floor; while the two higher floors each held several large rooms which we would use as bedrooms for the children and ourselves.

At least, the children shared one large room on the second floor, and Marguerite, Kate, and I resolved to share the largest of the rooms on the third floor. We would not be parted, Marguerite and Kate and I, and were grateful that the chamber contained a bed large enough to hold all three of us, as well as Kate's baby (and, I had no doubt, Marguerite's two children when they came to wake us each morning with their shrieks of joy).

The three of us, in bed, sharing love and warmth and companionship and, I hoped, enough power that we might form our own Circle.

As Eaving, I had hardly touched my powers during this life. I was waiting, I think, for whatever lay down the road ahead for me.

Now, with Marguerite and Kate close and loving, and already habituated in the Circle, I could do more. Enjoy more.

But for that day we merely settled ourselves, fed and loved the children and set them to bed as the sun sank, and then retired to our own chamber high in the house, there to disrobe and crawl into the vast bed.

"I can feel him on you," I whispered as we sat, our bodies lit only by the guttering flame of a single candle set on a chest. I ran my hands slowly over Marguerite's naked body, then Kate's, exploring the curves and bounties of each one, observing with pleasure the marks of their children on their bellies. "I can almost *smell* him on you."

Kate was nervous at this. "Do you mind?"

"No. I do not. I am glad that you and he both have managed to find some comfort. But, oh, how I envied you when your Circle reached out and touched me! I could feel the closeness between you, and I wished it so much for myself."

"And thus John Thornton," said Marguerite. She had stretched out on the bed atop the covers, close to both Kate and myself. One of her hands rested warmly on my thigh, where I sat cross-legged, the other on Kate's hip. We were all so close, so *together*.

"Aye," I said. "Thus John Thornton."

"Was he a good lover?" asked Kate, and I think the expression on my face was answer enough for her and Marguerite, for they both laughed, and Kate clapped her hands.

"He wishes this child was his," said Marguerite when she'd sobered, and her hand slid from my thigh to my belly.

I shuddered at its gentle movement. "Oh, aye. He begged me to allow him to acknowledge it."

Marguerite said nothing, but her hand slid back and forth over my belly, as if feeling the child within.

"You shall start to round out, soon," she said.

I put my hand over hers and pressed it against my flesh. "Kate, do you remember when you were Erith, and you and Loth took me to Mag's Pond?"

Kate grunted, no doubt remembering also the debacle of that occasion.

"I conceived my daughter that night, and lost her to Genvissa's ill-will seven months later."

I stopped, and they said nothing, waiting.

"This is she," I whispered. "Reconceived."

"Eaving," said Marguerite, "are you sure?"

"Oh, aye. I can *feel* it. My daughter, returned."

Kate, who, as Erith, had witnessed my sorrow at my daughter's earlier death, reached out a hand and very gently caressed my face. "Ah," she said, "this is good news, truly. A promise, for the future."

I hesitated. Since that night when first I had realized my pregnancy, I'd been torn between two conflicting emotions. Sheer joy, at this child's second chance at life, and a growing worry that no matter how hard I tried, I could not communicate in any means with her. Was there anything wrong with her, or was it . . . ?

"I fear so greatly for this child," I said, "sharing my womb with that . . ."

"That imp?" said Marguerite. "And *who* should *truly* fear, Noah? Your sweet growing daughter, or the imp?"

I laughed a little, for I thought she jested, but I sobered when I saw how darkly serious were her eyes.

"The imp?" I said. "*It* should fear?"

"Noah," Marguerite said, and she slid upright and, moving her hand from under mine, held me close as if she were the mother and I the child. "This child has been conceived for a reason. Yes, you and Brutus lay together, and did those things that tend to make babies . . . but this is a baby reborn. I think that she is here for a purpose, and I think that she is not as other babies, innocent and unknowing. Noah, she has been to the Otherworld and back. What has that done to her? What power has that given her?"

I did not respond, for Marguerite's comments had made me deeply uncomfortable.

"And she was conceived of two such powerful parents," Marguerite continued. "You, Eaving, goddess of the waters and of the fertility of this land. And *he*, Kingman of the Troy Game, and all else that awaits him. For all the gods' sakes, Noah, this baby is a gift, and I think you have yet to realize the full extent of that gift. The imp . . . ?" I felt her shrug slightly against me. "The imp is a mere nuisance compared to the power that I think comprises your daughter."

I put my own hands over my belly. "I try to feel her, to speak with her, yet I feel and see nothing."

"Sometimes that is the way is it," said Marguerite. "Whatever the power of the mother, she cannot penetrate her own womb."

I thought of the countless times I had seen my daughter within the stone hall, and said nothing. But I also remembered that I had always seen her at six or seven years of age, and that comforted me. She would live to be born, at least.

"She will live to command in her own right," whispered Marguerite against my ear, kissing me here and there between her words. "But for now, my sweet, I think we have better things to do than to worry about your child. She can take care of herself for this night, at least."

I laughed and put my cares aside, and turned to offer Marguerite my mouth.

Chapter Seven

Idol Lane, London

ROM TIME TO TIME WEYLAND SPENT A FEW HOURS in the evening in the Pit and Bull on Thames Street, just along from the Customs House. Here he drank his way through six or seven tankards of warm buttered ale as he sat at one of the larger tables, sharing the warmth and companionship of the tavern with whomever joined him. Most of the regular patrons of the Pit and Bull—mostly warehousemen, customs clerks, a few sailors, and the odd cowper—liked Weyland immensely (even though most knew that he kept a brothel, and some had even patronized it), although none was close to him. Weyland Orr related some of the best tales to be heard in London's taverns: yarns of long ago, concerning gods and demons, raptures and catastrophes, and, when he was in the mood, the best version anyone had ever heard of the ancient and beloved tale of the Trojan wars. Two of the customs clerks had pressed Weyland for many months now to write these tales down. "Put them out as pamphlets," they urged him, "and the London folk will snatch them up in scores."

But to this, Weyland Orr demurred. "Those Puritans who sit in Whitehall would throw me in Newgate for such a liberty," he'd say, "and then what would you do with your evenings over your ale in the Pit and Bull?"

Weyland enjoyed these hours, but they left him feeling empty. On this night he did not tell any of his tales, claiming a headache, but sat back—sipping his ale as one ear half listened to the chatter about him—and sunk into his own thoughts. Over the past year or two he'd become increasingly unsettled within himself. His life in his house in Idol Lane left him progressively more irritated. Jane, as with Elizabeth and Frances, was terrified of him (and most particularly of what he could do to her), but that didn't stop her cold, insolent silences, or her glances of sheer disdain. Frances was merely terrified, and almost literally shrank into a hunch-shouldered piece of insignificance whenever he was about. Elizabeth . . . Elizabeth was outwardly compliant, but Weyland sensed a great distance within her, as if she had managed to push him from her conscious world. The kitchen of the house was now entirely a woman's world, with the three women who haunted it, forming a coterie whose walls Weyland could not penetrate.

This should not have bothered him. After all, he kept these women within Idol Lane only to use them. Jane he needed to teach Noah the skills of the Mistress of the Labyrinth (and she damned well *would* teach Noah, or Weyland would flay the skin from her body, piece by soft, resisting piece); and Elizabeth and Frances were there to . . . well, to create atmosphere, if you will. Once Weyland dragged Noah from whatever false, comforting world she currently inhabited into his den, then he needed to debase and degrade her as quickly as possible so that he might work her to his will.

Once he managed to drag Noah from her false, comforting world. Weyland was impatient to move, yet concerned that any precipitous action would ruin yet once more his chances to snatch those kingship bands. He'd caused Cromwell's death, thus setting in motion the process by which Brutus-reborn could return to England; but that process looked as though it might stretch out over months, if not years. *Damn this modern preoccupation with politenesses and considerations!* In any former life, Brutus-reborn could simply have invaded and quelled; now he needed to bend knee and solicit.

Charles's reentry into England dictated the moment when Weyland would take Noah. Weyland was certain that Charles would know the instant Weyland took her, and, as wary as he was of Charles, Weyland was not going to leave himself open to . . . well, to whatever Charles might be able to throw at him. So Weyland intended to leave it until the last possible moment to rope Noah in.

Besides, snatching Noah just when Charles might think her safe, meant the greatest possible pain for Charles. The triumphant returning king would think she was out of harm's way, and then, just as he entered London . . . Well, Weyland had something very special planned for Charles as he made his triumphal reentry (yet once more) into London.

Weyland smiled into his ale, causing one of his companions to remark that he must be thinking of one of the women waiting for him at home.

"A woman," Weyland replied, "but not one that awaits me in Idol Lane."

Once he had Noah, then he had the bands. Once he had both bands and Noah, and Noah had been trained as his Mistress of the Labyrinth, then he had the Game.

And then, he had the world.

It all sounded so simple, and yet Weyland knew that such a prize could not be gained through simple means. He'd been outwitted twice before. He would not allow it to happen again.

* * *

ONCE BACK IN IDOL LANE, WEYLAND GLANCED INTO
the kitchen—Elizabeth and Frances had gone back to their tavern for the
night, and Jane was asleep—then took the stairs two at a time to reach the top
floor and his Idyll.

He was in a reasonably buoyant mood, due largely to the effects of the ale,
and he whistled as he moved about his sanctuary. He stripped naked, admiring
his body—at least in this life he had a body that was slim, unlike the dreadful
flab he'd had to carry about as Aldred—then stood before a mirror, running his
fingers through his thick fair hair to comb it flat.

Suddenly he froze, fingers in hair, mouth pursed in a now silent whistle.

A woman had appeared in the mirror, standing a pace or two back from
him. She was dressed in the ancient Minoan fashion, with a full, red silk skirt
and a golden jacket left undone to display her breasts. She had long, curly
black hair and a face of exquisite beauty, marred only by her expression of
vicious hatred. Flames licked at her feet, as if she had emerged from hell
itself.

In her arms she held a very small baby girl, naked and squirming.

Do you know what it is you lack in this false Idyll? she said, her plump red
mouth moving in a slow, exaggerated motion, as if this were a dream. *Do you?*

Weyland stared at her, his hands still frozen in his hair, unable in his shock
and horror to respond.

You lack a companion, Weyland. *You are alone. You are unloved. I never loved
you. I only pretended.*

And then, as Weyland started slowly to turn about, she hefted the child she
held in her hands, and tossed it squalling into the flames at her feet.

You are alone, Asterion, as always you were, and as always you will be.

"Ariadne!" he cried, reaching for her (or was it for the baby?) as he completed his turnabout, but she was gone, and Weyland was left standing in his
Idyll, gazing at nothing but emptiness.

He stood there, staring, for what seemed to him to be hours. *Ariadne.*
Where had *she* come from? And what was it she had said? *You are alone.*

They bit, those words, but Weyland would not allow them any truth. *Alone?*
He had always been alone. It had not troubled him to this point, and Weyland
refused to believe his solitariness could start to trouble him now. If he was
troubled and irritated, unable to settle or relax within his Idyll, then it was because he was impatient for the Game to begin anew in this life. Impatient for
those events to occur which would enable him to get his hands on the kingship
bands of Troy.

No, that vision had not been Ariadne. That had been the Troy Game, trying to unsettle him yet further. Weyland bared his teeth in a silent rictus of

bravado. The king was returning, thus the Game had struck out in a preemptive threat, hoping to clear the king's path.

What Weyland didn't want to contemplate, was how the Troy Game knew about his daughter.

CҺAPTER EIGҺT

WOBURN VILLAGE, BEDFORDSHIRE

HE HARVEST WAS IN, AND THE PEOPLE CELE-
brated with the Festival of Ingathering. A parade wound its way
through Woburn village on the weekend, and villagers danced in
the field and went to church to lay sheaves of grain on the altar as thanks to
God for their bounty.

Noah—Eaving—and her sisters celebrated in an entirely different manner.
This was a time of great power for Eaving. Pregnant herself, she blossomed as
the land ripened into harvest and as the creatures of field and meadow and
forest dropped their own young.

On the night of the Festival of Ingathering, Noah, Marguerite, and Kate
gathered in their bedchamber. Marguerite's two children were asleep in their
bedroom, while Kate's baby was fed and laid down between the two older children to sleep.

The three women sat in a circle in the midst of the bed. They were naked,
their hair unbound, their eyes thoughtful and introspective. This would be the
first time they had formed their own Circle.

"Will you go to . . ." Marguerite asked of Noah.

"Brutus-reborn? No. It is too dangerous. You have told me how Weyland
has used the Circle once to confront him. I do not want to risk that happening
again. Tonight we will walk the Realm of Faerie, using the power of the land
and of the waters which river it. That is magic foreign to Asterion. With luck,
we will stay safe from him."

Marguerite raised her eyebrows and nodded at Noah's belly, now gently
rounded with the child she carried. *The imp?*

"I will risk it," said Noah. "I am not willing to allow this imp to entirely control my life."

At that Marguerite reached for the box she had brought with her from the Continent, and she placed it before her.

"When Charles was fifteen and forced into exile," she said, not raising her eyes from the box, "he took with him a small piece of the land. It was instinctive, that snatching, but powerful."

She opened the box, and withdrew from it the dried piece of turf that had, until so very recently, accompanied Charles in all his travels while in exile. Charles had given it to Marguerite, saying that he and Louis would not form a Circle on their own, and that it was best now that the turf return home. *"I think we shall not be long in following it,"* Charles had said.

Now Marguerite held the turf cradled within her hand. Then she reached out and gave it to Noah.

Noah raised her eyes to Marguerite and Kate. "From now, until the ending of the Circle," she said, "I live and breathe and speak as Eaving."

A subtle change came over her as she said this. Her bearing and demeanor became both stronger and gentler, her eyes transformed from their normal deep-blue, into a dusky sage-green shot through with lightning flashes of gold. Her thick, richly colored hair, flowing down her back and over one shoulder, almost snapped as a surge of energy ran through it.

Her skin, so pale, now glowed in the darkened room, as if it were the moon itself.

Marguerite and Kate both took deep breaths, and bowed their head and shoulders to their goddess.

"Eaving," they said as one.

Eaving lifted her hands, and tossed the turf into the air. Magically, as it always had done for Marguerite, it transformed into the shimmering circle of emerald-green silk; but then, unlike what it had done for Marguerite, it fluttered down toward the three women, much larger than it had ever been previously.

Just before it settled over their heads, Eaving spoke.

"Let us greet the land as it rises to meet us."

THEY FOUND THEMSELVES BEYOND THE BEDCHAM-ber, standing atop a grassy hill in a gentle sunshine. All about them rolled many hundreds of forested hills, as if into infinity.

They stood within the Realm of the Faerie.

No longer naked, all three wore very soft, almost diaphanous, sleeveless loose-fitting robes of ecru, cream, and silver, the colors merging and shifting as each wearer breathed or moved. The material flowed down from the women's shoulders, draping softly over breast and hip, to a calf-length hemline that seemed to fade rather than to actually end. At one point the material was still visible; at the next, it appeared to dissolve; and at the next point it had vanished altogether.

"Welcome, Eaving," said a voice, and Eaving turned to see Long Tom standing a few paces distant.

Eaving smiled, and Long Tom came to her and kissed her briefly on the mouth, before greeting Marguerite and Kate in the same manner. Then, as he turned back to Eaving, the other two women gasped in surprise, for they found their little group surrounded by a crowd of the most magical creatures they had ever seen.

They were of similar colors as the women's own gowns, and thin and very short, the tops of their heads coming only to the level of the women's waists. They had very fine, copper-colored hair, and round eyes the same sage-green as Eaving's.

"Water-sprites," said Eaving, and touched individuals gently on the crowns of their heads, murmuring their names as they crowded about her. Several reached up delicate hands and stroked her rounded belly, but so soon as they had touched her, they turned away again, frowning.

Eaving herself frowned at this, and would have spoken of it, but Marguerite spoke first.

"Where do we stand?" she said, looking about her in wonder.

"We stand within the Faerie," Long Tom said. "It wakes about us as its gods move toward rebirth. This hill is The Naked, and it is the heart of the Faerie."

"And as the land wakes about us," Eaving said to Marguerite and Kate, "so is the Lord of the Faerie rising. Soon he will walk among us again."

Marguerite, rarely at a loss for words, hung her mouth open most unbecomingly.

Kate stared also, and although her brow creased she managed to keep her mouth in working order. "Who?" she said.

Eaving looked at Marguerite.

Marguerite's face cleared and she clasped her hands before her in a gesture of utter joy. "Of course," she said. "Coel! Coel-reborn. I should have known. I had felt something about him. Ah, no wonder he is so powerful in this life."

"Can he be with us here, tonight?" Eaving asked Long Tom.

"No. He will not come back to the Faerie until it is time for him to be crowned, and that cannot happen until he sets foot on the land. Now," he said in a graver tone, "where would you go this eve?" he said.

"I would visit my daughter," said Eaving. "I long to see her as you cannot imagine. Long Tom, is this possible? Can I use the Faerie to touch her?"

"You are not afraid of the imp?"

"I would visit the imp, as well, I think."

"Eaving, your daughter may not be what you expect."

"Marguerite said she would be different," Eaving said, "for she has been to the Otherworld and back, but she is my daughter, Long Tom, and I want only to love her."

"Will you love her, whatever she might be, Eaving?"

"Of course I shall love her!"

"The dead don't always return as you think they might," said Long Tom.

"She is my *daughter!*"

Long Tom sighed. "Very well. I can take you into the stone hall to your daughter."

He looked at Marguerite and Kate. "Sisters, would you watch?"

They nodded, each reaching out to touch Eaving as if in reassurance, then Long Tom took Eaving's hand, squeezed it, and said, "Walk down The Naked."

THE GIRL AND THE IMPS WERE ROUNDING A CORNER, walking from one maze of laneways across a narrow street into yet another maze, when the girl lifted her head.

"My mother!" she said, her voice hard. "She comes for a visit."

The imps started, and looked anxious.

"Do as I lead," the girl said to the imps, then her face assumed a look of complete innocence, and she grabbed an imp's hand in each of hers, and tugged them toward a nearby open doorway.

I DID AS LONG TOM SAID. I WALKED DOWN THE NAKED and soon meadow grass and flowers turned to marble underfoot, and the vast space of the land were replaced with the smaller—if still vast in its own right—space of the stone hall.

As I drew near to the central portion of the hall beneath the great golden dome, I saw two figures sitting cross-legged before each other in the heart of the patterned floor.

One was a stumpy, knobbled, blackened creature. My imp. I shivered, for this creature marred the beauty of the stone hall.

The imp sat as if deep in thought, his chin cradled in his hand, his brow furrowed, looking at the hands of . . .

My daughter.

I shivered again, but this time with happiness. There she sat, her hands spread apart before her, red wool twisted between them—and it was at the pattern this wool made that the imp stared.

The wool was nothing . . . But, oh, my daughter! She was so beautiful, a true amalgamation of Brutus and myself. Black curly hair tumbling down her back, ivory skin, my dark-blue eyes, a touch of her father's carriage, and his pride.

I slowed my steps, trying to calm my eagerness lest I scare her. As I approached, she raised her face, turning it toward me. "Mama!" she cried, and, allowing the red wool to fall from her fingers, leapt to her feet and ran to me.

Ah! At first she felt wonderful in my arms. Warm, alive, complete. Love over-whelmed me, and myriad other emotions.

She wriggled a little, and I let her go, and dropped to my knees before her, so that she should not have to crane her sweet face to look at me.

"What game is that you play, sweeting?" I asked, for want of anything better to say.

"Cat's Cradle," said my daughter. "Don't you know it?"

Of course I did, for Lady Anne's daughters had often played at it. But I had a feeling that the game Lady Anne's daughters had played, and what my daughter played, were very, very different.

Suddenly the feeling of warmth and love that had enveloped me when I first held my daughter abandoned me, and I felt hollow, and a little confused.

"Aye, I know it," I said to my daughter, trying to smile at her. "Are you teaching it to your friend?"

"Friend." I had no idea what else to call that dark hatefulness which now stood a pace or two away, peering intently at us. "Friend" was a somewhat uncomfortable compromise.

She turned a little and looked also at the imp. "Not truly," she said. "I challenge him to best it."

"And can he?"

She looked back to me, and grinned, and my heart thudded in that expression, for it was Brutus' mischievous smile, that which he used when he felt most sure of himself.

"Not yet," my daughter said.

"I came because I have missed you so much," I said, wanting to turn the conversation from the imp.

"I will be born this time," she said. "Don't you believe it?"

I stroked her cheek, and felt hurt when she moved away her face. "Yes, I believe it. I just want you to be safe."

"It is far more important that you be safe."

I felt more uncomfortable than ever. This was no child speaking at all.

"Be careful of the imp," I said, wanting only to mother her.

"The imp does not bother me," she said, rejecting not only the imp, but the mothering as well. Again I found myself fighting away that strange, uncomfortable feeling.

Almost as if she knew how I felt, my daughter leaned forward and kissed me on the cheek. "Are you walking the land tonight?"

"Yes," I said.

"Then know that the other imp lies quiescent tonight."

There was a movement behind the imp—my imp—and, yes, there stood another one, his expression dark and cross, and I knew that my daughter had been playing Cat's Cradle with both.

Again I shivered. What dark sorcery was going on within my womb?

"Genvissa-reborn—Jane Orr—lies alone," said my daughter, "with no one to love her. Go to her, Mama, for you shall both need to be friends if you are to learn the arts of Mistress of the Labyrinth."

My smile felt frozen. Dear gods, what did she not know? Tentatively, I touched her cheek again, then gathered her into my arms and hugged her tightly. "Be safe!" I whispered even as she wriggled in my embrace, and then both she and the stone hall and its impish inhabitants faded.

"YOU SAW," EAVING SAID, AS SHE STOOD ONCE AGAIN atop the hill.

"Yes," said Long Tom.

"We all did," said Marguerite.

"She is very knowing," said Eaving.

"She is your daughter," said Long Tom, "and as such you should love her, no matter what."

Eaving shot him a sharp glance. "I wanted . . ." she said, then turned her head aside, as if she could not bear to continue.

"What is this 'Cat's Cradle'?" said Marguerite to Long Tom, a little too brightly.

"A version of the Troy Game," said Long Tom. "She creates the winding path of the labyrinth between her fingers in red wool, and then challenges the imps to find their way from the heart of the labyrinth to its exit. They can't, for they are evil incarnate, and the Game's very purpose is to trap all evil within its heart."

"But what is my daughter doing engaged in this trickery?" said Eaving. "She should be just a child, a baby, innocent of all that has gone before."

"Eaving, do you not recall what I said to you earlier?" said Long Tom. "You should love her no matter what, even if she is not quite what you expected."

To that, Eaving made no reply.

Eventually Marguerite spoke. "Will you go to this 'Jane'?" she said. "To Genvissa-reborn?"

IN THE STONE HALL THE GIRL STOOD, STARING AT THE *space where her mother had vanished. The two imps stood at her shoulders, also staring.*

"I wouldn't trust that one, if I were you," said one imp.

"I have no intention of trusting her," said the girl, "for she carries not only the seeds of my victory, but those of my destruction as well. She shall have to be carefully managed."

She sighed, and, after a moment, the two imps followed suit and sighed as one, their black, bony shoulders heaving exaggeratedly.

CHAPTER NINE

JANE HAD TAKEN TO SLEEPING ON A PALLET CLOSE to the hearth in the kitchen. Weyland had made no objections. No doubt he found that amusing—look to what the great MagaLlan and Mistress of the Labyrinth had been reduced!—but Jane actually quite enjoyed it, as much as she could enjoy anything in this life. The kitchen was the warm heart of the household, and Jane found comfort there, alone in the deep of the night, that she found nowhere else.

Tonight was much as countless preceding nights had been. The two girls, Elizabeth and Frances, had finished their duties for the day close to midnight, and had gone home to the tavern's cellar rooms, shoulders hunched against the memories of the day. An hour after they'd departed, Weyland had gone upstairs to his den for the night and Jane was left in peace for her own bed.

But she hadn't slept.

Instead her thoughts had been given over to the Festival of Ingathering, and the memories that had invoked. Here, in this life, she was trapped within a city, but even so, the feels and smells and even the sights of the land were never far away. The celebration of the harvest had always been a huge festival during the age of Llangarlia, and one in which the MagaLlan, as the living representative of the mother goddess, Mag, had always played a large part. Harvest time was Mag's triumph: fertility come to fruition, life for the coming year.

Jane wondered if anyone remembered Mag now, or if Christianity had somehow managed to persuade people that no one but God, His Son, and all His saints were responsible. *How sad if that were true,* Jane thought, and she didn't even pause to think how extraordinary it was that she, Mag's implacable enemy, should consider such a thing.

No sooner had the thought crossed her mind than Jane went rigid, as a soft voice spoke into the kitchen.

"The people know in their souls. They know when they walk the country lanes and feel wonder at the sight of the flowers and the fragrant hedgerows and the waving grasses and the branches of trees rich with fruit. That is enough for me, that such a sight still cheers them, and lifts cares from their hearts."

Jane, who was lying facing toward the hearth, fought to control her panic. She knew that voice so well: Cornelia, Caela . . . and Mag, all in one.

Mag! Mag! Cornelia-reborn was the goddess-reborn!

It hadn't been her laundress, Damson in her previous life—not pitiful, clumsy Damson, at all.

It had been Cornelia-Caela. All this time.

Summoning all her courage, Jane slowly rolled over.

A woman stood on the other side of the room. She was stunningly lovely, as much in presence as in form and feature.

"I know you well," said Jane, amazed that her voice was steady. "And I saw you with Brutus. Why have you come?"

The goddess smiled. "You saw me with Brutus?" She put a hand to her belly, and Jane could see now its gentle roundness.

She was pregnant.

"I am Noah in this life," said the goddess. "Once Cornelia, once Caela."

"Noah is not your goddess name." Jane very slowly inched herself up into a sitting position.

"No. Do you want to know it?"

"Yes."

"It will give you great power over me."

Jane's mouth twisted. "Not enough to destroy you."

"You will tell Weyland," said the goddess. "That would be dangerous."

"I will not tell Weyland."

"No? Why should I believe that?"

"Because, knowing your goddess name, and not telling him, will give me some power over him."

"And you need that badly, I can see."

Jane's cheeks flamed, for she knew that the goddess referred to the frightful diseased pocks on her face.

The goddess walked over to Jane, then, gracefully, onto the flagstones of the floor by Jane's pallet.

"What are these the marks of, Jane?" she whispered, putting a hand to Jane's face.

Jane flinched away from Eaving's hand. *The pox, you sanctimonious bitch!* she wanted to scream, but instead the terrible truth came sliding over her tongue.

"They are the marks of my past."

The goddess tipped her face to one side, considering. "My name is Eaving," she said finally.

Jane drew in a slow breath. Eaving—the unexpected shelter, the god-sent haven from the tempest. Then Jane remembered what Caela had said to her in their previous life, the final time they'd met: *Swanne, if ever you need harbor, then I am it. If ever you need a friend, then I am it.*

Dear gods! She had been Eaving then, too! Who would have suspected it? Poor, mewling queen . . .

Jane opened her mouth, and instead of all the hatred and vileness that she was used to pouring out at this woman, she said, "Be careful. Weyland sleeps above."

"If he wakes then I will go."

"He will call you in. Gods, woman, you carry more in that womb of yours than Brutus' child!"

"I know I am to be Asterion's whore," Eaving replied.

"If you knew the full horror of it," Jane said, "you would not speak of it with such equanimity."

"Well, then, I am sure I shall know it soon enough."

"Why do you not sound fearful?" said Jane. "This"—her hand indicated the weeping sores on her face—"awaits you!"

"Neither of us truly knows what awaits us," said Eaving. "And do not worry overmuch about the imp in my womb, nor even in yours. They are otherwise occupied this night, and Asterion will not know I was here." She paused. "Jane, you saw me with Brutus?"

"Aye."

Eaving smiled a little, tenuously. "And yet you do not berate me for it."

"I appear to have lost my touch."

Now Eaving smiled more genuinely. "Jane, there are many wounds which need to be healed. Yours and mine prime among them."

"You want me to do *penance*?"

"It is not what I ask."

"I have no interest in healing, Eaving."

"I cannot think you truly mean that." Then Eaving bent forward, laid her lips gently against the worst of the sores on Jane's face, and in the next instant was gone.

* * *

JANE SAT UNTIL DAWN, SLEEPLESS, WONDERING THAT she had just spent a few minutes in a reasonably civil conversation with the woman she had hated bitterly for three thousand years.

What she found difficult to accept, what was astounding, was that Jane had to confront the truth that she no longer hated Noah.

CDAPGER GEN

WOBURN VILLAGE, BEDFORDSHIRE

ON CHRISTMAS DAY OF 1658, JOHN THORNTON knocked at the door of the house two up from Woburn Church. Noah answered the door, and smiled gently at their visitor.

John Thornton stood on the threshold, his hat in his hand, looking uncomfortable.

"A merry Christmas to you, Noah, and to you, ladies," he said, as he saw Marguerite and Kate appear behind her. "I hope the season brings you joy."

Noah smiled. "And to you also, John Thornton. I thought you would have celebrated Christmas with the Bedfords, in their private chapel. They always do it well."

"I, uh, I wanted . . ." *I wanted to come here, to see you.*

"You should forget me, John," she said gently.

"I cannot."

At the sound of agony in his voice, Marguerite stepped forward. "John Thornton. We have a goose simmering in a sweet, fragrant sauce on the hearth at our house. Will you join us for Christmas dinner?"

"Marguerite . . ." Noah said in a low voice.

"You would send the poor lovelorn man on his way with no warm food in his stomach?" Marguerite said, raising her eyebrows archly. "What harm can it do to feed him?"

"None, I suppose," said Noah and, smiling, she stepped back and waved Thornton inside.

THEY ATE IN THE WARMTH OF THE KITCHEN. JOHN Thornton realized that he had never enjoyed a meal such as this. The Christmas fare was traditional, but somehow tasted as if it had come to fruition in heaven's fields rather than in those of Woburn's acres, while the company was extraordinary. It was as if the women shared a companionship so deep and so mystical that every glance, every movement, every word, held far deeper meaning than John could ever understand. This strange underlying meaning did not perturb him, nor make him feel like an outsider. It was as if it were an added warmth to the dinner, an added depth, an added color. John Thornton felt as if he had been invited into a slightly different dimension, a deeper and vaster world than any he had ever known. It was almost as if the world he knew and understood was only a faded relic of a far older and far more brightly hued world, of which these women were strangely familiar.

Noah looked radiant—even more beautiful now, in midterm pregnancy, than she had ever been in his bed, and John found it difficult to look away from her.

He envied, desperately, the man she loved.

When the meal was done, and the children had run laughing into the front parlor to play at some game, Noah came to sit next to John. She smiled at him, then reached out, took his hands, and put them on her belly.

"Feel her?" she said. "She twists and turns, awaiting her birth."

John had never before touched a heavily pregnant woman. At first he felt embarrassed and hesitant, then the wonder of the child moving within Noah's body overcame him, and he pressed his hands the tighter to her belly.

He raised his eyes to Noah's, then froze, transfixed by her eyes.

Their dark-blue had faded, and now they were a soft green, streaked through with rivers of gold.

"My God," he whispered, "who *are* you?"

"She is Eaving," said Marguerite. "She is the fertility of the land, its waters and rivers, its breath, its soul. You have lain with her. Surely you have felt this?"

"Aye," he whispered, his eyes once again on his hands, still splayed over Noah's belly. "In her arms I have felt the land rise to meet me."

"If we have need of you, John Thornton, will you aid us?" said Kate.

"You are witches, all," he said, and sat back, removing his hands from Noah. "You are everything I have been taught to hate."

"And yet you do not hate us," said Noah. "How are we bad? How are we harmful?"

He did not answer, only looking at each of the women in turn.

"I cannot live without you," he finally said, to Noah.

"I cannot be yours," she said. "I am so sorry."

He looked away, keeping silent for a long time. Eventually he sighed, and spoke. "I will aid you, if you ask," said John, and Noah smiled, and leaned forward to kiss him softly on the mouth.

"The land," she said, "shall always rise up to meet you."

THE GIRL HAD LED THE IMPS OUT OF THE STONE HALL
and back into the twisting maze of alleyways. Now she directed them to a particularly dank corner. Here she sat, and indicated that the imps should do likewise.

"I said that I had the power to both trap and free you," she said as the imps sat, crossing their spindly limbs neatly, their bright eyes watching her with the utmost suspicion. "I said that I had the power to earn your love. Do you doubt any of this?"

"Of course," said the imp who sat to the girl's left. "We don't trust you at all. We know what you are."

"Ah," said the girl, her tiny face screwing up as if in thought.

"Your mother, on the other hand," said the imp sitting to the girl's right, "thinks you are a sweet little thing."

His brother giggled, a hand over his mouth to hide his pointed teeth.

"My mother shall love me well enough once she truly knows my purpose," said the girl. "Now, to that purpose—which is, of course, to destroy you, as your current master . . . as he thinks he is. I shall have the greatest pleasure in wrenching Weyland apart, for he has caused me innumerable troubles, but you and I can come to some small accommodation."

"Won't that destroy you?" said the imp to the right.

"Nay," said the girl. "I have grown way past such minor details. I am far different than ever I was, or was planned to be. Now, do you want to hear my proposition, or not?"

"We wish to hear," said the imps, as one.

"Firstly," said the girl, "I want you to continue to obey Weyland. I don't want him suspicious."

The imps glanced at each other, relief clearly etched on their faces.

"I want him to have no reason to know of me," said the girl, "so for the moment you may continue to dance to his orders."

"What is this proposition, little girl?" said the imp to the left. The last two words he spoke with a decided edge.

"You do my will, all of it, and when that will is done, you may be free. Completely free. To be and do what you will."

"But doesn't that contravene all that you are?" said the imp.

"It contravenes all that I once was," said the girl, "but not who I am now."

At that she smiled, and it was the coldest expression either imp had ever seen.

The imps looked once more at each other, then both looked back at the girl.

"*I think we might have an agreement,*" *said the imp to the right, while his brother nodded vigorously.*

"*A deal!*" *said the girl, and sounded that strange, chilled laugh of hers.* "*A deal!*"

"*A deal!*" *cried the imps, and laughed with the girl until the sound echoed up and down the alley, frightening the rats rummaging about in the refuse.*

"*A deal!*"

CHAPTER ELEVEN

BRUGES, FLANDERS

CHARLES SAT SPRAWLED IN A GREAT CHAIR UNDER the window of the parlor in the agreeable house he occupied on the rue Haute in Bruges. Outside, the late-February weather threw sleet against the window, but, for once, Charles didn't particularly care. He'd actually had enough money to pay for firewood this winter. In his right hand he held a letter.

Across the room Louis stood, waiting, very still. He hadn't wanted to disturb Charles until he'd read the letter. But, by the gods, it had been a quarter of an hour since Charles had opened it. *What did it say?*

Unable to wait any longer, Louis spoke quietly: "Well?"

"General Monck is receptive to the idea of my return," Charles said as Louis walked out of the shadows. "He is pleased that I have been conducting myself in the manner of a king. With dignity."

Louis laughed softly. "He has heard that you have removed your mistresses . . . but not that you've sent them to Woburn, nor with whom they now reside."

"But . . ."

"Ah, I *knew* there was a reason for this silence."

"He counsels that it may be many months yet before I can return by invitation. He hopes that disappointment won't make me think to invade. He reminds me of his military command, and their experience."

"If only he had half your experience," Louis said.

"What is past is past," said Charles, "and should remain so." He sighed, finally holding out the letter for Louis to read. "I should have known. My thirtieth birthday is yet many months distant. Fate, or the Game, or whatever, shall conspire to keep me from England's green shores a while yet."

Louis read the letter, then put it aside on a nearby table. "And Noah?" he asked, his voice very soft now.

"I have heard only that Marguerite and Kate and our children arrived safe, and that they now live with Noah in a house within Woburn village. More than that, I do not know."

"There must be more!"

"Louis, I am sorry. What can I say? I dare not write them, nor they I, and to try and touch them magically might harm them. Besides, Marguerite has the turf. We may no longer convene the Circle."

There was quiet for many long minutes.

"I wish . . ." both men said together; then they both smiled, a little self-consciously, and lapsed back into silence.

CHAPTER TWELVE

WOBURN VILLAGE, BEDFORDSHIRE

Noah Speaks

THE FINAL FEW WEEKS OF MY PREGNANCY WERE filled with girth, discomfort, swollen veins, and exhaustion. Not even Eaving, apparently, was allowed to escape every woman's burden during her final months and, indeed, I would not have wished it. This was a much-loved and -anticipated child—I pushed to the back of my mind any uncertainty I felt—and this discomfort would be forgotten the instant of her birth.

I tried not to think of the imp. I tried to believe what my daughter had showed me, that she could well manage both imps. But if I believed that, I had to accept that my daughter was not going to be quite what I wanted—an innocent, squirming child who existed only so I could love her.

On this night I lay restless and greatly uncomfortable. Marguerite and Kate lay together on the other side of the bed. I now slept so restively they preferred to keep their distance. Thus I was left, a great hulk breathing only with the most strenuous effort. I grew thirsty, and thought about finding myself some ale to drink—that would send me to sleep, surely—but moving was so difficult, the night so cold, and the kitchen so far, and down so many stairs . . .

I resolved to make the effort, no matter the difficulties, and threw back the bedcovers, swinging my legs to the floor and slowly pivoting my body about. But just as I was about to rise, I felt the most extraordinary—and most extremely unwelcome—sensation in my lower body.

It was not so much the pangs of labor—I had experienced those as Cornelia, and I knew well enough what to expect—but something much more debilitating.

The sense that someone else had taken over my lower body and was controlling my actions. I felt a twinge of fear, and tried to struggle to my feet, but my legs did not obey me.

Of their own accord—under the control of that "someone else"—they swung back onto the bed, then my body shifted so that I lay comfortably against the pillows.

My daughter moved in my womb, and I felt the opening to the birth canal relaxing for birth.

Gods, *she* was doing this!

I gasped—in shock, in disbelief, and in some measure of horror—and almost instantly Marguerite and Kate stirred on the other side of the bed.

"My lady," Marguerite said as she sat up and looked at me, "is it time?"

I nodded, taking a very deep breath.

Marguerite sat up, placing one of her hands over mine where they were splayed across my belly. "Is all well?"

"I do not know, Marguerite. This is not labor as I have known it previously."

"It is a special child," said Marguerite, meaning to comfort me.

"She is taking control," I said, "and I do not like it." At that I winced, for a wave of discomfort—not pain, not agony, just a strange discomfort—rolled up over my distended belly and into my chest.

Marguerite stared at me, then leaned over and shook Kate awake. "Noah," she said, "is giving birth."

"My daughter is birthing herself," I muttered between clenched teeth as another wave of discomfort—strange, irritating, and deeply unsettling—swept over me.

My legs drew up, and I groaned.

"Noah?" Marguerite said, now kneeling on the mattress at my side. "What should we do?" Kate had awakened, and moved about the bed so that she sat on my other side, on the edge of the mattress.

"None of us can do anything," I said, and then felt my body take a huge breath. *Ah!* How I loathed this lack of control! I had been entirely taken over, and it terrified me, for what it implied about my daughter.

My sweet, innocent daughter. That's all I wanted . . . *Please, gods, let it be what I receive!*

I took another breath, very slow and deep, and arched my back slightly.

"Is the pain—" Kate began.

"There is no pain," I said, and then arched my back again as that strange hateful discomfort swept over me. I could feel the child moving through my birth canal, could feel her head crowning, and yet there was no pain.

Just that total lack of control.

I cried out in frustration, and Marguerite, who had now shifted very close to me, reached down her hands, and drew forth my child from my body.

"Look!" she said, holding the child up before me. "Look!"

The baby stared at me with deep-blue eyes, perfectly aware. A calm, cool stare, tinged with what I thought might be triumph. This was no sweet child, no dependent being on whom I could lavish love and care. I tried to smile, but found it difficult. I rested one hand on my now flaccid belly. Where my daughter once had rested I felt only hollowness and loss rather than the ecstasy of a successful birth; and where my heart should have been, I felt only sadness and despair rather than the unconditional love every mother should feel instinctively for her child.

My daughter, still held in Marguerite's hands, stared at me, and her tiny brow seemed to wrinkle, as if in irritation. Maybe I was not the mother she had wanted . . . as I wondered that maybe . . . No. I could not think that at all. Not wanting this child went against my every instinct, both as Eaving, and as Cornelia-Caela-Noah. She was my daughter. I ought to love her.

None of this Marguerite or Kate noticed. Marguerite was now holding the baby in her arms, the umbilical cord severed, one fingertip tracing out the lines of the baby's face.

"She looks like a kitten!" Marguerite declared.

Once more I tried to smile, and this time somehow I managed it. "Then we shall call her Catling," I said, "not merely for her looks, but for the game she plays."

My heart felt like a great, still, cold rock in my chest.

CHAPTER THIRTEEN

IDOL LANE, LONDON,
AND WOBURN VILLAGE

One Year Later

WEYLAND GREW MORE IMPATIENT AND MORE nervy with each passing day. He spent most of the day, and half of the night as well, out in the city, listening to both gossip and hard news, trying (with every other person in London) to hear if Charles was on his way yet, if the king was to return. No one now doubted that he would return, but no one could know the *how* and the *when*.

Most of the citizens in London were torn between two emotions: joy—that the king would return—surely he would usher in a glorious golden age for the city and country both; and a deep anxiety—would the king exact revenge for the unfortunate murder of his father so many years ago?

Both anticipation and nervousness beset Weyland as well. There was, after all, a long history of debt and hatred between Brutus and Asterion, and Brutus-reborn in this life had considerably more reason to exact revenge than just Charles I's murder.

Weyland knew he could best Charles, but the weapon he could wield—Noah Banks—was one fraught with difficulties. Yes, Weyland knew he could control and contain Noah—she was his, after all; but he was also wary of her power which emanated from the land—and Weyland had no way of understanding it.

He didn't think she could break free from him, or manage to exercise her free will, but he wasn't completely sure.

Thus it was, in the last cold days of the winter of 1660, that Weyland decided to pay Noah a visit.

Just to be neighborly.

Just to be sure.

* * *

HE WENT IN PERSON, NOT IN SPIRIT OR GLAMOUR.
Weyland needed to feel and see and taste Noah, and he could do that only if
he went in the flesh. Woburn was not too great a ride away, and he could manage it in two days if he changed horses regularly and rode through part of the
night. He was young and strong enough to cope, and he was—Weyland himself was somewhat surprised to discover—jaded enough to relish the thought
of an excursion into the English countryside, as cold and as brittle as it
currently was.

He arrived in Woburn village in the early afternoon on a weekday in late
February. The air was icy and sharp, the road slick with frozen slush. The sloping high street of the village was deserted; who would be out in this weather?
The scent of Noah lay all about. Weyland could feel her, almost as strongly as
if they shared a bed and lay skin-to-skin. Her presence dominated the village,
although Weyland doubted all but the most gifted or sensitive could feel it.

He pulled his horse to a halt some ten or twelve paces from the church. At
this spot her presence was very, very powerful, and Weyland glanced at the
house a little farther up the street.

She was in there. By the gods, he could feel her breathing. She was sitting
at some needlework—for an instant Weyland's mind was flooded with the
memory of Caela with her ever-present embroideries and silks—and she was
at peace.

She had no idea he was close.

Weyland shivered, and put it down to the cold.

He dismounted, pulling the horse into the lee of the house. He drew in a
deep breath, and then whispered, infusing his voice with great power of
command.

Noah. Come to me, I demand it.

Instantly Weyland felt a flash of fear from her, and it relieved him. He sent
another demand, this one not composed of words, but of pure emotion: anger,
aggression, insistence.

He felt the needlework fall to the floor, and heard, as if he stood next to
her, Noah's voice as she mumbled some excuse or other to whomever it was
sat with her.

Then there were footsteps, straight to the front door, not even pausing so
she could gather to her a cloak or coat against the bitter cold.

Weyland smiled, and then shuddered again as chills ran down his spine.

The door opened, and a figure slipped through.

She hesitated as she closed the door, looking about, and Weyland had his
first sight of her.

It stunned him. He hadn't expected her to be so lovely. Her thick hair was tied in a simple loose knot which fell over one shoulder. Her face, pale even before she had come through the door, was now almost completely white with the cold.

Her blue eyes shone brilliantly in the winter light, and they were staring wildly at him.

Again Weyland trembled, and again he attributed it to the cold. Ignoring the knot in his stomach, he raised a gloved hand, and gestured slowly to her.

She swallowed, and then moved forward, stumbling a little, before coming to a halt some two paces away from him.

Her arms were now wrapped about her body, and she trembled violently in spasmodic shudders. She was not dressed for the outdoors, and Weyland knew she would be suffering badly.

"Noah," he said.

Her mouth moved, but no sound came out.

Dropping his horse's reins, Weyland stepped close to Noah, and cupped her chin in his gloved hand.

"Well-met, my lovely," he murmured.

"What do you want?" she said.

"You, of course," he said, and felt her flinch. Then her eyes hardened, and he saw defiance in them. For some reason it pleased him, although he knew he should punish her for it. Perhaps he *should* punish her for it.

Very slowly, Weyland leaned forward, and kissed her.

She stiffened, but he knew she would not pull away, for that would be to admit defeat. So Weyland took his time, drawing her against his body, very slowly exploring her mouth with his, tormenting her with softness.

"I remember," he murmured, pulling his mouth away from hers just enough so that he could speak, "taking your virginity when you were Caela. I shall enjoy our bedding even more, this life, I think."

"I am no virgin," she said. "I chose not to wait for your gruesome summons."

"You think I did not know that?" he said. "It is of no matter. I can but hope that your experience in this life has taught you some amusing tricks."

"Indeed," she said. "I shall be quite the skilled whore for you, Asterion."

Eyes narrowed, Weyland stepped back a little from her, although he kept a grip on one of her upper arms.

"I will . . ." he said, then stopped, not sure what it was he wanted to say.

One of her eyebrows raised, and, at the same time, Weyland became aware of the strength of her shivering. His horse had a small rug draped over its hindquarters, and Weyland busied himself for a moment, pulling the rug off and wrapping it about Noah's shoulders, using the time the action gave him to recompose himself.

"Thank you," she said.

"It shall not be long," he said, wishing now he hadn't become so weakened as to give her the rug. "Cromwell is dead, Parliament renders itself more incompetent each day, and the people in London's streets speak Charles's name with hope and joy." He stopped dead again, furious with himself at that last; for it had brought a flush of pleasure to Noah's cheeks.

"They do?" she said, and she smiled.

It was achingly lovely, that smile.

"He will never bring you joy and hope," he said. "You are mine now."

"I do not deny it."

"You shall come when I call."

"I shall."

Weyland realized that he'd lost all advantage in this conversation. *Damn her!*

"You will be my whore," he said, even more roughly than previously.

"I have no intention of escaping my destiny, Asterion."

"Do not call me that. I—"

"How should I call you, then, in this life? Beelzebub? Diabolos? Masshit? Asmodeus?"

"I am no biblical demon, Noah. It surely would not hurt you to remember that I was dragged into this Game as you were—not through my own actions, but by the betrayal of someone I loved." He paused, fighting down memory of Ariadne. "My name is Weyland. Weyland Orr."

Again she smiled. "It is a name that suits you, Master Orr."

Words bubbled in his throat. He wanted to tell her how he would hurt her, how he would debase her, how he would torment her until she screamed for mercy, and yet he said none of them.

"You are—" he began.

She looked a him, now fully in control of herself, her beautiful mouth curved in the hint of a smile that, however Weyland tried to view it, was in no manner sarcastic or patronizing.

"You are very lovely," he said, finally, and her smile once more broke through.

"And you are far prettier than ever you were as Aldred."

"Prettier than Brutus?"

Her smile faded, and Weyland almost hated her for it.

"No," she said finally.

"I will kill him, Noah. I will force you to give me his kingship bands, and then I will—"

She lay the fingers of one hand on his mouth. "None of us can ever know what the future holds," she said, "much less think to predict or control it."

"You will come to London when I call," Weyland said, trying very hard to regain the ascendancy in this dialogue.

"Aye, that I will," she said. "That is clear enough to me. If you want me to be your whore, Weyland, then I will do that."

He wanted her to scream and plead and beg, but she wouldn't do it. He wanted sullenness and resentment, hatred and revulsion, but he got none of it.

Instead, suddenly, and very horribly, Weyland realized he was staring into the eyes of an equal.

Somehow, poor lost Cornelia, poor humiliated Caela, had grown up.

"Let me go inside, I beg you," Noah said, "for I am frozen nigh unto death standing here."

Weyland breathed in deeply, immensely relieved at her words and at the consequent resurrection of his control.

He nodded, then quickly stepped forward, kissed her hard on the mouth, then pushed her toward the door of her house.

"Until London, Noah."

HE MOUNTED HIS HORSE AND KICKED IT INTO A CAN-ter down the slippery, icy high street of Woburn village before the door had even closed behind Noah. He'd needed to escape from her presence very, very badly.

A mile or so outside of the village he pulled the horse back to a walk, thinking over the encounter.

He was unnerved by what had happened. He'd thought Noah would be another Swanne-Jane; a woman powerful in magic, but weak in spirit. A woman who, despite her arrogant ways, could be humiliated with ease.

A woman he could despise.

Instead, Weyland had found none of that.

Damn her!

PART FOUR

THE SUMMONS

LONDON, 1939

*J*ACK SKELTON PUT THE CIGARETTE IN HIS MOUTH, *lit it, then handed it to Weyland. "Well?"*

Weyland took a long, appreciative drag on the cigarette. "It's Pen Hill," he said. "Noah loved this place."

"God damn it, tell me why you brought me here!"

Weyland tipped the cigarette toward the summit of the hill. "Harold came to her here and made love to her when she was Caela. That was just before the unfortunateness of Hastings."

Skelton's face tightened. He tipped out another cigarette from his pack, and lit it. "Yes?"

"Long Tom used to dance atop here."

"Weyland—"

"I wanted to show you the summit. D'you think you can get over these railings?"

Skelton shot him a black look, then leapt lightly upward, grasping the top of the railings and hoisting himself easily over.

At the curbside, Frank—who was now standing by the driver's window of the black sedan, talking to Piper—looked over, obviously appalled at the further time about to be wasted.

Within a moment Weyland Orr had joined Skelton, and together they slowly climbed the hill. It only took them a minute.

"It has shrunk and somewhat declined," said Weyland as they reached the top. Where the summit should have been, there was a dip of some four feet, and then the blank gray water of a reservoir. "Now the hill is used by the London Water Authority as a holding station for water before it is pumped farther into the City. Pity, really."

"A sad fate for a sacred hill," said Skelton. "Did you plan it? Do it to torture Noah? To torture the land?"

"Oh, it was done to torture the land," said Weyland, then took another long drag on his cigarette. "Effective, too. There are drowned stones at the bottom of this

reservoir, Jack. Murdered Sidlesaghes. But who now knows they are there, eh? Who cares, these days? But I didn't do this, Jack. You know who did."

Skelton didn't reply.

"Stella tells me you walked about London last night," Weyland said.

Skelton grunted.

"Did you see me, Jack? Parading about in all my bullish finery?"

Skelton dragged his eyes away from the water to Weyland. "You're far prettier this morning."

"I didn't move from my bed last night, Jack. As you know, my bed holds far greater pleasures for me than chasing you through the cold, heartless streets of London. You spoke to . . . well, I'm sure you know who you spoke to. But it certainly wasn't to me."

Jack Skelton stared at him, and then, with a muttered expletive, turned back for the cars.

CHAPTER ONE

WOBURN VILLAGE, BEDFORDSHIRE

Noah Speaks

OH, THE TERROR I'D FELT WHEN ASTERION APP-eared outside the house, and ordered me into the ice and snow to his side. It was terror, not only at the thought of his presence, but also at the fact that when he'd called I had no hope of resisting. I could do nothing but mumble some inane excuse to Marguerite who sat with me, and walk outside into the frigid weather wearing nothing but a light woolen gown.

There awaited Asterion, or Weyland Orr, as he now called himself. He loomed before me, a tall figure wrapped in a heavy cloak, thick scarves about his neck, and with his hands hidden within such bulky leather gloves that they appeared like mallets he would turn against me at any moment. Then I saw his face.

It was not what I had expected. Not in any manner at all.

His eyes were keen, and sharp, locked on my every movement. I knew they saw my fright, and for that I hated him more than ever I had previously. Then I saw their color, which was a soft hazel, and that disconcerted me, for I had never associated the concept of "softness" with Asterion at all.

Weyland Orr's face was, at first glance, all angles. A sharp, perceptive face to suit those eyes. But, like his eyes, it also had its softness. The line of his jaw was saved from angularity by its strength, his nose was saved from thinness by the regularity of its contours, and the inflexibility of his broad forehead was softened by a wisp or two of fair hair that fell forward and gave him, gods help me, a boyish air.

He was handsome, but not in any immediately striking way. It was only after you'd studied him for a few minutes that his features truly impressed themselves upon you.

His was a dangerous attractiveness, because it swept upon you unawares.

We talked. He threatened, I evaded or agreed, as necessity dictated. I tried to keep calm, although I dared not believe I was very successful.

He kissed me, and for some illogical reason Long Tom's directive to heal wounds came to my mind as he pulled me closer and deeper into that kiss.

He pulled the rug from his horse to keep me warm, and I wondered what terror he was trying to conceal from me with that action.

He let me go, the greatest cruelty, for I knew now as never before that shortly I would be lost. Shortly Weyland would call me to him, and I would be powerless to resist.

From this day on, his face haunted my dreams, and hardly a night passed that I did not wake, suddenly and terrified, staring into the darkness.

WOBURN VILLAGE MAY NOT HAVE BEEN THE CENTER of English society, but we heard most of what happened of note in the world. We heard the gossip in the market. We read the broadsheets that were sold for a penny apiece on Woburn's high street. And John Thornton visited and spoke to us of developments in the wider world.

Charles was to be restored. Parliament had worried to and fro about it for over a year until both public opinion and General Monck (at the head of his army) had forced their hand.

Charles was to be restored, and he was to come home in glory and to acclaim.

I could not help wondering how he felt about that, not only considering this life's experiences but those of his previous lives as well. He would worry, surely, about what Weyland Orr might have planned.

I tried as much as I could not to think of Weyland, but if he did not occupy my thoughts, then they were taken up with concern for my daughter—my strange, disturbing Catling. Oh, I had tried hard to love her. Sometimes, I almost succeeded. If, when I held her, I closed my eyes, and rocked her gently, and sang to her, I could believe she was a baby such as any other, who desired only to be held, and fed, and loved and protected.

But then her tiny mouth would close about my nipple, and she would feed from me, and I felt coldness and nausea grip my belly, and it was all I could do not to throw her away. If I looked down at her, as sometimes I steeled myself to do, I would find her blue eyes watching me unblinkingly.

At those times I rose abruptly, and handed Catling to Kate, and asked that Kate feed her.

My inability to love Catling troubled me greatly. Not merely because as a mother I felt I should love her, but as Eaving, I needed to love any child. I represented all mothers, the fertility of land and water and beast.

I could not feel such coldness toward any offspring, let alone mine.

Oh gods, I wanted to love her so badly! She was my daughter reborn, and I could not bear to think that I had lost her in a previous life only to reject her in this one.

I tried to keep my discomfort from Marguerite and Kate. I know they wondered that I did not laugh and sing with her, and so often passed her to Kate to feed.

When we spoke of it, as we did occasionally, I blamed my discomfort on Catling's amazing growth.

This was amazing (and, aye, disturbing) enough to satisfy Marguerite's and Kate's curiosity as to my apparent lack of bonding with Catling.

Indeed, as we could hardly hide the baby from the village, her growth was the talk of all Woburn.

Catling had sat up at two weeks, had crawled at three months, was walking at six months, and talking at seven. Now a year old, Catling was as accomplished as a five-year-old both in quality and in quantity of speech, and as tall and as agile as any four-year-old.

This daughter of mine wanted to waste no time on childhood. She rushed toward maturity.

Catling and I rarely talked, and then only to discuss the most mundane of daily chores: What gown would she prefer to wear this morning? Did she wish to attend the market with us? Would she prefer a plum or an apple with her morning breakfast?

She played happily with Marguerite's and Kate's children, and she appeared to do that required of a child (the giggles, the laughter, the tears when she fell over and grazed a knee), but she did other things also, most unchildlike.

She sat in corners, and sang to herself, softly, as she played Cat's Cradle with a length of red wool which she had begged from Marguerite.

She challenged the local vicar about the writing of the Gospels, claiming they were nothing but the fictionalized ambitions of a coterie of ruthless priests, until he was red-faced and discomforted. Eventually he asked me to please keep her apart from the other children.

She asked me once if the imp troubled me during my monthly menses, and said that if this was so, she could ensure he did so no more.

This was the one occasion we managed to bypass the mundane and almost spoke of what truly troubled or motivated us.

"Can you really control the imp that greatly?" I asked her.

"Of course," she replied, her eyes on her fingers as they twisted the red wool this way and that.

"What *are* you, Catling?" I said.

At that she raised her eyes, flat and emotionless. "Your daughter," she said. "What else?"

I said nothing, and so she continued with the inevitable, hateful question: "Do you love me?" she asked.

"Of course," I said, too quickly.

Her mouth twisted slightly. "Will you do anything I ask of you?"

I opened my mouth, but could not form the words. I sensed a trap here, so deep that if I fell in I might never manage to crawl out. So instead of answering her, I started, and looked toward the door. "Hark!" I said. "Is that Marguerite calling?"

And I hastened off, and thus did not have to witness the undoubtedly cynical smile that would have marred my daughter's beautiful face.

During this first year of Catling's life Marguerite, Kate, and I often formed a Circle, and walked the Faerie. These were times of great joy for me, and they comforted and compensated me for the loss of what I had expected in my daughter. Sometimes Long Tom asked after Catling, but the water-sprites never did, and I noticed that they backed away whenever Long Tom spoke her name, and I remembered how they had frowned when they had touched my belly when I was carrying Catling.

I asked them one night of this, and of what they had felt.

The sprite with the brightest copper hair replied, somewhat obliquely, "We revere you above all others, Eaving. We trust you above all others. Not her."

This also comforted me, and I laughed and embraced them, and they pretended to hate the embrace, and sprang away to dance joyously about me.

That was an enchanting night.

Apart from my disquiet about my daughter, life in Woburn was good for me. The village had come to accept my presence, as well as that of Marguerite and Kate and their children. We acted as seemly as we could. We made no fuss in the village, acted in most decorous manner, and enticed none of the village men into our house, and so the gossip abated, and soon enough the women of the marketplace began to natter cheerfully to us whenever we appeared among them, and to share with us the joys and hopes of their own lives.

We enjoyed that, Eaving and her Sisters, very much, and sometimes one or another of us would walk the meadows with some of the village women, and show them some of the wonders of the land. We would open their eyes, just very slightly, to the possibilities of the ancient ways, so that when time came for one of the meadow dances held on the solstices, or at the harvest festivals, they would the greater appreciate—and far better participate in—the natural rhythms of the cycles of earth, regeneration and rebirth. In our own way we returned the women gently back to the natural reverence of the land of ancient times and they, in turn, so influenced their husbands and children.

John Thornton continued to visit. He told me that the land rose to meet him now more than ever, and I was happy for him. Furthermore, when he told me that he had won the hand of a local squire's daughter, a woman named Sarah, then I was even happier, and wished him well in his marriage. His eyes were sad, but I knew that in time his memories of me would fade, and he would grow to delight in his wife.

Then, as if a god's blessing, word reached us in May of news which pushed to one side all my worries about Weyland Orr and Catling.

Matilda would shortly be joining with Charles, and then, gods willing, with us.

CHAPTER TWO

LISBON, PORTUGAL, AND
THE HAGUE, HOLLAND

HE INFANTA CATHARINE OF PORTUGAL, BETTER known in European circles as Catharine of Braganza, paused directly outside the closed door to her parents' drawing room, then gave a tight nod to the valet who stood standing waiting to open it for her.

Oh, please God, let this be the news she'd spent her life waiting for!

The door swung silently open, and Catharine entered in a quiet, graceful manner, showing none of her nerves. At twenty-three she was a small woman, barely five feet tall, delicate of build and of face, with fine white skin, large and widely spaced dark-brown eyes, and heavy black hair, which Catharine thought her best feature. Diplomats and ambassadors, in describing Catharine's best features, always ignored the hair and argued that her substantial dowry—Bombay, Tangier, and several million gold crowns—was indisputably her best feature. The dowry was certainly her best selling point to various princes about Europe.

But to all of them Catharine had said no. There was but one man she wished to marry, and until this year, it had seemed highly unlikely her father would ever allow it. Indeed, he had refused her lover's suit on several previous occasions.

But now . . .

The audience room was empty of all save Catharine's parents, King John IV and Queen Luisa de Guzman, and one man standing at the windows so that the light hid his features.

He bowed as Catharine entered, but as they had not been introduced, Catharine ignored him for the moment. She walked to where her parents sat side by side in chairs set by the hearth—if the occasion had been more formal, or their visitor anyone but their daughter, the king and queen would have been sitting on their thrones on the dais.

As it was, a small table to one side of Queen Luisa held the remnants of the tea of which Catharine's parents had been partaking, and sharing with the as-yet unknown man standing by the window, if the third cup was any indication.

"My lord father," Catharine said, curtsying deeply. "Madam mother."

She stayed deep in the curtsy until her father waved a hand, granting her permission to rise.

"Lord Edward Montagu," he said, indicating the man standing at the window. "The earl of Sandwich."

Please, dear God, let the earl not be here on some dreary trade delegation! Catharine prayed, again hiding expertly her inner turmoil as she held out her hand. The earl walked forward, bowed yet again, and kissed the backs of her fingers.

"Infanta," the earl murmured, and Catharine noted with renewed excitement how speculatively he regarded her.

"The earl and we," said John, "have been engaged in some discussion, first through our respective ambassadors, and latterly in person within this our palace."

"I had not known of your presence here, good sir," said Catharine, "else I should have made myself better known to you, and wished you well."

"You shall be pleased to hear of the nature of our discussions," said the king.

Catharine briefly closed her eyes, her hands clutching deep within the folds of her silken skirts. *Please, God, please . . . please . . .*

"It seems most apparent," her father went on, his voice languid, almost bored, "that the king of England in exile, Charles, shall no longer be very much in exile."

Please, God, please, please . . . I beg you . . .

"The earl," the king continued, "has brought to me reassurances from General Monck—you have heard of him?"

Catharine inclined her head.

"The general," said John, "has assured me that Parliament has set in motion the procedures necessary for restoring Charles to his throne. It shall not be many more months before Charles may enter England, not as a fugitive, but as its rightful king."

"Princess," said Montagu, "as a gesture of goodwill, Parliament, as well many notable private citizens of my country, have sent to King Charles a significant sum of money—"

"Sixty thousand pounds," said Queen Luisa.

"—as a true indication of their honorable intentions toward the king."

"Where once Charles languished in threadbare breeches," said King John, "begging money from every prince and duke in Europe to pay for his laundresses, he now lolls in silks and satins, threaded all about with seed pearls, and the princes and dukes of Europe line up to do him honor. Thus, I find myself quite prepared to reconsider King Charles's offer for your hand."

"Indeed, the earl's presence here," said Queen Luisa, "indicates, as I am sure you must by now be aware, that these negotiations have, on our part at least, been most truly successful. It only rests for you to—"

"Yes," said Catharine, in such a hurry that the word tumbled thickly from her mouth. "Yes, I agree. I wish to be his wife."

The earl grinned, and Catharine smiled back at him, her face dimpling prettily and relieving her of her usual aura of cool gravity.

"My queen," Montagu said, and bowed more deeply before her than he had done heretofore. *Bombay, Tangier, several million crowns, and a pretty smile as an added gift*, he thought. *My lord king shall be a happy man indeed.*

"YOU HAVE, PERHAPS," MURMURED CHARLES II, SOON-to-be-restored king of England, "some idea of how long I have waited for this moment." He had Catharine's hand in his, and raised it close to his lips as he spoke, but neither had regard for that movement, nor that kiss, but only for each other's eyes as they met.

About them the audience chamber in Charles's temporary palace in The Hague, was packed with members of Charles's court; statesmen and their wives of the States-General of Holland; and the court of Charles's sister, Princess Mary of Orange (her recently deceased husband, Prince William of Orange, had been among the most influential of Dutch noblemen).

The Hague was in a festive mood. After years of ignoring Charles, years of asking him to move on, years of denying him monies for basic housekeeping, years of wishing that the exiled brother of the princess of Orange would just go away, now the Dutch could not get enough of the suddenly wealthy and influential king of England. Monies, flatteries, fruits, and significant measures of gold were thrown his way as if Charles and his plight had never been found the least bit irritating.

Neither Catharine nor Charles had any thought for what was going on about them. Instead, both felt the profoundest sense of relief. Catharine, the last of the inner circle of Eaving's Sisters, was almost home, at last.

All they felt was relief and, as they gazed into each other's eyes, remembering what they had felt for each other in their last life: a not-unexpected desire.

Charles was the first to recall his duty. Catharine had arrived at The Hague only this morning, the earl of Sandwich escorting her from Lisbon (together with several shiploads of fineries, sugar, and, at Catharine's own request, an entire hold's worth of tea). Her most recent arrival notwithstanding, their marriage was due to take place within the hour—no one wanted to wait; least of all Charles and Catharine, after such a long delay—and, while gazing at his intended wife over their conjoined hands was all very sweet, there were matters which needed attending.

He kissed Catharine's fingers, then presented her to the assembled guests.

She curtsied, very prettily if not deeply (after all, she was soon to be their queen), and Charles beckoned forth a few of the more distinguished from among the assemblage. Catharine greeted each one with the deference due his titles and influence—and his potential influence over her future life—but it was the ninth and final man who truly caught her attention.

"Monsieur Louis de Silva," said Charles. "A most particular friend of mine."

"Monsieur de Silva," she said. "I am most pleased to acquaint"—*reacquaint*—"myself with you."

Louis bowed. "Madam, I wish you all happiness with your new husband, and joy in your new kingdom."

"I hope I shall have the chance to better acquaint myself with you, Monsieur de Silva, over the coming weeks and months."

"And I you, madam." This last, Louis accompanied with a dark, sultry look, directly into her eyes, that had Catharine fighting to dampen her smile.

"But for now," Charles said in an undertone, "she is *my* wife."

Louis's mouth jerked in a barely repressed grin. "Assuredly, Majesty. May I wish you great joy in your marriage."

And then he was gone, and the diplomats and ambassadors and assembled personages crowded about, and Charles drew Catharine to him, and they were married.

"THANK ALL THE DAMNED GODS IN EXISTENCE," Charles muttered as he watched the door to the bedchamber close, "that we are alone at last."

He sat with Catharine in a great and elaborately carved bed, a gift from the States of Holland. It was hung about with beautifully embroidered silken drapes, and accoutred in the most splendid of linens and comforts.

The marriage accomplished, the feast endured, and the "putting to bed" borne with as much grace as possible, the pair now found themselves alone.

And, surprisingly, suddenly shy in that aloneness.

"It has been so long," Catharine murmured. She sat on the other side of the vast bed, demure in a white linen nightgown that was feathered all about its square neckline with fine Dutch lacework. She did not look at Charles, but at her hands folded demurely in her lap.

"And so much to say," said Charles. He wondered why, when he had so gleefully shared his bed with Marguerite and Kate, he now found this moment so awkward.

"Do you worry," he said, after some considerable pause, "that Noah might not like to think that . . . you . . . and I . . . that she might feel some . . ."

"Resentment," Catharine said, her voice very low.

"Catharine," he said, and shifted across the bed to her side. He lifted a hand to her hair, and undid the ribbon that held her hair in a thick braid. "Catharine, I sent to Noah both Marguerite and Kate, together with their children that I fathered on them. She did not mind that—not from the reports I have heard—and she will not mind this, not you and I. Circumstances are such that it will be a long time before she and I shall be together again."

If ever, he thought, remembering so much of what had passed between them.

"Noah is not one," he continued, his fingers now combing out Catharine's hair, "to seethe with misplaced resentment."

Catharine had at last raised her face from the regard of her hands. "I have dreamed that she had a child."

He grinned, and Catharine saw in his eyes the deep love he had for Noah. "Aye."

"And it was fathered by . . ."

His grin broadened. "Aye, and within the most magical of Circles. And now that I have told you the truth, are you jealous? Resentful?"

She laughed. "No. I am glad for her."

"Then know that she shall be glad for us." He leaned through the distance between them, and kissed her brow. "Ah, Matilda-Catharine . . . How I desired you six hundred years past . . . How I desire you now . . . Speak to me no more of Noah, I pray you, but only of what you and I can make, here and now, in this bed."

And Catharine lifted her mouth to his, and let him ease her worries.

Chapter Three

Idol Lane, London, and Woburn
Village, Bedfordshire

SPRING OF 1660 WAS A MERRY TIME IN LONDON. The grim years of the Interregnum, or the Commonwealth, when gray austerity ruled and the youthful king languished in exile were well over, and Londoners prepared to welcome home their king. Royal crests on the chimney breasts of fireplaces were uncovered from the layers of concealing ash and plaster which had hidden them during Cromwell's years, and seamstresses and tailors set to sewing colorful pennants and banners to hang from every window on that glorious day when the king would set elegant foot once more within London's ancient walls. Youths set up Maypoles—long banned under Cromwell—in Smithfield so that maidens might dance about them. Church bells rang out wildly upon the least excuse, bonfires were lit in most public greens in and about the city, and many a citizen was observed to fall upon his knees in the street and drink to the king's health. That Charles's restoration coincided with the regeneration of spring was remarked on by all: England was moving toward a glorious new age and everyone would put well behind them that small unfortunateness of Charles's father's execution. This was the happiest period of May celebrations in living memory.

Charles himself excelled at diplomacy. In the first week of May he sent a letter to Parliament submitting himself as their servant. Parliament, in gratitude, sent Charles an extra £5,000 for his costs. Furthermore, in a gesture of goodwill, both Commons and Lords voted to ensure the burning of any books or pamphlets that were "against the king."

Everyone, king, Parliament, and commoner, strove to ensure that every bitterness be laid aside, and that only happiness would reign.

* * *

WEYLAND WAS GREATLY AMUSED. AT NIGHT HE SAT
with Jane in the kitchen of their house in Idol Lane, smiling cynically at the
duplicity of the English. "One day they strike the head from their king,
claiming he was a traitor to his country; the next, they dance drunkenly
about beribboned poles, thinking themselves lucky to submit again to royal
despotism."

Jane, her head bowed over the skirt she was trying to patch, said nothing at
all. It had been a poor day. Her legs and lower back had ached particularly
badly through the afternoon, her disease now grinding its inexorable way
through to the very marrow of her bones. The sores on her face, as did similar
ones on her hands and the soles of her feet, wept continuously of an evil, foul-
smelling effluent. She no longer walked, she hobbled. Almost everyone Jane
knew, save for Elizabeth and Frances, regarded her with a mix of contempt,
pity, and bleak hatred.

"Do you not find this mass hysteria at the coming of the king most amusing?" Weyland said. He sat across the table from Jane, the light from the single
lamp casting shadows about his face.

"I have forgotten what amusement is," Jane said. She wished he would let
her be, and retire to his upstairs lair.

Weyland's eyes narrowed. "Your life is truly pitiful, isn't it?"

Jane suddenly bundled up the skirt and slammed it down on the table. "Why
keep me alive?" she said. "Why keep me in this pain and humiliation? Why—"

"Why not?" he replied softly, and Jane put a shaking hand to her face as
tears sprang to her eyes. This was the worst of all, that he could so humiliate
her with a few soft words.

"Have you not had your satisfaction yet?" she said.

"No," he said. "Besides, you know I still need you. You need to teach
Noah . . . and once you have done that then I will set you free, broken and hollow, stripped of everything you hold dear. Perhaps I might even give you a few
pennies so you can buy a bowl of broth to warm you on your journey."

"You will never set me free. You will kill me so soon as I have done my task."

Weyland said nothing, merely kept his unblinking eyes on her, a small smile
playing about his mouth.

"I won't teach Noah!"

He gave a slight shrug of his shoulders.

"I—"

She never managed to reach the second word. Suddenly, agony swept
through her, and Jane doubled up, half sinking, half falling, from her chair to
the floor.

"If I want," she heard Weyland say in a soft, hateful voice, "I can keep you in this limbo of torment for years. Eventually you will have had enough, and you will do as I say."

Jane, doubled over on the floor, could do nothing but try to stifle her cries, and beat her fist uselessly over and over on the wooden floorboards.

Weyland watched her for a few minutes, then he looked up, and his eyes lost their focus, as if he were seeing something other than the kitchen in Idol Lane.

"Noah," he whispered. "Wake up, Noah. Idol Lane awaits."

Why wait for the king's elegant slippered foot to touch England once more? Why not act now, and forestall any plan Charles might have to save Noah?

NOAH STILL SLEPT IN THE LARGE BED, SANDWICHED between Marguerite and Kate. They had the room to themselves now, as Catling had, for several months since, slept with the other children.

Noah had slept well, for she and Kate had spent much of the day ferrying bread and cheese and ale to the men scything the meadows. They'd had hardly a chance to rest for almost the entire day, and so, once they'd come home and eaten the supper Marguerite provided, they'd been glad enough to fall into bed and to sleep.

In the early hours of the morning, Noah began to toss in her sleep.

She'd fallen from rest into dream.

SHE DREAMED SHE WALKED DOWN THE STRANGELY empty high street of Woburn village. She stopped, uneasy.

There came a sound from behind her, and to her left.

Noah turned about, then started, for there in the half-shadow of a doorway stood Weyland Orr.

"I'm sorry," he whispered, "but I do need to impress upon you my authority."

MARGUERITE WOKE THE INSTANT NOAH SCREAMED. She half jerked, half rolled to the edge of the bed, at first disorientated by the terrible sound that issued forth from Noah's mouth. Kate likewise had woken instantaneously, and now was twisted into a half-crouched position at the very head of the bed, staring at Noah.

Noah was tossing violently from side to side, her back arched, her head dug deep into the pillow, her hands clenched into white-knuckled fists at her sides.

Marguerite, fighting down her terror, inched her way across the bed toward Noah, laying a hesitant hand on her shoulder.

Noah screamed again, lurched forward so she sat upright, then bent forward, her arms crossed about her belly.

Marguerite stopped dead the instant she saw Noah's back. All three women slept naked—there was no linen to hide what was happening to Noah.

It looked as if something had run amok within Noah's body. On either side of her spine ran three parallel gouges, as if some clawed creature was raking her with its claws from within.

As Marguerite and Kate watched, appalled, the gouges slowly traced downward toward Noah's buttocks.

Noah convulsed, then screamed once more, her hands trying to reach behind her body to claw at her back.

Marguerite and Kate each grabbed at Noah's hands and arms, trying to push her down to the bed.

"Yes!" Noah screeched as—still bucking about wildly on the bed—she fought off both Marguerite and Kate. "Yes! I will come! I will come!"

Suddenly she collapsed to the bed, moaning and weeping.

Marguerite rolled her over so she lay on her side, facing Kate.

The terrible gouges had turned purple, filling with blood under the skin, but at least they had stopped gouging.

"Sweet heavens, Noah . . ." Marguerite drifted to a stop. She had no doubts at all what had caused Noah's agony.

"Weyland . . ." Noah managed. "Weyland has called me to him . . . he wanted me to know . . . what would happen . . . if I didn't . . ." She stopped, moaning.

"Mama."

Noah's cries had woken the children—now Catling stood in the doorway. Her face was calm, she was not scared, not even curious.

She knew precisely what had just happened.

Noah managed to raise her face, just enough to see her daughter. "You said once you could help with the imp," she said. "Stop him, please . . . Take away the pain."

"No," said Catling.

Noah let out a tiny sob, turning her face away from Catling, but Marguerite and Kate stared uncomprehendingly at the small girl.

"Why not?" said Kate. "Noah has told us of how you can manipulate the imp. Catling, surely you can—"

"I cannot," said Catling. "If I turn the imp now, if I make him stop hurting my mother, then Weyland will know. It is better that he doesn't realize. It is better that he thinks his imp under his full control."

Noah let out a sound that was half-sob, half-hiss. She still had her face turned away from Catling. "She is right," she said, very soft. "It is better that Weyland does not know."

Marguerite did not look away from Catling. "You can surely ease your mother's pain now, though. How will Weyland know of that? Aid her, Catling."

"I cannot," the girl said, yet one more time. "The hurt has been caused. I cannot take that back. Neither I nor the imp has healing powers."

Marguerite muttered something under her breath, then leaned her mouth close to Noah's ear. "I will help, darling," she whispered, and felt Noah tremble under her hand.

"But only this night," Noah whispered, "for in the morning I shall have to leave."

"No," said Marguerite. "Surely you can—"

She stopped appalled, as Noah screamed again. Even Catling flinched as her mother twisted frenziedly about the bed.

"You will leave in the morning," Marguerite ground out, understanding what was required. "We shall prepare you some food."

And, as suddenly as she had started, Noah fell still, although she continued to moan.

Marguerite met Kate's eyes above Noah's prone figure. "In the morning," she repeated, "but for now we can help."

WEYLAND SAT IN THE KITCHEN, STILL STARING SIGHT-lessly, Jane crumpled unconscious at his feet.

He'd had to do it. He'd needed to impress his authority upon Noah, most particularly after their conversation in the iciness of Woburn village.

But, oh, her screams.

He'd had to do it. Charles would be here soon, and Weyland did not want to wait until he'd set foot in England to snatch at Noah. That might be way too late.

Weyland wanted to be sure.

But, oh, her screams.

Abruptly he stood, stepping over Jane's prone form as he strode for the door and the stairs to his Idyll. Once Noah was with him, he would make sure she understood that every time she crossed him she would endure similar agony. Goddess or not, it didn't matter. Once the imps received their commands, then they . . . nibbled.

"She will learn soon enough," he muttered to himself, climbing the stairs three at a time. "She will learn to obey me, to do my will, and then there will be no need for the pain."

And with that, he comforted himself.

CHAPTER FOUR

CATHARINE WOKE, SCREAMING.

Charles lurched upright, sure that Weyland Orr had somehow managed to find his way under the sheets, and was even now engaged in ripping Catharine apart.

The door to the bedchamber opened, and several men stumbled in: a valet, a guardsman, and a passing nobleman. The valet carried a candle, and by its light Charles was able to see that Catharine was whole, if distressed.

He grabbed at the sheet and pulled it modestly over Catharine's naked breasts.

"My love . . . what is it? Wake up . . . A nightmare only, I assure you. Wake up!"

Catharine blinked, and seemed to come somewhat to her senses. Her hair was tumbled about her shoulders, her face pale, her eyes white and frightened. "Charles?"

"A nightmare," he said, but there was an underlying question to his voice.

"A nightmare . . ." Catharine said, her voice as riven with underlying meaning as his had been, and she looked significantly at the three men who now stood gape-mouthed at the side of the bed.

Charles turned to them, and smiled. "All is well, my friends. Catharine no doubt dreamed she'd been married to some German toad instead of to me. You may leave the candle, John, if you please."

There was polite laughter from the three, and they bowed, murmured a few well-chosen words appropriate to the occasion, and—the valet placing the candle on a table close to the bed—exited the chamber, closing the door behind them.

"Gods, Catharine, what has happened?"

"Weyland Orr has called Noah to him. He woke her, Charles, with pain so terrible that I felt a glimmer of it from this distance."

Charles had leapt from the bed as she spoke, and now paced naked to and fro at its foot. "Weyland has called Noah to him? But I have not yet set foot in England! Long Tom said he would not do this until I had set foot in England!"

"Charles—"

"Long Tom said he would not touch her until I had set foot in England!"

"Charles—"

"Catharine, we were supposed to save her! We—"

"Charles!"

He stopped his pacing, and stared at her.

"Send for Louis," Catharine said. "Now."

Charles stared one moment longer, then gave a curt nod, and strode for the door.

LOUIS MANAGED NOT TO RUN AS HE MADE FOR THE royal bedchamber, but it took all of his self-control. There might be many reasons Charles would send for him in the middle of the night, and Louis could not think of a single positive one.

The valet hurrying at his side sent Louis a sidelong glance, and Louis supposed that within the hour most of the people at Charles's court would know that the king had sent for his favorite French companion in the midst of the night.

Why? they'd whisper. Could our king not manage to service his wife as he ought, and thus called for de Silva? If the queen be pregnant this time next month, should we be watching at the child's birth to see if it cried in French, or in English?

Louis didn't give a damn about the undoubtedly ribald whispers. All he wanted was to discover the reason for the summons.

Finally they reached their destination. There was a small crowd standing about outside the bedchamber—Louis could see two physicians, as well Sir Edward Hyde, five Dutch noblemen, three serving girls, and at least seven guardsmen.

"Allow us passage!" the valet cried dramatically, and threw open the door and gestured Louis to enter.

Then, thankfully, he was inside, the door closed behind him, and he could see Charles sitting on the edge of the bed, and Catharine in its center, her pretty face pale and patently upset.

"What?" Louis said, starting toward the bed.

"Weyland Orr has taken Noah," Charles replied, and Louis stopped dead, still only halfway to the bed, his face slack with shock. "But—"

"I know, I know," Charles said, standing. "Not until I set foot in England, Long Tom said. But when has Asterion ever done what anyone else has planned for him? No, he must have suspected we'd try to rescue her ourselves, and so has forestalled us."

Louis looked to Catharine. "You felt this?"

She gave a single nod. "The imp . . . such pain . . . she can't resist. She must to London immediately."

Louis paled. "But she is still in Woburn village?"

"Yes," said Catharine. "But I have no doubt she'll leave soon, in the morning. She can't go through another attack like that again. If she doesn't move, Weyland will . . ."

Charles and Louis locked eyes, thinking over that *Weyland will* . . .

"If she's at Woburn, then I have time to get to her," Louis said.

"But—" Charles said.

"Damn it, Charles! We can't just sit here and moan! There are ships waiting at the wharves. On your authority I can command one to take me for England within the hour. If there is a good wind—"

"There will be," Charles said quietly.

"—then I can be at London within two days. Perhaps only thirty-six hours. It will take Noah at least that long to reach London by road. I can reach London before she does, waiting at the city gates, watching the road from Woburn. I can get to her before she reaches Weyland!"

"Gods, Louis," Charles said. "If Weyland realizes you are there . . ."

"And if he takes Noah?" said Louis. "What then, eh? If he has Noah, then he has the bands. If he can command her to London, then he can command her to fetch him those bands as easily."

Charles gave a slow, reluctant nod. "Very well. But, by all gods in existence, be careful! I'll move as fast as I can, set out for England myself within the next few days. Weyland Orr, if he senses anything, will think it is me moving."

"Write me letters of introduction. To Monck, to Parliament, to the damned passport inspectors, to the cursed street-sweepers if you must, but give me enough documentation to get me free access to London."

Charles turned for the desk set against one wall of the chamber. "Send for Hyde. He can aid me with the cursed passports and letters of introduction while you send to the wharves to wake the captain of the *Fair Polly*. He'll stand the best chance of getting you speedily and safely to London."

WHEN JANE FINALLY AWOKE FROM HER UNCONSCIOUS state, she only very slowly became aware of her surroundings.

The kitchen was dark; both the lamps and the fire had died.

She was cold, colder than she'd ever been in her life.

Her entire body ached. Everything, not just her belly. Her fingers, her head, her very bones. Her entire existence throbbed.

And yet, Jane was barely conscious of any of this.

Instead, she thought of something that had happened to her during that time when she had been in agony and when unconsciousness had not yet claimed her. Someone else had been there with her, sharing her pain.

Noah. Noah had been there, very faint, but there, writhing even as Jane writhed. Screaming, even as Jane screamed.

Sisters, finally, in agony, as they had never been when free of Weyland's imps.

Chapter Five

WOBURN VILLAGE TO

LUTON, BEDFORDSHIRE

Noah Speaks

HAD NOT EXPECTED THAT AGONY. THAT WAS FOOL-
ish of me, I am sure, but I truly had not expected it. As Caela,
whether as herself or in her glamour as Damson, I'd seen the terrible
effects of Swanne's imp on her body, and I'd seen the suffering in Swanne's
eyes. I should have known that Asterion would visit a similar anguish on me.

And yet, still, both the pain and the attack came as a shock. I'd harbored
the imp for so many years, through two lives, with little to show for it save
some discomfort during my monthly menstrual cycle, that when it did
strike . . . Oh, merciful heavens . . .

I could feel him crawling through my body. Feel him reaching out his claws
and raking them slowly down my inner back, delighting in my terror and pain.

Hear him giggling, the sound horribly distorted by its passage through my
flesh.

All I could think of was Catling's statement, once, that she could help if the
imp troubled me during my monthly menses. All I could think of was how
Catling seemed able to control the imp. All I could think of was that she could
now call a halt to this terrible tearing . . . this terrible agony.

That she didn't, came as no true surprise. She was right, of course, to say
that if she stopped the imp then Weyland would know that the black horror
was beyond his control.

But even so . . . To have her refuse to aid me . . .

Marguerite and Kate did what they could. Cool herbal poultices, and
love and compassion, applied in equal amounts, eased much of my suffering.
By dawn the overwhelming agony had gone, but my flesh still pained me

considerably. Marguerite said the welts on my back had bruised a deep-purple, and when she gently laid her fingers to one of them I yelped and jerked my body away.

Catling had returned to her bed for the night, but now came to me. At one point, when both Kate and Marguerite had left to prepare our breakfast, she said to me, "You are leaving for London today."

It was no question.

"Aye," I said.

"I shall accompany you," she said.

I said nothing. I wondered what she wanted, and what her purpose was. I wondered what *she* was.

But I was so tired from my night of suffering, so drained, and still so terrified at what might lie ahead of me that I said nothing. I knew full well that if I said no then Catling would nonetheless accompany me.

Marguerite returned eventually, carrying a fresh dish of herbs to apply to my back, and Kate came with her, bearing a tray of food for myself and Catling.

Both women were very quiet, very reserved. "I wish . . ." Kate began, as she handed me a bowl of a thick, warm porridge. She leaned back to her tray, hesitated, then handed a second bowl to Catling.

"Aye," I said, trying to smile at her. "I wish also."

"When will you go?" asked Marguerite. "And how shall you travel?"

"I will leave so soon as I have finished this porridge," I said, trying to keep the despair out of my voice. "And I shall take one of the horses, and Catling and I shall ride it well enough."

"But," said Marguerite, accepting without comment that Catling should accompany me, "traveling the roads to London for a woman and child is dangerous. I thought you would . . . walk the land."

She was being obtuse, but I knew what she meant. Why risk physical travel along the roads when I could use my power well enough to walk the land as Eaving?

"I do not want Weyland to see it," I said. "He knows too much as it is. I do not want him to see all that I can do. Besides, he wants me in London. He shall make sure I get there alive."

"Alive," Marguerite said, her tone harsh, "but not necessarily well and whole. We all know the extent of his cruelty and I can well believe he shall have several 'surprises' for you on the journey south. Sweet heavens, Noah, the journey will take you three days at least. Where will you stay? Who shall protect you? And Catling? What of her? You are so terribly injured you cannot look after yourself, let alone her. I—"

"Peace," I said. "I will travel to London, and both myself and Catling shall arrive there safely enough."

"And then?" said Kate.

I fell silent, not wanting to think of what would happen once my daughter and I achieved London.

And then?

I shivered, and turned my mind away from it. I would think no more of London, but only of the journey there.

I rose. "Marguerite. Will you aid me to wash? I do not want to set out unwashed."

She nodded, and, as she aided me first to bathe and then to don some loose-fitting underclothes beneath a lightly laced bodice and skirt, we talked of some of the necessities I should take with me in a pack.

Such preparations did not take long. What could I take, save a change of clothes for Catling and myself, as well as some food for the journey? If I traveled too heavily, then I risked not only slowing myself down, but exposing myself to theft. Better to journey light and poorly, than to invite attention.

We were all subdued. I felt sickened, not merely with the ache in my back, nor only for the fact I should so soon be leaving Marguerite and Kate, but for what I walked toward.

By the time dawn had made its mark, I was ready. The horse we had stabled at the back of the house was saddled and bridled and standing by the front door; Catling's and my small bag of belongings were tied behind its saddle. I took my daughter's hand and smiled, somewhat wanly, for Marguerite and Kate.

"It is farewell for the time being, then," I said, a little lamely.

Marguerite's eyes filled with tears.

I gulped, and then all three of us were crying, and huddled together in as close an embrace as we could manage.

"We will come to London after you," said Marguerite, once she had regained some semblance of control.

"Charles and Catharine shall be here soon," Marguerite continued, "and then all Eaving's Sisters shall be together, and near you. We will find a way to touch you and comfort you, Eaving."

I touched Marguerite's face, then Kate's. Then I turned for the horse, and managed to mount with as much grace as my painful back and voluminous skirts would allow me.

Marguerite handed Catling up to me—I settled her in the saddle before me—and then, with nothing more than a nod, I put my heels gently into the horse's flanks, and turned his head for the road, and we were off.

THAT DAY WAS BUT A GENTLE RIDE PACED AT A WALK. I had no heart for a joyous canter southward toward London, nor did I have the strength. With one arm about Catling at all times, and the other being tugged at constantly by the horse (who had patently decided to repay me for his early morning's awakening by leaning his head down into the bit the entire day), by midmorning my entire body ached, and my back throbbed horribly. The road was relatively quiet, for which I was greatly thankful, and Catling kept quiet, for which I was even more grateful. I did not think I could bear some false, daughterly chatter.

It was a dreadful ride. This was not merely because of my worsening aches, nor because of what I rode toward, but because I think I was finally forced to confront the fact that Catling was not all that she should be. Had her journey into the Otherworld and back to this changed her so much? Had she learned, perhaps, to hate me somewhere on that long and terrible journey? I didn't know what it was, I didn't know what was wrong. All I knew was that Catling bore me no more love than she bore the most inanimate pebble, and that I regarded her with disappointment, even some slight fear, rather than with love.

I had hoped for so much for and from this daughter. What I had instead was such a vast realm of disappointment that I felt a complete failure, as both a mother and as Eaving.

Thus we continued. The pain in my body grew increasingly worse, and eventually I had to grind my teeth together to prevent myself from begging Catling to do something about it.

By late morning we had passed through the town of Toddington. The town was bustling with market day, and it took a good hour for us to thread our way through the crowded streets. Every time someone jostled the horse I winced, and once a stab of pain so agonizing seared up my spine that I only barely managed to restrain myself from falling off the horse.

When we emerged into the countryside again I was weeping, not only with pain, but with fear: How was I going to continue on as far as London in this degree of pain? *Damn Weyland! He did not need to be so vicious!*

We continued on, Catling silent in the face of my obvious suffering. She gripped the pommel of the saddle with both her hands, as if she could not trust me to manage to keep hold of her, and she kept her face determinedly ahead, ignoring every gasp that escaped my lips.

Gods . . .

By late afternoon we had reached Luton, and I knew I could go no farther that day. I reined the horse in at a roadside inn, wanting nothing more than to be able to stretch out on a bed and close my eyes and somehow sleep away the aches and pain and worries.

But my day in the saddle, coupled with the injury to my back, meant that my muscles had cramped badly and, as I tried to lift Catling down, I felt myself waver before inexorably tilting over the horse's near shoulder.

Then, just before Catling and myself plummeted to the ground, I heard a
marvelously familiar male voice calling my name, and the next instant, strong
arms lifted both myself and Catling down, and I blinked, and looked into John
Thornton's dear face.

Chapter Six

Luton, Bedfordshire

JOHN THORNTON HAD ONLY BARELY HANDED THE reins of his own horse over to the stableboy when he heard the sound of another horse behind him.

He turned, then froze in shock as he saw Noah Banks and her daughter ride into the inn's courtyard.

In hindsight, he realized that it was not merely the shock of seeing them there, but the look of agony on Noah's face that had momentarily glued him to the spot.

Then he saw Noah teeter, her mouth open in horror as she realized she and Catling were about to tumble to the muddy surface of the courtyard, and he lunged forward, catching them only just in time.

One of his hands slipped about Noah's back as he steadied her, and she flinched away from him with a terrible cry.

"My God, Noah, what assails you?"

"Mama needs aid," said Catling. "She is not well. She cannot cope."

Thornton spared the girl a glance (and, by God yet again, how had a girl only some thirteen or fourteen months old, managed to grow to such height, and such clarity of expression?), then looked back to Noah.

She had steadied herself now, and proffered him an apologetic smile. "John. What do you here?"

I could well ask the same thing, he thought, but for the moment saved the question. "I am on my way to London. Lord Bedford has sent me there to prepare his townhouse for his and Lady Bedford's arrival . . . They are journeying down in a few days to greet the king on his arrival. Noah . . ."

"John, I beg you, Catling has spoken truly. Can you aid me to obtain a bed, and perhaps some manner of hot food? I am tired beyond knowing—"

"Noah," Thornton said softly, moving closer to her again and settling an arm gently about her waist, avoiding as best he could her back, "you are in agony. What has happened?"

"John, I beg you, a bed . . ."

Thornton gave her one more searching look, then acquiesced. "Catling, take my other hand. There is a room waiting for me, and you shall share it. No, don't protest, Noah. I have a feeling that if I allow you out of my sight then you shall slip away."

"I shall slip nowhere in this state," Noah muttered, but she made no more protest about the room.

Thornton looked to the stableboy, nodded at Noah's horse, indicating the boy should take care of him as well, then slowly led Noah and Catling inside the inn.

FAR DISTANT, ON THE GRAY HEAVING SEAS, A SHIP leaned into the wind.

At its prow stood Louis, alternatively glancing at the billowing sails and silently thanking Charles for sending such a propitious wind, and looking forward, straining to see the coasts and cliffs of the British Isles.

Farther back on the deck of the *Fair Polly* the captain stifled a yawn, then muttered to his first mate, "You'd think the hounds of hell were after him the way he begs us to make full speed."

The first mate shrugged. "So long as he pays us . . ."

The captain grinned, and jiggled his hand deep inside the pocket of his voluminous coat. "Handsome payment in king's gold already received, my friend. We'll all be dining well, once we reach London."

SWEET JESUS CHRIST! THORNTON SLOWLY PEELED Noah's bodice back over her shoulders so that her back lay exposed before him.

She must be in agony! He'd never seen wounds like this before, and could not think what had caused them, save that perhaps some foul villain had thrashed her with a lead-tipped whip.

As soon as they'd reached the room, and Thornton had closed the door behind them, he'd sat Noah on the bed and wordlessly, ignoring her protests, unbuttoned her bodice. He'd had no idea what he might find . . . but it certainly had not been this.

He spoke a single, soft word. "Who?"

"It is no one you—" Noah said.

"Who?"

"A bad man," said Catling, sitting on Noah's other side and looking at Thornton.

"Who?" he repeated yet one more time.

"John," Noah whispered, "there is nothing you can do."

In response, he leaned forward and very gently kissed the unmarked nape of her neck. "Who?" he whispered.

"John . . ."

He kissed her again, this time a little lower, and again on unmarked skin. "Who?"

"A fiend," she said. "His name is malevolence incarnate."

Again Thornton's lips touched Noah's back, lower yet, and she shuddered. "I shall kill him," he said.

Noah jerked away from his hands and mouth, pulling her bodice over her shoulders again. "John, no. Don't. Please. There is nothing you can do."

"Yes, there is," said Catling. "Reverend Thornton, if you please, we travel also to London. Will you accompany us? Mama cannot look after me herself. She shall fall, and fail. I cannot have that."

"You travel to London?" said Thornton, sparing Catling a sharp glance for her strange words. "Why?"

"I have a friend there, who has asked me to stay during the joyous time of King Charles's restoration," said Noah.

"And his name?" said Thornton, hating the tightness in his voice. He had thought to have put his need for Noah a long ways behind him. He had hoped that his new wife would make him forget his once-lover.

Forget how the land rose to meet him when he touched her.

Ah . . . how foolish he had been.

"Jane," said Noah softly. "Jane Orr."

Thornton cursed himself and his jealousy; as well, cursed the night the sixteen-year-old Noah had first come to his room. Better ignorance of her, than knowing her, and knowing he could never have her love.

"Catling," he said. "Will you go to the innkeeper's wife, and ask her for a bowl of warm water, with some mint steeped in it, and bring it to me? Your mother's back needs to be washed."

Catling nodded, rose, and left the room.

"I find it most strange," Thornton said, "that I should issue such a request to a child only just turned a year old and watch her walk from this room as might a five- or six-year-old child. Woburn gossips, Noah, about what could have bred such a girl on you."

"She had a most magical and powerful father," Noah said. Her voice was very soft, and she still sat so that he could see little of her save her back and shoulders.

"Most apparently," Thornton said. He hesitated, then added, "Whom you love greatly . . ."

She twisted about to look him in the eye. "What do you want to hear, John?"

He sighed. "I do not want to hear . . . Oh, Noah, I do not know what I want to hear." Hesitating, he reached out a hand, slipping it inside the back of her open bodice, caressing her breasts and belly.

"Don't, John," Noah said. "What do you want? To force such a sorely wounded woman to your will?"

He hissed, pulling his hand sharply away from her. "Where was your magical and powerful lover then, when you were so cruelly injured? Why cleave to him so faithfully, when it is I here with you now, and not he? Why love him so greatly, when it is apparent he has deserted you and your child?"

"You cannot understand," Noah said, then stopped, and began again: "I'm sorry for what I said. I was too tart."

He gave a hollow laugh. "You have made it plain enough to me that what we once had is now gone, Noah. But as you see, I am a weak man."

Noah took one of his hands in hers, waiting until it had relaxed before speaking again. "John, you promised to aid me if I should need it. Will you do so now?"

Thornton bit back his almost instinctive response: *Your lover is not here to aid you now.* He sighed. "Aye, of course."

"Accompany us to London, for we have sore need of your care. But—"

"Ah, that 'but.'"

"Once we have arrived, then leave me, John. Where I go, you cannot follow."

"You go to your lover."

She gave a small, sad smile. "I wish that were so, but, no, I do not go to him. He is lost to me for a long time, I think."

"I will accompany you to London, then, where I shall leave you. Noah . . ."

"I know," she said, and gave his hand a squeeze.

"I am lost in you, Noah. I was lost that first night you came to me. Lost in you . . ."

CHAPTER SEVEN

LUTON, BEDFORDSHIRE, TO LANGLEY HOUSE, HERTFORDSHIRE

THE NEXT DAY AT MIDMORNING THEY SET OUT from Luton. Noah looked much better for sleeping well; as well as for enjoying some good food provided by the innkeeper's wife. She appeared well enough to ride, so Catling rode behind Thornton, while Noah kept her own horse. It was a fine day, although there was a strong westerly wind blowing, and for the most part Thornton let his worries abate. Noah's back had looked much better in the morning, and he chose to believe that she was, indeed, visiting her friend Jane Orr in London, so that she might enjoy the festivities surrounding the king's restoration, due in only a week's time.

Noah had meant to travel to London via Watford today, but Thornton persuaded her to a slightly different plan. He meant to stay this night with friends who lived close to the manor of Bushey Park, just northeast of Watford. Thomas and Leila Thanet would provide much more comfortable accommodation than a crowded public inn and, Thornton argued, better care for Noah, should she need it.

Noah had not been sure of Thornton's suggestion—how would John explain both her and Catling?—but acquiesced after only a short hesitation. Thornton had argued that it would be safer for her and Catling if they stayed at the Thanets' Langley House, and to this, Noah had no counter.

The way from Luton to the Watford region was gentle and easy. They passed between ranges of hills on either side during the morning and, in the early afternoon, stopped in the fields of St. Albans, where they rested and partook of some food they'd carried with them.

"What shall you say to the Thanets about myself and Catling?" Noah asked as they stood up from their picnic, brushing down their clothes from the grass seeds and flowers which clung to them.

John Thornton shrugged slightly. "That you chose to accompany me to London to see your friend Jane Orr," he said. "Perhaps following the death of your husband." He looked significantly at Catling.

"I would prefer that you told them the truth," said Noah.

"What? That you are the scandalous companion of Lady Anne that so much of the county has gossiped about?"

Noah flushed, and Thornton fought away a twinge of guilt.

"Noah," he said, "it is best not to tell them *all* the truth. We need not speak of a deceased husband if you so wish—the Thanets shall merely assume it, and assume Catling is his child."

Noah hesitated a moment longer, then nodded. Thornton aided her to her horse, lifted Catling to his own, and then mounted himself, leading the way back to the road and the way south.

FROM THE FIELDS OF ST. ALBANS IT WAS BUT A TWO-hour ride at a sedate walk to where the Thanets lived in their large red brick house. Thornton told Noah and Catling that Thomas's great-grandfather had been a successful merchant during Queen Elizabeth's later years. With the riches he'd made from his business he'd purchased an estate just to the north of Bushey Park, and built Langley House in the flamboyant Elizabethan style. There the Thanets settled, selling their business, and engaging, over the next two or three generations, in a gradual process of gentrification.

"Thomas's father had represented the county in the House of Commons," Thornton said as they turned their mounts down the long drive toward the house. "Now Thomas hopes to do the same in Charles the Second's new Parliament."

"It shall be a grand new age," Noah said, but something in her voice made Thornton look at her sharply.

"You don't think so," he said.

She gave a slight shrug. "So much can always go wrong."

Thornton grunted. "You are a pessimist, indeed."

"Indeed," she said, and Thornton would have challenged her on that, but at that instant the front doors of the house opened to reveal a well-dressed man and woman, presumably the Thanets, hurrying to meet the man, woman, and child approaching the house.

"John!" Thomas Thanet exclaimed, catching at the reins of Thornton's horse as Thornton dismounted. They shook hands enthusiastically, then

Thornton stepped forward and kissed Leila Thanet's hand. "I am so happy to see you well," he said, glancing at her rounded, six-month belly.

Flustered, Leila stepped back from Thornton and looked to Noah, as well to the little girl still sitting behind the saddle on Thornton's horse.

"John," she said, her smile broadening, "you did not tell us you were bringing your new wife with you! What a wonderful surprise." She stepped over to Noah, who was staring at Leila with a shocked expression. "Welcome, my dear! You cannot know how happy we are to know that John has found his soul mate at last!"

Before Noah could open her mouth to protest, Thornton said, "She is my life, Leila. I cannot imagine existing without her."

NOAH WAS FURIOUS. SHE STOOD IN THE CENTER OF the large and well-appointed bedchamber to which Leila had led them (Catling, whom Thornton had explained was Noah's child from a previous marriage, had been taken to meet the Thanets' children), her face flushed and her posture stiff.

"You did not tell me you had married your Sarah! I thought only you had announced your betrothal!"

"I thought you would be pleased for me."

"I am! I am! But I would have not stayed with you in the manner I did if I had known you had married . . . And now the Thanets think I am your wife, and—"

"And if you tell them not, after having allowed Leila to show us to this private chamber, what shall she think? That I am disporting myself with some strumpet from Watford? Or a whore I picked up along the roadway?"

"*This,*" Noah waved her hand at the bed which took up almost half of the entire space of the chamber, "is a lie!"

Thornton sighed. "How can we now explain that—"

"Explaining *now* will take a greater skill at diplomacy than either you or I possess, I think. What should have happened, the moment Leila mistook me for your wife, was to set her to rights, *not* to stand there like a lovelorn donkey and say, 'She is my life. I cannot imagine existing without her.'"

"And that *was* the truth, Noah," Thornton said quietly. "To have said anything else would have been a lie."

Noah's shoulders slumped, her anger draining away. "Gods," she said, "how I have mismanaged this."

She turned away, walking to the bed and stroking the beautifully embroidered coverlet. "Here we are, arguing as if we are, truly, a married couple."

He said nothing, and she looked back to him.

"John, what will you say when one day the Thomas and Leila meet your true wife? And what shall *Sarah* say when she knows you have stayed here a night with a strange woman in your bed who you passed off as her?"

Thornton shrugged. "I shall think of some explanation." In truth, Thornton did not like to think what would happen once his new wife heard of this. He hadn't meant to say what he had when Leila had called Noah his wife . . . but the words somehow had slipped out and, as he had just said to Noah, they *were* the truth.

Noah rubbed a hand over her forehead, as if her head ached. "Well, at least we shall be gone in the morning." She studied the bed once more. "And thank the gods the bed is wide enough that we may keep fully half an acre between us during the night."

Thornton had noted not only Noah's hand rubbing at her forehead, but her slight wince as she had turned to the bed. "Your back. Noah. Does it pain you?"

"A little."

"I shall ask Leila for some soothing water and—"

"For sweet Christ's sake, John, you cannot let her see the welts! She will think you one who prefers to take his pleasures through pain rather than gentle caresses!"

"I shall wash your back myself," Thornton said. "And how could I manage this, if Leila did not think me your husband? You can afford no one else to see those wounds if you do not want them calling the sheriff so that your attacker might be taken into custody."

"Catling—" Noah stopped short, and Thornton wondered why she could not rely on Catling to wash her back for her.

"Catling is a wondrous child," said Thornton, "but those wounds need more care than what she can give."

Noah sighed, and sat down on the bed. "I have no concern for myself with these lies in which we have enmeshed ourselves, John, but for you. When the Thanets—when your *wife*—discover the deception you have played . . ."

"Then I shall live with the consequences," said Thornton. "Now, rest, for I am going to ask Leila for the water with which to soothe your back."

Chapter Eight

Langley House, Hertfordshire,
Idol Lane, London, and
The Hague, the Netherlands

THORNTON KNEW ALMOST SO SOON AS HE ROSE the next morning that they would not be riding anywhere that day. Selfishly, he was glad. Once he'd stepped from the bed, Thornton had opened one of the shuttered windows, expecting to see bright sunlight.

Instead all he saw was the unrelieved gloom of rain lashing against the panes of glass. He recalled the strength of the westerly wind of yesterday: a late-spring gale had blown in from the Atlantic and, if his experience were any judge, would take all day to blow itself out.

No one but a fool would try to ride in this.

"John?" Noah was sitting on her side of the bed, shivering in her thin linen nightgown. She reached for a shawl and wrapped it about her shoulders as she stood and walked over to join Thornton.

He nodded to the storm outside. "We'll be staying here this day."

"I have to keep moving, John."

There was a terrible tightness in her voice, as if she was frightened, and without thinking about it, Thornton put an arm about her shoulders and drew her in close.

Noah's eyes were fixed on the rain pelting against the window, and she didn't object to his touch.

"Noah," he said, his voice gentle, "no one should ride in this rain and wind. If you don't kill yourself, then you'll kill your horse . . . and, by God Himself, you couldn't want to take *Catling* out in this?"

She shivered again, and Thornton pulled her a little closer. "What are you frightened of?" he said.

To that Noah gave a small shake of her head. "I *have* to keep moving."

"Why? Will your friend Jane Orr pout and sulk if you be delayed a day?"

"Not her," Noah whispered, and before Thornton could ask her, *Who, then?* there came a knock at the door, and it opened before either Thornton or Noah could respond.

It was Thomas Thanet, wearing a thin, loose coat over his own nightgown. He grinned at the sight of Thornton and Noah standing so intimately close at the window.

"You'll be staying awhile, then," he said. "Poor weather in which to be traveling."

Thornton's arm tightened about Noah as he felt her start to move away. "Aye," he said, smiling easily. "Shall we stretch your hospitality to the breaking point?"

"We'll be glad of the chance to keep you a while longer," said Thomas. "Leila was saying to me last night that she regretted not having the chance to know Noah better. Why, my dear," he said, his eyes now on Noah, "before dinner she'll have pried from you every secret you harbor, I swear."

Noah smiled wanly, and Thornton felt her shiver once more.

IT WAS, ALL IN ALL, A DISMAL DAY.

Despite Thomas Thanet's initial cheerfulness, by the time everyone had breakfasted, the gray, frigid rain had affected the mood of the entire household. Catling retreated into a sullen silence; Noah responded only grudgingly to every question Leila asked; and Thomas Thanet himself descended into a fugue not unlike the outside weather.

"Your wife is *most* reticent," Leila Thanet confided to Thornton in the mid-afternoon. Noah had just taken Catling to the bed in the chamber she shared with one of the Thanet girls.

"She has had ill-news regarding a friend," Thornton said, now regretful that he'd put Noah in this position. He hadn't realized how greatly Leila would pester her with questions, and over the course of the day had noticed Noah's posture becoming stiffer and stiffer. He thought it might partly be due to annoyance at Leila's probing, but knew too well that her back was most likely paining her. The welts had gone down from when he'd first seen them, but they were obviously still extremely painful. Noah wore the bare minimum of clothing needed for modesty—her figure was good enough for her to manage without the corsets that most gentlewomen wore under their tightly laced bodices—but even the soft linens of her chemise and the light material of her bodice must have caused constant chafing against her back.

Not for the first time this day, Thornton thanked God that at least Noah was being removed into the relative safety of London from whomever it was at Woburn who had caused her injuries.

WEYLAND PACED BACK AND FORTH IN THE KITCHEN of his house in Idol Lane.

"She's not moving," he said.

"Dear God," Jane said, and lifted a hand from where she rolled out pastry dough on the table to wave it at the window, "look at the weather. This storm has enveloped half of England . . . *no one* is moving!"

"But I *require* her to move," Weyland said. His face was working, as if he battled something within himself. "She *can't* think she can get away with this. She *can't!*"

He lifted a hand—

"No!" Jane cried, starting away from the table to where Weyland stood. "Don't—"

She stopped, then dropped to the floor, clutching her belly, her face screwed up in agony, a single whimper escaping her opened mouth.

"*Don't* speak so sharp to me," Weyland hissed at her; then his eyes lost his focus, and he spoke a single word.

"*Noah.*"

And that single word was followed in Weyland's mind by a single, simple, telling phrase.

I'm sorry . . .

THORNTON SAW HER GO RIGID, SAW HER FACE GO bloodless, saw the panic and terror in her eyes, and, while he did not know the specifics of what was happening, knew he had to get her to their chamber as fast as he could.

Noah gave a terrible groan, then went rigid, her head straining backward, her back arched.

Both Leila and Thomas lurched to their feet, each exclaiming, but Thornton almost threw himself across the space separating Noah's chair from his, and grabbed her to him.

"Her head," he said. "She has the most profound attacks of brain ague."

It was the best he could think of on the spur of the moment, but it seemed to satisfy the Thanets immediate questions.

"No wonder she could not bear my questioning," Leila said. "Her head must have been aching all morning."

Neither she nor her husband seemed to notice that it was Noah's back that was the cause of her distress.

"John," Noah managed to gasp out. "John, please, our chamber . . ."

Thornton needed no other encouragement. He lifted Noah in his arms, trying his best not to touch her back, although she cried out harshly as one of his arms scraped across just below her shoulders, and made for the great staircase so fast as his legs could carry him.

"Not . . . not . . ." Noah said, and Thornton thought he knew what she was trying to say.

"She just needs some quiet," he said. "I'll let you know once the worst has passed."

And with that he was gone, Noah groaning desperately in his arms, and the Thanets were left to stand in the center of their hall, mouths agape.

JANE CURLED UP INTO AS TIGHT A BALL AS SHE could manage on the floor, hugging her belly, and thought she would die from the anguish. She writhed uncaring as her head, arms, and body hit the table legs. All she knew was the agony, all she knew was the suffering, all she knew was . . .

Something intruded into her blinding morass of pain. It was nothing recognizable, merely a presence, but Jane grabbed on to it without thinking or reasoning as to what it may have been.

It was a companion in pain.

Someone else who suffered and who, somehow, had forged a connection to her.

THORNTON KICKED OPEN THE DOOR TO THEIR BED chamber. Noah was now writhing in his arms, and biting her lips to keep from screaming out loud.

Catling had appeared at the head of the stairs, and now she shut the door as Thornton lowered Noah to the bed.

She rolled away from him instantly, and a terrible groan ripped out of her throat.

For an instant Thornton stood helplessly, not sure of what he should do. He glanced at Catling—she was standing at the foot of the bed, watching her mother with unreadable eyes—then Noah had rolled back toward Thornton, was reaching out to him with one hand, and was moaning and sobbing: "*Sweet gods in heaven, please, please, please . . .*"

Thornton grabbed her hand, wincing as he felt the bones of his own hand crush under her grip, then realized that blood stained the back of her bodice. Without thinking, he managed to extricate himself from Noah's grasp, grabbed the seam where it was laced closed at the back of her neck, and ripped the material apart down to her waist.

What he saw would haunt him for the rest of his life.

Sharp ridges ran down Noah's back from her shoulder blades to well past where her skirt was tied about her waist.

It looked as if . . . It looked as if something, some fiend, *was raking her from within.*

Thornton froze in horror.

Two claws emerged from the new welts appearing on Noah's skin down the right hand side of her spine, and Thornton knew then that whatever was *within* Noah was about to rip her to shreds.

"Oh, God, oh, God, save her," he gasped, and grabbed at her, trying to hold her arms, hold her to him, anything, so long as he did *something.*

"I can't help," he heard Catling say at the end of the bed, but Thornton paid her no attention as blood erupted from the terrible wounds in Noah's back, and spattered over his face.

SHE ROLLED ABOUT THE FLOOR, WEEPING IN HER MIS-*ery, yet still aware that someone else shared her pain.* "Noah? Noah? Is that you?"

"Who is this?"

"Jane."

"Ah, Jane, does your imp bite as well?"

Jane moaned. "Noah, run, if you can. Do not trap yourself as I trapped myself."

"I cannot run . . ."

"Noah . . ."

The presence faded.

"JANE!" NOAH CALLED OUT. SHE WENT RIGID IN Thornton's arms, then abruptly collapsed into unconsciousness.

Her body slowly relaxed.

"Thank God," Thornton whispered. He held her a moment longer, then sat up, kneeling on the bed. His face, chest, and arms were covered in blood. He looked at Catling, still standing, watching with apparent calm, at the foot of the bed. "Catling, *what just happened?*"

"Sometimes," Catling said, "my mother bleeds . . ."

Her bizarre words somehow frightened Thornton even more deeply than had the past few terrible minutes. "What can I do?" he said, his voice weak and trembling.

"Love her," said Catling, "and wash her back."

"The first shall be no burden at all," Thornton whispered, "and the last . . ."

He looked to Noah's back, now covered in fresh wounds down both sides of her spine, and shuddered.

CHARLES AND CATHARINE SPENT THE AFTERNOON of that day in a reception put on for them in The Hague by Mary, Princess of Orange.

It was a great, glittering affair, and both Charles and his wife were predisposed to enjoy themselves hugely. Last night a great fleet of ships had arrived from England, sent by Parliament to bring home their king in all the glory he deserved. All the officers and gentlemen of this fleet were at the reception this evening, dressed in silks and velvets and jewels, led by the General-at-sea, or Admiral of the Fleet, the Earl of Sandwich, Sir Edward Montagu.

Sir Edward was chatting to them now, describing how they should be met at Dover by General Monck himself, "Bearing all the love that both he and England bear for you, Majesty," Montagu said. He gestured forward a tall, well-built man with heavy-lidded but beautiful dark eyes, and long, curling black hair almost as luxurious as Charles's own.

"My secretary," Montagu said as the man bowed to Charles. "Samuel Pepys."

"Master Pepys," said Charles, as Pepys kissed first his hand, and then Catharine's. "I trust you enjoy the evening."

"More so I enjoy the thought of Your Majesty's return to England," said Pepys. "We have been the poorer for lack of your company."

Catharine laughed, clearly taken with the man. "You are a true gallant," she began, and then she froze, her eyes widening, as if some monster had nipped at her soul.

The next moment, just as Charles, Montagu, and Pepys all stirred in concern, Catharine's face regained its smile, even if her eyes remained clouded. "A passing trouble, only, my lords," she said, and politely requested Pepys to speak to her of her new home, London.

A few minutes later, as Montagu and Pepys moved away and the next guest stepped forward, Catharine leaned close to her husband and whispered, "Weyland Orr has struck again tonight, my love. Noah is in such agony as we speak that I do not think I can bear it."

"I will do what I can," Charles whispered hastily. "Can you manage a few minutes alone for us? Soon?"

Catharine nodded and, once the next guest had made his salutations, she put her hand to her cheek and spoke of a passing indisposition.

"A few moments in a side chamber, perhaps, my lord," she murmured to Charles, and, the deep concern for his wife evident in his face, the king escorted her through the throng—all standing back and bowing or curtsying as Their Majesties passed—to a small room just off the main audience chamber.

"How bad is she hurt?" Charles asked so soon as they were alone.

"Horribly so, my lord. But at least now the fiend has done with her. For the moment."

He was silent a moment, his face lined with worry. "Gods, Louis," he finally whispered. "Don't fail!"

CbAPGER NINE

HERE WAS WATER ALREADY STEEPING IN AN ewer by the hearth, for which Thornton was glad. He poured out a measure of the warm water into a bowl, took one of the towels that Leila Thanet had set out for Noah's and his use and, steeling himself, set to washing the wounds on Noah's back. He felt sickened, not at the bloodiness of the gashes down the right side of Noah's back, but at their very presence.

What evil had caused this?

Noah moaned whenever he touched her back, but there was little Thornton could do save continue to wash. The wounds needed to be cleaned, their bleeding needed to be staunched, and when he had finally done, and used a fresh shirt to lay against them, Noah managed a faint smile as she looked over her shoulder, and thanked him.

"Noah . . ." Thornton said, not knowing how to ask.

She sighed, turning her head back to look at the windows. Night had fallen now, but the rain still beat against the thick panes of glass.

"In the morning," she said, "I shall have to leave here and go to London."

"What is causing these injuries? Noah, what—"

"John . . ." She sighed again, and Thornton could see a tear run down a cheek.

Thornton looked from her to Catling. "Catling?"

"Catling," said Noah, before her daughter could answer Thornton, "will you go to Mistress Thanet and beg from her some warm buttered beer? And if she has some powdered bark of elm, then perhaps she could put a goodly measure of that into the beer. Tell her that the beer and the elm bark shall ease my aches somewhat. You can do this for me, at the least."

Thornton looked sharply at Noah at that last, but said nothing as Catling nodded and left the room.

When she had gone, Thornton shifted to the other side of the bed so he could see Noah full in the face. "Noah," he said. "Tell me."

DESPITE THE STORM WHICH HAD ENGULFED THE ship as she entered the mouth of the Thames, the *Fair Polly* had made good time, pulling into the wharf just below the Customs House in London by early evening. Louis de Silva, wrapped in a heavy coat, a broad-brimmed felt hat pulled down to his eyebrows, and with a small leather bag at his feet, stood waiting impatiently as the gangplank was lowered and the customs officials leaned into both the incline and the blowing wind to board the vessel.

"My good sirs," Louis said as the two men finally attained the deck. "I need to enter London as soon as may be possible. I have here passes and documents of entry from Charles II, as well letters of introduction from Admiral Montagu and Sir Edward Hyde. May I suggest—"

"May *I* suggest," said one of the customs officials, "that we view the documents from the comparative dryness of the captain's office? A letter signed by God Himself shall do you no good if this rain washes away His signature the instant you reveal it."

Louis ducked his head in agreement, and the three men slipped and slid their way into the captain's cabin.

None of them saw the tall, shadowy figure standing in an overhang of the Customs House, staring at the *Fair Polly*.

"HAVE YOU THE DEVIL IN YOU?" THORNTON ASKED.

Noah's mouth quirked. "One of his imps," she said, "set there as repayment for a great foolishness on my part. No, do not look so horrified, John. This burden is bearable, and shall become more so as time passes."

"I do not understand."

Noah reached out a hand, resting it on John's arm where it lay against the coverlet. "You do not wish to," she said. "Now, I beg you, strip away those bloodied clothes you wear, and pull the sheets about me, for I do not wish to explain to Mistress Thanet such a wash of blood from what she thinks to be a headache."

FINALLY FREED FROM THE QUESTIONS OF THE CUSTOMS officials, his passport and letter of introductions perused and then carefully held to the single candle in the captain's cabin to see if there was any secret writing contained within the paper, Louis slipped and slid his way down the gangplank to the almost equally slippery wooden decking of the wharf.

Home once more! Louis had not realized how glad he would feel. For a moment, ignoring the rain as best he could, Louis lifted his head and stared about him. The city was hid in an almost impenetrable gloom, but even so Louis could make out the spires of London's churches rising about the warehouses lining Thames Street. He turned westward, his eyes straining through the gloom for St. Paul's Cathedral. But there was nothing to be seen, not in this rain-pelted dark, and so Louis shrugged a little deeper into his coat and pulled the now sodden felt hat a little closer about his brow.

Louis started up Water Lane—a most appropriate name for current conditions, he thought—on the west side of the Customs House. He needed a place for the night, and there should be inns aplenty close to the wharves.

He did not see the shadowy figure break away from its hiding place and follow him at some twenty paces distance.

CATLING RETURNED WITH MISTRESS THANET, WHO carried a tray with three beakers of sweet, warm buttered beer and a concerned expression on her face.

"My dear," she said, setting the tray down on a table before advancing to the bedside, "how does your aching head?"

Noah managed a small smile, but Leila Thanet could see the effort it caused her. The woman was clearly ill, she thought, for her face was unnaturally pale and her eyes not only ringed with black smudges of exhaustion, but clouded with pain.

"The ache is bearable," Noah said. "I do apologize for the fuss I caused earlier."

"Do not think on that for now," said Leila Thanet. "I have brought your buttered beer. This beaker"—one of her fingertips touched the beaker nearest to Noah—"contains a goodly portion of the elm powder. I hope it eases your head."

"Then I thank you, Mistress Thanet," said Noah as Thornton moved to aid her to sit up a little, and lift the beaker to her lips. "This beer shall do me more good than anything might."

"Drink of it all," Leila Thanet said, "and sleep away your aches through the night."

Leila Thanet stopped, hesitated, then smiled once more at Noah, and left.

"She is a good woman," Noah said as the door closed. "I do not know of many who would do so much and ask so few questions. Ah, Catling, thank you for carrying my words to Mistress Thanet, and, oh, how soothing is this beer!"

Catling nodded, apparently somewhat pleased at her mother's thanks.

"Drink further," said Thornton, tipping the beaker so Noah could swallow the final dregs. "Then sleep."

She finished the buttered beer, then lay back, her eyes closing, slipping into sleep almost immediately. Mistress Thanet must have been generous indeed with the powdered elm bark, thought Thornton, grateful that Noah at least now had some respite from the pain.

He sent Catling to bed with her beer, then relaxed in the chair by the bed, his own eyes drooping.

LOUIS WALKED UP WATER LANE, GRATEFUL FOR THE protection the overhanging buildings gave him against the rain, but loathing the sodden muck—the curse of every city—lying in great, stinking piles on the street. At Tower Street he turned left, walking down to Hart Lane where he came upon a small tavern called the King Charles Rampant. As he entered, Louis noted the very freshly painted king's arms on the wall by the front door, and smiled at the thought that this name must only very recently been changed from something else.

Behind him, the figure which had been following Louis stopped, stared awhile at the tavern, then turned away, moving through the soaking streets of London until he reached the Guildhall. There he slipped inside via a small side door.

THORNTON WOKE VERY GRADUALLY, SLOWLY BECOMing aware of the room and of Noah's gentle breathing. He yawned, rubbed at his eyes with the heel of one hand, and then froze.

There was someone else in the room.

Thornton sat up sharply, his sleepiness gone.

"I mean you no harm," said a voice, and Thornton's gaze jerked to the window.

A man stood there. An ordinary man, of pleasant enough aspect, and dressed in good-quality clothes.

He smiled at Thornton. "I am a physician," he said.

"Mistress Thanet sent for you?"

The man hesitated, then nodded. "She said she had a guest who had . . . suffered."

Thornton stood up and offered the stranger his hand. "I am the Reverend John Thornton. I am . . . Noah's husband."

The man took Thornton's hand, raising his eyebrows a little. "Her husband?

I did not know she had a husband. She'd told me only that she'd . . . Well, well. A husband . . ."

He stopped, let go Thornton's hand, and walked over to the bed.

"I am afraid I did not catch your name," said Thornton. "And I do not think that you should—"

The man whipped about, seizing Thornton by the arm. "My name is not important," he said. "I am a friend."

Thornton opened his mouth, and then closed it again. *Yes. The stranger is right, his name is not important, and, yes, he is a friend.*

Slowly the stranger's grip on Thornton's arm loosened. He nodded to himself, as if satisfied, then turned back to Noah. "You shall tell her that Mistress Thanet sent for a physician."

"Yes," said Thornton.

The stranger stood a moment, looking down on Noah. "She is very beautiful."

"Yes," said Thornton, and something in his tone made the stranger turn and look at him with pity.

"You love her," he said.

Thornton sighed. "It will murder me, this love."

"Oh," said the stranger. "Not you." He bent down to Noah, and slowly uncovered her shoulders and back.

"She does not wake," murmured the stranger.

"She has drunk of buttered beer," said Thornton. "Infused with elm bark."

Again the stranger turned to smile at Thornton. "Buttered beer? It is my favorite."

Once more he bent to Noah, and now he carefully lifted away from her back the linen shirt that Thornton had laid there.

His face went very still at the sight of the terrible wounds. They had clotted, but still gaped; the flesh surrounding them was swollen and hard.

"They are very terrible," said the stranger.

"You said you were a physician. You said you could aid her."

"And so I shall." The stranger sat on the bed by Noah and, very gently, laid his hands against her back.

Noah murmured softly in her sleep, but did not otherwise move.

"I am sorry," the man whispered, so softly that Thornton only barely caught the words, and then the stranger's hands began to rub, very gently, up and down Noah's back.

Thornton watched them, only mildly curious at this strange action. The stranger's hands were very beautiful. They were large, yet elegant, with square palms and long, sensitive fingers. Thornton relaxed still further. They were the hands of a physician. There could be no doubt.

The stranger kept moving his hands, slowly, gently. As they moved, so the wounds closed over. The flesh was still red and swollen, but the angriness had subsided, and Thornton could see that even the swelling would subside within a few days.

"You have a remarkable skill," Thornton said.

The stranger's mouth twisted. "So I have been told." He paused, then lifted his hands away from Noah. For a long moment he sat there, staring at her; then, as gently as he had pulled them down, he lifted the bedcovers back over Noah's back and shoulders, then stood up.

"Tell no one I have been here, and tell Noah only what I have told you."

"That you are a physician, sent by Mistress Thanet."

The man's eyes gleamed with humor. "Aye. A physician with *uncommon* skill."

"'A physician with *uncommon* skill,'" Thornton repeated obediently.

The stranger stepped very close. "Tell me, Reverend Thornton, does she bring you bliss in your bedding? Is she . . . delectable?"

Thornton's eyes filled with tears. "She makes the land to rise up and greet me," he said; and at that, the stranger's face hardened, his eyes went flat and emotionless, and then, abruptly, he was gone, and Thornton was left standing alone by the bed.

Chapter Ten

LONG TOM WALKED INTO THE CAVERNOUS MAIN hall of the Guildhall, his steps soft and almost unheard in the empty, dim interior. He moved slowly down the open space of the hall to a balcony at its western end.

Some six paces before the balcony he stopped, and raised his eyes.

At either end of the balcony, standing on worn, ancient stones, stood two remarkable carved wooden figures of some eight feet in height, and well over five in girth. Each wore a suit of chain mail of wooden links, each clasped a weapon in its hand (one a spear, and the other a great sword), each had wild hair escaping from under the helmets and great beards that partially hid the statues' faces.

Each was quite something other than what it appeared.

They were Gog and Magog, the legendary protectors of London, and the stones the wooden figures stood on were the ancient stones of Gog and Magog which once had stood on the northern side of London Bridge.

Long Tom bowed, deeply, then spoke. "Greetings, brothers."

The wooden statues shifted, moved slightly, and then gained life. While they retained the forms of the statues, their faces beneath the helmets and beards became much clearer, and they were almost identical to Long Tom's own.

"He—" Long Tom began, but the creature who bore the name Magog interrupted.

"We know. We felt him arrive."

"He thinks to intercept Eaving as she goes to Asterion," Long Tom said.

Gog sighed. "We can understand his concern."

"He cannot be allowed to succeed," said Long Tom. "She *must* go to Asterion. It is her price, and, besides . . ."

"Besides," said Magog, "there is much for her to accomplish in his vile little dwelling."

"What do you need us to do?" said Gog, and Long Tom stepped forward, and spoke to them for long minutes.

JANE HAD MANAGED TO FIND AN ALMOST COMFORTable space on her pallet, the warmth from the hearth beating sympathetically over her battered and bruised body, when she heard Weyland's footsteps on the stairs.

"No," she whispered. "Please, gods, no . . ."

She had time for no more thought, for Weyland strode into the kitchen, leaned down to Jane, and buried a vicious fist into her hair.

"*He* is here!" he said. "Brutus-reborn! I can *smell* him! I leave this house for a moment, and *this*! Ah!"

"I—"

"Up, bitch, and tell me what you know!"

Jane screeched as he hauled on her hair, and she somehow managed to find her way to her feet.

"I know nothing," she said. "I have no—"

"You have a connection to him through those damned bands," Weyland said. "You have a connection to him through your role as Mistress of the Labyrinth by his side. You *must* know if he is here . . . *and* where!"

The only answer he received was a black stare of hatred.

"No answer forthcoming?" said Weyland. "Then allow me to force it out of you, my dear."

Once more his hand tightened within Jane's hair, but this time the fingertips became as if molten lead, and they sank into Jane's skull, burning through skin and bone.

"Take me to him!" Weyland commanded, and Jane, rent with agony, did so, her senses following the path left by the scent of the kingship bands which always trailed behind Brutus-reborn.

THE SCENE WAS EXTRAORDINARY. THE HARBOR OF *The Hague was lined with tens of thousands of people, most of whom carried torches.*

The harbor was alive with light, with sound, and with movement. The people cheered, raising their torches on high, staring out into the harbor where rode a magnificent fleet of ships. Many of these ships were firing their guns in a ragged, chaotic salute, the smoke and noise adding to the confusion and the gaiety.

"SEE!" HISSED JANE, AND THE VISION CHANGED SLIGHTLY.

NOW THEY WERE ABOARD A SHIP, THE ROYAL CHARLES, *and there stood Charles himself, Catharine of Braganza at his side, smiling and waving at the crowds.*

Charles turned to Sir Edward Montagu, commander of the fleet sent by Parliament to bring home their king, and he said, "Even though my feet do not touch the land of England, still nevertheless they touch home, standing as I do on England's timbers."

"THAT IS WHAT YOU SMELL!" HISSED JANE, KEEPING hold of consciousness only with the greatest of effort. "He stands with his feet on England's timbers, as if he stands on England himself. He *is* home, even if he has not yet alighted on England's shores."

Weyland grunted and, with a wrench, threw Jane back to her pallet.

She gave a great cry, her hands buried in her bloodied hair.

Weyland stood there for a while, his head down as if he stared at her, but with his eyes unfocused. Then, after some five minutes, he turned and left the room.

HE STOOD JUST INSIDE THE IDYLL, THE DOOR SWING-ing softly shut behind him, thinking.

Was that why he could sense Brutus-reborn so strongly? Because he was so close to home? So close that he *was* metaphorically home, now his feet had stepped onto the *Royal Charles*?

Or was it because Brutus-reborn had actually set foot on England's turf?

He wondered.

After a moment, his thoughts turned to Noah, and to the pain he had caused her this day.

He remembered how she had tasted, when he had kissed her outside her house in Woburn village.

How he had looked into her eyes and seen, not a terrified woman, but an equal.

He thought of her back, raked bloody by the imp.

He closed his eyes and, instead of dwelling on what *had* happened, thought only of what *would* happen, when Noah was here, in his house in Idol Lane.

When she was here, he wouldn't have to hurt her.

When she was here . . .

He opened his eyes again, his thoughts all on Noah. He had entirely forgotten about Brutus.

CHAPTER ELEVEN

LANGLEY HOUSE, HERTFORDSHIRE

Noah Speaks

I DO NOT KNOW WHERE I WENT TO IN MY SLEEP, BUT when I woke it was to discover that my flesh ached much less than it once had done, and that I could move more freely than I had anticipated.

And that was as well, for I knew I could not linger here another day.

I could not survive another attack as that last.

I saw John watching me. "I feel well," I said. "Do not fret."

"I have been worried," said John, and I could see that in his face as well as in the rough edge to his voice.

This is why I needed to walk away from you, John . . . But, oh, if he had not been here with me . . . If Catling and I had been sheltering out the storm in some dismal tavern . . .

If Weyland had struck on the open road . . .

The "if's" were too terrible to contemplate. I swear I have never been so grateful to have the company of a human being as I was for the company of John.

"Where is Catling?" I said, trying to inject some maternal concern into my voice.

"I sent her to sleep," said Thornton. "She was worried for you."

Worried? No, surely not. Concerned, maybe, but I doubt that worry came into it at all.

"Tell me," I said, taking his hand as he sat by me on the bed, "how is it my back has healed so cleanly? The wounds are stiff, and ache a trifle, but they do not pain me greatly. Why is this so, John?"

"A physician came. Mistress Thanet sent him."

I frowned. "A physician? An uncommonly good one, then."

"Yes."

Something in John's face worried me. A flatness, both to his features and to his voice.

"What was his name?"

"I cannot remember. I was concerned for you, and that filled my thoughts."

Perhaps, but strange nonetheless. I knew John's intellectual capacity intimately; that he should not remember a name was highly unusual. "Describe this man to me," I said.

John thought. "Well," he said eventually, "he was tall, and pleasant enough. He had keen eyes, and . . . Ah, I cannot remember."

Tall, pleasant enough, and with keen eyes. It was not a description I could use to pick someone out from a crowd.

A horrible thought suddenly occurred to me. "John! Mistress Thanet thought only that I had a headache. What will she think now, when the physician tells her that he cured not my painful brow, but my mauled back?"

"Do not worry. He came so late at night that I doubt he went from this bedchamber to discuss the details of your condition with Leila."

"But . . ." There were too many "but's." Leila Thanet had sent for a physician but had not accompanied him into the chamber, at the very least to introduce him to John. And all this had occurred in the middle of the night. Leila Thanet may well have sent a servant riding for the physician if she thought there was some life-threatening emergency, but for all she knew, I had but a painful headache.

And this strange, secretive physician with keen eyes had healed my back. At best, physicians soothed. They did not heal open and deep wounds. Not overnight.

Who?

I lay back thinking, and after only a moment the answer came to me. It must have been one of the Sidlesaghes, or even Charles, come from so far away in spirit. *He* would have been secretive, for he would not have wanted Weyland to know of his presence. I relaxed, relieved.

"There was one thing," John said.

"Yes?"

He colored slightly. "He asked if you brought me 'bliss' in bed. He asked if you were, ahem, 'delectable.'"

I stared. *That,* surely, was no question a Sidlesaghe would ask, and I could not imagine Charles asking it, either. Frankly, I couldn't imagine *who* could have asked such an intimacy. "And what did you say?"

"I said you made the land rise up to greet me."

My throat choked with emotion and I had to swallow so that I might speak. "And he said . . . ?"

"He said nothing, but his eyes hardened, and he vanished."

Not "left." Vanished. I was still worried about this stranger's identity, but at least my fears regarding Leila Thanet knowing the true nature of my affliction eased. This was, most certainly, *not* someone Leila Thanet had summoned.

I smiled at John, and squeezed his hand. "What this physician did was as nothing to what *you* have done for me over the past days and nights. If not for you . . . John, if not for you then I should be in despair. Despair cannot be healed as easily with power as can a few torn wounds. What you have done for me takes something far greater than the mere application of an unnatural power. I thank you."

He gave a nod, and a small smile, but he did not say anything, and I knew he had wanted so much more from me.

IN THE MORNING WE ROSE, DRESSED, BREAKFASTED, then took our leave of the Thanets (most apparently completely unaware of the physician's visit), and rode the fifteen miles or so southeast into London.

To Weyland Orr.

At one point, a mile or so south of Langley House, John reined the horse to a halt, and said to me, "Noah, is London the safest place for you? And this . . . this creature within you . . . Dear God, beloved . . . how can I—"

"John," I said, "be at peace. This woman I go to, Jane Orr, she is afflicted in the same manner as I. Individually we have no hope, but together we can overcome this dark trouble. I know it, and so does she. And I have many other friends in London. Marguerite and Kate shall join me soon, as yet others. Deliver me you must, and then you must leave me. If you do that, then one day I shall return, carefree and unburdened. If you do not, then I am lost."

"But you will never love me," he said.

I said nothing, and dropped away my eyes.

Chapter Twelve

London

OUIS DE SILVA LAY AWAKE MOST OF THE NIGHT, spending half his time worrying about Noah and the other half feeling London rising up through the timbers of the inn and the straw-filled mattress of his bed. The city felt like a wondrously familiar old friend, which Louis supposed that, indeed, it was. Land and London were now so well known to Louis, and he to them, that there was no sense of any discontinuation since Louis's last time in this land, and this. Six hundred years had passed, and yet it felt like only an hour or so ago that he had ruled over this land as its king, and it, and the city, had submitted themselves to him.

What Louis truly wanted, during that long night, was to set out and search the city—to be *doing*—but he knew that was pointless. For one, both the night and the storm meant Noah would hardly be out traipsing the streets. Secondly, Louis doubted Noah had had enough time yet to get to London from Woburn village. It would be normally a ride of two or three days: three, as the storm would have kept her trapped for at least a day. Presuming she was within a day of London, and presuming also the storm eased, she would likely be here today.

Knowing from where she came, Louis reasonably expected Noah would approach London via Holborn Road, entering the city through Newgate . . . but then, she might come via Smithfield, entering via Aldersgate . . . or even Cripplegate, if she got lost amid the twisting maze of streets about the dogleg in the city wall.

Damn! Louis lay there as dawn poked light about the shoddy shutters on the window of the chamber, and decided that a reasonable idea wasn't going to be good enough. Worse, he had no idea *where* she would go once she got to London. Vanish in the western parts of the city, or somehow thread her way into the crowded eastern quarters?

Or would the ground somehow rise up and swallow her the instant she got to the city walls?

Louis rose as soon as it was light, washed his hands and face, then threw on his breeches and doublet, hose and shoes, grabbed his hat and cloak, and slung his bag over his shoulder, trying to think optimistically. Noah wouldn't be hard to spot.

How many single women carrying a baby could there be, entering London on this day?

WEYLAND WAS UP THE SAME TIME AS LOUIS, DRIVEN by a similar impatience. *Noah was near.* He could sense every step closer that she came. Unlike Louis, however, Weyland had no intention of wandering the streets looking for Noah. She would come straight to him. There should be no need to go a-looking.

"Wake up," he said to Jane, with more good nature than usual as he entered the kitchen. "This shall be a day to remember. Your worst enemy is about to become my thrall as much as you."

Jane said nothing. She rose, straightened her bodice and skirt, and briefly laid a hand on her belly as she walked stiffly to the hearth to see to the fire. She was very pale, her eyes enormous in her increasingly cadaverous face, the sores on her forehead more prominent than normal.

Weyland sat down at the table, watching Jane as she set water to boil, then poured him a beaker of ale. She set it by his hand, then went to a cupboard, and pulled forth bread, cheese, a platter, and a sharp knife, which she also set by Weyland for his breakfast.

The knife had a most oddly twisted horn handle; it was the same wicked instrument which Asterion had first fashioned three thousand years earlier from the horns from his Theseus-murdered body, and it was the same wicked instrument which Cornelia had used to murder Genvissa, and later, herself, and which Swanne had used to murder Damson. It was now tired and worn, but Weyland kept it by him as a reminder of all that had passed.

He lifted it high, holding it up so that its blade caught the faint gleam of firelight from the hearth. "Will you be good, Jane, or should I hide all the knives?"

"Why be good? You'll just murder her, as you have every intention of murdering me."

"Jane—"

"Oh, *damn* you. I will not murder her! Satisfied?"

Weyland narrowed his eyes. That spite was nothing but Ariadne's blood coming to the fore. He considered making Jane regret her remark, but then decided to let it go. There were far more interesting matters to think on, and to anticipate.

"I will set her to sleep in the kitchen with you, Jane. I'd like you to become close."

Jane's face twisted, but this time she said nothing.

"Sisters, perhaps."

"Eat the bread and cheese before Frances and Elizabeth arrive and consume it for you," said Jane, sitting some distance down the table and nursing her own beaker of ale, but not touching the food.

"You *will* become her friend, Jane."

Jane hesitated, then sighed and nodded.

LOUIS MADE HIS WAY FROM HART LANE TO CORN-hill, and from there he walked westwards along Cheapside, his eyes the entire time on the rising hulk of St. Paul's on Lud Hill.

Gods, he thought, it was ugly. The Anglo-Saxon cathedral was long gone, and this, the Norman replacement. In its day (some three centuries previously) the cathedral had been beautiful enough, but time and decay had wrought their damage, as had a fateful lightning strike a hundred years earlier which had toppled the steeple.

Now the entire edifice looked tired and sad.

Louis paused outside St. Mary-le-Bow Church, staring down to St. Paul's, remembering how this location had looked almost three thousand years ago.

Little but rolling grasslands over the Veiled Hills, the sacred hills of Llangarlia, and ancient power that had seemed to seep from the very earth itself and drive the wind that had whistled between the hills and stirred both the grasses and the souls of all who stood on this ancient land.

Now? Crowded, dirty, narrow streets. Buildings leaning this way and that, so closely crowded together they blocked out the sun in many of the narrower lanes and alleyways. Animal and human waste befouled the cobbles of the streets. Men and women bustled everywhere, shouting and squabbling, even at this early hour. Dogs barked, while church bells hummed in the brisk wind. The rain, praise the gods, had vanished.

And yet even so, ancient power rose through the land beneath his feet. It was the power of the land and also the Troy Game that Brutus had brought to this land, and which was now as much a part of the land as Louis's heart was.

He resumed his walk, moving slowly toward the cathedral in the distance. It pulled at him, like it undoubtedly pulled at every one of those now caught up in the Game. Skirting the cathedral on its southerly aspect, Louis reached the ancient walls of the city. Here he had to decide which of the approach routes into London to watch: Holborn, or Smithfield? Which would Noah choose? And which of the gates would she enter? Newgate? Aldersgate? Crip-plegate? He couldn't keep an eye on all of them . . .

Coming to a decision, Louis set off for Smithfield, the great market to the northwest of the city. By the time he arrived the marketplace was bustling. Louis stopped at the edge of the marketplace, and looked about.

Finally he spotted what he wanted: a trader setting up at a stall which had good visual aspect to the roads leading away from Smithfield and to the city.

"Good sir," Louis said as he approached.

The man, while obviously wary of the Frenchman, nodded politely enough.

"I wonder if I might beg assistance from you, and possibly one or another or your apprentices."

The trader raised an eyebrow.

"I seek a woman—"

The man guffawed.

"Please, good sir, hear me out. My cousin is due into London today, and yet I have no idea of which gate she shall enter. I cannot watch all of them, and wonder if, in return for some gold coin—"

The man's gaze suddenly became a good deal more friendly.

"—you might keep watch out for her, and send one of your boys to alert me—I shall be at Newgate."

"How much gold coin?" asked the trader.

Louis lifted out his purse and counted out three heavy coins. "This, for now, and five more if you spot her."

The man's eyes widened. Eight gold coins in total was a small fortune. The Frenchman must want this woman very much—not for a moment did the trader accept the "cousin" tale. Well . . . for eight gold coins . . .

"What does she look like, then?"

Louis's face relaxed in relief. "Tall, slim, and beautiful, with silky dark-brown hair and skin paler than the moon. Deep-blue eyes. She shall have a baby with her . . . a toddler of some thirteen or fourteen months. A girl."

"They'll be traveling alone?"

"Aye. She'll have none with her." She wouldn't have wanted Marguerite or Kate to come, Louis reasoned. This would be a call Noah would answer alone, save for Catling. "She may not look well. She's had some illness recently."

The trader took the three coins. "Very well, then. I'll keep the lad"—he nodded at a boy of some fourteen or fifteen years—"about the market, watching for her. And if you'll show me one more gold coin now, I'll send another of my lads trailing after her, so you'll know where she's gone."

Louis handed over the coin, then shook the man's hand, knowing instinctively that he could trust him.

"Thank you." Then he was off, jogging back toward Newgate.

* * *

HOURS PASSED. THE SMITHFIELD TRADER, GOOD TO his word, and determined to earn the extra five gold coins, kept a keen eye on the passersby through the market, as well making sure his three apprentices kept a similarly close watch.

There was only one moment, in midafternoon, when he thought he may have spotted the woman. The description fit her perfectly, but she was accompanied by a man and a girl closer to six years than toddling age. The trader studied her hard, *almost* sent the apprentice for the Frenchman, hesitated, and then decided against it. The last thing he wanted was to drag the man away from his own watching post when clearly this woman, while physically similar, did not have the toddler or the solitariness upon which the Frenchman had insisted.

And so, unwittingly, John Thornton, Noah, and Catling passed by the man who might, perhaps, have saved them.

BY MIDAFTERNOON LOUIS WAS GROWING EVER MORE impatient and concerned. He was almost certain now that Noah would not approach through Newgate . . . and for the past quarter-hour or more had been plagued with a presentiment that she was very close . . . but northward.

In Smithfield.

Finally, unable to resist his intuition any longer, he abandoned his post by Newgate with a muttered curse, and jogged—then ran, after a minute or two— northward toward Smithfield.

THE TRADER WAS STILL ON THE LOOKOUT FOR THE woman (and plagued with a suspicion that the woman he'd seen with the man and girl might perhaps have been the one the Frenchman wanted) when Louis suddenly appeared before his stall.

"She's come through here," Louis said. "I *know* it. Are you sure you haven't seen the woman and child?"

The trader hesitated, and in that instant Louis *knew* he'd seen her.

"God damn you to hell," Louis growled, leaning over the stall so that the trader, truly frightened, took several hasty steps backward. "How long is it since she has passed? And why did you not send for me?"

"She was with a man," said the trader, stuttering in his nervousness. "And the girl she had with her was more like six years, not a toddler."

Louis did not understand why the child should appear so old, but the man *must* be John Thornton. Louis could barely credit his bad luck. "Which way did they go?"

The trader nodded in the direction of Cripplegate.

"How long since?"

"Not half an hour. And the traffic has been heavy, and the way through the gate slowed because of it. Like as not, they'll not have got far."

Louis stared at him soundlessly for one moment longer, and then he was off, running as hard as he could.

"What about my coin?" called the trader.

LOUIS RAN, DESPERATE. HE WAS TEMPTED TO GO IN the same direction he'd just heard Noah had gone . . . but he decided to risk a hunch.

What if she is traveling to St. Paul's?

Even if she wasn't going there as her final destination, St. Paul's would surely pull her as it had pulled him. And if the traffic was as heavy as the trader had said . . . then maybe he had a chance.

He darted down a side street and made for Aldersgate. From there he could cut through the backlanes and alleyways to St. Paul's (knowing the city like the back of his hand, even though he had not lived here for six hundred years).

Louis ran. He elbowed aside all who got in his way, and pushed over anything that had stalled in his path. The thought that Weyland might have her within minutes—*might already have her*—drove him to exertions which would normally have left him panting in a heap on the side of the road.

He got to St. Paul's, and stumbled about to the small section of churchyard on the northeastern aspect of the cathedral. Here he could see all the roads leading from Cripplegate converge at Cheapside.

He stood, one hand on a churchyard railing, his breath heaving in and out of his chest, and blinked the sweat out of his eyes.

Something made him look down to St. Mary-le-Bow, halfway down Cheapside.

There! He could see her, clinging to a horse, with the girl riding on a separate horse behind what must be John Thornton—

Louis took a deep breath, hope filling his soul, and stepped forward to run down Cheapside . . . *A few minutes and I would have her! Look, they are caught up in the snarl of traffic just beyond St. Mary-le-Bow!* . . . when a mighty hand fell on his shoulder.

"You shall *not* have her," growled a frightful voice, and Louis cried out in despair, and sank to his knees.

CHAPTER THIRTEEN

LONDON

E FELT ICE SLIDE THROUGH HIS BODY, AND HE blinked, and somehow regained his feet, stumbling in confusion, and saw that whomever—*whatever*—had grabbed him had mysteriously transported away from the churchyard of St. Paul's.

Moreover, he noticed, it (or *they*) had also managed to bring to his side his leather bag, which Louis vaguely recalled leaving tucked away in a niche in London wall by Newgate.

He blinked once again. He knew that he should be endeavoring to escape whatever prison his captor had brought him to; but, bizarrely, Louis was only able to think for the moment of what a methodical and neat mind his captor had.

To bring his bag from Newgate . . .

"You must truly want me gone," Louis muttered, and, with those words, finally his vision cleared.

He stood in a great hall, timber-ceilinged, stone-walled, flagstone-floored. At the eastern end of the hall rose a stunningly beautiful stained-glass window. Flags hung from the beams of the ceiling in neat rows down either side of the hall, and torches glowed in niches underneath the rows of windows within the two long walls.

Louis turned about, to the western end of the structure. He had an instant impression of a great wooden balcony that filled that end of the hall, but his eyes were instantly drawn to the two huge creatures standing before him.

They appeared to be carved of wood, yet they moved as if they were flesh. Their faces were almost obscured both by helmets and beards; chain mail (of wooden links, but nonetheless apparently impregnable) protected their chests; and each grasped a weapon—one a spear, the other a sword.

"Who are you?" Louis ground out. "*What* are you?"

The creature to Louis's right answered. "We are London's protectors," he said. "My name is Gog, and this is Magog. Once we were Sidlesaghes, but now are something other."

"I care not for your 'otherness,'" said Louis. "My God, what have you done? Noah is—"

"Noah is where she must be," said the creature named Magog. "What right have you to stop her?"

"I love her, and I—"

"Love is as nothing in this Game," said Gog.

"All I want is Noah—"

"What you want is neither here nor there," said Gog. "You need—"

"She goes directly to Weyland!" Louis yelled. He tried to move, but as he did so, Gog tipped out his spear and tripped him up so that he sprawled over the floor.

"You are very protective," said Gog. "One day you can make good use of it."

"Curse you! I—"

"And one day," Gog continued, "she *shall* be rescued from Weyland Orr's grip. But that day is not here. Be patient."

"He will murder her!"

"Oh, I don't think so," said Magog.

Louis was back on his feet, his face red, his eyes frightened and furious all in one, his fists balled at his sides. "He will torture her, he *has* tortured her. Don't you—"

"We revere her as much as you," said Magog. "But we are also willing to allow her to follow the paths that she must. We trust. Not only in Eaving, but also in the land, and in the Troy Game."

Louis started to speak, but the giant Gog put out a hand, and rested it in kindly fashion on Louis shoulder. "Look," the giant said; and, with a gentle pressure, turned Louis about so that he faced into the Guildhall.

JOHN THORNTON PULLED THE HORSE TO A HALT. They'd ridden from Cheapside down through several ever-narrowing alleyways until they'd come to this tiny, darkened lane that doglegged past the church of St. Dunstan's-in-the-East.

As Thornton looked down the lane the gloom intensified until there seemed nothing but blackness before him. "Noah—"

"It is where Mama and I must go," said Catling. "Jane is waiting for us."

"Jane and who else?" said Thornton.

"Jane is all that matters," said Noah. "John, please, if you do anything for me, then deliver me to that house. There, that one, just where the lane curves past St. Dunstan's."

The house was typical of most other houses Thornton had seen in the city: cramped; crowded out by the buildings on either side of it; its upper floors jutting into the laneway; heavy-beamed, lead-paned, tiny windows.

As Thornton studied the house, its street door slowly swung inward.

There was nothing inside, save further blackness.

"NO!" CRIED LOUIS, STRETCHING OUT HIS HANDS TO-ward the vision.

"You cannot interfere," said Gog, his voice deep with tenderness.

"I—" Louis could not continue.

"I know," said Gog. "I know."

"I WILL GET DOWN HERE, JOHN," SAID NOAH, "AND walk the last distance with Catling. There is no need for you to come closer."

"Noah, I can't—"

"This is something I and my daughter must do, John. Alone."

Noah slid down her horse's flank, pulling her skirts into order as she reached the ground. She lifted down her small valise, then helped Catling down.

Thornton jumped down to the cobbles. "Noah, will I ever see you again?"

Noah laughed, but Thornton could detect the thick edge of strain beneath it. "Why, of course, John Thornton. We shall meet again." She leaned forward, and gave him her mouth to kiss. "Be still, John. We shall be well enough."

"I will never see you again," he said, certain of that fact now.

Noah only looked at him, her eyes steady, then she lifted a hand, laid it briefly against his cheek, then took Catling's hand and, without a backward glance, walked down the last twenty or so feet toward the open door of the house.

Just before she entered, Noah paused and reached into her valise and pulled something out which, letting go Catling's hand for a moment, Noah slipped over her left wrist.

Thornton couldn't be sure from this distance what it was, but he thought it was a bracelet.

Then Noah turned and gave Thornton one last look as she took Catling's hand again.

Because of the distance between them, Thornton could not be certain of the expression in her eyes, but he thought it was either resignation, or a sadness so extreme it would have destroyed most people.

"Noah!" he called, and stepped forward, but as he called out, a white hand reached out from the darkness of the house, grasped Noah by the arm, and pulled her and Catling inside.

The door slammed shut, and Thornton winced.

"Noah," he whispered.

"SHE IS GONE NOW," SAID MAGOG. "GONE TO SOMEwhere you cannot yet reach. But be still, Louis de Silva. All will yet be well."

"I could have saved her!"

"No," said Magog. "As you are, you would only have doomed her."

Louis looked at the giant, his gaze full of hatred and despair.

"There is more reason yet that we brought you here," said Magog.

"What?" said Louis, raising an eyebrow in mock surprise. "Condemning Noah to slow destruction by Weyland's hand was not enough in a day's work for you?"

Gog reached out a massive hand and dealt Louis a hard rap across the face.

Louis staggered, barely managing to keep himself from falling to the floor.

"Your arrogance is overwhelming," said Gog. "You would do well to lose some of it."

"I would have done well by saving Noah," Louis growled, one hand to his nose, which trickled a little blood.

"If you had wrenched Noah away from her duty and her purpose," said Gog, "then Weyland would have destroyed not only her, but you, and all with whom you ally. What kind of fool are you, eh, to sally forth into London alone? Did you not think in your chivalrous rush that you might become the victim, as well as Noah?"

Louis said nothing, but merely stared at the giants with implacable eyes.

"There is something else you need to see," said Magog, and once again a giant's hand turned him back toward the cavernous space of the hall.

THE GLADE LAY COOL AND SHELTERED IN THE DAPpled light. A great pool of emerald water stretched across its center, while shadowy sentinel trees stood watch about its rim.

Partway between the water and the trees lay a white stag with blood-red antlers. His heart lay cruelly torn from his breast, but, as Louis watched, he could see that the heart continued to beat strongly, and the stag's flanks rose and fell with living breath.

There was a movement. The stag's head stirred, and raised a little. He snorted, and then gave a soft cry, as if calling to someone.

A man stepped forth from the shadowy recesses beneath the trees.

A king, for there was a halo of golden light about his head, as if a crown.

A king, tall and well muscled and with long black curling hair.

Charles.

He walked to the stag now straining to rise, and he lifted down a hand to its nose, and then suddenly blinding light filled the glade and, when it cleared, there stood the stag, as glorious as he ever would have been in his prime. His chest was healed, his stance was majestic, and he glowed with power and purpose.

"SEE," WHISPERED GOG. "THE STAG GOD HAS RISEN."

Louis could see nothing but the sight of Charles walking into the clearing. "I always knew it would be him," he said, his voice curiously flat. "Always. Whatever she said to me."

"Nothing counts for you in this life but that the Stag God rises," said Magog. "*Nothing counts but that!* Not the bands, not even Noah. Your purpose in this life must be *only* to ensure that the Stag God rises. Can you imagine, Louis, what an opponent the Stag God shall be, when he has not only his ancient powers of this land fully restored to him, but the powers of the bands as well? When he is not only Stag God of the ancient land, but Kingman of the Troy Game as well? Then he can challenge Weyland Orr, but not before."

"Not before," echoed Gog. "Never before that time."

"Noah shall survive until that moment, Louis. You must understand that it shall be the Stag God, and no one else, who must wrench her from Weyland's claws. *Do* you understand that, Louis?"

Louis said nothing, staring at the empty space where but a moment before he had seen Charles transform into the Stag God.

"Do you understand that, Louis?"

"Aye," Louis grated, as if he ceded away his life with each passing word. "I understand that."

PART FIVE

RESTORATION

LONDON, 1939

CHEY TURNED BACK FOR THE ROAD TO EPPING *forest, Frank barely able to contain his impatience and irritation, Skelton smoking nonstop. He sat so hunched down in his seat, and with his cap pulled down over his eyes, that even though Frank glanced at him several times, itching for conversation, he always turned his eyes back to the road, his words unsaid.*

With Piper's car still leading the way they drove through Higham Hill, then through Chigham, then yet still farther north until the great stretch of King George's Reservoir appeared on their left. On the right, in the distance, rose a long line of dark green.

Epping Forest.

Skelton kept his eyes ahead. He'd straightened a little in his seat as they approached the reservoir and he'd taken a fresh cigarette from its pack, although he had not lit it. Instead it tapped up and down, up and down, up and down, on his knee.

Frank glanced at it in irritation.

Skelton looked at him . . . and the tap-tap-tapping of the cigarette increased in tempo.

Frank opened his mouth, but just before he said anything, Piper's car swerved off on a narrow laneway to the right, heading eastward directly for the line of green.

Skelton glanced at the signpost at the head of the lane, surprised that it was still there. Hadn't the order gone out for all signposts to be taken down?

Then he started as he saw the name of the laneway: Idol Lane.

"Dear God!" he said. "Where are we going?"

"To the Old Man's house," Frank said. "I told you. Faerie Hill Manor."

"Are you certain this isn't Weyland Orr's house?"

Frank shook his head. "No. The Spiv hangs about, but the house belongs to the Old Man." He glanced down at Skelton's right hand.

Skelton looked down himself, and saw that he'd crushed the cigarette. He swore, and threw the ruined smoke out the window. "How far?"

"Not far," said Frank. "Look, see ahead? On that hill?"

Skelton leaned forward, trying to peer through the windscreen. There was a hill rising in the distance. It was not very high—covered in what appeared to be, from this distance, manicured lawns—and perfectly dome-shaped. On its summit stood one of those nineteenth-century Gothic fancies England was famed for, all towers and turrets and whimsical spires.

"Faerie Hill Manor," said Skelton softly, "atop The Naked."

CHAPTER ONE

IDOL LANE, LONDON
Noah Speaks

*J*ANE PULLED MYSELF AND CATLING INTO THE house and then closed the door behind us. We stood in a dimly lit parlor, its dark floorboards, heavy wooden sideboard and chairs, and shuttered window giving it an air of deep cheerlessness.

Granted, at that moment I did not need either floorboards or heavy furniture to impart any sense of cheerlessness. Yet, strangely, I also felt relieved. What I had dreaded for so long had finally arrived; I no longer had to anticipate it, I merely had to survive it.

We stood in that dark room, and stared at each other.

All our history—our battles and jealousies and hatreds as Cornelia and Genvissa, and then as Caela and Swanne—rose between us . . . and then somehow dissipated, as if neither of us had the courage or energy to deal with it at this moment.

Jane was dressed plainly but well in clothes that would have suited any well-to-do housewife, a fitted bodice and full skirt partly hidden by a voluminous apron tied about her waist. Neither apron nor full skirt did anything to hide her thinness.

Unlike the neatness of her clothes, her blonde hair was slightly unkempt, and then I realized it was deliberately left so, that the side wings of her hair might fall over her forehead and cheeks and hide, somewhat, the festering sores that marred her skin. If it was not for those sores, the fear in her eyes, and the lingering traces of pain that I saw shadowed in both her countenance and bearing, then Jane Orr would have been a lovely woman.

"You should have run," she said.

"I am sick of running," I said. I pulled Catling forward a step—she had been standing behind my skirts. "Catling, this is Jane Orr. She shall be our companion for some time to come."

Jane and Catling looked at each other, some degree of ill-will clearly passing between them. Catling, as I had so often bemoaned, was no innocent, and she well knew who Jane was.

Her murderess in her former life.

Jane gave a single nod.

Catling stared at her a moment longer, then looked about the parlor, affecting boredom.

Jane looked back to me. "*He* waits," she said.

I took a deep breath, and I am not ashamed to admit that it shuddered a little on its intake.

"Very well," I said, and Jane led us through the parlor to the door leading to the kitchen.

THIS ROOM WAS LIGHTER, BRIGHTER AND FAR MORE homely than the parlor, and that last was what surprised me most of all in the first instant I had to take it all in.

I had not expected Weyland's den to be "homely"—and I thought this must be Jane's doing, not his.

The kitchen was larger than the parlor, as befitting the most-used room of the house. There was a bright hearth, with irons holding pots and a kettle to one side of the fire. More bright-polished pots and baking dishes hung from the high mantelpiece on which rested some beautiful pieces of delftware.

Weyland must be doing well indeed.

There was a dresser, piled high with good plate, both pewter and pottery, and a table, and it was to this table, once I'd glanced elsewhere, that my attention was caught.

Three people sat there, two girls and a man.

I could not look at Weyland immediately—I did not want him to have the satisfaction of witnessing my frightened eyes alight instantly on him—and so I studied the two girls.

They were both staring at me with faces both frightened and fascinated. They were very young, perhaps nineteen or twenty, pretty, and yet with hard lines marring their mouths and foreheads.

I did not have to stretch my imagination to wonder what had caused that hardness in girls so young.

One of them was a redhead, her skin very pale and creamy and with freckles scattered over her forehead and nose. Her name was Frances, I later learned. The other was dark-haired and with black eyes shining with intelligence. She, as I discovered, was Elizabeth.

My eyes finally traveled to the man sitting at the head of the table.

I took a breath, and raised my chin.

Weyland Orr was of the same pleasant, even handsome, aspect that I'd noted when he'd come to Woburn village. Perhaps even more attractive, for here was no cold to pinch his cheeks and frost his breath. Now that he was not wrapped in a great cloak, I could see that he was a little too lean and his physique a little too rawboned for his height, but in some way that only added to his appeal. His face was striking—his bone structure was very strong, his forehead broad, his nose long and straight, his beardless jaw finely defined. His fair hair was worn long and neatly tied in a club at the nape of his neck, unlike the luxurious curls so many men affected. He was dressed well, his shirt of the finest linen, his doublet and breeches of a fine wool that had been dyed a soft-gray—a combination of colors which well suited him. He wore several gold rings, two on his left hand and one on his right, and a small gold hoop in his left ear lobe.

If I hadn't known what exactly he was, then I would have found his strong-boned face and rangy physique immensely appealing. Indeed, I am sure I would have liked him on sight, and I could imagine that if Weyland took that face and body into a tavern he would have the girls gravitating to him within no time.

Weyland was watching me with a glint of humor in those hazel eyes, then his lips parted, and I saw a glint of white teeth.

And then his eyes slipped lower, and I knew he had seen Catling.

"What's this?" he said. "A brat you picked up on the street to garner my sympathy? I don't remember seeing her when I—"

He stopped suddenly, and I wondered why he should be so surprised at not seeing her. After all, he'd been the one to call me out into the street when he'd come to Woburn village. Surely he hadn't expected me to drag out with me any children I might have had.

"My daughter, Catling," I said, thanking every god in existence that my voice did not quaver.

Weyland's eyes flew back to mine. "Daughter?" he said softly, and he gathered his legs under his chair, preparatory to rising. "I did not know of a 'daughter.'"

I raised an eyebrow, not dropping my eyes from his as, indeed, Weyland slowly rose.

It was a movement meant to intimidate, for he stared at me, his face cold, his eyes implacable, his movement very, very slow and deliberate. Like a dog, crouching for the attack.

"And where did you get a 'daughter,' then?" Weyland said, moving about the table toward me.

From the corner of my eye I saw Elizabeth cringe as he passed her, and Jane take a half-step back to allow him passage.

"From whoring about," I said. "I thought it best to get some practice in before I arrived." I wondered if Catling would have anything to say to that. But, no, she kept silent.

Weyland had reached me now, and I had to tilt my head even farther back to continue to meet his eyes. He was even taller than I remembered.

His nostrils flared, and his eyes narrowed. "I can smell a man about you now . . ."

"John Thornton," I said. "Reverend."

He laughed with what seemed to be genuine amusement, and perhaps even a little relief. "I know of him. He is a fine man." He appeared to be about to say something else, but he stopped himself, and instead reached forward a hand and rested it against my belly.

It was difficult, but I managed not to flinch.

"I have no doubt your dark incubus told you of him," I said. "I am sure that he got to know Thornton very well over the years."

Weyland's eyes dropped to Catling, who was doing a reasonable approximation of fear.

"And so this is his daughter, eh?"

I felt rather than saw Jane's eyes fly to me, felt her shock, and I prayed she would have both face and emotions under control by the next time Weyland thought to glance her way.

"Who can know?" I said softly. "It was very dark."

"You have as sharp a tongue on you, madam, as does Jane," Weyland said, and I am sure none in the kitchen could now fail to hear the threat in it. "Do you know how I soften *her* tongue?"

"With delightful cruelty, I should imagine," I said.

Something clouded his eyes, and he withdrew his hand from me. "I do not necessarily have to be cruel," he said. "Just do as I want."

I gave a short, disbelieving laugh.

"Cease!" he said, his voice so sharp that I stopped instantly. One of his hands raised to my face, and its warm fingers caressed my cheek and jaw. When he resumed speaking, his voice was very low, underscored with threat.

"I run a whorehouse here, Noah. Did Jane tell you that? Elizabeth and Frances let the men of London ride them, all for coin. So if there is food on the table, remember that it is *their* sweat and moans which has brought it to you."

"You have a most charming way with words, Weyland."

His face tightened. "I'm sure you won't mind contributing to the household upkeep."

I fought to keep my face neutral.

"As you will," I said, and, lifting my arms so I could reach the buttons at the back of my bodice, I began slowly to undo them.

There was a flash of something in Weyland's eyes—surprise, I suppose—but then he wiped all expression from his face.

"I have no intention," I said, "of disobeying my master."

And more of the buttons slipped free. For a moment my gaze crossed those of Elizabeth and Frances; both were rigid with either shock or fear, or maybe both.

My eyes went back to Weyland, and his mouth twitched, which surprised *me*. "Let me help you," he said, calling my bluff, and his hands tugged gently at my bodice so that it slipped free of my shoulders.

"You're not afraid that you might end your days with a face like Jane's?" he said.

"Jane's face is not her embarrassment to bear," I said.

The bodice and then my loosened chemise fell free to the floor, and every eye in the kitchen slipped to my suddenly bared breasts.

I was suddenly very sorry I had begun this. Defiance was all very well, but only if it achieved the effect you desired. In all other cases it was a miserable failure.

Weyland caught my eyes, and he smiled. Very slightly, but without any discernable sarcasm or spite.

I was more unnerved than ever.

He put one of his hands on my shoulder, then turned me about.

I heard Elizabeth and Frances gasp. They had not, obviously, expected to see the recently (and oh-so-strangely) healed wounds on my back.

Weyland put his hand against my back, gently, but its very presence was enough to make me jump. He was standing slightly to the side of me, so I could see his face, and I saw that his smile broadened very slightly at that evidence of my discomfiture.

Then his eyes caught sight of the ruby-and-gold bracelet on my left wrist, which I had put on just before entering the house. I don't know why I wanted to wear this jewel, only that somehow it seemed fitting.

His hand ran softly down the underside of my arm (causing me—gods help me!—to shiver), lifting it up so all in the kitchen could see the beautiful piece of jewelry.

"I remember this," said Weyland. "I once went to great trouble to give it back to you. You fainted, as I remember."

Silvius, as I thought then, riding the Troy Game to the acclaim of the crowds in Smithfield.

Harold and myself watching, not realizing we watched Asterion disporting himself before us.

"Yes," I said. "I fainted. I must have intuited somehow what maliciousness stood before me."

His face closed over, and he dropped my arm. His hands went to the laces of my skirt, and within the moment it had joined my chemise and bodice on the floor.

Now I was naked. Usually this condition did not discomfort me at all, but now, with Weyland standing so close to me, his hand running softly up and down my back, tracing those terrible welts, I felt terribly vulnerable. I tried to keep my bearing straight, my chin defiant, but I wanted nothing more than to wrap my arms about myself and hide my nakedness. There was want in Weyland's eyes, and it horrified me.

"These are terrible wounds, Noah," he said. Now only his fingertips were tracing up and down, a feather's touch.

The touch of a monster.

"Aye, and the more terrible for the malice which caused them," I said.

Again he appeared troubled, for his fingertips stopped momentarily, then resumed their gentle stroking.

"They were recently received, I believe," he said.

"Aye," I replied. I wondered what Elizabeth and Frances made of all this.

"And yet, see how well healed they are. How is this so, Noah?"

"A king came to me, and kissed them, and made them well."

His fingers caught at my skin, and pinched, and I had to stifle a gasp of pain.

"Speak the truth, Noah."

"I do not know. John Thornton said a strange physician came to me, and healed them."

"Is that so? Are you grateful to him?"

Gods, where was he going with this?

"Of course," I said. His hand—*those cursed fingertips!*—was now making me highly uncomfortable indeed, and as much as I hated to give him victory in this, I stepped away very slightly, bent down, picked up my skirts, and began, with trembling fingers, to relace them.

"Allow me," he said, and his hands brushed aside mine, and tightened the laces with several quick, practiced movements.

Then he turned me round so I faced him. One of his hands slid inside the waistband of my skirt, his knuckles rough against my belly, and he jerked me close.

I gasped, not because the rough pressure of his hand pained me considerably—which, indeed, it did—but because at the touch of his hand against me, at the feel of his hand gripping within my skirt, I was overwhelmed with vision.

A WOMAN, OF GREAT EXOTIC DARK BEAUTY, DRESSED IN a deep-red flounced skirt about a thickened and soft belly, as if she had just given birth, and with a golden jacket tied loosely about her waist, and left unbuttoned so that her full breasts remained exposed.

The Minotaur, standing before her, his body rent and torn as if by a sword, regarding her both with hate and with love.

She smiled at him, and brought her body close to his, as if in a lover's tease.

The Minotaur slid his hand in the waistband of her skirt, jerking her toward him, smiling at the wince on her face, and speaking words that Noah could not quite catch.

Their heads were very close now, her aristocratic beauty almost completely overshadowed by his dark and powerful countenance.

"I want you—" the woman began.

Asterion smiled, horribly, and his hand drew her yet closer.

"—to teach me your darkcraft."

I TENSED, WONDERING WHAT THIS VISION FORETOLD, and then, using all the self-will at my command, forced myself to relax against his hand.

"You *will* be my whore, Noah."

I was still under the lingering traces of the vision, and I understood that he had said this to Ariadne as well.

"I accept that," I said. "I am not here to shirk my duty." If he wanted me to scream and beg, then he should be disappointed.

He did not immediately respond. For a long moment he held my eyes, his hand warm against my belly, his presence completely dominating me.

He didn't have to shout or threaten. All he had to do was *be*.

Then the skin crinkled very slightly about his eyes. "Then you'd best get a good night's sleep," he said. "A morning's work awaits you."

He withdrew his hand, stepped back, and walked from the room.

Chapter Two

Idol Lane, London

THE REST OF THE DAY PASSED WITH RELATIVELY little incident. Noah dressed, and Jane set the table for dinner, ladling out from one of the steaming pots a vegetable-and-mutton broth and serving it up with crusty bread she'd baked that morning.

Weyland did not reappear for the meal—Jane told Noah that Weyland spent most of his time on the top floor—and, overall, Jane, Noah, Elizabeth, and Frances passed only enough words to ease the passage of the platter of bread here, the pat of butter there. Catling ate well, but Noah only picked at her meal.

Jane watched her out of the corner of her eyes as she spooned the broth into her own mouth.

She'd imagined this day for so long, through at least two lives—that moment when Noah could be trapped and made to suffer. And yet how strange that now she could only manage a vague sorrow that Noah had now been trapped.

I must indeed, she thought, *be losing my touch.*

But how silly it seemed, now, sharing this silent meal with Noah, to have spent so long in antagonism with this woman.

So pointless.

Jane simply didn't have the energy to feel much for Noah now—save a certain admiration for her earlier conduct. Jane was sure that Weyland meant to humiliate Noah the instant she'd stepped inside his domain. Yet nothing had happened as Jane expected. Noah had been both boldly defiant and tranquilly accepting. Weyland had been strangely mild.

After dinner Noah aided Jane to clean the kitchen, then sweep the parlor. At that point Elizabeth and Frances left for their tavern cellar, kissing first Jane, then Noah, on the cheek.

At that Noah smiled to herself a little. She had been accepted among the sisterhood of whores, it seemed.

Once they had left, Jane asked Noah if her back hurt.

"A little," Noah admitted, and Jane nodded to herself and, as Noah put Catling to bed on a small pallet under the window, prepared a cooling poultice.

It was only when Noah was sitting down at the table, her back bared so that Jane could soothe on the poultice, that Jane initiated a conversation other than to pass a word about the dishes, or the cleaning.

"Who *did* heal you?" she said, resting a hand lightly against Noah's skin. "There is power here in these scars, Noah. Who did this?"

Noah sighed. "I do not truly know. The man who was with me, John Thornton, said that a physician had come to me in the midst of the night, and healed me with his hands. When I questioned John about this man, he could barely remember his presence, let alone his name. His mind had been deliberately muddled."

"Who do you think?"

"I don't know. I'd thought the Sidlesaghes, but—"

"Who are the Sidlesaghes?"

Noah looked at her in shock, then explained. "They are the standing stones which comprise all the stone dances," she finished. "Ancient creatures."

"I had no idea," Jane said softly. "None."

"You did not want to see."

"And *you* did? I thought all you ever wanted as Cornelia was to find Brutus in your bed every night. You never looked past his . . . Ah! Don't patronize me, Noah."

Noah was silent a moment, then continued. "So if this physician was not one of the Sidlesaghes, then I thought perhaps Charles."

"You thought *he* would risk—"

"Why not? *Why not?*"

Jane sighed, and gave a slight shrug. "You are right. He might well have done that. He loves you dearly. But you don't think it was him, do you?"

"No. The man asked a strange question of John. An intimate question."

Jane raised her eyebrows.

"He asked John if I brought him 'bliss in our bedding.' If I was 'delectable.'"

Jane laughed, startling Noah. "Did John say yes?"

"Yes, he did." She paused. "Do you have any idea who it might have been?"

"No," Jane said after the barest of hesitations. "Tell me," she continued, "where are Ecub and Erith? I assume they have come back as well."

Noah glanced at the doorway.

"Do not worry," Jane said. "Once he goes into his dark den, Weyland rarely comes out for hours."

"They are reborn, and before they recently came to England lived with Charles as his lovers," said Noah.

Jane arched her eyebrows. "How does that make you feel?"

Noah shrugged, then winced a little as one of the welts flared up in pain. "I do not mind. They were good companions for him."

"Do you think they brought him bliss in *their* bedding?"

"There is no point to this conversation, Jane!"

"My, my, such a sharp tongue. Perhaps you mind more than you would have me believe."

Jane finished wiping on the poultice, then she laid soft linen clothes against it to keep the mixture in place. Both the women prepared for bed in silence; Noah helping Jane to lay out the pallets and blankets, and then, as they were crawling into their bedding, Noah spoke up again.

"Jane, what does Weyland have planned?"

"I don't know."

"And these imps? Gods, Jane, what does he plan to do with—"

"I don't *know!*"

Silence again, each woman lying awake in the dim light given out from the hearth, staring up at the ceiling.

"Noah?" Jane said eventually.

"Yes?"

"You did well earlier." Great praise indeed, venturing as it did between women who had spent the greater part of three thousand years hating each other.

"I needed to survive," Noah said. "If I came before him and trembled, then I would have betrayed myself."

"Your daughter," Jane said. "She is a strange one. Noah, I know when she was conceived. I know who got her on you. Catling should be but a toddler, and yet she looks five, or six. How is this so?"

"I do not completely understand Catling myself," Noah said. "She has power of her own—having walked the paths between this world and the next— yet she has rarely shown it to me. She is an island, complete unto herself. I do not know what she wants, or wants of me. I do not know why she is *here*. So to your question: Why has she grown so fast? I don't know. She is my daughter, and yet I do not know her."

"I do not truly like her."

Noah took a breath, as if to speak, but in the end remained silent.

"How strange," Jane said, "that we lie here now, side by side, and do not think to plunge daggers into each other's throats."

Noah bit her lip, then could not help a small smile. "Perhaps that is what Weyland hopes for," she said, and Jane laughed softly.

"How strange," she said, "that we lie here side by side and share a companionable jest."

"It is what we should have done so long ago," said Noah.

To that Jane made no immediate response. After some minutes, however, she rolled over to her side and propped her head on a hand so she could see Noah's face as she lay on the other pallet.

"Noah . . ."

"Aye?"

"What did you see when Weyland slid his hand into your waistband?"

Noah hesitated, then described her vision: the exotically beautiful woman, Asterion, the way they stood so intimately close . . .

"It was Ariadne, wasn't it?" Noah said.

"Aye," said Jane after a moment. "That was Ariadne, in the moments before she promised Asterion my soul, as those of my foremothers. That was Ariadne, in the moments before she destroyed my life and handed it to Asterion."

"Why did I see that?" said Noah.

Jane took so long to answer that Noah thought she would remain silent.

"I have no idea," Jane said eventually. "But I do know this . . . That vision was given to you by Ariadne, not by Asterion."

Noah drew in a sharp breath. "Ariadne sent me that vision?"

"Aye."

"Why?"

This time, Jane did not answer at all.

chapter three

HORNTON OPENED THE DOOR TO THE BROKEN Bough and surveyed the noisy crowd inside. Once he'd left Noah at the house in Idol Lane, Thornton had thought that all he'd want to do was to settle himself into the Bedfords' townhouse and go to bed early to try to ease his sore heart. But once Thornton had actually arrived at the townhouse and attended to his duties there, he'd discovered that he felt too unsettled to try and sleep.

So, uncharacteristically for him, he'd decided to visit a tavern, ease himself with a few tankards of beer and perhaps some hearty conversation, and then return for whatever sleep he could manage. Before he'd left Woburn the earl had recommended to him an establishment called the Broken Bough. Instead of the usual laborers, apprentices and roughened seamen looking for drunkenness and troubles, the tavern attracted the house servants of the nobles who had their townhouses along the Strand, the lawyers and barristers of the nearby Inns of Court, as well the occasional diplomat or ambassador visiting Whitehall.

Upmarket clientele or not, the tavern was nonetheless noisy and crowded, and Thornton hesitated in the doorway.

A well-dressed man, a German from the cut of his clothes and moustache, brushed passed him. He was carrying carefully several large tankards of beer, and the scent of the spiced and buttered alcohol instantly reminded Thornton of the previous night spent with Noah.

For no other reason, Thornton allowed the door to swing shut behind him, and made his way as best as he could through the crowd of well-dressed patrons to where the tavernkeeper took orders. There he parted with tuppence for a tankard brim-full of delicious buttered Lambeth ale—a rich, heady mixture only available to Londoners or those wealthy enough to import it into their locality.

"D'you know if there's a quiet corner somewhere?" Thornton asked of the tavernkeeper, taking a sip of his ale.

"Here?" said the man, and laughed. He was very thin, with a face which reminded Thornton of a old, genial horse: all long-nosed and -cheeked, and with so many folds about the corners of his mouth that it looked as though he'd been suckled as a baby on the hard steel of a bit.

Then, as Thornton took yet another sip, the man seemed to reconsider. "Well . . ." he said. "There's the space tucked away under the stairs. Room for a table and a couple of chairs. Warm place. Cozy. Usually. Late this afternoon, though, a damned Frenchman came in, ordered some spiced beer, and sat himself down there. Queer one, that. Cold. No one's been keen to take the spare seat at his table. That Frenchman's sat there for the past four hours, drinking beer after beer—and that having as little effect on him as if he'd been drinking water—and just sitting, glowering."

The tavernkeeper shrugged, the lines about his mouth folding deep in disapproval. "If you think you can bear the chill emanating from his person, and the glower in his eyes, then I'm sure that corner shall be quiet enough for you." Another pause. "Sweet Jesus, I hope he'd not sickening for something. The last thing I need in here is a plague-bearer . . ."

Thornton thanked the tavernkeeper, and decided to try his luck with the seat under the stairs anyway. A companion in melancholy, plague-bearer or no, sounded like the kind of companion Thornton needed.

At least he wouldn't try to engage Thornton in drunken, frivolous conversation.

Thornton eased his way through the throng, his ears catching the languages of a dozen different countries as he passed, heading for the rise of the stairs at the back of the tavern. When he'd got to within eight or nine feet, the final few bodies between him and his destination parted, and Thornton found himself looking on a man about thirty, half slouched in his chair under the stairs, and looking directly at Thornton.

The first impression Thornton had of the man was that he commanded great presence. He had an aura of authority about him—an aura so deep and so overwhelming, that Thornton thought it should have been commanded only by a king or emperor.

The second thing that struck Thornton was the sheer physical presence of the man. The Frenchman was handsome enough with an elegant body, long and lithe, exotic features, and dark, curly hair, although his sheer physical charisma went far beyond his comeliness. His black eyes burned, and Thornton thought that anyone spending any time with this man would eventually want only one thing—that those eyes should burn with fervor for he or she who beheld them.

The third thing that struck Thornton was that the Frenchman was almost as struck by him as Thornton was by the Frenchman. As Thornton looked, the Frenchman straightened himself in his chair, twisted his mouth almost as if he were about to snarl, and then tipped his head at the empty chair opposite.

"You've taken your time," said the Frenchman in good English and in a voice clear enough to reach through the noise of the tavern to reach Thornton. "I've had to drink the establishment half-dry in my wait for you."

Thornton went cold. He almost turned, and walked away.

"I want to speak to you of Noah," said the Frenchman, and Thornton, despite his reservations, made his way to the small table where, watching the Frenchman carefully, he sat down in the spare chair.

"What do you know of Noah?" said Thornton.

The Frenchman took a long draught of his beer—to one side of the table he had his own small bowl of spices and sugar to add as he wanted. He swallowed, wiped his mouth with the back of one hand, and set his tankard down.

"My name is Louis de Silva," he said. "The name will be meaningless to you, for I am but the bastard get of a feckless young count."

Thornton said nothing, simply gazing steadily at de Silva.

"I have been greatly befriended by your king, Charles," said de Silva. "And I am a great friend to him."

Still Thornton said nothing, but his thoughts were racing. *Charles's court in exile!* Suddenly, devastatingly, he knew who this de Silva was. "I sent a letter to Charles from Noah some two years hence," said Thornton. "You know, I presume, what it contained."

"Aye. The king has bastards everywhere."

Thornton winced, suddenly angry. "What do you want?"

"I want to know how you felt when you abandoned Noah this afternoon."

"I only did what she wanted."

"How did you feel, Thornton?"

"I felt *desperate!* Is that what you wanted to hear? Is it? I am a married man, de Silva, but I have loved Noah since she was sixteen. I felt desperate this afternoon, and I am desperate *for* her, as I have been for too many years to count, and yet I know I shall not ever have her. I wish I'd never met her, de Silva, for then I could have continued on my benumbed way through life, and never known what it was to love her, and to love life . . . and what it meant to love this land."

At that last, de Silva's eyes narrowed a little. "The land?" he said. "What could you possibly know about the land?"

"That Noah *is* the land in some ancient faerie way I cannot truly understand. De Silva, tell me, what do you know of Noah?"

"That you and I are companions in misery, John Thornton. You love her, and live in desperation that you shall never have her. *I* love her, and live in desperation that I shall never have her."

De Silva stopped, his eyes now on his tankard of half-drunk beer, his hands twisting it this way and that.

Thornton waited.

"I first met her when she was only fourteen or fifteen, Thornton," de Silva said, lifting his black eyes back to those of Thornton. "I loved her, too, although it did me little good but to cause misery and heartache."

Again Thornton felt a chill go through him. He recalled what Noah had said to him the night she told him of her pregnancy. A previous life, a lover, misery and heartache.

"And yet," de Silva continued, "there is a greater misery and heartache to come. I can *feel* it, here," he tapped himself on his chest. "Forget her, Thornton. Walk away from this. Walk away from London. Neither of us can do anything for Noah now. We're all far, far too late."

Thornton suddenly realized that de Silva was actually very drunk, although he showed little physical sign of it. But whether he was drunk from alcohol, or from despair, Thornton could not tell.

"Nothing counts in this life but that the Stag God rises," said de Silva. "Nothing. Not you, not me. Hardly even Noah. Nothing counts but that Charles rises anointed by more powerful, and more ancient, magic than that your archbishop shall daub on his brow. We're all irrelevant, John Thornton, save for Charles."

Thornton did not know what to say to the man. The depth of his despair appalled him.

He rose, his buttered beer forgotten. "May the land rise to greet you, Louis de Silva," he said, and as those words fell from his mouth, an unexpected vision filled his mind.

A great white stag with blood-red antlers raged across the sky, treading uncaring through the stars, and as he ran, so the land literally did rise up to meet him, filling the sky with forests and rolling meadows.

"Be well," Thornton said, as a final benediction, and then he was gone.

Behind him, Louis de Silva's head sank slowly until his forehead rested on the table.

Then, after a moment, he, too, rose, and left the Broken Bough.

LOUIS WANDERED THE DARKENED ALLEYWAYS OFF the Strand as it wound down toward Charing Cross. The day's events had exhausted him. He had failed to rescue Noah, he had been abducted by ancient giants and shown that he had no role to play in all that lay ahead—*no role to play in Noah's life*—and he had just been pitied by John Thornton, Noah's lover.

Could the day get any worse?

He'd wanted to castigate Thornton, but in the end had not.

He'd wanted to show him to what he'd left Noah—in the arms of the Devil himself—but in the end had been unable to.

What point driving Thornton into as deep a despair as himself?

Gods, what was he going to tell Charles?

FAR AWAY, ON THE OTHER SIDE OF LONDON, NOAH twisted and turned in her sleep on her pallet in the kitchen of the house in Idol Lane.

She dreamed twice.

First she dreamed of the running stag, and of the forests and tumbling streams, and of all that could be, if only she endured.

The second dream seemed an extension of the first, for she stood on The Naked. She was alone, but trembling in anticipation.

Soon a great Faerie lord would be striding up the hill, striding to meet her. He was strong and powerful and humorous, and he loved her more than life itself.

And she him.

She felt him approaching, and she cried his name.

And then woke in shock at the sound of that name.

CHAPTER FOUR

IDOL LANE, LONDON

*N*OAH AND JANE WOKE EARLY. NOAH LET CATLING sleep on until the noise of the rattling pots woke her, then she washed the child's face and hands, and dressed her, and set her at the table.

All this Jane watched from the corner of her eye as she tended the fire, and then set the morning's porridge to cooking. She was so used to having the kitchen to herself at this time of day that the presence of another woman and a child seemed most strange.

It was particularly strange, of course, that she should be sharing it so companionably with Cornelia-reborn . . . and the daughter that Jane, as Genvissa, had murdered.

In an instant Jane's eyes had filled with tears, and she had to stop stirring the porridge, overwhelmed by a sudden yearning for her own unborn daughter, who had died along with Genvissa.

"And that at my hands," Noah said very softly, suddenly appearing at Jane's side. "Jane, I am so sorry for what I did to you, and most especially for the loss of your daughter by Brutus. I had no quarrel with her, and yet I took her life also, when I took yours. That wrong is one of the reasons I am here now."

Jane shrugged Noah's hand away. "It is a loss long gone, Noah. Leave it alone."

"Nevertheless—"

"*Leave it!*"

"Jane, do you remember what I said to you in our last life, the last time we met?"

Jane remained silent, grimly stirring the porridge.

"If ever you need shelter, Jane, then I am it."

* * *

WEYLAND WAS IN THE PARLOR, ONE STEP AWAY FROM walking through the door into the kitchen. He froze as he heard Noah speak, then leaned back so that neither Jane or Noah would see him.

"IT IS MY NATURE—YOU KNOW THAT—AND I SHALL BE bound to any who ask it of me. Jane—"

"For all the gods' sakes, Noah, *leave it alone!*"

Noah repressed a sigh, and stepped away, turning to the table.

IN THE PARLOR, JUST OUT OF SIGHT, WEYLAND frowned. *Shelter?*

He backed away, silently, moving toward the stairs, and his Idyll.

JUST AS NOAH TURNED AWAY, THE KITCHEN DOOR into the side alley opened, and Elizabeth and Frances entered. Both were yawning, their clothes rumpled and awry, as if they had only just been pulled on, and they sat at the table with only nods as greeting to the other two women.

Jane set out bowls on the table as Noah and Catling also sat. She ladled out the porridge, a thick, sweet mixture liberally laced with raisins and nutmeg.

Noah waited until everyone had begun eating, then looked at Elizabeth and Frances. "Where do you sleep at night? Why not stay here?"

"Would *you* stay here if you had the choice?" said Elizabeth, her voice bitter, and Noah had to concede the point.

"We sleep in a basement chamber at a tavern on Tower Street," said Frances. "It is small, but comfortable enough, and the tavernkeeper is paid enough to keep his clients away from us."

"Time to yourselves must be precious," Noah observed.

Both Frances and Elizabeth shrugged, more interested in eating their breakfast than discussing the merits of solitude.

"One day," Noah continued, apparently not put out by their silence, "I shall show you the land."

Jane looked at her sharply, and Noah raised her eyes to her. "And you, too, Jane, should you wish."

"That might be dangerous," Jane said softly. "Step warily in this house, Noah. Do not allow Weyland to know any of your secrets."

Before Noah could answer, Weyland himself stepped through the door from the parlor into the kitchen. He looked well rested and cheerful, and his demeanor contrasted sharply with that of everyone else in the room.

Everyone at the table, save Catling who was still eating, had paused with spoons half lifted to their mouths.

Weyland grinned, and sat himself down. "'Secrets,' Noah?"

"I have a worldful of secrets, Weyland."

"Then I shall enjoy discovering them. Jane, hand me the jug of milk, if you please."

AS EVERYONE FINISHED, JANE AND NOAH ROSE, BOTH intending to clear the table.

"Noah," said Weyland, "sit down. Elizabeth, Frances, you may help Jane."

"But we have to . . ." Frances began.

"You are relieved of your duties for the day," Weyland said. "Noah shall cope, instead."

He looked at Noah, wondering how she would take this.

She was pale, but otherwise composed. "As you wish, Weyland." Then she looked at Catling. "Mind what Jane says, now. She shall be your mother for the morning, while I am earning our keep."

Weyland had to repress a grin. Noah was very good. He wondered how far she was prepared to take it.

"Jane shall be your mother for the afternoon and evening as well," he said, keeping his eyes steady on Noah. "Noah has more than enough to keep her busy for the entire day. Londoners are in a celebratory mood as they await their returning king. Apprentices are downing tools and counting out their coin, sailors abandoning their berths and preparing to spend their sea pay. And where else better to spend it, eh, than making love with some accommodating woman? Pretend a moan or two of pleasure, Noah, and they'll be so happy they'll pay an extra penny."

To her credit, Noah did not even look strained. Again, she inclined her head, and Weyland began to feel mildly irritated.

He turned his head slightly so he could see Jane. "Noah will need another poultice tonight, Jane. Although not for her back, methinks."

He smiled as Noah finally reacted. She'd gone paler as he'd spoken, and had shot a look of some concern at Jane.

Weyland wondered what had disturbed Noah the most. What he'd insinuated with his mention of the poultice, or the fact that he'd known about the poultice Jane had prepared for Noah the previous night?

I can see much leaning over the balconies of my Idyll, he thought. *More than ever you think.*

Noah regained her composure quickly. "I am ready for whatever you wish," she said.

Weyland smiled. *I doubt that very much, my lady.* "Good," he said, rising. "Noah, come with me."

HE LED HER UP THE STAIRS, LISTENING TO HER FOOT-falls behind him.

They were steady, and did not stumble.

If Weyland could hear Noah's footfalls, then he could *feel* her presence with every fiber of his being. It was as strong as when he'd felt it that day in Woburn village. A powerful, heady presence that disturbed him in some manner he could not quite define.

He was leading a goddess up the stairs of his house, leading her into whoredom. Who would break first? Noah . . . or himself?

He took her into the first room on the right at the head of the stairs on the first floor. It was a tiny room, dank and gray. The only furniture it possessed was a narrow bed clothed in creased, waxy sheets as filthy as the room.

"I'm sure you won't mind the grime," said Weyland, turning to face Noah.

Finally he was rewarded with a flicker of something in her lovely eyes.

Without thinking, he reached out, and touched her cheek briefly.

"Do you think to train me?" she said.

"I think to try and make you a little more desirable!" he snapped. From her cheek his hand went to her hair, and he pulled out pins, sending her hair tumbling to her shoulders.

She was still defiant, and it infuriated him. He pulled her close, and kissed her, hard and angrily, a contrast to the teasing softness of Woburn.

As abruptly as he had kissed her, he pulled back, keeping one hand clenched in her hair at the nape of her neck.

"A kiss is so intimate, don't you think?" he said. "More intimate than anything else a man and a woman can do with their bodies. No sweaty, frantic copulation can ever attain the sheer intimacy of a kiss."

"You're quite the poet."

Ah, she was deliberately goading him! He kept his face calm, and then pulled her to him again for yet another kiss.

This one was different from the first. This one was a brother to that he'd given her in Woburn.

This time, he felt her confusion.

Again he kissed her, first on the mouth, then on the neck, and then, his hands drawing back the material of her bodice, on her collarbone.

Finally he lifted his head. "What would hurt you more, Noah? To push you to the bed, and to there copulate with you? Or . . . to ask you for 'shelter'?"

Her eyes flared in naked panic, and she stiffened in his arms.

Finally he'd managed to disturb her. What was this "shelter"? Why was it so important?

"What would degrade you the greatest, Noah? What would *humiliate* you more than the other?"

He gave her a moment, a moment in which he could see her struggle for every ounce of self-control she owned, and then he smiled, smooth and easy, and stood back, letting her go.

"Why do you do it?" she said, and Weyland knew she was changing the subject deliberately. "Why degrade Jane and Elizabeth and Frances and gods alone know how many other women in this way? What pleasure can it possibly bring you?"

"Every time I degrade a woman, any woman," Weyland said, "I degrade *you.* That's what makes it so enjoyable, sweeting. That I have the power to take a goddess and turn her into a whore with every woman I force down to that bed beneath the sweating, hungry body of a sailor, or an apprentice, or some vicious soldier, angry and violent from the murder he has inflicted in the name of crown or country."

She was about to reply, but there came a sound from the front door, and Weyland cocked his head. "Unclothe yourself," he said. "I hear a knock at the door."

WEYLAND LED THE MAN UP THE STAIRS AND TO THE door of the room.

Noah lay on the bed, her face turned to the door. One of the filthy gray sheets was pulled up to her shoulders.

Weyland looked at her, but could find in her eyes and face no hint of fear or nervousness, so ushered the man into the room.

He was tall, and burly, with a huge pendulous gut.

And he was eager. He groaned with lust the instant he set eyes on Noah.

Weyland leaned against the doorjamb, feeling unaccountably tense.

The man almost stumbled in his haste to get to the bed. His hands fumbled with his breeches, his chest heaving in his anxiety, then he pulled out his erection.

Weyland saw Noah's hands whiten where they held the sheet.

The man reached down, his breath now a continuous rasp, and jerked the sheet violently away from Noah.

He pulled Noah's legs apart, knelt down between them, and—

Weyland grabbed him by the shoulder and hauled him off the bed. The man, furious with lust, leapt to his feet, and pulled back a fist, ready to strike Weyland.

Weyland's form shimmered. For a moment it appeared as if a man-bull stood there, and then it was gone, and all that could be seen was Weyland's fist driving into the man's face.

"Get out," said Weyland. "*Begone* from this house!"

The man had clambered back to his feet, and was slowly backing toward the door. His nose dripped blood, and his hands fumbled at his breeches. "I'll see you ruined for this, you foul whoremaster!"

Weyland took a threatening step toward him, and the man almost fell in his haste to get out the door.

"Ruined!" he cried, and he bolted down the stairs.

Weyland drew in a huge breath, then turned back to the bed.

Noah was now standing on the other side, the sheet wound about her.

"Get dressed," Weyland snarled, then he turned and left the room.

BARELY HAD HE REACHED THE BOTTOM OF THE STAIR-case when Weyland heard a commotion in the lane outside the house, and then a banging on the front door.

Weyland strode to the door and flung it open, half expecting to see the frustrated client there.

When he saw who it actually was, his mouth dropped open.

The deacon of St. Dunstan's stood on the step, his face flushed with excitement. Normally the officers of the church had nothing to do with their near neighbors—they knew well enough what service the members of this household provided—but now all that seemed forgotten in the deacon's excitement.

"The king!" he cried. "The king! The king!"

Jane appeared at Weyland's shoulder. "What *news* of the king, then?" she said.

"They say his ship lies off Dover, and that he shall land this very afternoon. Charles is *home!*"

And with that he was gone, and, from the sounds drifting down the laneway, most of London had by now heard the news.

The king was off Dover, and his feet would tread English soil once more this very afternoon!

Weyland pushed the door shut, then looked first at Jane, and then very slowly turned and looked up the stairs to where Noah stood at their head, still with the sheet wound about her.

"So your lover is home. How glad is your heart, Noah?" Weyland smiled, cruelly, intent on recovering all the ground he had lost when he tore the man away from Noah. "I think it is time we thought about preparing a small and very private reception for him, don't you think?"

Noah stared at him. Then she drew in a breath, visibly trembling.

"It was you who came to me and healed my back, wasn't it?" she said. "You are the strange physician."

CHAPTER FIVE

DOVER, SOUTHEAST ENGLAND

CHARLES II'S FLEET SET ANCHOR OFF THE SOUTH-eastern port of Dover during the evening of the twenty-fourth of May, 1660. Charles was in no hurry to land. He did not wish to appear anxious, nor as if he arrived in arrogance, nor even as if he were the invader and needed to rush ashore with blade drawn. The king had also had heard rumor that the reception at Dover still needed a few hours to arrive at its full magnificence. Thus it was he told his officers that they would spend the night at sea, breakfast, attend to some pressing matters of business during the morning (unlike the decades of his exile, Charles now had to attend to all the matters of state that needed the king's attention and decision), and then row ashore during the afternoon of the twenty-fifth.

There was one other public consideration in this dallying at sea. It lacked but four days to Charles's thirtieth birthday, and the king had expressed the wish that he enter London on his birthday, that being a fortunate coincidence, and a propitious one, at that.

Preparations for the landing commenced just after two in the afternoon. While there was a general, and highly excited, hustle and bustle on deck, Charles spent a quiet moment with Catharine in their cabin.

They were both accoutred splendidly for the occasion. Charles wore a deep-blue velvet suit with a sparkling silver-and-gold vest. Ribbons and jewels adorned all his fingers, as well the sleeves and cuffs of his coat and the buckles of his shoes and the wide band about the hat that currently sat waiting for the king's favor on a table. Charles's abundant, wavy black hair had been freshly washed and left to lie about his shoulders, his moustache had been freshly groomed: his entire appearance sparkled and snapped with authority and joy and majesty.

Catharine wore matching clothes, although the fabric of her gown was primarily the silver and gold of Charles's vest, and her accessories—ribbons, bows, and swathes of elegantly draped silk—were of the same deep blue velvet as her husband's suit. Her hair, like Charles's, had been freshly washed and groomed, and hung in heavy wings to either side of her face before rising into a complex knot on the crown of her head. Pearls and diamonds wove their way through her braids and about her delicate neck. Her fingers gleamed with diamonds, rubies and emeralds.

Her face, like that of Charles's, was taut and pale with worry.

"My God, Charles, what shall we find?"

"A people who shall acclaim us," he said.

"That was not what I meant."

He sighed, and turned to one side to pick up and fiddle with his broad-brimmed blue velvet hat. "I have not heard from Louis. Not from anyone." He looked back at his wife, and raised his eyes.

"And I have felt nothing. No echoes of pain or misery such as I felt two nights ago. I pray that Louis found her in time." She rested her hand on Charles's arm. "Charles, she *will* be well. Noah is a powerful woman. A *goddess*. No one knows that better than you. She will not be a pawn, even if Weyland has her."

Charles laid a hand against her cheek, then kissed her mouth, careful not to smear any of her carefully applied makeup. "I am well served in you as a wife," he said softly. "Whatever happens, with you at my side . . ."

"At the least we shall win for ourselves a kingdom," she said, and grinned. "And with considerable less fuss than the last time. Charles, put aside your cares, and keep that smile on your face, and go forth now and do what you must. Sitting here and worrying shall advance our cause not a whit."

"You are as wise as you are beautiful. *England* shall be well served in you as queen."

At that moment there came a discreet knock at the door, then it opened.

It could be only one person. James, duke of York, Charles's younger brother and Loth-reborn, had joined Charles just as he was leaving The Hague. James had spent most of the exile years with their mother rather than with Charles, but now, despite all that he denied his ancient allegiances, was as eager as Charles to end his exile.

"James," Charles said, and the door opened.

James, while dressed similarly to Charles, was a "not quite" copy of his older brother. He was not quite as tall, not quite so dark, his hair not quite so curly nor luxurious, his features not quite so handsome, and they exuded not quite so much power as did Charles's. Nonetheless, he exuded a particular peace, which Charles put down to his adherence to the Christian faith.

"It is time to go ashore," James said, a strange tightness to his voice.

"What, James," said Charles, "do you hear the thud of the stag's hooves on the forest floor?"

"Charles—" James began. He stopped, and Charles saw just how emotional his brother was.

"You are glad to be home," he said.

"Aye," said James. "I do not think I could ever bear to be parted from this land again."

Charles gave a small smile, although his eyes were wary, as they always were when dealing with his brother. "I am glad for it," he said, then he turned to Catharine. "Now, my darling, let us go to the deck, and endeavor to get ourselves into the admiral's barge with the least ruin to our finery as possible."

He gave Catharine his arm, and led her forth onto the deck.

After a moment, James followed.

MOST PEOPLE IN THE FLEET SEEMED TO THINK THAT they had a place clearly reserved for them in the admiral's barge, and it took almost an hour to manage to get both king and queen, several of the king's dogs, as well numerous officials, dignitaries, and courtiers into the barge and still leave enough room for the sailors who must perforce do the rowing.

Charles and Catharine sat about a third of the way down from the bow, shaded from the sun by a canopy and from the spray by artfully raised canvas walls to either side of the barge. Next to them sat the faithful Sir Edward Hyde (created earl of Clarendon as part of the king's morning business aboard) as well Sir Edward Montagu, while James sat just before them, his face continuously turned to the white cliffs and the swathe of green that topped them. More than anything else Charles would have liked to have had Louis at his side for this grand entry into England, but it was not to be. He took Catharine's hand, and squeezed it, and smiled for her.

She could clearly see the worry return to his eyes and, to distract him, she tilted her head to where Samuel Pepys sat toward the rear of the barge, scribbling away in what appeared to be a notebook.

"Master Pepys is ever the busy secretary," she said, and then looked to Montagu. "You are well served by Pepys, my lord."

"Oh, aye, Majesty," said Montagu, then sighed heavily. "No doubt he sits there now, going over my accounts, even on this day, of all that he might do them, and busies himself figuring how much I owe my creditors."

Charles laughed and, half rising from his seat, called out to Pepys. "What do you there, good Master Pepys? Is there not enough to entertain you on this day that you must worry at your lord's accounts?"

Pepys smiled and rose, bowing at both Charles and Catharine. "Not accounts at all, gracious Majesties! I take notes of all that happens about me, all that I see on this auspicious day. I keep a diary, and like to record all that I see as well all I do, sin or no."

Charles raised an eyebrow. "You record your sins? Truly? And what does your good wife say, Pepys, when she reads your diary while you are about your lord's business?"

Again Pepys bowed. "I write only in cipher, Majesty. There are few who could figure it, and my good Elizabeth most certainly not among them."

Charles laughed, and waved Pepys back to his seat as he sat himself. "A diary," he said to Catharine, half shaking his head.

"Well," she said, "he shall have many pretty things to write about today's celebrations, no doubt. And," she grinned, mischievous, "better a diary to record your victorious entry into your kingdom, perhaps, than years spent working a tapestry?"

Charles smiled at her reference to the magnificent tapestry that, as Matilda, she had caused to be woven to record her husband William's victorious campaign over the Anglo-Saxon forces.

Then Catharine's faced sobered. "Ah, I'm sorry, my love. I should not have laughed about Harold's—"

He kissed her mouth, silencing her apology. "You do not need to apologize to me," he said. "Never."

THEY REACHED SHORE SAFELY, SAVE THAT ONE OF Charles's dogs shat in the barge, which sent Pepys to more furious scribbling, and the rest of the barge into uproarious laughter.

"I am but a man," Charles said, disarmingly, as the laughter finally petered out, "and my dogs mess as those of any other men."

From the barge they managed the dry sand with minimum difficulty (Catharine smiling in delight as she was carried over the waves, sitting on the linked arms of two tall diplomats) where Charles immediately sank to his knees.

He grabbed two handfuls of the sand, and lifted them skyward. "I praise God in Heaven," he cried so that all might hear, "for my safe return to my beloved homeland, and beg Him to grant me the wisdom to guide my people bravely and well and in the manner to which He commends me."

To one side, Catharine nodded, murmuring an "Amen," glad that Charles had the presence of mind to set the scene for a rule guided by God's hand, and not as God's divine agent on earth, answerable to no one, which had been his father's fatal error. She also wondered at the action, knowing that among all those present, most were educated enough to know that William the Conqueror had done much the same thing when he first set foot on England's beaches . . . save that when William had seized his two fistfuls of sand, he had cried out, "See, England is mine!"

Her husband's diplomacy was second to none, but then, in both of his previous lives his tact and wisdom had been deeper than that commanded by most men.

From the beach the royal party made their way to a cobbled area that bounded the wharves. There awaited them a huge crowd waving flags and flowers; at their fore the mayor of Dover and the man to whom Charles owed his restoration: General Monck.

Monck stepped forward first and, stunningly, for none had expected this, dropped to his knee before Charles and kissed his ring before raising his face to the king and welcoming him with words of both loyalty and honor. Charles raised him gently to his feet, kissed him on either cheek, and spoke soft words of gratitude and admiration to him which made Monck's face flush with pleasure.

Then, once the mayor had greeted Charles, the ordnance of Dover Castle roared into life, and then after that, in quick succession, the ordnance of every military establishment, camp and castle, that had been lined out on the roads and upon the hills. At the deafening sound of the ordnance, great bonfires set out on the hilltops stretching from Dover all the way to the Tower in London leapt into life, so that the entire southeastern corner of England roared and shook and thundered and flamed in honor of their king.

Charles was home.

CHAPTER SIX

DOVER TO BLACKHEATH, KENT

CHARLES AND CATHARINE RESTED THE NIGHT IN Dover, both with terrible headaches from the noise of the ordnance. Next morning, their headaches dissipated, they proceeded by open coach through the port town and thence onto the road to Canterbury. Again, Charles and Catharine were dressed with considerable splendor as well as gaiety; they were happy, and they wanted all to see it. James rode just behind their coach, almost as richly dressed as Charles, and behind him came a great train of courtiers and nobles and soldiers, both mounted and on foot.

They traveled slowly. In part this was, again, because Charles wished to delay his arrival into London until his thirtieth birthday, but in part it was also necessity.

The roads were lined by local militia, resplendent in their uniforms, as well as people come to see their returning king; at times the crowds were so thick it was impossible for Charles's coach to have proceeded at anything faster than a walk. As the militia saluted, the people shouted and waved, sang and danced, and everywhere maidens threw handfuls of herbs onto the road before Charles's coach.

Charles appeared the epitome of gracious happiness. He smiled and called out good-naturedly to the crowds, thanking them for their grace in welcoming him. Sometimes he stood, and took Catharine's hand, and introduced her to the crowd as his "most divinely beautiful and gracious beloved, my wife, Catharine, your queen," and the crowds loved it as Catharine flushed.

By the night of the twenty-sixth they had reached Canterbury where Charles and Catharine attended service in the ancient cathedral, and the king met for the first time with his Privy Council. Here Charles took the opportunity to once again thank General Monck for his support and wisdom and advice, and present him with the Order of the Garter. They spent the night in

Canterbury, then proceeded in much the same manner the following day, the crowds and joy no less thick, to the town of Rochester.

From Rochester they made their way on the twenty-eighth of May to Blackheath, the windy plateau rising above Greenwich and only an hour or so by a fast horse from London. Charles was increasingly nervous, although he hid it well. At night, alone with Catharine, he worried that he'd not heard from Louis, nor even from Marguerite and Kate, who he had expected to be among the first to welcome him to England.

"They may be in London," Catharine had tried to reassure him.

"Dammit, Catharine! Louis knows I will be ill with worry!"

"Then perhaps he has Noah safely, but cannot move for fear of discovery."

"I pray it be so," Charles said.

At Blackheath Charles and Catharine took (or were offered on bent knee, rather) the house of a local dignitary that stood on the ridge of the heath and overlooked London in the distance. That evening, having somehow managed to extricate themselves from all hangers-on, servants, courtiers, clerks, and the sundry other officials that forever crowded about a king, Charles and Catharine stood at the window on the first-floor gallery which looked northwestward. It was a clear, calm evening, the setting sun silvering the gentle sweep of the Thames, and touching with gold the green trees and flowered gardens and meadows that stretched from the edges of Blackheath to the banks of the river some two miles distant.

Charles stood behind Catharine, gently cradling her against his body. He was almost physically ill with worry, but standing there, looking at what had been so unattainable for so long as it lay in the far distance, feeling Catharine's gentle warmth suffuse his body, he could almost forget his troubles.

"Catharine . . ." he said, nuzzling mouth against her neck.

She smiled, leaning her body even more firmly against his. "And wouldn't it be a tragedy, beloved, if Noah were to suddenly burst through those doors behind us right now?"

He laughed, his breath fanning out against her skin, making her shudder. "Noah would understand."

"Aye," Catharine whispered, her eyes now closed, her head tilted back so that Charles could run his mouth teasingly up and down her neck. "Charles . . ."

The doors behind them suddenly burst open and Charles and Catharine sprang apart as if someone had thrown a pail of icy water over them, before spinning about to face the door.

"My God," Charles whispered.

Louis de Silva stood there, his hands held out at his side, palm outward, his face the epitome of despair, explaining his failure more than ever words might.

"Louis," Catharine said, reaching out a silk-clad arm to him.

"I couldn't save her," Louis said, his voice breaking. "Weyland has her, now."

THEY SAT, THE THREE OF THEM, ON THE WINDOWSEAT, looking out to London. Louis told them as best he could of what had happened, how he had missed Noah because the giants Gog and Magog had spirited him away to the Guildhall, there to tell him that Noah needed to go to Weyland, and that Louis had no right to stop her.

"*I* had no right," Louis said. "Me. *No right.*"

"Louis—" Charles began.

"The giants showed me a vision," Louis said, and as he spoke he raised eyes filled with what looked like resentment. "They showed me the Stag God, lying in a glade."

Charles's face went expressionless, and, imperceptibly, he leaned back, as if putting distance between Louis and himself.

"He lay on the floor of the glade, cruelly injured. And then *you* walked in, Charles, in all your majesty as England's king, and there came a blinding flash, and when it had cleared, the Stag God stood there, healed and pulsing with a glorious ancient power."

Catharine felt Charles's hands tighten where they lay on her shoulders.

"The Stag God will rise, the giants told me, and nothing else matters save that. Nothing. Not even Noah's torture at Weyland's hands. She shall be saved, aye, but it will be the Stag God who shall rescue her. Not me. The Stag God, Charles. You."

"Do you mind?" said Charles, very softly and after a long moment's silence, his eyes steady on Louis.

Louis returned the stare, and then suddenly all the resentment and bitterness seemed to drain from him and his body sagged.

"No." Louis managed a small and infinitely sad smile. "Not truly. I would rather it had been me . . . But you . . . I can accept that. Save her, Charles. Please."

"The Stag God shall save her, and together he and Eaving shall save the land," said Charles.

He reached out a hand from Catharine and put it on Louis's shoulder. "Get some rest now, Louis. We all have a great day before us tomorrow. London."

"And somewhere within London," Louis whispered, still clearly distraught, "Noah. What shall *she* think, d'you think, when we ride past in golden, laughing glory, and she imprisoned in hell?"

* * *

MUCH LATER, WHEN CHARLES AND CATHARINE WERE
in bed, Charles sighed, and spoke sadly.

"Louis truly should learn to read visions better."

Her head nestled against Charles's naked chest, Catharine managed a small smile. "Louis was ever poor at reading vision, beloved. It is not the most widespread of arts."

Charles smiled, and kissed the top of her head.

"What shall you do?" said Catharine.

He was quiet a moment. "There is a crown to accept," he said, finally, "and I shall take it with glad heart."

Chapter Seven

The Realm of the Faerie

NIGHT INTENSIFIED OVER BLACKHEATH. ALL WAS still. As Charles and his entourage slid deeper into their dreams the heath beyond the windows appeared to ripple. For an instant—so fleeting that had you blinked, you would have missed it—the heath vanished and infinite rolling wooded hills replaced it. And then the heath was back. Still. Silent.

But altered.

Charles lay next to Catharine. Both moved restlessly, tangling the sheets about them.

In a chamber a little distant from the newly returned king and queen lay Louis, solitary in his bed, dreaming of that time he had first seen Cornelia standing naked in her father's megaron, defiant, beautiful, untouchable.

Still asleep, Louis began to weep.

COEL? COEL?

He woke, startled.

There was no one in the chamber save for himself. He took a deep breath to steady his nerves, then rose from the bed, tugging irritably at the sheets as they tangled about his legs.

"Coel," said a voice, and he looked at the Sidlesaghe who stood by the window.

"What is happening?" said Coel—for it *was* Coel, his body now returned to that finer and darker one he'd worn two and a half thousand years ago.

"See," said the Sidlesaghe, "the Realm of the Faerie awaits you."

Coel looked through the window.

Blackheath had vanished. Now the gentle wooded hills of the Faerie stretched into infinity beyond the windowpanes.

"Come," said the Sidlesaghe. "It is time. The king has returned."

Coel stepped forward, pausing briefly as he suddenly realized that although he'd slept in a linen nightgown, he was now wore trousers made of a fine, fitted leather, and walked through the open window, the Sidlesaghe directly behind him.

THEY CLIMBED THE NAKED, AND AS COEL CLIMBED, so the grass to either side of him, all about the hill, flattened itself in homage. Coel slowed as he observed this, shaken. He saw then that it was not merely the grasses which paid him homage, but also the trees on all the surrounding hills. As he climbed, so also did the trees at the corresponding height on the other hills dip their branches in deference.

As he climbed, so a great wave of deference dipped and swayed over all the hills of the Faerie.

"All over the land," said the Sidlesaghe, seeing the direction of Coel's eyes, and the shock on his face. "In the mortal world, so also do all the trees and grasses, as well the beasts of field and forest, pay their respects."

"How can I deserve this?" said Coel.

"Because you were born to it," said the Sidlesaghe, "but also because you have earned it, first as Coel, then as Harold, and finally now, as you live this life."

Coel shook his head, and they continued the climb in silence.

Just before Coel reached the top of the hill, the giants Gog and Magog loomed up before him, blocking his vision.

Coel stopped dead. "You stopped—"

"We had to," said Magog. "Surely you understand that?"

Again Coel shook his head. "It is so hard—"

Long Tom now appeared at Gog's shoulder. "Coel, if you wear the crown of the Realm of the Faerie, you must leave behind all your ties and promises to Eaving, as to the mortal world. Your *first* allegiance must be to the Faerie. Nothing else, *nothing*, must come first."

"If you cannot accept this," rumbled Magog, "then return to the world of the mortal, and to your dreams of Noah."

Coel stood, hands on hips, head dipped a little, thinking. Leave behind his ties to Noah? Oh, that would hurt, although Coel knew she would understand. But for so long he had been tied to her, loving her, wanting to protect and aid her. She had been his life, even more than the land . . .

"Don't you see?" said Gog softly. "Don't you understand? You can help her more as the Lord of the Faerie than you ever could as Coel, or as the man you are in this life. The Lord of the Faerie will be her rock in the turmoil ahead. *You* can be her rock."

Coel stood, still thinking. Eventually he raised his head. "I accept this for the Faerie," he said. "Not for Noah, even though I know this decision shall aid her. But this is for the Faerie, and for the land. My first allegiance shall be to the Faerie, and to the land."

As he said this a great weight fell from his heart, and Coel knew he had made the right decision, and for the right reason.

All three of the creatures standing looking down at him grinned. Then Long Tom bowed, followed closely by Gog and Magog, and they all stepped back, affording Coel a clear view of the summit of the hill.

It was filled with the throng of the Faerie: Sidlesaghes and badgers, shadows and dapples, cavelings and sprites, sylphs and giants. All manner of creatures packed the grassy space, all with their faces turned toward Coel as he ascended the final steps to the flat summit, all with eyes huge with elation.

And as Coel finally set foot on the summit, every single one of them dropped to their knees in homage.

And as they dropped to their knees, so the sunlight strengthened over Coel, illuming him in a shaft of gold.

"This day is but a formality," said Long Tom softly, at Coel's side. "You were, in truth, crowned that day you mounted Pen Hill to go to Caela. Do you remember?"

Coel nodded. "I was sick at heart then, and distraught, for I knew that death lay not far ahead of me. But even so, there was a great peace that came over my soul as I saw Caela. I thought she was my home."

Long Tom gave a very slight shake of his head. "*You* were her home, and her lord," said Long Tom. "*You* made her, that day. Never forget it."

There came a soft footfall behind Coel, and he looked, and smiled.

The reborn souls of Erith, Ecub, Matilda, and Brutus walked up the hill, and were now but a few paces from him. Each looked about them incredulously, and each of their faces, as their eyes alighted on Coel, softened into delight.

"He is a king," Long Tom said to them as they came to stand a pace away. "He is the Lord of the Faerie."

Brutus stepped forward, and enveloped Coel in a great hug. "I find myself most unsurprised," he said. He leaned back from Coel, and his expression sobered. "This is glad news, my friend," he said. "And lightens my heart away from its sorrow."

Coel nodded, knowing the man's pain, and then accepted hugs from the three woman.

"We shall lose you, shan't we?" Ecub said.

Coel touched her cheek gently with his thumb. "Never," he said. "Our bonds are too close for that."

"Faerie Lord," said Long Tom softly. "It is time."

Coel turned from his companions of so many lives, then walked slowly forward. He looked about, managing to catch in turn each individual creature's eyes, even though they numbered in the tens of thousands. Then he looked toward the eastern aspect of the summit, and saw there the throne and the crown of twisted twigs and red berries on its seat.

He stared, then he slowly smiled. "I have been gone too long," he said.

Long Tom's mournful eyes filled with tears. "Aye," he said. "For too long indeed."

As he spoke, so a copper-haired water-sprite and a pale-hued caveling, the two creatures nearest to the throne, stepped forward, bore up the crown between them, and carried it solemnly to Coel. They stopped some three paces away from Coel, and held out the crown.

Coel dropped to one knee, and bowed his head.

As he did so, so the crown rose, unaided by any hand, and settled on Coel's head.

The instant that it did, Coel's head snapped up, his eyes blazing. "There is something wrong," he said. "Something foul and dark has blighted this land."

Chapter Eight

Idol Lane, London

EYLAND KEPT THE FOUR WOMEN IN HIS house in Idol Lane during the three days it took Charles to reach London. Neither Frances nor Elizabeth were allowed to return to their tavern chamber to collect whatever they may have needed from their meager belongings. Weyland kept them in the kitchen, allowing them only brief trips to the small privy in the side alleyway, and keeping either Jane or Noah at knifepoint during those trips to make sure whichever woman had gone to relieve herself also returned.

Weyland was tense and anxious. Not merely because Charles was so close, but because he felt he'd left himself vulnerable after he'd refused to allow the man to rape Noah, and when she'd then realized he had been the one to heal her back. Since that day he'd barely spoken to her. He was determined, whatever else, to ensure that by the end of *this* day she would know her master.

The kitchen became a place of silence and a frightful, fearful anticipation. Frances and Elizabeth had no idea what was happening. They knew Weyland for a hard and sometimes cruel taskmaster, but of his greater being and mission they had no knowledge. Jane, normally composed and steady, became far more nervous in her demeanor. Noah was more serene, but her abnormally pale cheeks and bright eyes betrayed her inner tension.

Of everyone, Catling was by far the most calm and collected. She spent her days sitting on a stool in the corner of the kitchen. She played almost constantly with a length of red wool, twisting it this way and that between her fingers. At night she bedded down without complaint, and slept soundly through the night. For the most part, Catling was so quiet that everyone else forgot her presence for great lengths of time.

The women spent most hours of the day sitting about the table. Rarely were any words spoken. Certainly no one spoke of the approach of Charles. Frances and Elizabeth might not know the precise *who* of Charles, and *why* Weyland appeared so obsessed with him, but Jane had no doubt that they realized something terrible would occur when Charles did eventually enter the city.

What that terror might be, no one liked to think.

Unusually—for Jane, Elizabeth, and Frances had grown used to his absences in his strange hidey-hole on the top floor—Weyland spent the greater part of each day with the women, and even checked on them four or five times during each night. His constant presence (or the constant threat of his presence) added yet further to the already overwhelmingly tense atmosphere. By the time the day that Charles was due to enter London dawned, each of the women was so highly strung that she would jump at every noise, however mundane its source might be.

BEYOND IDOL LANE THE EXCITEMENT IN LONDON had grown to fever pitch by the twenty-ninth of May. Little work was done. London, as the entire realm, was waiting for its king with great anticipation. The streets were decked with flags and pennants featuring the royal standard, walls similarly daubed with colorful paint, taverns did a roaring trade (the only business, indeed, that thrived during this time of celebration), and, by the morning of the twenty-ninth, people thronged the street, calling out to each other to ascertain if someone had heard news of when the king might enter the city, and which route through the city he would take.

No one doubted that Charles would indulge both himself and his people with a celebratory parade.

None among the throng had any idea of how much Charles dreaded the day.

"CHARLES?"

Catharine, as was everyone in Charles's court and considerable entourage, was dressed in her finest apparel; in her case, a stunning gown made of cloth of gold, studded with jewels and laced so heavily about bodice and sleeves that Catharine found it tiring to lift her hand for any length of time.

Charles wore only breeches and a doublet (to be complemented later with a hat), but, *oh,* those breeches and that doublet. The breeches' material was black velvet, embroidered about waist and hip with golden threads and seed pearls. His doublet was of a stunning pure silver fabric, the finest lace seeded with rubies and diamonds at throat and wrists. It looked splendid even if, as Catharine knew, it was horribly uncomfortable to wear. From his left hip swung a great golden sword, scabbarded in jewels and finery.

The expression on Charles's face did not match the splendor of his clothes.

Charles and Catharine were alone for a few brief minutes before they proceeded to the huge procession awaiting them outside the house. It was almost the only time they had to themselves this morning, for barely had they awoken before their bedchamber was filled with the bustle of servants and courtiers, set to prepare their king and queen for the great day.

"Charles?" Catharine said again, placing her hand gently on an arm.

"Something terrible shall happen today," he said. "There is such a darkness over this land . . ."

"Noah will survive," Catharine said. "She *will*. Weyland won't kill her."

"I can *feel* it," Charles said, ignoring Catharine's reassurances. "Something dark. Something malevolent. Dammit, Catharine, all I want to do is to sneak into London in disguise and—"

"You know you cannot do that. Weyland expects you to ride glorious and triumphant into London, and thus, this you must do. You must act out your part, Charles, or else—"

"I know, I know," he said. "But, Oh gods, Catharine, I—"

The doors at the far end of the chamber opened, and James and Louis entered the room, almost as splendidly dressed as Charles and followed immediately by a gaggle of velveted and gilded noblemen.

"Do what you must, Charles. Do it for Noah," Catharine said hurriedly, then she stood back and put a smile on her face as the group reached them.

As she met Louis's eyes, Catharine saw there the same terror Charles felt. If he felt it too, then something terrible was surely about to happen.

Nausea suddenly overcame Catharine, and she lowered her eyes away from Louis lest she lose what little breakfast she had taken.

"Majesties," said the earl of Clarendon, bowing deeply. "It is time to depart."

"London awaits," said Louis, and his eyes locked to those of Charles.
London awaits.

THE TENSION INSIDE THE KITCHEN OF THE HOUSE on Idol Lane was palpable. Noah, Jane, Frances, and Elizabeth sat at the table, each woman sitting with her hands resting flat on the wooden boards of the tabletop, each pale, each with eyes that flitted about the room, each listening to the dim roar of the crowds that throbbed the streets beyond Idol Lane. Catling had retreated to a far corner of the kitchen.

Weyland leaned against the door frame, his eyes never leaving the women. He appeared relaxed, but Weyland was as tense as everyone else.

He was also torn. He knew what he had to do. Knew he *had* to do it.

Charles had to be intimidated with the most powerful weapon at Weyland's disposal, and that weapon was Noah.

Weyland knew he had to act fast, and he had to act decisively. He had to give Charles a very, very good reason to stay away from those bands, and to behave himself until Weyland managed to get his hands on them.

"Today," Weyland whispered very much to himself, "I hand to you that reason, Charles."

Yet every time he looked on Noah, his stomach knotted, and he silently cursed his weakness.

THE PROCESSION WHICH LED KING CHARLES II INTO London was almost twenty thousand strong. It consisted not merely of Charles and his immediate household, but of several thousand noblemen, the bejeweled lord mayor and all the aldermen of London, the ambassadors of a score of different countries with their own personal trains, several hundred gentlemen from the London guilds in velvet cloaks, red-cloaked and silver-sleeved sheriffs' men, courtiers, servants, and liverymen dressed in either purple liveries or coats of sea-green and silver, as well thousands upon thousands of horsed and foot soldiers who wore silver sleeves and scarves to complement their buff coats and shining helmets. Add to that the maidens who were to dance at the head of the procession, the jesters, the tumblers, the swordplayers, and the dogs and children and stray pigs that would inevitably attach themselves to the procession, and all who thought of the logistics of the situation knew that it would take the king many long hours to wend his way from his entry via London Bridge through the ancient city and around the curve of the Thames into the precincts of Whitehall and Westminster.

The shouting began the instant word spread that the king's horse had set hoof onto London Bridge.

The king was home!

"HE'S BACK," WHISPERED WEYLAND, FINALLY straightening in his doorway.

Jane and Noah glanced at each other, overcome with dread.

Weyland walked very slowly to stand behind Noah and Jane. He raised his hands, hesitated, clenched them as if to stop them trembling, then rested a hand on each of their shoulders, feeling their bodies go rigid. He truly only needed to do this to Noah, but Jane's torment would be just as useful to him.

And besides, those imps would be more useful on the streets of the city than lurking within the women's wombs.

"Brutus has returned," Weyland said. "Listen to the roar of the crowds! Imagine the fuss, the excitement, the *glory*. Fancy. But you know what. Eh? Do you know the truth of this magnificent, mighty day?"

He waited for an answer and, receiving none, tightened his hands.

"What *is* the truth of this magnificent, mighty day, Weyland?" asked Jane in a wooden voice.

"Because today Charles is going to learn just how helpless he truly is. He will—"

"Weyland, no," said Noah, twisting slightly so she could look up at him. "Don't do this, please. There is no need. Surely we can—"

Weyland's face closed over. "Be silent! Are you truly saying to me you don't want to rid your bodies of those black-hearted imps of mine?"

There was a terrible silence, both Noah and Jane hardly daring to breathe as their thoughts raced.

No, no, surely not . . .

At the end of the table, Elizabeth and Frances looked at each other, frowning. *Imps?*

Noah opened her mouth again, but before she could say anything Weyland's hands tightened to excruciating claws on both her and Jane's shoulders, and simultaneously both women screamed, arching their backs, then twisting and falling from their chairs to writhe in torment on the floor.

Weyland lifted his hands away as if he had been scalded, staring at the women. Finally he dragged his eyes away and looked at Elizabeth and Frances, both of whom had leapt back from the table in horror.

"Get some cloths," said Weyland said to them. *"Now!"*

Chapter Nine

London

CHARLES FELT IT INSTANTLY, A RIVER OF PAIN RUN-
ning down the street toward him. He'd only just crossed London
Bridge and was moving slowly through the shouting and waving
throng up Fish Street toward Lombard Street when Noah's agony hit him with
such physical force he groaned, and leaned forward in the saddle.

Almost instantly he straightened, managed with a herculean effort to put a
smile back on his face, lifted a hand to wave to the crowd . . . and swiveled in
the saddle of his white stallion, first seeing Catharine's appalled expression as
she sat in the coach immediately behind him, and then Louis's haggard face as
he sat his horse immediately behind Catharine's coach.

They felt it, too.

James, who was riding his horse just to one side of the coach, wore nothing
on his face but smiles and excitement, and Charles cursed him for his ignorance. This lack of empathy showed Charles as nothing else could have, that
the Stag God, land, and Troy Game had spoken: James, once Saeweald, once
Loth, had lost virtually all meaning in what battles lay ahead.

Another wave of agony hit Charles, and he winced, feeling his innards
cramp in sympathy inside him.

Gods! What was Weyland doing?

He is welcoming you, said Louis in Charles's mind, *in his own special way.*

Noah . . . Charles thought, and fought down his frustration that he could
do little to help her.

Weyland would like nothing better than to have the king vault from his
horse and tear his way through the street crowds, screaming for Noah . . .

I should have saved her, Louis said into Charles's mind, and Charles blinked
away tears for the guilt he knew Louis felt.

I should have saved her . . .

* * *

AS NOAH AND JANE THRASHED ABOUT THE FLOOR,
Weyland moved away several paces. He stared at them, his eyes wide, his face
covered with a faint sheen of sweat.

Frances and Elizabeth huddled against the farthest wall of the kitchen
They clung to each other, too terrified to do anything but watch the horror being enacted before them.

Weyland lifted his face from the women on the floor, looked to the two girls
standing clinging to each other, and suddenly screamed at them. *"Fetch cloths,
damn you!"*

The two girls took one look at Weyland's contorted face, then stumbled for
the small storeroom just behind the kitchen.

Weyland flickered a glance at Catling, who was sitting with commendable
composure in a corner. She appeared to be no trouble, and he wondered fleetingly
what kind of daughter she was, to watch her mother suffer with such impassivity.

He looked back to the women and, if possible, paled even further.

Both women were silent now, their eyes wide and staring, their mouths
contorted into rictuses of suffering, their bodies in spasms, their breaths heaving in harsh, convulsive gasps.

Frances and Elizabeth returned, bundles of rags in their hands.

"Get their clothes off them," Weyland said. "Then be ready to staunch as
best you can their bleeding."

He moved back to the door frame, leaning against the doorjamb, then folded
his arms, his eyes now resting on the hearth as if he found it fascinating.

Frances and Elizabeth bent down to Noah and Jane.

CHARLES FELT AS IF HE WERE BEING TORN APART,
and yet, worse than this shared pain, was the knowledge he could no nothing.

Desperate (and yet still sitting his horse and waving and smiling as if nothing more disturbed him than the worry that this crowd might keep him from
his roast beef), Charles did the only thing he thought he could do.

He reached out to Catling. *Help her, girl, help her!*

And he received back but the one word, spoken in the girl's unnaturally
calm mental voice.

No.

SOMEHOW FRANCES AND ELIZABETH, WORKING TO-
gether first on Jane and then on Noah, managed to pull and tear the clothes
from their writhing bodies.

When they'd done, and the women lay naked behind them, they paused to stare yet once more, horrified.

"For God's *sake*," Weyland said. "Attend to them!"

Elizabeth looked up at him. "Master, what can we *do?*"

Before Weyland could respond, Frances lifted her hands to her face, and shrieked.

Noah, who lay directly at the girl's feet, had partially raised herself and was now clawing at the small of her back. As Elizabeth and Frances watched, the skin over the base of Noah's spine suddenly swelled, as if it had developed into a gigantic bubo.

And then, as Noah screamed terribly, her hands now flailing at the floor, the bubo burst, and Frances and Elizabeth found themselves staring into the face of an impish creature, grinning at them with a sharp-toothed smile.

It put tiny hands to either side of the wound in Noah's back, and started to pull itself out.

Frances fainted, while Elizabeth staggered away, her feet slipping in blood, her body convulsing in desperate heaves as she vomited forth her morning's meal.

Weyland closed his eyes—*Pray to all gods that this will be worth the suffering!*—then forced himself to reopen them, and watch. He swallowed, knowing he had to act. This would not be worth the suffering if he didn't use it to best advantage. He sent his senses scrying out, seeing in his mind's eye Charles riding ashen-faced amid all the cheering crowds.

Using all of his strength, Weyland sent Charles a very personal message of welcome. *Greetings, king. Do you feel your lover's pain? Do you feel her body tearing apart? Fret not, for she will live. Just. Know that I only need her alive, I don't need her whole.*

CHARLES LITERALLY SLIPPED IN THE SADDLE AS WEY-land's loathsome words ripped through him, and only the quick thinking of the soldier walking at his stirrup managed to keep him on the horse.

The crowd suddenly hushed, thinking that their king had suffered a fatal brainstorm, but Charles managed to right himself and shrug a little, as if to say that he'd quite forgot himself in the excitement.

The next moment Louis was at his side, having spurred his horse forward.

"My God, Charles . . ."

"We can do *nothing* until this farce is over. He won't kill her, Louis. He won't."

Louis's face was a mask of horror—he didn't have Charles's strength of will to maintain a false smile. "She suffers so!"

Charles managed to reach out a hand and very briefly grasped Louis's forearm. "She will survive, my friend. *Know that she will survive!*"

"She'd be better dead," said Louis, then he allowed his horse to drop back level with the coach where, Charles presumed, he'd have the sense to say some words of comfort to Catharine, for she would be feeling this as much as Charles and Louis.

Curse Catling for not aiding Noah. Curse her!

JANE WAS SILENT—SHE WAS BEYOND SCREAMING— but her body whipped back and forth, back and forth over the floor, occasionally knocking into Noah, knocking over two of the chairs at the table, and coating herself in her own blood as well as Noah's.

Her belly mounded as if she carried a full-term baby inside her. Her imp roiled beneath her abdominal layers of skin and muscle. Elizabeth now sat with Catling. She had her arms wrapped tightly about her body, and watched with eyes numb with shock and horror at the frightful sight before her.

Catling remained calm, but her eyes were hooded, their expression unreadable.

Weyland straightened in the doorway. "Come here!" he commanded, and Elizabeth jumped, certain he meant her.

But instead the hideous black creature that had just pulled itself free of Noah's body looked up, its black eyes bright in its blood-coated face.

The next instant it was scampering over the floor and clinging to one of Weyland's legs with its two, spindly-fingered hands.

Weyland ignored it, instead watching Jane.

Her body spasmed, then suddenly, horrifically, her abdomen split apart.

A black head appeared, grinning, and then two thin, claw-tipped hands which dug themselves into the lips of the terrible wound. The imp pulled himself out, then sat up as the blood pumped from Jane's abdomen, looked to where Weyland and his brother watched him, and grinned happily.

He scampered over to join Weyland, who ignored him as he had the first.

Weyland took a deep breath, his face twisting slightly at the stink of fresh blood, and, motioning for the imps to stay behind, walked over to where the two women lay. For a moment he simply stood there, staring, his face expressionless.

Then he squatted down, and very gently felt Noah's wrist.

She did not move, lying so wan and still she could have been lifeless were it not for her irregular and shallow breathing.

Weyland's fingers tightened momentarily about her wrist, then he stood up, stumbling as he slipped in the blood on the floor.

"Elizabeth," he said, then snapped her name again when she did not immediately respond. *"Elizabeth!"*

The girl jerked her eyes to him.

"Rouse Frances," said Weyland, "then bind Noah's and Jane's wounds, and make them comfortable."

"But, master," whispered Elizabeth, "they will need a surgeon, surely. They are torn asunder! Frances and I cannot—"

"Do it!" snapped Weyland, and then, taking the hands of the imps, marched from the room.

A minute later Elizabeth heard their feet stamping and pattering up the stairs. She breathed deeply, summoning her courage, then managed to get to her feet and walk over to where Frances lay.

She gave her a hard shake by the shoulder. "Wake, for God's sake, Frances, *wake up!* I can't do this on my own!"

Catling watched as Elizabeth finally managed to rouse Frances. As they began their terrible task she made no move to aid them.

WEYLAND ESCORTED HIS IMPS UP THE STAIRS HIGHER and higher, until he reached the top floor.

The imps chattered between themselves, and wriggled about, as if uncomfortable at Weyland's grip, but he paid them no attention. He was numbed by what he'd seen downstairs.

What he'd *done* downstairs.

With every step he rejustified what he'd done.

Charles had to be contained.

Noah's suffering was the only means through which this might be achieved.

Charles had to be contained.

Noah had to suffer, it was the only way he could do it.

Charles had to be contained.

Noah was the only means by which he could . . . *Damn it. Curse it!* Why was he trying to justify himself? Gods, he'd murdered tens of thousands throughout his many lives. Why quibble now over the cries of one simple woman?

But hardly "one simple woman."

They reached the top of the stairs, and Weyland nodded at the door that led into his Idyll.

"There we shall rest," he said, "and you shall hear how you may aid me."

The imps nodded dutifully, and so Weyland led them forward.

The door swung open as they approached and, hesitating only slightly (never before had he led anyone into his Idyll) Weyland took the imps through.

He let go their hands once they were in the vestibule.

The imps stood, their mouths drooping open.

"Well?" said Weyland, trying to inject some cheerfulness into his voice.

The imps, their mouths now closed, surveyed the vastness.

"Don't like it much," said one.

"Too gaudy," said the other.

"Then find yourselves some shadowy corner and lurk," snapped Weyland, "for I find myself tired of you!"

So saying, he abandoned the imps, and strode off deeper into the Idyll.

CHAPTER TEN

IDOL LANE, LONDON
Noah Speaks

I HAD NOT THOUGHT EVEN WEYLAND CAPABLE OF such cruelty. This sounds naive, I know, but after I realized that it was he who had come to me and healed my back, and after I recalled how he had torn that repulsive man from my body . . . I had thought that perhaps the worst was behind me. I knew that he planned something terrible for Charles's return into London, but I had never thought he would do this: tear both Jane and myself apart, and use our agony to send Charles greeting on his arrival.

I had never thought . . .

I had never realized . . .

I had never *suffered* so as I did that instant Weyland set those terrible imps to tearing their way forth from Jane's and my bodies.

I felt that imp slash its way through every single one of my pelvic organs on his frightful journey to the base of my spine. I felt him rip me apart, and thus torment became my entire world.

Nothing else existed.

All thought of Charles fled.

All thought of the Game vanished.

I even forgot that terrible moment when Weyland had mentioned asking me for shelter (and *that* little piece of terror had occupied most of my waking hours during those days he kept us trapped in the kitchen). But I was so consumed by pain, the only thought I had was to hope that death would snatch me sooner rather than later. Nothing else mattered. All I wanted was the relief of death.

But of course death stood by and did nothing, for Weyland had better things planned for me. I would be kept alive, but in agony, because that would amuse him, and it would tear Charles apart.

What was it he'd spoken to Charles as I descended into hell? (And yet still Weyland had made sure that I caught this, too.) *Know only that I need her alive. I don't need her whole.*

I remained conscious until that moment the imp tore his way through my back. How can I describe what that felt like? I can't. There are no words for it. It would have driven me insane, I think, had it not been for . . .

Jane.

WHEN WEYLAND HAD SENT MY IMP ON ITS RAMPAGE while I'd been in Langley House, he'd also sent Jane into agony as well. Somehow we'd touched during that time, shared our suffering, and briefly comforted each other through that sharing.

It happened again this time as we both writhed about the floor of that kitchen, our bodies tearing apart about us. We met in some bleak wilderness of despair and anguish where, desperate, we touched and then clung to each other. It was somewhere beyond Weyland's knowledge. I don't know how I understood this, but know it I did . . . as also did Jane. We had not escaped our agony in this strange wilderness, but we drew some small measure of comfort from our shared suffering.

It wasn't much, and, eventually, it wasn't enough. We could feel our flesh tearing away from our bodies, feel our blood drain away, feel Weyland's eyes on us as we suffered. I think that we would have lost our minds, deliberately, as a means of escaping from the pain and horror, save that . . .

Save that, as we slid toward that great, welcome abyss of insanity, we heard a voice.

Follow me.

We paid it no attention. It had no meaning to what was left of our lives.

Follow me.

The voice was neither male nor female. We did not recognize it. We ignored it once more. That abyss before us was so tempting, and offered such an escape . . . Who cared if Weyland took my mind? I no longer did. He was welcome—

Follow me!

This time the voice roared through us. It was full of such power that we shrieked, and I felt Jane's fingernails tear through the skin of my shoulders.

Follow me, whispered the voice, and this time it was gentle and seductive, and, with no willpower left, Jane and I followed.

* * *

I BLINKED, THEN SCREWED MY EYELIDS SHUT. I WAS aware of two things: that I still clung to Jane, and that my pain was miraculously gone (strangely, the absence of pain was almost as painful as its presence).

I gulped in air and felt Jane do the same.

I tried to open my eyes again, and this time succeeded if only to almost close them again as I squinted against the bright sunlight. We were outside, but where? And how?

Slowly my eyes became more accustomed to the light, and, with Jane, I looked about.

"We're in Tower Fields," she said, her voice bewildered.

Indeed we were (my memory coming from my life as Caela rather than this life; the landscape, although much built over, had not changed greatly). We stood in the open space just beyond the northern walls and moat of the Tower of London. In the distance we could hear the roar of the crowds—somewhere farther to the west Charles was still engaged in his great parade.

"But *how* . . .?" Jane said.

"By my aid, of course," said a voice—*that voice which had saved us*—and Jane and I let go of each other and whipped about.

A woman stood some four of five paces away, surveying us with a small self-satisfied smile.

The style of her dress gave me great pause, for I was not used to seeing women dressed in the ancient Minoan manner standing about the grassy fields of London.

The woman wore a great flounced skirt of red silk that fell to just above her ankles, stiffened with many layers of petticoats, and a jacket of cloth of gold, embroidered with yet more golden threads and pearls and jade. It had three-quarter–length sleeves, wide stiffened lapels and a collar, and lay open to her waist where it was loosely tied with scarlet ties. She wore no blouse beneath it, and the open lapels of the cut revealed her bare, firm breasts.

She wore little jewelry save for a collection of thin golden bands about her right ankle and her left wrist.

Her face was stunning. Very finely boned, yet giving the impression of strength rather than fragility, the woman had a broad, high forehead, large and elongated dark eyes further emphasized with an outlining of kohl, gracefully arched and drawn eyebrows, and a full and sensuous mouth that was painted the same red as her skirt. Her skin was the same rich cream of her breasts.

A magnificent head of hair crowned all of this bounty. Very dark, almost black, it rippled in bright waves down her back and shoulders.

If I had been a king I would have lusted for her, for she radiated power as well as beauty.

If I had been a common man I would have lived in terror of her, for I would have understood that this witch had the power to destroy my life.

I also knew precisely who she was.

"Ariadne," I said, in as calm a voice as I could manage. "Well-met, at last."

She opened her mouth to answer, but just then Jane let out a shriek, and darted for her foremother. Her arms were extended, her hands clenched into claws, and I have no doubt that she meant to murder Ariadne so soon as she reached her.

It was a sentiment I could understand, even as I winced. It was Ariadne, after all, who had cursed Genvissa-Swanne-Jane with her promise to Asterion that should she or any of her daughter-heirs ever try to resurrect the Game, then she (or whichever of her daughter-heirs bore her blood) would become Asterion's slave.

Ariadne calmly held out a hand, turning it out heel down, palm outward, and said one single commanding word that emerged not as sound so much as a ripple of powerful emotion.

Jane stopped, so abruptly she collapsed into a heap about two paces from Ariadne. I stepped forward and aided her to rise. "Be still, Jane," I whispered. "This is not the time."

Then to Ariadne, who continued to regard us with a supreme equanimity that I greatly envied, I said, "Are we here in reality, Ariadne, or in spirit?"

"In spirit only," she said. "Your bodies still writhe about that dreadful kitchen floor. This was all I could do for you."

"Why?" I said.

"You were in pain, and I did what I could to save you." She gave a half-shrug, the movement one of exquisite grace. "I can do nothing to the injuries perpetrated upon your physical bodies—by now, surely, you shall be virtually lifeless—but I could save your sanity."

Now she looked at Jane. "I am sorry for what has happened, Jane. If not for my promise . . ."

"You have *no* idea of what I have suffered," Jane hissed.

"Yes, you are right. I can have no idea. And so I shall do my best to set things to right."

She paused, regarding us intently, then she smiled at me. The expression was cold, and predatory. "And well-met to you as well . . . Eaving."

I could not forget that Ariadne had once been the MagaLlan of Llangarlia as well as the Mistress of the Labyrinth, but I *was* put out by her knowledge of my goddess name. The surprise must have shown on my face, for her smile became genuinely amused.

"I have power, Eaving. I am not disinclined to use it to discover what I need."

"What are you doing *here*?" I said, gesturing about at Tower Fields and the built-up areas to the east and west of us. "And like *this*." Now I gestured at her clothes.

She laughed. "Oh, this is not the manner of dress I normally affect, Eaving. Generally I ensure I'm much less noticeable."

"You mean you're *living* here?" Jane said.

"I drift in and out, from time to time," Ariadne said. "I have an arrangement with the Gentleman of the Ordnance of the Tower."

I could well imagine what kind of arrangement she might have, but I wondered whether the Gentleman of the Ordnance of the Tower knew quite what he might have invited into his bed. And *why* should Ariadne want to be there? I opened my mouth to ask, but Jane got the question out first.

"Why are you back? For what purpose?"

Poor Jane. I imagine she was somewhat disturbed to discover that Great-great-great-granny Ariadne had been flitting about not four blocks from Idol Lane.

Again that fearsome, predatory smile. "For my place in the Game, of course, what else?"

I went cold. She couldn't possibly think that she—

"You have no right—" Jane began.

"I have *every* right," Ariadne said. "If not for me then neither of you would be toying with such greatness! If not for me, then neither of you would be—"

"Writhing about on a kitchen floor having our flesh torn apart," I said.

"Well, well, minx," said Ariadne, stepping closer to me and grasping my chin with one of her hands.

I could feel her fingernails digging into my flesh.

"Such spirit," she said. "What is your heritage, then, to spark so brightly? What was your name and heritage in your first life, before the Troy Game caught you in its web?"

Ah, if Ariadne knew my goddess name then surely she knew this. But for the moment I played along with her game.

"My name was Cornelia, and I lived in the city of Mesopotama, on the eastern side of—"

"I know where it was," she said. Her hand fell away from my chin. "An insignificant city. Dull. Who were you, Cornelia of Mesopotama? A servant's brat? A baker's bastard? A—"

Ah. She was needling me, and most successfully. "I was the daughter of the king, Pandrasus, and heir to the throne itself."

"Ah," Ariadne said on a long breath, although it was obvious none of this came as any surprise to her. Then, "Mesopotama was spared the Catastrophe.

Tell me, Cornelia-reborn, princess and heir to that long-lost throne, did you ever wonder why?"

Jane spoke then, and I was glad, for I had no answer to Ariadne.

"Aren't you afraid that Asterion—Weyland Orr, now—might find you wandering about the Tower, Ariadne?"

"The Liberty protects me," she said.

"The Liberty?" I said.

"The Tower of London exists under its own jurisdiction," said Jane. "It is free from the laws of London. This Liberty came into being after your last life, Noah. You would not have known of it as Caela." Yet still Jane looked puzzled, for that alone could not explain how Ariadne had managed to hide from Weyland's sight.

"Indeed," said Ariadne. "The fields and streets surrounding the Tower of London form their own jurisdiction. The Gentlemen of the Tower have even managed to claim all rights to the cattle and horses that fall off London Bridge, as well as the swans that wander into the Tower moat." She laughed prettily.

"But none of this explains why Weyland can't—" I began.

"*Think*, Eaving! What lies beneath the Tower?"

I frowned, then suddenly remembered. "The God Well!" It was where Brutus and I had been buried in our first lives, and where, as Caela, I had met William the night he had killed me.

"Aye," said Ariadne. "It took a little skill, of which I have a small measure, but I managed to entwine the power of the God Well with the legal entity of the Tower Liberty to form a protective ward. So long as I don't leave the Liberty, Weyland can't detect me."

I felt uncomfortable. As Eaving I should have sensed this, for Ariadne would have used her ancient knowledge of the land to manage it, and yet even *I* hadn't felt a thing. For the first time I had a true understanding of Ariadne's power.

"You will come back to me here," said Ariadne, "once your bodies have healed."

"Why?" said Jane.

"You know why," said Ariadne. Then suddenly she paled, and wavered on her feet. "I cannot hold you any longer," she said. "You must return now . . . but come back, come back in the flesh, come back to Tower Liberty . . ."

Her voice faded, and I saw the fields about the Tower waver and then vanish, and the next moment the terrible bloody stink of the kitchen of Idol Lane assailed my nostrils.

CHAPTER ELEVEN

WHITEHALL PALACE AND IDOL LANE, LONDON

CHARLES'S JOURNEY FROM LONDON BRIDGE TO his newly refurbished palace at Whitehall was a living nightmare. The procession took several hours to reach the palace and, even once there, Charles then endured two further hours of speeches in both the House of Commons and the House of Lords.

Through it all he smiled and waved, and spoke pretty and gracious words. It had been the most difficult thing he had ever done in . . . well, in all three of his lives thus far. Noah's pain had abruptly ceased when he was but a third of the way down Cheapside. Charles hoped it was because she had mercifully fainted.

Now, at ten at night, he and Louis and Catharine had finally managed seclusion within the royal apartments. The instant the door closed behind the last servant Charles sank down into a chair, dropped his wearied face into his hands, and muttered, "Gods . . ."

Louis was standing on the far side of the sumptuous chamber. He watched Charles for a moment, then turned to a table, meaning to pour himself a glass of wine. His hands were shaking so badly he dropped the decanter, sending red wine spilling over the beautiful parquet floor.

He swore, the obscenity rolling across the room, and Catharine gave a single sob, and sank to the floor by Charles's chair.

"Is she dead?" she said.

"Is she dead?" Charles said. "I do not know. Louis?"

Louis had been trying to pick up the larger pieces of the glass. Now he dropped them again, and walked over to Charles and Catharine, wiping his fingers over his once lovely silver doublet.

"No," he said. "She is not dead. Weyland would not allow her that mercy. She is alive . . . just."

"You must not blame yourself, Louis, for not—" Charles began.

"I blame those damned giants!" Louis yelled. "If not for them, if not for their cursed interfering—"

The door to the chamber opened, and Charles half rose, his face flushing as he prepared to shout at whichever servant had chosen this terrible moment to enter.

But it was no servant, and, as they saw who stood there, Charles swallowed his anger and walked over to where Marguerite and Kate stood just inside the door.

He embraced them fiercely, and then Catharine ran to them, and Marguerite and Kate enclosed her within their arms. Louis also came over, and in turn was hugged by the women.

"Oh," said Marguerite, "that we should meet under such circumstances. Matilda, it is so good to see you once more, but . . ."

"You felt it too, then," said Charles.

"Aye," Marguerite said. "We were riding into London when we felt it. Gods, Noah . . ."

"But are *you* well?" asked Charles. "And the children?"

"We are well indeed," said Marguerite, "if saddened by the day's events."

"And the children do marvelously," Kate finished. "They remain in Woburn village, Charles, with a kindly neighbor."

Charles nodded. "When matters have settled, I shall send for them to attend court."

"What natter this, of children and babies?" said Louis. "We should instead be talking of—"

"Louis," Marguerite said, "Noah knew that something of this nature was going to happen. She—"

"She had *no* idea that she would be torn apart, for what else could explain such pain?"

"She *needed* to be there," Marguerite said. "She needs to learn the arts of Mistress of—"

"Right now," said Louis, his voice dangerously soft, "I don't give a fuck about Noah learning the arts of the Mistress of the Labyrinth. I just care that she lies in agony, and none of us does anything save stand here and mutter *useless* words!"

To that no one had anything else to say.

IT TOOK ELIZABETH AND FRANCES HOURS TO CLEAN
and settle Noah and Jane as well as they could, and then to scrub the kitchen and themselves. As shocked and benumbed by events as they were, the two

girls nonetheless had managed to wash the two women, bind their terrible wounds as best they could with strips torn from a clean sheet, and move them to the pallets to one side of the kitchen.

They could do little else. Both women appeared as if dead; their skin cold, clammy and gray; their breathing hardly discernible. Neither stirred as Elizabeth and Frances worked over them, and both continued to seep blood; to the girls it appeared remarkable that they were alive at all, and it did not seem possible they would survive the night.

Once they'd done what they could for the women, the two girls set about cleaning the kitchen, which was nauseating work; the blood had jellified into several putrefying masses and had set rock-hard into the cracks and pockmarks of the flagstones so that it took backbreaking labor in the effort to scrub it out.

When the kitchen was clean, Elizabeth and Frances stripped themselves of their blood-soaked and wet clothes, and scrubbed themselves until their skin shone red and raw. Then, dressing themselves in some of Jane's petticoats and chemises they found in a chest (what spare clothes they owned were resting unobtainable in their chamber in the nearby tavern), and throwing shawls about their shoulders, they sat down at the table.

Neither spoke. Both were still so numbed by the horror of what they had witnessed they were literally incapable of speaking about it. Their minds could hardly process the events of the day.

There was only one thing they were sure of, one thing they had learned from this day, and that was, to run from this house was death. Neither doubted that Weyland would hunt them down . . . and now that they had seen what he could do when fully enraged . . .

Elizabeth and Frances had been under Weyland's thrall before this. Now they were so terrified of him, so sure that he was the Devil himself, they were virtually incapable of independent thought or action.

During all of this Catling had sat in her corner, her eyes following Elizabeth and Frances as they worked, but not moving or speaking.

As always, she had not lifted a finger to help.

THE NIGHT CLOSED IN. HIGH IN HIS IDYLL, WEYLAND could not see it so much as feel it.

But the gathering darkness was not the worst thing he could feel.

The entire building in which he sat throbbed with pain. It ran upward like fiery rivulets defying gravity, sharp and agonizing, pulsating with every beat of Noah's heart, searing into Weyland's heart and soul.

Damn her!

He sat in the chamber he used for his bedchamber, on the floor, back against the wall, knees drawn up. He sank his face into his hands, his fingers clenched into his hair, and groaned.

Damn her!

The night drew on, and grew colder.

The pain continued to slither up through the beams of the house, slicing into Weyland's bones.

The very soil beneath the house seemed to tremble, as if it wept.

A moan drifted up through the house, and Weyland knew it was not either of the women, but the land itself.

Weyland's hands grew whiter where they gripped his hair.

Finally, cursing, he rose to his feet, stiff and sore from his long hours sitting on the floor. He marched through the Idyll and into the vestibule, where the imps sat cross-legged on the floor, rolling dice and picking their noses.

"Stay here," Weyland said, and walked through the doorway into the house, slamming the door behind him.

FRANCES GAVE AN INCOHERENT CRY OF PURE FEAR as he strode into the kitchen, backing herself up as far as possible against the back wall of the room.

Weyland sent her a look of seething ill-will, then looked at Elizabeth.

She sat at the table, looking gaunt and wretched. She'd been resting her face in her hands, elbows on the table, and she merely raised her face and looked at Weyland as he entered.

Weyland shifted his gaze to where Jane and Noah lay. They were completely still, the blankets that covered them dark and heavy with their blood.

Weyland's jaw visibly clenched, then he jerked his eyes back to Elizabeth. "Come here," he said.

She tensed, her eyes almost starting from her head, but to her credit she did as he asked. Rising from the table, she walked stiffly to where Weyland stood.

He jerked his head at Noah and Jane. "I will need your help," he said.

Elizabeth gave a small nod. "Anything," she said.

Weyland's eyes grew harder. *"Anything?"*

"Anything for Noah and for Jane," said Elizabeth. "Not for you."

Weyland had lived many scores of lives, but nothing anyone had said to him had hurt so vastly as that simple statement from Elizabeth. He remembered how she'd wounded him years before, when he'd made love to her, and she'd spoken plain, unadorned words that had sent him reeling away. How had she this power, this simple girl? Where had she, this majesty?

"For Noah and for Jane, then," he said softly, "if not for me."

And he turned to the women.

Elizabeth drew a deep breath, and followed a step behind him.

THE GIRLS HAD STRIPPED NOAH AND JANE NAKED, although both wore bandages wrapped about their abdomens and hips. Between them Elizabeth and Weyland rolled Noah over onto her stomach, then Weyland ripped the bandage apart.

He stopped for a moment, still, staring at the wound. It was the size of a plate, stretching from hip to hip and almost to her waist. All the skin had gone, the bones of her spine and part of her pelvis lay bare, and blood vessels continuously seeped blood.

By rights she should not have been alive.

Weyland raised his head and looked at Elizabeth.

She raised an eyebrow.

Weyland held her stare a moment, then he sighed, and laid his hands upon Noah's back.

THEY MET ON A HILLTOP, AMID AN INFINITY OF HILL-tops. The grass was warm beneath their feet, the gentle breeze mild, and yet, even so, the tears on her cheeks felt like ice.

The very soil of the Faerie was moaning in grief.

"Why?" she said. "Why heal me? This is a greater torment than anything else you have done."

A muscle flinched in his cheek, and he turned away, pretending to study the forested hilltops which rolled away from him.

She wrapped her arms about herself. "This must be a trick. You are the Minotaur. You do not 'heal.'"

He whipped back to face her. "And why not? Am I such the black-hearted beast that I cannot aid?"

"You are a destroyer, nothing more. And if this man who stands before me is real . . . then you cannot be the Minotaur. A simple problem: Either you are the Minotaur, who has nothing for a heart save black ice, or you are an impostor, who pretends to be the Minotaur for his own purposes."

He came very close to her. "'A simple problem,' eh? Have I no ability to change? To feel? Tell me, are you still that shrieking harpy of a girl you once were, shallower even than the rivers of happiness that run through Idol Lane, or have you grown into something else?"

She was silent, and her eyes dropped away from his.

"And if you can grow," he said, "Why not me?"

There was a long silence, Weyland staring at Noah, she looking at the ground. About them the warm breeze wafted, gentle and caressing.

After a long moment Noah looked up and spoke words that were part prophecy, part bewilderment. "Weyland, Weyland, what are we doing? How can we stop? How can we stop?"

CHAPTER TWELVE

WHITEHALL PALACE AND IDOL LANE, LONDON

ANE DREAMED THAT SHE STOOD IN THE FIELDS outside the Tower of London.

Ariadne was not here. But the fact that Jane *was* here made her realize something that had niggled at her while she and Noah had talked with Ariadne. The ancient witch had used vast power to pull Noah and Jane to her—her power as Mistress of the Labyrinth. Jane stood in Tower Fields and frowned. Ariadne had used her power as Mistress of the Labyrinth to pull Noah and herself to this spot.

Jane knew there was something here she should grasp, but just before she actually managed it, she heard a soft footfall behind her.

She whipped about, sure it must be Weyland.

But it was a man, tall and brown-skinned, dark hair shifting slightly in the breeze, dressed only in a pair of leather breeches and wearing a crown of twigs and red berries on his head.

Jane knew who he was instantly, although she had never, in any of her lives, met him. Still, she once had been MagaLlan, and *she knew who he was.*

The Lord of the Faerie.

A vicious chill swept through Jane.

Was he here to murder her? What *other* reason? She took a half-step away, then halted as he spoke.

"I thought you were Noah," he said. "I felt . . . I wanted . . . I thought you were Noah. It was why I came."

Pain swept through Jane. She'd suffered terribly at Weyland's hands, but nothing he had done to her, not even when the imp had torn itself free of her body, had wounded her this deeply.

Everyone always wanted Noah, never her.

"I'm sorry," he said. Then his head tilted slightly. "Ah. You are Jane, yes? Weyland's sister?"

"You know well who I am."

He smiled. "Always the same Genvissa."

She frowned. Why speak of her as if he knew her?

He walked toward her. "Don't you know who I am?"

He was upon her before Jane saw through the aura of power that encased him and recognized his features. "Coel!"

She would have spun away—now she was more certain than ever that he would murder her—but he seized her arm. The instant his flesh touched hers, his face softened, and she saw real sorrow in his eyes. "Oh, gods . . . Weyland hurt you, as well as Noah. Tell me, Jane. Are you still alive?"

"Are you sure you are not asking if Noah lives?"

"I ask for both of you."

"I live. She lives. Barely."

His face relaxed. "That pleases me."

"That Noah lives, surely, but not that I—"

"I am pleased also that you live."

"I cannot believe *that*."

His hand moved from her arm to her shoulder, and then to the back of her neck. "I have had my revenge of you, Jane. We are even." Then he looked about. "What are these fields to you, Jane? Why stand here in your extremity, gazing at the Tower?"

"I do not wish to speak of it to you."

She thought he might object, but he didn't.

"I felt a great need to come here. Why, Jane, do you think?"

"I don't know." His hand was very warm on the back of her neck, and she wished he'd move it.

"The Faerie sent me here," he said. *The Faerie, the power that underlaid everything connected with the magical creatures of the land.* "I thought it was to meet with Noah. I had *hoped*—"

He laughed as he saw the expression on her face. "But here I have found you instead. It is not my day for luck, eh?"

She felt like spitting at him, and then, to her amazement, realized he was teasing her. She gave a small, unconvincing smile.

The hand at the back of her neck moved about, to the side of her face, to her forehead, sweeping back the wing of hair away from her sores.

"Ah, Jane. I am sorry."

His fingers slid over her poxed cheekbones, and she wished she had the strength to turn aside her face from them.

"The Faerie sent me meet you," he said. *"Why?"*

"To murder me. What else?"

The fingers were still working on her cheeks, then they slid back to her forehead.

"This disease has deep claws," he said.

She gave a nod.

Then suddenly she gave a yelp, and sprang back from his hand.

He laughed merrily. "Not anymore!" he said.

Jane had halted a pace or two away from him, staring. Slowly she reached up her hands to her face, and felt her forehead.

Her sores had closed over. Her brow was not quite smooth, for there were ridges and lines where the sores had closed . . . but it *was* healed.

Indeed, Jane felt well. Every bit of pain that had plagued her—not merely that which Weyland had visited on her over the past day, but *every* ache—had gone.

She opened her mouth, and then closed it, unable for the moment to comprehend what had just happened.

Suddenly there came the sound of beating wings. Jane flinched, and the Lord of the Faerie lifted his face. "Look," he said, and Jane reluctantly lifted her own face.

A magpie, all deep-blues and -blacks, hovered above them and, as they watched, slowly descended until it sat on Jane's shoulder. She tensed, but before she could move, the Lord of the Faerie held out his hand.

The magpie jumped from Jane's shoulder to his fingers, trilled a short phrase of some melodious, magical song, and then flew away.

Within a moment it had vanished.

"Aha," said the Lord of the Faerie. *"Now* I know why the Faerie sent me here. Well, well, Jane. Here's a turnabout for you and I."

"What do you mean?"

He answered with his own question. "Will you be coming back to the fields?"

She blinked at him, still disorientated by all that had occurred over the past few minutes.

"Yes," he said. "I can feel that you shall return. This place pulls you for some reason. Well, when next you come, meet me by the scaffold." He pointed to a spot at the northern extremity of Tower Fields. There, several man-high posts stuck up from the grass, half-rotted with age. A scaffold had once stood there, not used in generations.

"But—" she said.

"Meet me by the scaffold, Jane." There was power and authority in his voice, and so she merely nodded.

In the next instant he was gone, and her dream fading.

* * *

JANE ROUSED VERY SLOWLY FROM HER UNCON-
sciousness. She fought it, for the pain she knew would assail her the instant
she came to her senses, and for the further pain she was sure Weyland would
inflict on her the moment he realized she was no longer unconscious.

She could not believe that what had happened in dream would follow her
into waking.

But Jane could fight it no longer, and when she *did* wake, it was to find that
not only was there little pain, there was *less* pain than she had had to endure
every day for the past several years. The constant ache of her legs and spine
was gone. Her abdomen, torn apart by her imp, was merely aching slightly.

Gods, she thought, her eyes still closed, *the Lord of the Faerie did heal me!*

She could hardly comprehend it. *Healed*. Left without pain and the terrible
humiliation of those sores. Jane had thought never to be healed of her pox. A
life free of the pox had not once entered into even her wildest wishes and
hopes.

But it was not just the pox that had been healed. By rights Jane knew she
should be dead—no one, surely, could have survived the terrible torture of that
imp's exit. At the very least she should be assailed with agony.

But . . . nothing, save for those few aches and cramps.

Soft movements in the kitchen caught Jane's attention. Who was it?
Catling? Elizabeth or Frances?

Weyland?

A hand suddenly fell upon her shoulder, and Jane literally jumped.

She opened her eyes wide, staring, terrified, and saw that it was but
Frances, squatting down by her pallet and holding a tankard of what smelt like
warm ale.

"It is all right," Frances said softly. "He is in the streets, at Whitehall, gathering news of the king."

"Are you sure?" Jane said, her voice rasping out from her dry throat.

"I am sure," Frances said. "Here, sit up, and drink some of this."

Jane sat up, looking about the kitchen, clutching the blanket which someone had laid over her naked breasts. She felt a bandage about her abdomen,
but it felt whole. Looking about, Jane saw Noah was lying on a pallet just beyond Frances, and Elizabeth and Catling sat at the table.

Two youths also sat at the table, just beyond Catling, and Jane froze at the
sight of them.

The imps, made incarnate!

They had taken the form of boys of twelve or thirteen years of age, but, to
Jane, their origins were clearly visible in their sly faces and crafty, narrowed
eyes. They were very dark; their heads a tangle of dull, black, curly hair; with

swarthy skin pitted and blotched with adolescence (or perhaps natural malig-
nance); and thin arms and legs.

Which one, she wondered, was hers?

The one farthest from her grinned, showing sharp, pointed teeth, and Jane
had her answer.

She looked away, taking the tankard from Frances with shaking hands.

"How do you feel?" said Frances.

"I feel . . . well," Jane said. She glanced at Noah, then raised her eyebrows
at Frances

"She sleeps. She will wake soon."

"Frances, what do you know about—"

"Later," Frances said, and Jane made do with sipping her ale (either
Frances or Elizabeth had sweetened it with honey, and added a pinch of spice)
as Frances rose and rejoined the others at the table.

As Jane drank, the attention of those at the table turned to Catling, who
raised her hands from her lap.

Jane saw that she had a length of red wool twisted between the fingers of
each hand.

She's playing Cat's Cradle, thought Jane.

Then she caught a full sight of *what* it was twisted between Catling's fingers.

Somehow, the child had formed a labyrinthine design with her twists of
wool and, as Jane watched, the imp nearest Catling frowned, raised a long,
thin finger and slowly tried to trace a pathway from the center of the design to
the edge.

Jane went cold. *Cornelia's lost daughter be damned,* she thought. *That creature sitting there at the table is not her daughter at all!*

The imp got about halfway through the pattern, then his frown deepened,
and his finger stalled.

His lips pursed, and he muttered something that Jane did not catch.

Then his brother leaned over him, and tried his luck. His finger also stalled
at about halfway through the labyrinth, and he, too, frowned.

"Bother!" he said, quite clearly.

Catling smiled. "You admit defeat?"

The imps muttered between themselves for a moment or two, then one
sighed, and nodded. "We admit defeat," he said.

"Good," said Catling, and folded the wool away.

Something in Catling's actions clicked in Jane's mind. *Catling is playing the
Game with them!*

At that moment Noah stirred, and Jane, at least, was grateful not only for
the time it gave her to pull her thoughts together, but for the distraction.

She didn't want Catling looking at her face, and seeing there recognition.

Frances brought Noah a tankard of ale as well, and Jane saw that Noah seemed as puzzled by her current circumstances as was Jane. Indeed, Noah looked as well as Jane herself felt. Her color was good, and she wore no lines of pain on her face.

Jane saw the moment Noah caught sight of the imps. Noah froze, and then turned a little so she could see Jane. Her eyebrows rose, in clear question—*Why are we so well? And what do those imps at the table, sitting so casually?*

Jane gave a slight shrug. She turned aside her blanket, uncaring that both imps stared at her all-but-nakedness with boggling eyes, and stood up, feeling for her balance carefully. Finding that she could stand, she walked to the chest where she kept what few clothes she had, and lifted its lid. She drew forth some underclothes, and an old bodice and skirt. But, before she dressed, Jane lifted away the bandage from her abdomen, and stared.

There was a red gash running from her navel to her pubic hair, but, while it was red and angry, it had healed over.

Stifling her questions (not here, not with the imps present), Jane quickly dressed then turned to Noah, knelt by her side and, unasking, unwound Noah's bandage.

At the table, unnoticed, Elizabeth and Frances looked at each other.

Jane stilled as soon as she saw the wound. "It has almost healed," she said. "As is mine. The wound has mended, its edges neat and free of infection."

Elizabeth, who had been watching Jane and Noah, now spoke up. "Weyland healed you," she said. "Both of you."

Jane felt sick with regret and disappointment. Her dream of the Lord of the Faerie had been just that. A dream. *Weyland* had healed her.

She noticed Noah had gone white.

"I'd thought it was just a dream," Noah said. "Now I find he *did* heal me. And you. Oh, Jane, look! The sores on your face are quite healed!"

Elizabeth had risen, and came over to Jane, squatting down beside her. She lifted a hand and pushed back Jane's loose hair.

"They *are* healed," said Elizabeth. "All of them. And the aches in your spine and legs, Jane? Are they still there?"

Jane shook her head.

Elizabeth frowned. "Weyland healed the injury caused you by the imp, but he did not heal your pox. I remember particularly, because he made a remark that he didn't want you too grateful."

Jane stared at Elizabeth, and then very slowly smiled. *So my dream wasn't a fabrication! It truly happened!*

Elizabeth also smiled, responding to the sudden light in Jane's face. "What do you know, Jane? Tell us, how have these sores healed?"

Jane dampened her smile. "I cannot tell, Elizabeth. I was unconscious."

"You may speak of it," said Catling. "They won't tell."

"We won't tell," said the imps together, then both grinned, taking all the promise from their words.

"They *will* not tell," Catling said firmly, and the imps' smiles faded.

For an instant Jane almost believed her. She certainly believed that the imps would not say anything to Weyland, but then she realized she didn't want Catling to know about the Lord of the Faerie.

So Jane shrugged. "I truly don't know. It is a mystery to me."

LATER, NOAH AND JANE LAY DOWN ON THEIR PALLETS again, saying they needed to rest. The others—Catling, the imps, and Elizabeth and Frances—took themselves into the parlor, so that the two women might rest undisturbed. But instead of sleeping, Jane and Noah lay close together and conversed in low tones so that the group in the parlor would not hear.

"Jane," said Noah, "tell me. Who healed you of those sores? I do not believe this 'I do not know' of yours."

Jane took a long time to answer. "I dreamed," she said, "that I stood in Tower Fields, where we met Ariadne. A man came to me there." She hesitated. "The Lord of the Faerie came to me, Noah. Do you know who he is?"

"Yes. Long Tom spoke of him to me some years ago."

Jane felt disappointed. *Was there nothing Noah did not know?* "I was surprised to find he was Coel-reborn," she said, and was finally rewarded with a look of utter shock on Noah's face.

Noah took a deep breath, and managed to speak.

"Yes, of course. It fits. Jane, in our last lives I saw him crowned with light atop Pen Hill, and I also saw the Sidlesaghes doing him homage in his crowning in Westminster Abbey. And when he came to me on Pen Hill, then he was the one to induct me into my full self. I had never before now realized the true significance of all this. Now it all makes sense."

"He healed me," said Jane. "He touched my face, and my sores were gone."

"If the Lord of the Faerie walks," said Noah, "then it means the Stag God is close to rising."

"*Who?*" Jane said, very soft, leaning her head so close to Noah that they might have been lovers.

"You know who it must be," said Noah, as softly.

Of course. Jane battled her emotions; then, finally, she said, "And does Weyland know this?"

Noah paused. "I hope not," she said. "But . . ."

"Aye, 'but' . . ." said Jane. "I do not know about you, Noah, but I am heartily glad to have that creature gone from my body. I feel . . ."

"Free," said Noah. "Light." She took a deep breath, and Jane heard it shudder in her throat. "Jane, do you think that Weyland still has the same control over us as he did when those imps were inside our bodies?"

Jane thought a moment. "Oh, aye," she said, her tone bitter. "I can feel it in here." She tapped her breast. "A blackness. A bleakness. He can still control us, Noah, if not with such suffering." She paused. "Noah, why did he heal us?"

Noah took a long time to answer. "I don't know," she said finally.

They both fell silent for a time. They might be healed, but were still exhausted both physically and emotionally.

Eventually, Noah spoke again. "Jane, what is Ariadne doing back? And in *London* itself? For all the gods' sakes, do you think she wants to take control of the Troy Game?"

"Instead of *you*, do you mean?" said Jane, allowing a small measure of bitterness to creep into her voice.

"Whether I do or not, Jane, is your choosing. I shall not ask, nor beg for you to teach me the ways of the Labyrinth, and whatever you do choose, then I shall accept."

"Well, then," said Jane, "perhaps I shall keep my powers as Mistress of the Labyrinth, eh? I shall wait for whoever wins the battle to be Kingman, and dance with him the Flower Dance, and live forever wrapped in the immortality of the Game."

To that Noah made no reply, but merely looked at Jane with sad eyes.

That look of pity infuriated Jane. "I may not have my teeth at your throat this very instant," she snapped, "and I may not control the respect and fear that once I did, but do not think I am so well disposed to you, nor so desperate, that I shall hand to you my powers as the Mistress of the Labyrinth with little more than a shrug!"

Noah sighed, and looked away.

WEYLAND MADE HIS WAY THROUGH THE CROWDS outside Whitehall. It seemed that most of London was here, thronging the streets, dancing where there was space, drinking where there was not. The palace itself was guarded from the revelry by units of the army.

Weyland managed to maintain a semblance of joy—anything less would have drawn immediate attention to him—but his thoughts were far from the celebration going on about him. Yesterday had been exhausting. First the horrific birthing of the imps, then the healing. Noah and Jane had still been unconscious when he left the house this morning, for which he had been grateful.

He didn't want to face them, or any of the questions.

He didn't want to face Noah. Not just yet.

He certainly didn't want to think too deeply on that strange vision he'd had, of standing atop the hill, looking at Noah, at the tears coursing down her face . . .

Weyland forcibly turned his thoughts to what he needed to accomplish today. Yesterday had served its purpose; today he needed to send another message to Charles.

After several hours of pushing and shoving through the crowds, Weyland found himself standing before the high iron railings that ran about the Great Courtyard of Whitehall Palace. He managed to find himself a secure place close to the gates where the crowd would not jostle him too much, and wrapped his hands about the upright iron posts, staring at the buildings.

He thought that Whitehall had to be the most ugly collection of buildings he'd ever seen. The palace complex had grown haphazardly over a hundred and thirty years: a hall here, a dormitory there, courtiers' quarters somewhere else, a cockpit for entertainment, a garden for pleasure, a chapel for salvation. Weyland had never been inside, but he'd heard from several sources that the king's and queen's quarters were each a series of barely coherent rooms that were often cold and drafty. Fifty years ago, during the time of James I, the king's daughter actually had to bed down in the tennis court. James's son, Charles I, had commissioned a complete new plan of the palace, meaning to rebuild it.

Of course, his head had come off before he'd been able to sign the work order.

Weyland didn't envy Brutus-reborn this ugly monstrosity. He preferred his home in Idol Lane.

His Idyll.

He suddenly thought of the imps. He'd left them in the kitchen, not merely to suitably intimidate the women, but because Weyland was sick of their constant whining about the Idyll. He regretted ever taking them in there.

Frankly, he had come to regret ever creating them in the first instance. They'd served their purpose, and perhaps now he could send them off to wander the streets.

He grinned, a little wanly. They'd certainly manage to create mischief among this throng.

A light flickered in one of the windows of the nearest palace building—it was now close to dusk—and Weyland's mind returned to the task at hand.

The light in the window grew stronger, and shadows moved behind it. Courtiers and servants, Weyland thought, tending to the needs of the king.

And, by all the gods of hell, Weyland could *smell* Charles. A few hundred yards, at the most, separated them. He was so close. Weyland could feel the power of the Kingman as it filtered through the walls of the palace.

Feel his bare limbs as they cried out for the kingship bands of Troy.

Feel his *despair*—Charles had been deeply affected by the Noah's agony. *Good.* Tomorrow Weyland would drive the message home, make *sure* Charles understood it.

Weyland turned his attention from Charles and sent his senses scrying out over London. Could he now feel the bands? Had they responded to the presence of their Kingman?

He went very still, shutting his eyes.

Yes! There! Stronger than ever Weyland had felt them before in this life. The bands had indeed woken at the nearby presence of their Kingman.

They were awake, and they could be taken.

Now all Weyland had to do was to keep Charles away from them.

And from the forest.

Weyland knew many, many things, and one of the things he did know was that the Stag God meant to rise in this life. It was something Weyland had managed to glean from Mag in that life when Charles and Genvissa had first created the Game. Mag had planned for the Stag God to rise again, and it was in this life that it was supposed to occur.

Weyland meant to take every step necessary to ensure he didn't. Genvissa should have made sure of the Stag God's murder three thousand years ago. This life, Weyland would rectify her mistake.

Once again Weyland looked at the palace. The evening was settling in now, the golden, joyous light behind the windows of the palace ever more prominent.

Charles was within.

Now Weyland felt the tiniest measure of fear. Charles was so much more powerful in this life, and Weyland would need to be very, very careful. It would be tempting to assume a disguise—a glamour, such as he had had in his previous life as Silvius—and try to enter Charles's court to see the king for himself. But Weyland thought it would be a mistake now, he was unlikely to get away with that particular trickery again.

Still, he had the perfect messenger. All he had to do was ensure that Charles knew she was on her way.

Weyland drew in a deep breath and held it for one moment. Then he gathered his power, and sent a single thought pulsating toward the palace, through the walls, through to Charles . . .

THE KING SAT IN A HUGE AND MAGNIFICENTLY carved chair in his reception room, courtiers crowded about him, music and women and wine abounding. The gaiety of the chamber was astounding, the colors magnificent, the richness almost unbelievable. *All those years,* he thought. *All those years in penurious exile, and now . . . this.*

His women were here. Kate and Marguerite were circulating among the guests, Catharine was at his side, looking cool and beautiful in her jewels and silks. Louis was here, tense and still angry, but managing to be courteous to all who addressed him. His air of suppressed anger made him appear exotic and mysterious, and he formed a second center of interest after Charles himself. Once a nobleman and his wife had been introduced to their king, and had passed a few words, then inevitably they gravitated to Louis, and sought his company for a short while.

As Charles's eyes drifted about the chamber, he suddenly tensed.

Listen well, Brutus! I shall be sending a whore to you tomorrow. Her name is Jane. Make sure you receive her.

There was a movement to one side, and Charles looked.

Louis. His face pale, his eyes bright with emotion. He had heard, as well.

"Charles?" Catharine said, concerned.

"Weyland," Charles murmured, his eyes shifting about the chamber. "Somewhere close."

She drew in a sharp breath. "Does he . . ."

"He calls me Brutus," said Charles.

Catharine relaxed, just a little. "Indeed," she said. "Who else?"

Before she could say more, Louis was at their side.

"He said that he is sending a whore to me tomorrow," said Charles. "He said her name is Jane."

"Genvissa," Louis said.

"Yes," Charles said. "Genvissa. Weyland's sister, and, now, messenger."

"He's told you so that you can inform your guards to expect her," said Catharine.

"At least he thinks well enough of me," said Charles dryly, "that he feels the need to warn. He does not think I am so corrupt that a whore turning up at the front gate asking to visit should be automatically sent through."

"What does he want?" said Catharine.

"Perhaps," said Louis, "he is sending Jane to ask for the keys to the front door of the Game."

Charles became aware that the entire chamber was watching them—the tenseness on the dais was obviously palpable. He smiled, and waved, and laughed, and the chamber slowly relaxed.

"Put a smile to your face, Louis, for the gods' sakes!" said Charles. "If you walk from here with that glower on your face my guests shall think that I have just received word of a renewed outbreak of the plague."

The expression on Louis's face did not alter appreciably. "Charles—Jane will know. The instant she sees you, she will *know*."

Charles nodded. "Aye. She will know. But I think we shall have no need to fear her."

Louis laughed, a hollow, cynical sound. "No need to fear *Genvissa*? The day that happens, the world shall have turned upside down indeed."

Chapter Thirteen

Idol Lane, London

EYLAND WORKED HIS WAY SLOWLY BACK up the Strand, past St. Paul's, then down Cheapside to Idol Lane. It was full night now, and even though it was a day since Charles's arrival in London, it seemed as if the celebrations had not slackened in the slightest.

Of course, the continuation of the festive mood had been aided in no small part by the Venetian ambassador's generous gift of free wine to all who thronged up and down the Strand. Weyland himself had stopped and drunk a good measure of the fine French wine—now he felt the slightest bit lightheaded as he made his way to his house.

He wondered if Noah was awake. One part of him hoped she was, another hoped not.

HE ENTERED THE KITCHEN, AND STOPPED DEAD.

Jane was at the hearth, as she normally was this time of the day, stirring at a pot over the flames. She glanced at Weyland as he entered, and he saw a shadow of uncertainty in her eyes.

Her face was pale, and there were dark rings under her eyes, and Weyland saw that she held herself stiffly, but Jane was looking remarkably whole.

Too whole? There was something about her . . . but Weyland could not immediately place it, and so for the moment turned his attention to the table.

There sat Noah, together with her strange daughter, Frances and Elizabeth, and his two imps.

Like Jane, Noah was holding herself with obvious stiffness, and Weyland saw that her clothes were left loose about her back. But otherwise she, too, looked well.

She raised her face and looked Weyland in the eye.

Unlike Jane, Noah did not lower her gaze away from his.

"And a good evening to you, too," said Weyland as he entered the room. He glanced at Catling, sitting playing with a tangle of red wool in her lap, then he looked to his imps, and raised an eyebrow.

They returned his gaze with faces swathed in innocence.

Weyland walked to the table, and sat down.

"Well?" he said to Noah. It was not the wittiest of comments, but Weyland didn't want to lead the conversation.

"You are a strange man," Noah said. "To so wound us, and then to heal us. Why? So we are made strong enough to suffer once more for your pleasure?"

Weyland didn't answer. He'd suddenly realized why Jane looked *too* well.

"Your poxed face is all but healed," he said, looking from Noah to Jane. "Why is that so, Jane?"

She shrugged disinterestedly. "Perhaps it was the faeries, Weyland. It certainly wasn't something I accomplished on my own."

Weyland continued staring at Jane, hoping his regard would make her uncomfortable enough to proffer a better explanation.

Jane kept on stirring the pot. She remained silent.

"I preferred your face poxed, Jane," Weyland said quietly. "It suited my purpose better that way."

Jane well knew that tone of voice, and she stopped stirring and visibly stiffened. "You must have expended more power than you thought, Weyland, and healed all of me, not just my belly. Perhaps you misjudged. Do not blame *me* for my smooth skin!"

"There is far more in the land than you know," Noah said, and Weyland whipped his gaze back to her. "You are a foreigner, and not privy to its ways."

"As are *you!*" Weyland snapped. "Don't patronize me, Noah."

She didn't reply, merely held his gaze calmly.

After a moment Weyland looked back to Jane. He considered her, then rose, walked over, and dealt her a heavy blow across her face so that she fell to the floor.

"I need you to look a little morose," he said, "for the duty I have for you in the morning."

Then, without a backward glance, he left the kitchen.

NOAH AND JANE LAY ON THEIR PALLETS BEFORE THE hearth. It was very late at night, and the household was quiet. Elizabeth, Frances, and Catling were abed in one of the bedrooms upstairs, the imps likewise in a different bedroom, and Weyland shut within his own chamber at the very top of the house.

Jane and Noah lay still, each awake, staring at the shadowy ceiling above them. There would have been silence between them save that Jane's breathing came harsh and thick—Weyland's blow had injured her nose and it now dribbled a little blood and clear fluid. The left side of her face had also swollen, so that her left eye, now black-and-blue, was almost closed.

"Jane?" said Noah softly. "We need to talk."

Jane sighed.

Noah tuned her head, looking at Jane. "How can I make amends to you, for what I did? For taking your life?"

"Oh," said Jane. "Now I see. We're going to forgive each other, fall into each other's arms weeping in new-formed friendship, and then I, grateful wretch that I am, shall hand to you my powers as Mistress of the Labyrinth. Yes?"

"Jane—"

"Gods damn you," Jane said softly. "What do you *mean,* 'amends'? There are no 'amends' to be had between you and I. We have done each other enough damage to call the score even, I think. There is no forgiveness to be given or accepted."

Noah was silent, and Jane almost smiled. All Noah's carefully laid plans, shattered. *Beg forgiveness from Jane, make her your friend, and hope that, in gratitude, she'll hand over to you her powers of Mistress of the Labyrinth.*

Gone.

There was no forgiveness to be begged, no gratitude to be ladled about.

"I am not going to teach you the ways of the Mistress of the Labyrinth," said Jane, now watching Noah closely. "Would you like to know why?"

Noah raised an eyebrow.

Jane had to admit some grudging respect for Noah's composure. "Because it is what Weyland wants."

"*Why?* And how can you be sure? Has he said as much?"

"Yes," said Jane. "He has been plain about it. I teach you to be a Mistress of the Labyrinth, and then I walk free. *Ha!* I die, more like. But, yes, he wants me to teach you. Thus he throws us together in the kitchen each night, hoping that we shall magically bond through some shared sisterly magic. He wants you to become Mistress of the Labyrinth." Jane managed a cynical laugh, which, coming as it did from her deformed face, sounded both harsh and despairing. "Amusing, isn't it?"

Noah stared, clearly shocked.

"Oh," said Jane, "surely you don't need me to explain *that,* as well? Do you think he would want *me,* when he could have *you*? Do you think he'd be satisfied with just a mere Mistress of the Labyrinth when he could have one that also commanded goddess power as well? For the gods' sakes, Noah! Were you to learn the craft of the Mistress, then you'd be the most powerful Mistress of the Labyrinth that ever was! *I* know that, *I* can admit that, and you may be sure that Weyland knows it, as well. He wants to be Kingman. He wants you at his side."

"I had not thought—"

"Then *think,* damn you. *Think!* Everyone always underestimates Weyland. In this life I, at least, am determined not to make that mistake again."

"If you did teach me the ways of the Mistress, would Weyland know?"

Jane nodded. "Yes. He would feel the growing power in you. He is as attuned to the ways of the Labyrinth as is the Kingman."

"Then we must find some means to—"

Jane hissed in frustration. "I am *not* going to teach you! *I am not!* I may have been beaten into a pulp more times than you've managed breakfasts, but I still have my pride left!" She paused, gathering her composure.

"Besides," she continued in a more even tone, "I somehow think my teaching you would be all but useless." Her mouth quirked, now finding the entire situation intensely amusing. "As useless as is my selfish determination not to teach you the arts of the Labyrinth."

"I don't understand you."

Jane studied Noah for a long moment before she answered. During the day, Jane had finally realized what it was that had worried at her when Ariadne had pulled both her and Noah to Tower Fields. "Because it is hardly necessary," Jane said eventually.

The confusion in Noah's face deepened.

"I have had some time to think this evening," said Jane, "and I find myself confused. Ariadne expended much power to bring both you and I to her side yesterday."

"Yes?"

"It was a very particular power she used, Noah."

"*Yes?*"

"Ariadne used a particular aspect of her power to call to us. It was an aspect only used between Mistresses of the Labyrinth—or those women who, while not trained, have been born with the potential within them. Women who already have the blood of the Labyrinth within them. No one else can respond to it or be touched by it."

Jane paused, looking at Noah.

Noah was still confused.

"You are incredibly silly for a goddess," Jane said. "Don't you yet understand? How foolish can you *be*? If it had been Elizabeth writhing on that floor with me, then Ariadne could not have pulled her spirit away. Ariadne used a power that calls *only* to trained or born Mistresses of the Labyrinth; that's why it was so powerful and effective. But she should only have been able to reach me. Not you. So tell me, little Cornelia, incompetent Caela, uncomprehending Noah—if uncomprehending you truly are—how is it that *you* also ended up standing in Tower Fields? *Eh?* How was it that Ariadne could also snatch *you* from that writhing agony on the kitchen floor?"

CHAPTER FOURTEEN

IDOL LANE, LONDON

I DO NOT KNOW WHAT YOU MEAN," SAID NOAH IN A low voice, as both women bent over the breakfast preparations. "Of what do you accuse me? I know nothing of the arts of the Mistress of the Labyrinth. Nothing. For the gods' sakes, Jane . . ."

"I said all I needed last night. Do not speak of it *now*, I beg you! Not when the house wakes about us!"

Noah's mouth folded into a thin line, annoying Jane.

"Don't dare to condescend to me, Noah! At least *I* know precisely what it *is* that you birthed—" Her eyes slid to Catling, playing at the table with her red wool.

"Jane? *What do you know?*"

But Jane pretended to not hear, and instead looked to the pot Noah was supposed to be stirring continuously.

"Don't let the porridge burn!" she snapped, grabbing the ladle out of Noah's hand.

"Ladies, ladies," said Weyland from the door, and both women stiffened. He walked into the kitchen, his imps at his heels. They clutched at the hem of his three-quarter–length cream-colored linen coat and grinned slyly at the women.

Weyland glanced at Jane's face, paused—during which time Jane stiffened even further—then gave a slight nod as if satisfied and sat down at the table.

At that moment Elizabeth and Frances came in from the side alley after a trip to the privy. The two girls looked at Weyland and the imps, then at Noah and Jane, and then sat down at the opposite end of the table, glancing at Weyland with open hostility.

The imps glanced at Catling playing with her wool, then sat at the table at the far end from Elizabeth and Frances. They placed their hands flat on the tabletop, then, simultaneously, looked over to where the porridge had just been rescued from a burned fate and licked their lips.

Weyland shot them an irritated glance.

Jane and Noah served up breakfast, adding a platter of freshly baked bread to the fare, and pouring out warmed, weak beer for everyone to drink.

Then they sat down themselves and Weyland, dipping a piece of bread into his porridge and taking a bite, regarded Jane speculatively. She tried not to react, but could feel her heart pound, and a tickle of sweat started down her spine.

Weyland swallowed his mouthful, and addressed Elizabeth and Frances instead, eyeing their borrowed clothes.

"Where are your clothes?"

"When we cleaned up, um, after . . ." said Elizabeth.

"Get to the point," Weyland said.

"After we'd cleaned the kitchen, we found our skirts and bodices ruined with blood. We had to throw them out. Our spare clothes are at our lodgings, and you said that we couldn't—"

"You could surely have saved the clothes," said Weyland. "They cost me good money."

"Money that *Elizabeth* and *Frances* had paid for with weeks spent on their backs and half of London's apprentices heaving over them," Jane said. She did not look at Weyland.

His eyes, hooded and guarded, swung back her way for a moment. Then he glanced at Noah, and whatever he saw in her face made his cheeks color slightly. His mouth thinned, then he dipped a piece of bread into his porridge, and chewed and swallowed it. "You have my permission," he said to the two girls, "to return to your lodgings and collect what clothes remain to you. While you are there, you may tell your landlord that you shall not be returning, and that he may hire out his dismal cellar to some other desperates, if he so desires. Remind him that I have paid your rent until Michaelmas, so do not allow him to trick more coin out of you."

What coin? thought Elizabeth, but kept her eyes cast down so that Weyland should not see the expression in her eyes.

Weyland scrapped out the last of his porridge with his spoon, fed it into his mouth. "You and Frances may take the first bedroom at the top of the stairs," he said. "The bed is large enough for the two of you."

"And perfectly foul," said Noah. "If Elizabeth and Frances are to live here—"

He looked at her once more. "I will give you coin, Elizabeth," he said, his eyes not leaving Noah's face, "to purchase some new linens while you are out."

"And coin enough to buy a chest for their clothes, and candles and pewter to make the room liveable," said Noah. "And I'm sure they could do with some material to make some better clothes for themselves than what they own now."

Weyland stared at her, his eyes hard, then gave a curt nod.

Everyone sat in silence for several minutes, Catling still playing with her wool, the imps staring about with their bright eyes, Jane and Noah making a show of eating some breakfast, and Elizabeth and Frances sitting tense and watchful, as if they were waiting only for a signal from Weyland before bolting out the door.

Weyland sipped at his ale, ate a little more bread, and then spoke. "I have decided to discontinue our business activities," he said. "All this whoring has ceased to amuse me."

"Then let Frances and myself return to our homes in Essex," said Elizabeth.

"Not yet," said Weyland.

Elizabeth shared a glance with Frances, opened her mouth, and then subsided. She had pushed her fortune far enough for the day.

"You *will* return from your outing today, Elizabeth," said Weyland, his voice still low, fixing each of the girls in turn with a steady eye. "You and Frances both."

They did not reply, looking everywhere but at Weyland or his imps.

"You *will* return," he repeated, his tone even lower.

Elizabeth was the first to drag her eyes back to him. "Yes," she said. "We will return."

Weyland smiled. "Good." His attention shifted to Jane. "Now, you may recall I said I had a duty for you this day."

He pushed his chair back suddenly, as if he were going to rise, and Jane flinched.

Weyland's mouth curved in a very small smile. "Once you have cleaned this kitchen, I want you to set off down to Whitehall, and visit with the king."

Everyone in the kitchen, imps and Catling included, looked at Weyland in astonishment. He grinned at their undivided attention, then winked at Noah, who was looking aghast.

"He shall receive you," Weyland continued, looking back to Jane. "Knowing Brutus, my love, he's probably already smoothing the bedsheets in anticipation. No, wait . . . I forgot . . . He didn't exactly fall into your bed in your last lives together, did he?"

Jane's face tightened. Weyland always instinctively knew the best barb for the occasion.

And Brutus. What would he say when he saw her this way? Her face battered, her shoulders slumped with years of degradation . . . How could she face him? By the gods, once she'd been so powerful, so beautiful. He'd loved her, lusted for her. And now . . . to come before him in this state . . .

Jane realized Weyland was staring at her, and by the satisfaction apparent in his eyes she knew he understood her humiliation.

"You will go before the king, before magnificent Charles, before resurgent Brutus, and you will give him three messages."

He waited, and after a moment Jane dipped her head stiffly in acceptance.

"Good. First you may offer Brutus my hearty congratulations on regaining the throne. He must be very pleased. You will say this to him."

Jane jerked her head in assent again.

"Second, you shall tell him this: 'Do not think to attempt to locate the bands, fool, for I have Noah, and I will do to her what I have done to you, should you try to find your damned kingship bands.' Do you understand?"

Again Jane gave a single jerk of her head.

"He is *not* to attempt to find those bands, for then I will slaughter Noah—not *kill* her, you understand, but steep her in such misery and humiliation and degradation, that she will wish herself dead. I will do to her what I have done to you. *Do you understand?*"

"Yes! I understand."

"There is a third message. Tell the fool this, also: 'If you go near the forests, King, if you so much as eye a single tree, or step within its shade, *I will make sure that Noah suffers for an eternity.*' If he stays away from both the bands of Troy, and the forests, then I will keep Noah well."

Jane glanced at Noah. *He knows. He knows about the Stag God—*

Silence! Noah all but shouted in her mind. *Not here!*

A slow grin lifted the corners of Weyland's mouth, and he looked between Jane and Noah. "This is going to be a most pleasant day," he said. "I *do* wish I could be a fly on the audience chamber's walls. Or do you think Brutus shall receive you in his privy, Jane? It's the only proper place for you, don't you think?"

Jane hung her head, and her swollen eye stung miserably as a tear squeezed its way out. Then she flinched as Weyland leaned over the table and wiped it away.

"Remember all I have said, Jane. Oh, and enjoy the day. You don't get out much."

Chapter Fifteen

Whitehall Palace, London

*J*ANE WALKED UP IDOL LANE. SHE HAD NEATENED herself as much as possible—although the state of her face (swollen, bruised, scabbed, black-eyed) meant that she was a sorry sight indeed.

A passing youth glanced at her, and then hurried on, not quite managing to stifle his snigger, and Jane colored as she turned down Little Tower Street and then eventually down an alley running parallel with Cheapside.

Oh Gods, that once she had walked this way when she had been beautiful and powerful, and all who had passed her had bowed in respect.

Now, here she walked, a bedraggled, humiliated prostitute, off to visit Brutus.

A king.

How would he regard her? With pity? Revulsion? Surely not with respect.

A sudden, horrible thought occurred to Jane: Were Ecub and Erith there as well? Would they smile in satisfaction, and send cruel barbs her way?

Jane forced herself to think of Noah to take her mind away from how Ecub and Erith, not to mention Brutus, might treat her. She'd meant what she said to Noah the previous night: Ariadne should *not* have been able to pull Noah to her side with the power that she used. Noah was not a trained Mistress of the Labyrinth, so that meant only one thing.

She must have it bred within her. *Gods, how had* that *come about?*

Jane crossed into the square about St. Paul's and, without a glance at the cathedral, walked down toward Ludgate and Fleet Street. She felt numb. Jane's one piece of pride remaining had been her ability to deny or grant Noah powers as Mistress of the Labyrinth as *she*, Jane, chose. *If you want me to teach you the craft of the Mistress of the Labyrinth, then do this, or be that, or grant me this wish.*

Now even that had been taken away from her.

Even Noah didn't need her anymore. Sooner or later Noah was going to realize that she barely needed to snap her fingers to assume her powers as Mistress.

But why? Why? And how long had Noah been carrying this potential? Had she, even as Cornelia, been harboring the power of the Labyrinth?

How? How?

Jane was walking past Charing Cross now and her steps slowed. It was now but a short walk to her total mortification. She made the effort to straighten her spine, square her shoulders, and bring her emotions under some kind of control.

Finally managing to attain some semblance of calm, Jane walked to the gates of Whitehall palace. There was a crowd gathered, composed of curiosity seekers and supplicants, and Jane had to shove her way through so that she could speak to the guards.

And how was she going to argue her way past them? Impress them with her regal bearing, her pride, her damned, cursed *power*?

"I am Jane Orr," she said, as she finally managed to stand before them. "I have come to present my respects to His Majesty, King Charles."

The four guards looked her up and down, glanced among themselves, and then, stunningly, one of them shrugged and opened the gate enough for her to slip through.

"Follow me," said another, and, stupefied (*had Weyland arranged this?*) Jane trailed a pace or two behind the guard as he led her into the palace.

Tears threatened again as she walked as softly as she could manage through the palace. Never had she felt so shabby, so unworthy, as she did in this royal building. Everywhere was gilt, or marble, or rich, dark, carved wood dressed with silk and velvet.

Everyone she passed, stopped and stared, their eyes round, their mouths open.

Aghast.

Jane stiffened more with each step, her head held unnaturally high, her eyes focused straight ahead, wondering if some of those exquisitely clothed courtiers were even now sending for the servants, to wash and scrub the path where Jane had trod.

What manner of king, they would be thinking, *would want this in his presence?*

The guard led her into grander and grander apartments, until they reached a series of massive rooms that opened one into another. It was, Jane realized, the end of her journey. Here, the final approach to the king, the series of waiting and audience rooms, where, in each succeeding chamber, the hopeful supplicant would be vetted by increasingly senior members of the king's household privy chamber, to be judged and either allowed to continue on her pilgrimage to the royal person, or to be cast aside, and asked to leave the palace forthwith.

Here, even more people stared at her: those waiting, or those already told their application to be received by the king had been unsuccessful. Here they stood or sat, watching as a tattered, thin, beaten prostitute was shown through chamber after chamber without any examination.

Why, oh why, Jane thought, *couldn't the guard have brought me to Charles via some unknown way, some servant's passage?*

Then Jane realized that Charles had wanted this, had wanted her to suffer the ultimate humiliation.

He'd wanted her to endure this open shame, this public crucifixion.

He'd wanted her paraded her as entertainment through his palace as . . . What? Triumph on his part? Malice? Punishment?

As the guard brought Jane to a halt outside the final doorway leading to the king's private audience room, the royal parlor, Jane briefly closed her eyes. It had come to this, all the promises and ambitions and power of three thousand years before.

Hatred, revenge, humiliation.

"You may enter," said the richly dressed man whom the guard had addressed. The man, probably the palace chamberlain, lifted an eyebrow at her, and pointedly stepped back . . . then pulled a snowy handkerchief from his coat pocket and held it to his nose.

The doors swung open, and Jane, hating herself more than she thought humanly possible, entered.

KING CHARLES'S PRIVATE AUDIENCE ROOM WAS smaller than Jane had initially expected.

It was also dimmer, and she had to stop a few paces inside the doors and blink, trying to refocus her vision.

There were only a few lamps burning which, combined with the fact that the heavy drapes at the windows had been pulled closed, meant the room was as dark as twilight.

The chamber gradually came into focus. Its walls were hung with rich green damask silk which matched the drapes at the windows. The domed ceiling was ivory, and richly gilded. The accoutrements of power were everywhere: the gold glinting from ceiling and chairs and tabletops; the richness of the oriental carpets on the solid mahogany floors; the oil portraits of King Charles I and his queen, Henrietta Maria, as well the current Charles's grandfather, James I; the all-pervading sense of power in the room.

It was that sense of power that brought Jane to her senses. She glanced about, orientating herself. There were two women standing almost hidden in the drapery by the window.

There was a man—dark, tall, lithe—standing to one side of the dais. He had a hand on his sword, and his face was swathed in dark anger.

Coel? she wondered, and her heart beat faster as she recalled that strange dream she'd had while unconscious after Weyland's attack. She looked at the man again, wondering at the anger on his face.

Finally, Jane looked to the dais. There were two thrones atop it, and Jane looked first to the queen.

She was tiny, and dark, and sat sitting forward, her arm propped on the arm of the gilded throne, resting her delicate chin on one hand. She wore a speculative expression on her face, and Jane could see strength and determination there as well.

Jane felt her mouth go dry. That was Matilda-reborn. Queen again, at Brutus' side, and once more witness to Jane's mortification.

Finally, Jane looked at Brutus himself: Charles II of England.

There was something "hidden" about him. Jane's eyes were now accustomed to the dimness of the room, and she should have been able to make him out as clearly as she had Catharine, his queen.

But much of Charles remained hidden. She could *feel* him, feel the power of the kingship bands about him (and yet even that was muted, as if also hiding behind some enchantment), but she could make out little else about him save for his overall height and the vast richness of his clothes.

He made an expostulatory sound, as if Jane had somehow annoyed him, and rose.

Scared almost to death, Jane sunk to her knees—wishing she had thought to do this the instant she'd entered the chamber—and hung her head low.

Perhaps this way he won't see how terrified I am. How ashamed I am. How—

"Jane," he said, and she literally jumped at the kindness and gentleness in his voice.

She shifted her eyes forward, and saw a pair of beautifully tooled scarlet boots.

She lifted her gaze a little higher, and saw the fine cut of his silken-and-velvet breeches.

Still higher, and Jane saw the richly brocaded and jeweled doublet he wore, saw the lace that cascaded from their cuffs, saw the gems on the fingers of his hands as they rested relaxed on his hips.

Still higher, and she saw his face.

And in that moment, as she heard herself gasp and as she heard everyone else in the room step forward and move to encircle her, Jane was absolutely certain that she was a dead woman.

She looked into the handsome face of Charles II, looked at his black, curling hair, felt the aura of the golden bands of Troy emanate from his flesh, looked at the power in his dark eyes.

Looked at the knowledge in them.

And recognized him.

"You're not Brutus," she said.

PART SIX

THE FAERIE COURT

LONDON, 1939

OTHER!" SAID FRANK AS THEY DREW UP BEFORE
the house. Piper's car had come to a halt some ten feet before them,
and about that car, as now also about Frank's, were gathered what
appeared to Skelton to be a small army of policemen with a few military officers
thrown in for good measure.

"Does 'the Old Man' always go in for such security?" Skelton asked dryly as he
wound down his window and handed out his military identification papers to the
policeman standing there.

"This isn't for the Old Man," said Frank. "Looks like the Boss has come as well."

Skelton almost screamed with frustration, and might have done so, save that
just then, the policeman handed him back his documents.

"Very good, sir," said the policeman. "If you'll just follow me."

Skelton climbed out of the car, and looked about. There was a flight of stone
steps leading up to the house's portico. Weyland Orr already stood at their head,
several small housedogs fussing about his legs.

He was grinning at Skelton, obviously enjoying the spectacle of the American
being detained for a check of documentation while he, Asterion, was allowed
straight through.

Skelton jerked his cap straight on his head, gave his jacket a tug to pull out as
many wrinkles as possible, and envied Weyland his easy sartorial elegance. Skelton
ran up the steps, his gait light and graceful, and brushed right past Weyland.

Behind him he heard Frank and Piper mutter something as one of the waiting
officers asked them to come about the back.

Whatever was awaiting Weyland and Skelton inside, Frank and Piper would
not be a part of it.

They're no one reborn, *Skelton thought.* They're just bit players, unaware of
just what kind of web they've been caught within.

He was just reaching out for the cedar-and-glass doors, intending to push right
into the house without waiting for Weyland, when one of them opened and a
woman stepped through.

It was Stella Wentworth.

Genvissa!

He'd seen her not eighteen hours previously, huddled under a lamp on the Embankment. There she'd looked beautiful.

Here she looked stunning. Her black hair was glossy and left loose to hang down in waves to her shoulders. Her well-cut lavender suit hugged her figure, as did her silken stockings to her shapely calves.

"Major Skelton," she said, offering him nothing more than a casual tip of the head. "We've been waiting."

"Your lover detained me," he said, and looked back over his shoulder.

Weyland Orr had vanished.

"My lover awaits you," Stella said softly, and she stood back, holding open the door.

CHAPTER ONE

IDOL LANE, LONDON
Noah Speaks

EYLAND SENT ELIZABETH AND FRANCES TO collect their belongings as soon as Jane had gone, then he nodded to the two imps and Catling to leave as well. I sat there and looked on, and raised no objections, telling Catling only to be good, and not to stray too far.

I felt no great care at sending her off to play with two such evil companions.

Weyland and I sat at that table, listening to the rattle of departing feet over the parlor floor, and then the sound of the front door opening and closing.

"You were surprised," he said without preamble, "when I told Jane to tell Charles not to go near the forests."

I said nothing, not knowing what to say. If he knew that, then he knew too much.

He knew the significance of "shelter," I was sure of it, and if he knew *that*, then I was lost. Everything was lost.

And yet why did I not feel afraid? For an instant I recalled that strange vision he and I had shared when he'd healed me, then I forced the memory aside.

"Jane told me not to underestimate you," I said.

He smiled, an easy, friendly expression that sat well on his attractive boyish face. "Jane is a very wise woman. The question is, though, can she overcome her dislike of you enough to teach you the craft of Mistress of the Labyrinth?"

Weyland leaned forward slightly across the table.

I leaned back in my chair, the movement instinctive, and saw something in his eyes at my reaction that almost looked like . . . regret. Perhaps even hurt.

I tried not to allow myself to be persuaded. After all, I'd learned a long time ago that Asterion was a good actor.

"Let me tell you something of my origins," he said, "for I would you came to know me better. Do you know of where I came, of how I came to be?"

"You were trapped in the heart of the Great Founding Labyrinth of Knossos," I said, wondering at this history lesson.

"Yes, but from where did I come? Who were my parents? What my origins?"

"How does this matter?" I said. I'd never seen Weyland like this, disarming, almost soft, although when he wore his glamour of Silvius he had often been humorous and teasing.

"Do you not want to know who I am?" he said. "Do you not want to know *why* I act as I do?"

"You want power, and you will stop at nothing to achieve it," I said. "Murder. Destruction. Chaos. *Agony*, whenever you can cause it!"

Again, that *cursed* memory of the few minutes Weyland and I had stood on the hill came back to me. *Weyland, Weyland, what are we doing? How can we stop?*

"And where do you think all that came from, eh?" Weyland's air of boyish charm vanished completely. "Who taught that to me? Ariadne. What was I before she betrayed me, Noah? I was an object of disgust and shame, which was why I was imprisoned in the Labyrinth in the first instance . . . Ah!"

He sat back, looking away. I could see the muscles in his jaw working, and I thought that he was, truly, upset. He spoke again, his voice once more soft, and he did not look at me.

"I was conceived when Minos' wife, Pasiphae, fell in love with a white bull. Imagine the manner of woman she must have been, to fall in love with a *bull*."

He hated his mother, I thought, and then my mind fled to my own lover, the white stag, lying so desolate in his glade, and my heart broke for Pasiphae.

"She was determined to copulate with him," Weyland continued, "no matter the injury to herself. She had a craftsman, Daedalus, construct for her a wooden cow with a convenient opening, I would imagine, at the appropriate spot. She then inserted herself into the cow, her legs down its back legs, her body within its body, and had a servant bring the bull to his 'cow,' whereupon the bull mounted it."

He paused, probably thinking of that bestial moment, and for some reason I looked at his left hand which still rested on the table. I'd seen his hands before, surely, but I'd never really looked at them. It was a surprise, this hand. Large and square, but with fine skin and long fingers, tipped with well-kept nails.

It was a sensitive hand. A gentle hand.

"I heard that she screamed when the bull entered her," he said, his voice now very low, "and begged the servant to pull the bull away. But the bull was strong, and intent on taking his pleasure. Can you imagine, Noah, the sight of it?" He turned his face to me, and I recoiled at the hatred I saw there. "The bull, grunting and thrusting atop Queen Pasiphae."

I closed my eyes briefly. I *could* imagine, all too well. Was this from where he got his dark power? I wondered. Power engendered by that terrible, tearing, agonizing, *stupid* mating?

If only Pasiphae had known what she was conceiving. If only . . .

"And thus, I was engendered in agony and horror. My mother hated me, thinking only of the pain and the humiliation. Her husband, King Minos, loathed me . . . no doubt thinking of the humiliation of the gossip running up and down the streets of Knossos: 'They say she fornicated with a bull, and that her child has been born so malformed that its mother cannot bear to gaze upon it.' And that was true enough, for I was born malformed, born with the head of a bull, the head of my *father*." He spat the word out, and I realized at that moment that *none* of this was acting; this pain was all too real.

"Minos determined to hide me away," Weyland continued. "It is said he instructed Daedalus to build a labyrinth, and then to place me within it, so that none might ever see my face again, save those that were sent to their deaths. But that is not strictly true. Knossos already had a labyrinth, the Great Founding Labyrinth, and it was into that they placed me—Daedalus merely was the fool sent to place the mewling infant into its heart. And there I stayed, and there I grew, and all the food they ever sent me, Noah, was human flesh. Twice a year, in batches of terrified youths, pissing themselves in fear. Do you blame me for eating?"

My mouth was dry. I could not respond.

"Everyone regarded me with loathing. Everyone. There was no one, Noah, to offer me any kind of shelter at all."

There! Again! He was watching me carefully as he spoke that last, and I knew he saw my panic.

"No one," he said very softly, his eyes intense on mine, "to offer me any kind of love."

I managed, somehow, to swallow, and that gave me the courage to speak. "But, Ariadne . . ."

"Ah, yes. Ariadne. My sister. My lover. She was born eight years after myself . . . I assume the time difference was because it took Minos some time to bring himself to mate with a woman who had betrayed him with a bull. Anyway, Ariadne was born, and grew, and became the most powerful Mistress of the Labyrinth that had ever been."

"And, as part of her duties, she met you."

His expression softened. "Aye, she met me. She came to me, not only from curiosity, although that was certainly part of it, but driven by compassion as well."

That, I found most implausible. *Ariadne,* driven by compassion?

"We became lovers, and, oh, how I *did* love her! She was the only one I'd ever known who did not look on me with fear or loathing. She made me laugh." He paused. "She made me feel wanted."

Weyland stopped, caught in his memories, and I stared at him, fascinated by this tale of rejection and horror.

He saw me watching, and smiled, and it caught at my heart, it was so sweet. "We had a child . . . did you know?"

Now he'd stunned me, and for some reason I felt a shiver of premonition. "No," I managed. "I didn't know."

"A little girl. Perfect. She had no bull nose, no horns, but merely tangled black hair and the loveliest of faces. Ariadne let me hold her. Once. Just once."

Tangled black hair and a lovely face. Just like Catling. I shivered again with that strange fearful premonition.

"And then?" I said, trying to distract myself from my thoughts.

"And then one day, perhaps a month after her birth, Ariadne came to me and said she had sent the girl away. She was ashamed, not of the girl—"

Again I closed my eyes briefly.

"—but of the man who had got the child on her."

"Where did your daughter go?"

"I don't know. I never saw her again, and Ariadne never spoke of her."

Oh, gods . . . I was so confused now I didn't know what to think. *This,* the dreaded Minotaur? *This,* the frightful beast evil incarnate? I knew that Asterion was most likely constructing this to sway me, to make me sympathize, to make me pliable . . . but there was something deep within me that screamed that this was *truth.*

"But then Ariadne met Theseus," I said. I needed to get past that child.

"Ah, yes, Theseus. She met him, she wanted him. And so she sent him to me, and he slew me, and then he betrayed her, and this entire . . ." He waved a hand about, trying to find the right word. ". . . debacle was created." Again Weyland looked at me, and what I saw there I thought was as real as anything I'd ever read in anyone else's face. "Do you blame me for what I do, Noah? Do you blame me for fighting with all my might to prevent myself being thrown back into the Labyrinth?"

"Then walk away! We shall let you be, Brutus and myself. Walk away!"

"No!" His hand—that sensitive, long-fingered hand—thudded into the table. "The instant the Game is completed, then so shall I be incarcerated once more into its heart."

"Then you must be true malevolence," I said, "for otherwise that should not be your fate."

He said nothing, just looked at me.

"Why cause myself and Jane all this pain?" I said. "Why *tear* those imps from us? Why, if not that you act out of hatred and maliciousness?"

"I did that," he said, "because I am nothing but what the Labyrinth made me."

Now my emotions swept back the opposite way they had run. This *had* been all a lie, uttered to confuse me.

Weyland sighed, and lowered his eyes. "I began this crusade against you and Brutus and Jane and all else involved in this bitter Troy Game," he said, "out of malevolence and hatred. But do you know what, Noah?"

I raised my eyebrows.

"I am tired of it, Noah."

I gave a small, disbelieving smile.

"Why else should I have healed you?" he said.

"To trap me," I said. "To make me think you had a better nature."

He sighed. "I cannot blame you for thinking badly of me."

He stopped, looked at me, smiled in a strange, funny little manner, then he leaned over the table, closed the distance between us, and kissed my mouth softly.

I did not move, and I told myself that this was because I was terrified into stillness.

He leaned back, and I turned aside my face. I would not look at him.

Again Weyland sighed. "You are free to come and go as you wish, Noah. I will not prevent you. I ask only that you do not see Brutus, that you sleep your nights here, and that you spend time with me. That you come to know me."

Freedom to come and go? This was a trap, I *knew* it.

He smiled, soft and sad. "It is no trap, Noah. All I want is for you to have the freedom you need. To learn from Jane the ways of the Labyrinth."

"You want me to become a Mistress of the Labyrinth?"

"Of course," he said. "Can you imagine it, Noah? You and I, Mistress and Kingman? *I* can. I lie awake nights imagining it. Imagining you and I . . ."

He leaned forward, and kissed me once more—my cheek this time, as I had my face averted.

"Do you remember," he whispered, his mouth brushing my flesh with every word, "when we met in dream on that strange hilltop?"

I wished I had the strength to deny it. "Yes," I said.

He had moved about the table now, and was sitting on a chair next to mine, and his hands, so gently, had turned my face to his.

"When you said to me, 'Weyland, Weyland, what are we doing? How can we stop?' Remember? I do. Those words have not once left my mind since you uttered them."

He kissed me yet once more. On the mouth again, very gentle.

"Noah, what did you mean with those words?"

I began to cry, as I had on the hilltop, and Weyland began to kiss away the tears. He moved closer still, and all I could think of was his presence and his nearness, and I was horrified that I did not find them fearful, nor unwelcome.

What did I mean?

"What did you mean, Noah?" he whispered. Another kiss, just behind my left ear this time.

"I—"

There was the sound of the door opening, and then came Elizabeth's and Frances's low voices, and Weyland muttered a soft curse, and sat back from me.

chapter two

YOU'RE NOT BRUTUS," SHE SAID. "YOU'RE NOT Brutus." There was a slightly hysterical ring to her voice, and Jane had to forcibly shut her mouth lest she babble those words over and over.

Charles sank down to his haunches before Jane, his eyes watchful. Louis, Marguerite, Catharine, and Kate moved close about him, their eyes similarly on Jane; Louis had his sword drawn.

Jane found it difficult to breathe. Any moment, she knew, she would feel the blade of that sword through her neck.

Wielded by Brutus. *Gods, somehow Coel and Brutus had swapped identities!* The *why* of it Jane could understand—this way Brutus had free rein to do whatever he needed while Weyland, the fool, watched Coel-reborn like a hawk. But how? *How?*

"You are Coel-reborn," she said to Charles, using every ounce of courage she possessed to utter those words. "You are not Brutus." *You are the Lord of the Faerie.*

Aye, he responded, *but of that we will not speak, for the moment.*

"Aye," Charles said aloud. He was studying her face, noting its new abrasions, the broken nose, the closed eye, and he frowned at them.

"Jane," he said, "is Weyland still ignorant of this deception? Does he think me Brutus-reborn?"

She nodded, the movement jerky and slightly uncoordinated.

Louis moved in closer, so close that Jane could smell the steel of the sword. He made a sudden movement, which made Jane flinch, then squatted down also, so he could look her in the face.

"I won't tell him," she said, garbling the words in her fear. "I won't!"

"You want us to believe you?" said Catharine. "*You?* Lady Snake?"

"Don't trust her," said Marguerite. "She was always the lying bitch."

Jane averted her eyes again, and she hugged her arms about herself, crouching a little lower to the floor. "I will not tell him," she whispered. "Please, believe me."

"You have spent hundreds of years teaching us *not* to believe you," said Louis, his voice very low, his eyes burning into her huddled form. "You would be better dead, for all you have done to Coel, and to Cornelia-reborn. Dead, we can surely trust you. Alive? I am not so sure."

He shifted a little, only to readjust his balance, but Jane cringed at his movement.

Charles stood. "I want to speak with her alone," he said. "If you could leave us, please."

"Charles," Louis said, rising also. "I should be here. I—"

"*Leave us*, Louis!" Charles said. Then he added, softer: "She is terrified, Louis. I will do better on my own than with this circle of vehemence about her. Sisters, please, leave us. I can accomplish what we need."

Louis looked at Catharine, Marguerite, and Kate, then he nodded, glanced once more at Jane, then shepherded the women before him toward the door. Charles paced slowly about the chamber until the door closed, then walked back to where Jane knelt, and extended down to her his hand.

Very slowly, tremulously, Jane took it, and rose.

Almost immediately she sank into a curtsy again.

"I do not," she said, looking up to him, "honor you as king of England, for which I care very little, but as—"

"I know," he said. "Jane, do not speak of the Faerie here. Not now. When next you go to Tower Fields, then we shall speak when you meet me by the scaffold. But not here."

"Yes, my lord."

Charles burst into laughter. "'My lord'? Oh, that I should hear *that* from your lips! Hark, is that the sound of Genvissa and Swanne turning over in their cold, cold graves?"

Jane smiled apprehensively. He was teasing her again, as he had when they'd met in dream.

"In the realm of the mortal, you may call me Charles when we are alone, and any variety of honorifics of your choosing when we are in public. But when I come to you in the Realm of the Faerie . . . then . . ." He paused, his brow creased as he thought. "Well, when we are alone you may call me Coel."

Again that apprehensive smile, and a little nod.

"Good." He still held her hand, and now he raised her to her feet, and he pulled her close. His fingers touched her cheek.

"When did he do this?"

"Last night. He was not well pleased that my face had healed. He wanted me ugly for you."

"Ah, gods, Jane, I am sorry. I had not thought he would punish you for that."

"You have not lived with him these thirty and more years."

Charles reached out a hand, and she flinched.

"I will not hurt you," he said, and very gently ran his hands over her swollen cheekbone and then her nose.

"Oh, gods . . ." she said, the breath shuddering in her throat. "Don't."

He withdrew his hand and let her go, standing back a pace. "You *are* sure that Weyland thinks I am Brutus?"

She nodded. "I don't understand. You *feel* like him. You have the aura of the kingship bands about you, and only Brutus has that. How can this *be*? Dear gods, Charles, you had me fooled as much as you have Weyland."

"It was a simple deception, but a much-needed one," Charles said. "Louis and I were conceived at the same moment, born the same day. Our souls are thus easily confused, especially when we are together."

"But the aura of the bands . . ."

"In our last life, when I had died at Hastings—"

Jane winced. *She* had caused his death.

"—Caela stopped me on my journey into the afterlife. She gave me two of the bands to take with me to the Otherworld. They and I are close, now. I cannot use them, or wield their power, but their aura clings to me. That has made the deception possible."

Jane wondered again how Charles could allow her to live, having told her so much.

"I am *not* going to kill you, Jane."

She started to cry. "Why not? Why *not*? I have killed you twice over, and you have taken my life but once. You are owed a death."

"I am sick of death," he said, very gentle, "and I think you have suffered enough in this life to settle whatever lies untallied between us. I meant what I said in Tower Fields. There is no score to settle. Jane, I do not hate you."

"You should."

He studied her a moment before continuing. "Jane, you may owe me nothing, but you do owe the land."

Of course, Jane thought. *I knew there would be a revenge somewhere.*

"You tried to murder both Mag and Og, and all but succeeded. For that, I'm afraid you shall have to do reparation. Not death, but some degree of penance. The land itself demands it. It is why the Faerie sent me to you in the field. The magpie came, and demanded it."

Her face twisted, and she looked away.

"Bitterness does not become you," Charles said.

"It comforts me," she said, her voice very low.

"Well," Charles said, "of how the Faerie might judge you, we will not speak within these man-made walls."

It will be a windswept moor, Jane thought, *or a forest. There I shall be judged.* She trembled, thinking of how harsh that judgment was likely to be.

The silence grew longer, and Jane grew more uncomfortable. Then, suddenly, she remembered why she was here.

"Oh gods, Charles, Weyland has sent me here with messages for you, and I have forgotten them completely!"

"Then relay your messages, Jane."

"He has sent you three messages. One: Weyland offers you his hearty congratulations on gaining the throne. He thinks you must be very pleased."

Charles quirked an eyebrow, but said nothing.

"Two: Weyland says that you must not attempt to locate the bands, for he has Noah, and he will do to her what he has done to me should you attempt to find your kingship bands. He says he will 'slaughter' Noah, not kill her, but steep her in such humiliation and degradation that she will wish herself dead, should you so much as lay a hand to those bands."

"Really. And what is the third message?"

"That if you go near the forests, if you so much as eye a single tree, or step within its shade, he will make sure that Noah suffers for an eternity."

"Then I had best keep away from both bands and forest, hadn't I?"

She looked at him, then suddenly laughed. It was weak, but it was a laugh, and somehow it lifted a great weight from Jane's heart. "My God, Charles, if Weyland ever realizes that you're not—"

"He must not realize, Jane."

"And he will not from me."

Charles nodded. "I know . . . Noah? How is she? We did not speak of it overly when we met in dream."

"She is well now. Weyland . . . Weyland healed her, and me. Not my pox— that is your doing alone—but the wounds I suffered in birthing the imp."

Charles frowned. "Why? Why would he do that?"

"Perhaps he wants us to believe he suffered from guilt. I do not know the true reason, but I am sure it is malicious."

Charles's frown deepened, then he gave his head a slight shake.

"Jane, I know what kind of a house Weyland runs. Noah . . . has he . . . ?"

"Prostituted her? He tried. But something happened. I don't know *what,* for Noah has not spoken of it to me, but"—Jane could not help an ironic twist of her mouth—"be assured, your lover has not yet been tarnished with that same brush which has blackened me."

"She is not my lover," Charles said mildly. "But be assured I am pleased to hear she has not suffered your fate."

Jane's face hardened a little.

"For the moment," Charles continued, "I am but grateful to hear that *both* of you are well . . . although your face . . ."

Once more his fingers touched it.

"Don't heal the marks," she said, standing back. "If Weyland sees, he will know that you are—"

"He will merely think that Brutus has more power than he'd thought," said Charles. "Here, let me take from you the pain."

His fingers rubbed gently, and, miraculously, all the pain and aches vanished.

"It still looks red and swollen," said Charles, "but you shall not suffer from it."

"Thank you," she whispered.

"Now, what else? What other news?"

Jane thought. "The imps," she said after a moment. "They are now incarnate. Did you know?"

"DEAR GOD," LOUIS SAID MUCH LATER, WHEN Charles rejoined him and Catharine in the royal bedchamber. "You let her leave? You told her the *one* secret that—"

"She knew," Charles said mildly. "There was no need to tell."

"But to let her go . . ." said Catharine. "I hope you did not also reveal to her your Faerie crown!"

Charles gave her a sharp look. "Misery has changed her. I do not think she will tell Weyland."

Louis grunted. "Did you ask her about Noah?"

"Aye. She is well enough." He paused. "Weyland healed both Jane and Noah after that horrific day. I do not know why."

Louis, as everyone else present, visibly relaxed in relief.

"Thank all the gods of creation," said Catharine. "But . . . I know he runs a brothel. He hasn't—"

"Set Noah to work for him?" Charles said. "Apparently he tried, without any success. Noah is not yet entertaining the masses of London, and is not likely to. Jane said Weyland has decided to cease his whoremastering."

Louis said nothing, but Charles could see by the tightness of his jaw and the glint in his eyes that he was angry.

"Weyland sent me a message," Charles said. "Of three parts." He briefly related them.

"He knows that the Stag God is to be reborn?" said Marguerite.

"Aye," Charles said. "Weyland is not to be underestimated."

"Anything *else*?" said Louis.

Charles shook his head. "That was it. Stay away from the kingship bands and the forests, or else Noah suffers. But I learned more from Jane. That agony we felt during our processions through London. It was the imps, tearing themselves free of Noah and Jane's bodies."

Catharine gave a slight cry, her hands raising to her mouth in shock, while Louis cursed, low and cruel, and looked away.

They talked of what Jane had said for some time, then Louis left, claiming to be tired, although the others knew that he needed to be alone for a time.

Once the door had closed behind him, Charles looked to the three women.

"Amid all of the celebrations that we shall attend this week," he said, "I think I shall add one other. A very private celebration, I think."

Catharine, standing closest to Charles, raised an eyebrow.

"I shall hold a Council of England," said Charles, and as he spoke his features altered very slightly, his face becoming slighter and darker and assuming the aspect of the Lord of the Faerie. "Using the magic of the Circle, and convening atop The Naked. I shall summon the Faerie folk, and the water-sprites, and the Sidlesaghes, and even Louis's hated giants."

"And Noah?" said Catharine.

"And even Noah, if she is able," said Charles. "Jane, too, if she can manage."

Marguerite hissed. "You trust Jane way too greatly, Charles. Gods, man! She has murdered you *twice*!"

"And will not again, I think," Charles said. "If anything, Genvissa, in all of her lives, has always hated to be predictable."

CHAPTER THREE

IDOL LANE, LONDON

VEN AFTER TWO DAYS, LONDON REMAINED IN celebratory mode. The Venetian ambassador's wine stores might have dried up, but most of the taverns stayed open well into the night and offered cut-price ale and beer, while the coffeehouses were packed with those wanting to hear news of what the king had done, who he had knighted, and if he'd happened to have opened the royal coffers enough to ensure that the streets of London should be paved with gold forthwith. Gossip spread like fire from one Londoner's tongue to the next. Royal mistresses had been spotted on every street corner, royal bastards from every palace window.

Royalty had been reclaimed, and London reveled in the pageantry and color and, overall, the excitement of the restored court at Whitehall.

Jane hurried home, not wanting to be distracted into the celebrations. She was walking up Ludgate, concentrating on what she would say to Weyland, when a small white hand reached out from a darkened doorway and snatched at her.

Jane recoiled, but the hand had a good hold, and it pulled her close into the darkness of the doorway's overhang.

"Jane," said a voice, and Jane went rigid with recognition.

Catling stood there, still in the form of a small girl, but with vast knowledge and power burning from her eyes.

"Jane," said the girl again, as Jane stared at her. "Jane—you want to reveal me to Noah, don't you?"

"Why not?" Jane managed, feeling the infinite threat emanating from Catling. "She has a right to know."

"Tell her, and I will destroy your future."

If Jane had been frightened when she had realized Charles's deception, then it was nothing to what she felt now. *This* creature standing before her could create more havoc than five wrathful Asterions. Terrified, Jane nonetheless managed a sneer. "*What* future?"

"If you manage any hope in this life, then I will *destroy* it, Jane. *Do not tell Noah who I am!*"

"She will find out soon enough."

"She doesn't want to see past the hope of her daughter."

"You fool!" Jane said. "She will inevitably discover your true nature, and then what? She will turn against you with everything she is."

"She will see the necessity of what I have done soon enough. She is a sensible woman."

Jane stared at Catling, wondering how the creature could not see what would inevitably happen. "She is a mother," Jane said softly. "That is her nature, before anything else. All she wanted was her daughter to love. Would that have been too much trouble for you to arrange?"

And with that, Jane pulled her arm from Catling's grasp, and stepped back into Ludgate.

JANE ARRIVED BACK AT IDOL LANE WELL INTO THE evening, having dragged her feet after her encounter with Catling as she considered what to do.

Elizabeth and Frances had long returned, and were upstairs in their bedroom, trying to cleanse it of the scent of years of sexual slavery and transform it into something more habitable. Catling and the imps were also home, playing quietly in the parlor with felt balls and linen skittles stuffed with rags.

Weyland sat at the kitchen table, reading the description of the king's triumphant entrance into London from a just-printed broadsheet, a small smile on his face.

Noah was at the hearth, where she had been cooking meat and pastry for their evening meal. Now she stood, staring at Jane, her hands wiping themselves slowly on her apron.

Weyland looked, then raised one expressive eyebrow in question.

"I thought Brutus-reborn would kill me," said Jane, brushing past Noah and taking her own apron from a hook to one side of the hearth.

"Brutus-reborn is not a tolerant man, it seems," Weyland said, looking at Noah as he spoke.

She averted her eyes.

"But," said Weyland, his eyes now back on Jane, who had elbowed Noah away from the cooking, "most apparently your fears were mistaken."

"I gave the king your messages," said Jane, frowning as she poked at Noah's attempt at savory meat encased in sweet pastry.

"And?" said Weyland.

"He will not go near the bands, nor step foot in the forests," said Jane. "And he sends his thanks to you for your hearty congratulations on his restoration."

"He fears for Noah," said Weyland. "He still loves her."

"Aye to both," said Jane.

Weyland gave a soft laugh, apparently emanating from genuine humor rather than forced bravado. "The fool. He has no idea . . ."

At that he finally managed to catch Noah's gaze, and Jane was astounded to see that Noah blushed before hurriedly looking away. *Gods!* What had happened here while she was gone?

"And how *is* Charles?" said Weyland. "Of what manner of man is he in this life?"

Jane paused in her examination of the meat pastry. "He is more powerful than you believe," she said. "When I knew it, I feared more for my life than at any other time, or in any other life."

"Even more than when *I* have threatened you?" Weyland said.

"Aye," Jane said quietly. "I could not believe . . ."

"Believe *what?*" Weyland said.

"How powerful he is. How he has grown," Jane finished.

Weyland leaned back, watching her speculatively. She *had* been afraid, he could smell it about her. But now . . . He frowned, puzzled. Now he sensed an excitement about her that he hadn't expected.

"*Was* Brutus glad to see you?" he asked.

She gave a short laugh. "He drew his sword, and waved it at me."

Weyland roared with laughter. "Then he has not changed so much as you imply, my dear. Come now, has he sent any messages for his sweet Noah?"

Jane glanced at Noah, who was watching her with bright, intense eyes.

"No," Jane said.

Weyland shrugged a little. "Well then, now that you've returned, perhaps you can fix whatever it is Noah has done to that pastry. A goddess's skill, most apparently, does not rest in the culinary arts."

AT WHITEHALL, LOUIS HAD SOUGHT PRIVACY WITHIN A small antechamber to the king's public audience chamber. No one was here now—all had gone to the great feasting hall. No doubt Charles and Catharine were there, as well Marguerite and Kate, and, likely, James.

Louis sat on a bench seat thrust against the rear wall of the chamber. It was a plain chamber, even with its decorations of carved wooden panels of a far earlier period, dark and somber, and it suited Louis's mood.

Seeing Jane—Genvissa—had brought back memories. Too many memories, and too many of them bad.

There came a step at the door, and Louis lifted his head, more than half expecting Charles.

But it was a Sidlesaghe. Louis had seen them on only a very few occasions, first when, as William, he had brought Caela's body to Ecub at St. Margaret the Martyr's Priory, and then once or twice during this life, when Long Tom had appeared when Charles led the Circle, and at Coel's crowning atop The Naked.

This was not Long Tom, but clearly one of his kind. "Louis de Silva?" he said.

"Yes?" said Louis.

"You are required to attend a Council of England, to be held atop The Naked, on the night after next. Attend."

He held out one of his extraordinarily long arms, and Louis saw that in his hand he held a rolled-up parchment that was tied—not with ribbon or cord—but with what appeared to be woven green light.

"The king bids me attend," Louis said, unable to keep a tinge of bitterness out of his voice.

"The Stag God must rise," said the Sidlesaghe. "You must be there."

Louis stared at the parchment, then abruptly reached out and took it.

"You *must* be there," the Sidlesaghe said again, his words now underscored with command, and Louis nodded curtly.

"I shall be there. Do not fret. I will do this last one thing for Charles and for Noah, and then let me be in peace, I beg you."

The Sidlesaghe's mouth twitched, as if he wanted to smile, and then, as Louis wished, he was gone, and Louis was left to his self-absorbed solitariness.

JAMES, DUKE OF YORK, BROTHER TO KING CHARLES and once–heir apparent to the powers and mysteries of the Gormagog of Llangarlia, rested in his bed in his luxurious bedchamber, one hand lying comfortably on the breast of Anne Hyde, the daughter of Sir Edward Hyde.

He didn't love Anne, but he respected her, and liked her immensely (she had more wit than most of the court women he met) and, most importantly to James, Anne had no connection at all with Games, Minotaurs, or dead and dying or newly risen gods, and thus had never acquired the (to James) enormously bad habit of constantly referring to past lives to justify what she did in this one.

For her part, Anne was desperately in love with James, and James had to admit the slightest degree of guilt in taking her to his bed. She was of the nobility; she was of high education and wit; and here she was, destroying all hope she could have for a virtuous life and a subsequent good marriage.

She looked at him and smiled shyly—this was their first time at bedding, and Anne had been a virgin.

"I am sorry if I hurt you," James said, kissing her softly on the bridge of her nose.

"No," she said. "You did not—"

She stopped, then suddenly tensed in James's arms before giving a small half-shriek of total dismay.

Then she was sliding under the covers, pulling them to her chin, and staring wildly at James's side of the bed.

James rolled over, sure that they'd been discovered by Anne's father.

Well, he thought, Hyde was a mere earl, while James was a prince and a duke. If nothing else, he should manage to pull rank fairly easily on the aggrieved father.

But the creature that stood there was not to be outranked at all—and most certainly not by James.

James took one look at the Sidlesaghe, and cursed. *Jesus Christ! How would he explain this to Anne?*

"Greetings, Lady Anne," said the Sidlesaghe, bowing slightly as he saw Anne's eyes peeking at him from over the top of the coverlet.

Then the Sidlesaghe turned his attention to James. "Greetings, Loth."

"'Loth'?" said Anne. "James, who *is* this?"

"What do you here?" James said, sitting up in bed.

The Sidlesaghe extended a hand, holding a rolled-up parchment tied with emerald light. "Your are hereby invited, Loth, to a Council of England to be held atop The Naked on the night after next. Be there."

"What?"

The Sidlesaghe patiently extended the invitation once more.

"I have nothing to do with . . . Sidlesaghe, I am not among those who now battle this particular Game. I have chosen Christ over my past allegiances—"

Anne was now regarding James with huge eyes.

"—and renounce all former rights and privileges that I had. I want nothing to do with—"

"*Be* there," said the Sidlesaghe.

"I—"

"You still have the power. You *must* be there."

James sighed, and rubbed at his eyes. *God. Would he never escape this?*

"No," said the Sidlesaghe, softly. "Not until the Troy Game is played to a conclusion."

Highly reluctantly, James reached out a hand and took the parchment.

"How do I find my way to this . . . 'Naked'?" Despite himself, James felt the smallest twinge of curiosity.

More of Anne's face emerged from the coverlet. "May I come?" she said. All fear had vanished from her face, and now she looked more curious than anything else.

"No!" James cried.

"You're a faerie creature," Anne said to the Sidlesaghe.

He smiled, and inclined his head slightly.

"And Charles's court is going to convene at this . . . 'Naked'?" she said.

"Anne . . ." James began.

"England's Faerie Court, aye," said the Sidlesaghe.

"That's enough!" James yelled.

"You may come, madam, if you wish," said the Sidlesaghe. "The invitation shall include you as well."

Anne sat up, forgetting in her excitement that her breasts were totally naked.

"For God's sake!" James muttered, hauling the coverlet up to her shoulders.

"But," the Sidlesaghe continued, his voice now rigid with warning, "you shall tell no one of this invitation. *No one.*"

She nodded. "I will tell no one."

James groaned.

"She shall make you a fine wife," said the Sidlesaghe.

"I—" James said, then stopped, knowing that any denial spoken now would devastate Anne. He'd only wanted to bed her, not wed her . . . and most definitely had not wanted to get her caught up in the machinations of the Troy Game.

"I am so tired," James finally said, meaning that he was not physically tired, but that he was tired of everything he had been battling for three thousand years.

"Then I shall share your weariness," said Anne, one of her hands on his upper arm, and she very gently kissed his cheek. Anne may have understood very little of the hidden meanings and depths behind this strange conversation, but she felt as if she suddenly knew James a great deal better.

"Be there," said the Sidlesaghe. "Do it for all that once you were, and can yet be."

Then he was gone, and James was left sitting in bed, Anne Hyde at his side, staring at the enchanted invitation in his hand.

"WHAT CAN YOU TELL ME?" NOAH SAID VERY SOFTLY, lying on her pallet beside Jane.

Jane, who was obviously awake, did not immediately reply.

"Jane . . ."

"Charles was not quite all I had expected."

"Ah."

"'Ah'? You *knew?*"

"Yes."

"Why did you not tell—"

"Would you have said, if our positions had been reversed?"

To that, Jane said nothing for some time. She lay there, seething that she'd been left to think that Brutus-reborn was Charles, when all the time he'd been Louis. Oh, intellectually she knew the reasons why she hadn't been told. But, emotionally, Jane could not help the hurt at knowing she'd been deliberately left unknowing.

"And you?" Jane finally said. "How did you spend your day, Mistress Noah? It seemed quite the domestic scene I came home to this evening."

"We talked."

"Oh, aye. But of what?"

Noah hesitated. "Of what he wants."

"Aye? And that is?"

"Me," said Noah softly.

At the softness in Noah's voice, Jane rolled over and looked at Noah. "And this surprises you?"

"No. You were right. He wants me to become the Mistress of the Labyrinth so that he and I can together control the Troy Game."

"Well," said Jane. "As for learning the craft of Mistress of the Labyrinth, then I shall see about that. I—"

At that moment both women jumped nervously. A tall figure had appeared from nowhere at the foot of their pallets.

"I come bearing an invitation," said the Sidlesaghe.

CHAPTER FOUR

THE NAKED

The Realm of the Faerie

AT THE STROKE OF MIDNIGHT, AS INSTRUCTED BY his invitation, Louis de Silva rose from the chair where he'd been waiting, and opened the door of his bedchamber. By rights, there should have stretched a long, nondescript corridor beyond that door. But now Louis saw a wide and long meadow that stretched toward The Naked.

Louis stared into the Faerie. He would have stood there indefinitely, save that a Sidlesaghe materialized at his side, and extended his hand into the faerie meadow in obvious invitation.

"Come forward, Louis de Silva, for you are greatly wanted."

Louis slid a cynical sideways glance at the Sidlesaghe, then walked forward into the faerie meadow leading to The Naked. Louis was surprised at how fast they approached The Naked. One moment it seemed as if they were miles from it; the next, they were leaning into its gentle slope.

"Will Noah be here?" Louis asked.

"Aye," said the Sidlesaghe, "unless by misfortune the Bull stops her. But we think not. We think that the Bull will sleep well through this night. He knows nothing of faerie things."

As do I know nothing, thought Louis, *and yet still I am here*. His nerves increased. Noah—*Eaving*—would be here tonight. How could he bear it, seeing her go to Charles?

"You should have loved her earlier," said the Sidlesaghe, "and then you would not now feel so dejected."

Irritated at the Sidlesaghe's too-easy reading of his most intimate thoughts, Louis merely grunted. He could see many other creatures approaching, or already climbing The Naked, some escorted by Sidlesaghes, others singly or in small groups. When Louis and his Sidlesaghe attained the summit, it was to discover almost the entire Faerie folk already there.

The Sidlesaghe touched his elbow gently. "Now, Louis de Silva, do follow me, and greet your host." ·

They walked forward through the throng. The summit of The Naked was peopled here and there with individuals and groups of the strangest folk Louis had ever encountered: Sidlesaghes in great numbers; water-sprites; women who looked of human origin, but who exuded such power Louis could hardly dare to allow his eyes to rest for too long on any one of them; various creatures of forest and moor and mountain—foxes, badgers, bears, wolves, moles, elk, hares, aurochs, creatures of both this world and lost worlds; the giants, Gog and Magog, standing and laughing with a group of ethereal creatures the Sidlesaghe murmured to him were snow ghosts; and strange lumpen gray men called movles that the Sidlesaghe told Louis were the souls of the very mountains themselves.

"And these exist beside us in the ordinary world?" asked Louis, feeling completely out-of-place. *Gods, he had so much to learn about this land!*

"Aye," said the Sidlesaghe. "But who has eyes to see, these days?"

Louis caught sight of Eaving's Sisters then, standing a few paces away, and they smiled at him, and curtsied as one, which he hadn't expected. Marguerite came over, and kissed him softly on the mouth. "I am glad you came, Louis," she said. "The night would have been lost without you."

Then, before Louis could reply, she returned to Catharine's and Kate's side.

The Sidlesaghe smiled at them, and motioned Louis to keep walking forward.

"Who are the women?" said Louis, nodding to one of women who exuded such strange power. She was a small, dark fey creature, watching Louis and his companion Sidlesaghe with much curiosity.

The Sidlesaghe bowed slightly in the woman's direction, and she inclined her head and smiled. "She is Mag, of whom you must have some passing acquaintance."

Louis jerked to a halt, staring at her. "Mag? But—"

"All the great mother-goddesses depart from their ordinary life, if goddess life can ever be so called, and come here, to dream and laugh," said the Sidlesaghe.

Louis shook his head slightly. Again he thought, *How could all this have been, and continue to be, and I not ever realize?*

He was still shaking his head when he saw James standing to one side, Anne Hyde standing with him. *Anne?* Louis thought bemusedly. James looked as stunned as Louis felt; Anne merely looked fascinated. She was also so excited that she had her hands clasped tightly before her like a small girl: when she saw Louis she grinned and actually jiggled up and down on her feet for a moment.

Dear gods, thought Louis, his sense of unreality deepening. *Who else shall I see here?*

"The Lord of the Faerie," murmured the Sidlesaghe at his side, and Louis tore his eyes away from James and Anne and looked forward.

At the eastern end of the summit stood a throne, and before it, had been scattered a great circle of leaves. In the center of this circle of leaves stood a man, dressed simply in leather breeches but wearing a crown of twisted twigs and red berries.

"Go," whispered the Sidlesaghe, and Louis stepped forward, his eyes locked on the Lord of the Faerie's face.

Coel. Louis could hardly believe the power and dignity—as well as a deep sense of peace and tranquillity—that radiated out from the Lord of the Faerie. Louis walked forward, hardly daring to breathe, and bowed as he stopped before the Lord of the Faerie.

The Lord of the Faerie stepped forward and took Louis into a tight embrace. "I thank every god and faerie creature that exists and has ever existed that you have come tonight," he said into Louis's ear, his arms hugging the man even closer to him. "I know the difficulty this has caused you."

Some of Louis's discomfort eased, and he returned Coel's embrace tightly. "Know that I wish you well," Louis said.

The Lord of the Faerie laughed, and leaned back, his hands now holding Louis's shoulders. "I *am* glad you came," he said. "I could not have done without you."

Louis smiled—a little wanly—and would have spoken, but then the Lord of the Faerie's eyes focused on someone over Louis's shoulder.

"And here she is," the Lord of the Faerie whispered. "How I shall love her, I think, my Faerie Queen."

His hands dropped away from Louis, and Louis turned about.

And went still.

Noah—*Eaving*, for she came in her goddess form—and Jane walked toward them, still at some distance, but Louis had eyes only for Eaving.

He had never seen a woman so stunningly beautiful, nor seen a woman exude such immense power, as did Eaving. She wore the face and figure of Noah—the long glossy brunette hair, the ivory skin, the slender limbs and body—but was incalculably *something else* as well.

In part this was due to her faerie raiment, but in large measure her goddess power shone forth from her eyes. In all her lives, as Cornelia, as Caela, and as Noah, Louis had known her to have the loveliest deep-blue eyes he'd ever seen on a woman.

Now they were a sage-green, shot through with blue and slivers of gold.

Eaving came slowly, for she stopped to greet various members of the Faerie, as well as guests, as she walked. Mag she embraced with evident delight; with James she placed a soft hand against his cheek, gracing him with a quiet word or two; she introduced herself to a still-excited Anne Hyde with a kiss to either cheek; Eaving's Sisters she hugged tightly; the water-sprites were greeted with a laugh and a wave of the hand; and Gog and Magog with an elegant incline of her head and a smile.

All the time Jane trailed a few steps behind, turning her face away from Mag, and from Eaving's Sisters.

Eventually, Eaving stopped a pace or two away from where Louis and the Lord of the Faerie stood. She looked first to Coel, and then, slowly, to Louis.

She inclined her head, and smiled, and said, "Greetings, Brutus. How do you?"

He blinked, disorientated by her naming him as Brutus, and then he looked down and, rather than wearing the silvered doublet and breeches he'd set out in, Louis saw that he was indeed dressed as Brutus in the white linen waistcloth and the strapped boots.

All the better clothed to hand over my power, he thought; and then Eaving stepped past him and fell into the Lord of the Faerie's arms.

chapter five

The Naked

The Realm of the Faerie

*J*ANE FOLLOWED EAVING ACROSS THE SUMMIT OF
The Naked, as astounded as Louis had been.

How had she never known this existed? How could she have
been so blind?

No wonder they picked Cornelia, she thought.

Frankly she was stupefied to find herself here at all. She thought she would
have been close to the last person invited to this Faerie assembly (well,
second-to-last; Jane thought that Weyland might actually be slightly more reviled than she). But then, had she been invited here only to be judged? To be
condemned and belittled?

Eaving stopped here and there to greet members of the Faerie with obvious pleasure. Jane followed, her movements stiff, her eyes averted. When Eaving stopped to greet Mag, Jane could barely breathe. Surely she would be
struck down now?

But nothing happened, Eaving moved off, and Jane followed, burning with
humiliation as she felt Mag's eyes on her. Jane could hear the whispers, feel
the fingers pointed at her back, and shivered under the weight of so many
stares of cold hatred.

In an effort to distract herself, and to concentrate on something *other* than
how much people loved Eaving and loathed herself, Jane looked forward to
where Louis stood with the Lord of the Faerie. Jane's heart beat a little faster
when she saw Coel, for he seemed to her to be her only friend, and her only
hope of refuge in this nightmarish assembly.

Louis looked as out-of-place as she felt herself, dressed in his court finery,
and with that same slightly disorientated cast to his eyes that Jane was sure
she must also exhibit. She blinked, and in that moment Louis's appearance

rippled and altered. Now he stood in the same place, still staring at Eaving, but dressed as Jane had first seen him so long ago, when he had been Brutus and she Genvissa.

He hadn't taken Brutus' form: he remained as Louis, taller and leaner than Brutus had ever been, but he was now dressed as a Trojan prince.

Save for the golden bands of Troy. His limbs were naked.

Eaving came to the central space, spoke briefly to Louis, and then stepped up to the Lord of the Faerie, and was enveloped in his tight embrace.

Then, as Eaving stood back, the Lord of the Faerie looked at Jane, smiled, and held out a hand. "Jane," he said.

She hesitated, and his hand waggled a little impatiently.

Tense, Jane stepped forward—and received as tight an embrace as Eaving had.

"When will you start to believe," the Lord of the Faerie whispered into her ear, "that I have no intention of murdering you?"

"If not you, then most of the gathered throng here would be happy to wield the knife," she said.

He placed his palm against her cheek, very briefly. "I have welcomed you here," he said, "thus there shall be no murdering. Although if I were you, I would stay out of Mag's way."

Then he motioned Jane and Louis to one side and, taking Eaving's hand so that she stood at his side in the center of the circle of leaves, addressed those atop The Naked.

The creatures gathered were now congregated into one mass a little distant from where the Lord of the Faerie and Eaving stood in their circle of leaves.

"Behold!" the Lord of the Faerie cried. "The Faerie Court convenes!"

The assemblage roared, and Jane jumped.

"I bid you welcome, one and all," the Lord of the Faerie continued, "for you are all beloved to this land." The Lord of the Faerie paused, and Jane swore that his stature literally grew an inch or two as he studied the throng before him.

"We convene tonight for one most magical reason—to witness the anointing of he who is to rise as the Stag God."

Jane saw Louis frown, then look away, as if irritated.

"A man most ordinary, and yet extraordinary," said Eaving.

At this point Eaving gazed at the Lord of the Faerie with such emotion that Jane was not surprised to see Louis's expression turn angry. She felt a moment's sympathy for him; what the Lord of the Faerie and Eaving did here was cruel, to say the least, as they flaunted their love and power before Louis.

"It matters only," Eaving said, turning away from the Lord of the Faerie and dropping his hand, "that he accept the responsibility for the Ringwalk, the track of the stag through the forests, and accept the challenge that his rising shall encompass. Brutus, once William, reborn again as Louis de Silva, will you accept the responsibility of the Ringwalk, and the challenge of your rising?"

Jane looked to Louis, and knew then that she was truly alone in the world. Everyone else moved ever forward into greater power, and into a greater understanding with, and connection to, the Faerie.

Only she, of all, slid ever backward toward irrelevance and dismissal.

HE THOUGHT IT WAS A CRUEL JEST, THAT SOMEHOW this was his punishment for all the hurt he had done to Cornelia and Caela. He thought that this was the true purpose of the Faerie Court, to humiliate and torment him, and that at any moment the expression on Eaving's face would turn from loving joy to terrifying contempt.

Brutus, once William, reborn again as Louis de Silva, will you accept the responsibility of the Ringwalk, and the challenge of your rising?

Louis staggered a little, unable to comprehend that Eaving could have said that as anything but a contempt-ridden jest. He stared at her wildly, then looked about the cathedral, wondering if he dared to run, and if the throng would part for him if he did.

If they parted, would they laugh as he ran past? Pepper him with malicious jests?

How could Eaving and the Lord of the Faerie think that he would willingly hand over his powers as Kingman to the Lord of the Faerie after *this* particular piece of spite?

"Louis," Eaving said, very soft. She had walked close to him now, and the expression on her face had changed, as Louis was sure it would, but not into terrifying contempt—rather, into an even greater depth of compassion.

"How could you not have known?" she said, so close to him now that her breath played over his face. She leaned against him, her hand warm on his chest. "I tried to tell you so often, but you would never listen."

How could you not have known? whispered the assembled throng of faerie creatures. *How could you not have known?*

Louis still could not speak, nor raise his hands to Eaving. He looked beyond her to where the Lord of the Faerie stood, a empathetic expression on his own face.

"How could you not have known?" the Lord of the Faerie whispered.

"I—" Louis began, drifting to a close, not knowing what to say. His mind still could not grasp what had happened, or that Eaving now leaned so close against him.

"Will you run the forests?" she murmured. "Will you trace the Ringwalk?"

Will you run the forests? whispered the throng. *Will you trace the Ringwalk?*

"Will you be the land?" said the Lord of the Faerie, now also very close.

Will you be the land? echoed the throng.

"Come dance with us," murmured Eaving.

Dance with us.

"Come dance with me, into eternity."

Come dance with us, into eternity.

"Walk this land with me, run its forests, be my Kingman, be my stag. Complete the Troy Game with me, and dance with me . . . dance with me . . . dance with me . . ."

Dance with her, be her lover, dance . . . dance . . . dance . . .

Louis realized he was trembling, so badly he wondered he did not fall to his knees.

"I cannot . . ." he stumbled.

Eaving withdrew enough so that her magical eyes could look deep into his. "Is it that you do not want to, or that you do not think yourself able?"

"How can I? Gods, I am not what you *want*."

"You are everything that this land needs."

He wanted to believe her. He wanted to shout, *Yes!* And yet . . . why did she not speak words of love? Why did she not promise herself to him? Why was *he* not everything that *she* wanted?

Now she was kissing his brow, his cheek, his ear, and Louis wondered why she would not look at him.

"The Lord of the Faerie shall show you the way of the Ringwalk," said Eaving, her fingertips trailing down his naked chest.

"Oh, aye," murmured the Lord of the Faerie, now standing almost as close to Louis as was Eaving. "And when you are risen, and the Stag God runs the Ringwalk, then shall you and Eaving be joined together in the Great Marriage, and so shall the land be whole once again."

The Great Marriage. Louis could remember Genvissa telling him of it when he'd been Brutus. When the goddess of the waters joined with the god of the forests in the Great Marriage, then, and then only, would the land be whole.

"Is that what you want?" Louis asked Eaving, and she leaned back, and her eyes glinted and sparkled.

"What else?" she said.

Louis relaxed. He had been shocked. His thoughts had tumbled in disarray. She loved him. She wanted him.

He took Eaving's face between his hands. "We will dance the final Dance of the Flowers," he said, "and then we will walk forward, together, into eternity."

"Yes," she whispered, and if there was a shadow in her eyes as she said that, then Louis merely thought it the reflection of the throng gathering close about them.

"We will all walk with you about the Ringwalk," whispered the Faerie folk now encircled about them. "Into eternity."

Eaving leaned back a very little again, and put a hand against his cheek. "Brutus," she said, "will you accept the responsibility? The challenge? Will you face the Ringwalk?"

Suddenly Louis felt the strangest sensation in his chest, and it took him a moment to realize it was joy.

"Yes," he said. "I do so accept."

He cradled Eaving in his arms, and kissed her as he once should have kissed her when they'd stood beneath the night sky at the Altar of the Philistines, so long ago, and felt that newfound joy in his heart deepen into a hope he had not realized, until now, that he'd abandoned many years before.

When she pulled back from him, he did not think it anything other than her desire to share her joy with the assembled Faerie folk.

CHAPTER SIX

THE NAKED

The Realm of the Faerie

*J*ANE LOOKED AS LOUIS DREW EAVING CLOSE, AND kissed her. She felt cold and empty. Useless. A nonentity in this congregation where everyone seemed to have a purpose but her.

What was I, she thought, *but a pawn in all of this? I can no longer delude myself that I began this, with Brutus as a willing, lustful confederate. We were all manipulated by something larger, and much darker. I was merely a piece, moved by some other, vaster purpose.*

"We have all been pawns, in our own way."

Jane turned her head. The Lord of the Faerie was standing by her side, his attention all on her rather than on Eaving and Louis.

"That is so easy for you to mouth," she said. "What have you gained from this but joy? I have slid the other way. I am tired, Coel. I don't want to play any longer. Let me go, I pray you."

The Lord of the Faerie's face crinkled a little, as if in puzzlement. He lifted a hand, and brushed it softly against her cheek.

"Strange words, indeed, for Genvissa. For Swanne."

"They are long dead," she said turning her head slightly away from his contact. "I hope they stay that way."

"But *you* still have a role to play," the Lord of the Faerie said.

Jane's face twisted. "Ah, yes. I must hand over my powers as Mistress of the Labyrinth, mustn't I? And how can I refuse, eh? There stands the delightful couple, god-reborn and god-apparent, and all I need to do to complete the happy union is to give Eaving what she needs to make herself and her lover the most powerful divinities in creation—gods *and* players of the Game."

"That was not what I meant."

Jane looked at him, hating it that all her bitterness and disappointment must be written plain across her face. "Really? Then what is my role? To bake the cake for the Great Marriage? To ensure that the floor is swept and the sideboard dusted? To—"

"Jane," he said, "still that harsh tongue of yours for just a moment." Taking her hand, he led her a little way from the throng. When they stopped, he pulled her close so that he could speak quietly in her ear.

"Do you remember," he said, "when you were Swanne and I Harold, how well we suited each other in those first years of our marriage?"

"*You* never suited *me*."

He laughed. "You were blind."

"What do you *want* from me?"

"Do what's best, Jane. Do what's best."

Her mouth tightened into a thin line. She knew what that meant. *Hand over your powers of Mistress of the Labyrinth*. If only he knew how little she would be needed even for that.

"Jane, I talk of that time when you come to meet me by the scaffold. Then you must do what's best."

"Why, Coel? What could you possibly want of me?"

His hands moved to her face, turning it so that she faced him squarely, and then the Lord of the Faerie lowered his mouth to hers, and kissed her gently.

"I will watch for you by the scaffold, Jane."

She pulled away from him. "Don't."

"Don't . . . what?"

"Don't toy with me, Coel. Don't torment me."

The skin about his eyes crinkled. "Do what's best, Jane. Not for you, but for the land. And . . ." The fingers of one hand trailed down a cheek, then traced about her jaw line. "And, do what's best for me and for you, and for the both of us."

She was confused. She didn't know what he meant. "Coel—"

He drew away from her, looking over her shoulder. "Ah. I must go."

He brushed past Jane, his fingers very briefly brushing against her hand, and walked to where Eaving and Louis stood a little distance away, where they had been watching the Lord of the Faerie and Jane.

Jane turned, hesitated, then followed him.

Louis, his arm about Eaving's waist, was talking to him.

"What do I do?" he said. "Gods, Charles—Oh dear gods, that is not what I should call you, is it?—my mind is still so numbed. I can't think . . ."

He broke off, and shook his head as if to express his bewilderment, but Jane could clearly see his happiness, and it made her feel worse. Once she had so wanted this man, wanted what she and he could achieve together. Now he loved, and was loved by, another, and planned his ambitions and his future about her.

The Lord of the Faerie put his hand on Louis's shoulder, and spoke in low tones to him, and as he did so, Eaving pulled herself gently from Louis's grasp, and came to Jane's side.

"We should go soon," she said, her strange, enchanted eyes soft. "We have risked our luck this far. I would not have Weyland come down from his lair and find us gone."

"*I* should go," Jane said. "*You* appear to have found your haven."

At that, Eaving's face turned aside very slightly. "None of us ever truly knows what our haven is," she said, very soft, "until we fall in through the door one bright day."

"Well, I, for one," said Jane, "am sick of—"

Before she could finish, she felt the unmistakable power of Ariadne touch her. The Naked dissolved abruptly about them, all the throng vanished, and she and Eaving were standing once more in Tower Fields.

CHAPTER SEVEN

TOWER FIELDS, LONDON

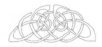

"WELL, WELL," SAID ARIADNE, "WASN'T THAT A pretty little scene, then?"

It was deep night, and cold, and so Ariadne had set herself a little fire amid a cleared space in the grass. She stood directly behind it, allowing the light of the flames to wash over her. Jane thought it made Ariadne look particularly malevolent, and realized this was a carefully staged scene.

So, Jane thought, *Ariadne has used her powers of Mistress of the Labyrinth and pulled us back again. Myself and Noah.*

Jane glanced at her, and saw with a little shock that she had indeed returned into Noah—although still she held herself with the pride and honor and power that she commanded as Eaving.

"You saw?" said Noah, showing no confusion at Ariadne's precipitous actions in pulling her to this spot once more.

Ariadne smiled a very little. "I see most things," she said. "Come, sit with me"—Ariadne sat herself gracefully on the ground as she said this, patting her hands to either side—"and partake of the wine and fruit I have brought to share."

Noah hesitated, then walked about the fire to sit on Ariadne's right, Jane seating herself on the witch's other side. Ariadne moved back slightly, so that Noah and Jane could the more easily see her face, and they hers. With her movement, Ariadne had changed the seating pattern so that the three woman and the fire formed a rough circle.

"So," said Ariadne, reaching out a hand and very briefly touching Noah's face. "You've finally managed to tell your Brutus about his—um . . . How shall I say this?—anticipated forestal divinity. He seemed shocked." She shrugged. "I would consider it worrying that it has taken him all this time to realize."

She cocked her head to one side, and smiled brilliantly. "But then, that isn't my problem, is it? My problem is you, Noah. Or Eaving. Whomsoever you happen to be at present. Everyone appears to expect you to become Mistress of the Labyrinth, but Jane appears unwilling to teach you."

Jane opened her mouth, but was forestalled from speaking when Ariadne held out a hand, palm-upward, commanding her to silence.

"Jane," Ariadne continued, "is also concerned about how I've managed to haul you here along with her, Noah. The power I use for this particular piece of magic is only supposed to touch trained—or women bred to be—Mistresses of the Labyrinth, after all. So, Jane is anxious to know why you're sharing this space with us. I'd like to hear your explanation for it, as well. If you don't mind."

Again, that cocked eyebrow.

"I have no explanation," said Noah.

The eyebrow went even higher. "Oh, come now, Noah. I really want to know why—"

"You are not surprised to see me here," said Noah, her voice and manner calm. "If there is a reason for my presence, then you already know it."

"Ah," said Ariadne softly, "you are no fool, are you?"

Instead of answering Noah's implied question, Ariadne turned her attention to Jane. "All seem to expect you to hand over your powers, Jane. Noah has wanted it for years. Brutus wants it. He'd like nothing better than to be able to complete the Troy Game with the great love of his life . . . ahem, *lives*. This strange enigmatic Lord of the Faerie also seems to expect it, if I read his words to you this evening rightly."

"If you can interpret his words, then I'd be glad to hear it," said Jane.

Ariadne ignored her. "I'm sure the Troy Game is falling over itself wanting Noah to learn her arts as Mistress of the Labyrinth."

At that Jane looked way. *So that was why Catling came to Idol Lane! Of course . . . She should have realized it earlier.*

"So, Jane," Ariadne continued, "the question is, shall you teach her?"

Jane now studied Ariadne, unable to read the witch's face. What did she want to hear?

"No," she said eventually.

"Good answer," Ariadne said, very soft. Her eyes switched back to Noah. "Jane shall not teach you, Noah. *I* shall. Jane *could* teach you, surely. But if *I* teach you, then I can turn you into the most powerful Mistress of the Labyrinth that has ever been. More powerful even than myself, if you can believe it." She laughed prettily. "After all, you shall combine both labyrinthine arts with those of Eaving and of the land, shan't you?"

Noah's face was such a confusing mix of emotions that Jane might have laughed if she hadn't been so angry. *Ariadne, to teach Noah? Why? Why?*

And why *was* it Ariadne could spirit Noah here in the first instance?

Jane looked back at Ariadne, and was not surprised to find her foremother watching her with an amused look.

"What is it about Noah, Ariadne? Why is she here? Why take such an interest in her? *What is in it for you?*"

Ariadne answered the last of Jane's questions first. "Revenge," she said. "Revenge is in it for me. I want to put Asterion away once and for all, and I want to see the Game flowering in all its glory and majesty. Noah is the one to do that."

"But surely—" Jane broke off, wondering how to put her question so that it didn't make her sound spiteful or vindictive.

"Why not one of my own blood, Jane? After all, it would take one of my own blood to be able to better my own skills, eh?"

Now Ariadne turned her eyes away from Jane and looked at Noah very, very carefully. "I have no intention of teaching anyone *but* my own blood, Jane," she said.

For a moment there was a silence, Ariadne and Noah staring at each other, Jane looking between the two of them.

"No," Noah whispered.

"Did you not realize, Jane," Ariadne said, her eyes not moving from Noah, "that Noah is as much my daughter-heir as you?"

"What?" Jane said. She felt as if her heart had stopped. *What?*

No, Noah said, whispering the word with her power.

She moved as if to rise, but Ariadne reached out and snapped her hand closed about one of Noah's wrists.

"If you're here with me tonight," said Ariadne, "if you have been a part of the Game since you were the whining little Mesopotamian princess, if it was *you* that Mag chose to hide within, and to be reborn within . . . then why was that? *What was that?* Because you just happened to be around? Because you just happened to be handy to the whims of gods?" Her head whipped about, and she stared at Jane. "And you, Jane. Why did you so instinctively hate her? Why work so assiduously to remove her? Why fear her so greatly?

"Why, why, why?" Ariadne said, her voice softening a fraction. "Why, why, why, for all of this . . . if not for the fact that *you,* Cornelia-Caela-Noah, are as much my daughter as is Genvissa-Swanne-Jane?"

CHAPTER EIGHT

TOWER FIELDS, LONDON
Noah Speaks

HY, WHY, WHY, FOR ALL OF THIS . . . IF NOT FOR the fact that you, Cornelia-Caela-Noah, are as much my daughter as is Genvissa-Swanne-Jane?

Oh, I loathed Ariadne then. I *reviled* her. And not so much for the import of those words, what they meant or would come to mean for my life, but because they had wiped out in one foul sentence all the joy of Louis's realization at the Faerie Court. All I had wanted to do was to return to my pallet in Weyland's kitchen and revisit every wonderful faerie moment of that court.

But no. This witch had to ruin it with her one, single devastating sentence.

"Ah," said Ariadne very softly, "you know it, don't you?"

"No," I said. "I know *nothing* of it!"

She let go my wrist and reached behind her, pulling forth a basket that I had not noticed. She took out a cloth, spreading it before her, then produced a small bowl of fruit and a flagon and several glasses. She filled the glasses, handing one to myself and one to Jane, took a healthy sip from her own, settled herself comfortably, then began a lovely little tale of love and betrayal that I found horrifying, not merely because of its content, but also because I had so recently heard it from Weyland's mouth.

"I became Asterion's lover when I was, oh, perhaps thirteen or fourteen," Ariadne began, taking another mouthful of her wine, "and just learning the skills of Mistress of the Labyrinth myself. He fascinated me, and I fancied myself in love with him." She paused, looking at Jane over the rim of her glass as she took a sip. "*You* loved him in your last life. You should sympathize."

"He bewitched me," Jane said. "That was not true love."

Ariadne shrugged, not put-out by Jane's answer. "Well, I found the feel and taste of that bull's mouth running over my body quite stimulating—"

I shuddered. *He was her half-brother!*

"—so . . . animalistic. Better than a man."

"Until you met Theseus," I said.

Ariadne looked at me sharply. "I am talking currently of Asterion, my dear, not Theseus. Pay attention. So, as I was saying, I found his attentions reasonably stimulating. And I was young, and perhaps a little foolish, and so when I was eighteen I allowed myself to fall pregnant to him."

"You sent the baby away," I whispered. "A month after she was born. You were ashamed of her."

"Yes. How did you know of that? Goddess intuition, perhaps? Or some memory from your—"

"No," I said. I put my hands over my ears. I did not want to listen. *I did not want to hear this!*

Yet still her words penetrated inside my skull.

"Yes, well, I did send her away. After all, I'd fornicated with my own brother, and, frankly, the attraction of that bull mouth was starting to pall by then. I still needed the patronage of my father King Minos . . . He would not abide such an abomination in his palace. So I sent the child to—"

No! No! No!

"—Mesopotama, a silly little place, but the king was prepared to take the girl in so she could be raised in his court and subsequently marry his son. He did not know of her fatherhood. All he knew was that she was the daughter of the Mistress of the Labyrinth of Knossos . . . and thus a powerful little minx to marry into his family."

No!

"For the love of all the gods in heaven, Noah. You were Mesopotamian, but you wore the fashions of the Minoan court. Mesopotama escaped the wrath of my Catastrophe. You were plucked out of obscurity by the man destined to go on and establish the Troy Game. Did you never think back and put all these pieces together? Did you never ask Brutus why he chose you so precipitously? Did he never say to you, 'I was god-struck, my dear, and simply had to have you?' Did you never wonder *why*, when it was so apparent he hated you, he kept you close? Did you not even *once* stop to think why you, this tiny bellyaching spoiled little brat, was indeed so god-blessed? Why you became so tightly embroiled in the Troy Game with nary a thought about it in your witless, *addled* little mind? Did you *never once* wonder why it had picked *you*?"

Her eyes were slightly bulging at this point, and I think Ariadne was aware of it, for she stopped, and patted at her cheeks with fingers cooled in her wine.

"You were blood," Ariadne continued, her voice and manner far more re-strained now. "You were chosen."

She looked now at Jane, at whom I could not myself even dare to look. "There was always more at work here than you and your ambition, Jane. There was the Game, as well, always the Game, as there is now."

I was trembling, unable to accept any of this.

No, there was only one thing I was unable—*unwilling*—to accept.

That I was descended of Ariadne and Asterion. That I was of their blood. Everything else was meaningless in my mind. That was all that mattered.

An hour ago I had thought my dreams almost complete.

Now I could see them lying shattered across the summit of The Naked.

What would Louis say when he knew? What vile words would he spit when he knew I was the daughter of . . . *No!* No, I could not even think of it!

Oh gods . . . I felt nauseous, and wondered if I would vomit my supper all over Ariadne's pleasant little picnic.

"Am I not a good-enough foremother for you?" said Ariadne, that damned eyebrow of hers raised again.

My hands were shaking. I clasped them tightly in my lap, and bent forward over them, unable to look at her any longer.

"And me?" said Jane. She sounded lost, and I spared a moment's sympathy from my own misery for her. She had thought herself Ariadne's daughter-heir. The one and only. The favored. And now she had discovered that Ariadne had kept a spare, set aside all this time.

And *what* a spare. *Cornelia-Caela-Noah.* I could have laughed if I hadn't been in so much pain.

"My dear," said Ariadne, and I felt her move, saw her shadow as she leaned over and patted Jane on the arm. "I did not plan this, as much as you may think it. I was truly ashamed of my daughter with Asterion, and was glad I'd sent her away. At best I thought that if I never had another child, then perhaps I might recall her . . . if only I could overcome my revulsion."

Revulsion. Oh, my line was *repulsive.*   •

"When Theseus arrived at Knossos," Ariadne continued, "I fell instantly, stunningly, in love with him. I threw myself at him, begged him to take me, conceived a new daughter the instant he lay with me. I was thrilled. *Now* I had a daughter-heir I could be proud of. Of course, Theseus proved a little disap-pointing, but I cleared that problem up nicely."

Cleared that problem up nicely. Murdered tens of thousands, destroyed lives, lands, cities, cultures. Problem solved.

"When I took my new daughter to Llangarlia," Ariadne continued, "when I planned to resurrect the Game in that land, I still had no thought for my first daughter, and whatever heirs *she* may have borne. I had my daughter. I had my ambition. Frankly, I don't think I actually thought of my first daughter again during my lifetime."

"What was her name?" I ground out. I could not bear to hear this child being dismissed so callously. Gods, Ariadne had borne a daughter—had she never once loved her? Cared for her?

Weyland had loved her, I was sure of it. I truly don't think Weyland could have fabricated that sentiment he showed me when he talked of her.

I was looking at Ariadne now, and she gazed at me with an air of bewilderment.

"I never gave her one. *Why?* She was just a daughter I meant to abandon—" *Abandon!*

"—I had no thought to *name* her."

"Does . . ." I began, then stopped to gather the courage needed to ask this question. "Does Weyland know who I am? Does he know that I am his blood?"

A line appeared between Ariadne's perfectly drawn, arched brows. "Weyland?" she said. "No, I don't suppose so. Why should he?"

I didn't know. Why had Weyland told me of his daughter if he hadn't known?

"Anyway," Ariadne said, returning to Jane and her question. "Your foremother, my second daughter, was always intended to be my true heir. Her line was my true line of power—or so I intended. I didn't ever think of my first daughter and what her line might be doing."

"But you spared Mesopotama from the Catastrophe," I said. *When would this witch stop lying?* "You *must* have thought of her."

Ariadne looked a little uncomfortable. Clearly she did not like being caught amid her web of lies.

"I might have decided to spare her and her line, just in case," she said finally. "But it was always my second daughter whom I meant to bear my line and my ambition and my power. The Game thought differently."

"And so now you are going to teach Noah the ways of the Labyrinth," said Jane. "Maternity regained. How pleasant for you."

Ariadne studied Jane for a long moment, and I was struck by how calm, how deeply mysterious, her black eyes now looked.

"Yes," she said. "I am. I was mistaken. It was my first daughter who truly carried the line of power, the ultimate power. Oh, you and your foremothers were powerful, Jane. But none of you would ever have been as powerful as Noah is destined to become."

She looked at me now, and, terrifyingly, I could see that the words she spoke now were complete truth. "Noah-Eaving will become the most powerful Mistress of the Labyrinth in history, more powerful than even myself. She will command all manner of magic. Her magic as Eaving. Her magic as the Mistress of the Labyrinth, counterdancer to the most powerful Kingman who has ever lived, Brutus, reborn Stag God."

She paused, and somehow I knew in that silence a storm was gathering that would tear apart not only my life, but all lives associated and entangled with mine.

"And through the blood of her forefather," Ariadne whispered—that whisper reaching throughout eternity and into all of my past lives and all of my future ones, "Noah will command the power of the darkcraft as the greatest Darkwitch that has ever lived."

I tried to shut out her voice, but I could not. I could not.

"I had to win my command of the darkcraft, Noah," Ariadne said. "But you have it inherent within you, if only you care to look. It is in your blood, as much as is the magic of the Mistress. That is why I will train you, and teach you all I know. You are the only one alive, the only one who has ever lived, who can put away Asterion once and for all. Who can trap him in the dark heart of the Labyrinth. He has grown too powerful for me, or for my line through my second daughter. You are the only hope left, Noah. Goddess, Mistress of the Labyrinth, and Darkwitch rising. You, and only you."

Chapter Nine

I T WAS VERY EARLY MORNING, AND MOST OF THE palace was still asleep. In the king's inner privy chambers, however, both the king and queen and their most private inner circle were awake, if exhausted.

Charles and Louis sat alone in the king's bedchamber to either side of an unlit hearth; Catharine, Marguerite, and Kate were in the outer chamber. Facing each other across the fireplace, the two men reclined in chairs covered with fabulously woven scarlet–and–lime-green silken brocades, each dressed only in linen breeches, their chests and arms and feet bare. Both held a beautifully cut glass goblet of wine.

Charles showed little sign of interest in his wine, his right arm hanging relaxed over the arm of the chair, dangling the glass from his fingertips so that it caught glints of light from the two candles burning from wall sconces. He was watching Louis, who looked, as if fascinated, into the empty grate, very carefully.

"How do you, Louis?" he said. "How has this past night altered you?"

Louis grunted softly. "Do you need to ask?" He sighed, and set his wine down on the floor. "Gods, Charles, I do not know how to answer that. Impossibly glad and relieved, that I am not forgotten, and still have a part to play in what comes. But, oh, what a part. What a role. Tell me . . ." He looked at Charles directly for the first time since they'd returned, and sat down. "Did Noah—Caela, as she was then—feel this way when she first discovered that she did not merely carry Mag in her womb, but *was* all that Mag had been, and more besides?"

"I do not know," said Charles. "I was unknowing when this happened to her. When I did remember, then what little time we spent together was not wasted in talking of such matters." His mouth twisted a little. "It was Asterion, in the guise of Silvius, who talked with her, and heard her fears and her uncertainties."

There was a moment's silence.

"I wish I could have spent longer with her last night," Louis said.

"You have your own journey to undertake," said Charles. "It will not involve her for the longest time. And Noah needs to learn the ways of the Mistress of the Labyrinth."

"Do you think Jane will teach her? I saw Jane only briefly, but what I *did* see of her, bespoke only bitterness."

Charles thought a moment, introspective. "She's changed. I think Jane no longer cares so much for power, nor for the Game. I think Noah will be taught the ways of the Labyrinth. Have no fears for that."

Louis shot Charles a cynical look, and Charles grinned. "Truly, Noah *will* learn," he said. "Trust me, and do not concern yourself with worry over it. For the moment, think only of yourself, and your journey."

Louis spread a hand out to his side, indicating his helplessness and confusion. "How, Charles? *How?* I still cannot believe that I was chosen all this time. How could this land choose *me?*"

"Indeed, I have spent these past hours wondering the same thing," said a new voice, and both Charles and Louis straightened in their chairs and looked to the door.

James stood there. He clicked the door closed behind him, and walked slowly to where the other two men sat.

"I have had the strangest night," he said. "I have dreamed the strangest things. My world has been turned upside down."

His face was largely expressionless, and neither Charles nor Louis could read him. Charles glanced at Louis, then looked back to James.

"Will you sit, brother," Charles said softly, "and talk with us?"

James hesitated, then took a chair that stood closer to the bed, as ornately furnished as those Charles and Louis sat in, and dragged it closer to the hearth, finally setting it down between the other two, and at some little distance from them—that distance telling Charles and Louis far more than James's face did.

James spent some time thinking, then he raised his face and looked at Charles. "I thought you were Brutus."

"The deception was intentional," said Charles, "although it was meant for Weyland rather than for you. The fact that you were also misled was of concern to me."

"You did not tell me!" James said. "Not of the Brutus deception, and . . . God, not that you were the Lord of the Faerie." Suddenly James seemed to realize who he was snapping at, and he made a move to apologize, but Charles waved him to silence.

"You should have known of both matters," Charles said. "But you, Loth-reborn, did not know. *That* told me volumes of you, James. You turned your back on me, on the land, and on the role you had to play. You turned to Christianity, and fought to *forget,* and you succeeded marvelously."

"Why the deception?" James said, ignoring what Charles had said, and ignoring for the moment the greater revelation that Charles was the Lord of the Faerie.

"Until last night," Louis said, "*I* would have told you that it was because I needed the time and space and anonymity to gather in the golden bands of Troy. But now . . ."

"The true reason, which Louis has only just realized," said Charles, "was that Louis would need the time and the space to assume the mantle of the Stag God. The bands could wait until he had attained his full powers. Weyland needs to think that Brutus sits useless and frustrated in this . . ." Charles waved a hand about. ". . . sumptuous, decaying palace. Thus the deception. Weyland will concentrate on me—I shall gnash my teeth in irritation at my immobility from time to time to keep him happy—while Louis . . ."

James turned dark eyes now burning with anger and resentment on Louis. "*You.* Brutus. To become the Stag God. I cannot believe it."

"And there we find ourselves in some considerable agreeance," Louis muttered.

"*I* find your distaste difficult to accept," said Charles to his brother. "You have run as hard as you can in this life from the responsibilities of your past lives. Why now sit there and moan, eh? What care *you?*"

"But *Brutus* . . . to run as Stag God over this wondrous land!"

"And again I ask," Charles said, his tone now dangerously low. "What care you?"

James slid down slightly in his chair, refusing now to look at either Charles or Louis, staring straight ahead at the fireplace. He did not answer.

"I want you to care," Charles said. "I *want* you to have some say in what happens to this land, to Louis, and to myself. That you *do* have some role is obvious, for the Sidlesaghes invited you to the Faerie Court.

"James, you may have run all your life from your responsibilities, but this land still needs you. *You are still wanted.* Louis will need you, James. *I* need you. The Stag God himself will need you. For the next few months, at the very least, your loyalty to your Christian god shall be severely tested."

"I will not—" James began.

"What?" said Charles. "Are you about to say that you will not aid us?" He leaned forward, staring intently at James. "Are you truly saying to me that the land means nothing to you? That its health and survival means nothing to you?"

He paused. "Or is it that you're jealous, eh? Didn't you want this for your-self once? To be the Stag God–reborn?"

James's eyes jerked back to his brother. "How did you—"

"Kate told me. She said that in your previous life as Saeweald you'd har-bored ambitions to be Eaving's lover, to be the Stag God–reborn. Is that true?"

James dropped his eyes to his hands resting in his lap.

"None of us have any say in what we grow into," said Charles softly. "Not me, not Louis, not even Noah. All of us have accepted what we have, or will, become. As must you."

"And what am *I* to become?" said James bitterly. "Nothing! I am but some-one to hand over power, not to attain it. When I was Loth, my father and Gen-vissa conspired to keep me from power, and all my successive lives have shown me is that everyone else conspires in the same manner, no matter how much they protest themselves, my friend!"

"Then take the dammed initiative and *seize* power, you cursed fool!" Charles all but shouted, making both James and Louis jump and stared at him.

Charles leaned even farther forward in his chair, fixing James with eyes narrowed and passionate. "I need you, the land needs you, and even Louis needs you. Curse you, James. Louis murdered *me* in a former life. Am I sitting here sulking? Nay. *Nay*. If ever you want to see the stag run the forests again, James, then you need to help. If not for the land, then for yourself, for you shall be aiding yourself most of all. I am sure that your crucified lord shall har-bor no grudges. He seems the forgiving sort. He'll take you back again, if you want. But help us, James. *Help us*." Charles gave a quirky smile. "I am certain you shall enjoy your duties."

Then he sat back in his chair, all his passion and energy spent. Charles sighed, shook his head very slightly, then seemed to remember he held an almost-full glass of wine in his hand (albeit some of the wine had spilled on the floor during his impassioned speech), and he raised the glass to his mouth, and drained it.

"Why was Anne Hyde at the Faerie Court?" he said. "Don't misunderstand me. I like and respect her and do not begrudge her presence at all . . . but why should the Sidlesaghes deliver *her* an invitation?"

"She was with me when the Sidlesaghe came," mumbled James, his atten-tion once again riveted on his hands.

"With *you*?" said Charles. "But it was my understanding the Sidlesaghes ex-tended their invitations very late at night, when all were abed."

James said nothing.

Charles glanced at Louis, then looked back at James. "She was in your bed?"

"And what of it?" James said, finally raising his eyes to Charles's.

Charles slammed his fist down on the arm of his chair, making both Louis and James jump yet again.

"Damn it!" Charles said. "Anne Hyde is the only daughter of my most respected adviser; she is a noblewoman, and a virtuous one. What in your god's name did you mean, taking her to your bed? Now she has lost all that is most precious to her—her virginity and her reputation—and ruined her chance for a great and noble marriage."

"I did not force her!" James said.

"You could have perhaps refrained from issuing the invitation in the first instance," Louis murmured.

"Oh, fine words from *you*," James snarled. "Did you ever ask Cornelia what she wished when you forced her to your bed?"

"Enough," Charles said tiredly. "James, you will marry Anne. I will accept no other course of action."

"*Marry* her? But—"

"You took her to your bed, and for all you know, she may be carrying your child," Charles said. "I want no hint of scandal about this court and about my name. Gods, I have only just returned after more than half my life spent in exile—the last thing I need is my younger rake of a brother deflowering half the court while I try to run the country with an even hand!"

James dropped his eyes, but said nothing.

Louis looked at him, then at Charles. "Charles," he said. "What do I do? Where do I go from here?"

Charles seemed as glad of the change of conversation as Louis was to make it. "I will take you to the forests," he said. "And show you the Ringwalk. From there, we step onto the Ringwalk—with James, I hope—and we do as fates dictate."

"But," said Louis, "Weyland will know that you—"

Charles shook his head. "I will walk the Ringwalk with you as the Lord of the Faerie, Louis. Not as Charles. Weyland will not know. He has no sympathy with this land. He has no idea of the Lord of the Faerie's presence and he will not recognize the Lord of the Faerie's movements, or know when he walks abroad. Dear gods, half the land's faerie creatures could crawl under Weyland's nose and he wouldn't know they were there . . . James—"

James dragged has eyes back to his brother's.

"James, did you *truly* have no idea that the Lord of the Faerie walked, or that I was he?"

James hesitated, then shook his head. "I may harbor a bitter soul, but in this I am happy for you, my friend. I can think of no safer harbor for either the Lord of the Faerie or this land than in your soul."

At that, Charles smiled. "James," he said, very softly. "If the Lord of the Faerie asks for your aid, will you give it?"

James took a long time in replying. "Yes," he said finally. "I will aid you, if you promise that I may walk away in peace at the end of it."

Charles gave a short laugh. "I doubt that any of us shall get any peace at the end of this, brother."

CHAPTER TEN

IDOL LANE, LONDON

NOAH SAT DOWN HEAVILY AT THE TABLE IN THE kitchen of Idol Lane, and Jane, after a moment's hesitation, sat down opposite her. There was no one else in the kitchen this early. Noah had her elbows resting on the table, her hands clasped tightly before her—to stop them trembling, Jane thought.

In truth, she felt like trembling as well. Ariadne had borne an earlier daughter.

And had told no one.

Until now.

And *what* a daughter. Cornelia's foremother. How . . . amusing.

Jane raised a hand to her forehead and rubbed at her brow, unconsciously tracing out the faint marks where the ridges and hollows of her sores had once festered. What fools they had all been, Ariadne as much as anyone. How could Ariadne have thought that a second daughter born to Theseus would have had more potential than a daughter born to the Minotaur himself! *Sweet gods . . .* Noah had the dark power already within her! *She*, at least, did not have to prostitute herself to Asterion in order to try and get some of the precious darkcraft for her own.

Or was this what Ariadne had planned all along? A wave of all-consuming hatred for her foremother washed over Jane. Ariadne had toyed with lives . . . had toyed with *Jane's* life, as with all her previous lives.

And had toyed with Noah's life. Jane looked over at Noah, who was still staring at the tabletop, her face wan and strained.

"Well," said Jane in an even, if tired, voice. "So now *you* are to carry the strain of Ariadne's ambitions. Congratulations."

Noah raised her eyes to Jane. "You think I wanted *this*?"

"I know you didn't, and, frankly, I am somewhat pleased to discover that I am not wearing *your* shoes."

Noah gave a very small smile. "I will have no hesitation in offering them to you."

Jane chuckled, and gave her head a little shake, as if to clear her thoughts. "What a night, eh?" Then her smile faded. "Will you tell your lover, then, what you are?"

Noah's face went white. "Louis! Oh, what will he say when he discovers this? And Charles? Merciful heavens . . . neither of them will trust me! The blood of the Minotaur runs in me . . ."

"And Weyland?" Jane said softly.

Noah's hand snaked across the table and grabbed Jane's. "Promise me you will not tell. Please. Not Weyland. Not *anyone*. I . . . I have to think this through first. I cannot face . . ."

You cannot face what Louis will do, Jane thought, *when he discovers you are more Darkwitch than Mistress of the Labyrinth, more Ariadne than Eaving.*

And what would Weyland do?

Jane shuddered. Suddenly she felt a tremendous relief that she, at least, had been shouldered off the path of power. If only she could just walk out that door, and lose herself amid the gathering London crowds.

Would Weyland let her go if he knew about Noah?

"So," said a voice, "Ariadne has spoken to you, finally. At least *someone* shall be teaching you the craft of the Labyrinth."

Both women turned. Catling had just entered the kitchen, her hair tousled from sleep, but her eyes bright and knowing. Jane could not help but give another small shudder.

Poor Noah, to think she believed this creature her daughter.

"You knew?" Noah said softly, staring at Catling.

"Mother—"

"Don't 'Mother' me! I have had *enough* of this pretense. How did you know?" Without waiting for an answer, Noah whipped her head back around to face Jane, and her hand, still about Jane's, suddenly tightened. "You told me that you knew precisely what it was I had birthed. Tell me now, I beg you, and hand me all my shocks in one day. By the gods, I cannot go through another day like this."

Jane glanced at Catling.

"Jane—" Catling began. "Do not—"

"Catling is not your daughter, Noah," Jane said, still looking at the little girl. "You have suspected it for a long time, I think. What daughter is *this*, eh? No, Catling is—"

"*Jane!*" Catling said again, her voice seething with warning.

"Do you think I care for your threats?" Janes said to the child. "What care I that your secrets are shared? Noah . . ." Her voice softened, and she looked back at Noah. "Catling is not your daughter, although she assumes the glamour of her. Catling is the Troy Game *incarnate*. The Troy Game made flesh. *Your* flesh, and that of Brutus-reborn's. Child of the Mistress and Kingman *it* has chosen. Here to meddle and manipulate. Here, apparently, to ensure that someone teaches you to be what *it* needs—a Mistress of the Labyrinth."

Jane had not thought that Noah's face could get any whiter, but somehow it managed the feat.

And then it suffused with red, and Jane saw Noah's eyes glitter.

Suddenly Noah stood up, sending her stool skittering against the far wall, stepped up to Catling, and dealt a sharp blow to the girl's cheek. "You hateful little—"

"Don't!" Jane said, rising herself, and grabbing at Noah's hand before she could strike Catling again. "You will do not any good, either to yourself or to this land!"

"What I have done has always been for the best," Catling said softly, her eyes on Noah. "Sometimes it is not easy to see, but—"

"I thought you were my daughter!" Noah said; and very slowly, agonizingly, sank to her knees. "*I thought you were my daughter!*"

Jane knelt down and put her arms about Noah's shoulders. After all the shocks Noah had received in the past hours, *this* coming on top of them was probably just too much to bear.

Noah was weeping now, and she looked up and stared at Catling. "Why weren't you honest with me?"

Catling shrugged. "It wasn't important . . . and I had to be careful, after all."

"Don't think that now I will do what you want, what you have manipulated me into—"

"You must," said Catling evenly. "For this land, for the good of—"

Noah spat out an obscenity, and Jane almost reeled back in shock. "I will *not* be your pawn!" Noah said.

"You will do what is necessary," Catling said. "You have no other choice."

"Does my daughter still live somewhere? Within you? Trapped elsewhere?"

Catling hesitated, then shook her head. "No. She died, truly, that night that Genvissa swept her from your body."

"You led me to believe . . . Mag led me to believe . . . All those visions of my daughter in the stone hall. I was to have her, eventually, once all had succeeded."

"You led *yourself* to believe," Catling said. "There was never any hope for your daughter. She was lost thousands of years ago, Noah. *Accept it.*"

"*I* led myself to believe? I will not 'accept' that. I saw my daughter—or was it you all this time?—in the stone hall long before I ever became pregnant with her. I have been tricked. *Tricked*. And this trickery was laid down almost three thousand years ago. You have been planning this deception for almost *three thousand years*. You just wanted to *use* me."

She lunged forward, and Jane thought then that Noah would have reached out and clawed Catling's eyes from her face if Jane had not physically held her back—and even that took every ounce of strength she could summon.

"I would have done everything for this land, had you but asked," Noah shouted. "*Everything!* Why wrap me about in so many lies and secrets? Why feel the need to force my hand? Why lead me to believe I could have my daughter back?" She paused, then almost screamed the next: "*Why lead me to believe I could ever* have *a daughter?* Was it Genvissa who murdered my daughter, you hateful, *hateful,* piece of creation, or was it *you* all along?"

"Shush!" Jane said. "Weyland will hear!"

"All I have wanted," said Catling, "all I have ever needed, was to make sure that all plays out as *I* want." Suddenly she seemed not the little girl at all, but something massive and ominous that filled the kitchen with its power. "What you wanted was totally unimportant."

"Get out," said Noah, very low, staring at Catling.

"Noah—" Jane began.

"Get out," Noah said. Her voice was low, but it was trembling with power, and with hatred. "*Get out!*"

Catling looked once at Jane, bleakly, as if promising retribution. Then she turned, and left.

CҺȺPͲЄR ЄLЄVЄN

IDOL LANE AND WHITEHALL PALACE, LONDON

OMETHING HAD HAPPENED DURING THE NIGHT, something powerful, but Weyland did not know what it was.

"What have you been doing, Noah?" he whispered as he walked silently from the Idyll. Had he revealed too much? Had he been too kind?

Had she taken advantage?

He paused at the door to Elizabeth and Frances's room, putting a hand to its wood.

They were still there. Asleep and unwitting.

Weyland dropped his hand, and looked to the head of the stairs.

He could hear voices from the kitchen. Noah's voice, raised. Jane's, soft and cajoling.

Weyland raised an eyebrow. *Jane—soft and cajoling?*

There was a movement behind him, and Weyland turned.

The two imps had appeared, both with worry lines creasing their faces.

"What is it?" Weyland said softly.

"Catling is gone," said one.

"Run away?" Weyland said. He felt a slight sense of relief. He hadn't liked the girl. Not at all. She wasn't the kind of daughter he thought Noah would ever have bred.

"No," said the other imp. "Gone, chased by angry words. Her mother sent her away."

Weyland gaped. *Dammit, this had happened while he slept?* "Why did Noah chase her daughter away?"

Both the imps shrugged, although they looked discomforted and awkward. *What did they know?*

Weyland stared at them a moment longer, then he turned and ran lightly (but, oh, so silently) down the stairs, crossed the parlor, and entered the kitchen.

Noah and Jane were sitting huddled together on the floor before the hearth. Both looked up as he entered, Jane looking shocked, Noah angry and distraught all in one. Her face was tear-streaked, her eyes swollen.

"What has happened here?" Weyland said.

"We live in *your* house," Jane said tartly. "You must expect tears now and again."

"Catling has gone," Weyland said, watching Noah as he said the words.

She turned her face away, her expression now wooden.

"Jane," Weyland said softly, not moving his eyes from Noah, "you may leave us now."

"Weyland—" she said.

"Leave us!"

Jane gave Noah's shoulders a squeeze with her hands, stood, sent Weyland a baleful stare, then brushed past him.

A moment later he heard her cross the parlor and start up the stairs.

Weyland walked over to where Noah sat on the floor, and held out a hand.

Very reluctantly, Noah slowly reached up her own hand, took his, and allowed Weyland to aid her to rise.

He pulled her close, noting well how she averted her face from his, and laid a hand lightly on her waist. *Gods, how she trembled!*

"Why?" Weyland said, very soft. "Why send Catling away? She is only a child, Noah. *Your* child . . ."

Noah said nothing, but, if possible, turned her face even more from his.

"What did she do?"

"I have had a poor night, Weyland. I would like to be alone."

"Tell me." His face was so close to her now that his breath brushed her ear as he spoke.

She tensed.

"Tell me," he whispered, pulling her yet closer. "What could be so bad that you sent away a little girl?"

She laughed shortly, the sound harsh and grating. "Perhaps I have more of Ariadne in me than you imagine, Weyland. Perhaps I, too, can send a daughter away."

"You are nothing like Ariadne. You loved your daughter."

"She did not wish to be loved."

"Noah . . ."

"I did not want her here, Weyland! Can you not understand that? How could I want a daughter trapped with me in this . . . in this . . ."

"But you brought her here willingly."

"I changed my mind."

"What happened during the night? Everything is . . . different."

She finally looked at him, her eyes overbright, her smile strained and hard. "Jane has finally agreed to teach me the ways and traps of the Labyrinth, Weyland. Aren't you pleased?"

Weyland narrowed his eyes. "Truly? How . . . courageous of her."

"How courageous of me to accept," Noah muttered. She was stiff and unyielding in his arms, but suddenly Weyland did not care. Finally she would become his Mistress, and Weyland was never so glad of anything in his life. They would dance together, control power together . . .

"I am glad," he murmured, and kissed her cheek, and then, softly, lingeringly, her neck. When she pulled away he did not try to hold her back.

"Perhaps," he said, "we should fetch those kingship bands today."

"No. Not yet." She was several paces away now, her face averted.

"No?" He moved over to her, taking her arm as she tried to evade him. "Noah, don't make me force you. Please."

She turned her face yet farther away, and said nothing.

"You know, surely, that the hold I have over you is as strong as ever it was when the imp rested inside you? That I can—"

At that she looked at him. "I don't believe you will do that again. I don't think you are capable."

A complete stillness fell between them.

Weyland could hardly bear it. He wanted to scream at her that, *Yes!* he was capable. That, *Yes!* he could send her shrieking to the floor any moment he chose. That, *Yes!* she was *his* creature as much as ever she had been.

And yet not a word left his mouth.

"Weyland," Noah said softly. "It would be better to leave the bands until I attained my full powers as Mistress of the Labyrinth, surely?"

He did not answer, nor did he shift his eyes from hers.

"Leave the bands for the time being, Weyland. Believe me, Charles will not try to take them."

He did believe her, although he fought against it. She was telling the truth. Charles would not try to take the bands.

"If I asked a price for leaving the bands be," he said, "would you agree?"

There was the faintest glimmer of panic in her face, then she had control over herself again. "What price?" she asked.

"A terrible one," he all but whispered, and he leaned close to her, his mouth brushing hers.

And then he let her go and walked away, leaving Noah staring after him.

* * *

ONCE JANE HAD PASSED THEM ON THE UPPER LAND-
ing, the imps scuttled down the stairs and out the front door.

What had gone wrong? Why had Catling left them?

Idol Lane was all but empty, but the street beyond was half-filled with
people hurrying early to market. The imps went this way and that, finally discovering Catling waiting for them under the overhang of a wool-sorting house.
She played with her red wool, and appeared unconcerned.

"Is it over?" one asked, breathless with worry. "Has—"

"Our pact still stands," she said. "I will do for you what I promised. Now,
hurry back to your master's house, but come when I ask."

Both imps grinned, immensely relieved. They turned, leaving Catling
standing under the overhang of the wool-sorting house.

WEYLAND CLIMBED THE STAIRS TO THE FIRST FLOOR
of his house in Idol Lane. His movements were slow, his expression
thoughtful.

Noah had sent Catling away? It still didn't make sense to him, nor, if he
were honest with himself, did Noah's sudden dramatic pronouncement that
Jane had decided to teach her the ways of the Labyrinth. It was what he
wanted—*gods, it was what he wanted*—but . . . There had been something else
in that room this morning. Something distracted about Noah, something desperate in her eyes. Whatever it was, it had to be serious if it had caused her to
send away her only child, and to beg of him that the bands be left until she had
attained her full powers as Mistress of the Labyrinth.

In a sense, Weyland could understand why she had asked that. Whatever
happened, Noah would not want him to get his hands on the bands. *That* request had been in character.

But to send her daughter away . . .

Her *daughter*?

If Weyland knew anything about Cornelia-Caela-Noah it was that she
loved children. He hadn't been surprised to find she'd had a child in this life,
although he had been surprised to find she'd drag her into his house . . .

Yet now the child was gone. Thrown out with vicious words.

That was not Noah at all.

Something was happening. Something he couldn't quite glean or scry out,
and that made him wary.

Weyland reached the top of the stairs and paused outside the door to Elizabeth and Frances's chamber. He lifted a hand and rested it against the wood,
fingers tapping slowly, thoughtfully.

Then he opened the door and stepped inside. Both girls were sitting on the bed, staring at him with wide eyes.

"Pack whatever you need," Weyland said. "I have no need of you here."

"We can leave?" Frances said. "Return to Essex?"

"That was not what I said. Look lively now, don't sit there. *Pack!*"

Another glance at each other, and then the girls rose and began to fold what pitiful belongings they had.

Weyland leaned against the doorjamb, studying them, grateful that he hadn't so overworked them that they were rendered completely undesirable.

"You're going to the palace at Whitehall," Weyland announced.

"The *palace*?" said Elizabeth.

"Yes. You are to find yourselves employment there. And you *will* find yourselves employment there. Once ensconced within the royal household, which you shall achieve by this evening," Weyland's tone gave the girls no doubt that he would brook no delay in this schedule, "then you shall be my eyes and ears. You will note what our good king Charles eats, when he farts, and what he does to while away the time when not drafting royal proclamations."

"But Weyland," Elizabeth said, "every girl in London wants a place within the royal household. How can we—"

"For God's sake, Elizabeth, you're a trained whore! Offer yourself. I'm sure he'll snap. You're still young and pretty enough."

Elizabeth and Frances glanced at each other again, and Weyland saw their uncertainty. He sighed, and his posture relaxed a little. "Do this," he said, "and you will earn my gratitude. Watch the king for me. Be my eyes and ears. Insinuate yourselves into his graces, and if you do this, if you do it *well*, then I shall consider you free of all bonds and obligations to myself."

"Can we trust you?" said Frances.

"No," said Weyland softly, "but what choice do you have? Remember what happened to Jane and Noah when they crossed me. You *will* do this."

Both the girls had paled, and Weyland nodded, satisfied. "Go," he said. "I've had enough of you lingering about Idol Lane."

He stared at them a moment longer, ensuring they were properly cowed, then left the room, leaving the door open. He continued up the stairs toward the Idyll, hearing the girls move about their chamber, whispering. He would use the imps to keep an eye on them, make sure they did as he asked.

He opened the door to the Idyll and walked inside, his face relaxing the instant he crossed the threshold.

Now there was just Jane, Noah, and himself left within Idol Lane—discounting the imps who Weyland thought he might leave to scamper about the streets until he needed them.

Weyland smiled, the expression making his face surprisingly soft. Just Jane, Noah, and himself.

And, once Jane had done her task and taught Noah the ways of the Mistress of the Labyrinth . . . just Noah.

Weyland stood, and looked about the strange place he called his Idyll. "I think it is about time," he said to no one in general, "that I introduce Noah to my own world. *Our* world, one day."

Then, stunningly, after all these years, the Idyll suddenly felt complete. He could *feel* it, almost as a sigh of contentment running through the Idyll.

Weyland went very still, hardly daring to believe what he felt. "I will bring Noah to you," he whispered.

Again, that strange, eerie sigh, as if of contentment, as if of *satiation*.

The Idyll had been waiting for Noah.

All this time, the Idyll had been waiting for Noah. *She* was what would make it complete.

Weyland sank to his knees, his hands over his face.

KING CHARLES II WAS HOLDING COURT WITHIN HIS main audience chamber when he halted in his conversation with the Venetian ambassador just long enough to murmur a few hasty words to one of his valets. The servant hurried away, and Charles resumed his conversation as if nothing had happened.

Seven hours later, when it was late night and Charles had retired to his private chambers, he called to him the same valet, and spoke again a few quiet words.

The valet nodded, as he had earlier in the day, and left the chamber.

Twenty minutes later he returned, bringing with him two ill-dressed girls.

"Elizabeth," Charles said, "and Frances." As the valet left, Charles advanced on the two stunned girls, who remembered their manners just in time to make hasty curtsies.

"Your Majesty," Elizabeth said, stumbling over the words. "I cannot imagine why . . . how . . ."

"Why I knew you had stepped forth within my palace court, and then had you brought before me, so privately?" Charles said.

Elizabeth nodded.

Charles smiled, gentle and kind. "Lovely ladies, I am far more than you think."

"You are our majestic king!" said Frances, feeling she needed to say something, and blushing for the stupid naivety of her words.

Charles's smile widened. "Indeed," he said. "England's Faerie King."

Then, as the two girls watched wide-eyed, his form shimmered and changed, and Elizabeth gave a startled "Oh!" as the Lord of the Faerie materialized before her. Both Elizabeth and Frances scuttled back several steps.

"Welcome to my court, ladies," the Lord of the Faerie said, leaning forward and kissed each softly on the mouth. "I am sure I know why you are here. Weyland sent you, yes?"

The girls nodded, still too dumbstruck to answer with their voices. Some of their fright was beginning to pass, and their regard now was more stunned curiosity than fear.

"What provoked this?"

"There was an argument in the kitchen this morning," Frances managed to say, amazing herself that she actually *had* managed to speak. "We were not there, but we heard some of what happened. Noah sent her daughter away, threw her out of the house. The next thing, Weyland sent us here. Your Grace, *who* are you?"

The Lord of the Faerie opened his mouth to answer, but in fact it was Elizabeth who spoke, her voice full of wonder. "You are the Green Man," she said. "The lord of the forests."

The Lord of the Faerie smiled, pleased. For centuries the simple folk had worshiped the Lord of the Faerie as the Green Man, honoring him every May Day with dances and song and branches gathered from the woods. "Aye," he said. "That is one of my names, although my realm stretches far farther than just the forests."

Elizabeth smiled, the expression making her beautiful. She sank once more into a deep curtsy. "My great lord, I am your servant!'

"And I!" cried Frances, aping Elizabeth's curtsy.

"What may I do to please you?" asked Elizabeth, looking up at the Lord of the Faerie with shining eyes.

"Only that you do as I ask," the Lord of the Faerie said. "Now, tell me, do you know who Eaving's Sisters are?"

The girls glanced at each other, then shook their heads.

The Lord of the Faerie smiled. "Then I have some introductions to make. Come. You are about to be inducted into a sisterhood far greater than the one you have known hitherto."

CHAPTER TWELVE

IDOL LANE, LONDON
Noah Speaks

I WAS NUMBED BY ALL WHICH HAD HAPPENED. THE terrible agony when Weyland had set the imp to tearing his way free. Weyland's subsequent healing of me. The story of his daughter.

Our shared vision atop the hill, where we both said too much.

Weyland's two terrifying references to "shelter."

Set against the uncertainty and terror of Weyland was the wonder of the Faerie Court, and the moment when Louis, *knowing*, finally had held me in his arms—and I had somehow, for some reason, held back from him.

In my current state I didn't feel like exploring why I might have done that.

Then, so quickly following on that, Ariadne, telling me I was of her and Asterion's blood. That I was a Darkwitch. That I was something that Louis and Charles both would naturally revile.

Then, Catling. My daughter, the lie.

The Troy Game, making sure I did what it wanted. Nothing counted but what *it* wanted.

Yet more—Weyland, talking to me of a terrible price. I had told him that Jane was to teach me the ways of the Labyrinth (I could hardly tell him about Ariadne, could I?) merely to distract him from questioning me too closely about Catling. Then he had wanted the bands. I had hedged (*For all the gods' sakes, I had wanted some space to think! Some time—was that too much to ask?*), and then he had sprung, trapping me.

My entire world was utterly devastated. There was not a single element left that I could understand, or which existed to save me.

Amid all this chaos, where I drifted so vulnerable and fragile, stepped a savior. Someone who offered *me* shelter, and time, and all the space I could ever need.

At a terrible price.

PART SEVEN

Noah's Terrible Price

LONDON, 1939

*J*ACK SKELTON HAD SEEN HOUSES LIKE THIS IN HOLLY-
wood movies, but even Hollywood's versions did nothing to prepare him
for the sheer beauty and elegance of the building in which he found
himself.

The front doors led into a small antechamber where waited a uniformed footman waiting to take any coats and bags. The antechamber then opened out into a
magnificent domed entrance chamber with a grand staircase rising in graceful spi-
rals into the heart of the house. The floor was marble, the fittings rich, glowing mahogany and crystal, the atmosphere one of studied elegance and stillness.

He heard Stella come up behind him, and he turned to look at her. "What is
Weyland doing here? For God's sake, he—"

"He is welcomed here, Ringwalker."

"This is a pretty turnabout," Skelton hissed. "Are you still his whore, then?"

Stella went white, and her eyes glittered. "Everyone else has moved forward,
Brutus. Why can't you?"

He took a step toward her, a hand outstretched, but stopped as he heard two
sets of footsteps coming down the stairs.

He whipped about.

Two men walked toward him. The one in front was in his early fifties, tall and lean
with an ascetic face under thinning brown hair. He was dressed in what Skelton called
"casual uniform," military trousers and shirt under a civilian red woolen pullover.

"Jack," said the man, holding out his hand.

Skelton took it, but, instead of shaking the man's hand, bowed his head over it
in a gesture of deep respect. "Faerie Lord," he said. "You must be the Old Man."

The Lord of the Faerie grinned. "Absolutely, old chap. Glad to see you, don't
you know?"

He laughed at the expression on Skelton's face. "I am glad to see you, Jack.
More than you can possibly know." His face sobered. "You cannot imagine the
pickle we find ourselves in."

"If you've invited Weyland Orr into the Faerie then I'm not bloody surprised," Skelton muttered.

"I think you know my companion," the Lord of the Faerie said, turning about and waving the other man forward.

Skelton looked, and went still with shock.

The Lord of the Faerie's "companion" explained the security outside.

He was George VI, king of England, and John Thornton—reborn.

"Jack," said the king, stretching out his own hand. *"More salubrious surroundings within which to meet than the Broken Bough, I should think."*

Chapter One

The Llandin

"**SEE," SAID THE LORD OF THE FAERIE SOFTLY. HE** had his hand on Louis's shoulder, and could feel the man trembling.

They stood atop Parliament Hill near Highgate. Once called the Llandin, it was the senior among the sacred hills of the ancient land.

It was late at night. London stretched in the distance, a sparkling of tiny lights by the moonlit gleam of the River Thames. To the east and west tiny hamlets likewise twinkled as people lit candles and lamps for the night.

None of this did the Lord of the Faerie and Louis de Silva see. Instead, there stretched before them the ancient, faerie landscape. Forests crept down from the north and the east. Tiny laneways and roads, winding barely visible in the moonlight. The sweep of the river, far vaster in its ancient form than it was in seventeenth-century England.

The river also twinkled. Deep within its depths water-sprites cast their eyes upward, catching the moonlight and refracting it back to the two men atop the Llandin. As the sprites' eyes caught the moonlight, so also did the tens of thousands of bronzed axes lying on the riverbed. They had been cast there over hundreds of years in order to honor the great goddess of the waters so that both land and women would burgeon with new life.

The river was *alive* with light.

Strange, primeval beasts nosed among the river meadows, occasionally raising their snouts and sniffing the air, knowing that magic was afoot this night, and nervous with anticipation.

Shadows were everywhere, haunting not only field and forest but also the few tiny human encampments dotting the meadows.

"When is this?" Louis asked softly. He remembered the time Genvissa brought him to this hill and showed him the land, and what he saw now was different even to that. Far, far older.

"Many millennia ago," the Lord of the Faerie said.

"Is this when you first walked?"

The Lord of the Faerie turned his strange, light eyes to de Silva. "There has never been a 'first time' in my walking," he said. "I have always been. If there have been trees, then there, also, was me. I have taken many forms, not just this man-shape. I have imitated the shape of the great toothed birds that once nested in the trees of a far more primordial time. I have taken the form of the tiniest of moles and vetches. Now this man-form appeals to me, for it mirrors the shapes of those who play the Troy Game."

Louis shivered. "You do not play the Game, do you?"

"No. I am one of the very few who has not been caught within its twists and turns."

"And thus you can see what others cannot?"

The Lord of the Faerie's teeth gleamed. "Do not ask me what I can see," said the Lord of the Faerie, "for it shall do you no good."

Louis studied the face of the Lord of the Faerie. He could see Coel in there, but only just, and he wondered if Coel would ever survive in—

"What if Coel was always me?" said the Lord of the Faerie. "I rarely walk, only when needed. But I always *live*. Somewhere. In someone. Besides, would you begrudge Coel a death in me?"

The Lord of the Faerie paused, then laughed softly at the expression on Louis's face. "You would," the Lord of the Faerie said. "That surprises me . . . and comforts me. Fear not, Louis-William-Brutus. Coel shall always laugh during the day. But on some nights . . . or on some desperate Faerie concern . . . then I step forth in my true form. What better for a king of England, eh?"

"None better," said Louis. "Lord of the Faerie, what happens tonight? What do I do?"

"You step forth on the Ringwalk, my friend."

"What *is* this Ringwalk?"

"It is the path the Stag God takes over the land and through the souls of its inhabitants." Once more the Faerie Lord extended his hand over the landscape. "See."

The once random scattering of lights over the landscape had resolved themselves into a pathway of twinkling lights. It stretched from the foot of the Llandin, from the Holy Oak, east and then northward, leading deep into the forests.

"What happens when I set foot on the Ringwalk?" Louis said.

"That, my friend, is up to you," and the Lord of the Faerie's hand gave Louis a very gentle push toward the hill as it sloped down toward the Holy Oak.

Louis hesitated, then he turned his back and set off down the hill.

The Lord of the Faerie smiled, cold and feral. "Die well, my friend," he whispered. "Die well . . . or die not at all."

CHAPTER TWO

IDOL LANE, LONDON

*L*ATER THAT NIGHT WEYLAND ASKED JANE ONCE
again to leave Noah and himself alone in the kitchen. Weyland
had been fiddling about by the hearth, and as Jane left the room
he moved back to the table where Noah sat, sitting opposite her.

"I'm sorry," he said.

"For what?" Noah said.

"For whatever happened with Catling. She has done something to hurt
you," he said.

"What care you if I hurt or not?" she said.

"I find I care very much, Noah."

She stared at him. Very slowly, his eyes not leaving hers, Weyland gently
took one of her hands in his.

Noah tensed, but did not withdraw her hand from his.

"I am glad Jane will teach you the craft of the Mistress of the Labyrinth,"
he said.

"You shall be able to use me splendidly, then."

He gave a short laugh. "Learning the ways of the Mistress will make you
more beautiful, more desirable. Any woman would be enhanced by learning
the craft of the Mistress of the Labyrinth. *You* will be graced. I find I look forward to that very much."

"I will never love you, Minotaur. Do not think to trick *me* into love!"

"Then I shall harbor no expectation of your love." His mouth
quirked again. "Although I still find myself confused by what you said atop the
hill."

"Then forget it, I pray you!"

Weyland let go her hand and looked about the kitchen, as if seeing it for
the first time.

"This is a poor room," he said finally. "A poor place to sleep." He glanced at Noah, and saw panic light her eyes.

"I find it warm enough, and pleasant," she said.

He grinned. "Nevertheless, I would prefer that you spend your nights with me from now on."

"No."

"I said I would ask a terrible price of you, Noah, for leaving the bands to lie undisturbed until you learned the art and craft of the Labyrinth. This is it. Your choice. Spend your nights with me, or I will force you to fetch the king-ship bands."

She stared at him, clearly appalled.

"This price is not so terrible as you may fear, Noah. Let me deal plain with you. Spend your nights with me—I am demanding no sexual favors or comforts from you—and I will agree that the bands can stay where they are until you have completed your training, *and* I will give you and Jane the complete freedom you need so you can learn from her teaching. See what a good humor I am in? I have even given you a bonus."

"You think I should believe you?"

"I do not play with words. I will not force you to any sexual play that you do not want. That you do not *ask* for. But we will lie together side by side, and talk, and share sleep. For this you receive your freedom to do what you must, and you receive my word that I will not force you to take the bands until you have finished your training. It is a bargain, Noah."

"Why?"

Because I want you. "Because I want to know you better, and I want you to know me."

Noah frowned, and Weyland could see her trying to fathom the trap.

"No trap," he whispered.

"With you there is always a trap."

"No trap." *Not for her, maybe.*

She was silent, still thinking; then, with some obvious reluctance, she nodded. "Very well."

"We must seal the bargain with a kiss."

"You said no sexual play I did not ask for!"

"It is but the conclusion of a pact, Noah, and common enough. Come now, a kiss."

He leaned across the table, and laid his mouth very gently against hers. He let it go at that, waiting, and was rewarded when she sighed, and moved her mouth more firmly under his.

He increased the depth of his kiss, but still kept it undemanding, and, very, very slowly, he felt her relax under his mouth.

Oh gods, he had not felt this way since Ariadne first offered herself to him. All these thousands of years, all the women he had taken, and raped, and forced, and squandered, and he had never kissed, nor been kissed with this sweetness, until now. Until Noah . . .

"Dear heavens, Noah! What are you doing!"

Noah sprang back from Weyland's mouth as he forced down a curse, sat back down in his chair, and turned about.

Jane stood in the doorway, looking at Noah with such an expression of astonishment on her face that Weyland thought she looked like a little girl who had caught her parents in frenzied sexual congress.

"I had not thought that *you* . . . with *him* . . . !" Jane said. "No wonder he asked me to leave the room."

"It was not what you think!" Noah said.

"Noah shall be spending her nights with me from now on," said Weyland casually, enjoying the renewed expression of astonishment, tempered with horror, on Jane's face. "A platonic agreement, naturally. Noah agrees to this because it shall please me so much that I will allow both you and she as much freedom as you need to teach and learn the ways of the Labyrinth."

If possible, Jane gaped all the more at Noah. "You told him—"

"I told Weyland that you had agreed to teach me the craft of Mistress of the Labyrinth," Noah said.

Jane managed to close her mouth. "Oh."

"And I am most pleased," Weyland said. "Most pleased."

Jane shot him a dark look.

"He would know anyway," said Noah, still looking hard at Jane. "Why *not* tell him?"

"Precisely," said Weyland. "And now, I see that it is late, and I am tired. Noah, we should go to bed, I think."

Weyland looked back to Noah. *Her* face had closed over, and Weyland knew that she wondered what lay ahead of her, in that unknown den above them.

"It shall not be as you fear," he said softly.

Chapter Three

The Ringwalk

*L*OUIS WALKED DOWN THE HILL. HE WAS UNSETtled and nervous, more by the glimpse of the potency of the ancient power of this land as it emanated from the Lord of the Faerie than what might happen to him this night.

The Holy Oak loomed before him, and Louis stopped beneath its ancient, spreading branches and looked to the small pool formed from the spring that bubbled forth from the rocks at the foot of the tree.

The pool—the place from which he'd rescued Cornelia from Loth and Erith, and from where he'd carried her back to their home, and conceived with her their daughter.

There was a movement before him, and Louis looked up. A fox had emerged from the undergrowth and was standing directly before him, staring into his eyes with his own unblinking yellow orbs.

Then the fox turned, and walked down a pathway which led from the pool into a small grove of trees.

The gravel and earthen floor of the path glowed with a faint luminescence. *The Ringwalk.*

Louis took a deep breath, and stepped forward after the fox.

EVERYTHING CHANGED.

The first thing Louis noticed was that his clothes and shoes had vanished, leaving him naked.

The second thing he noticed was that the forest had changed. The trees seemed different. Foreign.

Louis frowned, puzzling it over as he walked deeper into the forest.

The third thing he noticed was that it was now daylight rather than night.

And warm. Hot, even, as if this also was a foreign land rather than—

"Oh, sweet gods!" he muttered, coming to a stop, staring almost frantically about him.

The fox had vanished, and now there was nothing about him save the forest, and the warm scented air, and the soft touch of a breeze across his naked and now goose-bumped flesh.

Louis knew where he was, and that knowledge terrified him.

He was in the Italian forests outside his birthplace of Alba on the River Tiber.

Where he had hunted and killed his father, Silvius.

Louis circled about on the path, his heart pounding. *What trickery, this? What meaning, this?*

Louis felt the first stirrings of true fear, something he'd not felt since he'd been Brutus, and faced with a life of (as he'd thought then) mediocrity.

"And would I take that mediocrity now, in preference to what awaits me down this trail?" he asked himself, still circling slowly, his eyes wary.

No, he thought. *Never.*

Louis turned back to the path, and strode down the Ringwalk.

To either side of him reared great trees, thick with leafy branches and trailing ivy, the way between their trunks obscured with shrubbery and nettles. Apart from the sounds he made, there came little evidence of other inhabitants of the forest, whether bird or animal or other, watching eyes.

It was very calm.

Very still.

Very . . . *waiting.*

It irritated Louis, this silence, this emptiness.

"Come, take me, if you will," he said, then repeated it louder, shouting it into the forest. "Come, take me, if you will!"

"Is that what you wish?" came a soft, lilting voice; and Louis started, for the voice was that of his mother when he had lived as Brutus. She had died in his birth, and by rights Louis should not recognize it at all, but the instant he heard that voice, he *knew.*

Is that what you wish?

"Yes," he whispered. "That is what I wish."

The instant the words had fallen from Louis's mouth, there came from a far distance a sound that sent a chill down Louis's spine.

The haunting call of the hunting horn, echoing through the trees.

The horn was so far remote, and so distorted by echoes, Louis had no means of knowing how far and in what direction it lay. But this he did know: that horn signaled the start of the hunt, and the quarry was himself.

Louis grimaced. *Yes,* he had said. *That is what I wish.*

He recommenced his progress down the Ringwalk.

For a time all seemed peaceful, although the forest almost literally quivered with tension.

And then, almost apologetically, came a sound from behind Louis.

A single footfall.

A single hunter.

Silvius.

CHAPTER FOUR

THE IDYLL, IDOL LANE, LONDON
Noah Speaks

HE TOOK ME BY THE HAND AND LED ME UP THOSE damned stairs into the loft of the building.

Once we attained the top landing, we stood before a plain wooden door. Weyland glanced at me with amused eyes, knowing full well my lack of enthusiasm, then he opened the door and, still holding my hand, pulled me inside.

The door closed softly behind us. For a moment there was blackness, and it disturbed me so much that I actually moved closer to Weyland, needing the reassurance of his warmth and presence.

"Light," he said, very low, and within a heartbeat soft lights glowed in a score of places.

They did not flare suddenly into life, but gently pervaded the dark with their luminescence, as dawn lightens the land toward the end of night.

My first impression as the lights slowly intensified was one of space. We stood in a great sandstone-columned vestibule with a fan-vaulted ceiling, and with a flooring of vivid blue, gold, and scarlet tessellated tiles. The vestibule's outer walls were pierced with graceful arched open doorways leading into balconies, walkways, bridges, and long elegant arcades and cloisters. Beyond the doorways and balconies I could just make out a jungle of domed and spired buildings, their gilded tiles glinting under some enchanted sun.

It was a city, all in this tiny upstairs chamber of Weyland's house in Idol Lane, and the vestibule its central hub.

My eyes were, I think, impossibly wide. I looked to Weyland, and he smiled very gently at the expression on my face.

"What did you expect? A stinking, dismal cave, full of the musk of Minotaur?"

My face flamed. It was precisely what I *had* expected.

He laughed, and squeezed my hand before letting it go and walking farther into the vestibule.

"I call this," he said, swinging back to look at me, "the Idyll. It is my retreat from everything that people expect of me, or fear from me, or consider me."

What people feared of him, or considered him? For that, surely, he had no one to blame but himself. I stared at him, and he made a face.

"You think all of this is a trap, don't you."

"Is it?"

"I don't know," he replied.

No other answer could have unsettled me more.

I distracted myself by paying more attention to my surroundings. The air was strange—warm, slightly humid, and sweetly spiced.

It was not *English* air.

"Where is this?" I asked.

"The tiny chamber above the kitchen in—"

I made a noise of exasperation, and he smiled. "It is an amalgamation of the best of all that I have seen over the past three thousand years. I have taken the best and most beautiful from cities in Egypt and Persia and faraway China."

"This is the heart of the Labyrinth," I said, indicating the central hub in which we stood (I experienced a moment of renewed unease as I said this, for as I turned about, I could not see which door it was that led back into the house below). "You have merely re-created your own home, your *original* home, Weyland, if perhaps slightly more salubrious."

"Ah, Noah," he said, walking very close now. "You *are* perceptive, are you not? Aye, this echoes the heart of the Labyrinth, but with one crucial difference."

"Yes?"

"I know the way out. And you don't."

Paradoxically, at last I felt on firmer ground. *This* was the Minotaur I understood.

CHAPTER FIVE

THE FOREST

ILVIUS!

Louis stopped dead.

Who else but the father he'd murdered when he was but fifteen for the golden bands of Troy about Silvius' limbs?

This is no way to found a Game, Silvius had said to Brutus when he'd founded the Troy Game with Genvissa. *You cannot found a Game on the corruption of my murder.*

So what was *this,* then? Silvius come to exact retribution? Was this what the Stag God demanded?

Louis ran lightly forward. He was not scared so much as angry, and not running away so much as finding time and space in which to think. His father Silvius, trapped in the heart of the Game all these thousands of years, was coming to murder him, to set the Game to rights, to enable Louis, as Brutus-reborn, to rebirth as the Stag God.

Why run from it, then?

Why this anger?

Louis's footsteps slowed. Throughout his lives as Brutus and then William, the Troy Game had been steeped in murder. Asterion's, to start with, and then Ariadne's murder of so many in the name of revenge. Silvius' murder, by his own hand. Genvissa's death. The death of his daughter with Cornelia. Coel's murder. Caela's. Swanne's. Harold's.

Blangan.

Blangan. Gods, how many years was it since Louis had given her a single thought? She'd been the reviled mother of Loth, elder sister of Genvissa, exile from Llangarlia, brought back to the land by Brutus only to have her heart torn out in the center of Mag's Dance by her son.

What was it about that death? Louis frowned, trying to remember what it was Genvissa had told him about it. She'd manipulated Loth into murdering Blangan, not so much to rid herself of Blangan (although that was a true bonus for Genvissa), but because she'd wrapped this murder within so much dark magic that Blangan's murder effectively caused the Stag God Og's murder.

When Loth tore out his mother's heart, he also tore out Og's heart.

Louis stopped dead on the pathway, breathing heavily, although more from inner turmoil than from any effort. He heard the footfalls farther down the way—Silvius, hunting him—but for the moment he paid them no concern.

He knew what was going to happen, and why.

He knew what part both Silvius and James—Loth-reborn—had to play.

And it terrified Louis.

Why all this lack of courage to face your own death, Brutus, when it was but a simple matter to arrange my murder, and to execute it?

Louis straightened and spun about, all in one movement.

His father, Silvius, stood fifteen or sixteen paces behind him.

It was Silvius in his prime. He stood straight and tall; tightly muscled; skin bronzed with good health; crisp, curled black hair tied with a leather thong at the nape of his neck; white waistcloth beaded with scarlet and emerald and tasseled in gold.

Both eyes stared at Louis, dark, liquid, intense.

About his limbs shimmered six bands of light—Silvius might no longer have the bands, but their legacy still gleamed about his arms and legs.

Silvius held a hunting bow in his hands, a single arrow strung and ready for flight. He had no other arrows.

Louis stared at that arrow, unable now to keep his fright contained, then looked at his father. "Silvius—"

Silvius bared his teeth. *Run! Run! I am the hunter, and you the hunted. I will not kill a standing prey, for there is no honor in that. Run! Run!*

Louis looked at his father a single moment longer, his eyes wild, then he turned and ran.

Behind him Silvius grinned, and raised the bow to his shoulder.

Then, the bow still held to his shoulder, he also began to run, save that he moved with a curious high-stepping gait, his back straight, his arms held almost at shoulder-height in order to keep the bow in position, his head high and unmoving, his eyes sighted down the length of the arrow.

It was as if Silvius did not so much *run* down that forest pathway, but *dance.*

Ahead of him, panting now, Louis ran as desperately as he could. What if the true test was *escaping* his father's justice?

There is no escape for you, murderer.

Louis slid to a halt, staring wildly ahead. Just as that new voice had spoken inside his mind he'd run into the opening approaches to a wide and pleasantly shaded glade.

Standing in the center of the glade was a man, hobbled and knobbled, crippled and distorted, a terrible mixture of Loth and Saeweald.

In his hand, dangling loosely at his side, this nightmarish creature held a knife, a long, wicked blade.

Louis looked over his shoulder, certain that Silvius was, at any moment, about to run into him.

But instead he heard his father call out from behind some intervening shrubbery.

Hark! Hark! Is that a stag I hear crashing about in that leafy gloom?

No!" Louis screamed. He tried to duck, to turn aside, to run, but before his brain could send that message to his muscles, the shrub before him parted, as if by magic, and a single arrow sped through it.

No! Louis screamed in his mind, one of his hands instinctively raised to his face, and in the next instant the arrow thudded into him, punching straight through the palm of his hand and embedding itself in his left eye.

The force of the impact sent Louis sprawling to the ground. He writhed, in agony. The arrow had skewered his right hand to his left eye, and as he moved the hand, instinctively trying to pull it away, it tugged at the arrow, making its barbed point wriggle deeper and deeper into Louis's orbit, scraping against bone and nerve endings.

He screamed, his back arching off the forest floor, his heels thudding frantically on the ground.

A man stepped up to him, and Louis knew it was his father. "For all the gods' sakes," he screamed, his voice now hoarse with pain and fear. "Do it! Do it!"

No, said Silvius.

"For gods' sakes . . ." Louis moaned. "Please, push this arrow in, and kill me. *Do it now! Now!*" *Oh gods, the agony, the agony . . .*

No.

CHAPTER SIX

THE IDYLL, IDOL LANE, LONDON
Noah Speaks

ON'T FRET," WEYLAND SAID, WITH A CHARMING grin to take away any sense of sarcasm. "This is no trap. If you want to leave, then I will show you the way. But it is, in its own way, a manner of test. A Mistress of the Labyrinth would know the way out. If you learn well, then eventually you won't need to ask me for guidance every time you want to leave." Then he nodded at a blue-tiled archway to my left. "In this Idyll, tonight, that is the way back into the house of Idol Lane."

" 'Tonight'?"

"Every time you enter the Idyll it is slightly different, slightly dissimilarly reconfigured. Not much, but enough to confuse."

"You have built yourself a tricky haven."

"And do you blame me? With all these gods and witches and Kingmen and Mistresses and gods-know-what-other faerie creatures out to trap me?"

I could not answer that, and I found his gaze too direct, too challenging. I looked away, hating it that he'd forced me to that evasive action.

"Noah . . ." He moved very close now, our linked hands pressed warm and tight between our bodies. "Do *you* want to trap me?"

"Of course. Every time you set that imp to work within my body I cursed you, and wished you every foul fate I could devise. I will see you trapped once more within the heart of the Labyrinth, Asterion, if it is the last thing I—"

He kissed me, stopping the flow of my words.

I pulled my mouth away.

"I am sorry for that imp," he said, very soft.

"No," I said. "You enjoyed it."

He kissed my neck, my ear. "When I set him, yes, of course I did."

I flushed, remembering that night he'd taken on the glamour of Silvius, and taken my virginity within the stone hall.

"And when, in this life, you were far distant from me, then yes, I am afraid I enjoyed it when I set the imp to work. I knew it caused you pain and sorrow, and that fed my hatred of you."

"And *this*," I said, meaning his closeness now, his kisses, "does *this* feed your hatred of me?" Sweet gods, he knew how best to use his mouth. *Damn it, this man was my forefather!* I battened down my thoughts. I couldn't let myself think of this now, not with Weyland so close.

He stood back, watching me curiously. "I don't hate you now, Noah. If I hated you, then I would never have brought you to my Idyll."

"You want to manipulate me, to use me."

"That is why I brought you to Idol Lane, yes. But that has changed. It is what I no longer want."

My face set in hard, disbelieving lines.

"For millennia, Noah, I hated the very thought of love. I distrusted it." His voice became very soft. "But what if I had been mistaken? What if love provided, not a trap, but a shelter?"

I went cold. *There, again, the use of the word "shelter."* All he had to do was to ask *me* for shelter and I would be lost. My goddess name *meant* "shelter," it defined who I was. If he asked for shelter, then I would need to give it. Worse, Weyland was defining "shelter" in terms of love. *I need shelter, Noah. I need love.* All he had to add to that was, *Give it to me, I ask it of you,* and I *would*—both shelter and love, for Weyland had bound the two concepts together so tightly they could not be separated.

How did he know? How?

I tried to feel panic, *fought* for panic, but in the end all I could summon was a quiet calmness at the prospect. Perhaps that was resignation.

Perhaps.

Weyland stepped back, although he still held my hand loosely. "Come to bed, Noah, and talk with me awhile."

"We can talk here well enough."

His mouth twitched. "When we lie side by side, naked, then there can be no secrets between us. *That* makes for good conversation."

I stared at him, and he laughed at the expression on my face.

HE LED ME TO A CHAMBER SEVERAL ARCHWAYS AND bridges and cloisters distant from the entry vestibule. The chamber was intimate, although not claustrophobic, with a domed ceiling painted a deep-blue and patterned with pink and scarlet flowers rioting amid soft gray-green leaves. It was beautiful, and I think I might have embarrassed myself by staring at it a moment too long. I lowered my gaze eventually, and saw that directly under its apex stood a circular bed loosely draped with silken sheets and scattered with soft pillows.

"There is a washing chamber through there," Weyland said, indicating a small arched doorway to one side, "and a closet stocked with robes and linens through there." He nodded to another doorway. "There is nothing you can lack for. Save Brutus, of course."

His voice became tighter at this last, and I glanced at him, surprised by this evidence of jealousy. He hadn't been jealous when he'd lain with me as Silvius when all I'd thought about was Brutus.

But now he was. *Why?*

Weyland was disrobing, laying his shirt and breeches carefully atop a chest to one side of the bed.

I averted my eyes and turned my back, twisting my arms behind me to undo the buttons of my bodice. I could have used the washroom, but that would have admitted defeat.

The next moment I heard him step up behind me, and then his hands brushed mine aside, and he deftly undid the bottoms of both my bodice and skirt.

"They will need to be hung," I said, thinking to take them from his hand and into the clothesroom where I might escape his presence, even for a moment. But Weyland paid me no attention, draping the clothes over a chair which had mysteriously appeared just to our side.

I closed my eyes, gathered my courage, and stepped out of my chemise and petticoat, and then my underdrawers.

"Where is the bracelet, Noah?"

I held up my left arm, and, lo, there it twinkled. It came and went largely as I summoned it.

He touched it, and it vanished.

That startled me, for it was not of my doing.

"I did not like Cornelia," he said. "Perhaps we can do without the bracelet."

I nodded, and glanced at the bed. Thank the gods it had silken linens for me to hide my nakedness beneath.

In the instant before I bolted for the bed I felt his hand caress my back, running lightly over the scars the imp had made, and I flinched away.

"You said you would not touch my naked body."

Abruptly the warmth of his hand vanished. "I apologize. Now, come to bed, Noah, and talk to me before we sleep."

I turned and walked the few steps to the bed, climbing in and sliding the silk sheet over me, trying not to appear as if I rushed, but knowing from the amused gleam in his eyes that he had well noted my hurry.

He lay down beside me, not bothering to hide *his* nakedness.

"Of what do you wish to speak?" I said.

"Ah, how formal you are."

He lay close to me, not touching, but I could feel his warmth even so.

"Talk to me of Catling, Noah," he said.

My eyes filmed with tears. *Damn him.* That hurt was too recent for me to talk of it unemotionally.

"Noah?"

Ah, gods, if that care and concern in his voice was forced pretense, then he was a far better actor than I had ever given him credit.

I heard and felt him turn over.

"Was it because she was not a daughter of Brutus that you disliked her?" he said. "You always seemed so detached from her. I found that odd."

"You never commented on it," I managed to say.

His voice was amused. "Being an evil Minotaur, I had other things on my mind than mother-daughter relationships."

"Do not jest about it!"

"Noah, I'm sorry. What could she have done that has caused you so much distress?"

How to answer that? *Well, Asterion, you see, I brought the Troy Game itself into your house, save that I did not know she was the Troy Game, because I thought she was my beloved daughter.*

"I lost a daughter once," I said.

"I did not know," he said. There was infinite sympathy in his voice, and no question. He had left it up to me as to whether or not I continued.

Naturally, at that sympathy, and that tact, I began to babble.

"In my life as Cornelia, Brutus hated me, had gone to Genvissa, and I thought that the only was to get him back was to fall pregnant to him. I did, a daughter . . . Oh, I wanted her so much! I wanted someone to love me, my son was all Brutus' child, and I thought that even if I lost Brutus to Genvissa completely then I would have his child, and she would love me . . ."

I stopped, aware not only that was I babbling nonsense but I was crying openly, and completely unable to stop myself. All the emotions of the past few days had bubbled to the surface at Weyland's kindness (false kindness it may have been, but at this point any kindness at all had the power to undo me). One of my hands, dangerously trembly, dashed at the tears, and I continued relentlessly on my road to utter destruction.

"I was seven months pregnant, Brutus had abandoned me completely. Genvissa thought to rid herself of me, and of the child. One night she . . . she . . ."

"You lost your daughter through Genvissa's malevolence."

"And my own life as well . . . But Mag came to me, and saved me, and set me on the road to . . ."

"To my utter destruction. Yes. But the daughter? Mag did not save her?"

I had never thought of that. Mag had saved me, but not my daughter. *I* was the more severely damaged of the two of us. If Mag could have saved me then she could have given breath to a seven-month infant.

She could have saved my daughter, and yet she didn't.

"No," I said. "No. And I thought . . . I believed I would have my daughter back one day . . . and Catling . . ."

"Catling was not what you expected."

I couldn't talk about it. I put my hands over my face, hating my tears.

With a sigh, Weyland moved closer and gathered me into his arms.

"Noah—" he began, kissing my brow in comfort rather than passion, and then . . .

Then it was if the chamber vanished. And all I could see was Silvius, leaning down to Louis, driving an arrow through Louis's hand, and deeper and deeper into Louis's brain.

I gasped, unable to help myself, and Weyland's arms tightened about me.

CHAPTER SEVEN

THE FOREST

*D*O IT NOW!" LOUIS SCREAMED, ONLY WANTING TO feel that arrow slide into his brain so he could embrace oblivion and death. "For gods' sakes, Silvius, *do it now!*"

Silvius took firm hold of the arrow with both his hands, and pushed down. Louis tensed, terrified, yet glad it would soon be over.

Silvius pushed the tip of the arrow into the bone of Louis's left orbit, and twisted, grinding the arrowhead slowly deeper and deeper, mangling bone and nerve endings both.

If Louis had thought he was in pain before, then this was suffering such as he'd never known. The pain in his hand was bad enough as the shaft of the arrow twisted slowly through flesh and bone, but what the arrowhead did to his skull was indescribably agonizing.

Worse was the terrible knowledge that Silvius knew what he was doing. That he could have easily sunk that arrowhead through the rear of Louis's orbit and deep into his brain, killing him instantly, but that he chose not to.

Louis's left hand beat uselessly at Silvius, his feet kicked more uselessly. None of the blows made any difference. It was as though Silvius was totally insubstantial save for those terrible hands, gripping the shaft of the arrow.

Thus you have brutalized me for three thousand years, Silvius whispered into Louis's mind. *Thus have I suffered.*

Louis managed to speak. "I . . . killed you . . . instantly. There was no . . . suffering . . ."

There was no suffering? To see my own beloved son come up to me, his face expressionless, to see him look at the arrow, look at my kingship bands, and then look back to the arrow in my eye with an expression of such murderous ambition on his face, that all I had ever been, all I had ever loved, was murdered with that single look?

That *was not suffering? Do you know what it is like, Brutus-William-Louis, to be murdered by that person you have loved the most?*

He ground the arrowhead back and forth, back and forth, scraping terrible grooves into Louis's orbit.

"Father . . . kill me now. *I beg you!*"

You think this is suffering? *Do you not know that your greatest suffering, your greatest despair, is yet to come?*

And then, dimly, gradually, Louis became aware that someone else was standing at his side, and he knew it was James.

And he knew what James held in his hand, and, perhaps understandably, Louis thought that the greater suffering Silvius referred to, would be at the hands of James.

Chapter Eight

The Idyll, Idol Lane, London

Noah Speaks

I SAW ALL OF THIS, AND WAS APPALLED BY LOUIS'S suffering, as much also by James's need for revenge.

And yet I was still wrapped in my tears and all that long-buried pain that had cruelly bubbled to the surface.

And all through that terrifying scene of Louis's suffering, I was conscious of truly only one thing:

Weyland's arms about me, and his silent comfort. I didn't know if he could scry out my thoughts—the gods alone knew that Weyland had the power to somehow sense, if not share outright, the vision I experienced—but I think he would have reacted if he had. I think I would have known if he were there with me.

All he did was lie beside me, and hold me, and try and comfort me.

I pulled back a little from the vision, and stirred. He leaned back, and pushed away some of my hair that had fallen over my face. "I lost a daughter," he said. "Not so painfully as you did, but for years I wondered if she was dead or, if she lived, if she was well, or if she suffered in life, or if—"

I didn't hear the rest of what Weyland said, for a memory had suddenly filled my mind. Long Tom, speaking to me when I was but a child, and on my way to my life at Woburn Abbey.

"*Old wounds must be healed,*" Long Tom said. "*All of them.*"

"*Old wounds?*"

"*The wounds caused during your first life: not those caused only by you, but those caused and suffered by* everyone *caught in the Game.*"

I caught my breath. Gods, gods, *gods!*

Wounds must be healed, all those caused and suffered by everyone *caught in the Game.*

"Weyland," I said. "I am so sorry."

Then I reached my hands up, and slid them into his hair, and pulled his face down to mine.

We kissed, once, twice, and then again and again, and I felt a shiver of desire at the base of my spine. "Weyland," I said on a breath, and that was all I said for a very long time.

JAMES SQUATTED DOWN BESIDE LOUIS, STILL WRITH-*ing beneath his father-held arrow.*

James raised the dagger in both hands high above Louis's heaving chest, then plunging it down, down, down . . .

The sickening crunch of bone . . .

Louis screamed, terribly, terribly . . .

I SAW ALL THIS, AND SOME SMALL PART OF ME SUF-fered with Louis's suffering, and yet most of me was concerned with the moment *I* was caught in, and the man I was with.

"Noah . . . are you certain?"

I answered him with my mouth against his, and my hands, on his body.

LOUIS COULD NOT STOP SCREAMING, EVEN THOUGH *the knife had lacerated both his lungs, and air now bubbled up through the blood that welled around the blade.*

"Here it is," said James, almost conversationally, and he plunged his hand into the frightful cavity in Louis's chest.

I SORROWED FOR LOUIS, WISHED THAT HE COULD undergo his rebirth as Stag God in some way other than that he currently endured.

But, oh, there was very little for me now but Weyland, and the sweetness and warmth and overweening comfort of our lovemaking.

JAMES GRUNTED WITH EFFORT, THEN RAISED WITH *some difficulty his hand.*

It held a beating heart.

* * *

I CRIED OUT, AND CLUTCHED FRANTICALLY AT WEY-
land. His hands ran over me, everywhere, his mouth following, and I felt him
trembling, and somehow that touched me deeply, that he should tremble
so . . .

LOUIS WAS SOMEHOW STILL ALIVE, ALTHOUGH DESPER-
ate. His left hand, the one that wasn't pinned by the arrow, waved weakly in the
air, begging his father to push that arrow deeper, to murder him finally.
*   Silvius hesitated, then, with a look of immense love on his face, leaned all his*
weight on the shaft and pushed the arrowhead deep into Louis's brain.

I CRIED OUT ONCE MORE, FOR AS THAT ARROW HAD
pierced into Louis's brain so Weyland had slid deep into me. He was murmuring, meaningless, soothing words, and I wept, and hugged him to me, feeling
Louis's relief at death enveloping him at the same time as my body dissolved
into sweet relief. I let my body go limp, let my mind free, let Weyland hold me,
closed my eyes, and felt nothing but the warmth of his arms about me and
heard nothing but the sound of his voice, whispering my name.

WE LAY FOR HOURS, SO IT SEEMED, SWEATY AND RE-
plete, our bodies still tangled, our hands now and again stroking at the other,
caressing, exploring. Occasionally we kissed, deep and velvety.
    We did not speak, and for that I was grateful, for I did not know what
words to use. All I knew was that somehow I had done something right.
    All I knew was that I had stepped forth on a path so dangerous that I could
not know where it would lead me, or him, or any that I loved.
    Eventually I opened my eyes, and saw Weyland's face a few inches away,
looking down gently at me.
    "What are you thinking?" he said.
    "That the paths of the Labyrinth are most twisted indeed," I said, and
pulled him back down to me.

WE MADE LOVE A FURTHER THREE TIMES THAT NIGHT.
Very gently, very sweetly. When, finally, we lay exhausted, I allowed my mind
to drift back to something Silvius had said to Louis.
    You think this is suffering? *Silvius had said.* Do you not know that your great-
est suffering, your greatest despair, is yet to come?

I wondered if *I* was to be that suffering, and I thought if that were so, then so be it. I had had enough of guilt.

THE LITTLE GIRL SAT, ARMS ABOUT HER LEGS, CHIN REST-
ing on knees, on the gently sloping roof of a warehouse in Thames Street.

She stared toward Idol Lane, but she saw none of the rooftops or chimneys or steeples that rose between her and it.

Instead she saw Noah, writhing in pleasure beneath Weyland's body.

"Fool!" whispered the girl. "Would you destroy everything that can be, out of spite? Do you truly think that Weyland could be what you need?"

Something moved beside her, and she turned her head slightly. It was one of the imps.

"We have a problem," said Catling.

"Yes?" said the imp, his eyes gleaming.

"It appears that my erstwhile mother has developed a 'closeness' with Weyland."

"Really?"

"We must turn her away from him."

"How?"

Catling smiled. "With something that should cause you great pleasure, my friend."

"What is it?"

Catling laughed softly at the eagerness in the imp's voice. "Something I need you to fetch from Holland."

Chapter Nine

Idol Lane and Whitehall
Palace, London

HE WHITE STAG WITH THE BLOOD-RED ANTLERS
lay deep in the center of the Troy Game, his heart cruelly torn from
his chest and left to lie beating weakly against his bloodstained pelt.
The stag's heart beat. Once. Weakly.

Then it beat again, far more strongly, it jolted, and the stag quivered, and groaned.

And then, suddenly, the stag's chest was whole, his heart vanished once more within his body, and the stag's legs were thrashing wildly against the smooth green grass, and he lifted his head . . .

And then he was gone, running through the forest, and the heart of the Troy Game was still and empty.

WEYLAND WOKE EARLY, AND DRESSED. HE STOOD FOR a few minutes, watching Noah sleeping, his face expressionless, then he left the chamber and walked a little deeper into the Idyll, thinking.

Dear gods . . . He hadn't expected Noah to succumb so quickly. He had planned so intricately, maneuvering her to the point where she would agree to spend her nights next to him in his bed. From there Weyland had expected that it would take weeks, perhaps months, of gentleness and closeness and a gradual easing of suspicion before she might allow him to touch her, and before she might allow herself to enjoy it, and to respond.

But instead . . . instead . . . *Oh gods, that "instead"!*

Weyland reminded himself to be cautious. Had there been anything wrong with last night? Anything false?

Had Noah succumbed too quickly? Had she been trying to hide something from him?

She had *appeared* completely honest with him, too emotional to spin intricate lies. But still . . . it didn't hurt to be wary.

After all, he'd loved and trusted Ariadne, and look to where that had brought him.

Weyland sent a silent call out to his imps, asking them to meet him in the kitchen of Idol Lane. He had no idea if they'd appear—Weyland felt his control over those imps was not quite what it should be—but should they turn up, then he had a duty for them.

One that could perhaps still that niggling doubt in his mind.

Having decided on a course of action, Weyland relaxed. He paused on one of the balconies of his Idyll, recalling every moment he and Noah had shared last night.

"Where are we going, Noah?" Weyland whispered. "Where are we going? How can we stop? How can we stop?"

LOUIS FLOATED IN HIS OWN MAGICAL EXISTENCE, neither alive nor truly dead. He could feel the arrow still within his eye, feel it piercing into his skull, feel it scraping back and forth, back and forth, in random sharp patterns across the inside of his cranial cavity. It was not painful, merely . . . irritating.

He felt also the great gaping hole in his chest, feel the magical currents wash in and out of it, feel them pull away clots of blood and slivers of bone.

He found that irritating, too. He just wanted to breathe, to control his own body, and his own fate.

This drifting within enchantment, neither alive nor dead, annoyed him beyond measure.

In an effort to calm himself he thought of Noah. Where was she this night? Did she know of his journey? Louis could not help but think that she must. She could not have been unaware. Had she knelt in prayer? Watched with helpless anxiety?

Was she now rejoicing, knowing that surely, *surely,* it would not be long before he could be with her, god to her goddess, true lovers, finally.

He smiled, and then the smile vanished, as what felt like a cruel taloned hand reached into his chest, grabbed at whatever remnants of flesh remained there, and hauled him into a fiery cauldron.

* * *

WEYLAND KISSED NOAH AWAKE, LEFT HER A TRAIL OF
ivory silk through the Idyll to the door she would need to find her way back into
the house once she had done, and said he would see her downstairs, so soon as
she had bathed and dressed. When he emerged into the house on the first-floor
landing it was to observe with some surprise that all was as he'd left it last night.

Somehow he'd thought all of existence should have been altered after what
they'd shared.

He smiled, his entire face softening, and he ran lightly down the stairs, and
walked through the parlor and into the kitchen.

Jane, as ever, was standing at the hearth, stirring at their breakfast. She
started a little at his entrance, watching him warily.

"Noah?" she said.

"She shall be down shortly," Weyland said, sitting at the table and surprising himself, and Jane even more, by suddenly grinning widely at her.

He couldn't help it. He'd felt such a surprising surge of happiness, for no apparent reason, that the only outlet he could find for it was an inane grin at Jane.

She stared at Weyland, then looked abruptly away.

"Are my imps about?" he said, finally managing to bring his expression under some degree of control.

Jane inclined her head to the door leading into the small alley. "Playing at
hoop and ball. They arrived earlier."

They had *answered his call! Good.* Weyland snapped his fingers, and almost
immediately the kitchen door opened and the two imps poked their heads
about it.

"Master!" they cried.

"I have a duty for you this morning," Weyland said.

As one they raised their eyebrows, their expressions eager.

"Go to Whitehall, and seek out Elizabeth and Frances. Ask them if anything of note happened within the palace last night. Concerning the king, perhaps. They will know what I mean."

Once the imps had scurried away, Weyland rose and walked over to Jane.

"Jane? Did *you* feel anything last night? Anything 'of note' that you might
like to mention?"

"What do you mean?" She studied him. "Surely, perhaps, I should be asking
that of *you*?"

Again Weyland grinned, the expression so unforced, so natural, that Jane
blinked in surprise. "Would you be surprised to hear," Weyland said, "that
Noah and I—"

He stopped abruptly at a step in the door. Noah entered and cast Weyland
a sharp look, then walked over to the dresser and lifted down the dishes they'd
need for their breakfast.

Jane looked to Noah, then back to Weyland, and her eyes widened at the expression she saw there.

Dear gods! That was softness in his eyes!

Hastily turning her back, not wanting Weyland to see her confusion, Jane stirred vigorously at the porridge.

ALL HIS PAIN AND CONFUSION AND IRRITATION VAN-ished, and, as he felt solid ground beneath his feet, Louis opened his eyes.

And found himself standing in his father's private chamber in his childhood home in Alba.

Silvius' chamber was so private, that Louis, as Brutus, had only ever been in it five times throughout the first fifteen years of his life (before he had murdered his father and had been expelled from Alba). Those five visits had all been for the same reason: he'd done wrong, and Silvius had summoned Brutus to inform his son of his disappointment.

Brutus had loathed those summons. Silvius could have raged at him, or meted out punishment, but he had done neither. Silvius would merely stand, gazing out the open door that looked out over a small courtyard, before slowly turning as Brutus entered and, very softly, explaining his disappointment.

Now, as Louis opened his eyes and was overwhelmed by a long-forgotten sense of deep discomfort and shame, he wondered how much those terrible, shame-filled visits had been behind his decision to push that arrow down, instead of pulling it out.

Louis's next thought was . . . *Am I here for another discourse on disappointment? Has Silvius stored up three thousand years' worth of disappointments to "discuss" with me?*

He glanced down at his ruined chest, rubbed away the dried blood that caked his left cheek and jaw, and straightened, looking about with the one eye remaining to him.

The chamber was as he remembered it. Tiled in softly colored mosaics, it was barely furnished save for a couch set close to the window, a desk clean of any pens or parchments, and a low wooden chair set against the wall.

Louis automatically looked to the light-filled doorway which led to the courtyard, expecting to see, as he always had, the shadow of his father, slowly turning about to study his son.

There was nothing. The doorway was empty of everything save light.

Louis turned slightly to look behind him at the doorway which led back into the house.

Nothing. The chamber was empty save for himself.

"Father?" Louis said, once more facing into the chamber. "Silvius?"

Silence.

"Father?"

Silence . . . Save that this time, there was a change in the light at the court-yard door—as if someone moved deep within the courtyard.

Louis walked forward, silently and carefully. He reached the doorway, then, unable to stop himself, turned (*slowly, slowly*) and looked back into the chamber.

For an instant he saw a shadow, the boy-child Brutus, standing sullen and resentful as he waited for his father to speak.

Then the shadow shimmered and vanished, and Louis turned, and, taking a deep breath, stepped into the courtyard.

The courtyard was almost as spare and empty as Silvius' chamber. There was a small tree, a wooden bench beneath its shade, and, just beyond the bench, a large pond.

Silvius was crouched by the pond, crumbling a piece of bread into the fishes' gaping mouths as they broke the surface in their boiling, bubbling, frantic crowd.

Louis stared, not knowing what to do or say, but then Silvius rose, tossed in the final piece of bread for the fish to squabble over, and turned to look at his son.

"I have been so blessed in you," he said, and, walking forward, embraced Louis.

WEYLAND HAD GONE TO THE MARKET ABOUT HIS OWN business, and Jane and Noah were left alone.

"Well?" said Jane.

Noah frowned, as if puzzled.

"Why is Weyland so cheerful? Gods, Noah, I have never seen him so . . . carefree."

"Perhaps he is happy, knowing he has me trapped within his den at night. You should be grateful, Jane, to sleep so undisturbed in this kitchen."

Jane narrowed her eyes. "And what *is* in that den, Noah? Is it gray noth-ingness? Is it terror-ridden nightmare? Or is it . . . ?"

Noah hesitated, sliding her eyes away from Jane's direct gaze.

"Noah?"

Noah ran her tongue over her lips, meeting Jane's gaze once more. "He calls it his Idyll, Jane. It is a place of beauty." Her voice softened. "Beauty be-yond anything I could have imagined. It is not like this land. It is . . . ."

Her voice drifted off, and for one crazed moment Jane thought Noah had been going to say, *It is Asterion.*

"It must be a trap," Jane said.

"No," Noah said, and in her eyes Jane saw a faint reflection of the same delight she'd seen in Weyland's. Faint, but there.

"You lay with him!" Jane said.

"No! Gods, Jane . . . No. I did not. We lay together side by side, and we talked, but we did not . . . No. If I look . . ." Noah hesitated, and Jane saw again the tip of her tongue sliding over her lower lip. "If I look content, and perhaps even joyful, then it is merely the memory of Weyland's Idyll." Her voice slid into the defensive. "It *was* beautiful, and remarkable."

"I had no idea you were this gullible, Noah."

"Well then," Noah said, "there is another reason I should look joyful." Noah glanced about the room, moved yet closer to Jane, and whispered into her ear: "Last night Louis began his journey."

It was a dangerous thing to say, even so blandly put, but Jane knew instantly what she meant. "Ah!" she said on a breath. "I knew I felt something last night! Has he completed . . . his journey?"

Noah gave a small shake of her head. "There is a way to go yet."

"Then we should be careful," Jane said.

"Aye."

"Noah . . ."

"Aye?"

"Tomorrow morning we must begin our own journey."

Noah stilled.

"Ariadne spoke to me," Jane said. "Last night. While you slept. Chastely. With Asterion."

LOUIS LIFTED HIS ARMS AND HUGGED HIS FATHER TO him fiercely until Silvius laughed, and managed to pull back a little.

"Well," Silvius said, "it is finally time you came through that door and into the courtyard."

Louis realized suddenly that Silvius had both his eyes, and that he, also, could see with two eyes. He put a hand to his chest, and felt it whole.

He looked back to Silvius. "You said you had been so blessed."

"Brutus was what *I* had made him. I should more than have expected that arrow through the eye, that surge of ambition. But what you are now, and what you shall become . . . *that* you have made yourself, and it is that making which has blessed me. You are a son to be proud of, Brutus, and I could not have asked for one better."

Louis's eyes filled with tears. "Will you come back with me, Silvius? When I can find my way out of this damned enchanted existence? Tell me that this is not the last that I shall see of you. I would like my father back."

"And you shall have him. There is certainly nothing better I would like than to live out my life beyond the magical portals of the Troy Game." His face now lost all trace of humor. "I would like *Silvius* to walk the streets of London, not that foul glamour which Asterion created."

Louis looked about. "Where do I go from here?"

"Forward," said a new voice, and Louis turned to see Long Tom standing just inside the door that led into Silvius' private chamber.

Long Tom held out his hand, and Louis walked forward.

As he drew closer to the doorway, he saw that beyond lay not Silvius' chamber, but the forest.

ELIZABETH WAS SETTING OUT ONE OF CATHARINE'S gowns when another of the queen's women, Lady Northard, entered and informed Elizabeth, with a sniff, that there were two disreputable boys waiting in the servants' courtyard to speak to her.

Elizabeth thanked her, then walked swiftly to the courtyard, trying to still her nerves. *What could they want?*

She found the imps waiting for her in a shadowed corner of the courtyard.

"What is it?" she said, taking care not to stand too close to them.

"Weyland wants to know," said one, "if you have anything interesting to report on Our Majesty the king's movements last night. Did anything of note take place?"

Little beast, Elizabeth thought, but was careful to keep the distaste off her face.

"No," she said. "He spent a quiet night in bed with his queen."

"And how could you be so sure of that?" said the other imp. "Did you hide behind the curtains, and peep at them while they fornicated?"

"They spent the night together. In bed. I saw this for myself, for early in the morning, well before dawn, the queen called me to her side—'twas my turn, last night, to sit awake in case she needed me—in order that I might empty her chamber pot, for she'd passed a particularly foul—"

"Yes, yes," said the second imp, wrinkling up his nose into a score of shadowy lines. "It is the king we are interested in, not the queen's bodily stenches."

"In that case," said Elizabeth, "I shall tell you that the king lay awake, concerned for his wife."

"Concerned at the reek, more like," the first imp muttered. Then, louder, "And you are sure indeed that it was he? Not some stable-lad pretending to be the king?"

"It was he," Elizabeth said, her voice calm, her eyes steady.

The imp nearer to her reached out suddenly, and closed sharp-nailed fingers about her wrist. "Really?" he said softly, and Elizabeth felt darkcraft seethe through her.

She gasped, sure that her lie would be discovered, but the imp only peered intently at her for the moment, then sighed, nodded, and withdrew his hand.

"It was a horrid reek, indeed," he said to his brother. "The king quite lost all lustful thoughts he had for his queen."

Then the imps both looked at Elizabeth. "Don't get too comfortable," said the first imp. "Weyland might always want you to come home, you know."

At that they were gone, and Elizabeth leaned momentarily against the wall in sheer relief.

Then she smiled, remembering what had happened last night when the Lord of the Faerie returned to the chamber.

He had greeted Catharine, then Marguerite and Kate, and had then turned first to Elizabeth and then to Frances, kissing each girl warmly on the mouth.

"He will never know," he'd said. "Tell him, if he probes, only that my lady wife needed you to empty her chamber pot, and that as you did so, you spied myself, sleepy, in the bed."

"WELL," SAID THE FIRST IMP, "I'LL POP BACK TO IDOL Lane, shall I, and tell Weyland what she said?"

"Aye," said his brother. "And then hurry down to the wharves, for there awaits us a berth on the *Woolly Fleece*, bound for the Low Countries. Weyland shall see us no more for the next week or so, I think."

chapter ten

The Great Founding Labyrinth
Within the Tower of London

"T OMORROW MORNING," SAID JANE TO WEYLAND that evening as they sat at supper, "Noah and I must leave you for the day. It is time she began her training."

His gaze was hooded and watchful. "Very well. That was part of the bargain I made with Noah. If she lay by my side at night"—those eyes slid Noah's way for a brief moment—"then she and you had your freedom to do what you needed. Tell me, where do you go?"

"You do not need to know," Jane said. "It is a matter which concerns only Noah and myself."

Weyland looked intently at Jane for a moment, but eventually he nodded. "I am pleased you do this, Jane."

"Are you not in the smallest bit concerned at *what* I might teach Noah?"

Weyland laughed. "You forget I *know* you, Jane, I know every piece of you, every thought you've ever entertained, every ounce of power you think to wield. I know what you are capable of, and what you are not. So, no, I am not in the least concerned. You can do no harm."

An hour later, he took Noah by the hand and led her upstairs to his Idyll.

JANE LOOKED CAREFULLY AT NOAH THE NEXT MORN-ing, but saw nothing in her face save some excitement intermixed with apprehension. Having breakfasted—Noah eating very little—they departed, walking down Idol Lane to Thames Street and then turning left toward the Tower.

"Where will we meet Ariadne?" said Noah as they approached the Tower. The complex loomed before them, the original Norman fortress now known as the White Tower rising from amid a motley collection of roofs, all bordered by ill-repaired walls that sprouted shrubs here and there throughout their height, and punctuated by gloomy bastions, the entire complex surrounded on three sides by a stinking, stagnant moat, and on the fourth by the Thames itself.

"She said she would wait for us by the Lion Gate," Jane said, referring to the medieval gate and towers that guarded the bridge over the moat which gave access to the Tower.

As she spoke, they turned the final corner, walked up the incline leading up Tower Hill, and saw the Lion Gate directly.

A woman and a man stood there, arm in arm, the woman of a great dark exotic beauty and clothed in red silk (the gown of contemporary English design, not ancient Minoan), the man dressed in the uniform of an Officer of the Tower.

Ariadne, and her lover, the Gentleman of the Ordnance.

"What's *he* doing here?" Noah said as they approached.

"Presumably she needs him to get us inside," said Jane.

"But why—" Noah said, and then could say no more, for they stood before the Lion Gate, and Ariadne and her gentleman advanced toward them.

"My friends!" Ariadne said, and, taking first Noah's—then Jane's—face between her hands, kissed them each soundly on both cheeks. "I am so glad you could come!" Then, almost without drawing breath, she said to Jane, "Thank you for bringing Noah, Jane. You may return toward dusk to collect her again."

Almost panicked, Noah said, "You cannot go home, Jane! Weyland thinks that you—" She stopped, looking at Ariadne's lover, regarding the women before him with amused blue eyes.

"I am not that silly," Jane said. "I shall spend my day about Tower Fields, gathering flowers." And with that she was off, striding briskly along the western perimeter of the Tower complex toward Tower Fields.

Ariadne put her arm through Noah's, and turned her toward the waiting man. "Noah, may I introduce my protector, Frederick Warneke, who is the Gentleman Officer of the Ordnance."

Noah dipped her head slightly at the man. "Gentleman Officer, I am most pleased to meet you. An unusual name, and most certainly not English." She raised an eyebrow.

"My father was a German merchant," Warneke said. "He settled here many years ago."

"Ah," said Noah. "Did he prefer London to his home, then?"

"Very much so," said Warneke. "He liked to say it was his spiritual birthplace."

Noah laughed, liking the man. He was plain of aspect with thinning fair hair and a luxuriant ginger moustache, but with such lively, humorous blue eyes that they lifted his presence from the ordinary to the attractive.

Warneke led Ariadne and Noah through the Lion Gate and then across the bridge toward Bell Tower and into the Inner ward. The Tower complex was filled with many buildings: the ancient Norman keep, the White Tower, which dominated the entire site; medieval halls and residences; more recent armories and storehouses; barracks for troops; galleries and chapels; and a few large open spaces consisting of stretches of green and squares of gravel. Warneke nodded at a long building to their left. "My quarters," he said, "where you may refresh yourself if desired."

Noah hesitated, looking to Ariadne for guidance.

"Noah and I have much to talk about," she said. "We shall walk awhile in the grounds, and once we feel the pangs of hunger and thirst we shall return."

Warneke gave a small bow. "Then I shall return to my duties," he said, and without further ado walked briskly across the Inner Ward toward a long line of armory buildings set against the northern wall of the Tower.

"For all the gods' sakes," said Noah, once Warneke was out of hearing range. "What—"

"He thinks only that you are my kinswoman who has a great curiosity about the Tower. Generously—for he is a generous man—Frederick has agreed that I may show you about the complex from time to time, so long as we stay away from the supply and ordnance stores."

"And what does he think that *you* are?"

Ariadne smirked. "A fine woman, who contributes more to his life than ever he thought possible."

Her arm tightened about Noah's. "Now, come with me, and walk the pathways toward the Great Founding Labyrinth. As you take your first step, accept that you will never, *never* be able to go back. You will either succeed on this quest, Noah, or you will die."

JANE WALKED ACROSS TOWER FIELDS UNTIL SHE CAME to the scaffold. She paused by the rotten posts, resting her hand on one of them, looking about.

Would the Lord of the Faerie remember?

"Of course, Jane. I have been waiting for this day."

Jane spun about, and saw the Lord of the Faerie emerge from the other side of the scaffold, a small smile on his face.

"Noah has gone to Ariadne?" the Lord of the Faerie asked.

"Yes. Why did you want me here?"

"Because you need to decide where you will go, Jane."

You need to decide where you will go. Jane decided she had never heard a more weighty, doom-raddled statement.

"What are my choices?" she asked.

"Come with me," the Lord of the Faerie said, extending his hand to her, "and walk awhile."

Jane reluctantly slid her hand within his.

His fingers entwined with hers. They were surprisingly warm and soft. Jane had been expecting something else. Something hard, perhaps.

She sighed, and allowed the Lord of the Faerie to lead her forward.

Within a moment she gasped, for Tower Fields abruptly vanished, and she found herself walking among the wild, ancient forests of Llangarlia. The Lord of the Faerie's hand tightened about hers as he realized her shock, but he said nothing, merely leading her farther along the forest path.

They walked for some time before Jane became aware that there were creatures behind the crowded trees, darting behind the trees, whispering, always keeping themselves just out of sight.

She tensed, and came to an abrupt halt, pulling her hand from that of the Lord of the Faerie's. "There is something *else* in the forest," she said.

"Aye," said the Lord of the Faerie. "There are other things in the forest."

"What are they?" Jane said, looking about her.

"Your choices," said the Lord of the Faerie quietly.

Jane went still, hardly able to breathe. Suddenly she felt very, very afraid. "What do you mean? *What* choices?"

"Jane, do you want to live, or do you want to die?"

Jane opened her mouth, then closed it slowly, staring at the Lord of the Faerie. "I want to live," she said, her voice low.

"Do you want to live *free* of your past, Jane?"

"I cannot," she said. "I am trapped, as are we all."

The Lord of the Faerie shook his head slowly, smiling. "No. It is your choice. Do you want to live, free of your past, and free of all the ambitions that have trapped you?"

Yes! Jane wanted to scream at him, frightened by the terrible intensity of her emotions.

"Yes," she whispered.

"There is a price."

Jane felt the old, familiar rage rise within her.

And then, suddenly, strangely, the rage died, leaving her feeling empty and ill. "I have always known there would be a price," she said.

Again the Lord of the Faerie gave a gentle smile. Once more he took her hand.

"Are you willing to pay the price?" he said.

Jane did not speak for a long time. She was not hesitating, as such, merely absorbing all the implications of the conversation, and thinking that, not so very far away, Noah was engaged in her own transformation, and Jane did not envy her one whit. She realized that this moment was a gift; one she thought she'd never receive.

"I am willing," she said.

Somewhere, deep within the forest, something terrible screamed.

"THE GREAT FOUNDING LABYRINTH?" NOAH SAID. "BUT that was on Knossos, and was destroyed when—"

She stopped suddenly.

"Really?" said Ariadne softly, and looked very deliberately at the White Tower which rose a little distance away.

Noah gasped in shock. As she had looked, so the White Tower had vanished, replaced by something dark and winding, and so monstrous, so frightening, that she had to look away again immediately.

"The Great Founding Labyrinth can be re-created anywhere, at any time, in any convenient structure," said Ariadne. "All trained Mistresses of the Labyrinth can do it. It is how the arts of the Labyrinth spread so far about the ancient world, for not all Mistresses could be trained on Knossos. When it came time to teach my daughter-heir, my *second* daughter, in Llangarlia, then I used the Meeting Hall on Thorney Island to re-create the Great Founding Labyrinth. Genvissa was taught by her mother in the same manner. Now, the White Tower, which sits directly atop the ancient God Well, serves my purpose better."

"I cannot look at it," Noah said softly.

"Not yet, no," said Ariadne, "for to gaze upon it for any length of time will kill you. But rest easy, Noah, for I shall not call it back until much deeper into your training. Eventually, of course, we shall enter it, and it shall be the site of your Great Ordeal."

" 'Great Ordeal'?"

"Your final test, my dear, to determine whether or not you have the strength and the courage to become a Mistress."

Noah dared glance toward the White Tower again, visibly relaxing when she saw that it had resumed its normal aspect. "Others cannot see what you just did?" she said.

Ariadne shook her head. "What you and I do within the Tower complex shall be for our eyes only." They were walking about the green-grassed area to the west of the White Tower, walking toward the chapel. "Now, we can waste no more time, for there is much to be accomplished today. Tell me, if you dare, what you know of the Labyrinth."

"It is a protective enchantment," Noah said, after a moment's thought. "A magical form which traps evil at its heart, thereby lending protection to the city it is created to safeguard." She glanced once more to the White Tower.

Ariadne raised her eyebrows. "A perfect textbook explanation," she said. "If bland and lusterless. Noah, you were literally bred within the Labyrinth—at least, your ancient foremother was, and you carry her blood in full measure—so, now, tell me what your heart, your bowels, your *soul* tells you about the Labyrinth."

She stopped, pulling Noah to a halt, and rested one of her hands flat against Noah's chest, the touch of her long elegant fingers burning down to Noah's skin.

Noah flinched, but the touch freed something within her. "The Labyrinth is powerful and alive and it *throbs*," she said. "It . . . It *is* my body!"

Her eyes widened as she said this, and Ariadne laughed, less in amusement than in genuine respect and with some measure of relief. *Yes, she had it within her. A power so vast that Noah would eventually—not even in some distant future, but soon—wield so much power that . . . well, that the earth would stop its spinning if she so chose to command it.*

JANE FELT MORE THAN HEARD IT. THOUSANDS OF creatures, converging toward her.

The shrubs beneath the trees quivered, then whipped from side to side, and before Jane could draw a single, shocked breath, she found herself surrounded by tens of thousands of creatures.

Faerie folk, all gazing at her with flat hatred.

"Their recompense is your price, Jane," said the Lord of the Faerie. "For two lives you have conspired against them, against the land, against the goddess of the waters, and planned and all but executed Og's murder. You have caused Eaving countless miseries through two lives. You have been a dark, malignant presence in this land, Genvissa-Swanne-Jane, and for this you must pay recompense."

Suddenly his hand tightened about Jane's. "Are you still willing to pay the price?" he asked.

No! she wanted to scream.

"Yes," she said. "Yes."

His hand loosened. "I had not thought you would agree," the Lord of the Faerie said, and Jane looked at him, at the tone of wonder in his voice.

"I am sick of myself," Jane said.

"That is a terrible thing," said the Lord of the Faerie. Then he looked up, looked about at all the Faerie folk there gathered, and said. "Shall we convene?"

The forest vanished about them.

"TELL ME," SAID ARIADNE AS THEY STOOD IN THE center of Tower Green, which stood just to the west of the White Tower. "Where do you think the Labyrinth lives when it does not loom dark and malevolent before us?"

Noah frowned. She looked away, as if staring at the distant chapel, but Ariadne knew she did not see stone and mortar, but the spaces deep within her own psyche.

"It lives all around us," Noah eventually said.

"How do you know that?" *Come on, girl. Tell me the ultimate secret!*

"The Labyrinth is life," Noah said. "The Labyrinth is creation."

Ariadne's eyes filled with tears. It had taken her weeks to fathom that secret, weeks of training and meditation and damned, terrifying ordeals.

And here Noah had won it from the thin air, without even stepping inside the Great Founding Labyrinth.

She *had* been born to this.

Ariadne again hooked her arm through Noah's, turning her to walk once more across the green toward the chapel.

"The Labyrinth *is* creation, yes," Ariadne said. The women's hips rubbed now and again as they walked, and Ariadne reveled in it, the touching and the closeness. *Oh, to have bred such a daughter-heir!* "The Labyrinth is the result of the marriage of life and the globe, this earth, and of life itself. The Labyrinth is reflected in the twistings of our brain and bowels, in the secret passages of our veins, the flow of our blood through our bodies. It mirrors the dance of the stars through the heavens, and the twistings of our own earth through the strange night skies."

"And the Mistress of the Labyrinth?" Noah said. "How does she manipulate this? How does she gain ascendency over this power? How does she *use* it?"

"Dancing the Labyrinth re-creates the harmonies of life, Noah. The harmonies of the movement of the stars, the earth on which we live, the recurring patterns of the seasons and the tides, the twistings of rivers and streams and of the breath through all living things—all of these harmonies thrum through every living being. The ultimate Mistress of the Labyrinth 'dances the Labyrinth,' and in so doing, controls all these separate yet entwined harmonies. In controlling them, she manipulates them."

Ariadne paused, pulled Noah to a halt in the shadow of the chapel and eyed her carefully. "The greatest Mistress of all, my dear, controls the power of the earth and the stars, of the sun and moon, of the seasons and tides and the breath and purpose of every living thing. Do you think yourself capable of that?"

Noah responded with her own question. "And you, Ariadne? How much of this did *you* control?"

"A fraction, Noah, but enough to effect the Catastrophe."

"And Genvissa?"

"A fraction of what I managed."

Noah took a deep breath, and Ariadne knew that she was thinking through the possibilities . . . and the responsibilities.

"*Am* I capable, Ariadne?" she said.

"You are born of both myself, the greatest Mistress of the Labyrinth hitherto, and of the creature who lived at the dark heart of the Labyrinth. You are, separately, also the goddess of the waters and the cycles of the seasons. I do not think that coincidence. Of all women who have aspired to be the highest among the Mistresses of the Labyrinth, you have the greatest potential. Whether or not you attain that potential is up to your own courage and determination."

"What does my training consist of, Ariadne?"

"Of learning the dance. Of learning to manipulate the power of the Labyrinth, of *creation*, without allowing it to rope out of control, or to manipulate you or control you."

"And the Game? What part does this play in the power of the Labyrinth?"

"The Game is the single way the ancients found to use the power. The original Mistresses and Kingmen learned to use the power of the Labyrinth to create the protective enchantment you know as the Game. In your case, the Troy Game."

"Is the Game only capable of protection and safeguarding?" Noah said.

"No. The Game is as capable of great evil as it is of great good. The Troy Game, that which Genvissa and Brutus left unfinished, has roped out of control. It is all of that power I have spoken of, and it is out of control."

"Gods," Noah whispered.

"Yes," Ariadne said, "gods, indeed. There is very little else now that can stop it."

"WE'RE BACK AT THE NAKED!" JANE SAID.

Indeed they were. Jane looked about as she stood at the Lord of the Faerie's side, astounded at the stunning view of rolling, wooded hills. When she'd been here previously, when Louis had been told of his destiny, she'd not thought to look about at the landscape.

A movement caught her eye, and she looked down.

All the creatures which had surrounded her within the forest were walking slowly up the sides of the hill.

There were giants, Sidlesaghes, cavelings, sun-dapples, moon-shadows, snow-ghosts, water-sprites—a host of faerie creatures that Jane had only ever glimpsed as Genvissa, and then only at the height of some of the most powerful rites that she and Gormagog had conducted.

This was stunning—and terrifying, for every one of the faerie creatures had flat, hateful eyes, and every one of them was trained on Jane.

She took an automatic step backward.

"Are you sure you want to do this?" the Lord of the Faerie said, his hands catching at her shoulders and holding her still. "Are you so very, very sure that you want to face their judgment in return for your freedom?"

Jane was *not* sure at all, but she couldn't back down now. Not in front of Coel and what he had become.

"I am sure," she said; sure only that her "freedom" actually meant death.

"Then stand on your own," he snapped, letting go her shoulders, and taking a step back from her.

Summoning all of her courage, Jane stood as upright as she could, straightening her back and shoulders in a flash of her old arrogance.

The next ten minutes—as the bleak-eyed creatures slowly ascended the hill—were the slowest in her life. The Faerie folk drew close, their first rank standing only two paces away from Jane, almost completely encircling her save for a passage they left clear through to where the Lord of the Faerie had sat on his throne on the eastern edge of the summit.

"My Faerie folk," the Lord of the Faerie said, once they had all come to a halt, "here stands before you a woman you know well. She has been a Maga-Llan, a Darkwitch, a wife, a whore, and through all her lives she has sought to do the Faerie as much damage and death as possible. Yet here she stands, willing to pay recompense to you so that she might live in freedom. What say you? Will you accept her recompense?"

"Aye!" shouted the great throng, and Jane winced, not so much at the sound, but at the *hatred* she felt washing over her. *Gods, why had she agreed to this?*

"And your price?" said the Lord of the Faerie, his low voice carrying clearly across the entire summit. "The price you demand of this Darkwitch whore?"

A water-sprite stepped forth. "I speak for all," he said, staring at Jane.

"Yes?" said the Lord of the Faerie. "Name the price."

The water-sprite held his flat, hateful stare at Jane for a long moment, then suddenly, stunningly, he grinned, and held out one of his spindly arms.

A magpie fluttered down from the sky, coming to roost on the water-sprite's arm.

"We want you to learn to carol," the magpie said. "We yearn to hear once more the Ancient Carol of the dawn and the dusk."

"THAT SHALL BE ENOUGH FOR THE DAY," SAID ARIADNE. "You have done far better than I'd dreamed."

Noah blinked, looking about. Somehow most of the day had passed, and now late-afternoon shadows stretched across Tower Green.

"You need to go back to your house in Idol Lane," said Ariadne, "and think about what you're doing."

"What do you mean, 'what I am doing'?"

Ariadne lifted her hand once more to Noah's chest. "I can feel it within you," she said, her voice soft, her eyes hard. "Asterion's seed. You lay with him, Noah. Why did you do that?"

"The same reason you did," Noah replied, flatly enough that Ariadne knew she was lying. "Because he felt good to me."

"He is a good lover, is he not?"

"Aye, he is a good lover."

"He was desperate when first I had him," said Ariadne. "I was his first. I imagine, however, that he's gained some experience since then."

"In coupling, yes," said Noah. "But not in love. Of that he has never had experience."

Ariadne hissed. "Be wary where you tread, girl! Couple with him if you must, for whatever reason you wish. But, gods, girl, do not speak of *love* in connection with the Minotaur!"

Noah remained silent.

Ariadne drew in a deep breath. "There are few people who would accept this with the same equanimity that I have, Noah. It is dangerous."

"Really? But am I not a product of such 'danger'?"

Ariadne laughed. "Oh, yes, you are a product of my own lustful cuddlings with the Minotaur. *Aye.* I can see what a daughter of mine you truly are." She sobered. "*Be careful.* Use him; do not allow him to use you. And think, also, do you not have this Stag God lover awaiting you? Your Kingman? Why jeopardize that with an affair with Asterion?"

"I do not have to justify this to you, Ariadne."

Ariadne's eyes narrowed, and she nodded to herself very slightly. *Oh gods . . .*

JANE GAPED, UNABLE TO BELIEVE WHAT SHE HAD heard. Behind her, the Lord of the Faerie, laughing merrily. All about her the

Faerie folk were laughing, and she thought that perhaps this was a great jest on their part; that at any moment their laughter would reveal it for what it truly was—malicious retribution.

"We want you to carol," said the Lord of the Faerie, and Jane jumped, for suddenly he was standing at her side. "We want you to carol in the dawn and the dusk, and lighten all our hearts. You shall spend an eternity paying your recompense, Jane, but I think you will do very well at it."

Jane stared at him. Her eyes had filled with tears, and the Lord of the Faerie had become nothing but a misty blur, and the great crowd of Faerie folk were little more than an undulating ocean surrounding her.

"I can't sing very well," she finally whispered.

The Lord of the Faerie bent his head down, and kissed her—and it was for Jane the greatest kiss she could ever have imagined, for it was full of nothing but laughter and mercy.

"Then we shall teach you," he said, lifting his mouth away from hers.

NOAH AND ARIADNE DRANK AN ALE WITH WARNEKE in his chambers before he escorted them back to the Lion Gate. There Noah and Ariadne found Jane waiting for them, standing patiently a few paces away in the shadow of the wall.

"Have you been bored, sweeting?" Ariadne said. She did not move from beneath the Lion Gate.

"Deeply," Jane said, walking over and looking at Noah. "You're still alive, then?"

"Deeply," said Noah, and Jane's mouth twitched, and then smiled.

CHARLES SAT IN HIS MOST INNER AND PRIVATE OF HIS chambers in Whitehall, Eaving's Sisters gathered about him.

"Well?" asked Marguerite.

Charles smiled, soft and warm. "She is learning the ways of the Labyrinth," he said.

"And *Jane* teaches her?" said Catharine, her tone incredulous.

Charles looked at her, then raised a hand and twisted a finger about one of her dark curls which had escaped a pin. "Of course," he said. "Who else?"

AT THE WINDOW, UNBEKNOWNST TO ANY IN THE ROOM, the little girl smiled, and then stepped back from the window and faded away.

CHAPTER ELEVEN

THE GREAT FOUNDING LABYRINTH
WITHIN THE TOWER OF LONDON, AND
IDOL LANE, LONDON
Noah Speaks

NOAH, MISTRESS OF THE LABYRINTH. THAT ALLI-
ance of name and title had a certain ring to it. Most certainly it had
been something I'd needed to achieve for well over a lifetime so
that I could be Mistress to Brutus-reborn's Kingman and complete the Troy
Game.

What surprised me was that once I began to learn the ways of the
Labyrinth, then I *wanted* it as well. Badly. Ariadne said it was my "blood" coming out. I'd been bred to this; thus, once my eyes were opened, and I realized
my potential, then I could not wait a single moment before I reached out with
both hands and seized that potential and that heritage, and made it mine.

The power of the Labyrinth was sublime, exciting, sexual, enlivening, addictive. I could not get enough of it. I *wallowed* in it. I was proud of my natural
abilities, and lived for Ariadne's smile, her nod, her rare, *"That was well done,
Noah."* For six visits Ariadne took me about the White Tower (although to our
perception it rose above us in a twisting mass of darkness rather than white-
washed ragstone) in meandering circles, but we did not enter it. Ariadne did
not so much teach me, as draw forth from me understanding that I had not realized was there, and which made me wonder if indeed I had been bred for this
task, rather than having it thrust suddenly upon me. Then, at the end of my
sixth visit, I realized that Ariadne had not been leading me in meaningless
perambulations about the White Tower at all, but in clearly defined patterns.

As we had walked, so we had re-created the windings of the Labyrinth.

I exclaimed, and told Ariadne of my realization, and she smiled, and patted my arm, and said, "So. Now you are ready."

On my next visit to the Tower, Ariadne took me inside the White Tower itself. Here—although only our eyes could see it—entwined in representative form the harmonies of stars and tides, moon and brain, blood vessel and forest path. Here, I would learn to control and, eventually, to manipulate these harmonies.

The Labyrinth of creation.

It was terrifying and exhilarating, all in one.

Managing the power within the Great Founding Labyrinth was not easy. As eager as I was, even with the heritage I had, I found it a troublesome task. To even open myself up to the harmonies was to allow so much apparently chaotic discord to flood my being, that I found it difficult to concentrate for longer than two or three minutes. Ariadne told me my initial training was to enable me to cope with this flood of sensory information, then later stages would enable me to control and manipulate it.

To rebuild the Labyrinth to my own needs.

"Previous Mistresses of the Labyrinth, and Kingmen, have rebuilt it only for reasons of protection," Ariadne said to me one day as I sat on the outer steps of the White Tower, nursing my aching head in my hands. "It was all we knew how to do. You? You may go much further, do more with the labyrinthine enchantments than any before you."

She shrugged, seemingly disinterested. "And maybe not."

Ariadne may have affected dismissive indifference on occasion, but there was one thing about me which fascinated her—and myself, come to that.

I was not simply Noah, long-lost daughter-heir returned to Ariadne, nor even an Asterion-bred Darkwitch. I was also Eaving, goddess of the waters and fields and fertility of the land, and, as Eaving, I had a peculiarly strong bonding with the labyrinth. I was deeply attuned to the seasons and the turning of the tides and the year, and this meant I was even more greatly attuned to the harmonies of the labyrinth than might otherwise have been. Eaving complemented what natural skills I had as Mistress of the Labyrinth, and my increasing skills as Mistress of the Labyrinth complemented my abilities as Eaving.

"I should never have been so dismissive of my role as MagaLlan," Ariadne said thoughtfully one day as we walked back to share our usual ale with Frederick Warneke. "Imagine what I might have achieved, had I truly realized how complementary were the land and the labyrinth."

I shot her a dark, cynical look. Ariadne controlling both powers as goddess and labyrinth would have sent the stars themselves into a panic.

And myself? Was I worthy of panic?

"Ariadne," I said, "should I use the darkcraft within me? What *of* this dark heritage? I am terrified of using it . . . or of it using me."

"The darkcraft is not to be feared, Noah. It will be a better lover to you than any man ever could be. Even Weyland."

I could not smile. The truth was that just the thought of having the darkcraft inside me was terrifying. What would it do if ever I unleashed it? What did it *feel* like? Would it corrupt me? Would it alter who I was as Eaving, and as a Mistress of the Labyrinth?

If I was unsure about the darkcraft, then I was terribly uncertain about the Troy Game itself. I still had no true idea of *why* the Game had decided to emerge as flesh incarnate; and the fact that Catling was "loose" in London worried me from time to time. My faith in the value of the Troy Game to this land had been severely undermined. I most certainly no longer believed in "the one true way." I was no longer ready to accept that there was merely *the one path,* and that it was my duty as female representative of all things good and fair to walk its straight and narrow boundaries.

I was learning that life, like the labyrinth, and like creation itself, is made up of varied subjective interpretations.

I was realizing that for any one problem there were many solutions, many paths which could be trod.

All this meant but one thing: I was no longer prepared to accept without question the future that the Troy Game had mapped out for me.

I was becoming . . . independent. A strange state, for me.

Partly this was because of the Troy Game's—*Catling's*—unnecessary deception. The utter cruelty of that deception had cost the Game dearly in terms of unquestioning loyalty. There was now no "unquestioning" about it, and even the loyalty, on some days, had to be questioned.

And, partly, my new independence of thought and my questioning of my old loyalties, was because of Weyland Orr.

Asterion.

EACH AFTERNOON AFTER I'D BEEN TO THE TOWER (perhaps twice a week), Weyland would kiss me, taste the growing power in my mouth, and smile at both myself and Jane.

Each night he and I repaired to the Idyll. Each night we talked, then we went to that sumptuous bed.

Each night, invariably, we made love.

And we talked, far into each night. There were a few nights where neither of us slept, and then in the morning we would be irritable and cross with each other, and with Jane. Ironically, our bickering on these mornings tended to set

her suspicions to rest for a while, because she could not believe such a squabbling couple could be involved in any matter of the heart.

Any matter of the heart.

This was not what I had meant to achieve that night I first lay with Weyland. I had convinced myself (in the heat of the moment when possibly I was
grasping for any excuse) that this was a matter of healing of an ancient wound.
But the *sex* was not the healing. No, the healing of Asterion's wounds was
something infinitely more dangerous.

Those wounds needed true companionship. Those wounds needed trust.
Those wounds needed love.

Over three thousand years I'd had a pitiful handful of lovers—Brutus and
Harold; then Asterion, once, in his glamour of Silvius; and finally John
Thornton—but Weyland made me forget them all. There was no pining for
Brutus whenever I was with Weyland.

There was only Weyland.

One night we lay, sweaty, slightly out of breath, recovering from the heat of
our passion. Weyland's hand was slowly tracing its way up and down my back,
sending delicious little thrills of pleasure through my body. Then, on one downward sweep, his hand went much lower than it had previously, and it rubbed and
bumped over the ridged scars left after that hateful imp had eaten its way out.

His hand jerked away, and he went very still.

"Why?" I said. "Why be so malicious? You didn't need to cause us so much
agony. You didn't need to tear Jane and myself apart in order to impress
Charles."

Weyland kept his hand very still for a long time, and did not move it again
until he finally spoke. "I was fed hatred from the time of my birth. My mother,
leaning over my cradle, spitting at me. King Minos, devising the worst possible
means to keep me caged. The population of Knossos, of *all* Crete, invoking my
name to frighten their children."

His hand was now running from the nape of my neck, down my back, over
my scars, about my buttocks, slowly, caressingly, and then up again, traveling
as leisurely on its return as it had on its journey thither. I was trembling, partly
at what Weyland was saying, mostly at his hand.

"Hate became for me not merely a means of existence, but the very *nature*
of existence. It became more than that. It became a vehicle, a means of achiev-
ing my ambitions, and it became a safe place to hide."

A glib-enough explanation on the face of it, but there was something about
Weyland's voice and the way his eyes wouldn't meet mine, that made me realize he was telling me the actual way it had been for him. For a man such as
Weyland, this opening and sharing was painful and dangerous, and so I kissed
his mouth, and stroked his face, and after a moment or two he continued.

"It is no excuse, not to such as you, but it was who I was." He paused, and finally allowed his eyes to meet with mine. "Hate is something too easy to fall into, Noah. It is . . . addictive. Safe. It demands nothing save that it be fed."

"Do you still hate, Weyland?"

"Not here, not with you."

I gave a soft, somewhat breathless laugh. "I am so very afraid of you, Weyland. Of what we are doing."

Weyland, Weyland, what are we doing? How can we stop? How can we stop?

"On some days," he whispered, "I am nauseous with fear. All I want is to force you to get those bands for me, to force you to my will . . . and yet . . ."

"What is different about this life, Weyland? Why these doubts and hesitations now?"

"You," he said without hesitation. "I had no thoughts for Cornelia, she was merely a piece to be moved on the chessboard. I despised Caela. But you . . ."

"I have grown a little."

"You have grown a great deal. But . . ." His thumb traced about the borders of my face, over my forehead, about my cheekbone, around my jaw. "Ah, Noah, I have never encountered such a jewel as you. Not in any life. Not in any place I have traveled." His voice changed, became full of laughter. "You are still my concubine . . . but freely now. Not forced. That has been a strange lesson for me to learn—that I can achieve more through granting freedom than through forcing with fear."

Aye, still his concubine. And more dangerously trapped now than ever I was with his imp inside me.

We were quiet for a while after that, touching and stroking, kissing now and again, moving closer to lovemaking once more, but as yet too indolent to be bothered.

I eventually spoke, thinking to use the intimacy of this moment to ask something about one of my deepest fears. "Weyland, talk to me of the darkcraft. I had thought you might try to apportion some of the blame for your actions on that. 'See, I am consumed with dark power. I am its slave.'"

He laughed, rolling over on his back. "I wish I *had* thought of using it as an excuse. Would you have accepted it?"

"No. I would have loathed you for it."

His smile died. "The darkcraft is but power, Noah. It imparts no moral values, and has no destination or objective of its own. What I have done, in all my lives, is my own burden to bear. Not that of the darkcraft."

"So . . . the darkcraft does not corrupt?" I held my breath, waiting for that response.

His mouth twisted slightly. "Not unless he who wields it is corruptible."

I relaxed. I had the darkcraft quiescent within me. *It* would not corrupt me . . . not unless I was myself corruptible.

So, *did* I trust myself? *Was* I true?

And true to *what*?

Weyland was now watching me quizzically. "Why these questions? And why these emotions I see rolling over your face?"

I tried to distract him with humor. "I merely wanted to know precisely what I shared a bed with."

Something in his face changed. "Well, my lady Noah, perhaps you should experience *precisely* what it *is* you share a bed with."

Weyland's hand touched me again, but this time it was as if a different man had touched me . . . no, as if a different *world* had touched me.

"Weyland!"

"You want to know what the darkcraft is, Noah? Then let it love you, let it lie with you, let it *inside* you." His body was resting full-length and firm against mine now, his hands were at my back, my shoulders, my breasts. "Let *all* of me make love to you, Noah."

THUS BEGAN A JOURNEY, AN EXPERIENCE, FROM which it took me days to recover and to regain my equilibrium. Weyland took me down the paths of the darkcraft, allowing it to envelop me, consume me, wash through my very soul.

It was the most frightening, exhilarating, joyous, dangerous, unbelievable encounter of all of my lives.

Initially I was terrified, for power such as I had never imagined swept through me.

Worse, I could feel that as-yet untried and unopened potential deep within myself responding to it, wanting to join with it, and I dared not allow it. Because then, not only would Weyland realize I had kept such critical knowledge from him that he would never trust me again (*and why was that so important, eh?*), but because I knew instinctively that if I did allow it, then Weyland and I would be joined by forces so powerful that I would never be able to break free from him again.

But as the moment passed, and I became a little more used to Weyland's darkcraft washing through me, I realized that, first, I could keep my own potential quiescent without too much trouble; and second, I was enjoying this experience so greatly that, frankly, I did not want to put a halt to it. Ariadne was right, this *was* the greatest lover imaginable.

Warm, dark, caressing, safe.

Exciting. Stimulating. Erotic. Addictive.

Use it, Weyland whispered in my mind, *to make love to me.*

And so I did. I growled, feeling his darkcraft bubbling through me, and I sank my teeth into his shoulder. He laughed, and began to do things to me that, had I been told of them by another, would have shocked me to the core.

But now . . . Now, Oh gods . . . now . . .

We did not so much make love, as we *reveled.*

ON A LATER NIGHT, WHEN WE LAY QUIET, I ASKED Weyland why he had made the Idyll, and why in this house. It was a night of exploration, and, as neither of us could sleep, it was a good-enough topic of conversation.

"I purchased this house years ago," he said, "after hunting for many months. I found better houses than this, more spacious, grander, more solidly built, but this house . . ." He paused.

"I walked into this house," he resumed softly, "and it called to me. I walked up the stairs, and entered the chamber at the very top of the house." Again he paused, remembering. "It was if it spoke to me, and offered me possibilities."

"What kind of possibilities, Weyland?"

He was silent a long time, and I wondered what it could be that was so difficult for him to say.

"It offered me a home," he finally said, so low I barely heard him. "Safety. Peace. Comfort."

Tears sprang into my eyes. "Then I thank you for bringing me here," I said.

I had my hand on his chest, and I felt his breathing slow, and deepen.

"This place was waiting for you," he said.

I closed my eyes, unintentionally squeezing out two of those gathered tears.

"Do you know what this place is?" I asked. I doubted he did, for it had taken *me* weeks of climbing these stairs every night to realize the significance of both house and Idyll, and Weyland did not have the same understanding as I.

"What do you mean? This is the Idyll, sitting within my house in Idol Lane."

"And where does this house sit?" I said. "Where does Idol Lane sit?"

"I don't know what you're asking me, Noah."

Again I closed my eyes briefly, and wondered why I was about to speak. *Weyland, Weyland, what are we doing? How can we stop? How can we stop?*

"Weyland, this part of London covers Cornhill."

"Yes?"

"In ancient times, in Llangarlian times, this was known as Mag's Hill."

His hand, which had been stroking my neck, suddenly ceased.

"The goddess hill," I said, my voice now almost a whisper. "*My* hill. Idol Lane follows exactly the ancient mystery track to the summit. This house sits close to the top of the hill, but the top floor, where we are now, is level with the summit. Weyland, you have built your Idyll figuratively, and almost literally, on the summit of the goddess hill. Every time you climb the stairs to the Idyll you metaphorically climb into the realm of the goddess. Yes, this place was waiting for me. *I* am what makes it complete."

We did not speak for a long time.

Finally, just as I was drifting into sleep, I heard Weyland whisper, "Noah, Noah, what are we doing?"

THERE WAS A DARK CORNER TURNED THAT NIGHT, but whether it was toward the light, or into greater darkness, I do not know. Even then, I think, I knew there was no turning back for me.

CHAPTER TWELVE

IN THE REALM OF THE FAERIE; THE GREAT FOUNDING LABYRINTH WITHIN THE TOWER OF LONDON; AND IDOL LANE, LONDON

*L*OUIS DREAMED, BUT THIS WAS AS NO DREAM he'd ever experienced as a man, nor even as a soul waiting impatiently through hundreds of years for rebirth. He dreamed as if he were awake; that is, he existed as if in a dream, but he knew this was no dream.

This was enchantment and magic and power such as he'd never encountered previously, not even when he laid down the foundations of the Troy Game with Genvissa.

Louis ran the Ringwalk. He sometimes ran as a man, but more often he ran as something four-legged, far more powerful and swifter than a man.

He ran as the white stag with the blood-red antlers, and he ran through dream and reality, through land and mist, through time past and time future, and he ran until his heart pounded frantically in his chest, and he ran *because* he had a heart to pound frantically *in* his chest.

And he was glad.

Sometimes Louis ran alone, but more often than not, other faerie creatures ran beside him.

Sidlesaghes, in their thousands, sometimes singing, sometimes silent.

The Lord of the Faerie. Laughing, sharing laughter.

Sometimes his father, Silvius, and Louis did not know if Silvius accompanied him because Louis was his son, Brutus-reborn, or if because Louis was Silvius' longtime companion, the stag, risen from his death.

As Louis ran the Ringwalk, he learned. Rather, as Louis ran the Ringwalk, he absorbed. He absorbed the memories of all those who had run as the Stag God previously, and he understood that somehow Noah had undergone the same process when she had become Eaving. He discovered he could remember back to the dawn of life, back to the primeval world, back to when he, the white stag with the blood-red antlers, was nothing more than an ambition, a dream, a needing.

He remembered that first day he'd taken form, slithering free of his mother's birth canal, dropping to the forest floor—not on his side or belly, as did other fawns, but on his four feet, running from the moment of birth.

Born for the Ringwalk.

He remembered those who had hunted him, and those who had protected him. The Faerie folk who had been his friends and lovers, and the creatures who had hated him and who had tried to kill him: other gods, frantic druids, fearful Christian priests.

Of them all, only the Darkwitch, Genvissa, had almost succeeded, and from that the stag had learned—he had only one true enemy, and that was the Darkwitch.

Louis ran the Ringwalk, and as he ran, he changed.

LIFE IN IDOL LANE TRANSFORMED. JANE, WHO HAD lived there all her present life, had known only humiliation, day after day, year in, year out. Now, something else replaced that humiliation. Tolerance. Amusement.

Friendliness.

Generosity.

Her reward, for teaching Noah the ways of the labyrinth.

She didn't trust it, this new world of Idol Lane. She was terrified of what would happen when Weyland discovered that it was not her teaching Noah, but Ariadne. But for the time being, for this brief time when Weyland relaxed and the house became bearable, almost likeable, Jane determined to enjoy it.

Where once Jane had been a prisoner of the house, allowed out only when Weyland sent her on some closely watched chore, now he tolerated her coming and going virtually as she wished.

Noah did not often choose to leave the house on those days she did not go to the Tower to learn from Ariadne. Jane wondered if it was because she was fearful of meeting Catling somewhere in the streets, or if she just preferred to stay close to Weyland. Whatever the case, Jane took whatever chance she could to wander the byways and nooks of London. She rarely saw anyone she knew, and few people recognized her now that her face had healed, and she walked with more pride than Jane the whore had ever managed.

Weyland largely left Jane alone. She'd been the butt of his viciousness all through the years when there was just herself and him (until Elizabeth and Frances, the procession of broken girls through the house had meant little to either Jane or Weyland). Now, Weyland had something else to amuse him— Noah. Jane wasn't sure what Noah had done. (*Had* she slept with him? Jane puzzled over it, and then decided she didn't truly care one way or the other. If she had, then that was Noah's damnation, and the woman could deal with it herself.) Every evening that they returned to the house from the Tower, Weyland would take Noah in his arms, and kiss her, and taste the rise in her power, and would then smile and relax, well pleased. He was happy, he was sure of himself, and so he left Jane alone.

Thus, there being no one to disturb her, Jane slipped deeper and deeper into her own world. Or, rather, she sank deeper and deeper into the world of the Lord of the Faerie. Rather like Weyland and Noah (had she known it), Jane existed in her own little realm of happiness. Jane spent most of her waking hours thinking of nothing but the Lord of the Faerie and what the Faerie Realm offered her. Release, freedom, a new life. And something else, something Jane hardly dared think about. She felt like a girl again, her heart thudding whenever she reflected on the Lord of the Faerie, her breath shortening whenever she remembered a way in which he had glanced at her, or the manner in which he had held her hand, and she would spend hours trying to interpret these tiny gestures in the best possible light.

Release, freedom, a new life, and possibly—*possibly*—love.

And all for a song.

When she had left the Faerie, and its Lord, he had said to return to him the next time she and Noah came to the Tower. "We will show you the Ancient Carol," he said, "so that you may best know how to greet dawn and dusk."

What the Faerie asked of her *was* simple (and yet so complex within that simplicity), and what they offered rich beyond expectation . . . but first Jane had to escape Weyland. He could still control her, should he so want.

He could still *kill* her, and Jane was very afraid that he would do just that, the moment Noah had completed her training and Weyland felt that Jane was superfluous to his needs.

This single fear regularly interrupted her otherwise happy reveries with a stomach-knotting terror.

Freedom and hope lay proffered before Jane, but between her and that offer lay that single insurmountable hurdle.

Weyland Orr.

* * *

THREE DAYS AFTER NOAH'S INITIAL TRAINING SES-
sion (and Jane's strange ordeal atop the summit of The Naked) Ariadne called
them back to the Tower.

It was three days too long for Jane. The instant Ariadne met Noah at Lion
Gate (her lover not in evidence this time), Jane turned her back and walked
to the rotting scaffold, and then beyond. She could barely contain her
excitement—*the Lord of the Faerie awaited!*—and the moment she reached the
scaffold she looked about, breathless, her eyes wide.

"I remember when you were Swanne," a gentle, amused voice said behind
her, "you could not wait to be *rid* of me."

Jane spun about. "Coel!"

He was leaning, arms folded, against a massive tree trunk two paces away.
(Tower Fields had again vanished, replaced by the ancient forest.) He straightened as Jane came over, and took her hands and kissed her mouth.

"Welcome home, Jane," the Lord of the Faerie said, very softly.

HE CONVEYED HER TO THE NAKED. ON THIS OCCA-
sion, both the summit and the slopes were bare of anything save grass, the
Lord of the Faerie's throne set to the eastern portion of the summit, and the
magpie sitting on an arm of the throne.

"Master Magpie," said the Lord of the Faerie, "shall be your songmaster."

At that, he let go her hand and stood back, and Jane felt a pang of great
loneliness. But she took a deep breath, and stepped forward, and the magpie
smiled (its beak curving most marvelously), and bowed its head, and spoke.

"Welcome, Caroler. Have you come to learn the ways of the dawn and the
dusk?"

Jane's sense of loneliness abated as curiosity and eagerness filled her.

"What have I missed all these years?" she said, looking down at the magpie.

Life, came the Lord of the Faerie's whispered reply in her mind. *Joy.*

"And thus," said the magpie, "you shall greet the dawn and dusk with life
and joy, and with majesty and reverence, so that both the day and the night
shall grace the Faerie. Is this something you can accomplish?"

"I wish to," said Jane, and that appeared to be the right answer, for the
magpie smiled once more, and then began to hum. It was but a simple phrase,
repeated over and over, but Jane could hear a great complexity running
through it. She frowned, concentrating, and wondering if she could ever master its intricacies.

"Sing it," the Lord of the Faerie said, and Jane jumped slightly, for suddenly he was behind her, his hands resting lightly on her shoulders.

"Sing it," he whispered. "Complete your penance."

And so Jane, drawing a deep breath to steady her nerves, opened her mouth, and began to sing.

She'd never thought she had a good singing voice, but somehow the melody she sang, that simple repeated phrase the magpie had hummed to her, created a richness of its own. To her stunned surprise, Jane heard the complexity she'd recognized in the magpie's voice repeated in her own, yet ten times over, so that the phrase became redolent with meaning and imagery, even though she sang only with tone and not with words.

Jane stopped suddenly, amazed.

The magpie and the Lord of the Faerie laughed, the magpie flapping his wings, the Lord of the Faerie sliding his hands down Jane's body to her waist, turning her about, and kissing her once more.

"Each time you come back to The Naked," he said, "Master Magpie shall teach you another phrase of the Great Song until you have accomplished it all, and then, who knows? I loved you once, maybe I shall again."

"Don't taunt me," she whispered.

"I only offer possibilities, Jane."

Another moment of silence, in which they looked at each other, and then looked away.

"Jane . . ." the Lord of the Faerie said, his voice drifting away. Then he sighed. "It is time to go. Noah has done for the day."

ARIADNE ASKED JANE, MANY TIMES, WHERE SHE WENT while she and Noah spent their time within the Tower, and Jane affected a bored air, and said that she did little but wander about the grassy spaces of Tower Fields plucking at flowers.

At this, Ariadne always rolled her eyes, and Noah looked at Jane as she delivered her *"I spent the day being bored"* explanation, and Jane wondered if perhaps she had some idea of what truly happened. But Noah did not question her closely, and so they continued, Jane and Noah traveling every few days to the Tower. There Jane would watch Ariadne and Noah disappear inside the Lion Gate, then she would walk to the scaffold.

There, always, waited the Lord of the Faerie, and he would take her to The Naked. There, each day, Jane would learn a new phrase of the Ancient Carol, and fall a little deeper into hope, and even deeper into love.

Chapter Thirteen

At Sea on the *Woolly Fleece*

HE MASTER OF THE *WOOLLY FLEECE* WAS SOME-
what bemused by his two strange saturnine passengers, but they
had paid well enough, and the master had been at sea for too
many years to question gold coin placed in his hand. The two youths—Tim and
Bob, they called themselves—kept to themselves, bunking down with the
sailors in the hold at night, and, strangely, crouching under the deck railing at
the very prow of the ship during the day. The master thought they looked like
hunched black monkeys as they huddled there, drenched with sea spray,
bright eyes peering ahead.

They had sailed from the Pool of London ten days ago, making good time
to The Hague where over three days they'd offloaded their cargo of wool, then
reloaded with fine woven cloth from Flanders and Venice. During these three
days the two youths had absented themselves from the port, reappearing but
an hour or two before the master was to shout the orders to cast off for England. He'd regarded them critically—as he did all passengers and sailors after
a stay in the Low Countries—but they were bright of eye, and quick of movement, and he could see no sign of the sickness within them. If it *was* there,
then doubtless it would appear on the voyage back home, and if that were the
case, well then, the master would take care of it as he took care of all passengers or crew who happened to show signs of fever, or exhibited any lumps under their armpits or groin.

A regretful smile, and a quick shove off the deck. The rolling gray sea was,
so far as the master of the *Woolly Fleece* was concerned, the best remedy of all
for the plague.

But these two youths appeared well enough. They carried with them two
small casks, which the master duly inspected.

They were packed with black feathers.

The master raised an eyebrow at the youths.

"We have a mistress," said one of them, "inordinately fond of her feathers. The best of the black are to be found here, in the Low Countries."

It was the strangest response the master had ever heard, but harmless enough, so he shrugged, and walked away.

An hour later, the *Woolly Fleece* was on her way back to England and her home port of London.

"WELL?" SAID CATLING. SHE SAT ON A BALE OF WOOL (part of the cargo awaiting the *Woolly Fleece* which would, within a day or two, be on her way to Flanders with this particular consignment).

The two imps stood before her, each with a cask under his arm.

"Collected from the very pits of the contagion," said one.

Catling smiled, and jumped lightly down from the bale. "Good," she said. "You may begin tonight. Not all, mind, just a handful here and there. I want this to spread slowly. Innocuously. Next week, a handful or two more, elsewhere."

THE TWO IMPS CROUCHED ATOP A SECTION OF THE crumbling medieval wall of London by Cripplegate. They had one of the casks between them. They sat there for several hours, absorbing the night, watching as lights winked out in houses, and the streets emptied of the last of the tavern customers.

In the very early hours of the morning, one of the imps inserted his long, thin dark fingers under the lid of the cask and carefully opened it, placing the lid silently to one side.

He looked at his brother, blinked slowly, then gave a slight nod.

His brother lifted out a small handful of the black feathers.

"Go where you will," he whispered, "and enjoy."

Then he put his mouth to his open hand, and blew.

The feathers lifted out into the night, drifting this way and that, north and south, east and west, until, one by one, they dropped slowly, like soft sooty ashes, over the tenements of London.

Each one fell in a direct line, ignoring the wind, and each one fell, without fail, directly down a chimney to settle on the ceramic covers—called curfews— placed by householders over the coals for the night.

There, they clung to the handles of the curfews, ready to be taken up in the morning by whomever it was wished to relight the fire.

* * *

EIGHT DAYS LATER, A GENTLE PHYSICIAN BY THE NAME of Nathaniel Hodges was called from his house in Watling Street to treat a young man who lived in a narrow laneway running off the churchyard of St. Botolph Aldersgate. The moment Hodges saw the black swellings in the young man's armpit he knew with what he dealt.

Hodges stepped back from the bed, and sighed, and shook his head at the man's wife. "Pray," he said, "and keep him comfortable. It is all you can do."

From the house, Hodges went straight to his local alderman and reported that, regretfully, the plague had returned to London.

Two nights later, Catling sent the imps to the parish of St. Giles-in-the-Fields, where they clung to the steeple of St. Giles, and cast their feathers into the night.

TWO WEEKS LATER, REPORTS DRIFTED INTO THE PRIVY Council about the growing numbers of deaths due to plague. Fifteen hundred people in the parish of St. Giles-in-the-Fields had died within the past eight days alone, and the Council took the precaution of setting wardens at street junctions at the borders of the parish to prevent people leaving the plague-ridden area.

And then there was the area surrounding Smithfield. Although the first cases of the plague had been reported from there, the outbreak hadn't been as heavy as that at St. Giles-in-the-Fields. Now, however, it was growing, and creeping steadily through the ancient alleyways and lanes of the city.

Worst of all were the reports on the weather. It was unusually warm for the time of year, and dry, and with strong westerly winds. Historically the plague was always at its deadliest during hot dry spells when the wind blew in from the west.

The Council prepared itself for the worst, and sent a report to the king.

Chapter Fourteen

Whitehall Palace, London

ELIZABETH WAS SPREADING WASHING TO DRY IN ONE of the small, inner courtyards of Whitehall when a servant came over and whispered in her ear. Elizabeth paled, but she nodded, set the washing to one side, and hurried to the servants' courtyard where she found the imps lurking in a shadowy corner.

"What is it?" snapped Elizabeth.

The two imps, masquerading as usual as disreputable street youths, both raised their eyebrows. "Snarly lady today," observed the first imp.

"Has she a fever, then?" said the other. "Do her armpits swell and discomfort her under the tight sleeves of that sweet bodice?"

"What *is* it?" Elizabeth said again.

"We come," said the first imp, "because we carry a message from your one-time lover, Weyland. Remember him?"

Elizabeth's lips thinned. "Yes?" she said.

"Don't fret," said the second imp. "The message is not for you. These are words that Weyland wants you to carry to the king, our great lord almighty Charles, Majesty, benevolence, defender of the faith, high prince of righteousness, et cetera, et cetera, et cetera."

Elizabeth's mouth tightened yet further, but she said nothing.

"Tell him," said the imps as one, their voices perfectly matched in bleakness, "that if the Londoners grow buboes, then it is because Weyland has planted the seeds. Tell Charles that Weyland is spreading his horror over London to show Charles his might, and to demonstrate that Weyland is unconquerable. Tell Charles that Weyland thinks that all this digging of graves in the churchyards and fields and orchards of London will surely scare out those kingship bands . . . yes?"

The imps' voices had become singsongy, but that did nothing to diminish the horror of what they imparted. "Tell Charles, that he is to gather in the kingship bands of Troy, and hand them to you, so that you may hand them to Weyland. Only then will the death halt. A simple enough message, yes?"

Elizabeth had taken two steps back as they spoke. "This is vileness," she said.

"This is the way it is," said the first imp, "vile or not." Then the imps were gone, and Elizabeth was left standing alone in the shadowy corner of the courtyard.

ELIZABETH WALKED SLOWLY THROUGH THE PALACE, dragging her feet, unable to hurry this ghastly message to Charles. Inevitably, however, her grudging feet drew her close, and she asked admittance of the king's guards in a soft, hesitant voice.

Elizabeth was of Charles's inner coterie, and the guards allowed her into the king's private apartments without hesitation.

Charles was sitting, together with Catharine, Marguerite, and several of his older bastard children, under an apple tree in the private courtyard off his apartments. The instant Charles saw Elizabeth's face he waved the children to a far corner to play, then beckoned her close.

"What is it?" he said quietly.

"Weyland has sent a message," said Elizabeth, not looking at Charles, so ashamed was she to be the one Weyland had chosen to bring this before the king.

"Aye?"

"Weyland has caused the pestilence which spreads through the city and its fields. He says the death will not stop until you gather in the kingship bands, and hand them to me, so that I may pass them to Weyland."

Marguerite hissed. "We should have known this outbreak was Weyland's handiwork. Such foulness becomes him."

For the moment Charles ignored Marguerite's comment. He reached forward, and took Elizabeth's hand, making her look at him. "I do not hold you to blame for such grim news, my darling," he said. "Do not fear."

"What can we do?" said Catharine. "*You* cannot gather the bands."

Charles and Marguerite exchanged a look. Two of them Charles could very well gather, but this they did not remark upon.

"Dear gods," Catharine continued, "the plague will spread and spread, inching its dark way into the soul of every Londoner. What can we do? Louis . . . Louis should—"

"Louis cannot be disturbed from his transformation," said Charles. "Not unless it be for the direst reason."

"This is not 'the direst reason'?" Marguerite said.

"And what of Eaving?" said Catharine, too consumed with her worries to take much note of what anyone else said. "She is trapped within Weyland's den, and may not move until Jane has taught her all she needs to know of the labyrinth. Gods, what is happening to her?"

Charles's eyes flickered at that, but he said nothing.

"Weyland is the foulest creature ever to draw breath," said Marguerite. "It will be a blessed day indeed when Eaving can escape him."

NOAH AND WEYLAND HAD SPENT THE ENTIRE DAY within the Idyll. They had touched, and kissed, but had not made love. Instead they talked, of whom they had been in former lives, and what they had seen. By the late afternoon Noah was feeling restless—these remembrances had not always been comfortable—and so, Weyland trailing behind her with a smile on his face, she embarked on a far-reaching exploration of the Idyll.

Noah had known the Idyll was large, but had not suspected it was *this* vast. She explored for what felt like hours, and what she saw convinced her that in acreage alone (not even considering power and enchantment) the Idyll was far larger than London itself.

Chamber emptied into chamber after chamber, balconies led to eerie walks along battlements that made Noah dizzy, stairwells rose and fell with apparent abandonment.

At last, growing tired, Noah paused, and Weyland took the opportunity to gather her in his arms.

"What do you think, then," he said, "of what I have built atop the goddess hill? Is it a fine-enough shelter for you?"

She tensed in his arms, and Weyland regretted the tease. Should he just finish it now, then, and just *ask* for shelter?

Noah had put a bright, false smile on her face, and Weyland sighed, and let her go.

She turned—a little too abruptly—and walked through yet one more door onto a balcony that overlooked a vast vista.

Noah stopped the instant she saw what lay beyond the balcony. "What made you create *this*?" she said.

Weyland looked over the balcony to where stretched a succession of wooded hills, rolling into infinity. Mist drifted in the valleys and dips between the hills and scarlet and blue birds dipped slowly and gracefully in and out of the mists.

"Don't you remember this?" he said. "That night I healed your back in the kitchen? We met in vision then, in this strange land. It was so lovely . . ."

Noah was looking at him strangely. "And so you re-created it here?"

He shook his head slowly. "I did not make this, Noah. It just appeared one day. I thought *you* had made it."

Now she was staring as if she were frightened. She took a half-step back, and Weyland reached grasped her arm, terrified she was going to run.

"Noah?"

Noah made a visible effort to relax, and she offered him a sunny, false smile. "You must have dreamed of it, and made this without thought."

"The only thing of which I dream," he said, "is of what you said to me in that vision."

She stared at him a moment longer, then abruptly she pulled her arm from his hand, and left the balcony.

Chapter Fifteen

By the Scaffold in Tower Fields

ONE MORNING JANE WENT TO THE SCAFFOLD IN Tower Fields to find the Lord of the Faerie waiting for her. Unusually, however, his face was creased with worry and he did not immediately take her to The Naked.

"Jane," he said, leaning to kiss her.

"What is it?" Jane could hardy breathe for apprehension.

"It is not you," the Lord of the Faerie said. "Do not fear. Jane, there is plague in London."

"Yes, I know. Noah and I have heard reports. But it is to the west of London, yes? We have seen no sickness in our walks to the Tower."

"It is spreading. Jane—"

"Do not worry overmuch, Coel. Plague comes and goes. It has been seven or eight years since the last outbreak, so surely if it has arrived now it is not surprising."

"This is a vicious outbreak, Jane. Worse than ever." He paused. "There has been nothing said within Idol Lane of it?"

"Noah and I have talked of it. You know Noah, far better than I do . . . She worries about it, and wishes she could somehow wish it away . . . but you know that she can't . . ."

The Lord of the Faerie nodded. Noah, as Eaving, would not interfere in the natural cycle of life and death. Sadness and disease was as much a natural part of life as was happiness and health.

But there was little "natural" about this outbreak, was there?

"Weyland has said nothing?" the Lord of the Faerie said.

"No."

The Lord of the Faerie chewed his lip. "Jane, I have received a message from Weyland. He said that he had caused the plague, and that he would only call his dogs of pestilence back, once I—as Charles—gave him the kingship bands."

"*Weyland* sent you that message?"

The Lord of the Faerie gave a single nod.

"How?"

"He sent his imps. They spoke to Elizabeth, and she related their message."

Jane thought. *The imps?* Dear gods, she hadn't seen them about the house for weeks, and she could have sworn that Weyland hadn't given them a thought, either.

But . . . the plague. *That* had Weyland's handiwork written all over it. Jane shuddered. "He has been so pleasant. *Too* pleasant. I should have known he would do something like this."

"You must tell Noah. She needs to know."

Jane nodded. "That news, at least, should get her out of his bed."

"What?"

"Noah has been sharing Weyland's bed. It was his price so that myself and Noah could have the freedom we needed to teach and learn the arts of Mistress of the Labyrinth."

The Lord of the Faerie's face had gone ashen, and Jane felt a deep stab of jealousy. *He still cared for her.*

"Noah *says* that she and Weyland share nothing else but the bed. That they do not make love. But . . ."

" 'But'?"

"I do not know, Coel. Weyland appears too content. And Noah denies too strongly."

He gave a shake of his head. "What is happening? To what darkness has Noah been exposed?"

Jane felt a confusing mixture of fear and jealousy wash through her. Suddenly Noah was all the Lord of the Faerie could think about.

"Perhaps we should rescue her," the Lord of the Faerie said. "Take her from him. Pull her back into the Faerie, where she shall be safe."

Jane turned aside her face.

"But still . . ." the Lord of the Faerie said.

" 'But still'?"

"Long Tom, the Sidlesaghe, once said to us that Noah *had* to go to Weyland. That was something in this life she had to endure. When I was merely Charles, and not fully aware of what *else* I was, I thought, with Louis, that we should try to prevent Noah going to Weyland. Louis tried, and failed. Now, with all the wonder of the Faerie to draw upon, I sense that perhaps Long Tom was right. Noah needs to be with Weyland, although . . . dear gods, what you say about her sharing his bed . . ."

"Coel, if you take Noah away from Weyland he will kill me."

"Jane? *Why?*"

"Because he will need an outlet for his spite, and because he will think I have failed to teach her the ways of the labyrinth."

"He doesn't know that Ariadne . . ."

"No, and I for one am not about to tell him. It would be my death sentence."

"Jane, talk to Noah. Tell her Weyland has caused the plague. Then ask her advice."

Jane looked away, sure that whatever happened, it would end with her death.

"Very well," she said.

BUT JANE DID NOT IMMEDIATELY TALK TO NOAH OF the plague. Noah was too encased in the lingering memory of her training that afternoon when they walked home, so that she was in no mood for conversation, and so soon as they had arrived home, Weyland was there, kissing Noah, and then leading her away, up to his den on the top floor.

The next day Jane barely saw Noah at all, and then only in the company of Weyland.

It was almost three days later—days when they hadn't gone to the Tower so that Jane could talk to Noah privately—that Jane finally found Noah alone.

"Noah," she said. "I have heard news about the plague that you need to—"

"Jane," Noah said urgently, taking Jane's hands, "the plague is dreadful, yes, but for the moment there is a more urgent matter. I need to see the Lord of the Faerie. Can you arrange it?"

Jane stared at her, not overly surprised that Noah knew of her meetings with the Lord of the Faerie, then relaxed. The Lord of the Faerie could tell Noah. It would be better, all in all, coming from him.

"Yes," she said. "I can."

Chapter Sixteen

The Great Founding Labyrinth
Within the Tower of London, and
Idol Lane, London

Noah Speaks

*M*Y DAYS WERE CONSUMED WITH ARIADNE AND her teaching, my nights with Weyland. I thought of little else. I'd heard reports that the plague had reappeared within London, and was sad of it, but knew also that I could not interfere with its dark progress. Sickness and death were in their own right an intrinsic part of life. Every living creature—whether faerie or mortal—must endure pain and sorrow and often untimely death. I did not like the plague, but I understood it. It was one of the necessary sadnesses of life that somehow made life the sweeter—should you manage to hold on to it.

I went every third or fourth day to the Tower of London to continue my training with Ariadne. I no longer was frightened of the Great Founding Labyrinth (that which masqueraded as the White Tower), but nonetheless maintained a healthy respect for it. Its power exhilarated me, and the knowledge that with every visit I came to understand it better, came closer and closer to being able to manipulate it for myself, became almost as addictive as a drug. I swear I almost dragged poor Jane through the streets on our way to the Tower . . . although I noticed she never complained about it.

Better even than furthering my study with Ariadne—*dear gods, to what pits I had fallen!*—was making love with Weyland. Sometimes (not often, for I did not wish to arouse his suspicions) I asked him to use the darkcraft when we made love, and I reveled in it. I used it to discover more about my own potential . . . but mostly I just reveled.

I liked it.

This cold dark power was addictive.

As addictive as Weyland. It was not just the sex that I found so enthralling, it was the sheer *intimacy* of our relationship. Each of us was, bit by bit, allowing the other one deeper into our soul. We began sharing secrets, remembrances, and beliefs that both of us normally would have kept to ourselves. I talked of some of my darker, stupider moments as Cornelia. He talked of some of the horrors he had visited on people, on entire cities, and shared with me how he had felt during these slaughters.

It was not what I expected.

We began to share ourselves, high in that Idyll that Weyland had built. There were still shocking moments, times when I pulled back—like that day I explored the Idyll, and found that Weyland had somehow managed to build it to the very borders of the Realm of the Faerie. *How? How could he have done that?*

So I would draw back, but then, inevitably, I would slide into his arms again, fascinated by him, and enthralled by what he revealed of himself.

Falling ever deeper into Weyland Orr.

I began to trust him and, inevitably, I began to betray all that I had ever been, and all I had ever promised to do.

I no longer thought of myself entirely as Noah, or as apprentice Mistress of the Labyrinth. There were moments, hours, sometimes even days, when, as I strolled through the myriad complexities of the Idyll with Weyland at my side, that I thought of myself only as "Darkwitch rising."

MY SLIDE INTO COMPLETE BETRAYAL BEGAN SO IN-
nocuously. We'd eaten with Jane in the kitchen, retired to the Idyll, bathed, and had then gone to bed. We hadn't made love, for tonight I felt uncommonly tired, and Weyland was content merely to hold me as we both slid into sleep.

I fell almost immediately into a profound, and profoundly disturbing, dream.

I was trapped in the heart of the labyrinth, trapped by *Catling*. I could feel the labyrinth closing in about me, feel it imprisoning me, and I fought with all I had, but to no avail.

The labyrinth had me trapped.

Why should the labyrinth do this to me? I *was not evil.* There was no reason to *trap* me.

I became aware that I was covered in a sticky, warm, thick liquid. It irritated me, and unnerved me.

A light very gradually grew about me, and I looked down to my hands, and saw that I was covered in blood.

I gagged, for the instant I realized what I was smothered in, so the smell of the coagulating blood hit me.

As I doubled over, retching, I saw the body of my daughter lying on the floor. Not Catling. My *daughter*. That sad little wrapped bundle that Loth had put in my arms that night so long ago when Genvissa had forced her from my body. A tiny baby, too young to breathe on her own.

I crouched down, and turned back the covers from the baby's face, hoping against hope that somehow this time she was alive.

But she wasn't. She was cold, her white flesh marbled with gray.

Dead . . . as she had been for almost three thousand years.

I began to cry, and it was then I realized where the blood had come from.

I was weeping blood, weeping away my life over the corpse of my daughter, and over all that could have been.

"NOAH!"

Weyland's voice jolted me out of the dream. For an instant I resisted, wanting to reach down and touch my daughter again, but then I woke, and in waking I still wept—but salty tears now, rather than blood.

But, dear gods, it felt as though those tears were wrenched from the very pit of my soul. I turned in Weyland's arms, buried my face against his chest, and sobbed hard enough to rattle every house in London.

He held me for the longest time, rubbing my shoulders, murmuring my name, saying none of those pathetic platitudes that the witless use: *It was only a dream. You're awake now. Come, I'm here, no need to be afraid.*

Finally, when I had quieted a little, he stroked the hair back from my brow, and said, "Tell me."

"Catling had me trapped in the heart of the labyrinth. Why *me*? I was covered in blood. And there . . . there . . . on the floor . . ." I had to stop, and sniff, and try to steady my breathing.

"'And there . . . '?" He kissed my cheek softly, reassuringly.

"There, on the floor, was my daughter. Dead. Oh . . . gods . . . *dead!*"

"Catling?"

"No. My *daughter*."

"Ah," he said. "The daughter you lost to Genvissa."

I nodded, too upset to speak of it.

"And *Catling* had you trapped. I thought you said you were trapped in the labyrinth."

I was silent a long time, realizing my mistake. I thought about how I could lie convincingly, and finally I decided I'd had enough of lies when it came to Catling.

"Catling was my daughter in name only," I said. "I bore her, but she was never a *daughter* to me, although I only discovered it after I'd come here, to you."

He waited.

"Catling was a trick," I said.

I felt rather than saw Weyland's eyes harden with speculation.

"She was the Troy Game made flesh," I said. "The Troy Game used me to assume living, breathing life. *That* was what I'd seen in my visions. Not a loving, natural daughter." I stopped, looking at the soft blues and purples of the ceiling, and wondering how Weyland would react to this. Fury? Triumph? Hate? *He'd harbored the Game within his house and had not known.*

I saw from the corner of my eye that Weyland stared at me, then he abruptly lay down and rolled onto his back, staring at the ceiling as I did.

Then, stunningly, he began to laugh: softly and, from what I could discern, with true humor.

"I had the Troy Game incarnate within my house," he said, eventually, "and I did not know. What trickery, eh? What trickery."

"*I* did not know," I said, wanting him to believe that I had not kept this a deliberate secret for too many weeks, "until that night I cast her from this house."

Now he turned back to me. "You were angry that night, almost incandescent with rage. Why?"

"Because I realized then the depth and length of the deception. Not merely that the Game used the false promise of a daughter to manipulate me, but that it *did* manipulate and deceive me. When I realized what Catling truly was, then I realized what the Game is truly capable of."

"But still you want your daughter," Weyland said, very soft.

"Yes," I said, weeping once more. "Yet she was only ever a lie."

"I'm sorry," he said, and pulled me close and held me until, once more, I had managed to stay my tears.

"Do not trust your imps," I said.

"Why not?"

"She has both of them under her control."

He drew in a sharp breath. "Why tell me?" he said. "Why tell me what Catling truly is, and that she controls the imps?"

Why had I? "Because I wanted to pay the Game back some of the pain it had dealt me," I said, and, stunningly, realized it was true. *There, Troy Game, I've told your archenemy what disguise you wear.*

He burst into loud, genuine laughter, pulling me close and rolling me over and over in the bed until I thought we would fall out.

"You have a fine career as a wicked witch ahead of you, my love," he said finally, when we had stopped rolling about and he lay atop me, pinning me to the mattress, his face close to mine. He kissed me, and I ran my hands through his hair, and then we were smiling at one another, enjoying the joke.

The joke. I had just told Asterion that the Game walked incarnate. The "joke."

And I did not care. It had actually made me feel a little better.

"I'm sorry about your daughter," he said.

"Aye, I know."

"And I never did like Catling."

I laughed. "Thank you."

He grinned, slowly, his eyes watching me very carefully. "What is this, then? Are we not supposed to be enemies? Patrolling opposite sides of that great chasm of ambition that divides us?"

"Perhaps we share an enemy," I said, and then a chasm *did* open, save that it had opened under my feet, and not between Asterion and myself.

"Gods, Noah," he whispered. "What are you saying?"

"I don't know. I don't know."

Weyland was watching me with troubled eyes. He lowered his face, and kissed me, and said,

"Noah? Will you be my shelter?"

THERE. THERE. HE HAD ASKED IT OF ME AND I COULD not refuse. I knew why he had chosen this moment—laughter notwithstanding, Weyland would have been truly shaken by what I had just revealed. Thus he had moved swiftly to consolidate his control over me, knowing he had lost control elsewhere. He had asked me for shelter. I wondered that the stars were not screaming, or that the land was not twisting and turning, or that I could not hear the Sidlesaghes moaning atop their blasted hills.

But all I could hear was Weyland's gentle breathing, and all I could feel was his body atop mine, his weight on mine . . . and a profound sense of relief, that finally he had asked me, and I need not fear the question anymore.

A profound sense of relief, that finally I would be able to say, "I had no choice. He asked of me shelter."

"YES," I SAID. "I WILL BE YOUR SHELTER."

THE NEXT MORNING I ASKED JANE TO ARRANGE A meeting between myself and the Lord of the Faerie. I needed him to arrange a meeting between Louis and myself.

I needed to know where I was going.

CHAPTER SEVENTEEN

THE REALM OF THE FAERIE

HE LORD OF THE FAERIE TURNED, HIS FACE breaking into a smile, and held out his arms.

Noah ran into them, hugging the Lord of the Faerie tightly. Jane watched, careful to keep her emotions from spilling forth onto her face. Ostensibly they'd been off to do more training—that is certainly what Weyland thought—but instead of going to the Tower, Noah had used her own powers to transport Jane and herself to The Naked.

"Noah, what is it?" the Lord of the Faerie said. "Why do you need to see me so badly?"

"Am I not allowed to see you from time to time?"

"Noah . . ."

She sighed. "I need to see Louis. Badly. Very badly. You are the only one who can arrange that for me."

"But he has not completed the transformation. And you—"

"I know! Gods, Charles—or whatever I should call you—I need to see him. *Badly!*"

"What is it? What is so wrong?"

The tip of Noah's tongue wet her lips. "I need to speak with Louis."

"Is it Weyland?"

"No. Please, can you arrange it?"

"It is the plague, isn't it."

Noah frowned. "The plague? No, I—"

"I would have thought that the fact Weyland has sent plague to consume London would have been reason enough, Noah."

"What?"

The Lord of the Faerie sent a querying look to Jane.

"I did not tell her," Jane said, her voice low. "I'm sorry. I did not have the courage."

The Lord of the Faerie looked back at Noah, and sighed. "Weyland has caused this malevolence. He sent his imps to Elizabeth with a message for Brutus-reborn: 'Gather in the kingship bands, and hand them to me, and then only will the death stop.'"

Noah stepped back from the Lord of the Faerie. "No. I cannot believe that. He would not . . . No . . . Weyland could not have done this."

The Lord of the Faerie stared at her. *"You cannot believe it?"*

Noah looked bewildered. Veins of color stained her pallid cheeks, and she clasped her hands together, wringing them about. "I can't believe that he would do such a thing. The imps . . . No. *No.* He doesn't control the imps. You said the *imps* sent the message?"

The Lord of the Faerie nodded, still watching Noah carefully.

"The imps are not in his control anymore. If the imps have sent a message, then that message is from the Troy Game, not from Weyland."

The Lord of the Faerie did not immediately respond. He stood, his eyes on Noah, his chest drawing in deep, slow breaths as he thought.

"Noah," he said eventually, "why would the Troy Game send plague to visit London? The Game is dedicated to protecting the city from evil, not instigating it. Its very purpose is *protection.* This plague stinks of Weyland, not of the Troy Game."

Noah had regained her composure. "I no longer believe the Troy Game is dedicated only to protection. I think that it has infinite capacity for harm. It wants completion, and it will allow nothing now to stand in its way."

"Noah," Jane said, very slowly, very deliberately, "what are you saying?"

Noah looked only at the Lord of the Faerie. "I need to see Louis more than ever. *Soon.* Can you arrange it?"

The Lord of the Faerie nodded, his eyes intense as he gazed at Noah. "I can do it. But, by all the gods, Noah, it will be dangerous. Interrupting his transformation . . ."

Noah smiled, very sadly. "Danger is all about us."

THE LORD OF THE FAERIE SAT ON HIS THRONE ATOP The Naked. He was alone. Not Jane, not even the magpie, kept him company.

He thought on Noah, and as he thought, so the fingertips of his right hand thrummed slowly against the armrest.

She was walking a dangerous path. The Lord of the Faerie was not sure if Weyland had corrupted Noah away from her allegiance to the land, or if her closeness to Weyland had enabled her to see the dangers about them far more clearly than he could himself.

There was a bleakness hanging over the land, somehow infecting it. The Lord of the Faerie had felt that on the day of his crowning, the instant the crown had settled on his head. Then, he'd thought it was, as always, the presence of Asterion.

But what if it was not? What if the alliance between land and Troy Game was not beneficial, but cancerous?

The Lord of the Faerie sat on his throne, looking out over the rolling infinity of wooded hills and wondered which might prove to be the more deadly. Noah? Or the Troy Game?

The Lord of the Faerie's fingers stopped thrumming as he came to a decision within himself.

It might be highly dangerous path, but in a previous life, when he had been Harold, he had promised to walk that path with her.

All every path needs is a companion with which to share it.

He sighed, and rose from his throne.

CHAPTER EIGHTEEN

IDOL LANE, LONDON

Noah Speaks

J WAS DEVASTATED AS I ABSORBED WHAT THE LORD of the Faerie told me—that Weyland had sent the plague to further his ambition to acquire the kingship bands.

For an instant I believed Coel, but then my benumbed brain screamed at me that it was the *imps* who had delivered the message to Charles, and I knew that Weyland now had little or no control over the imps.

At least, I *thought* Weyland had no control over them. He rarely saw them. They occasionally had come to the house, and I knew Weyland occasionally sent them out on a mission. But then, he had not known that Catling had control of them until very recently.

Maybe the message *had* come from him.

I defended Weyland stoutly to Coel, but in my own mind I was no longer so sure.

Would he have done this?

A few short months ago I would not have doubted. The use of plague to force Brutus-reborn's hand would have stunk of Weyland.

But Weyland had promised me that he would make no move on the bands until I had attained my full powers as Mistress of the Labyrinth. Then I could retrieve the bands. I had believed Weyland's promise.

Should I have done that?

When we left The Naked, Jane and I did not go directly back to Idol Lane. Instead, we sent our senses scrying through London.

I felt the difference instantly. Death and disease was not unknown to me. As Eaving, goddess of the waters, I felt it constantly as it appeared here and there about the land. That was unwelcome, but always, always a part of the natural order of things.

This plague was different. It was black and terrible, as always, but it was also completely *unnatural*. It had no place within the natural cycle of life and death. If I had not been so absorbed within Weyland and within learning the ways of the labyrinth then I would have realized this long before.

"Dear gods," I whispered. "This stinks of deceit!"

"Aye," Jane said. "Weyland's deceit, surely."

I did not answer. She had far more reason, far more *right*, to blame him than myself.

"Do you truly think it is the Game and not Weyland?" said Jane. She was watching me very carefully now.

"The plague stinks of Catling, Jane. Surely you can smell it?"

"No," she said. "I can't. I am curious, Noah, why you are so desperate to blame Catling and not Weyland. What has he done, then, to merit such belief?"

WE RETURNED TO IDOL LANE, JANE STILL WAITING for a response to her question.

She did not get it. In truth, I don't know if I *could* have answered it. Why feel so wretched that Weyland *might* have set this plague? Should I not have expected it of Weyland, the great Minotaur?

I hadn't expected it of the man I had come to know.

Unless that man was a lie.

I felt miserable, and I wondered if my promise to shelter Weyland was the reason I kept insisting that it could not have been him to cause this plague.

Or was it that I was so in love that I was completely blind?

WEYLAND WAS, AS USUAL, WAITING FOR US IN THE kitchen. He rose, and, as usual, kissed me. Then he frowned, for he felt no increase in the power of the labyrinth.

"You did not learn today?" he asked.

"No," I said, and looked significantly at Jane.

She threw me one of her sharp glances, but withdrew into the parlor, and, a moment later, up the stairs, and I turned back to Weyland.

"I was distracted," I said. "By the spreading evil that has London in its clutches."

He shrugged, disinterested.

That made me furious. "I am Mag's successor, Weyland! I *am* this land—do not expect *me* to shrug and turn away!"

"What has caused this temper, Noah? You can hardly blame me for the plague."

I said nothing, staring at him.

"What? You *do* want to blame me for the plague?" He gave a short laugh. "Why not lay at my heels the blame for every woman who has died in childbed, or for every cat which has become lethally entangled in the wheels of one of the city's dung-carts, or for every child dead of fever?"

"Have you caused this spreading sickness, Weyland?"

He was studying me very carefully now. "Noah, why fret so, over 'blame'?"

"Have you caused this spreading sickness, Weyland?"

He stared, silent, then spoke. "No. I had thought very little of it until your hysterics this evening."

He was treating me like a child, and I was furious. "You are being blamed for it."

Again, that short, humorless laugh. "What care I? No doubt I am blamed for most ills that beset the world."

"And for that you can hardly blame anyone but yourself."

He put his hands on my shoulders, his eyes searching mine. "Why are you so upset, Noah?"

"I thought you might have set the plague to gain yourself some advantage." *To gain the kingship bands of Troy,* but I could not say that.

"Ah. Having heard of the plague, you immediately leapt to the conclusion that I had caused it. I thought we understood each other better than that, Noah."

"It is rumored," I said, "that you sent a message to Charles via the imps, saying that you would not stop the plague until he handed you the kingship bands."

"How would you know what had been whispered to Charles, Noah?"

"Because . . . it was just a rumor, Weyland."

Oh, he could have forced it out of me. I could see the *want* simmering along with anger within those intense, hazel eyes.

He wanted to. So badly.

And he didn't. He just gave a single nod, and stepped back. "I have not caused the plague, Noah. You know I haven't, for did you not tell me how it is that Catling controls the imps?"

"But . . . But this message was passed to Charles some time ago, before you knew about Catling. I wondered . . . I knew you still used the imps from time to time, and I thought you may have used them for this message. I had to ask."

"And *do* you believe me, now that I have given you my answer?"

"I wish . . ." I said, and watched the disappointment gather in his eyes.

cbΔpϚꓰꓳ NIɴꓰϚꓰꓳN

Atop The Naked,
in the Realm of the Faerie

 E BECAME AWARE OF ANOTHER PRESENCE, SO VERY gradually that Louis wondered if the presence had been there for hours, perhaps even days, before Louis had truly taken any notice of it.

It was an irritating presence, if only because it was so persistent.

Louis . . .

Louis . . .

Louis . . .

It was the Lord of the Faerie, and because of that, Louis slowed on his journey through the Ringwalk, and eventually halted. *What is it?*

Noah needs to see you, to talk with you.

We can talk enough once I have completed my journey. Why now?

Louis, it is urgent. This should not wait.

What is it?

It is Asterion.

Ah . . . He nodded. *I will see her.*

THEY MET ATOP THE NAKED. LOUIS WAITED IN THE center of the summit, a vastly different man than he'd been when last he'd been there. Now there was a wild stillness about him that made any who regarded him deeply uncomfortable.

Not that there were many to observe him. Louis was alone save for the Lord of the Faerie, who sat his throne on the eastern edge of the summit.

Noah appeared in her goddess form, walking up the slope, close to the summit. One moment she was not there, the next she had all but arrived.

Louis, watching, realized that she moved like a dancer, which was something new for Noah. He recognized the movement instantly, for it bespoke her training in the arts of the labyrinth. At that he felt a great relief. All would be well. She was transforming, as was he. When both were done, and the Great Marriage accomplished, then nothing could stop them in their goal to complete the Troy Game.

"Louis," Noah said, coming directly to him. "How do you?"

She leaned forward and kissed him, not waiting for an answer. When she pulled her mouth away from his, her eyes shone even brighter. "The Ringwalk has truly become your home."

"As the labyrinth had become yours," he said, gathering her once more into his arms for a longer and far deeper kiss. "Noah, what is it?" he said, as she pulled back. "What has Weyland done?"

She rested her hands on his chest. "Louis, leave the matter of Weyland, for the moment. First, I must tell you news of our daughter."

"She is not harmed? Weyland has not—"

"What has happened to Catling is most certainly no doing of Weyland's," Noah said. "Louis, Catling is *not* our daughter."

"But we conceived her." He smiled slowly. "Unless I imagined that afternoon we spent in your bedchamber of your father's palace in Mesopotama."

"We were tricked." Noah closed her eyes, took a deep breath, and then looked directly into Louis's eyes. "Catling is the Troy Game incarnate. It used us, used our bodies, to gain flesh and breath."

He did not answer her verbally, but his entire being became still, and yet more watchful.

"The Game took the shape and form of our daughter, she who we lost, and pretended to *be* her, and—"

He stopped the flow of words with a finger to her lips. "Noah, I am so sorry. I had no idea." He pulled her to him, and cuddled her, knowing she would feel this deception greatly.

Yet, as he held her, Louis frowned, puzzled. His perceptive powers were far stronger and far more finely attuned than they had been when he was merely Brutus. Now, as Noah leaned against him, and wept, he felt something from her.

Something that stank of the taint of Weyland.

He pushed her away a little, so he could see her face.

"Louis," she said, very low, "plague is infesting the land. A terrible pestilence. Deliberately sent."

"Weyland—"

"I think the Troy Game has caused it."

Again, Louis wondered what it was that he felt from her. What was this strange taint within her flesh and spirit? "Why would the Game wish to do that?"

"To force me to its will."

Louis frowned. What did she mean by that? "Weyland has caused this plague. Surely." *Gods, my love, tell me that you also believe this, and stay my fears.*

She shook her head. "I fear that the Troy Game has grown into a terrible being, Louis. The land suffers. Listen to me, I beg you."

He wanted to listen to her, very badly. Here she stood within the circle of his arms, the woman he loved before all others, his true mate, and she wept because her daughter had been torn from her yet once more, and she worried that what they were supposed to protect and nurture, the Troy Game, had turned sour.

But . . . still . . . that strange, subtle taint . . . and her refusal to believe that it could be Weyland who had caused the plague . . .

Worse, he could feel a slight stiffness in her, as if she wanted to withdraw from him.

"Noah, this plague is not the Troy Game's doing. The plague is Weyland's handiwork, certainly. The land needs the Game."

"I am no longer sure that the Troy Game is what the land needs."

That shocked him, but he tried to stay reasonable. She was, after all, upset about her daughter. "The Game is not always pleasant, Noah. Surely you have learned that already from your training within the labyrinth. But it is not evil. It cannot be. It will not harm the city it has been formed to protect. That is not its nature."

"Louis, please, *please* listen to me. Consider what I say . . ."

"Gods, Noah, how can you think the Game more evil than Weyland? I felt your agony the day Charles entered London. Have *you* forgotten it? What spell has Weyland cast over you, that you so willingly believe that this malevolence gripping the land is the Game's doing, and not his?" He suddenly whipped her about, and pulled away the diaphanous material that clothed her back. He stared, then laid a hand gently against the scars that marred her flesh. "He does this to you, my love, and you think him worthy of *belief*?"

She twisted around, away from his touch. "I am talking of the Troy Game, Louis. Not Weyland."

He reached out a hand to her face, trying to reach her with both touch and love. "Noah, think, I beg you. How can you believe Weyland—*Asterion*—before the Troy Game?"

"Louis, do you believe *me* before the Game?"

He hesitated, and she drew back from him, her eyes round, terrified, lost. "Noah . . ."

But she was gone, and Louis was left standing in the middle of The Naked, his hand outstretched.

THE LORD OF THE FAERIE CAME TO HIM, AND STOOD by his side.

"That was not so well done, Louis. She needed you to believe her."

"How can I believe her, my friend? She lives within Weyland's den. She could be his mouthpiece—"

The Lord of the Faerie started to say something, but Louis held up a hand and silenced him. "No. *Listen* to me. I mourn with her about the child. I know how much she wanted a daughter, and how much she mourned the one who was lost. I can understand how she feels betrayed by the Game, and its winding ways. But I also feel something else from her. A closeness with Weyland. Gods, I can almost *smell* it. There is something happening between her and him. I don't know *what*, but I do know it. Can I trust the Game, my Faerie friend? Perhaps not. But I also wonder about Noah. I love her, I want to love her . . . but I think Weyland has turned her."

There was something else, but for the moment that possibility so terrified Louis he could not elucidate it.

He thought he had felt the power of a Darkwitch rising, as if seeping from the very pores of Noah's skin.

CHAPTER TWENTY

LONDON BRIDGE

Noah Speaks

BELIEVE ME," WEYLAND HAD SAID TO ME, AND I couldn't.

"Believe me," I had pleaded with Louis, and he hadn't.

All this disbelief, tearing my life apart.

All I wanted was a firm footing somewhere. Someone, or something, in which I could believe.

I wandered for a time, first through the Faerie and then through London, knowing Weyland waited for me, and knowing he was undoubtedly fretting and edging closer to doing something unpleasant with each minute that passed, yet even so, I was determined to discover some means by which I could find that elusive firm foothold.

I wandered as Eaving, and thus very few people realized my presence. But some did. A gaggle of wide-eyed children who stopped their ball game as I passed. I smiled at them, and one or two, braver than the others, returned it.

A carter, hunched exhausted over the reins, started and stared as he passed.

I inclined my head, and smiled for him also, and the exhaustion lifted from his face.

A vicar, who went white, and who reminded me of John Thornton for no other reason than their shared calling.

He passed, stumbling and staring, and I turned aside my head . . . and, as I did so, thought of something I *could* do.

I stood very still, thinking furiously, realizing I had found a means by which I could discover the origins of this plague. Whether it was Weyland or Catling, knowing the truth would enable me to move forward: the truth would show me the right path to tread.

But, oh, this was so dangerous. It would upset and frighten many people, but it was so . . . daring.

And for the first time in my life, in my many lives, I felt like embracing the "daring."

It was not something my enemies, known as well as unknown, would expect me to do.

I began to walk toward London Bridge, my stride now filled with purpose.

There was someone with whom I needed to speak.

LONDON BRIDGE WAS A CROWDED, JOYOUS PLACE. IT leapfrogged across the river from Southwark to the city itself in a series of leaning, creaking, ponderous piers. These piers were so wide and thick they acted as a partial dam to the river—the water level on the eastern and seaward side of the bridge was a full four feet lower than the level on the western side. The river banked up and then swept through the narrow openings between the piers in a series of tumultuous waterfalls. Boats that wished to travel upriver generally had to wait for high tide, while those wishing to continue on downriver under the bridge dared an exciting ride under the bridge.

Not a few were capsized during the dangerous passage.

River-watching—hanging over the side of the bridge and shouting at those daring enough to attempt the passage beneath—was a favorite pastime for those living on, or traveling over, the bridge, and one I enjoyed myself. Not so much for the pleasure of watching daring boatmasters undertake the hazardous travail of the bridge passage, but because scores of water-sprites played around the piers and upon the small islands on which the piers had their foundations. The city fathers spent much angst, and many pounds each year, trying to keep the narrow passages between the piers clear of the branches and refuse which swept down the river and stuck between the piers (cow and horse carcasses creating the most blockage), intensifying the damming effect of the bridge. But no sooner than one dredging effort had been made than, within days, the problem was as bad as ever it was.

London's aldermen and councillors had no idea that mischievous water-sprites spent much of each night carefully putting back all the branches and carcasses they could find. The sprites adored the wild waters created by the bridge's piers, and loved chasing the boats through.

Mortal dredging efforts were always going to be in vain.

I walked to the central portion of the bridge—that part free of the houses, shops, and chapels which had been built atop the bridge for virtually its entire length—and leaned over the balustrade. The water below was thick, green, and foaming as it tumbled about, seeking a way under.

I could see the copper glints of water-sprites' hair as they darted within the water, and within moments they became aware of my presence, and floated to the surface. There they bobbed calmly, apparently unaffected by the turbulence of the water, and stared up at me with their bright-green eyes.

I need to speak with our Faerie Lord, I said to them. *Will you send word?*

They waved in response, and slipped under the water again, and were gone.

I leaned back against the balustrade, relaxing, thinking, and watching the people passing.

An old woman saw me, and nodded companionably.

A nobleman, riding by on his gloriously trapped steed, saw me. He paled in shock, but recovered enough to grace me with a salute, which must have surprised most of his retinue and half the bystanders who watched him.

A small dun dog, trotting from Southwark through to London on his own canine business, interrupted his journey long enough to snuffle about my feet before giving a small yelp of recognition and deference and continuing on his way.

Soon enough, the Lord of the Faerie joined me.

"NOAH," HE SAID, APPEARING AT MY ELBOW AND LEANing down to kiss my cheek.

I turned my head, and offered him my mouth, and was happy that he accepted the invitation without hesitation.

"You cannot blame Louis," the Lord of the Faerie said, "for not abandoning his loyalties and ambitions and needs as Kingman all in one moment. Each life, Noah, you have undermined his world. I think he is growing tired of it. He does not know what you will do next."

For the Lord of the Faerie, that little speech constituted a considerable chastisement. But it was true enough, and I nodded, accepting what he said.

"I do not blame him," I said, "although I confess a considerable disappointment. Not at him. At circumstance, I think."

We stood there in silence for a little time, enjoying each other's company, both of us, I think, remembering all that had been between us.

I took one of his hands in both of mine. "Do you remember, so long ago, when we made love atop Pen Hill and you promised to me that you would be a companion along my path ahead?"

"Aye," he said. His eyes were very gentle as they looked into mine. "I have had reason to revisit that day recently, as well."

I was not surprised. The Lord of the Faerie must have had some inkling of where my feet—let alone my heart—had been taking me. "Do you believe that what I do, I do only for the good of the land?"

"Aye," he said. "I do. I trust you, Noah."

Oh gods, I was so blessed in him! "Coel," I said, calling him by his most ancient and beloved of names, "I want to bring Weyland through into the Faerie Realm."

I THINK DAYS MIGHT HAVE PASSED AS HE STARED AT me in shock. I could not read his emotions, because the instant those words were out of my mouth his face shut down completely, and his hand went cold and stiff in mine.

"Coel," I said, "I need to know for certain who is causing this plague. This sickness has infected the land as well as its people. You and I both know that if I bring Weyland to the borderlands of the Faerie Realm, then, if he is guilty, the land will reject him the instant his feet touch the land. It will not allow the architect of this pestilence entry into the Realm of the Faerie."

"The Faerie will not allow him entry in any case."

I thought that it might (for how else could the Faerie have allowed Weyland to build his Idyll to its very borders?), but for the moment I said nothing about that. "My lord of the Faerie," I said, "I need you to grant dispensation for him. I need to *know* if he is the one who has blighted land and city with the plague. This test will eliminate or damn Weyland once and for all, and it will show me if *I* have taken the right path, or one so blighted that I risk all of creation. This is a test as much of me and my choices as it is of Weyland. My lord, and my love, please, *please,* tell me you understand why I ask this."

"Noah, Louis said he could smell Weyland on you. He said you stank of Weyland's taint."

I felt cold. "Then all the more need for this test," I said softly, holding the Lord of the Faerie's eyes.

"Are you his lover, Noah?"

I took a deep breath. "Yes."

He let his breath out on a hiss. "To what depth, Noah?"

"That is what I need to find out."

"Noah, you ask me to risk the Faerie. To bring Weyland there. To bring *Asterion* into its sacred borders . . ."

Dear gods, what would he say once he realized that I was a Darkwitch, and of Asterion's bloodline?

I decided I needed to tell the Lord of the Faerie more. "Weyland is almost there already. Atop his house in Idol Lane he had built a magical realm, his Idyll. My lord of the Faerie, it reaches to the very borders of your Realm. Furthermore, on the night that Weyland had torn myself and Jane apart, we met in vision on The Naked. I do not know if we were truly there, or if it were merely dream but still . . . I think there is some connection between Weyland and the Faerie, something even he does not realize, and we need to know what it is. Please . . . Please allow this; for, if nothing else, we need to know the nature of the threat that this land faces, whether it be Weyland . . . or something else."

He heaved a great sigh, but eventually he nodded, and for that I loved him more than ever. I had upset Coel's world more than once, too, but *his* love and belief had never wavered.

"Gods, Coel," I said. "Thank you for this!"

"When?" he said.

"Tonight."

CHAPTER TWENTY-ONE

THE REALM OF THE FAERIE

EYLAND WAS MORE UNSURE OF HIMSELF than he had ever been, in all of his myriad lives. Every instinct screamed at him to rein Noah in, to wrap her about with power, to force her to his will. Over the past two days those instincts had screamed louder than ever: Noah had too much freedom; she was not necessarily going to learn the skills of the Mistress of the Labyrinth as she had said she was; she was possibly in contact with Brutus-reborn; and—gods, gods, *gods!*—she had brought the Troy Game incarnate into this house, and told him that his precious imps were now under its control.

If it had been anyone else, Weyland knew he would have slaughtered them without a second thought.

Intellectually, Weyland knew that granting Noah tolerance and freedom worked more in his favor than any force or fright he could have used.

Intuitively he knew that asking for shelter had somehow bound Noah more tightly to him than any enchantment he could have used. Weyland did not know the *how*'s and *why*'s of it, but he *knew*, just as surely as he knew that he needed those kingship bands in order to win out against Brutus-reborn.

Emotionally, Weyland was not sure that he could bear to use force on Noah anymore, and that realization scared him more deeply than anything had for three thousand years.

Not since Ariadne had betrayed him.

Love. Who could trust it?

He'd loved Ariadne, and with such a vast intensity that even now it hurt to recall its strength. She'd been the only one to regard him without loathing, to offer him her body for love, to give him a child. And then she had snatched it all back.

The child, gone because it had humiliated Ariadne.

Love, taken from Asterion and handed to Theseus.

Weyland remembered that day, lying on his bed in the heart of the labyrinth, when he'd heard Ariadne's soft footfall. He started up, a smile on his face, thinking she'd come back to him, but then Ariadne had entered holding the hand of a man she graced with her smile, and whom she addressed as Theseus.

"Take the beast, for I am weary of him," Ariadne had said to her new lover, and Theseus started forward, a sword raised.

Asterion tried to defend himself, but he had no sword, and Ariadne used her arts as Mistress of the Labyrinth to negate his powers.

That is what love accomplished. Humiliation. Betrayal. Murder.

But, oh . . . Noah. There was something happening there, something growing within him, and Weyland was terrified that it might be love, come again to betray him.

"Weyland."

He started, literally jumping from his chair at the kitchen table onto his feet.

Noah stood before him . . . but it was a Noah he'd not ever seen before.

Her hair, thick and dark, flowed free down her back, moving slightly within the stillness of the kitchen as if it had a life of its own.

Her clothes—the tired bodice, the heavy skirts, and the thick leather shoes—had all vanished, and instead Noah stood clothed in a raiment of cloth that looked as if it were made of flowing waters: part green, part gray, part shimmery silver.

Her face—it was still Noah's face, but vastly different. Now it radiated magic, and her eyes . . . Oh, her eyes, they had turned from dark-blue to a sage-green, shot through with gold and silver.

Weyland's first thought was that he had never seen such a vision of loveliness and power.

His second was that she had come to betray him.

Brutus was waiting outside, with a sword.

"Weyland," she said, her voice far richer and deeper than usual, "will you come walk with me?"

He was tense—so tense he barely could have moved, had he wanted to. "What is happening?" he said.

"The land is walking," she said, and Weyland felt a thrill of the supernatural vibrate through his bones.

"What is happening?" he said again.

"The land is walking," she repeated, and this time she held out her hand.

Her arm was round, and firm, and glowed with a wonderful luminescent creaminess.

"You are going to betray me," he said, and in defense he began to summon his power, to call it screaming to the surface.

In an instant she was upon him, the hand which had been outstretched now clasping one of his, her body held close against his, her face, so near to his own, her mouth, almost upon his.

"No," she breathed. "Let go your power, let go your fear. Trust me."

Weyland felt the power radiating out from *her*. A memory sprang into his mind, that time he'd met with Mag—Noah's predecessor—in the stone hall. He recalled how contemptuous of her he'd been, how weak and insipid he'd thought her power.

But Mag was as *nothing* compared to Noah. The being who stood so close to him now was a giant in comparison. *Her* power was so vibrant and so unfathomable Weyland knew he could never plumb its depths even had he a thousand years in which to attempt it.

It terrified him, and he wondered if he should destroy it.

Then she laid her mouth against his, and kissed him.

Weyland closed his eyes, part frightened, part lost. Her body pressed closer against his, and Weyland felt its warmth, and felt the rolling of the meadows and the waters within it.

She leaned back a fraction, and Weyland was appalled to hear himself moan.

"Come walk with me," she said. And then, softly, "Trust me, Weyland. I am not Ariadne."

No! No! No! his instincts screamed at him. *Everything* within him shrieked, *Danger! Danger!*

And yet there was one small place, one small haven within his soul, that said, *Trust her*.

"Come walk with me," she whispered against his mouth, and the next moment she stepped back a little, her hand tugging gently at his, and Weyland found himself following her.

SHE LED HIM THROUGH THE KITCHEN, AND THROUGH the empty, barren parlor.

She led him to the front door, which she opened with the gentlest of touches of her free hand.

She led him through the open door, and into something so extraordinary that for the moment Weyland forgot his fears, and merely stared.

"We stand," she said softly at his side, "on the borderlands of the Faerie. Welcome to the land, Asterion."

Weyland stared at the vista before him. He and Noah stood on what appeared to be the rise of a small hill. Before them rolled a series of rolling hills, carpeted with thick, almost impenetrable forest, wisps of mist floating about the treetops, birds dipping in and out of the mists.

In the far distance rose great purple peaks gilded with snow.

During his many lives, Weyland had seen a score of stunning landscapes which had momentarily touched him. They, however, could not hope to compare with this. It was not so much what Weyland saw, but what he *felt*.

The sense of a land so ancient it was virtually incomprehensible.

A wildness of power, drifting through the trees, and throbbing up through his boots from the very soil beneath him.

A sense of permanence so extraordinary, Weyland doubted that even if he threw all the power at his command at this land, it would not touch it.

A loveliness, so great he felt as if he would weep. He realized that this was the same landscape he'd seen in that vision he and Noah had shared— *Weyland, Weyland, what are we doing? How can we stop? How can we stop?*—but now that he stood here in reality it was incomparably more potent.

"Noah . . ." he said, at a loss as to what to call her, for "Noah" did not manage in any manner to encompass all that she now was.

So soon as he had spoken, and so abruptly it left him breathless, Noah pulled her hand from his, and stepped back four or five paces. She was distancing herself from him, and Weyland was certain now that it was because she was about to attack him.

Then she looked down at the ground.

He followed her eyes.

A small hand suddenly shot up out of the turf, grabbing Weyland's left ankle.

He gave a yelp, and started back, knowing that she *had* brought him here to destroy him, that she was as much a betrayer as ever was Ariadne, and once more he called forth his darkcraft, meaning to use it in any manner he could to—

The tiny hand let go his ankle, hovered a moment in the air, then patted at his boot, as if in approval.

Noah laughed, the sound both merry and so vastly relieved, Weyland would not have been surprised if she had wept with the force of it.

Weyland stared at Noah, then looked back down at the turf . . .

. . . where a small, white-bodied and copper-haired creature was pulling itself free of the soil.

"It is a water-sprite," said Noah. "One of my servants, and closer to the land than . . . oh, than almost any other creature save myself and one or two others."

"What is going on?" said Weyland, totally confused but somehow incredibly relieved. There *had* been danger present, he was sure of it, but now it had somehow miraculously vanished.

"You have been welcomed . . . I think," said a man's voice, and Weyland spun about.

Behind him stood a man dressed simply in leather breeches, and wearing a crown of twigs and red berries. He radiated infinitely more power than did Noah.

"The Lord of the Faerie," said Noah.

Weyland was not sure if he was supposed to speak or not, but this strange Lord of the Faerie forestalled any attempt he may have made.

"The soil does not reject him," the Lord of the Faerie said to Noah. "You have your answer." He relaxed, and smiled. "Thank the gods. We *all* have our answer, though how it may be, I do not know."

Noah looked at Weyland, smiling with such loveliness that Weyland himself relaxed even further. This had not been a betrayal, but a test. *But a test of what?*

A cool hand slipped into one of his, and Weyland jumped. It was the water-sprite, smiling up at him.

"He is among us, if from a great distance," said the sprite, and the Lord of the Faerie gasped.

"It cannot be!" he said.

"Ah," said Noah, "but it can. It *can*."

"What did the sprite say?" said Weyland. "What did he mean?"

Noah raised her eyes from the sprite to Weyland. "He said that you were among us." She paused. "What he *meant*, was that you are *one* among us. That you, too, are of the Faerie folk, if from a very distant land and time. Weyland, was that truly a bull which mated with your mother? Or was it a god?"

Noah suddenly laughed, the sound rich and merry. "If poor Cornelia can find herself standing here, Weyland-Asterion, then there is no reason why you cannot, too."

CHAPTER TWENTY-TWO

THE GATEHOUSE, PETERSHAM

THEY WALKED DOWN A STRAIGHT GRAVELED path, an overgrown park to either side of them. They walked mostly in silence, sometimes exchanging a meaningless comment or two. By and large, both were lost in their own thoughts: Noah relieved and happy in that relief, Weyland somewhat confused and disconcerted.

"What just happened?" Weyland said, eventually.

"I took you to the edge of the Faerie world," said Noah, "which exists side by side with the mortal world. There are, in essence, *two* lands, the mortal and largely unaware, and the Faerie. Each of these worlds exist side by side, but also exist interwoven."

Weyland considered what she had said. Two lands, two worlds. He had only been aware of *one*. An icy finger of sheer fright stirred about in his bowels. *What had been going on, of which he had not been aware?*

"A great deal," said Noah softly, and Weyland came to a halt, catching at Noah's elbow so that he could stare at her.

"The Troy Game . . ." Weyland said.

"The Troy Game is largely of the mortal world," said Noah. "When Brutus and Genvissa constructed the Game they did not use any of the Faerie in the Game's creation."

"But now?"

"But now, as I grow as both goddess of the waters and as Mistress of the Labyrinth, the realms of the Faerie and the mortal world grow ever closer. The battle for the Troy Game, Weyland, shall be fought through both worlds."

"Then why take me there? Surely I, the Great Enemy, should have been left in ignorance of the Faerie?"

"There was a straightforward reason for me to take you there," she said, finally, turning to resume her walk along the path, and forcing Weyland to follow. "And there is a not-so-straightforward reason."

"The straightforward reason was to 'test' me?"

"Yes."

"And this 'test' was . . ."

"To see if you had caused the plague, or not. If you had, the Faerie would have rejected you."

Weyland considered this. She had not believed him when he'd said he hadn't created this pestilence which gripped London. For a moment he considered a minor sulk over the matter, then grinned a little to himself. Over their past three lives he'd given her every reason not to trust him.

"And thus I passed," he said. "Does that make you happy?"

She glanced at him, half smiling herself. "Oh, yes, it does."

"And the second reason you wanted to take me into the Realm of the Faerie?"

She paused, and Weyland understood that what she was about to say would be difficult for her.

"Because I needed to be sure that what I was doing was the right thing. That the path I had taken was a true one."

"And that path, Noah . . . ?" he said softly.

Again she stopped, Weyland coming to a halt himself.

"My goddess name is Eaving, Weyland. That is who stands before you now."

He stared, and, as he remembered all the languages he'd learned during his various lives within England over the past three thousand years, then everything he'd intuited about asking her for shelter fell into place. "Gods," he said, "your name means 'shelter'!"

She smiled dryly. "Aye. The unexpected shelter from the haven. The name dictates my nature. I must shelter any who ask me for it."

He stared, his mouth hanging open.

"You did not know?" she said.

Weyland gave a small shake of his head. "I overheard you and Jane talking about shelter, and knew that it was important . . . but I was not sure why. All I knew was that whenever I mentioned 'shelter' to you, then a look of part fear, part resignation, came into your eyes. I used it instinctively . . . Eaving." He paused, thinking, then looked at her with sharp, calculating eyes. "What hold does that give me over you?"

"In its own way, a far greater hold than that of your imp."

"Tell me what it means, precisely."

She hesitated, the tip of her tongue touching briefly at her lower lip. "It means that I cannot betray you to Brutus-reborn. To do so would be to violate the trust of the shelter."

"And has *he* ever asked you of shelter?"

Her eyes became brighter. "Yes."

Weyland felt a jolt of sheer jealousy surge through him. "Have you slept with him, in this life?"

She resumed walking. "Sheltering does not imply answering every question you might have, Weyland."

He wanted to seize her, to shake the answer out of her, and was dismayed at how easy he found it to ignore the urge. "Eaving—"

She was walking again, and he had to take three or four quick steps to catch up with her.

"Weyland," she said as he reappeared at her side. "You know none of this land's magic, and recognize little of its beauty. And yet you could build your Idyll to the very borders of the Faerie. You are such a strange man." She gave an odd little laugh. "You have passed your test, and I also, and to celebrate I thought I would bring you to this place, which is special to me."

He realized she wanted to change the subject, and for the moment he was prepared to allow it. "Is this part of the Faerie?" he said.

"What do you think? What do you *feel*?"

"No. It is not part of the Faerie."

"You are right. This is a beautiful spot, but it is not part of the Faerie. We are just beyond the village of Petersham, a place nestled in a great curve of the Thames. Do you feel it? The closeness of the river?"

She waited, and after a moment he gave a single nod.

Noah—he knew that in this guise she was Eaving, but somehow he could only regard her as "Noah," and knew that name was, in its own right, as magical as "Eaving"—smiled, pleased. "See this path," she said. "Is it not particularly lovely?"

He looked down the path, studying it. It was made of well-packed gravel, and very long and straight. To either side grew small, immature trees and shrubs studded among the waist-height grass. Weyland thought it had the feel of both man and nature, and because of that, had a prettiness that was particularly attractive.

"This path is what remains of a great drive," said Noah. She nodded to her left. "Beyond that hill lies a magnificent house. Once this was its drive. If we walked back for a half a mile we would come to padlocked and rusted iron gates that are five paces wide and eight tall. Some fifteen years ago the people who lived in the great house decided to build themselves a new drive, a new approach to the house, and this new drive winds manicured and tamed some three or four miles to the west of us. *This* drive has been left to do as it willed."

"Why show this to me?"

"Because this is a beautiful place to me, and because at the end of this

drive, hidden among the grasses and trees, is a small gatehouse, gone to ruin—
or gone back to the earth—as has this drive. I want to take you there."

"Why?"

"To heal wounds."

"What wounds?"

She put a hand on his chest. "We all have accumulated wounds, Weyland.
All need to be healed."

"Noah . . . *Noah* . . ."

"Come with me, Weyland." Taking his hand once more, she led him down
the overgrown driveway.

THE GATEHOUSE WAS A SIMPLE STRUCTURE. BRICK-
walled and built on the octagonal, it had but one room, open to the elements
now that the glass had been removed from its seven windows, and the door
taken off to more useful purposes.

"See," said Noah, halting with Weyland in the open doorway and looking at
the leaves and dried grasses scattered over the tiled floor. "It has many walls,
and many openings, but it is no labyrinth, no Game, no Idyll. It is a simple and
good-hearted structure, with no traps, sitting warm and forgotten by mankind.
This is a good place."

"For *what*?"

"For healing my heart, and yours," she said, and came to him, and kissed
him, and drew him inside the gatehouse.

LATER, AS THEY LAY ENTWINED, WEYLAND THOUGHT
he could perhaps feel the faintest of thrums vibrating through the tiles on the
floor. Perhaps it was the worms, disturbed by his and Noah's recent lovemaking. Perhaps it was just his imagination, perhaps just wanting.

And perhaps there was something beneath him that he could truly feel, lying here on tile above earth, a goddess in his arms. Either Noah, or perhaps
his short trip into the Realm of the Faerie, had woken something hitherto unknown in him.

Already languid in the aftermath of lovemaking, Weyland relaxed even further, drifting into a semidreamlike state. Noah lay with her back pressed
against his chest and belly, warm, her own chest gently rising and falling within
the circle of his arms.

"Weyland," she said, very soft.

"Hmmm?"

She turned within his arms. "Do you know," she said, a note of wonder in her voice, "that you are the only man whom I have ever shared a bed and a house with, who has ever treated me with even a modicum of respect and of friendship?" She paused, and when she resumed speaking, laughter had replaced the wonder in her tone. "I speak, of course, of that time *after* you tore that damn imp from my body."

He did not reply for a minute or two, and when he did, his voice was heavy with regret. "I wish I had not done that. I wish . . ." *I wish I had thought sooner that friendship and respect would win more from you than pain and terror.*

"We all wish," she said softly, "and yet all that wishes ever achieve is to expose our sorrows."

Again, a silence, then Weyland spoke.

"Do you know," he said, the fingers of one hand very gently stroking her shoulder, "that you are the first woman I have ever *liked*? It is a strange feeling, this 'liking.'"

Her mouth twitched. "I have made Asterion 'like,'" she said. "I am a witch indeed!"

CHAPTER TWENTY-THREE

IDOL LANE, LONDON

Noah Speaks

HERE WAS A GREAT CORNER TURNED THAT day. I finally decided I could trust Weyland, and I finally decided I could trust myself. I had stepped down the right path, even if it was a strange, sometimes frightening, and totally unknowable one.

I learned also, however, that Weyland had hidden depths. That somehow he also had the Faerie in him, and that likely it had come from his strange father. A bull? Truly? Or had it been a god disguised as a bull, which would explain why Asterion's mother had been so severely smitten? The heavens alone knew how much those impractical Aegean gods liked to cavort about in animal form, seducing women here and there.

I also decided, finally, that the Troy Game was likely far more malevolent than Asterion had ever been. We had all been trapped by it, deluded into thinking that it would defend us, and be some great protective amulet from all manner of evil.

Instead, the Game *was* all manner of evil, and the land's alliance with it had been a sad mistake, and one we might yet all live to regret.

Still further, I learned something more from that day, but it took a few weeks for the lesson to sink in.

I learned that going to Weyland, opening myself to him, had been no mistake. It had been something that I *needed* to do.

It had been the right thing to do.

Three weeks after we had made love in the gatehouse in Petersham, I realized I was carrying his child. I realized not through any physical symptoms, but because, unlike my experience with Catling, I was able to communicate with the growing life within me. One day, a day so extraordinary, a new soul reached out to me, and spoke.

A daughter.

I wept. I wept for joy and I wept for all the pain I knew I would cause to those I loved, because suddenly my path opened up before me with an intense clarity that left me reeling, and because, finally, I would have my daughter.

Not she whom I had lost as Cornelia—I knew and accepted now that she would never come back to me—but a daughter conceived with a man I loved.

That shocked me. I think I must have loved Weyland for months, but had never dared admit it to myself.

Weyland, Weyland, what are we doing? How can we stop? How can we stop?

I was a goddess, I was Eaving, and I understood from the very depths of my soul that I did not ever conceive by accident or whim, but because it was something I wanted.

And I only ever wanted to conceive with a man I loved.

For the first time in three thousand years I felt at peace, and it was a wonderful place to be.

TWO DAYS AFTER I REALIZED I WAS PREGNANT I FOUND my way out of the Idyll by myself for the first time. This had little to do with my approaching maternity, and everything to do with my growing skills in the way of the labyrinth.

Weyland watched me, a little concerned, but proud also. *Pride—not satisfaction.*

That made me happy, but I did not yet tell him of my pregnancy. For the time being I wanted to enjoy it for myself.

"Noah the mother," I murmured to myself that evening, standing alone before the sheer waterfall that served as a mirror in Weyland's spectacular "washing chamber."

Noah the destroyer, for that was the only way I could ever protect my daughter, and the land.

PART EIGHT

DARKWITCH RISING

LONDON, 1939

*J*ACK SHOOK THE KING'S HAND. "WHY ARE YOU back?"

George VI smiled sadly. "I loved Noah. Why else?"

Skelton looked about. "Is she here? Is she upstairs somewhere, cavorting with Weyland?"

The Lord of the Faerie took Skelton's elbow, guiding him through double-doors to their right, ignoring his question.

"We need your aid, Jack," the Lord of the Faerie said. "Desperately."

"We've a problem," the king said, falling into step beside Skelton.

"And, naturally," said Stella, now a step behind the men, her high heels striking sharply against the hard floor, "it involves Noah. When haven't the entire world's problems involved her?"

Skelton glanced over his shoulder at her. Stella sounded exasperated, but nothing more. Apparently her ancient hatred of Cornelia had vanished.

"Jack." The Lord of the Faerie drew him to a halt just inside the double-doors. "How much loyalty do you owe the Troy Game?"

Skelton looked at the Faerie Lord carefully. "What do you need me to say, Coel?"

"Would you put Noah before the Game?"

Skelton lowered his eyes. "Does she remain corrupted?"

"You have never truly loved her, have you?" said George VI, softly.

Skelton made a sound of exasperation. He would have said something, but just then came a soft cry. A wail, as if a young girl cried gently.

He looked into the drawing room of the house, where the Lord of the Faerie had led him.

There was a huge stone fireplace in the far wall, a fire within, burning brightly.

And before it, sitting on the carpet with her legs neatly tucked underneath her, was a girl of some sixteen or seventeen years.

Some part of Skelton's brain registered that she was lovely, and that she *reminded him of Cornelia when first he'd seen her, but his eyes were drawn immediately to her hands and wrists.*

They were held out before her as if tied, and to Skelton's startled gaze it appeared as if they had been bound with red-hot wire.

"This is Grace," said the Lord of the Faerie quietly, "and we love her dearly, even though she is our doom."

CHAPTER ONE

THE BONE HOUSE, ST. DUNSTAN'S-IN-THE-EAST,
IDOL LANE, LONDON

Noah Speaks

*I*T WAS THE NIGHT BEFORE CHRISTMAS, AND WEY-
land had brought me to the bone house of St. Dunstan's-in-the-East
to celebrate. He had decorated the chamber warmly for the Christian celebration: scores of guttering candles were set askew among the piles of
bones on their shelves; a table, set in the clear space of the center of the chamber and spread with good glass and silverware, all entwined with holly and
mistletoe; golden silk, draped over the chairs set at each end of the table; a
skull, taken from the trove stacked against the east wall, set squarely in the
center of the table and overflowing with candied fruits.

Soft music filtered through the bone house. The choir were at song about
the altar of St. Dunstan's, the muted sound of their voices riddling through
the cracks of the church and monastery walls, and all the dark, unknown
spaces between, before trickling out from the joints of the bones tumbled
higgledy-piggledy about the shelves and the outer edges of the chamber.

Weyland was watching me, trying to gauge my reaction to this interesting
spectacle.

I slid a glance his way from the corner of my eye. "The bone house," I
said. "How sweet. This can only be *your* very peculiar sense of humor,
Weyland. You might have honored me at Christmas Eve in a hall decked with
gold and jewels. Instead, you have brought me to this dusty establishment."

He grinned, stepped forth, took my hands, and kissed me softly on the
mouth. "I knew you would appreciate the effort," he said, and kissed me the
harder when I laughed.

The past three months since I had taken Weyland to the gatehouse near Petersham had been easy ones for me, which I had not anticipated. I had been distraught at first, discovering Catling's true nature, and then at Louis's reaction, and all this sense of sadness and betrayal coming immediately after I'd learned I was Ariadne's long-lost daughter-heir, and Asterion's get, to boot. There had been so much to cope with, and think through.

Now I was at peace with myself and with where I was going.

I knew what *I* had to do, and I also knew that it would enrage both Louis and the Troy Game when they learned what I proposed.

For the moment, then, it was best I kept my plans to myself.

"Will you sit?" said Weyland, and he pulled out one of the chairs for me, and I sat, arranging the heavy folds of the deep-red velvet gown as I did so. A few weeks hence Weyland had returned to the house in Idol Lane accompanying a cart laden with bolts and bolts of silks, velvets, linens, laces, ribbons, buttons, and sundry feminine fancies, and in those times when we were not otherwise engaged, Jane and I had happily sewn ourselves some garments a good deal prettier than we'd possessed heretofore. It had been just one more happiness to add to my general sense of well-being and contentment that had come over me these past months.

Weyland sat at the other end of the table, smiled at me, poured me some wine, and then waved a hand.

A gray wraith appeared from the shadows, bearing a platter of steaming food.

My mouth hung open, and my heart stuttered a little in my chest.

"One of the bone chamber's inhabitants," said Weyland softly, watching my reaction carefully as the wraith came to the table, set the platter down, bowed, and then vanished back into the shifting shadows from whence it had come. "Come to serve us on this celebratory night."

I took a deep breath. "You surprise me," I said.

"Good," he said. Then he grinned again. "You have constantly surprised me, so I am most glad I have managed something to make even your beautiful mouth drop in astonishment."

I laughed. "You can talk with the dead?"

"I have been dead, and returned," he said. "As have you. But I was dragged back from death by the ancient Crone of Death at Ariadne's request. That first time I was not reborn. I came direct from death. I still have a good rapport with the realm of the dead."

I took a good sip of wine. Weyland could drag back the dead if he wished. *Fabulous.* Then I laughed again, softly, shaking my head.

"If only the good monks and priests and worshipers in St. Dunstan's knew what went on not twenty feet from their fervor," I said. "The earth goddess, being entertained by the black-hearted Minotaur, and waited on by the souls of the dead. It is a good Yuletide gift, Weyland. I appreciate it."

"Then allow that appreciation to whet your appetite, Noah." He preferred to call me Noah than Eaving, and somehow I liked that. He preferred the woman before the goddess. "Eat on, I pray," he continued, "for the kitchens of the dead are a long way to send back this food to be reheated."

We ate, talking now and again of inconsequential things. Laughing here and there. Enjoying, as had become habitual between us, the other one's company.

It was only when the wraith had removed our plates and passed about the skull of candied fruits, that Weyland broached what must have been bothering him, not only this night, for the months past.

"What is Brutus doing, Noah?"

I put down my piece of fruit untasted. "I cannot tell you that, Weyland."

His mouth twisted, and he looked away. A silence fell between us for a few minutes, and I was unsure how to break it.

"You will betray me," he said finally. We always came back to that, eventually.

"No," I said. "I will not betray you."

His eyes slid back my way. "You will not? *Why* not? I thought that Brutus' love was all you lived for. Is not my betrayal a condition of his love?"

"When I lived as Cornelia, all I lived for was Brutus' love. When I was Caela, all I lived for was what the Troy Game and what Mag wanted me to do on their behalf. This life . . . Oh, in this life I started out accepting that all I wanted was Brutus' love, and that all I lived for was your defeat and the triumph of the Troy Game. But now . . . no."

He looked disbelieving and cynical, and I did not blame him for that.

"I've changed," I said, meeting his eyes, "and in the process discovered things about myself that have astounded me. Weyland, I am not going to blindly do what the Troy Game wants, and I am not going to blindly do what Brutus wants, but I am going to do what is right for me, and *for this land.* This land, Weyland, is what I hold most allegiance to. Not the Troy Game. Not Brutus."

Why didn't I point out that I would not do what Weyland *wanted? Did I not want to say it, or did I not want to do it?*

"But you will not tell me what he is doing," he said.

"No. Neither will I betray you to him, Weyland."

He regarded me steadily, the illumination from the candles catching the glint in his eyes. "I could force you. I still can, you know. The presence of the imp was immaterial. You *are* my creature. I can force the information from you."

I continued to hold his eyes, more sure of him now than I had ever been. "You won't," I said. "You will not force me."

He affected one of his old sneers.

"Don't," I said softly. "That is not the Weyland you have shown me these past months."

He dropped his eyes, and one of his hands fiddled with a piece of holly on the table.

"What I have seen in the past months has turned my heart, Weyland."

"Don't," he said.

"I will not betray you," I repeated. "I am not Ariadne. And *that* is my Yule-tide gift to you, Weyland. My promise: I will not betray you."

He would not look at me, his hand still fiddling with that irritating piece of holly.

"Will you fetch me the golden kingship bands of Troy?" he said, thinking he knew the answer.

"Yes," I said, and his startled eyes flew up to meet mine. I laughed. "In a manner of speaking. I will fetch them and bring them to the Idyll, and there I will place them. But I will not hand them to you. They will be safe in the Idyll."

"Hand them to me."

"No. I will remove them from where Brutus-reborn can reach them, and I will secrete them in the Idyll. You will not be able to find them, but they will be closer to you than to him. And I can only bring four of the bands. Not all six."

He raised his eyebrows.

"I sent two of the bands into the Otherworld, and I do not know where they are. Even your wraiths would not be able to find them. It was a foolish thing for me to do, perhaps . . . but it means that neither you nor Brutus can achieve all of the bands."

"Who *can* find those two?"

The Lord of the Faerie, I thought, but would not tell him this. "A friend," I said. "One of the Faerie folk, and one who has the best interests of this land in his heart, as do I."

He sat, thinking. "Noah, why do you do this?" he said eventually. "Why promise not to betray me? Why bring four of the bands to the Idyll now, when you had made me promise to wait until you'd gained your full powers as Mistress of the Labyrinth? Why treat me as if . . ."

I rose and moved about the table. "Why treat you as if I regarded you with love, Weyland, rather than hatred?"

He flinched at that word, "love," and I wondered at the fact that we had both steered well clear of it for so long. I came to him, and sat down in his lap.

"Why do we never speak that single word, Weyland?" I said, shivering with pleasure as his arms slid about my waist, and sliding my own about his shoulders. "Why do we avoid it so assiduously?"

He was looking down, as if fascinated with the patterns in the silk of my skirt, and did not answer.

"Why are we so afraid of love?"

He took a deep breath, and closed his eyes.

"I will not betray you, Weyland," I whispered. "How can I, when I love you so deeply?"

Oh gods, those words had been sitting in my throat for weeks and months, choking me, standing in my way, impeding all my progress. How sweet it felt, now, to say them to this man.

To Asterion.

His eyes were still tightly closed, and I wondered what thoughts consumed him. I put one of my hands on his head, and stroked gently at his hair. *I will not betray you, Weyland. I will not betray you.*

"Weyland, Weyland," I whispered. "Where are we going? And why *should* we stop?"

Tears forced their way between his tightly closed eyelids, and coursed down his cheeks. His arms about me tightened, and I was suddenly very afraid for him, that he should be this terrified of being loved.

"Weyland," I said, and I took one of his hands, and put it on my belly.

"I have your daughter in there," I said. "Your daughter, and mine. Not a re-born daughter, or a re-creation of the ones we have both lost, but a new child. One made for both of us."

He tensed, his hand rigid on my belly.

"I am not Ariadne," I said. "I will not betray you to another Theseus, nor will I ever take this daughter away from you. This child heals wounds, Weyland. Your wounds, and mine."

He finally dared enough to open his eyes, and raise to mine. *"Why?"*

"Because I loved and trusted you, Weyland."

He was looking at my belly now, his hand still rigid. "I am so scared . . ." he whispered. "I had not thought this would happen."

"I know." I pulled his head against my breasts, and for the longest time we sat there, cradled together, he and I and the child we had made growing within me, as the voices of the church choir filtered about us and two wraiths from the halls of the dead cleared the table, and set out port wine for us to drink, should we so desire.

CHAPTER TWO

IDOL LANE AND EARL'S
COURT STATION, LONDON

EYLAND STOOD, STARING AT NOAH, IN THAT strange reserved manner he had when he was at his most wary.

"I have arranged the driver and carriage to meet you on Thames Street," he said. "As you asked."

She smiled, briefly putting the palm of her hand against his cheek. "Then I do thank you, Weyland."

"Brutus—"

"He will know. He won't act."

"Are you sure?"

She paused, and Weyland could see that she was not sure at all. "I will come with you," he said.

"No, Weyland. I can *only* do this by myself. The band will remain hidden if it senses you nearby."

Weyland repressed every natural instinct he had to insist that he accompany her. He took a deep breath.

"Very well," he said. "Gods, Noah . . ."

"I *will* come home, Weyland. Trust me."

The frightening thing was, he thought, that it was too easy to trust her. Too easy to believe in her.

Too easy to love her, and risk all.

Weyland gave a weak smile, and she leaned forward and kissed him. "I will bring back the band, Weyland . . . and I will *not* bring Theseus with it."

At that, Weyland felt so weak with fear, with sheer vulnerability, that he actually felt physically nauseous. Noah knew too many of his weaknesses. She knew what horror it had been for him to see Ariadne leading Theseus by the hand into the heart of the labyrinth, and knew that the horror had not so much been fear, but that soul-destroying knowledge of treachery by someone he had loved without reason.

She kissed him again, briefly, and then she was gone, leaving Weyland standing at the head of the stairs, staring after her.

THE CARRIAGE AND DRIVER WERE WAITING AT THE junction of Idol Lane and Thames Street as Weyland had promised. Noah spoke softly to the driver, waited for his nod, then allowed him to settle her into the carriage.

The driver climbed to his seat, picked up reins and whip, and clucked the pair of bay mares into motion, and they were off.

They drove west along Thames Street, then worked their way to Fleet Street and then the Strand, which they followed to Charing Cross. From there, they turned right up Haymarket Street and then west along Piccadilly and Portugal Street into the open countryside. Fields and orchards, covered with a dusting of snow, stretched on either side; the market gardens of Earls Court, where they were headed, were sure to be smothered in either slush or mud.

But as they drove, a change came over the countryside and, indeed, in the vehicle in which Noah traveled. The sound of the horses' hooves faded, as did also the dark-cloaked figure of the driver. The carriage grew a roof, where before it had none, and its motion changed from rolling and rocking into a far smoother action.

Noah was riding in one of the strange black machines she had seen on several occasions in her previous life, when she had moved the bands for the first time. She tensed, unhappy with the strangeness of the vehicle, but knowing it had to be endured.

The countryside closed in. Tall, dirty, stuccoed buildings rose to either side, shutting out any view of what fields may have been left behind them. People in strange clothing bustled along footpaths, while about Noah rushed many similar vehicles to the one in which she was trapped.

She leaned forward on her seat, and opened the small glass window between her and her driver, who didn't seem in the least perturbed to be in control of a conveyance far different to the one he had started out driving.

As he heard the window slide open, the driver turned his head slightly, and, with a jolt of surprise, Noah saw that he'd turned into one of the gray wraiths of St. Dunstan's bone house.

"Madam?" he said.

"Turn left down Earls Court Road," she said, "and drop me off at the station."

He nodded, and Noah sat back, slightly fascinated despite her initial uneasiness by the style of housing along the roads down which they drove. So substantial, such big windows and porticoed entrances, so . . . staid.

And the roads. Noah was used to the crowded streets of London, but never had she seen traffic move so fast. She remembered the time in her previous life when she'd had to cross to Gospel Oak Station, and had frozen in the middle of the road, terrified by the traffic.

Fortunately, the driver pulled up at the footpath right by Earls Court Station (apparently breaking some kind of honor code as he did so, for several of the black monsters blared screeching horns at him as he crossed in front of them), and Noah was spared another crossing.

"Wait for me," she said to him as she climbed out of the vehicle (making several attempts before she worked out how the door opened), straightened, and with no apparent hesitation, walked into the gaping entrance of Earls Court Underground Station.

There was an initial low-ceilinged vestibule, then the station opened out into a large concourse which overlooked the railway platforms themselves. To her right there were five windows, at which people queued; directly before her were stairs leading down to the platforms; and to her left was a small teahouse.

There were several small tables set out here, and at one of them sat a very tall man dressed in a tightly belted coat and with a soft hat pulled well down over his eyes.

Before him, on the table, stood a steaming cup of tea.

Noah drew in a deep breath, steadying herself, then walked over to the table.

It looked as if the man was asleep, and Noah stretched down a careful, silent hand, reaching for the cup and saucer.

The man—*the Sidlesaghe*—raised his face to her, his eyes large and mournful.

"What do you, Eaving? Why take the golden band of Troy now?"

Her hand closed about the saucer, and it shifted fractionally toward her.

The Sidlesaghe put his large, long-fingered hand over her wrist, and the cup and saucer slid to a halt. "Eaving—"

"Friend," Noah said softly, "release the band to me, please."

"Eaving, we fear what you do."

"I will shelter it," she said. "I promise this."

Reluctantly the Sidlesaghe lifted his hand, and Noah slid the cup and saucer toward her, then lifted it into her hands.

Instantly it transformed into one of the heavy golden bands of Troy, emblazoned about its outer diameter with the icon of the stylized labyrinth with the spinning crown above it.

Noah gave the Sidlesaghe a nod, and then she was gone.

THE JOURNEY BACK TO IDOL LANE WAS THE PRECISE reverse of her journey through time and space to Earls Court. The wraith was waiting for her in his vehicle at the curbside—he leapt out to open the back door for Noah so she could sit inside.

The wraith set the black vehicle in motion, and drove northward to Kensington Road where he turned right and headed back into the city.

As they drove, so the great dirty stuccoed buildings faded away, and the winterfields appeared once more before, while at the junction of Portugal Street and Piccadilly, the townhouses of suburban London began to appear. As the outer transformation took place, so also did that of the vehicle in which Noah traveled. The horses reappeared, the roof and confining walls of the black monster slid away, and Noah was left, grateful, to sit in the open carriage in the cold sharp sunlight of a winter's day.

All the while she kept close hold of the band.

All the while she kept shut out, as much as she could, the soft cries of Louis that prodded at her mind from his magical journey through the Ringwalk.

Why, Noah? Why? Why? Why?

"Because I choose," she whispered.

NOAH OPENED THE FRONT DOOR, AND LOOKED UP the flight of stairs.

Weyland was still standing at their head, as if he had not moved the entire time she'd been gone.

"Jane?" Noah said softly.

"Gone to market," Weyland replied. "Noah—"

"I have it," she said, and held it forth.

Weyland visibly sagged, and Noah realized how tense he'd been. She walked up the stairs, faced him, and held it out so he could see.

Weyland swallowed, then reached out a hand and touched it.

The instant his fingers made contact with the metal he sprang back, with a soft exclamation.

"What is it?" Noah said.

"It bit me!" Weyland said, looking between the golden band and the tips of his fingers, which were reddened and slightly swollen.

"Then I shall have to keep it safe," she said, "if it will not allow you to touch it."

"Noah—"

"I will shelter it, Weyland."

"And when I ask for it?"

"Then I shall bring it forth, and we can see again if the band shall allow you to handle it. It will not go far. Trust me."

Weyland opened his mouth to say something, but just then the front door opened, and before either he or Noah could react, Jane entered, looked up the stairs, and gave an audible gasp of horror. "Noah! *What have you done?*"

Noah sent a quick, hard look at Weyland—*Let me speak with her, Weyland, I beg you*—and then she was running lightly down the stairs, one hand clutching the band, the other held out in appeal to Jane.

But Jane did not see. She slammed the front door closed and marched through the parlor into the kitchen.

"Jane . . ." Breathless—and that through shock rather than through exertion—Noah stood in the doorway between kitchen and parlor, watching Jane as she thumped goods out of her basket onto the table.

"I cannot *believe* what you have done!" Jane said.

Noah took a step into the room. "Jane—"

"You are giving Weyland the bands of Troy? You are *giving* them to him?"

"No," said Noah. "I am taking them into my own hands."

"Ha!" said Jane.

"I am no longer willing to allow the Troy Game to dictate what happens, Jane. The bands are too valuable to allow to lie about."

Jane stopped what she was doing and stared at Noah. "Has the power of the labyrinth gone to your head, Noah? Have you lost what little wits you possessed? I *saw* you! Standing there, holding out one of the bands to Weyland! How many of the other bands does he have? How many betrayals have you managed before I saw *that* particular little touching scene?"

"Jane—"

"What have you done, Noah?"

"For all the gods' sakes, Jane, it is not what it seems!"

"No? Then explain it to me."

"I—"

Noah got no further, for at that moment Weyland appeared behind her, and, sliding his arms about her waist, drew her close back against him.

Noah winced and closed her eyes, as if she could not believe Weyland's actions. *Not now, Weyland, not now . . .*

"Noah and I have become . . . close," said Weyland. He was sick of pretending. Moreover, some part of him felt that if he *pushed*, then he would discover sooner rather than later if he had left himself critically open to betrayal.

Jane was staring at the pair before her as if she could not believe *this* further development, either.

"You *have* been sleeping with him," Jane whispered. "You lied to me."

Before Noah could stop him, one of Weyland's hands had cupped her very slightly rounded belly. "She's carrying my child, Jane," he said. "A real child. Not an imp."

Jane gaped, her face white.

"Jane," Noah said, wriggling out of Weyland's grasp. "Please, I need you to trust in what I am—"

"Trust?" Jane said. "*Trust?* Wait until Brutus hears what—"

"Jane!" Noah's voice snapped out from the distance between them. "Jane, I beg you . . ." *Keep silent about this, Jane. Please!*

"Why?" Jane said, very soft. She'd caught the unspoken words.

"Jane, I need you to keep this secret for me." *I need you to keep* all *my secrets, and tell no one.*

Jane glanced at Weyland. He was looking between them, but Noah was using her powers as Eaving to send her thoughts, and Jane was fairly sure Weyland could not catch them. *You want me to keep silent about the fact you are handing Weyland the bands,* and *carrying his child? You have lost all your wits, indeed.*

"Please, Jane," Noah said. *Keep this secret for me.*

"Why, Noah?"

"Because I ask it, Jane, and because . . ."

"Yes?"

"Because, Jane, as a favor to me, Weyland shall grant you your freedom when I have completed my training as Mistress of the Labyrinth. He will have no further need of you then. He will let you go."

"I *will*?" Weyland said.

"A bribe?" said Jane. "How tasty."

Noah inclined her head very slightly Weyland's way. She didn't look directly at him, but somehow the movement conveyed such emotion, and such appeal, that she might as well have thrown herself to her knees.

"Do this for me, Weyland, and for our daughter," she said, her voice low. "Promise that you will grant Jane her freedom once I have attained full powers as Mistress of the Labyrinth. Why not? What need shall you have of her, then? Grant me this boon, Weyland, I pray you."

Weyland looked at her, a look of such hopelessness passing over his face as he did so that Jane was momentarily stunned; then he looked to Jane.

"Very well," he said. "Your freedom, Jane, once Noah ceases to need you."

Jane didn't know what to do or say. She'd never dared even to consider the notion of freedom because she'd been certain, all this life, that Weyland would eventually kill her once he'd done with her.

All the time she'd been learning the Ancient Carol in the Realm of the Faerie, she'd feared that Weyland would murder her before she could escape entirely into the Faerie.

Could she trust his promise now? Freedom?

Gods, freedom . . . Jane suddenly wanted it so bad she felt it as a ache in her belly.

But was freedom worth what Noah asked her to do?

Noah wanted her to keep Noah's secrets for her. And *what* secrets, and from so many people? Hide from all (*save the Lord of the Faerie; at least he knew this*) that it was Ariadne who taught Noah, not Jane. Hide the fact that Noah was Ariadne's blood daughter-heir. Hide the fact that Asterion was her forefather. Hide the fact that Noah was a Darkwitch bred and born. Hide from the Lord of the Faerie and from Louis, as from all their allies, that Noah was handing the bands to Weyland. Hide from the Lord of the Faerie and from Louis the fact that Noah was pregnant with Weyland's child. If and when any of these people found out what secrets Jane had been keeping . . . gods, she *would* be dead.

But, by the gods, what she would achieve if she succeeded.

Freedom.

Freedom to do as she wished.

Freedom to be what she wanted, where she wanted. Freedom from the Troy Game and all it meant.

Freedom to stand behind the throne on the summit of The Naked, to carol in the dawn and the dusk.

Freedom to stand and watch the Lord of the Faerie as he lifted his eyes to hers, and smiled.

She swallowed, looked at Weyland, then nodded at Noah. "Very well," she said. "I will do it."

Weyland smiled, but Noah didn't, and, looking at her, Jane realized that Noah knew the risks Jane was taking.

"Thank you," Noah said, and Jane looked away, not knowing if that "thank you" was enough.

chapter three

IDOL LANE, LONDON

HE LORD OF THE FAERIE KNEW NOAH HAD shifted a band. The next time Jane saw him, which was two days after Noah had asked her to keep her secrets (*all her damned, cursed secrets*), the Lord of the Faerie greeted her by the scaffold, kissed her, and asked instantly why Noah had moved a band. Was Weyland forcing her to it? Was she in danger?

"Weyland is not forcing Noah," Jane said. "Noah told me she was 'sheltering' the band, and that you were not to worry."

The Lord of the Faerie nodded. "Ah. Then I shall not worry. Noah is sheltering them."

Frankly, Jane didn't know *what* Noah was doing with them, but if Noah was witless enough not only to sleep with Weyland, but also to fall pregnant with his child, then she wasn't at all certain that Noah wasn't also handing Weyland the kingship bands.

"Coel," she said. "Noah has made Weyland promise that once she has completed her training as the Mistress of the Labyrinth, then I can have my freedom."

The Lord of the Faerie stared at her, then his mouth slowly curved in a smile. "Has she, now? Do you believe him?"

Jane meant to say something bland, but all she managed to do was burst into tears. She was terrified that Weyland *didn't* mean it, that he was taunting her, and that the day Noah finished her training would be Jane's death day.

The Lord of the Faerie pulled her to him, and cuddled her close. "You will be well," he murmured. "You *will* live to stand behind my throne."

Jane tried to calm herself. One of the Lord of the Faerie's hands was stroking up and down her back, and she slid her arms about him, and rested her face against his shoulder, and dared to believe that all would, indeed, be well.

But how could it? *How could it?*

What would happen when she told the Lord of the Faerie *all* that she knew? Noah, a Darkwitch. Noah, a descendent of Ariadne and Asterion. Noah, carrying Asterion's child.

What would the Lord of the Faerie do when he knew all that? Would he loathe her? Throw her from the Realm of the Faerie?

And what possibility freedom in the first instance when Weyland found out that not only was Ariadne—his mortal enemy—teaching Noah, but that Noah was herself descended of Ariadne and Asterion, *and* was a Darkwitch besides?

"I know more than you think, beloved," the Lord of the Faerie said softly, his hand still stroking, and Jane began to weep once more, softly, despairingly. *He couldn't possibly know it all.*

"Trust me," he whispered.

Jane wanted to. She wanted to more than anything. But she was too scared. She was caught in a web of lies and deceit, and she was certain that, sooner or later, that web would strangle her.

OVER THE NEXT WEEKS NOAH RETRIEVED THREE more kingship bands. While Jane did not see her with another of the bands, she knew because the Lord of the Faerie remarked on it on each occasion.

"Noah retrieved another band yesterday, Jane. She is sheltering it?"

"Of course," Jane said, knowing that is what the Lord of the Faerie wanted to hear. In reality, Jane had little idea what was happening to the golden bands of Troy. She saw Noah only infrequently: Noah and Weyland spent most of their time in his den (*their* den, Jane supposed) when Noah was not at her training with Ariadne, and both Noah and Weyland made sure that Jane never surprised them as she had on that first occasion. For all Jane knew, Weyland and Noah spent their time sitting in the Idyll, playing hoops with the damned things.

Whenever Noah went to Ariadne, Jane went to The Naked and learned more of the Ancient Carol from the magpie. She threw herself into her learning, using the magic of the music to empty herself of all her fears. From time to time the Lord of the Faerie asked her what was wrong, but she always evaded his questions.

At home in Idol Lane Jane hummed to herself as she stood over the hearth, using the music to blot out the faint sounds of Weyland and Noah.

Gradually, as the months passed, Jane grew more withdrawn, and far thinner than ever she had been. The kitchen of Idol Lane had grown into a lonely, desolate space.

* * *

NOAH'S PREGNANCY PROGRESSED. JANE SAW RELA-
tively little of her (mostly on their way to and from the Tower of London), but
what she did see, showed her a woman blooming in anticipation of her forthcoming child. Sometimes they talked, briefly, of the baby. Succinct as these
conversations were, Jane had no doubt how greatly Noah loved her child, and
how greatly she anticipated her arrival.

It made Jane fear for her. To love this deeply, to *want* this badly . . . It left it
too easy for Fate to step in with its ruinous quirks, to destroy hope, and to rav-
age love.

Jane wondered how Noah explained the baby to Ariadne, or if she even felt
the need to explain it. Noah would need to give birth to the baby before she
underwent the trial of the Great Ordeal, the culmination of her training as a
Mistress of the Labyrinth. Noah could cope with learning the arts while pregnant without harming the baby, but she could not undergo the Great Ordeal.
That would be too dangerous to both mother and child.

So Jane counted the months of Noah's pregnancy. When she gave birth and
then underwent the Great Ordeal in the Great Founding Labyrinth, so would
Jane be free.

When Noah gave birth, so would Jane be free.

When Noah endured the Great Ordeal, so would Jane be free.

If Weyland kept his word.

CHAPTER FOUR

THE TOWER OF LONDON
AND IDOL LANE, LONDON

Noah Speaks

*A*RIADNE KNEW THE FIRST TIME I CAME TO HER after I conceived that I was carrying Asterion's child. She was angry and deeply frightened, which disconcerted me.

"Why bring Asterion's child to the labyrinth?" she demanded.

"Because she happens to be in my body, and this is where I need to be at the moment," I replied.

Ariadne stared at me, her fury unabated. "You are a Darkwitch—"

"Not that I've ever touched the darkcraft," I murmured.

"And you have bred back to the father who gave you the darkcraft in the first instance. Imagine what this child shall be!"

"Loved. Cherished. Wanted," I said, although Ariadne's comments somewhat dismayed me. I hadn't thought of that. Darkcraft, bred twice as powerful in this child. Twice fathered by Asterion . . .

Yet when I was with Weyland, all the doubts fell away. My pregnancy both terrified and exhilarated him. Although I knew Ariadne's betrayal had damaged Asterion, his constant fear that I would do the same all over again made me realize just how deeply Ariadne *had* wounded him. He wanted this child, yet was terrified in the wanting. It made me feel humble . . . and scared, lest I should misstep and hurt him when all I had wanted to do was heal.

This child would mean a great deal to both of us. I am not sure precisely what Weyland thought to receive from our daughter—unconditional love? respect? Not obedience, for he knew he could command that through fear—but all I anticipated was that simple joy of a child's unquestioning love.

At night, when we lay naked together in the Idyll, Weyland would place his hands on my swelling belly, an expression of wonder intermixed with fear on his face as he felt our daughter move. I had never seen that expression on Brutus' face. Never.

Weyland was vulnerable. Brutus never had been. Not where our children were concerned. They were merely commodities.

"What will you name her?" he asked me one night when I lay half propped-up on pillows. My belly was so huge now that this was one of the few ways I could find comfort to rest.

I smiled, and ran my fingers softly through his hair. "You name her," I said.

He raised his face to me then, happiness and wariness competing for dominance. The joy of *He could name his daughter!* tempered with *What does Noah hope to gain from this?*

"Why me?" he said.

"Why not? Just allow me the right to sulk if I don't like it."

He laughed, and the joy won the battle of his face. "I wish . . ." he said, his voice drifting to a close as he thought of all the things he could have wished for.

"We all wish," I said, and thought of all the things that could have been.

I WENT INTO LABOR ON MAY DAY, WHICH GAVE ME immense joy. My daughter would be born on the rise of spring, which was cause for great celebration.

Unlike my labor with Catling (*with that foulness which had pretended to be my daughter*) this labor was painful and debilitating and undignified—just like all true labors should be. Weyland was so horrified he ran from the Idyll and fetched Jane—that he brought Jane into the Idyll was a true indication of how unsettled he truly was.

In her lives as Genvissa and Swanne, Jane had borne many children and, frankly, was far less interested in me than she was in the Idyll. To Weyland's dismay she kept wandering out of the bedchamber to explore other areas. I imagine that Weyland's creation as drastically altered her perception of him as it had altered mine.

How could a creature of pure, innate evil create such a magical world of beauty?

Eventually Weyland managed to drag her back to my side, where Jane sighed, sat down, and prepared to wait.

"Is there not something you should be doing?" Weyland said, his voice cold, as a touch of the old malevolent bully emerged.

"Waiting is all any of us can do," said Jane. "Except, on Noah's part, to curse, which is her right."

I laughed . . . and then did indeed curse as a red-hot vise closed about my belly.

My daughter was born ten hours later, just as the sun set on London. Jane was a good midwife (as she should be, with all her own experience) and the baby herself did all that was asked of her. Still, it was painful, and messy, and sweaty, and I swear I was never so glad of anything as I was the instant I felt my daughter slide free of my body into Jane's hands.

At that point Jane did something extraordinary.

She began to sing. Just softly, under her breath, but it was the most beautiful melody I had ever heard. I stared at her, and Jane looked sideways at me.

Slyly, which was Jane all over.

"Your daughter is at the dawn of her life," she said. "I was caroling her in."

I knew then what she was doing with the Lord of the Faerie. My mouth dropped open (although maybe it was already open, for I'd been grunting and huffing far more than was dignified), then I collected my senses, and managed to pull my mouth into working order.

"Thank you," I said simply, but, I hoped, meaningfully.

Jane knew. She reddened with pleasure, then bent back to the baby.

I struggled up, more or less supported by Weyland, who was less help than he was astounded and overcome by the baby's birth, and watched Jane as she wiped our daughter's mouth and nose clean of mucus, rubbed her chest until she gave a startled little cry, and then handed her to me, the umbilical cord still binding us.

Oh, she was perfect. I cradled her in my arms and felt that instant bonding, that overwhelming love, that I had never felt with Catling.

Weyland stared, too scared, I think, to touch.

Eventually I lifted one of his hands and put it on the baby girl's head.

"She looks like me," I said. "Which is a mild relief."

He smiled, just a little, too overwhelmed as yet to manage anything save astonishment, and then jumped as Jane cut the cord.

"Let me wipe her down," Jane said, and I gave her the baby.

Weyland made a small sound, almost like a baby mewling.

"She needs to be wiped down and wrapped," I said, and he settled and waited more or less patiently until Jane brought the baby back.

I took her, cradled her, kissed her, and then without hesitation held her out for Weyland to take.

I have never seen such love on anyone's face as I have on his, at that moment when the weight of the baby settled into his arms.

"She's . . ." he said, unable to find the right adjective.

I smiled, looking at him rather than our daughter. "Aye."

"I can't believe . . ."

"I know," I said.

Weyland ran a finger very gently over the child's face.

"What will you call her?" I asked.

He raised his eyes to mine, and grinned. "Is that fear I hear in your voice, Noah?"

I smiled. "What name, Weyland?"

He looked back at the baby. "Grace."

I could have cried. I think I *did* cry, and I swear I saw Jane wipe something from her eyes as well. Grace. *Oh gods, aye.* She graced us all.

LATER, AS WEYLAND WALKED ABOUT THE BEDCHAM-
ber, cuddling our daughter, Jane came and sat by me.

"You are very clever," said Jane, softly, so that Weyland could not hear. "He will do anything for you now."

"I did not do this to be clever," I said. "I did not do it because I hoped to manipulate Weyland. I did it because of what this child demonstrates."

"And what is that?" Jane asked archly, reminding me so much of her arrogance as Swanne.

"Reconciliation," I said. "Healing." My mouth twitched with emotion, and I almost began to weep once more. "Grace."

I paused, looking to where Weyland held Grace. "Love."

She looked at me, her eyes hard with cynicism. "And what will Weyland do, do you think," she said, so soft now I had to strain to hear her, "when he learns all you have kept from him? When he learns of your true paternity, and maternity?"

I held her gaze, unintimidated by the inherent threat in her words. "Then he will hold his daughter, and gaze upon her, and know that the past need never direct the future. *That* is in our own hands."

She snorted, rose, and attended to the cleaning of both myself and the bed.

TWO MONTHS LATER ARIADNE STOOD WITH ME BE-
fore the malevolent, writhing, rising darkness that was to ordinary eyes merely the White Tower, and said, "You're ready."

CHAPTER FIVE

THE RINGWALK AND THE WHITE TOWER

*H*E RAN, AS HE HAD BEEN RUNNING FOR AEONS. But there was a change, now, in his running. Whereas, so far back as he could remember, his feet had occasionally slipped on the Ringwalk, or his stride had felt a little constrained, or he had been ever so slightly aware of a pull in a tendon in his off foreleg, or near hind . . .

. . . *or he had lain within the heart of the Troy Game so close to death that there was no difference* . . .

. . . now his stride extended effortlessly, and he was not aware at all of the ground beneath his feet although he knew he still ran the Ringwalk.

He felt . . . *alive.* Aware. Knowing. Energized. Brimming with promise and life and magic and wonder.

Ready.

He leapt, and as he leapt, so worlds cascaded past under his feet, and the sun bowed in homage at his passage.

NOAH STOOD AT THE DOORWAY TO WHAT THE WHITE Tower had become—the living Great Founding Labyrinth. Her figure slim and lithe two months after the birth of her baby, her face calm, focused, beautiful, Noah was dressed in nothing but an ankle-length white linen skirt.

Her hair was left unbound down her back, her arms and hands and neck were bare of any jewelery, her lovely face was left unpainted.

All about them walked the officers and men of the Tower of London, engaged in their normal duties.

None saw anything save two women strolling arm in arm slowly about the grounds.

Noah stood, regarding the doorway of the Great Founding Labyrinth. The tower rose above her—huge, threatening, throbbing with a thundery dark-blue glow.

"Enter," said Ariadne. "If you do not survive, I will look after your baby for you."

Noah gave a little smile. "She shall know no mother but me, Ariadne." Then she looked back at the doorway, her face relaxing, concentrating.

After a moment of almost complete stillness, Noah's hand went to the linen wrap bound about her waist, and with a swift, economical movement she undid it, and discarded the wrap.

Naked, she stepped into the Great Founding Labyrinth.

HIS STRIDE FED BY HIS JOY, THE STAG GOD STRETCHED out his legs, and bounded over hill and dale, meadow and crag. This was *his* land, and he could have burst for the joy of it. As he ran, memories and images jumbled about in his mind: running as a fawn through the forest; his hand, forcing the arrow into his father's eye; mating the doe that stood silent and waiting in the dappled shade; standing before the girl called Cornelia, but knowing, this time, what and who she was to him; dancing in complex steps through passages of darkness; juggling golden limb-bands until they spun in an intricate dance through the great spread of his blood-red antlers.

Below him, men and beast alike raised their eyes skyward, and gasped.

NOAH WALKED INTO THE GREAT FOUNDING LABY-rinth without hesitation. She had done this so many times now that it was a second nature to her, and she paid no mind to the swirling stairs and ladders and passages, the promises and delusions that power sent to disarm her. Instead she reached out with her own power, and began slowly to spiral in the entwined energies of tide and river, star and moon, bowel and seashell, until she had surrounded herself with a pulsating ball that consisted of a myriad lines of light and power. This was the labyrinth, that which bound all life from birth to death, and which, now, Noah sought to bend to her own will.

Be as I am, she whispered to it. *Do as I will.*

Instantly, every one of the myriad lines of light and power turned black, and the ball which surrounded Noah solidified into a mass of darkness, and hid her from life. Breath. Existence.

Everything.

* * *

IN THE KING'S GREAT AUDIENCE CHAMBER OF WHITE-
hall Palace the furniture had been pushed against the walls, the carpet had
been rolled away, the shutters closed and bolted, the doors likewise. Two lone
lamps glowed on opposite walls. The space of the chamber had been bared,
and in its center sat a Circle, its members sitting cross-legged, their hands
clasped, their heads slightly bowed in concentration.

The Lord of the Faerie's presence dominated the Circle, the deference of
every other member indicated by subtle body language and facial expression.

Once, Charles had led Circles composed only of himself, Marguerite,
Kate, and sometimes Louis.

Now, the Lord of the Faerie convened a Circle made up of the original
Eaving's Sisters, but also including the reformed whores Elizabeth and
Frances, as well Long Tom and fifteen of his fellow Sidlesaghes and the two gi-
ants, Gog and Magog.

I can feel him running, said the Lord of the Faerie. *Can you? Can you?*

NOAH STOOD WITHIN THE SPHERE, THE DARK HEART
of the labyrinth, and considered.

This is not as I will, she said.

It is what you have, said the dark heart.

No, said Noah, *what I have is this!*

She flung wide her arms, her head falling back, and both power and sound
burst from her. Very gradually her body twisted to and fro in sinuous, liquid
movements, and the black heart of the labyrinth bulged and creaked.

My name is Noah-Eaving, said the entity standing in the heart of the
labyrinth, *and I am both the goddess of the earth, the mother of life, and the mover
of waters, and I am also your Mistress, the weaver and dancer of mysteries, and
thus I command you: Do as I will, and not as you wish.*

There came a great moan, and then, in a sudden, brilliant burst of light, the
black sphere exploded, shooting bolts of light and incandescent globules into
the larger structure of the Great Founding Labyrinth, exposing the goddess
that stood in its center, naked and throbbing with power, head back, arms outstretched, eyes as black as a witch-night, her hair snapping wildly in the powers that twisted and turned with the sphere.

She smiled, staring overhead, and said, *Welcome.*

HE LEAPT OVER THE MOON, VAULTED THE SUN, TWIST-
ed within the stardust of the heavens, and then looked down.

Below him lay a vast blue-green-gray lake, and deep in its waters he saw a great witch, naked, standing with her head thrown back and her arms out-stretched.

Dance with me, she whispered.

ARIADNE FLINCHED, FEELING MORE THAN SEEING what had happened within the Great Founding Labyrinth.

She looked briefly about, wondering that, about her, the life of the Tower continued so calmly. Then a movement caught her eye, and she looked forward once more.

Noah walked toward her. Her eyes were black pools of mystery, and her body was clothed in a garment which appeared to be made of flowing green water with the stars twisting within its depths.

"Who are you?" whispered Ariadne, *knowing* the answer, but needing to hear it confirmed.

"I am Noah," said the woman standing before Ariadne. "Goddess, Mistress of the Labyrinth, Darkwitch Risen. Entwined."

THE LORD OF THE FAERIE GAVE A GREAT, CHOKING cry, his head snapping back on his shoulders.

An instant later everyone else within the Circle cried out also, their bodies twitching.

When another moment had passed, and the members of the Circle managed to draw breath and calm themselves, they saw that a naked man stood in the center of the Circle. He looked like Louis, and yet not. He wore Louis's face and body, and yet rising from his twisting dark hair was a set of blood-red antlers, and from his eyes shone a fierce wildness that made most of the onlookers drop their own gazes away from his.

"Who are you?" asked the Lord of the Faerie. "What have you become?"

The man that was once Louis, and who had once lived as Brutus and then William, turned slowly about to face the Lord of the Faerie.

"My name," he said, his strong, low voice reverberating about the chambers and through the souls of everyone present, "is Ringwalker."

CHAPTER SIX

IDOL LANE, LONDON

SHE WALKED THROUGH THE DOOR FROM PAR-
lor into kitchen, and both Weyland and Jane, sitting at the table,
the baby in Weyland's arms, instantly recognized the difference
in Noah.

There was something about her, such a dark knowingness, that she could
have done nothing but succeeded in her Great Ordeal.

Jane wondered why Weyland could not see Noah's darkcraft screaming
forth. She understood that until Noah actually used her darkcraft it would not
be readily apparent, but still . . .

Perhaps there were none so blind as those who loved.

Noah halted at the head of the table; she looked at Jane, and then at Weyland.

"Let her go," said the being that was Noah. "I am all you need."

Jane tensed, terrified that although freedom was but a word away, Weyland
would surely kill her. *He wouldn't let her go. He wouldn't.*

"Go," said Weyland, staring at Noah.

Very slowly, hardly able to breathe for fear, Jane rose to her feet. She
inched about the table, her eyes never leaving Weyland, who just as unblinkingly regarded Noah.

As Jane reached the head of the table, Noah put a soft hand on her arm
and drew her close for an almost inaudible whisper. "Tell the Lord of the
Faerie that . . . Tell him . . . Ah, tell him that above all I am Noah and that I
am for the land. Tell him that."

And then Jane was gone, running for the front door.

SHE LAY IN WEYLAND'S ARMS, LISTENING TO HIS
breathing, and to that of her baby in the cot by the head of the bed.

About them the Idyll floated, wrapping them in peace.

She lay, thinking, unable to sleep. The Noah that she had been, had almost transformed during her Ordeal. Something had altered and twisted within her during that transformation, and Noah was not entirely sure that she liked it.

Or that she could even recognize it.

She sighed, and was about to rise, perhaps to wander the Idyll awhile, or just sit and hold Grace in her arms, when she felt it.

A pull.

A tug.

Imperative.

Noah sat up, looking about frantically, wondering if . . . *Oh gods, no, surely he could not do that!*

By her side Weyland roused directly from full sleep into clear-headed wakefulness. He sat up, glanced about, then looked at the woman at his side. "Noah? What is it?"

"Weyland . . ."

"*Noah?*"

"Weyland, let me go, I pray you. Just for an hour or so. I will return."

"Who is it? Who calls you?"

She looked at him, her eyes huge and dark in the dim lighting of their bedchamber.

"Brutus," Weyland breathed.

"Let me go to him," Noah whispered.

Weyland did not immediately reply. He stared at her. "You want me to let you go to *Brutus*?"

"I will not betray you."

There was something in her expression or manner, or voice, or perhaps all three, that made Weyland want to believe her.

But what was Brutus doing, reaching into the Idyll like this? What power had he obtained to enable him to do so?

"How is Brutus able to reach out to you within the Idyll?" he said, softly, dangerously.

She dropped her eyes away from his.

Cold fear slid through Weyland's belly. "Noah . . . *How can Brutus reach you within the Idyll?*"

"Let me go to him, Weyland. Please. I will return."

"Why should I believe you?"

"Because I have promised it to you," she said. "Because I will leave our daughter here with you. But most of all . . ."

"Yes?"

She reached out a hand, and cupped his cheek very gently. "Because I love you," she said. "Because I am your shelter and thus I *must* return. Do you know, Weyland, how well you trapped me with that single, simple question?" She smiled, softly and sadly. "And do you know, Weyland, how much you *didn't* need to ask me for shelter? That I was trapped already?"

Weyland gazed at her, his eyes stricken. "If you do not return, you will destroy me."

Again she gave that sad smile. "I know."

"Then go. *Go!*"

SHE FLED, THROUGH THE DREAMLIKE DOMINION OF the Idyll, through the shadowy walls of London, through the dim meadows and fields that bordered the city, through the night and through reality, until she stood on the borderlands of the Realm of the Faerie.

There, standing under the spreading branches of the Holy Oak Tree, stood the one who had every reason to consider himself her lover, her mate, and her husband.

"Louis," she said, very soft, drifting to a halt a pace or two away from him.

"That was once my name," said the man-god.

She regarded him, partly to give herself some time to think, but mostly to drink in the changes within him. His overall aspect was dark, his bearing full of promise and majesty, his essence a still watchfulness. His face and hair reminded her most of the man Brutus he had once been, so long, long ago. His hair remained long and black, snapping with wiry, wild curls. His eyes similarly dark and wild, but with such depths now . . . Ah, such depths . . .

She glanced once more at his limbs, almost as if she expected to see there the faint marking of the golden kingship bands of Troy, which had once graced them.

"What are you called now?" she said, her eyes returning to his face.

"Ringwalker," he said, and, closing the distance between them, gathered her into his arms, and kissed her.

"Eaving," he whispered. "Dance with me, be my lover, into eternity."

She sighed, and he felt her stiffen within his arms. Not much, just very, very slightly, but he felt it.

"Why not?" he whispered.

"So much has changed."

"Eaving . . . I know you question the Troy Game. But now *we* can take control. Now *we* can—"

"Do you truly think that the Troy Game will allow us to control it *now*, Ringwalker? It has been free from interference for two and a half thousand years." She leaned back in his arms, regarding him. "I do not think we should complete the Troy Game. I don't think we would ever be able to control it, not even who we are *now*. I do not believe the Game ever meant to protect this land, Ringwalker. I think it means to consume it."

"No, no, the very essence of the Game is protection."

"The very essence of the Game is bleakness."

Ringwalker felt a terrible hollowness yawn open inside him that threatened at any moment to turn into panic. "Noah, where has this misgiving come from? Have you and I not worked to this very end? Have you and I not died for it, more than once?"

"So much has changed."

Ringwalker let her go, standing back a pace. "There is a darkness in you, Noah. What is it?"

She slid her eyes away. Ringwalk felt his hollowness turn to true fear. "I am only what I have always been, Ringwalker," she said. "Do you not remember, how once you related to me how Membricus, your ancient lover and adviser, told you that I was Hades' Daughter, that there was a dark shadow within me? That darkness has always been there. Once you hated me for it. Now, if you wish to love me, you must accept it."

"No. Don't try to fool me. That darkness is Weyland's touch. I smelt him on you when you came to me during my transformation. Now I can smell him on you more strongly than ever. What has he done to you?" He paused. "Noah, have you turned to Weyland? Have you betrayed me, as Swanne did in our previous lives?"

She tilted her head, her eyes now direct on his, and full of boldness. "I have not done what Swanne did in her previous life. I am not that foolish."

Ringwalker did not know what to think. He had thought she would fall into his arms. Hadn't that been what she promised him when she'd told him of his heritage? *Dance with me*, she'd whispered.

Now, it was all indecision and "maybe."

And all stink of Weyland.

"Where are my kingship bands, Noah?"

Again that soft, sad smile at his "my." "I have sheltered them, Ringwalker. Do you know what that means?"

"Aye. I know what your name means. You are the shelterer. That is your name and your very nature."

"Aye."

"But where are they?"

"They are in the Idyll. Do you know what that is?"

"No." He shifted, sick of her evasiveness.

She sighed. "It is a beautiful place."

"Fetch them for me, Noah. I need them."

"No."

"Why not?"

"I cannot give them to you, Ringwalker. It is too dangerous. I fear the Troy Game's strength, once you win control of the bands. I think giving *you* the bands will be handing the Troy Game way too much power."

"Damn it, Noah, *what is wrong?*"

She looked away, and he saw that her eyes had filled with tears. Anxiety now turned to fear.

"Weyland *does* control you, doesn't he? You are *his,* aren't you? Everything you have said to me here has been designed to protect him!"

Again that chin tilt. "You know what my goddess name means, yes? You know what Eaving means?"

"Yes. Now, *answer* me, curse you!"

"Very well. Ringwalker, you need to know that Weyland has asked me for shelter. I will not betray him, even if it is you who asks it of me."

Then, as Ringwalker stared at her, now shocked beyond horror, Noah turned and walked away.

WEYLAND SAT ON THE EDGE OF THE BED, HIS BODY tense, a sheen of sweat on his skin. His eyes rested on the baby asleep in her crib as if he expected her to somehow vanish at any moment.

She said she would return.

Weyland tightened his hands about each other. He had a terrible urge to let loose his dark power, to track Noah down, to destroy . . .

What was he thinking? What had he become to so allow love to distract him?

And was he more afraid of what he had become, or what he might revert to, if he lost her?

"Weyland."

He leapt to his feet, jerking about; Noah had walked back into the chamber. She gave him a small, tired smile, and bent down to their daughter.

"She sleeps," she said.

"Aye. She has not woken."

"Weyland . . ."

He swallowed.

"Weyland . . . I know you want to control the Game. But have you ever thought about destroying it? Completely?"

He stared.

"It will destroy this land, Weyland," she said, "and it will destroy us. It cannot be allowed to reach its full potential."

He could not speak.

"Weyland?"

"You came back," he whispered.

She gave a half-sigh, half-sob, and walked over and wrapped her arms about him. "I said I would, and here I am."

"What did Brutus want?"

"Me."

"But you came back."

"Yes."

His arms slowly lifted themselves and embraced her. They clung to each other for a long moment.

"Weyland? Will you help me destroy the Troy Game?"

He sighed. "It will eat you, Noah."

"Not if you help me."

"What will your Brutus have to say about that?"

She gave a small, unconvincing smile. "I hope that he will help, too. I think it will take all three of us to destroy it now."

Weyland shook his head as if in disbelief.

"Weyland? If the Troy Game is destroyed, then we will be free. Free of this damned dance that has trapped us all."

Again he sighed. "Yes, I will help you destroy the Game, but I think you are naive in thinking that will free your precious land. I think that if we destroy the Game, we will also destroy the land." He turned around and looked at Noah. "I think the Troy Game is going to take us all, Noah. The moment it realizes that you are prepared to betray it, I think it will take us all."

Chapter Seven

Cheapside and Whitehall Palace, London

*J*ANE FLED, EVERY STEP FARTHER SHE TOOK AWAY from Idol Lane, the more she believed that she might, *might,* actually manage to escape.

She had reached Cheapside, a wild-eyed, frantic woman, before she came to her senses. She supposed she'd been heading for Charles at Whitehall, but then she realized her stupid error.

There was only one place Jane wanted to escape to.

Only one person she wanted to be with.

Eaving's Sisters could have Charles the king. Jane wanted no one but the Lord of the Faerie.

She had to get back to the scaffold in Tower Field. Surely he would be there, waiting . . .

"He's not even *thinking* of you at the moment, bitch," said a voice writhing with venom, and Jane's heart almost stopped in her chest.

She spun about, knowing in the pit of her soul that she was dead.

"You told Noah what I was," said Catling, emerging out of the shadows, the two imps hanging close behind her shoulders. "You poisoned her against me. If it wasn't for you, she'd be mine, now."

"No," Jane whispered, one hand held out piteously. "Let me—"

"I asked you not to tell," said Catling, drawing closer. She only took the form of a tiny girl, but somehow her presence loomed about Jane like a great, dark malevolent cloud. "I said you'd be sorry."

No! Jane screamed in her mind, but before she could put voice to her terror, Catling clicked the fingers of one hand, and the imps scuttled forward.

* * *

CHARLES SAT IN THE GREAT, ORNATELY CARVED, gilded, and velvet-padded chair in his audience chamber, his face propped in a hand, three fingers thrumming incessantly against his cheek. It was deep night.

About the king, either seated casually or standing about the chamber, were those people and creatures Charles most trusted, valued, and loved. Among them were Marguerite and Kate, his earliest companions; Catharine, his wife; Elizabeth and Frances, somewhat newer companions; Anne Hyde, now married to James the duke of York, and some five months pregnant; James himself, looking nervous and unsettled; the giants Gog and Magog; and Long Tom and a half a dozen Sidlesaghes.

Charles's fingers tapped back and forth, back and forth, the crown of his head blurring between glossy black hair and the twisted crown of twigs and berries with each breath that he took. The Lord of the Faerie was not far away.

"Where *is* he?" Marguerite suddenly said, her nerves getting the better of her. "Dear gods, Ringwalker should have returned with Noah by now."

Charles glanced at her. Ringwalker should indeed have returned by now, aye, but frankly, Charles was not greatly surprised that he hadn't returned with Noah.

He was also worried about Jane. Noah had completed her training. Had Weyland let Jane go? Charles wished he could just rise and go down to Idol Lane, but there was too much else happening. This was a night of power, and for the moment Charles was not sure where he would most be needed.

"There is nothing to keep her with Weyland," said Catharine. She had been seated in a chair close to Charles; now she rose and paced back and forth, her heavy silken skirts rustling with the sound of a dark wind through the forest. "She is *Eaving* and she is *Mistress of the Labyrinth*. With all the power at her command, and with her lover calling her, there is no reason *at all* why Ringwalker should not have returned with Noah—and with the bands of Troy—by this late hour."

"The imps . . ." offered Kate. "Might they . . . ?"

Silence. Elizabeth and Frances looked at each other, remembering all the vilenesses they had seen those imps commit.

"Noah is now too strong for the imps," said Charles, his entire form now blurring gently between his mortal appearance and that of the Lord of the Faerie.

"I fear for her," Long Tom said softly.

"You do well to fear," said Ringwalker, suddenly appearing out from the shadows behind Charles's chair, "although whether that fear should be for Noah, or of her, I am not certain."

"Ringwalker!" Charles leapt from his chair.

Ringwalker looked about at those gathered. "She would not come with me," he said.

"Why not?" cried three or four voices as one.

Ringwalker paused a long moment before answering. "Weyland has asked her for shelter."

Charles drew in a sharp breath, but it was Marguerite who spoke. "How did he know? How—"

"How do *I* know this?" Ringwalker said. "All *I* know is that I asked her to come with me. I begged her, and she would not. She returned to Weyland."

"She can *never* move against him now," said Marguerite. "She *must* shelter him! Oh gods . . ."

"There is more," Ringwalker said. "I sense a darkness within Noah that cannot be explained merely by her promise to Weyland."

Charles frowned. "'Darkness,' Ringwalker?"

"Believe it, if only because I tell you of it, Charles. There is a—"

"Dear gods," said Charles, suddenly starting as if he'd been jabbed. "It is not Noah we should be fearing for this night, but *Jane!*"

SHE STRUCK OUT AT THE IMPS WITH EVERYTHING SHE had—limbs, hands, feet, teeth, and all the power she could muster.

But that power was nothing. Catling was now too potent. For every ounce of power that Jane poured forth, Catling dampened it with twice as much.

What have I done? thought Jane as the imps began to bite. *What did Brutus and I do?*

How did we go so terribly wrong?

And then the pain began, and Jane suffered as she had never suffered before.

They'd been so very wrong, she and Brutus. It was not Asterion who was the malignant evil which needed to be contained.

It was the Troy Game.

CHARLES CRIED OUT, *SCREAMED* OUT: "JANE!"

"Charles?" Ringwalker said, grabbing him by the arm.

"I can't go to her!" Charles cried. "I can't . . . Something is keeping me back! Something—"

"*I* am keeping you back."

Charles turned about so quickly Ringwalker almost lost his grip on the man.

Catling stood just inside the door. "Jane's dead," she said. "Poor Jane. Those imps *do* have a terrible appetite."

No one spoke. Everyone stared at Catling.

"Do not mourn her," Catling said. "Listen instead to Ringwalker," she said. "There is truly a terrible darkness within Noah, and Jane was concealing it from all of you. For that, she had to pay."

"What in gods' names do you mean?" Charles all but shouted.

"Noah is a Darkwitch," Catling said. "Have you not felt her rise these past months? *That* is the darkness you felt, Ringwalker."

There was a stunned silence. Everyone stared at Catling.

"What do you mean," said Marguerite eventually, enunciating every word very carefully, "a 'Darkwitch'?"

"Why, Ecub, my dear," said Catling said, moving forward slowly, deliberately. "Did you not know that Noah is as much Ariadne's daughter-heir as Jane was? And that Jane knew this, and conspired against all of you to keep Noah's foul little secret?"

"That is not true," said Ringwalker. His voice was flat.

Catling gave a small smile. "Oh, I was as shocked as you when first I learned it. But hear this. Ariadne had two daughters. An elder one whom she sent as bridal goods to Mesopotama, where she became Cornelia's foremother; the younger one by Theseus became the foremother of Genvissa, or Jane, as she is—*was*—in this life. Thus the Minoan clothes Cornelia wore, Ringwalker. Did you never once wonder why she wore Minoan fashion in a Greek court?"

Ringwalker did not answer.

"That does not make Noah a Darkwitch," said Catharine, "even if what you say is true."

"Oh, what I say is true enough," said Catling. "But, oh, did I not mention who fathered that girl on Ariadne?"

No one spoke.

"Asterion," said Catling. "Asterion fathered her."

"No!" Ringwalker cried.

"Aye!" hissed Catling. "*Aye!*"

"Could this be true, Ringwalker?" Charles asked.

Ringwalker did not answer, keeping his gaze on Catling.

"*Could this be true?*"

Ringwalker spun about, wanting to deny everything he had just heard. "Gods curse you, Charles! The moon could have been her father, but that does not make it so!"

"Noah *is* a Darkwitch!" Catling said. "*You* felt it, Ringwalker. *You* said she had a darkness within her!" She paused, then continued more moderately.

"Noah is the most powerful Darkwitch that has ever been, because it has been bred into her by the greatest wielder of darkcraft, Asterion himself. It was not something learned, or given. Noah's darkcraft is inherent. Think of this: Noah is goddess, Mistress of the Labyrinth, *and* Darkwitch. More powerful, even, than Ariadne. Do you still, truly, want to adore her as you have?"

"And you." Catling stared at Charles. "Do you truly want to champion *Jane*? She knew this for months, and yet she said nothing. She conspired to protect Noah, conspired to keep all of you witless and unknowing. Conspired against the Game. Against me."

"I will not believe this," said Marguerite, low and angry. She walked forward until she stood with Ringwalker, staring fiercely at Catling. "If Noah was all of this, then Jane would never have taught her the ways of the labyrinth. Damn it! I *knew* Jane through her two previous lives and I cannot believe she has changed so much in this one. Jane would not have wanted to create a being far more powerful than herself. That goes against her very nature."

A very small smile played over Catling's face. "Jane did not teach Noah. You only assumed that she did."

To one side, Charles's face had gone expressionless.

"Ariadne taught her," Catling said.

Again that perfect, still, horrified silence.

"Did you not know?" Catling continued. "Ariadne has been living these past years within the Tower of London. *She* has been the one teaching Noah."

"No!" Marguerite cried, her hands over her ears. "No! Curse you, Catling! Why should any of us believe you? Why should we believe you, when—"

"Because Noah has given Weyland the four kingship bands she has retrieved. Worse, she has given Weyland a daughter. She has given Weyland everything: child, kingship bands, and her love and allegiance. She is your enemy now. Believe it."

The silence this time was catastrophic. The faces that stared at Catling reflected—variously—anger, fright, fragile disbelief, and confusion.

Ringwalker was the first to find his voice. "She told me the bands were in a place called the Idyll."

"The Idyll is Weyland's own creation," said Catling. "If the bands are in the Idyll, then Weyland has them. Be assured of that."

Long Tom stepped forward. "I will believe none of this," he said, very soft, "until I hear it from Noah's own lips."

"When she can find the time to raise her mouth from that of Weyland's," Catling said, "I am sure she will be more than happy to confirm all I have said."

Then she looked at Ringwalker. "If you ever want to salvage your part in the Game," she said, "in what *I* have to offer you, then you need to take Noah from Weyland sooner rather than later. Perhaps then something of her can be salvaged. On the other hand," she looked at Long Tom, and at Eaving's gathered Sisters, "if you want the land to wither under Weyland's overlordship, then let Noah continue with him, by all means."

And with that, she vanished.

"Jane!" Charles said, and then he, too, vanished.

chapter eight

On the Path to the Otherworld

THE PATH TO THE OTHERWORLD WAS VERY BEAUTIful, paved with warmth, walled with comfort, lit with hope. For the first time in any of her lives Jane felt totally at peace.

She found this sense of enveloping peace bewildering, for she had not managed her freedom after all. She would never stand behind the throne of the Lord of the Faerie and carol in the dawn and the dusk.

Death had found her first, as she'd always feared.

It was just that the Troy Game had wielded the death, not Weyland.

How odd. The world gone topsy-turvy.

Death gone topsy-turvy.

The path to the Otherworld was strangely unpopulated, because she knew that tens of thousands were dying of plague, and there would surely be the usual elderly morbidities, and those women dead in childbirth, and the children run over by carts . . .

But perhaps everyone got their own path. Jane didn't truly care. All she wanted was to walk forward, walk closer to the soft light ahead that radiated succor.

Escape from it all. Finally. Jane drew in a deep breath, and—

"Jane!"

She paused, frowning. The voice came from far behind her, and it aggravated her, for she wanted to maintain this sense of well-being, and the voice sounded like it—

"Jane!" The voice was far closer.

Curse it! Jane put her hands to her ears.

"Jane."

Now the voice was but a few paces behind her, and infinitely gentle.

Jane . . .

She turned around, weeping.

The Lord of the Faerie stood there, one of his hands outstretched.

"Come back, Jane."

"No!" Jane pressed her hands more firmly against her ears.

"Jane, come home."

"Home is waiting for me ahead!"

"No, Jane. Home is with me."

"How is it that you can tread this path, then, Coel? Are you dead as well?" she finally lowered her hands from her ears.

"I learned these paths in my last life. That is how I returned, and—"

"Murdered me."

He laughed. "And murdered you, yes. But now I offer you life, Jane. Will you take it?"

Her mouth turned down. "My body is all ripped and broken."

"Your body is whole and beautiful, Jane. Look."

Jane looked down upon herself.

Her tears became sobs. Her body was indeed whole, and far more beautiful than she had ever known it to be in her life as Jane.

"Comb out your hair, Jane, and see that also," the Lord of the Faerie said softly.

She put her hands to her hair, and discovered it long and thick. She drew her hands out, slowly, looking at the strands as they ran silken through her fingers.

They were golden, silvered, and rosy, all in one.

She wore the hair of . . . of . . .

"You wear the hair of a Caroler, Jane—the color of the dawn and dusklight. Dear gods, Jane, I need you to carol in the dawn and the dusk. How can you stand before me, and weep, and say you want only to walk away? How can you abandon the Faerie for the oblivion of the Otherworld?"

"I lied to you," she said, "You know that now. I can feel it. You know how I deceived you, and—"

"I love you," the Lord of the Faerie said, very gently. "I know you lied to protect Noah."

"You love me because I protected Noah?"

"I love you because I discovered a beautiful woman. I *knew* it for certain that day you stood before the Faerie on the summit of The Naked, and offered your throat for their revenge."

"But you love Noah."

"I will always love Noah. But that is a soft and gentle thing now, not the raging want that once it was. I am her overlord, and her companion on the road. I am not her lover. Not anymore. Nevermore."

She relaxed, as if for the first time in thousands of years. He did not want Noah as he had once wanted her; he still loved her, but it was a quiet and quiescent thing now. Jane could understand that.

"I have a message for you from Noah," she said.

"Yes?"

"She said to tell you that above all she is Noah and that she is for the land."

He smiled, and Jane saw he was vastly relieved. "I am more than glad to hear that. Catling has been telling some nasty tales."

"Catling murdered me," said Jane. "She set her imps to me."

The Lord of the Faerie went very still. "I know. But why?"

"In revenge, because I was the one who opened Noah's eyes to Catling's true nature."

The Lord of the Faerie hissed, and Jane lowered her eyes, not wanting to see the anger there.

"It was a foul day," he said, "when the Game concluded its alliance with the land."

"Can it be stopped?"

"Do you *want* the Troy Game stopped, Jane?"

"I want nothing more to do with it!"

"Then take your place behind my throne, and in the place in my heart which I offer to you. Then you may deal only with the Faerie, and with my heart. A bargain . . . yes?"

Still she stood, too scared to take the step.

The Lord of the Faerie sighed, stepped forward, and took one of her hands. "Come with me," he said, "and carol in the day and the night, and be my Faerie Queen."

He pulled her close, and she was unresisting.

"Come with me," he said.

"*Yes,*" she whispered.

And then she lifted her face to the light, and she began to carol.

Chapter Nine

RINGWALKER, MARGUERITE, KATE, AND CATHA-rine, together with Long Tom, retired to Charles and Catharine's bedchamber.

They sat in a tight circle of chairs before the fire, trying desperately to make some sense of what Catling had said.

"Surely you believe none of this," Catharine said to Ringwalker. "That child was full of hate, not truth."

Ringwalker did not answer her. All he could think of was how what he'd felt from Noah, married *entirely* with what Catling had said.

"Ringwalker," Marguerite said, "trust Noah, *please*. We know nothing of what has occurred within that house on Idol Lane, nothing of what Noah has endured, or even of what she has learned. We should trust her . . . please."

"None of this tale can be proved or disproved until we have Noah among us," Long Tom said. "I am sure there is an explanation for all of this."

"I, for one, do not like Catling," Marguerite said. "The Lord of the Faerie has told us how distressed Noah was when she learned the truth about Catling."

"I am also wondering if I should have believed so implicitly in what the Game—" Long Tom began, but Ringwalker interrupted him.

"Still, all these words! They are useless. I am going to take Noah. Seize her from Weyland's house. Catling was right enough about that. We cannot allow Noah to linger with Weyland any longer."

Take her, Marguerite thought, her heart sinking. *Seize her. Not "Rescue her."*

"That is too dangerous!" Long Tom said. "You are not yet ready to—"

"What?" said Ringwalker. "Should I sit here and allow Noah to succumb completely to her foolishness?"

"Can't you give Noah the benefit of the doubt?" said Catharine.

But Ringwalker was not listening to Catharine, nor to what he had felt for Noah, nor was he even recalling what Catling had said to him. All he could see, all he could remember, was that day in Mesopotama, so many thousands of years ago, when he had been Brutus, and Noah had been his hated wife, Cornelia.

BRUTUS AND HIS TWO COMPANIONS MEMBRICUS AND Assaracus stood on the beach of the bay just west of Mesopotama. Almost one hundred black-hulled ships bobbed at anchor in the waters before them, crowded so closely together there was scarcely an arm's breadth between their sides. Soon, Brutus would be able to embark for Troia Nova with the Trojans.

He turned a little and caught sight of a figure standing atop the walls of Mesopotama.

Even at this distance he knew who it was.

Cornelia.

Beside Brutus, Membricus hissed as he, too, recognized the figure.

Cornelia moved a little, and as she did so, a shadow suddenly poured from her and slithered down the city walls and across the ground to where the three men stood.

It touched Brutus, enveloped him in its gloom, and traveled no farther.

"Sorcery!" Membricus said, grabbing Brutus and pulling him to one side.

But as Brutus moved, so the shadow moved, and Brutus could not escape its touch.

Membricus hissed again. "She is a witch, Brutus! Beware!"

"'Witch'?" said Brutus. "Surely not, unless hatred and scheming can brew sorcery of its own accord."

"Kill her," said Assaracus flatly.

"She carries my son."

"Brutus, listen to me!" said Membricus. "See this shadow? Do you remember, when we stood atop that hill overlooking Mesopotama, that I said I could see a darkness crawling down the river toward the city? It came from Hades' Underworld. Look at this shadowy darkness crawling toward you now. Brutus, can you not understand what I am saying?"

Brutus glanced at his wife—she still stood, watching them, and it seemed that in that moment the shadow deepened about them—then looked back to Membricus. "No. I can't. What do you mean?"

"Cornelia was born and raised and fed by the evil that crawled out of Hades' Underworld down the river to Mesopotama," Membricus said. "She is Hades' daughter, not Pandrasus', even though he might have given her flesh. If she continues to draw breath, then I think—I know—that she has the power to destroy your entire world."

* * *

RINGWALKER SAT IN THE KING'S BEDCHAMBER WITH-
in the palace of Whitehall, staring into the flames of the fire, and remembered.

She is a witch, Brutus! Beware!

His mind formed the word *no,* and his lips shaped it, but no sound came
forth.

She is a witch, Brutus!

All these years, and now Ringwalker wondered if Membricus had been
speaking the truth.

She *was* a witch. But she was Asterion's daughter, not Hades'.

Asterion's daughter, and now his lover.

A Darkwitch. The Stag God's only true enemy. The one with the power—
born, bred, and taught—to destroy his entire world.

"I am going to take her," he said.

OUTSIDE, CROUCHED WITHIN A SHADOWY CORNER
of the great courtyard, Catling conferred with the two imps.

"There is nastiness afoot," said Catling. "Evil."

"Besides you?" said one of the imps.

Catling grinned. "Besides me. But listen to me, my best boys. We have a
problem. You were right to say that Noah was not to be trusted. Even now she
plots to destroy me, with Weyland her axeman."

The imps hissed, their eyes widening and glinting in the dim light.

"You need to do something!" one of the imps said.

"Of course," said Catling. "I'm really going to pinch her where it hurts. But
I need you to do something for me, and I need you not to fail."

The imps raised their eyebrows.

"I need you to sneak back into the Idyll," said Catling. "There's a sweet
baby there. She's going to be all that we need to bend both Noah and Weyland
to our will."

CHAPTER TEN

THE IDYLL

Noah Speaks

*J*DON'T KNOW WHAT I'D EXPECTED FROM LOUIS— Ringwalker, I should now call him—but what *else* could I have expected from him? I could not blame him. He'd known, even if I had not said as much, that I was Weyland's creature.

He had thought I was to be his partner, and I had turned my back on him, and on the Troy Game for Weyland.

Treacherous Cornelia, come to full flower in Noah.

I did not know what to do to make it right with him. Yet I would have to, for, as I had said to Weyland, it would probably take all three of us to destroy the Troy Game.

All three of us, working in concert.

In truth, the moon would turn to cheese before that ever happened, and for that, I had only myself to blame.

I didn't know what to do, but I decided that one thing that would make a fine start was to begin speaking the truth to Weyland. I could not bear to have him turn against me as well.

WHEN I CAME BACK TO THE IDYLL, I TOOK WEYLAND, and I led him to the bed and there, lying with Grace wriggling between us, I spoke. "I need to talk."

Weyland tensed.

"I have been to Brutus-reborn," I began. "You know this."

"Yes."

"You felt his power."

"Yes."

Oh, those single, curt words. They fell like stones on my heart.

"Weyland, I am telling you this because of two things, and I want you to know what those two things are before I—"

"What two things?"

"I am your shelter, and I must point out to you what shoals lie in your path."

"Very well. What is the second?"

Gods, but he was tense! Grace was starting to fret, sensing her father's deep anxiety.

I reached out a hand and allowed my fingers to drift gently over his face. "The second reason I want to tell you about Brutus, is because of what lies between us, Weyland."

"Yes?"

"A love, Weyland, that I had never expected. And, oh, it is so fragile. I fear greatly for it, and for me."

"Just spit it out, Noah! Don't put me through this *hell* of indecision!"

"Brutus-reborn has transformed into the Stag God."

He went rigid, his eyes widening, and I could see that he had to use every particle of self-control he had not to leap out of the bed away from me.

Stupidly, at this critical moment, all I could think of was how, if Weyland had been Brutus, how he *would* have leapt out of the bed.

"How?" The word hissed between us.

I closed my eyes briefly. "Brutus-reborn is not Charles. That was a deception. Instead, Brutus lived as a minor French nobleman within Charles's court. You were meant to focus entirely on Charles, which—"

"Gave Brutus the time and space to transform. *Oh dear gods, Noah!* How long have you know this?"

"Always." I whispered the word.

"Why tell me *now*?"

I flinched at the coldness in his voice. "I brought the bands here so that Brutus could not take them, Weyland. When I went to him, he demanded them of me. I refused."

Weyland stared at me, then he uttered an obscenity and rolled away, sitting on the side of the bed.

His back was toward me, stiff and angry. "You will betray me. You *have* betrayed me."

"No. *No!*"

And then another voice, one which ripped all that fragile love between Weyland and myself apart:

"But of course she will betray you, Weyland. Betrayal is in her very blood. Didn't you know that?"

I gave a low cry and sat up, one hand drawing the sheet over Grace, as if that could protect her.

Ringwalker stood framed in one of the beautiful arched doorways, naked, tense, and with a great spread of blood-red antlers rising from his curly black hair.

Weyland gave a strange, incoherent cry, and flung himself at Ringwalker, the force of the impact sending them rolling into the chamber beyond.

THE IMPS MOVED THE INSTANT WEYLAND ATTACKED Ringwalker. As Noah moved to the doorway, watching aghast as the two battled, the imps scuttled unseen and silent from a shadowed corner to the bed, where lay the baby.

One tried—mostly unsuccessfully—to make happy faces at Grace. The last thing they needed was for the baby to start to squall, and attract her mother's attention.

The other imp reached forward.

Between his hands he held an intricate web of red wool.

He slipped the twisted strands of wool over both the baby's wrists, binding them tightly.

Then the imps stood back, desperate to be gone, but needing to know that Catling's hex had worked successfully.

The baby waved her bound wrists before her, mildly puzzled.

Suddenly the wool glowed into red-hot lines of power, flashed, then sank into the baby's flesh.

Within an instant they were gone, and the imps breathed in sheer relief, and vanished also.

Grace stared at her wrists, still waving back and forth in front of her face.

Her face creased, and her mouth wavered.

And then she began to scream.

I MADE A SOUND, BUT WHETHER SHOUT, CRY, OR roar, I am not sure. All I knew was that my entire world was about to be destroyed.

And I did not know what I should do. I stood in the doorway, watching Ringwalker and Weyland battle, and hesitated.

As I hesitated, Grace screamed, a cry of pure fear.

I whipped about. She was lying on the bed where I'd left her, waving her arms about before her, obviously terrified at the sounds coming from the other chamber.

I ran back and grabbed her, holding her against me so tightly she was in danger of suffocation. Then I turned back to the battle, screaming at

Ringwalker and Weyland, trying to tear their attention away from each other to me.

It was impossible.

I can hardly describe what I saw as once again I stood in the doorway.

Both Ringwalker and Weyland maintained their human forms, although both forms blurred now and again as each warped power through his flesh and into the flesh of the other. Not merely their forms, but almost their every movement was blurred.

They were intent on tearing each other to pieces. There was no finesse about this, no elegance, no dignity, no majesty. Two men, yet beings far more powerful than any mortal man, punching and grappling and shoving and roaring and twisting and pummeling and biting and raking. It was a bitter, hateful, vicious, brutal exchange fed by raw emotion and long-nurtured hatred.

Ringwalker drew on his powers as both Kingman and Stag God, although he was as yet so new to the realm of the forest that his powers as Stag God–reborn were muted and uncertain, and nowhere near as natural to him as those of Kingman.

Weyland fought with everything he could draw on as Minotaur. He fought with darkcraft, and with enough vicious, murderous resentment that it could have darkened the moon all by itself.

He also fought with the power of four of the golden bands of Troy.

I have no idea how Weyland did this, or even if he was aware of it. Somehow, merely having the bands so close to him within the Idyll imbued Weyland with extra power, and it was enough that he was in danger of murdering Ringwalker. He'd driven Ringwalker to the floor, pinned him against a far wall, and was standing over him, pounding him with his fists about his head and neck and shoulders.

Ringwalker resisted as well as he could, but Weyland had driven him so far down that it would be all but impossible for him to rise against Weyland's rain of blows.

Blood dripped down Ringwalker's nose and chin, and spattered across his chest.

One of Weyland's fists drove into Ringwalker's neck, and I heard something crack, and Ringwalker cried out.

"Weyland!" I screamed. "Stop! I beg you! Stop!"

Hugging Grace—still screaming in terror—against my breast, I ran as close as I dared. It was not just the physical violence which frightened me, but the power that roped between the two men. A fistfight would not have done much damage to either one of them, but each drove home with power behind each strike, and it was that which was proving so deadly.

Especially to Ringwalker. He had slumped to the floor now, and I cursed him for his damned stupidity. *What had he hoped to accomplish by coming here?*

Weyland took a half-step back and, clasping his hands together into one gigantic fist, raised it above his right shoulder, preparing to drive it down into Ringwalker's skull.

They paused momentarily at the apex of their swing, and I saw power *glowing* from Weyland's fists.

"No!" I screamed, and without any care for either myself or, indeed, for Grace, threw myself down over Ringwalker's form.

"Damn you!" Weyland cried, but his fists unclenched, and the power drained from them, and he reached down to grab me and pull me out of the way.

But just then Ringwalker came to his senses and, seizing my shoulders, pulled us away from Weyland's reach.

"Did she tell you, fool," Ringwalker rasped as Weyland started forward, "that it was not Jane who taught her the craft of the labyrinth, but Ariadne?"

No!

Weyland stopped dead.

"What?" he whispered, staring at me.

"Did she tell you, fool," Ringwalker continued, "that she is as much of Ariadne's blood as Jane was; that she is descended from—"

No! Weyland could not hear this now, not like this.

I twisted in Ringwalker's grip, and I swear I hit him as hard as Weyland had been doing but a moment ago. "No!" I hissed.

"She is a treacherous bitch," Ringwalker hissed. "Ariadne taught her well."

Oh gods, where had Ringwalker found these words? Nothing could have wounded Weyland more, nor more easily cut away that fragile trust we had built between us.

Weyland was staring at me, his face an absolute mask of horror. "Is it true?" he whispered. "Did Ariadne teach you?"

"Yes, but—"

He gave an incoherent cry of loss and betrayal, and there was so much agony in it that I cried out, too.

Then I felt Ringwalker's hands tighten about my shoulders, and I knew what was about to happen.

"I am not Ariadne!" I screamed as Ringwalker's power enveloped me, and I felt myself being torn away from the Idyll.

I am not Ariadne!

Just before Ringwalker pulled me from there entirely, I lifted Grace in my hands, and tossed her toward her father.

I am not Ariadne!

The last thing I saw was Weyland, snatching his terrified daughter from midair, his face twisted with hate, or loss, or perhaps both.

CHAPTER ELEVEN

WHITEHALL PALACE, LONDON

HAT WAS THAT I SAW?" RINGWALKER SAID. "A baby? I cannot believe that—"

"Enough," said Noah, her voice tired. "I want none of your judgment."

They faced each other in a highly private chamber of Charles's palace in Whitehall. To one side the Lord of the Faerie sat in a throne (with a strange incandescence rising behind it), Marguerite, Kate, and Catharine standing to each side of him, and Long Tom and several other Sidlesaghes yet farther back.

"I just want to understand," Ringwalker said, and Noah's eyes flashed at him.

"No. You don't want to *understand* at all. You want me to justify myself, and I have no intention of doing that."

"You are a Darkwitch," Ringwalker said. "Trained in the ways of the labyrinth by Ariadne. Bred of Ariadne, and Asterion himself. Lover of Weyland. Mother of his child. Spiller of secrets into his mouth. Is there *anything* in that list you wish to deny?"

Noah's chin tilted. "Am I on trial?"

"You are not on trial," the Lord of the Faerie said, and Noah glanced at him gratefully, her eyes widening very slightly as she saw the incandescence behind his throne.

"Is that so?" said Ringwalker. "I *think* that she is—"

"Noah is not on trial," the Lord of the Faerie said again.

Ringwalker stared at him, the muscles in his jaw working with anger, and Noah spoke softly into the silence.

"I did not know of my heritage, Ringwalker. It is nothing I can help. Ariadne trained me because there was no one else. Jane would not do it. And as for Weyland—I became his lover because Weyland, believe it or not, has wounds that need to be healed as well. I stayed his lover, because . . ."

Noah's voice drifted off, and everyone stared at her.

She looked about, then shrugged. "I stayed his lover because it felt right to me."

"And bred his *child*?" Ringwalker said.

"I have given birth to a daughter." Noah looked to Long Tom. "Do you remember, Long Tom, when you came to me in this life many years ago? You said that in this life I needed to heal wounds. Well, my place in Weyland's bed, and the daughter I gave him, do just that."

"What wounds?" Long Tom asked. "What wounds are these you needed to heal?"

"Weyland was wounded as much as anyone in pursuit of this terrible Game. He was loved and betrayed, his daughter taken from him. That was what shaped the Minotaur, not natural evil."

"And undoubtedly this is why," Ringwalker said, "filled with this spirit of generosity, you have handed four of the bands of Troy to Weyland."

Noah smiled, very sadly. "I have not given them to Weyland. I am sheltering them."

Ringwalker took two angry steps forward, jerking his chin up and to one side to show Noah the vicious red marks about his neck. "See these? They were inflicted by Weyland wielding the power of the kingship bands! This was—"

"If Weyland had been truly wielding the power of the kingship bands," Noah said, "you would not be here now."

"Noah." The Lord of the Faerie stood up, walking slowly over to her and taking both her hands in his. "Noah, tell us what it is you do, and why."

"I do not trust the Troy Game," Noah said. "I am not dancing to its tune anymore."

"Fine words," said Ringwalker, "and doubtless put in your mouth by Weyland."

Again that soft, sad smile. "No. Words put in my mouth by knowledge, Ringwalker."

"You are for the land," said the Lord of the Faerie. "And you are the same Noah you have always been."

Noah's eyes flickered toward that strange incandescence behind the throne. "Jane gave you my message?"

"Aye."

"And you trusted it?"

The Lord of the Faerie smiled, his hands tightening about Noah's. "Aye."

Noah breathed out a long sigh of pure relief. "Thank you, Coel," she whispered.

Then she looked to Long Tom. "Long Tom, you have been my friend through two lives. You were the one to show me how the land and the Game had contracted an alliance. Do you still support this alliance?"

"It no longer tastes so fine to me," Long Tom said, "but neither does this alliance you have made with Weyland."

"There is something I should say about Weyland Orr," said the Lord of the Faerie, dropping Noah's hands and looking about the group. "Firstly, he did not cause the plague, and, secondly," the Lord of the Faerie drew in a deep breath, "he is of the Faerie himself."

Several of the group gave disbelieving cries.

"How do you know this?" said Ringwalker.

"Noah brought him to the Realm of the Faerie, with my permission. This is when we both discovered that Weyland hadn't caused the plague, and that he was of the Faerie himself. The Faerie accepted him, although it was greatly uncomfortable."

"Catling caused the plague," Noah said. "The Troy Game itself is engaged in murdering as many Londoners as possible."

"Why?" cried Ringwalker. *"Why?"*

"In an effort to turn me against him," said Noah. "Who knows what the Game will do, now that ploy has failed? Ringwalker, do you truly think the Troy Game wants to subjected to bit and bridle? *I* don't think so. *I* think much of the evil which has gripped England and London is just as much the Troy Game's doing as that of Asterion, or any other malevolent entity."

Now Noah looked back to the Lord of the Faerie. "I will do what is best for the land, but I will *not* do what is best for the Troy Game. Not anymore." She stepped closer to the Lord of the Faerie, placing her hand softly against his cheek, and once more calling him the name by which she'd first known him so many lives ago. "Coel, I am this land before anything else. Before my love for you, or for Ringwalker. Before my duties as Mistress of the Labyrinth. Before what I feel or owe to Weyland. And very, very definitely, before what the Troy Game has planned for me. Once, perhaps, the land and the Game were wedded in harmony, but I no longer think this the case. Please, trust me in this."

The Lord of the Faerie lifted his own hand, and pressed hers the tighter against his cheek. "I will trust you, Noah. I do not like this, not at all . . . gods *damn* it, my love, be careful in what you do."

Ringwalker's face twisted. "Asterion has a fine champion in you, Noah." He turned, walked away several paces, then vanished.

CHAPTER TWELVE

WHITEHALL PALACE, LONDON

J CAN UNDERSTAND," NOAH SAID TO MARGUERITE, Kate, and Catharine, "if you do not wish to support me."

"You ask us to support a stranger alliance than we could ever have imagined," said Marguerite.

"What I do, I do for the land," Noah said. "Everything is subsumed to this."

"But Weyland . . ." Kate said, shivering a little and wrapping her arms about herself like a child.

"I had always thought him foul," Noah said, "and there can be no doubt he has done foul things. And yet . . ." She shook her head as if *she* could not believe what she was saying.

"Do you love him?" Marguerite said.

"Love?" Noah gave a short, humorless laugh. "Oh, aye, whatever 'love' is. I loved Brutus-now-Ringwalker for many lives, over thousands of years. All uselessly, I think. All he has ever wanted is the Troy Game, whatever words of love he has spoken to me."

"Noah," said Catharine, very gently. "Ringwalker is distressed beyond words. All he has wanted, for so very long, is to be one with you. Now you deny him this, and turn instead to the Minotaur. He is angry, and for the time being he will accept nothing of what you say. Do not blame him for his pain."

There was a silence, and Noah dropped her eyes and looked away.

"Noah," said the Lord of the Faerie, "you say that you are for the land, but the land cannot have the goddess of the waters and the god of the forest at odds, each with the other. If the land is to survive, then you need to make the Great Marriage with Ringwalker."

"And so I will," she said, "once he decides to walk with me and not against me."

To one side Marguerite gave a great, exaggerated sigh. "Why do I have the feeling that this dilemma is going to pursue us through the next *twenty-five* lives?"

"Noah," the Lord of the Faerie said, "please do not turn against Ringwalker."

"Before anything else," she said, "I am for the land. That shall come first, always, before Ringwalker, before the Troy Game, and even before Weyland." She cast her eyes about the entire group. "Trust me, please."

And then, before any could respond, she vanished.

"GODS . . ." MARGUERITE SAID ON A LONG BREATH. Then she raised her face to the Lord of the Faerie. "My lord? What should we do?"

He was still staring at the spot where Noah had vanished. "I swore once that I would be her companion on the road to her destination. I am no longer sure what that destination is . . . In truth, I think that destination may be the most terrifying objective I could possibly imagine. But . . . But I said I would be her companion, and so I will be. And you?"

Marguerite looked at Catharine and at Kate, then spoke for all three: "If she is for the land, then we are for her. Even if, as you say, she takes us on a journey more strange than we could ever have thought."

From far, far away, came two simple, whispered words. *Thank you.*

WEYLAND.

"Go away!" he hissed. He stood in the kitchen of the house in Idol Lane, clothes strewn about, food scraps littering the surface of the table and the floor, windows shuttered against the light.

Weyland.

He held Grace in his arms, his touch gentle. "No. You shall not have her!"

I am not Ariadne.

Then, suddenly, she was there, giving Weyland a brief smile before reaching out to touch Grace's short bright curls. Noah's face relaxed and gentled at that touch, and she drew close, her eyes entirely on the baby.

"May I hold her?" she asked Weyland.

He stiffened, then reluctantly handed her to Noah.

Noah's eyes flew to his, and she gave him a lovely smile. "Thank you."

Weyland very gradually relaxed as he watched Noah murmur to their daughter. "Don't take her."

"I won't. I came only to see her, and you."

"I did not think you would come back."

Again she raised her eyes to his. "I am not Ariadne."

"I thought Ringwalker—" Emotion choked his throat, and Weyland could not finish the sentence.

"I am sorry you heard about Ariadne in the manner that you did," Noah said.

"Why didn't you tell me?" Weyland wanted to rail at her, to scream and kick and punch, but he was too exhausted . . . and too scared.

"I was frightened," Noah said. "Frightened of all I had heard. Frightened of you. Secrets became my survival. If it gives you any pleasure, then know that Ringwalker is as angry as you have a right to be."

"What do you mean, 'all you had heard'?"

Noah went very still, her eyes now entirely on Grace. "There is more you should know."

Weyland felt the pit of his stomach fall away.

Noah took a deep breath, finally looking at Weyland. "Ariadne sent your daughter away."

"Yes."

"She sent her to a tiny city in western Greece called Mesopotama."

Weyland's face went very still, but in his chest his heart hammered as if it rang out the dawn of doom.

"Her daughter, *your* daughter, was my foremother."

His face sagged in stunned disbelief. For long moments his mind could not grasp what she said. Noah was standing before him, their child in her arms, staring at him with a face white with apprehension, telling him that . . . that *she was bred of his daughter?*

She opened her mouth to speak, but Weyland waved a hand at her, silencing whatever she'd been about to say, and sat down on a chair with a thump. He turned away from Noah, resting his elbows on the table and his face in his hands.

Noah was born of his daughter. Of him, and of Ariadne.

Weyland began to shake, great tremors that wracked his body. Behind him, he heard Noah start to weep, and to babble out words that made no sense.

He heard a thud, and knew she was on her knees at his side, begging him to look at her.

There was another sound, a high-pitched screaming, and he knew Grace was wailing.

Noah was born of his daughter. Of him, and of Ariadne.

He took several very deep breaths, managing to stop his tremors, but not yet able to look at Noah and their daughter.

Their daughter, twice bred of him, and of Ariadne.

He became aware, very slowly, that Noah was crying out his name, over and over, her voice thick with sobbing, and that one of her hands was clenched in the material of his breeches.

He took another great breath, managed somehow to quiet the racing of his heart, lifted his head, turned about a little in the chair, and looked down on Noah's grief-ravaged face.

He felt very calm, and very sure of himself.

And, for the first time in countless thousands of years, at total peace with who and what he was.

"No wonder," he said, "that I love you so greatly."

THERE WAS A SPACE OF TIME IN WHICH NOTHING WAS said. Weyland slid down to the floor beside Noah, took her in his arms, and let her cry herself out as he rocked her back and forth. He crooned softly to her, and to their daughter, until eventually both lay quiescent and quiet in his embrace.

When that silence had stretched into an infinity, Weyland kissed Noah's brow, and spoke. "Imagine what the good vicar of St. Dunstan's shall say when he hears that I have been fornicating with my daughter-heir, so close to his house of God."

"You are angry," Noah said.

"No," he said. "I am not. I am at peace. I know who you are, and what you are, and I do not think there can be anything more you can tell me that could shock me."

She tensed. "Weyland, I have the—"

"Darkcraft within in you. Yes, I understand that. No wonder you kept asking me to use it in our loving. You were exploring it, yes?"

"Yes," she whispered. "I'm sorry that I didn't—"

"I should have felt it. Dear gods, no woman has ever been able to withstand the amount of darkcraft I poured into you. Not even Ariadne." He paused. "Tell me, does Brutus know this?"

"Yes."

She could not see it, but Weyland smiled, and closed his eyes in contentment. He felt on solid ground with her, for the very first time. "He rejected you."

"I turned my back on him."

Weyland tilted her face up so he could see it. "Truly?"

"Aye. Truly."

He studied her a moment, then he lifted his arm from about her, took Grace from her, and rose, resting the baby carefully in a cradle which rested to one side of the hearth.

He turned back to Noah, who watched him apprehensively, then he undressed until he stood naked before her.

"I am going to make love to you," he said, "and in the doing I am going to pour into you all the darkcraft of which I am capable, and, when I do this, *you* are going to set your darkcraft free, and thus, for once, we are going to be honest with each other, and we are going to know each other for who and what we truly are."

* * *

AND THUS HE DID, AND THUS I DID AS HE COM-
manded. If I hadn't, I would have died under the onslaught of his darkcraft.
I needed to loose my own darkcraft in order to negate his and in order to keep on
living.

The darkcraft, rising. It boiled and bubbled and seethed and scalded forth, and
it met and entwined with Weyland's, and suddenly I felt whole and complete. If
there had been any doubts left, then now they crumbled.

That initial mating, that initial meeting of dark powers, was vicious and hard
and cruel and it tore the breath from my body.

But when I (and he also, I think, for he had never before coupled with a woman
with darkcraft innate within her) became more used to it, then frenzy and appre-
hension turned to serenity and certainty, and we reached a strange, peaceful
plateau. There, struggle turned to languidness, and there we rested.

And there, eventually, we became aware of a third presence.

Our daughter, Grace, bred from two parents with darkcraft for blood, reaching
out to us, and loving us.

"YOU NEED TO LEARN TO USE YOUR DARKCRAFT
slowly," Weyland said as he lay entwined with Noah.

Neither cared, nor were even aware, of the cold stone flagging.

"If you let the darkcraft free again with such little inhibition, and I am not
with you, and you are not used to it, then it may well destroy you."

She kissed his chest, one of her hands running down his flank. "Then stay
with me."

"Noah, the Troy Game will come after us. We have to—"

"I know." Now she sighed, and sat up. "Weyland, I must move, and soon."

"*We* must move, and soon."

She smiled. "Aye. *We.*" Then her smiled faded. "But we cannot move against
the Game right now. We have not the power to murder it. We need . . ."

We need Ringwalker.

"We need to consolidate," Weyland said, although he knew what she had
meant. "And *you* need to learn."

Noah lifted her face and looked across to where Grace lay in her cradle, then
she looked back to Weyland. "I must go. There are those I need to talk to."

"I know." He reached out a hand, sliding it slowly over a shoulder and
down one arm. "We will wait for you."

chapter thirteen

WOBURN PARK, BEDFORDSHIRE

*J*OHN THORNTON WOKE SUDDENLY, HIS HEART
thumping.

Someone was in the bedchamber.

He rolled his head over to check his wife, Sarah.

She was sleeping soundly.

There was a soft sound by the window.

Thornton turned his head to look.

Noah stood there, her mouth curving in a smile. "Hello, John."

"Lord God!" Thornton said in a hushed voice. "What are you doing here?"

Noah glanced at Sarah, still soundly asleep. "Come to visit, John. Perhaps, if you'd like to put on a shirt and breeches, and some stout shoes, we can walk in the park."

Then she faded away, and John was left staring at the frosted window. He took several deep breaths, then, very carefully, he extricated himself from the bed, gathered his clothes and shoes, and left the bedchamber.

JOHN THORNTON STILL TUTORED THE EARL AND
countess's younger children, but now that he was married, with children of his own, the earl had given him a house on the estate. It stood just on the edge of Woburn Park, under the trees, where it overlooked the gentle rolling hills, and where the deer wandered past twice a day on their journey to and from the lake to water.

Thornton loved the house, for it represented the chance for him to build a marriage and a family with Sarah.

Here he could try to forget Noah, and all she had been and might have been to him.

Consequently, by the time Thornton had struggled into his clothes, grabbed a cloak, and left the house as quietly as he was able, he was in a state of combined high anxiety and righteous anger.

He had wanted to forget Noah as best he was able. He had thought she had forgotten him.

So what now was she doing, appearing in his bedchamber in the middle of the night? God, but if Sarah had woken and seen her . . .

By the time he had stomped down the front path, Thornton was in a temper such as he rarely achieved. He had achieved a kind of fragile peace in his life, and with this single visitation Noah had murdered it forever. He would spend the rest of his life wondering if she would appear again, keeping alive that fragile, terrible hope that she might actually return his love.

"John . . ."

Noah stood just beside him, smiling. "I am sorry to wake you so."

"What do you want?"

"There is a bench under that tree. Will you came sit with me?"

"Dammit . . ." But she was already moving toward the tree, and Thornton had no choice but to follow her.

Once he reached the bench, Thornton stood a moment looking at her. She was in her most magical form, the green eyes shot through with gold, the strange diaphanous robe that *should* have left her half frozen with cold but which instead seemed to clothe her in warmth.

She was lovely, far lovelier than Thornton had remembered, and he had thought his memories too beautiful for truth.

He sat down with an angry thump, which Noah ignored. She took his hand and held it in her lap, and the warmth that had enveloped Noah now encased Thornton.

"I need to talk to you," she said.

"Really?"

"I have missed you, John."

"Do not do this to me, Noah."

"I need to talk."

"God, woman, you have half of England's men trailing after you. Could you not talk with one of them?"

"I find myself at a crossroads."

He didn't answer. He was looking now, not at Noah, but at the distant shape of a tree. He concentrated on it with all his might, praying that he would somehow survive this night without his life falling apart about him.

"You will never escape me, John."

"Don't do this," he whispered.

"John, I am in a bind."

Again he didn't reply.

She drew in a deep breath. "There is something I want to tell you."

He still refused to look at her.

"It is a story," she said, "which goes back three thousand years. If I tell you this story, I risk trapping you within it."

"Then why take this risk?"

"Because I need your advice very badly. John, I need your permission to tell this tale. I need you to know the risk I am taking with your future . . . lives."

John stared at her.

"We all come back, John. Life after life. If you are caught up in the Game that has ensnared me, then you will become ensnared in my life also."

"I already *am* ensnared, Noah." Then he sighed. "Just tell me this damned story."

And so Noah did. She sat for over an hour, talking, sharing with him her growth through her different lives, and growth of the Troy Game which had not only ensnared her, but most of England besides. She told him of Brutus, and Coel, of Eaving's Sisters, of Catling's true identity, and of Asterion, and how she had either loved or hated all of them.

She told him of how she had come to love Asterion in this life.

She told him of her true origins, and of the darkcraft seething through her blood.

"You appear very content with yourself," said Thornton, as her voice drifted into silence. "Why tell me all of this? *Why are you here?*"

"Because I need your permission for what I am about to do."

"Why *my* permission, Noah?"

"Because you represent to me the mortal world. And for what I am about to do, I need to know that I have its understanding and permission."

"And you are about to do . . . what?"

Noah told him, and Thornton's face, already pale, became completely colorless.

"Why ask permission for *that* piece of foulness, witch?"

"John, don't, please."

He looked away from her, staring into the moon-dappled landscape. "My life would have been so much more peaceful without you in it, Noah."

"It would have been a tame thing, John."

He smiled slightly, wryly, and gave a small shake of his head. He would never be free of her, and in some strange way, he found himself grateful. She was right; his life would have been a tame thing indeed if she had not been at its heart.

He sighed. "I understand what you are going to do, but, oh God, how can I condone it? How can I grant you permission?"

"There will be little loss of life, John. If any. There will be material devastation, there will be grief, but not for loss of loved ones."

"You can manage that?"

"Yes."

He sat awhile, before finally speaking. "This is the only way?"

"It is the only way I can think of."

He sat again in silence for some time. "Very well," he eventually said, his voice flat, as if he thought that with this, he betrayed his God, "you have my permission."

Her hand touched his. "Thank you, John."

"And as for the father of your new and *only* daughter . . . Do what you have to. I think he will be a far better lover to you than . . . well, than I could ever have been."

"You are a generous man, John, and I shall be everlastingly grateful to you."

"Noah . . ."

"Yes?"

"If I come back again, as you intimate I will, then I hope to God I will lead a happier life than ever I have in this one."

Her face paled, and he was glad that at last she knew how badly she had hurt him.

Chapter Fourteen

Idol Lane, London

Noah Speaks

O H GODS, POOR JOHN. HOW I HAD HURT HIM. I would make certain, for I knew I had the power to do it, that in his next life he would be happy, and love, and be loved.

I felt easier now, having spoken to John about what I wanted to do. I would also need to speak to the Lord of the Faerie, for this plan needed the permission of both mortal and Faerie, but I thought he would agree, if as reluctantly as John.

My decision had come to me slowly, so slowly I could not recall when over the past day or so I first considered it, but now it felt as though the idea had always been with me: To stop the Game in its tracks, if I could not actually kill it. To give me the time I needed to grow and learn. To give London the time it needed to become . . . that final battlefield.

I needed to move quickly. Catling would surely be aware of what I planned, and the gods alone knew what measures she might take in countermeasure.

So, from John, I went back to Idol Lane. Weyland was still in the kitchen, our daughter still in his arms, but his face was lighter, and his posture was more relaxed than the last time I had come to him here.

I hoped he was getting used to this—the knowledge that I would, always, return.

"Weyland," I said, giving him a kiss and then bending to brush my lips against Grace's curls. Weyland handed her to me, and then he enfolded both of us in his arms, and held us tight, and I did love him for that, because he knew instinctively how greatly I needed it.

"Weyland . . ." I said again.

He leaned back, looking at me quizzically. "Noah, what are you planning?"

I told him, as I had told John.

Weyland gave a short, disbelieving laugh. "What a true daughter—and lover—of mine you are. But . . . you will need to the darkcraft to accomplish this."

"I know. Will you aid me?"

He smiled, gently. "Always."

I took a deep breath, I was so happy. But first . . . "We need to make sure Grace is protected, and I need to speak with the Lord of the Faerie."

He nodded, and so we left the house on Idol Lane.

At that moment I was happy, and sure of myself.

WE WENT THEN TO LONDON BRIDGE, WITH OUR daughter, and stood, leaning over the side, looking into the waters, and waited.

The Lord of the Faerie joined us within minutes. He glanced at Weyland at my side, took a longer look at Grace in my arms, then his eyes settled on my face.

"This is a strange and frightening path you take," he said. "I stood behind you as you talked with John, and heard."

"Then you know I need to ask your permission also."

"Gods, Noah, what you plan . . ."

"Coel, if I don't act, then the Troy Game will destroy the land, and then reach into the Faerie and take that, too. It is evil beyond knowing. I need to act before it destroys us all. Coel, as you have ever loved me, then grant me your aid and your permission."

He rubbed at his eyes, fretting, then finally nodded. "Yes. Yes to both. What may I do to help?"

"Can you take our baby, Grace, and keep her safe? I do not think Catling can yet reach into the Faerie . . . can she?"

He shook his head. "No. For the moment, it lies beyond her. Very well . . ." He reached out, and took Grace from me.

Weyland had gone very tense at my side, and I realized that, apart from Jane, this was the first time he'd allowed anyone else to hold his daughter.

The Lord of the Faerie realized Weyland's tenseness. "I will watch over her, and all the Faerie folk besides," he said. "We shall be watchers . . . We will not be imprisoners."

Thank you, Coel. Weyland needed to know he will get his daughter back.

"What else do you desire of me?" the Lord of the Faerie asked.

"To watch over these," I said, and held out my hands at the same time I sent a summons of calling into the house in Idol Lane.

The four kingship bands of Troy that I had taken over the past year materialized on my palms.

Weyland gave a start. "Noah, no!"

"Weyland," I said, "Coel will watch over them. When I ask, he will hand them back."

I was looking at Weyland as I said this, but from the corner of my eye I was aware that the Lord of the Faerie was watching him very carefully. Whether he knew it or not, Weyland was facing a critical test that would either earn him the Lord of the Faerie's trust, or his suspicion.

It was a battle. Weyland had wanted those bands for so long he'd forgotten what life was like without his desperate need for them. To hide them within the Idyll was one thing. To hand them to the Lord of the Faerie was another.

Then Weyland gave a short little laugh and addressed the Faerie Lord. "I am trusting you with my daughter, but hesitate to trust you with these four damned pieces of gold. I can't believe it. Take the bands, Faerie Lord, but take care of my daughter before all else."

The Lord of the Faerie smiled, then he gave a short nod.

The bands vanished from my hands, and the next moment reappeared as four golden ribbons, one about each of Grace's limbs.

Weyland and I both laughed at the sight. Somehow, those golden ribbons about our daughter's limbs reassured us as almost nothing else might have done.

"Well," said the Lord of the Faerie, "now that I hold your entire future in my arms, what else could you possibly want from me?"

"I need to ask this of Charles, the king," I said.

The Lord of the Faerie smiled. "I will pass him the message."

"There is a man who has been commissioned to draw plans for the rebuilding of St. Paul's. His name is Christopher Wren."

"I know him. He has a good heart, and can persevere, no matter the difficulties."

"Coel, will you, as Charles, be his friend? Will you trust him, give him free rein as much as you are able?"

"I can. What else?"

I drew in a deep breath. "I need the aid of Gog and Magog, and of the water-sprites."

"You do not need to ask my permission for their aid."

"Nevertheless . . ."

He smiled once more. "Speak to them. They will do whatever you wish."

"Thank you."

His smile died, and he glanced again at Weyland. "Noah, you *must* speak with Ringwalker. You *must*. You owe him this, at least."

"Do I? Why, Coel?"

"Noah, he loves you. He—"

"I loved him for thousands of years while he ignored me. And now he still wants to believe in the Game more than in me. Coel, I do not know where we will go, or what we will do, but I—"

"Talk to him!"

I didn't want to. I didn't know how I would feel, or where my emotions would pull me.

And I wasn't sure if I could trust him. Ringwalker was too close to the Game, unable yet to see beyond it.

"Talk to him," Coel whispered, and, very reluctantly, I gave a single nod.

I LEFT WEYLAND WAITING FOR ME ON THE BRIDGE while I went into the dreams of the man I had mentioned to the Lord of the Faerie, Christopher Wren.

I took him through the realm of the dream into the stone hall, that vision which had both plagued and comforted me over thousands of years.

"Who are you?" Wren said to me as I escorted him down the hall. Even as I asked, his eyes were darting about, staring first at the columns and then at the great dome that soared above us.

"Master Wren," I said, "who I am, does not matter. I am merely a messenger."

"What is your message?" he said, not even pretending to look at me anymore. Instead, he was standing entranced under the dome, head cricked back, staring upward.

"This," I said softly, "is London's heart, and it will be your monument. Build it, I pray, and let none stand in your way in the doing."

"The cathedral chapter will never stand for it," he said. "It's not English enough."

"You have a powerful ally—the king. *He* will stand behind you. Do this, Christopher Wren."

Finally he looked back at me. "Why? What purpose does it suit for you?"

"This?" I stood, looking about as I had not done for many long years. The stone hall. How much had happened here? How many seductions? How many lies? How many murders? "This, Sir Christopher, is going to become the most wondrous casket in history, the coffin of so many hopes and dreams and ambitions, that it would take a lifetime to number them all."

And with that, I left him to his dreams.

* * *

I HAD ONE FINAL TASK THAT NIGHT. I CALLED TO ME
Gog and Magog, and the water-sprites who tumbled joyfully amid the raging
torrent under London Bridge. I spoke long and seriously to them, and, eventually, all nodded—the giants reluctantly, the sprites with the most marvelous
joy.

Mischief was about.

I RETURNED TO WEYLAND, AND WITH HIM WENT BACK
to the house in Idol Lane.

We sat at the table in the kitchen, a table about which so much had happened and so much had grown, and we waited for the following night.

While we waited, Weyland talked. He did not stop for almost twenty-four
hours, and he talked of nothing but the darkcraft.

CHAPTER FIFTEEN

LONDON

EYLAND AND NOAH LEFT THE HOUSE AT DUSK the next day. They stood outside for a moment, close together, looking up at the house.

"For the house," said Weyland, "I care nothing. But what of the Idyll?"

"Whatever happens," said Noah, "the Idyll will survive. We may need to build ourselves some new steps, but the Idyll will survive."

He lowered his gaze from the house to her face. "Are you ready?"

Noah gave a wan smile. "No. I feel sick to the stomach at what I must do. But do it I will. I am sick of dancing to the Game's tune. Now *I* will construct the dancing floor, Weyland, and fashion it to my own needs."

"Catling is about," he said. "I can sense her."

"Catling is *all* about," said Noah. "She is under our feet and in the air that we breathe."

Weyland grasped her hand in his. "Noah, be careful."

She squeezed his hand. "I have you, and all of Faerie, with me. How can I fail?"

Weyland had opened his mouth to reply, but before he could get out the first word there came a sharp and commanding step from the Tower Street end of Idol Lane.

Weyland and Noah turned to look.

And stiffened, their interlocked hands now tight, their faces guarded.

It was Ringwalker.

THE LORD OF THE FAERIE CRADLED THE BABY GRACE in his arms, speaking soothing words to her, and carried her into the Realm of the Faerie. The woman who had once been called Jane, and who was now known simply as the Caroler, met him at the foot of The Naked.

"It is Grace!" the Caroler said, raising her eyes to the Lord of the Faerie's face.

He gave a wry smile. "We are to baby-sit."

Then the Caroler saw the ribbons about the baby's limbs. "Dear gods, I can understand that Noah might want to secrete the bands within the Faerie, but *Weyland*?"

"He agreed, and thus undermined every notion I had formed of him. The world is turning into a strange place, my love."

"What is Noah planning?" the Caroler asked.

The Lord of the Faerie told her, and the Caroler shuddered. "Catling will eat her," she said.

"Then we must pray for her, and pray that either Noah, or Weyland, may overcome Catling."

The Caroler gave a small shake of her head. "They both have the darkcraft within them. She will *eat* them. That is her nature!"

The Lord of the Faerie went white. "What can we do? We can't just stand here and—"

"Hold the baby?" The Caroler laughed, the sound a lilting reflection of the Ancient Carol. "I think that is precisely what we should do. I think Grace may be the only thing that may save Noah." She paused. "And Weyland, besides, should we wish."

RINGWALKER WALKED SLOWLY DOWN THE LANEWAY toward where Weyland and Noah stood. He walked in his mortal form, as Louis de Silva, but there was no mistaking who and what he was, for power— and anger—radiated from him as if he burned with the heat of the sun.

"I wish I had never entered the cursed city of Mesopotama," he said. "I wish I had never set eyes on you. I wish I had never—"

"Loved me?" Noah said. "I am sorry, too, Ringwalker, that you left it this long."

The words stopped, and they stared at each other.

"You were both doomed, always," said Weyland. "Do not now blame each other for it."

"Do not *dare* to—" Ringwalker began.

"Weyland is right," Noah said. "We were always doomed, Ringwalker. The Troy Game could construct many things, and manipulate more, but it has no idea of love, does it? Whatever you and I might have been, Louis, was murdered at the start by the Game."

There were tears in her eyes as she finished, and it seemed to drain Ring-walker's anger. "Noah, I am sorry. What can I do? You and I must . . . We must . . ."

"We must do many things," Noah said, "but we are going to have to do them without those bonds of love which once we thought awaited us. I hope that we will walk on parallel paths, but I don't think our paths will ever converge. Not now."

Ringwalker's eyes moved to Weyland. "Did you plan this?"

Weyland gave a grunt of humorless laughter. "I planned to use her, Ring-walker. I planned to destroy you through her, and then obliterate her. I planned to laugh in the doing. But what has this life wrought for any of us, save to demolish all ambitions and turn all plans into dust?" He paused. "Ring-walker, the prize is not Noah, not for either of us."

Ringwalker cocked an eyebrow, his face set and hard.

"It is *life*," Weyland said. "Freedom from the Troy Game. Its death is the only way any of us can live. Its death is most assuredly the only way any of us can live freely."

"He's right," Noah said softly.

Ringwalker was looking back at Noah. "You need me for that." He strode the distance between them, and took her chin roughly in one hand.

Weyland made to move, but Noah gestured to him to stay where he was.

"I know that," she said. She did not move to free herself from Ringwalker's grasp.

"You and I," Ringwalker said, giving her chin a little shake, "are the King-man and the Mistress of the Labyrinth. We control the Troy Game—"

To one side Weyland gave a short, derisory laugh.

Ringwalker's face tightened. "*We* control the—"

"No, we don't," Noah said. "*It* thinks to control us."

Ringwalker let Noah's chin go. "You want to destroy it."

Noah gave a small nod.

"You won't succeed."

"Not without you," she said.

Suddenly all of Ringwalker's anger and hurt boiled to the surface. "Why plead for me," he spat at her, "when you have *him*?"

And, with that, and with a final look of such fury that Noah had to avert her eyes, Ringwalker vanished.

THEY WALKED DOWN IDOL LANE TO THAMES STREET,
then walked west until they reached Pudding Lane just before Fish Street Hill.

There they stopped, both peering through the gathering darkness up the lane.

"Why here?" said Weyland.

"Because every dance must start somewhere," said Noah, and she walked into the darkness.

The moment she vanished into the gloom of Pudding Lane, water-sprites seethed up from the Thames, clambering over the wharves and docks that lined the river. There they lingered but a moment, taking only enough time to orientate themselves, before they scuttled forward and vanished into the myriad alleyways that connected the city with its wharves.

In the Guildhall, Gog and Magog stirred, and sighed, and took up spear and sword.

CHAPTER SIXTEEN

LONDON

*P*ARTWAY UP PUDDING LANE STOOD A LARGE
house owned by a merchant supplier called Thomas Farriner. He
rose during the night to empty his bladder, then, driven by some
presentiment, walked through the house, checking each of his ovens and
hearths in turn.

All were safe, either covered with ceramic curfews, or with their coals
smothered under a thick layer of ash. He paused for the longest time before
the baking oven, staring at it, unable to shake off his foreboding.

The baking oven stared back at him, cool and innocent.

Farriner chewed his lower lip, checked for the fourth time that the door to
the oven was tightly closed, then walked yet one more time about his house, this
time checking not only the hearths and ovens, but that all windows were tightly
shuttered against drafts.

All was well.

Finally, Farriner went back to bed, lying down beside his wife, and closing
his eyes.

He was unable to sleep.

Yet, even so, Farriner did not hear the soft footfall of the goddess within
his house, and did not hear her open the baking oven's door, and whisper into
it words of power and darkcraft.

The merchant stirred only a half-hour later, when the flames had already
taken hold, and he heard their vicious crackle sweeping up the stairs.

He leapt to his feet, and raced to the head of the stairs.

The entire lower half of the house was encased in flames. As he stood, staring, too shocked and appalled for the moment to move, he heard the dull thud
of an explosion in his cellar as tubs of tar and of fine brandy exploded.

"Get your wife," said a soft voice in his ear, "and your children and maidservants, and escape as quickly as you may, through the attic window into your neighbor's house. There, hasten to raise the alarum, and tell your neighbors to gather their goods, and flee."

Farriner stared at the lovely woman standing at his elbow. He thought she might be an angel, or perhaps—far more likely—a temptress risen with the flames from hell.

"Why?" he whispered. "Why have you done this?"

"To level the dancing floor," she replied, "and to rebuild it to my needs. Now, go! *Go*, for the Death Crone creeps up your stairwell in those flames."

With that, Farriner fled, screaming to his wife and children and servants.

In later weeks, when Parliament convened an inquiry into the fire, Farriner only told them that he had risen during the night to check the ovens and hearths.

He did not mention the woman, or what she had said to him, for he well understood that, in the hysteria and the search for a scapegoat following the Great Destruction, there were some things better left unsaid.

OVER THE NEXT TWENTY-FOUR HOURS NOAH AND Weyland moved slowly through the city. Noah was exhausted, and Weyland stayed close by her side. He did all he could to support her, but he could not help her, for Noah used all three aspects of her power to control the flames which now ravaged through the eastern portion of London: her darkcraft to fuel the flames, and to speed the unnatural easterly wind that fanned them; her powers as Mistress of the Labyrinth to dictate what path the flames must take; and her powers as Eaving, goddess of the waters, to slow the flames enough that citizens had time to escape from their homes, not merely with their lives, but with all their belongings as well.

London was tinder-dry. Its buildings were largely constructed of timber and lathe plaster, and its cellars—particularly along the waterfront—were packed with casks of inflammable materials: pitch, spirits, canvas, hemp, and rope. By rights the city should have exploded.

That it didn't, and that over the three days the fire crept slowly westward only six people lost their lives, was due almost solely to Noah's efforts in keeping it constrained; and secondly, to Gog and Magog's tireless labors to whisper into people's minds, to encourage them to leave, and to herd them ever forward into safer fields.

The Great Fire was constrained, but not containable.

As Noah and Gog and Magog fought to save lives, the thousands of water-sprites who had crept into the city at the start of the fire worked tirelessly (and with the utmost joy, for this was mischief such as they adored) to make sure no one could put the fire out.

London had burned on many occasions, and thus the city was well prepared for that moment when first the alarum was screamed into the night.

The lord mayor arrived on the scene and, while he privately commented to a friend that he thought a woman might piss the fire out, he nonetheless made sure the fire watches were roused and the fire engines summoned. Both watches and engines duly arrived, bucket brigades hastily set up, and fire engines carried with much huffing and puffing up stairs to attack the fire from above.

But, unseen by all those who thronged the streets—either fleeing or crowding about to gawk—water-sprites wriggled everywhere. Their tiny, deft, sharp fingers sprung leaks in the leather buckets and pushed wads of sodden tobacco into the machinations of the fire engines, so that they stopped. Others wormed their way into the city's reservoirs and turned the cocks, so that all supplies of emergency water to the city were halted.

When, in desperation, the fire watches started to pull down buildings in order to create firebreaks, the water-sprites took great lungfuls of air, and blew fireballs into the sky so that fire rained down behind the firebreaks.

The fire spread, slowly, inexorably, west- and northwestward, consuming almost the entire part of the old city, and setting the dead in the city churchyards to flaming like candles. Gradually, the fire moved in a pincer movement toward the cathedral of St. Paul's.

On the third day, Tuesday, as the crackling flames drew near to the cathedral, Catling roused, and hissed.

Then she picked up her length of red wool, and twisted it through her fingers.

SINCE THE START OF THE FIRE, ST. DUNSTAN'S-IN-THE-East had been guarded by the scholars of Westminster School, led by their dean, John Dolben. Tense and wary, they were nonetheless relieved as the fire spread ever westward, away from the ancient church.

On Tuesday morning, flames crept eastward, against the prevailing wind, directly for Idol Lane. It was as if some malevolent hand directed them, for surely no natural fire could move thus.

Nothing that the watch at St. Dunstan's did, managed to stay the flames. They were so concentrated in one snapping, frenzied river of fury which was so inexplicably *purposeful* that Dolben finally ordered the scholars to stand back. It was better to watch the ancient church burn than to lose lives.

They gathered in the churchyard, somber youths and men, their faces drained and smudged with soot, as that strange river of fire roared into Idol Lane.

"God have mercy on all of us," muttered Dolben, "for I fear the Devil himself directs that fire."

The fire had flowed to a point just north of the church. Then, as all watched, it suddenly, violently, inexplicably, exploded eastward.

Directly into Weyland Orr's house.

The house detonated with such a frightful roar that the blast threw Dolben and his scholars off their feet—at least five of the scholars fractured limbs or skulls as they impacted headstones. By the time Dolben gained his feet, shaking his head clear of the effects of the blast, Orr's house had vanished inside a tower of flame.

The next instant, the top of the house erupted as if it were a volcano. Flames and molten stone burst over the entire area, and Dolben threw himself once more to the ground, sure that this time he would be killed.

And yet once again not only he, but all his charges, survived.

Unbelievingly, Dolben raised his face out of the hot earth.

Before him Orr's house had vanished, as had the bone house attached to it.

And there was a small lick of flame peeking almost apologetically out of the timber struts of the church spire.

"To work!" screamed Dolben, as he stumbled in his haste to rise to his feet. "To work!"

Eight hours later, the spire had collapsed into crumbled ruins and some of the outer buildings had been destroyed, but the main body of St. Dunstan's-in-the-East had been saved.

Whatever malevolence had sent that hell-driven river of flame into Idol Lane had apparently found something else to play with.

ARIADNE STOOD ATOP THE WHITE TOWER, AS SHE had for three days and nights, wrapped in concealing magic, watching as the fire spread eastward. She was clothed in her ancient Minoan finery, her red skirts and black hair whipping about her in the wind. The flames cast rosy shadows on her white skin, and reflected the bright fear in her eyes. "Ye gods, Noah," she whispered. "Be wary!"

WEYLAND FELT IT FIRST. A TUG. TINY, YET INSISTENT.

They were standing on one side of Ludgate Hill, just below St. Paul's, watching the flames march relentlessly forward. Noah was concentrating, her body shaking with the effort, trying to hold back the flames enough so that the hordes of people darting about like ants before the flames could get out of the way, and save their precious belongings. Both Noah and Weyland were masked in magic, their forms hidden by the hot shadows thrown forward by the fire.

"Noah," he said, and instinctively grabbed her shoulders.

It was only just in time.

The next instant Noah wailed as she felt something grab within her belly, and then both she and Weyland were hauled forward, through the crowds, dragged forward, forward, forward, up Ludgate Hill and through the open western doors of St. Paul's.

Catling had called.

Chapter Seventeen

St. Paul's Cathedral, London

"WELL-MET!" THE LITTLE GIRL SEETHED AS NOAH and Weyland finally came to a halt before her. She'd pulled them before the altar where, in the rosy glow cast by the approaching fire through the stained-glass windows of the cathedral, Noah stood only because Weyland had her by the shoulders.

Otherwise, exhausted, and so totally drained, emotionally, physically and magically, Noah would have slumped to the floor.

"You think yourself so clever," said Catling. She was still in the form that Noah had last seen her, a beautiful black-curled little girl with porcelain skin and dark-blue eyes, garbed in a black dress with a tight bodice and a full skirt that rustled about her like the flames in the streets outside.

"You think to outwit me," the girl continued, and took a step toward Weyland and Noah.

Her eyes, blue a moment before, now reflected red and angry with the light filtering through the windows.

Noah struggled to stand upright, and Weyland's hands tightened on her shoulders.

"You and I," Noah said in a voice surprisingly strong, "shall meet indeed within this place, but we both know that now is not the time, nor the place."

Catling hissed, but Noah continued.

"I no longer dance to your merry jig, Catling. *I* will control the dancing floor, and the patterns that it weaves. Not you."

"You couldn't control the death of a cockroach, weakling," said Catling. "Look at you! You'd fall if it were not for the hands of your companion in hell."

"*I* have a lover," said Noah quietly. "He makes me whole. What do you have, save—"

"I have your destruction in my hands," said Catling, "and I intend to wield it as I want." Her right hand suddenly jerked up, and in response the fire in the streets outside roared.

The windows flamed as the fire leapt into the sky.

There came a light pattering on the lead roof high above them, as if the rats who lived between its joists had decided to flee.

"The roof is afire," said Catling conversationally. "We're all going to burn."

Noah and Weyland tried to take a step backward, but neither could move.

Catling's smile became a rictus of triumph. "You must know where we are," she said. "We stand high above that ancient labyrinth that Genvissa and Brutus carved into the summit of Og's Hill. Where they gave birth to *me*. They were good creatures. Precious. Reliable. *Obedient*. You? You're nothing. I wish I had never bothered with you. I wish I had never thought to use you. But never mind, for we stand over the dark heart of the labyrinth, and surely you both know what that means."

Noah again turned her eyes to Weyland, and they were agonized.

We stand over the dark heart of the labyrinth.

"Trapped," whispered Catling. "Trapped by the Troy Game. Unable to find your way out. Your powers as Mistress of the Labyrinth and as Eaving shall not aid you here, Noah. You're all Darkwitch, that's all that counts, and that's all that will eventually destroy you."

"You speak arrogant nonsense!" Weyland said. "Destroy Noah and you destroy any hope you have of being completed! You may be able to manipulate Ringwalker, but he's useless to you without Noah!"

"When did I say *I* was going to destroy Noah?" Catling said. "I just need you both in my dark heart. There's something there I need to show you."

There came a dim roar from high above, and all three involuntarily lifted their eyes.

Ragged lines of fire, glowing red, had zigzagged across the wooden struts supporting the lead roof.

The roof groaned, and something hot and foul-smelling splattered to the floor just to the left of Noah.

She jumped, and Weyland cursed. "Let her go, you fool! If she dies in here, with you, then—"

"No one is going to *die!*" Catling hissed. "We're just all going to *suffer* a little. I'm going to teach you a lesson, Noah, and I want to make sure you will remember it well."

Another globule of molten lead dropped down from the roof. It was much larger than the last, and much closer, and it spattered over Noah's gown.

The material, weakened and dried by three days of the heat of the fire, burst instantly into flame.

Noah shrieked, and Weyland beat at the flames with his hands, but he could do nothing, and within a moment Noah was enveloped in a pillar of fire.

Five or six more globules, as large as buckets, spattered down from the roof, striking all three struggling forms far below.

All three glowed, and then Catling and Weyland burst into fire, to complement Noah's already burning form.

Welcome to the dark heart of the labyrinth, Catling whispered as they burned. *Do you feel at home yet, Darkwitch?*

CHAPTER EIGHTEEN

THE REALM OF THE FAERIE AND ST. PAUL'S CATHEDRAL, LONDON

HE LORD OF THE FAERIE AND THE CAROLER stood atop The Naked. The Faerie Lord rocked the baby in his arms, but even his soothing voice had no effect on the child, for she screamed and writhed.

"Noah burns," said the Caroler. "I knew she would, once Catling got her hands upon her. Weyland dies, too." She paused. "Agony. *He* endures agony, for once."

"We must do something!" the Lord of the Faerie cried.

"We can do nothing," said the Caroler. "We are of the Faerie, and we cannot reach into the heart of the labyrinth." She lifted her head, and looked to the west. "See? The sun sinks. Soon I shall have to carol in the dusk, and—"

"*Noah burns!*" the Lord of the Faerie shouted. "Has that no meaning for you?"

The Caroler sighed. "Then lift up the child, Coel, and set her free."

IN ALL HIS PREVIOUS LIVES (SAVE, OF COURSE, HIS first) Weyland had controlled the manner of his own death. He had slipped quietly and gently into death, and had then, as soon as practical, organized his reemergence back into life (save, of course, for this last, which the Troy Game had controlled). Death and rebirth was, for him, a gentle and predictable transition, one which caused no anxiety or suffering.

This was different.

This was anguish beyond Weyland's experience, beyond his imagination, beyond comprehension. The fire rippled over his body like a wave, then spread tiny, insistent fingers of flame into every one of his orifices, and through every single one of his pores.

Through all this, far worse was living in tandem with Noah's suffering.

Catling had reserved the worst for her.

A GIRL WALKED THROUGH ST. PAUL'S. THE CATHEDRAL was alive with fire. The roof had gone, and flames roared through the nave with the force of a hurricane, before swirling about the altar and then lifting up in great, thick ropes into a sky heavy with smoke and thunder.

The girl walked as if she were aware of none of this. Indeed, the fire seemed as unaware of her as she was of it, and touched not a hair of her head, nor scorched a single inch of her pale skin.

She was a lovely girl, on the verge of womanhood, still a little long of limb, but with an exquisite grace about her that bespoke a career, perhaps, as a dancer.

Or a lover.

As she walked, the girl talked. She carried on a conversation with someone unseen. Every so often her eyebrows would raise in question as she talked, then her face would fall into repose as she waited for a response, and then she would nod gravely, as if accepting the answer given as wisdom incarnate.

She addressed the person she spoke to as "Grandmother Ariadne," and sometimes she laughed, as if Grandmother Ariadne had said something particularly witty. Sometimes she frowned, if only a little, as if Grandmother Ariadne had mouthed something faintly heretical.

Overall, she accepted what grandmother Ariadne said, for she was a wise girl, and knew she currently stepped into parts unknown.

She was Grace, as she would eventually be, and she was coming to find her parents.

Above, thunder cracked, and then roared.

Grace walked on, darkcraft incarnate.

Shapes reeled about her.

Trojan maidens and youths, long dead, twisting in their lovely Dance of the Flowers.

Poiteran marauders, daubed in blue, thrusting sword and spear into shrieking victims.

Genvissa's daughters, dying alongside Brutus and Cornelia's sons.

Roman centurions, marching in solemn procession.

Tall, broad-shouldered Vikings, carrying torches that outshone even the leaping flames about them.

Christian priests, carrying foreign magic on crosses.

Normans, dark-eyed and -visaged, surrounding their triumphant king.

Londoners, past and present, burning like the fierce candles used to light the Yuletide log.

Grace walked on through this dancing, burning throng, serene and lovely, her hands clasped gently before her. Her mouth was still now, for she had heard all that Ariadne had to say.

She walked toward where the altar had once stood, then, in a sudden, swift movement, Grace bent to the floor—*a floor running with fire*—and picked something up.

It was a length of red wool.

She held it out before her with one hand, holding it by one end, studying it, her beautiful head cocked ever so slightly to one side.

The length of wool twisted and cavorted in the heat.

Grace slowly reached out her other hand, watching the snapping, winding length of red wool carefully, then she suddenly grabbed out and grasped the bottom end of the wool and snapped it straight.

With that single motion, Grace drew out all the twistings and meanderings and cavortings of the wool so that it stretched from hand to hand in one continuous, direct length.

A shriek echoed through the cathedral.

It had come from far below.

NOAH AND WEYLAND WERE DEAD, THEY KNEW IT, BUT Catling had made sure that they still existed in all the agony she'd visited on them during their dying. Over and over they relived their suffering as they burned, and their flesh melted through the cracks in the stone flooring of St. Paul's, down and down, into the heart of the labyrinth.

Enough, Catling said finally, and Noah and Weyland found they were able to breathe again and that, amazingly, they stood within the dark heart of the labyrinth in flesh, and as whole as if they had never burned.

They could see nothing, for a great darkness enveloped them.

"Weyland?" Noah gasped, and the next moment she felt his arms about her.

"Are you well?" he said.

"Yes. You?"

"Aye. I—"

"Oh, stop this gabble," said Catling. "It is very pretty, but we are about to have a visitor, and there is no time to waste on precious endearments. Listen. *Listen!*"

Noah and Weyland clung to each other, still gasping for breath, desperate to escape and yet feeling such a great weight of hopelessness falling about their shoulders that they knew they'd never be able to accomplish their freedom.

"Listen!" Catling cried one more time, and this time they heard it.

Footfalls, as if someone descended down a great flight of stairs.

Gradually the footfalls grew ever louder until they rang through the darkness.

Then, suddenly, crazily, came the sound of a door creaking open.

Light flooded into the dark heart of the labyrinth, and Noah and Weyland had to momentarily shut their eyes against its brightness.

When they opened them again they saw a young woman standing silhouetted in a door frame.

Behind her rose a stairway, and both Noah and Weyland knew where those stairs led.

Into the Idyll.

Noah gave a soft cry. "No! Grace, no!"

"Oh," said Catling, "I'll not murder her. Never. Not precious baby Grace. Indeed, I'll do *everything* I can to keep her alive. But look, see, and know how greatly I have trapped you."

At that moment Grace gave a cry, and her arms sprang forward, as if some power other than her own controlled them, and her wrists jerked together, as if they were bound.

Glowing red lines encircled her wrists, and, as Noah and Weyland watched, horrified, the lines closed about Grace's wrists, and the girl shrieked.

"Listen to me, and listen well!" Catling hissed, holding Noah and Weyland back with her power as they struggled to reach their daughter—by now slouched in the doorframe, weeping as the agony tightened about her wrists.

"I have bound Grace to me," Catling continued, her words searing into Noah's and Weyland's minds. "Whatever you do to me, you do to Grace. Destroy me, and you destroy Grace. Complete me, and you allow Grace to live. Oh, and I forgot to mention: Anywhere that Grace has been, and anything that she has touched, is likewise bound. Has she been to the Idyll, Noah? Have you ever taken her on a tour of the Faerie? *Has the Lord of the Faerie cuddled her to his breast?*"

No! Noah wailed.

"*Aye!*" Catling said. "So *now* do you remember your duty, O great Mistress of the Labyrinth? If you destroy me, then you destroy not only Grace, but this land, this city, and the Idyll and the Faerie besides."

No . . .

"Complete me," Catling went on, "and Grace lives, and this land and the Faerie and the Idyll live as well. Under my dominion, of course, but at least they live. Now go. *Go!* Level the dancing floor as you wish, ensure your stone hall is rebuilt as you will, but know always that there is only one thing you can ever do if you want Grace and *everything* that you hold dear to survive . . . and that is to dance the final Dance of the Flowers with Ringwalker."

She paused, and for a moment the only sound was the harsh breathing of Noah and Weyland, and the terrible cries of Grace, lying in the doorway, her wrists bound with agonizing vileness.

"You cannot undo what I have done, Noah. No one can. Grace is bound to me, and everywhere she walks is tied to her fate. Now . . . *go!*"

There was an instant's hesitation, and then, as the bands of fire about Grace's wrists vanished as abruptly as they'd appeared, Weyland grabbed Noah and together they stumbled toward the open door and their daughter.

EPILOGUE

London 1666–1675

J T WAS DIFFICULT TO COME TO GRIPS WITH THE
enormity of the disaster. As the fires slowly burned out, people
picked their way back through what was left of the streets of London. In many cases the streets themselves no longer existed. Buildings had
collapsed the length of several blocks or more, entirely filling the open space
of streets with blackened, scorched, foul-smelling bricks and stones and half-
consumed timbers. In some places the fire had been so intense the stones had
melted, in other places buildings were left half-standing with dangerous un-
supported stone walls swaying in the incongruous blue skies.

There was very little left of any home which had stood in the fire's path.
Goods and valuables, history and emotions, all had been devoured by the
flames. People were stunned and uncomprehending, unable to envision how
they might ever manage to rebuild their lives.

Only a few men summoned any degree of decisiveness in the initial days,
and among them the king was first. Charles was everywhere, organizing, com-
mending, sympathizing, releasing funds from the royal purse, and from stores
for food and materials for shelter. He had spent the three days of the fire in
London itself, directing his guards to aid the firefighting efforts, handing out
golden coins to any who would help in pulling down buildings in an effort to
create a firebreak. By the time the fire had burned itself to a standstill, Charles
looked tired and disheveled, his clothes were sooty and water-soaked.

Yet still he did not rest. He paid for food to be sent to the homeless sheltering in Moorfields, then went there himself and addressed the hopeless
crowd, assuring them that London would rise from the ashes better and
stronger than ever. He consulted with architects, engineers, surveyors, and set
them to drawing plans. He bullied Commons into setting up parliamentary
committees to establish strict laws regarding the rebuilding of London.

He called Sir Christopher Wren before him, and spoke quietly to him, and set him to rebuilding St. Paul's.

"As your vision requires it," the king said to Wren quietly.

Wren looked startled. "You know of . . . ?"

"Aye," Charles said. "She came to me, as well." He put his hand on Wren's shoulder. "Listen to me, Wren. Many people will oppose what you shall build. It will be different. Innovative. Alarming. But between us, we will persevere. We must. Sir Christopher, St. Paul's *must* be rebuilt the way you were shown."

"I understand," Wren said. "It will be my life's work to accomplish it."

FOUR DAYS AFTER THE FIRE WAS FINALLY QUELLED, the king stood amid the ruins of St. Paul's. The lead roof had melted entirely away, in places running down stone walls; in others, collecting in great lumpy masses amid the rubble strewn along the floor of the nave. The walls had partly collapsed, the stained-glass windows had shattered and exploded in the heat, all the memorials and side chapels were gone. The great Norman cathedral of St. Paul's was nothing more than a shapeless, dangerous, teetering mass of leaning walls and piles of rubble.

Charles had come to the cathedral with a score of courtiers and guards, but he had waved all but one of them away as he picked his way through the rubble. Louis de Silva was the only one he wanted to accompany him into the dark heart of the cathedral.

Louis and Charles walked slowly and carefully through the rubble. They did not speak, and, although to the watchers it appeared that it was the king and the courtier who walked through the ruins, in reality Charles and Louis slipped into the Faerie almost so soon as they had stepped out alone.

Now, in the heart of the cathedral, standing before what had once been the altar, the Lord of the Faerie and Ringwalker stood, looking down at a jumbled pile of scorched bones.

"Is it . . ." Ringwalker said.

"Noah?" said the Lord of the Faerie. "No. She is safe. For the moment."

"Then, to whom do these bones belong?"

"Not to whom, Ringwalker, but to *what*. They are a warning of what will come if you and Noah do not complete the Troy Game." He paused. "They are the bones of all our hopes and dreams."

Ringwalker stood in silence for a long time, his eyes not leaving the pathetic jumble of bones.

"What can we do?" he whispered finally.

"I do not know," said the Lord of the Faerie.

* * *

*IN THE REALM OF THE FAERIE, NOAH SAT WITH HER
baby daughter in her lap. Behind her, his hand on her shoulder, stood Weyland Orr.
Before them stood the assembled mass of the Faerie folk, as well as the Lord of the
Faerie and the Caroler.*

Noah looked down on her daughter, and wept, and all wept with her.

*They had flung everything they knew at the baby, every power at their com-
mand, and yet still, faint red lines of fire glowed about her wrists.*

She had been their joy. Now she would prove to be their doom.

*All Noah could think of, as she sat there and wept, was her prophetic request to
Christopher Wren:* Build me a casket, Master Wren. Build me a coffin of hopes
and dreams.

And so he would, save that now the cathedral would prove her *casket, and not
that of the Troy Game's.*

1675

After years of wrangling, of planning, of heartache, of arguing and of desperate pleading, Sir Christopher Wren finally had the approval of the city and
church officials to rebuild the ancient cathedral church of St. Paul's in a cruci-
form layout with a magnificent dome.

On this day in the second half of the year, Wren stood on the site of the de-
molished cathedral. It had taken nine years, and far more lives, to bring the
scarred, charred walls down. Now, Wren could start the intricate work of laying out the foundations.

It was an important day, and a crowd had gathered to watch. Wren, hatless,
his curls blowing a little in the breeze, walked slowly about the leveled site, finally choosing a spot where one day would rise the great dome as that place
most suitable from which to measure out the rest of the cathedral.

Impatient, his booted foot tapping, Wren called to a nearby laborer.
"Bring me a stone, a flat stone, so that I may the more permanently mark
this spot."

The man hurried off, conscious of everyone's eyes on him.

To one side of the churchyard was a pile of flat stones. The laborer grabbed
one, and hurried back to Wren.

"Humph." Wren took the stone, turning it over in his hands.

He stilled as he saw the stone's front surface, and a chill of supernatural
awe ran down his spine.

The stone was an old tombstone, broken and scorched in the Great Fire.
But despite the dirt and ash which coated its surface, Wren could clearly read
the single word inscribed there.

Resurgam

I will rise again.

Wren breathed in deeply, trying to still his emotions. Then he raised the broken tombstone high above his head, showing it to all gathered about, and shouted, "Resurgam! Resurgam!"

Resurgam!

As the shouting died down, a movement at the edge of the crowd caught Wren's eye.

A little girl, not more than five or six, stood there. She was very lovely, with black snapping curls cascading down her back and with deep blue eyes in her pale face.

Shadows danced about her eyes and form, and for a moment Wren felt coldness evelop him.

In one hand she held a large rolled up sheet of paper, which she allowed to unravel once she realized she'd caught Wren's eye.

See here, she said in his mind, gesturing to the paper with her free hand, *I have a plan here for you. A plan of London as it should be rebuilt. It shall be our Game, yours and mine alone. Will you play?*

GLOSSARY

ALBA: ancient, and now vanished, city on the banks of the River Tiber in Italy.

ANCIENT CAROL: that which is sung by the CAROLER within the FAERIE to welcome in both dawn and dusk.

ARIADNE: ancient MISTRESS OF THE LABYRINTH in Knossos in Crete at the GREAT FOUNDING LABYRINTH. She was the half-sister of ASTERION, the Minotaur, and also his lover. She betrayed him to Theseus.

ASTERION: the ancient Minotaur who inhabited the GREAT FOUNDING LABYRINTH in Knossos on Crete. Murdered by Theseus, and recalled from death by ARIADNE, he has ever since been locked in a battle with BRUTUS for the kingship bands of TROY and control of the TROY GAME. In this current life he is known as WEYLAND ORR.

BANKS, NOAH: CORNELIA re-born and EAVING, the goddess of the waters. In her previous life she was Caela, wife to Edward the Confessor, and in her first she was CORNELIA, wife to BRUTUS.

BEDFORD, EARLS OF: see RUSSELL.

BRAGANZA, CATHARINE OF: Princess of Portugal, and wife to CHARLES II.

CAROLER, THE: the songstress who carols in the dawn and the dusk in the REALM OF THE FAERIE.

CARTERET, MARGUERITE: daughter of the governor of Jersey, Marguerite became CHARLES II's mistress when he was in exile and bore him several bastard children.

CATASTROPHE, THE: after Theseus left ARIADNE, she responded by destroying much of the ancient Aegean world in revenge. This is known as the Catastrophe.

CHARLES I: King of England 1625–1649. Executed by Parliament at the end of the English Civil War.

CHARLES II: son of CHARLES I and HENRIETTA MARIA, lived most of his youth in exile following the ENGLISH CIVIL WAR. Regained the throne in 1660.

CLARENDON, EARL OF: See HYDE, EDWARD.

COEL: a man of the Bronze Age and a friend and lover of CORNELIA.

COMMONWEALTH, THE: that period in England between the death of CHARLES I in January 1649 and the restoration of his son CHARLES II to the throne in mid-1660.

CORNELIA: wife to BRUTUS when the TROY GAME was first constructed. Now she lives as NOAH BANKS.

CROMWELL, OLIVER: Protector of England during the period of the COMMON-WEALTH, leader of the Parliamentary forces against the royalist forces during the ENGLISH CIVIL WAR.

CATLING: daughter of NOAH BANKS.

CIRCLE, THE: the means whereby three or more people can recreate the ancient magic of the STONE DANCES.

DANCING FLOOR, THE: literally the labyrinth as it is carved into rock or stone. The MISTRESS OF THE LABYRINTH and the KINGMAN use the dancing floor to raise the Game from the labyrinth. Dancing floors—labyrinths—could be found in many medieval European cathedrals.

DOLBEN, JOHN: Dean of Westminster School.

EAVING: the goddess of the waters who takes the mortal form of NOAH BANKS. In the Anglo-Saxon language, Eaving meant "shelter," or, "the unexpected haven from the storm."

EAVING'S SISTERS: in *Gods' Concubine* EAVING was reborn in Caela (now NOAH BANKS). She drew fiercely loyal women about her who became known as Eaving's Sisters. Chief among them is Ecub, reborn now as MARGUERITE CARTERET; Erith, Judith in her previous life and now reborn as KATE PEGGE; and Matilda of Normandy, now reborn as CATHARINE OF BRAGANZA.

ELIZABETH: a prostitute working in WEYLAND ORR'S brothel in IDOL LANE.

ENGLISH CIVIL WAR: CHARLES I, like his father, believed in his divine right to rule (i.e. he believed he was answerable only to God). In a country which had long believed the king was subject to his nobles before God, this attitude caused great friction, resulting in civil war between the forces of the king and Parliament between 1642 to 1646. From 1646 to 1649 CHARLES I was held captive by Parliament until his eventual execution in January 1649.

FAERIE, LORD OF THE: an ancient being who watches over the FAERIE. He is often confused with the Green Man, an ancient mythical figure in English village culture closely associated with the forests, and with the May-tide celebrations. Figures of the Green Man, or the Lord of the Faerie, can be found carved into the decorations of a myriad English (as European) cathedrals and churches.

FAERIE, REALM OF THE: the faerie world which exists side by side with the mortal world. Governed by the LORD OF THE FAERIE.

FELTON, BESS: a goodwife of Easthill, who took in NOAH BANKS after her father's death.

FOX, SIR STEPHEN: one of CHARLES II'S companions in exile.

FRANCES: a prostitute working in WEYLAND ORR'S brothel in IDOL LANE.

GARDIEN, HELENE: mother of LOUIS DE SILVA.

GOG: one of the legendary giant protectors of London, closely associated with the Guildhall (you can still see him there); his brother is MAGOG. Once a SIDLESAGHE.

GOG MAGOG HILLS: a line of hills a few miles south of the town of Cambridge.

GREAT FOUNDING LABYRINTH, THE: the original labyrinth in Knossos on Crete, where was imprisoned the Minotaur ASTERION, and where ARIADNE betrayed him to Theseus.

GREAT ORDEAL, THE: whenever a woman is trained as a MISTRESS OF THE LABYRINTH, she must undergo a final test to determine whether or not she is capable of controlling the powerful sorceries of the labyrinth. It is the Great Ordeal, and not all novice Mistresses of the Labyrinth survive it.

GREAT MARRIAGE, THE: the formal union between the STAG GOD and the goddess of the waters (see EAVING), signifying that forest, water, and land exist in harmony.

HAMPSTEAD HEATH: lying in the north-west of modern-day London, the Heath comprises 800 acres of parkland and woods; Parliament Hill rises in its south-east quadrant. To its east, close to the village of Highgate, are a number of natural springs which in the seventeenth century became popular for medicinal purposes.

HENRIETTA MARIA: French-born wife of CHARLES I, mother to CHARLES II, Queen of England.

HENRIETTE-ANNE, PRINCESS: daughter of HENRIETTA MARIA and CHARLES I, and sister of CHARLES II.

HYDE, ANNE: daughter of EDWARD HYDE.

HYDE, EDWARD: advisor and friend of CHARLES II. Later Earl of Clarendon.

IDOL LANE: one of London's many remaining medieval lanes, Idol Lane is now a fairly mundane passageway watched over by office blocks and CCTV cameras. It does, however, bear an exploration if ever you're in London.

JAMES, DUKE OF YORK: younger brother to CHARLES II, eventually James II 1685–1688 before he was deposed. Loth-reborn.

KINGMAN, THE: the TROY GAME is constructed and controlled by two people, the MISTRESS OF THE LABYRINTH and the KINGMAN. The Kingman was traditionally the king or ruler of the city which needed to be protected by the Game. In TROY, the original Kingman was Aeneas, and his descendant Brutus later took on the role.

KINGSHIP BANDS OF TROY, THE: when Brutus originally constructed the TROY GAME with Genvissa, he used the power of the ancient and magical six kingship bands of Troy he wore about his limbs. But when CORNELIA killed Genvissa, and ASTERION threatened to invade, Brutus took the kingship bands and hid them about London as part of a protective enchantment. Ever since then both Brutus-reborn and ASTERION have competed in the effort to locate them. In book II, *Gods' Concubine*, Caela (Cornelia-reborn and NOAH BANKS in this book) took them and hid them in different locations about London. Possession of the bands enables the wearer to control the TROY GAME.

LIBERTY OF THE TOWER: See TOWER LIBERTY.

LLANGARLIA: the ancient name of England during the Bronze Age (about 1500 BCE).

LONG TOM: a SIDLESAGHE, and a close friend of Noah Banks, particularly in her previous life as Caela. In medieval and early modern England, individual standing stones were often called Long Tom.

LONQUEFORT, SIMON GAUTIER, MARQUIS DE: French nobleman, father of LOUIS DE SILVA.

MAG: goddess of the waters in ancient LLANGARLIA, now reborn in NOAH BANKS as EAVING.

MAGALLAN: the priestess who acted as living representative of the goddess MAG in ancient LLANGARLIA.

MAGOG: one of the legendary giant protectors of London, closely associated with the Guildhall (you can see him there); his brother is GOG. Once a SIDLESAGHE.

MARY, PRINCESS: daughter of HENRIETTA MARIA and CHARLES I, sister of CHARLES II, and wife of William of Orange.

MESOPOTAMA: In the Bronze Age Mesopotama was a Dorian city on the River Acheron on the west coast of Greece. It was ruled by Pandrasus, who was CORNELIA'S father.

MISTRESS OF THE LABYRINTH: the TROY GAME is constructed and controlled by two people, the MISTRESS OF THE LABYRINTH and the KINGMAN. The Mistress is an ancient office which derives from the great founding labyrinth in Knossos in Crete. In previous lives Genvissa, reborn as Swanne (now JANE ORR), has been the Mistress of the Labyrinth.

MONTAGU, SIR EDWARD, EARL OF SANDWICH: General-at-sea, or Admiral, of the English fleet which sailed to bring home CHARLES II to England.

NAKED, THE: the greatest of the holy sites within the REALM OF THE FAERIE, and the site of the LORD OF THE FAERIE'S throne.

OG: see STAG GOD.

ORR, JANE: sister to WEYLAND ORR, and a prostitute working at her brother's brothel in IDOL LANE, London. She is Genvissa reborn, who lived her last life as Swanne, wife of Harold of Wessex.

ORR, WEYLAND: procurer and brothel keeper living in Idol Lane in London. ASTERION reborn.

PARLIAMENT HILL: once known as the Llandin, it is the most sacred of the sacred VEILED HILLS of ancient Llangarlia. Parliament Hill is still easily accessible from Hampstead Heath, and has an ancient circle just to one side of its summit.

PEN HILL: one of the ancient sacred VEILED HILLS of Llangarlia. Pen Hill has now vanished underneath the nineteenth-century urban sprawl (and waterworks) of London.

PEGGE, CATHERINE (KATE): Erith-reborn and one of CHARLES II's mistress when he was in exile. Kate bore him at least one child.

PEPYS, SAMUEL: secretary to SIR EDWARD MONTAGU, and noted diarist.

RINGWALK, THE: the medieval term for the path of the stag through the forest.

RUSSELL, LADY ANNE: wife to WILLIAM RUSSELL, Earl of Bedford. Her maiden name was Anne Carr.

RUSSELL, WILLIAM: fifth Earl of Bedford. Husband to LADY ANNE RUSSELL.

ST DUNSTAN'S-IN-THE-EAST: one of the medieval churches of London. Named after St Dunstan, a martyred Saxon archbishop of Canterbury, it was first built sometime in the thirteenth century, was partly destroyed during the Great Fire of London in 1666 (its steeple was rebuilt by Christopher Wren), and destroyed again during the Blitz of World War II. The steeple has been rebuilt, and the bombed and burned walls have been left standing as a memorial.

ST JAMES PALACE: built by Henry VIII in Westminster in the sixteenth century the palace remained as one of the monarchy's principal places of residence for over 300 years.

STAG GOD: one of the ancient gods of the land of LLANGARLIA, the Stag God is particularly associated with the forests. For aeons he was known as Og. Now that he is to rise again, he will take a new name.

STONE DANCES, THE: the ancient circles of standing stones which dot the British Isles. See also the CIRCLE.

SIDLESAGHES: ancient magical creatures of the land who often take the form of standing stones within the STONE DANCES.

SILVA, LOUIS DE: bastard son of SIMON GAUTIER, Marquis de Lonquefort, and his mistress, HELENE GARDIEN, and friend to CHARLES II.

SILVIUS: father to BRUTUS, murdered by BRUTUS in the forests outside Alba in Italy almost three thousand years ago.

SPIV: an early twentieth-century term for a black marketeer.

THANET, LEILA: mistress of Langley House near Bushey Park, north of London. Wife to THOMAS THANET.

THANET, THOMAS: master of Langley House, near Bushey Park, north of London. Husband to LEILA, and long-time friend of JOHN THORNTON.

THORNTON, REV. JOHN: tutor to the Earl and Countess of Bedford's (see RUSSELL) children at Woburn Abbey.

TOWER FIELDS: During the medieval period and up to the end of the seventeenth century, the complex of the Tower of London was surrounded on its north-west and north-east sides by the gentle slopes of Tower Hill (see the VEILED HILLS). These open grassy areas were known as Tower Fields. In the north-western portion of Tower Fields stood the crumbling remains of a medieval scaffold.

TOWER LIBERTY (OR LIBERTIES, OR LIBERTY OF THE TOWER): until the nineteenth century the Tower of London and a small area surrounding it was free from the jurisdiction of the City of London. The Tower Liberty had its own court-house and prison, and the Gentlemen (or Officers) of the Tower claimed certain rights, such as the beasts that fell off London Bridge, all swans which floated below the bridge, as well the right to exact some tolls on goods traveling on the Thames past the Tower.

TOWER STREET WARD: London was anciently divided into administrative wards. Tower Street ward covered the extreme south-eastern corner of London. It contained IDOL LANE, ST DUNSTAN'S-IN-THE-EAST, the Custom House and many of the wharves along the Thames.

TROY: the fabulous city of Troy sat on the western shores of Anatolia (modern-day Turkey). Paris, son of the Trojan king Priam, stole away Helen from her husband, Menelaus, King of Sparta, precipitating the Trojan war in which the city-states of Greece united against Troy. Although it survived a long Greek siege, Troy was eventually destroyed due to a combination of hubris, the betrayal of the gods, and Greek cunning. Those Trojans who survived the destruction scattered about the lands of the Mediterranean, either as refugees or slaves.

TROY GAME, THE: the ancient protective sorcery which draws on the power of the ancient labyrinth in order to protect a city. In *Hades' Daughter* Brutus and Genvissa constructed the Game, but were unable to complete it when CORNELIA murdered Genvissa. Now the Game has taken on a life and power of its own, and wishes only to be completed by the KINGMAN and MISTRESS OF THE LABYRINTH.

VEILED HILLS, THE: the six sacred hills of LLANGARLIA, clustered above the Thames River in the area now known as London. The six hills were: Tot Hill (where now stands Westminster); the Llandin, the most sacred of the hills (now called PARLIAMENT HILL); PEN HILL; Og's Hill (Ludgate Hill); Mag's Hill (Cornhill); and the White Mount (Tower Hill; see TOWER FIELDS).

WHITEHALL PALACE: situated on the northern bank of the Thames between Westminster and Charing Cross, and formerly known as York Palace; Whitehall Palace was extensively renovated by Henry VIII, with various buildings and chambers added by every monarch following. By the time CHARLES II was born in 1630 the palace was a warren of some 2,000 rooms centered about the Great Courtyard. The palace burned to the ground in 1698 when a Dutch laundress lit a fire to do her washing; all that remains now is the Great Banqueting House (outside of which CHARLES I lost his head).

WOBURN ABBEY: home of the RUSSELL family, earls and later dukes of Bedford. The site was once a medieval abbey, the lands given to the Russells by the monarchy after the dissolution of the monasteries in the sixteenth century. Woburn Abbey is open to visitors for much of the year, and if you ask nicely, the curator might show you an engraving of the Abbey as it would have been in the seventeenth century.